MW01697622

THE WORD & THE VOID

Also by Terry Brooks

SHANNARA

First King of Shannara

The Sword of Shannara
The Elfstones of Shannara
The Wishsong of Shannara

The Heritage of Shannara
The Scions of Shannara
The Druid of Shannara
The Elf Queen of Shannara
The Talisman of Shannara

The Voyage of the Jerle Shannara
Ilse Witch
Antrax
Morgawr

High Druid of Shannara
Jarka Ruus
Tanequil
Straken

The World of Shannara
(with Teresa Patterson)

The Magic Kingdom of Landover
Magic Kingdom for Sale—Sold!
The Black Unicorn
Wizard at Large
The Tangle Box
Witches' Brew

Sometimes the Magic Works:
Notes From a Writing Life

Star Wars®: Episode 1
The Phantom Menace

Hook

Armageddon's Children

THE WORD & THE VOID

RUNNING WITH THE DEMON
A KNIGHT OF THE WORD
ANGEL FIRE EAST

Terry Brooks

SFBC®
FANTASY

This is a work of fiction. Names, places, and incidents either are a product of the author's imagination or are used fictitiously.

RUNNING WITH THE DEMON Copyright © 1997 by Terry Brooks
Printing History: Del Rey hardcover, September 1997.
Del Rey paperback, July 1998.

A KNIGHT OF THE WORD Copyright © 1998 by Terry Brooks.
Printing History: Del Rey hardcover, August 1998.
Del Rey paperback, June 1999.

ANGEL FIRE EAST Copyright © 1999 by Terry Brooks.
Printing History: Del Rey hardcover, October 1999.
Del Rey paperback, September 2000.

First SFBC Fantasy printing: September 2006.

Published by arrangement with:
The Random House Publishing Group
A division of Random House, Inc.
1745 Broadway
New York, NY 10019

Visit the SFBC at http://www.sfbc.com
Visit Del Rey at http://www.randomhouse.com/delrey/

ISBN 978-0-7394-7547-8

Printed in the United States of America.

CONTENTS

RUNNING WITH THE DEMON

TO JUDINE

FOR SHOWING ME EVERY DAY WHY THE JOURNEY IS MORE IMPORTANT THAN THE DESTINATION.

PROLOGUE

He stands alone in the center of another of America's burned-out towns, but he has been to this one before. Even in their ruined, blackened condition, the buildings that surround him are recognizable. The streets of the intersection in which he finds himself stretch away in windswept concrete ribbons that dwindle and fade into the horizon—south to the bridge that spans the river, north to the parched flats of what were once cornfields, east toward the remains of Reagan's hometown, and west to the Mississippi and the Great Plains. A street sign, bent and weathered, confirms that he stands at the corner of First Avenue and Third Street. The town is eight blocks square, two blocks in any direction from where he stands, petering out afterward in dribs and drabs of homes that have been converted to real-estate offices and repair shops or simply leveled to provide parking. Farther out lie the abandoned ruins of two supermarkets and the mall, and down along the riverbank he can see the broken-down stacks and rusted-out corrugated roofs of what is left of the steel mill.

He looks around slowly, making sure he is in the right place, because it has been a long time. The sky is clouded and dark. Rain threatens and will probably fall before night. Although it is noon, the light is so pale that it seems more like dusk. The air and the earth are washed clean of color. Buildings, streets, abandoned vehicles, trash, and sky are a uniform shade of gray, the paint running from one into the other until nothing remains but shadows and light to differentiate any of it. In the silence, the wind moans softly as it rises off the river and whips down the empty streets. Twigs, leaves, and debris skitter along the concrete. Windows gape dark and hollow where the plate glass has been broken out. Doors hang open and sag. Smears of black ash and soot stain the walls where fires have burned away the wood and plastic veneer of the offices and shops. Cars hunker down on flattened tires and bare axles, stripped of everything useful, abandoned shells turning slowly to rust.

The man looks the town over as he would a corpse, remembering when it was still vital.

A pack of dogs comes out of one of the buildings. There are maybe ten of them, lean and hungry, quick-eyed and suspicious. They study him momentarily before moving on. They want nothing to do with him. He watches them disappear around the corner of a building, and he begins to walk. He moves east toward the park, even though he knows what he will find. He passes the bank, the paint store, the fabric shop, Al's Bar, and a parking lot, and stops at Josie's. The sign still hangs over the entry; the enamel is faded and broken, but the name is recognizable. He walks over and peers inside. The furniture and pastry cases are all smashed, the cooking equipment broken, and the leather banquettes ripped to shreds. Dust coats the countertop, trash litters the ruined floor, and weeds poke out of cracks in the tile.

He turns away in time to catch sight of two children slipping from the alleyway across the street. They carry canvas bags stuffed with items they have scavenged. They wear knives strapped to their waists. The girl is in her teens, the boy younger. Their hair is long and unkempt, their clothes shabby, and their eyes hard and feral. They slow to consider him, taking his measure. He waits on them, turns to face them, lets them see that he is not afraid. They glance at each other, whisper something punctuated by furtive gestures, then move away. Like the dogs, they want nothing to do with him.

He continues up the street, the sound of his boots a hollow echo in the midday silence. Office buildings and shops give way to homes. The homes are empty as well, those that are still intact. Many are burned out and sagging, settling slowly back into the earth. Weeds grow everywhere, even through cracks in the concrete of the streets. He wonders how long it has been since anyone has lived here. Counting the strays, the dogs and the children and the one or two others that linger because they have no place else to go, how many are left? In some towns, there is no one. Only the cities continue to provide refuge, walled camps in which survivors have banded together in a desperate effort to keep the madness at bay. Chicago is one such city. He has been there and seen what it has to offer. He already knows its fate.

A woman emerges from the shadows of a doorway in one of the residences, a frail, hollow-eyed creature, dark hair tangled and streaked with purple dye, arms hanging loose and bare, the skin dotted with needle marks. Got anything for me? she asks dully. He shakes his head. She comes down to the foot of the porch steps and stops. She trots out a smile. Where'd you come from? He does not respond. She moves a couple of steps closer, hugging herself with her thin arms. Want to come in and party with me? He stops her with a look. In the shadows of the house from which she has come, he can see movement. Eyes, yellow and flat, study him with cold intent. He knows who they belong to. Get away from me, he tells the woman. Her face crumples. She turns back without a word.

He walks to the edge of the town, a mile farther on, out where the park waits. He knows he shouldn't, but he cannot help himself. Nothing of what he remembers remains, but he wants to see anyway. Old Bob and Gran are gone. Pick is gone. Daniel and Wraith are gone. The park is overgrown with weeds and scrub. The cemetery is a cluster of ruined headstones. The townhomes and apartments and houses are all empty. What lives in the park now can be found only in the caves and is his implacable enemy.

And what of Nest Freemark?

He knows that, too. It is a nightmare that haunts him, unrelenting and pitiless.

He stops at the edge of the cemetery and looks off into the shadows beyond. He is here, he supposes, because he has no better place to go. He is here because he is reduced to retracing the steps of his life as a form of penance for his failures. He is hunted at every turn, and so he is drawn to the places that once provided refuge. He searches in the vain hope that something of what was good in his life will resurface, even when he knows the impossibility of that happening.

He takes a long, slow breath. His pursuers will find him again soon enough, but perhaps not this day. So he will walk the park once more and try to recapture some small part of what is lost to him forever.

Across the roadway from where he stands, a billboard hangs in tatters. He can just make out its wording.

WELCOME TO HOPEWELL, ILLINOIS! WE'RE GROWING YOUR WAY!

John Ross woke with a start, jerking upright so sharply that he sent his walking staff clattering to the floor of the bus. For a moment, he didn't know where he was. It was night, and most of his fellow passengers were asleep. He took a moment to collect himself, to remember which journey he was on, which world he was in. Then he maneuvered his bad leg stiffly into the aisle, jockeying himself about on the seat until he was able to reach down and retrieve the staff.

He had fallen asleep in spite of himself, he realized. In spite of what that meant.

He placed the walking stick beside him, leaning it carefully against his knapsack, bracing it in place so that it would not slide away again. An old woman several seats in front of him was still awake. She glanced back at him briefly, her look one of reproof and suspicion. She was the only one who sat close to him. He was alone at the very back of the bus; the other passengers, all save the old woman, had been careful to take seats near the front. Perhaps it was the leg. Or the shabby clothes. Or the mantle of weariness he wore like the ghost of Marley did his chains. Perhaps it was the eyes, the way they seemed to look beyond what everyone else could see, at once cool and discerning, yet distant and lost, an unsettling contradiction.

But, no. He looked down at his hands, studying them. In the manner of one who has come to terms with being shunned, he could ignore the pain of his banishment. Subconsciously, his fellow passengers had made a perfectly understandable decision.

You leave as many empty seats as possible between yourself and Death.

Friday, July 1

CHAPTER 1

"Hsst! Nest!"

His voice cut through the cottony layers of her sleep with the sharpness of a cat's claw. Her head jerked off the pillow and her sleep-fogged eyes snapped open.

"Pick?"

"Wake up, girl!" The sylvan's voice squeaked with urgency. "The feeders are at it again! I need you!"

Nest Freemark pushed the sheet away and forced herself into an upright position, legs dangling off the side of the bed. The night air was hot and sticky in spite of the efforts of the big floor fan that sat just inside her doorway. She rubbed at her eyes to clear them and swallowed against the dryness in her throat. Outside, she could hear the steady buzz of the locusts in the trees.

"Who is it this time?" she asked, yawning.

"The little Scott girl."

"Bennett?" *Oh, God!* She was fully awake now. "What happened?"

Pick was standing on the window ledge just outside the screen, silhouetted in the moonlight. He might be only six inches tall from the tips of his twiggy feet to the peak of his leafy head, but she could read the disgust in his gnarled wooden features as clearly as if he were six feet.

"The mother's out with her worthless boyfriend again, shutting down bars. That boy you fancy, young Jared, was left in charge of the other kids, but he had one of his attacks. Bennett was still up—you know how she is when her mother's not there, though goodness knows why. She became scared and wandered off. By the time the boy recovered, she was gone. Now the feeders have her. Do you need this in writing or are you going to get dressed and come help?"

Nest jumped out of the bed without answering, slipped off her nightshirt, and pulled on her Grunge Lives T-shirt, running shorts, socks, and tennis shoes. Her face peeked out at her from the dresser mirror: roundish with a wide forehead and broad cheekbones, pug nose with a scattering of freckles, green eyes that tended to squint, a mouth that quirked upward at the corners as if to suggest perpetual amusement, and a complexion that was starting to break out. Passably attractive, but no stunner. Pick was pacing back and forth on thc sill. He looked like twigs and leaves bound together into a child's tiny stick man. His hands were making nervous gestures, the same ones they always made when he was agitated—pulling at his silky moss beard and slapping at his bark-encrusted thighs. He couldn't help himself. He was like one of those cartoon characters that charges around running into walls. He claimed he was a hundred and fifty, but for being as old as he was, it didn't seem he had learned very much about staying calm.

She arranged a few pillows under the sheet to give the impression that she was still in the bed, sleeping. The ruse would work if no one looked too closely. She glanced at the clock. It was two in the morning, but her grandparents no longer slept soundly and were apt to be up at all hours of the night, poking about. She glanced at the open door and sighed. There was no help for it.

She nudged the screen through the window and climbed out after it. Her bedroom was on the first floor, so slipping away unnoticed was easy. In the summer anyway, she amended, when it was warm and the windows were all open. In the winter, she had to find her coat and go down the hallway and out the back door, which was a bit more chancy. But she had gotten pretty good at it.

"Where is she?" she asked Pick, holding out her hand, palm up, so he could step into it.

"Headed for the cliffs, last I saw." He moved off the sill gingerly. "Daniel's tracking her, but we'd better hurry."

Nest placed Pick on her shoulder where he could get a firm grip on her T-shirt, fitted the screen back in place, and took off at a run. She sped across the back lawn toward the hedgerow that bordered the park, the Midwest night air whipping across her face, fresh and welcoming after the stale closeness of her bedroom. She passed beneath the canopies of solitary oaks and hickories that shaded the yard, their great limbs branching and dividing overhead in intricate patterns, their leaves reflecting dully in the mix of light from moon and stars. The skies were clear and the world still as she ran, the houses about her dark and silent, the people asleep. She found the gap in the hedgerow on the first try, ducked to clear the low opening, and was through.

Ahead, Sinnissippi Park opened before her, softball diamonds and picnic areas bright with moonlight, woods and burial grounds laced with shadows.

She angled right, toward the roadway that led into the park, settling into a smooth, even pace. She was a strong runner, a natural athlete. Her cross-country coach said she was the best he had ever seen, although in the same breath he said she needed to develop better training habits. At five feet eight inches and a hundred twenty pounds, she was lean and rangy and tough as nails. She didn't know why she was that way; certainly she had never worked at it. She had always been agile, though, even when she was twelve and her friends were bumping into coffee tables and tripping over their own feet, all of them trying to figure out what their bodies were going to do next. (Now they were fourteen, and they pretty much knew.) Nest was blessed with a runner's body, and it was clear from her efforts the past spring that her talent was prodigious. She had already broken every cross-country record in the state of Illinois for girls fourteen and under. She had done that when she was thirteen. But five weeks ago she had entered the Rock River Invitational against runners eighteen and under, girls and boys. She had swept the field in the ten-thousand-meter race, posting a time that shattered the state high school record by almost three minutes. Everyone had begun to look at her a little differently after that.

Of course, they had been looking at Nest Freemark differently for one reason or another for most of her life, so she was less impressed by the attention now than she might have been earlier.

Just think, she reflected ruefully, how they would look at me if I told them about Pick. Or about the magic.

She crossed the ball diamond closest to her house, reached the park entrance, and swept past the crossbar that was lowered to block the road after sunset. She felt rested and strong; her breathing was smooth and her heartbeat steady. She followed the pavement for a short distance, then turned onto the grassy picnic area that led to the Sinnissippi burial mounds and the cliffs. She could see the lights of the Sinnissippi Townhomes off to the right, low-income housing with a fancy name. That was where the Scotts lived. Enid Scott was a single mother with five kids, very few life options, and a drinking problem. Nest didn't think much of her; nobody did. But Jared was a sweetheart, her friend since grade school, and Bennett, at five the youngest of the Scott children, was a peanut who deserved a lot better than she had been getting of late.

Nest scanned the darkness ahead for some sign of the little girl, but there was nothing to see. She looked for Wraith as well, but there was no sign of him either. Just thinking of Wraith sent a shiver down her spine. The park stretched away before her, vast, silent, and empty of movement. She picked up her pace, the urgency of Bennett's situation spurring her on. Pick rode easily on her shoulder, attached in the manner of a clamp, arms and legs locked on her sleeve. He was still muttering to himself, that annoyingly incessant chatter in which he indulged ad nauseam in times of stress. But Nest let him be. Pick had a lot of responsibility to exercise, and it was not being made any easier by the increasingly bold behavior of the feeders. It was bad enough that they occupied the caves below the cliffs in ever-expanding numbers, their population grown so large that it was no longer possible to take an accurate count. But where before they had confined their activities to nighttime appearances in the park, now all of a sudden they were starting to surface everywhere in Hopewell, sometimes even in daylight. It was all due to a shifting in the balance of things, Pick advised. And if the balance was not righted, soon the feeders would be everywhere. Then what was he supposed to do?

The trees ahead thickened, trunks tightening in a dark wall, limbs closing out the night sky. Nest angled through the maze, her eyes adjusting to the change in light, seeing everything, picking out all the details. She dodged through a series of park toys, spring-mounted rides for the smallest children, jumped a low chain divider, and raced back across the roadway and into the burial mounds. There was still no sign of Bennett Scott. The air was cooler here, rising off the Rock River where it flowed west below the cliffs in a broad swath toward the Mississippi. In the distance, a freight train wailed as it made its way east through the farmland. The summer night was thick with heat, and the whistle seemed muted and lost. It died away slowly, and in the ensuing silence the sounds of the insects resurfaced, a steady, insistent hum.

Nest caught sight of Daniel then, a dark shadow as he swooped down from the trees just long enough to catch her attention before wheeling away again.

"There, girl!" Pick shouted needlessly in her ear.

She raced in pursuit of the barn owl, following his lead, heading for the cliffs. She ran through the burial mounds, low, grassy hummocks clustered at the edge of the roadway. Ahead, the road ended in a turnaround at the park's highest point. That was where she would find Bennett. Unless . . . She brushed the word aside, refusing to concede that it applied. A rush of bitterness toward Enid Scott tightened her throat. It wasn't fair that she left Jared alone to watch his brothers and sisters. Enid knew about his condition; she just found it convenient now and then to pretend it didn't matter. A mild form of epilepsy, the attacks could last for as long as five minutes. When they came, Jared would just "go away" for a bit, staring off into space, not seeing or hearing, not being aware of anything. Even the medicine he took couldn't always prevent the attacks. His mother knew that. She knew.

The trees opened before her, and Daniel dove out of the shadows, streaking for the cliffs. Nest put on a new burst of speed, nearly unseating Pick. She could see Bennett Scott now, standing at the very edge of the cliffs, just beyond the turnaround, a small, solitary figure against the night sky, all hunched over and crying. Nest could hear her sobs. The feeders were cajoling her, enticing her, trying to cloud her thinking further so that she would take those last few steps. Nest was angry. Bennett made the seventh child in a month. She had saved them all, but how long could her luck hold?

Daniel started down, then arced away soundlessly. It was too dangerous for him to go in; his unexpected presence might startle the little girl and cause her to lose her balance. That was why Pick relied on Nest. A young girl's appearance was apt to prove far less unsettling than his own or Daniel's.

She slowed to a walk, dropping Pick off in the grass. No point in taking chances; Pick preferred to remain invisible anyway. The scent of pine trees wafted on the humid night air, carried out of the cemetery beyond, where the trees grew in thick clumps along the chain-link fence. In the moonlight, the headstones and monuments were just visible, the granite and marble reflecting with a shimmery cast. She took several deep breaths as she came up to Bennett, moving slowly, carefully into the light. The feeders saw her coming and their lantern eyes narrowed. She ignored them, focusing her attention on the little girl.

"Hey, tiny Ben Ben!" She kept her voice casual, relaxed. "It's me, Nest."

Bennett Scott's tear-filled eyes blinked rapidly. "I know."

"What are you doing out here, Ben Ben?"

"Looking for my mommy."

"Well, I don't think she's out here, sweetie." Nest moved a few steps closer, glancing about as if looking for Enid.

"She's lost," Bennett sobbed.

A few of the feeders edged menacingly toward Nest, but she ignored them. They knew better than to mess with her while Wraith was around—which she fervently hoped he was. A lot of them were gathered here, though. Flat-faced and featureless, squat caricatures of humans, they were as much a mystery to her now as ever, even after all she had learned about them from Pick. She didn't really even know what they were made of. When she had asked Pick about it once, he had told her with a sardonic grin that as a rule you are mostly what you eat, so the feeders could be almost anything.

"I'll bet your mommy is back home by now, Ben Ben," she offered, infusing her voice with enthusiasm. "Why don't we go have a look?"

The little girl sniffled. "I don't want to go home. I don't like it there anymore."

"Sure you do. I'll bet Jared wonders where you are."

"Jared's sick. He had an attack."

"Well, he'll be better by now. The attacks don't last long, sweetie. You know that. Come on, let's go see."

Bennett's head lowered into shadow. She hugged herself, her head shaking. "George doesn't like me. He told me so."

George Paulsen, Enid's latest mistake in the man department. Even though she was only fourteen, Nest knew a loser when she saw one. George Paulsen was a scary loser, though. She came a step closer, looking for a way to make physical contact with Bennett so that she could draw the little girl away from the cliff. The river was a dark, silver shimmer far below the cliffs, flat and still within the confines of the bayou, where the railroad tracks were elevated on the levy, wilder and swifter beyond where the main channel flowed. The darkness made the drop seem even longer than it was, and Bennett was only a step or two away.

"George needs to get an attitude adjustment," Nest offered. "Everybody likes you, Ben Ben. Come on, let's go find your mommy and talk to her about it. I'll go with you. Hey, what about Spook? I'll bet your kitty misses you."

Bennett Scott's moppet head shook quickly, scattering her lank, dark hair in tangles. "George took Spook away. He doesn't like cats."

Nest wanted to spit. That worthless creep! Spook was just about the only thing Bennett Scott had. She felt her grip on the situation beginning to loosen. The feeders were weaving about Bennett like snakes, and the little girl was cringing and hugging herself in fear. Bennett couldn't see them, of course. She wouldn't see them until it was too late. But she could hear them somewhere in the back of her mind, an invisible presence, insidious voices, taunting and teasing. They were hungry for her, and the balance was beginning to shift in their favor.

"I'll help you find Spook," Nest said quickly. "And I'll make sure that George doesn't take him away again either. What do you say to that?"

Bennett Scott hugged herself some more and looked fixedly at her feet, thinking it over. Her thin body went still. "Do you promise, Nest? Really?"

Nest Freemark gave her a reassuring smile. "I do, sweetie. Now walk over here and take my hand so we can go home."

The feeders moved to intervene, but Nest glared at them and they flinched away. They wouldn't meet her gaze, of course. They knew what would happen if they did. Nevertheless, they were bolder than usual tonight, more ready to challenge her. That was not a good sign.

"Bennett," she said quietly. The little girl's head lifted and her eyes came into the light. "Look at me, Bennett. Don't look anywhere else, okay? Just look right at me. Now walk over here and take my hand."

Bennett Scott started forward, one small step at a time. Nest waited patiently, holding her gaze. The night air had turned hot and still again, the breeze off the river dying away. Insects buzzed and flew in erratic sweeps, and, not wanting to do anything that would startle the little girl, Nest fought down the impulse to brush at them.

"Come on, Ben Ben," she cajoled softly.

As Bennett Scott advanced, the feeders gave way grudgingly, dropping down on all fours in a guarded crouch and skittering next to her like crabs. Nest took a deep breath.

One of the feeders broke away from the others and made a grab for Bennett. Nest hissed at it furiously, caught its eye, and stripped it of its life with a single, chilling glance. That was all it took—one instant in which their eyes met and her magic took control. The feeder collapsed in a heap and melted into the earth in a black stain. The others backed off watchfully.

Nest took a deep, calming breath. "Come on, Bennett," she urged in a tight whisper. "It's all right, sweetie."

The little girl had almost reached her when the headlight of the freight train swept across the bayou as the lead engine lurched out of the night. Bennett Scott hesitated, her eyes suddenly wide and uncertain. Then the train whistle sounded its shrill, piercing wail, and she cried out in fear.

Nest didn't hesitate. She grabbed Bennett Scott's arm, snatched the little girl from her feet, and pressed her close. For a moment she held her ground, facing down the feeders. But she saw at once that there were too many to stand against, so she wheeled from the cliffs and began to run. Behind her, the feeders bounded in pursuit. Already Pick was astride Daniel, and the barn owl swooped down on the foremost pursuers, talons extended. The feeders veered away, giving Nest an extra few yards head start.

"Faster, Nest!" Pick cried, but she was already in full stride, running as hard as she could. She clutched Bennett Scott tightly against her, feeling the child shake. She weighed almost nothing, but it was awkward running with her. Nest cleared the turnaround and streaked past the burial mounds for the picnic ground. She would turn and face the feeders there, where she could maneuver, safely away from the cliffs. Her magic would give her some protection. And Pick would be there. And Daniel. But there were so many of them tonight! Her heart thumped wildly. From the corner of her eye, she saw shadows closing on her, bounding through the park, yellow eyes narrowed. Daniel screeched, and she felt the whoosh of his wings as he sped past her, banking away into the dark.

"I'm sorry, Mommy, I'm sorry, I'm sorry," Bennett Scott sobbed, a prayer of forgiveness for some imagined wrong. Nest gritted her teeth and ran faster.

Then suddenly she went down, arms and legs flying as she tripped over a road chain she had missed vaulting. She lost her grip on Bennett Scott and the little girl cried out in terror. Then the air was knocked from Bennett's lungs as she struck the ground.

Nest rolled to her feet at once, but the feeders were everywhere, dark, shadowy forms closing on her with wicked intent. She turned to mush the handful that were closest, the ones that were foolish enough to meet her gaze, ripping apart their dark forms with a glance. But the remainder converged in a dark wave.

Then Wraith materialized next to her, a massive presence, fur all stiff and bristling, the hairs raised like tiny spikes off his body. At first glance, he might have been a dog, a demonic German shepherd perhaps, colored an odd brindle. But he was deep-chested like a Rottweiler, and tall at the shoulders like a boxer, and his eyes were a peculiar amber within a mass of black facial markings that suggested tiger stripes. Then you recognized the sloped forehead and the narrow muzzle as a wolf's. And if you looked even closer, which if you were one of the few who could see him you were not apt to do, you realized he was something else altogether.

Scrambling over each other in an effort to escape, the feeders scattered like leaves in a strong wind. Wraith advanced on them in a stiff-legged walk, his head lowered, his teeth bared, but the feeders disappeared as swiftly as shadows at the coming of full sun, bounding back into the night. When the last of them had gone, Wraith wheeled back momentarily to give Nest a dark, purposeful glance, almost as if to take the measure of her resolve in the face of his somewhat belated appearance, and then he faded away.

Nest exhaled sharply, the chill that had settled in the pit of her stomach melting, the tightness in her chest giving way. Her breath came in rapid bursts, and blood throbbed in her ears. She looked quickly to find Bennett. The little girl was curled into a ball, hiding her face in her hands, crying so hard she was hiccuping. Had she seen Wraith? Nest didn't think so. Few people ever saw Wraith. She brushed at the grass embedded in the cuts and scrapes on her knees and elbows, and went to collect her frightened charge. She scooped Bennett up and cradled her gently.

"There, there, Ben Ben," she cooed, kissing the little girl's face. "Don't be frightened now. It's all right. Everything's all right." She shivered in spite of herself. "It was just a little fall. Time to be going home now, sweetie. Look, there's your house, right over there. Can you see the lights?"

Daniel winged past one final time and disappeared into the dark, bearing Pick with him. The feeders were scattered, so the owl and the sylvan were leaving, entrusting the return of Bennett Scott to her. She sighed wearily and began to walk through the park. Her breathing steadied and her heartbeat slowed. She was sweating, and the air felt hot and damp against her face. It was silent in the park, hushed and tender in the blanket of the dark. She hugged Bennett possessively, feeling the little girl's sobs slowly fade.

"Oh, Ben Ben," she said, "we'll have you home in bed before you know it. You want to get right to sleep, little girl, because Monday's the Fourth of July and you don't want to miss the fireworks. All those colors, all those pretty colors! What if you fell asleep and missed them?"

Bennett Scott curled into her shoulder. "Will you come home with me, Nest? Will you stay with me?"

The words were so poignant that Nest felt tears spring to her eyes. She stared off into the night, to the stars and the half-moon in the cloudless sky, to the shadows of the trees where they loomed against the horizon, to the lights of the buildings ahead where the residences and the apartments began and the park came to an end. The world was a scary place for little girls, but the scariest things in it weren't always feeders and they didn't live only in the dark. In the morning she would talk with Gran about Enid Scott. Maybe together they could come up with something. She would look for Spook, too. Pick would help.

"I'll come home with you, Ben Ben," she whispered. "I'll stay for a little while, anyway."

Her arms were tired and aching, but she refused to put the little girl down. By the time she reached the crossbar blocking the entrance to the park and turned left toward the Sinnissippi Townhomes, Bennett Scott was fast asleep.

CHAPTER 2

Robert Roosevelt Freemark—"Old Bob" to everyone but his wife, granddaughter, and minister—came down to breakfast the next morning in something of a funk. He was a big man, three inches over six feet, with broad shoulders, large hands, and a solidity that belied his sixty-five years of age. His face was square, his features prominent, and his snow white hair thick and wavy and combed straight back from his high forehead. He looked like a politician—or at least like a politician ought to look. But Old Bob was a workingman, had been all his life, and now, in retirement after thirty years on the line at Midwest Continental Steel, he still dressed in jeans and blue work shirts and thought of himself as being just like everyone else.

Old Bob had been Old Bob for as long as anyone could remember. Not in his boyhood, of course, but shortly after that, and certainly by the time he came back from the Korean War. He wasn't called Old Bob to his face, of course, but only when he was being referred to in the third person. Like, "Old Bob sure knows his business." He wasn't Good Old Bob either, in the sense that he was a good old boy. And the "old" had never been a reference to age. It was more a designation of status or durability or dependability. Bob Freemark had been a rock-solid citizen of Hopewell and a friend to everyone living there for his entire life, the sort of man you could call upon when you needed help. He'd worked for the Jaycees, the United Way, the Cancer Fund, and the Red Cross at one time or another, spearheading their campaign efforts. He'd been a member of Kiwanis, the Moose, and the VFW. (He'd kept clear of Rotary because he couldn't abide that phony "Hi, Robert" malarkey.) He'd been a member of the First Congregational Church, been a deacon and a trustee until after Caitlin died. He'd worked at the steel mill as a foreman his last ten years on the job, and there were more than a few in the union who said he was the best they'd ever known.

But this morning as he slouched into the kitchen he was dark-browed and weary-hearted and felt not in the least as if his life had amounted to anything. Evelyn was already up, sitting at the kitchen table with her glass of orange juice laced with vodka, her cigarette, her coffee, and her magazine. Sometimes he thought she simply didn't go to bed anymore, although she'd been sleeping last night when he'd gotten up to look in on Nest. They'd kept separate bedrooms for almost ten years, and more and more it felt like they kept separate lives as well, all since Caitlin . . .

He caught himself, stopped himself from even thinking the words. Caitlin. Everything went back to Caitlin. Everything bad.

"Morning," he greeted perfunctorily.

Evelyn nodded, eyes lifting and lowering like window shades.

He poured himself a bowl of Cheerios, a glass of juice, and a cup of coffee and sat down across from her at the table. He attacked the cereal with single-minded intensity, devouring it in huge gulps, his head lowered to the bowl, stewing in wordless solitude. Evelyn sipped at her vodka and orange juice and took long drags on her cigarette. The length of the silence between them implied accurately the vastness of the gulf that separated their lives.

Finally Evelyn looked up, frowning in reproof. "What's bothering you, Robert?"

Old Bob looked at her. She had always called him Robert, not Old Bob, not even just Bob, as if some semblance of formality were required in their relationship. She was a small, intense woman with sharp eyes, soft features, gray hair, and a no-nonsense attitude. She had been beautiful once, but she was only old now. Time and life's vicissitudes and her own stubborn refusal to look after herself had done her in. She smoked and drank all the time, and when he called her on it, she told him it was her life and she could lead it any way she wanted and besides, she didn't really give a damn.

"I couldn't sleep, so I got up during the night and looked in on Nest," he told her. "She wasn't there. She'd tucked some pillows under the covers to make me think she was, but she wasn't." He paused. "She was out in the park again, wasn't she?"

Evelyn looked back at her magazine. "You leave the girl alone. She's doing what she has to do."

He shook his head stubbornly, even though he knew what was coming. "There's nothing she has to be doing out there at two in the morning."

Evelyn stubbed out her cigarette and promptly lit another one. "There's everything, and you know it."

"You know it, Evelyn. I don't."

"You want me to say it for you, Robert? You seem to be having trouble finding the right words. Nest was out minding the feeders. You can accept it or not—it doesn't change the fact of it."

"Out minding the feeders . . ."

"The ones you can't see, Robert, because your belief in things doesn't extend beyond the tip of your nose. Nest and I aren't like that, thank the good Lord."

He shoved back his cereal bowl and glared at her. "Neither was Caitlin."

Her sharp eyes fixed on him through a haze of cigarette smoke. "Don't start, Robert."

He hesitated, then shook his head hopelessly. "I'm going to have a talk with Nest about this, Evelyn," he declared softly. "I don't want her out there at night. I don't care what the reason is."

His wife stared at him a moment longer, as if measuring the strength of his words. Then her eyes returned to the magazine. "You leave Nest alone."

He looked out the window into the backyard and the park beyond. The day was bright and sunny, the skies clear, the temperature in the eighties, and the heat rising off the grass in a damp shimmer. It was only the first of July, and already they were seeing record temperatures. There'd been good rain in the spring, so the crops were doing all right, especially the early corn and soybeans, but if the heat continued there would be problems. The farmers were complaining already that they would have to irrigate and even that wouldn't be enough without some rain. Old Bob stared into the park and thought about the hardships of farming, remembering his father's struggle when he'd owned the farm up at Yorktown years ago. Old Bob didn't understand farming; he didn't understand why anyone would want to do it. Of course, that was the way farmers felt about fellows who worked in a steel mill.

"Is Nest still in bed?" he asked after a moment.

Evelyn got up to pour herself another drink. Bob watched the measure of vodka she added to the orange juice. Way too much. "Why don't you lighten up on that stuff, Evelyn? It's not even nine o'clock in the morning."

She gave him a hard look, her face pinched and her mouth set. "I notice you weren't in any hurry to get home last night from telling war stories with your pals. And I don't suppose you were drinking tea and playing shuffleboard down there at the hall, were you?" She took a long pull on the drink, walked back to her chair, sat down, and picked up the magazine. "Leave me alone, Robert. And leave Nest alone, too."

Old Bob nodded slowly and looked off again out the window. They had lived in this house for almost the whole of their married life. It was a big, sprawling rambler on two acres of wooded land abutting the park; he'd supervised the building of it himself, back in the late fifties. He'd bought the land for two hundred dollars an acre. It was worth a hundred times that now, even without the house. Caitlin had grown up under this roof, and now Nest. Everything that had meaning in his life had happened while he was living here.

His eyes traveled over the aged wood of the kitchen cabinets to the molding and kickboards and down the hall to the paneled entry. He had even been happy here once.

He stood up, weary, resigned, still in a funk. He felt emasculated by Evelyn, helpless in the face of her fortress mentality, adrift in his life, unable to change things in any way that mattered. It had been bad between them for years and it was getting worse. What was going to become of them? Nest was all that bound them together now. Once she was gone, as she would be in a few years, what would be left for them?

He brushed at his thick white hair with his hand, smoothing it back. "I'm going downtown, see if there's anything new with the strike," he said. "I'll be back in a few hours."

She nodded without looking up. "Lunch will be on the table at noon if you want it."

He studied her a moment longer, then went down the hall and out the front door into the summer heat.

It was another hour before Nest appeared in the kitchen. She stretched and yawned as she entered and helped herself to the orange juice. Her grandmother was still sitting at the kitchen table, smoking and drinking and reading her magazine. She looked up as Nest appeared and gave her a wan smile. "Good morning, Nest."

"Morning, Gran," Nest replied. She took out the bread and stuck a couple of slices in the toaster. Thinking of Bennett Scott, she stood at the counter and rolled her shoulders inside her sleep shirt to relieve the lingering ache in her muscles. "Grandpa around?"

Her grandmother put down the magazine. "He's gone out. But he wants to talk with you. He says you went into the park last night."

Nest hunched her shoulders one final time, then slouched against the counter, her eyes on the toaster. "Yep, he's right. I did."

"What happened?"

"Same as usual. The feeders got Bennett Scott this time." She told her grandmother what had happened. "I walked her to the front door and handed her over to Jared. You should have seen his face. He was so scared. He'd looked everywhere for her. He was about to call the police. His mom still wasn't home. She's a dead loss, Gran. Can't we do something about her? It isn't fair the way she saddles Jared with all the responsibility. Did you know he has to make all the meals for those kids—or almost all? He has to be there for them after school. He has to do everything!"

Her grandmother took a deep drag on her cigarette. A cloud of smoke enveloped her. "I'll have a talk with Mildred Walker. She's involved with the social-services people. Maybe one of them will drop by for a chat with Enid. That woman checks her brains at the door every time a man walks in. She's a sorry excuse for a mother, but those kids are stuck with her."

"Bennett's scared of George Paulsen, too. Next thing, he'll be living there."

Her grandmother nodded. "Well, George is good at showing up where there's a free ride." Her eyes shifted to find Nest's, and her small body bent forward over the table. "Sit with me a moment. Bring your toast."

Nest gathered up her toast and juice and sat down. She lathered on some raspberry spread and took a bite. "Good."

"What are you going to tell your grandfather when he asks you what you were doing in the park?"

Nest shrugged, tossing back her dark hair. "Same as always. I woke up and couldn't get back to sleep, so I decided to go for a run. I tucked the pillows under the covers so he wouldn't worry."

Her grandmother nodded. "Good enough, I expect. I told him to leave you alone. But he worries about you. He can't stop thinking about your mother. He thinks you'll end up the same way."

They stared at each other in silence. They had been over this ground before, many times. Caitlin Freemark, Nest's mother, had fallen from the cliffs three months after Nest was born. She had been walking in the park at night. Her state of mind had been uncertain for some time; she had been a very fragile and mercurial young woman. Nest's birth and the disappearance of the father had left her deeply troubled. There was speculation that she might have committed suicide. No one had ever been able to determine if she had, but the rumors persisted.

"I'm not my mother," Nest said quietly.

"No, you're not," her grandmother agreed. There was a distant, haunted look in her sharp, old bird's eyes, as if she had suddenly remembered something best left forgotten. Her hands fluttered about her drink.

"Grandpa doesn't understand, does he?"

"He doesn't try."

"Do you still talk to him about the feeders, Gran?"

"He thinks I'm seeing things. He thinks it's the liquor talking. He thinks I'm an old drunk."

"Oh, Gran."

"Its been like that for some time, Nest." Her grandmother shook her head. "It's as much my fault as it is his. I've made it difficult for him, too." She paused, not wanting to go too far down that road. "But I can't get him even to listen to me. Like

I said, he doesn't see. Not the feeders, not any of the forest creatures living in the park. He never could see any part of that world, not even when Caitlin was alive. She tried to tell him, your mother. But he thought it was all make-believe, just a young girl's imagination. He played along with her, pretended he understood. But he would talk to me about it when we were alone, tell me how worried he was about her nonsense. I told him that maybe she wasn't making it up. I told him maybe he should listen to her. But he just couldn't ever make himself do that."

She smiled sadly. "He's never understood our connection with the park, Nest. I doubt that he ever will."

Nest ate the last bite of toast, chewing thoughtfully. Six generations of the women of her family had been in service to the land that made up the park. They were the ones who had worked with Pick to keep the magic in balance over the years. They were the ones who had been born to magic themselves. Gwendolyn Wills, Caroline Glynn, Opal Anders, Gran, her mother, and now her. The Freemark women, Nest called them, though the designation was less than accurate. Their pictures hung in a grouping in the entry, framed against the wooded backdrop of the park. Gran always said that the partnering worked best with the women of the family, because the women stayed while the men too often moved on.

"Grandpa never talks about the park with me," Nest remarked quietly.

"No, I think he's afraid to." Her grandmother swallowed down the vodka and orange juice. Her eyes looked vague and watery. "And I don't ever want you talking about it with him."

Nest looked down at her plate. "I know."

The old woman reached across the table and took hold of her granddaughter's wrist. "Not with him, not with anyone. Not ever. There's good reason for this, Nest. You understand that, don't you?"

Nest nodded. "Yep, I do." She looked up at her grandmother. "But I don't like it much. I don't like being the only one."

Her grandmother squeezed her wrist tightly. "There's me. You can always talk to me." She released her grip and sat back. "Maybe one day your grandfather will be able to talk with you about it, too. But it's hard for him. People don't want to believe in magic. It's all they can do to make themselves believe in God. You can't see something, Nest, if you don't believe in it. Sometimes I think he just can't let himself believe, that believing just doesn't fit in with his view of things."

Nest was silent a moment, thinking. "Mom believed, though, didn't she?"

Her grandmother nodded wordlessly.

"What about my dad? Do you think he believed, too?"

The old woman reached for her cigarettes. "He believed."

Nest studied her grandmother, watched the way her fingers shook as she worked the lighter. "Do you think he will ever come back?"

"Your father? No."

"Maybe he'll want to see how I've turned out. Maybe he'll come back for that."

"Don't hold your breath."

Nest worried her lip. "I wonder sometimes who he is, Gran. I wonder what he looks like." She paused. "Do you ever wonder?"

Her grandmother drew in on the cigarette, her eyes hard and fixed on a point in space somewhere to Nest's left. "No. What would be the point?"

"He's not a forest creature, is he?"

She didn't know what made her ask such a question. She startled herself by even speaking the words. And the way her grandmother looked at her made her wish she had held her tongue.

"Why would you ever think that?" Evelyn Freemark snapped, her voice brittle and sharp, her eyes bright with anger.

Nest swallowed her surprise and shrugged. "I don't know. I just wondered, I guess."

Her grandmother looked at her for a long moment without blinking, then turned away. "Go make your bed. Then go out and play with your friends. Cass Minter has called you twice already. Lunch will be here if you want it. Dinner's at six. Go on."

Nest rose and carried her dishes to the sink. No one had ever told her anything about her father. No one seemed to know anything about him. But that didn't stop her from wondering. She had been told that her mother never revealed his identity, not even to her grandparents. But Nest suspected that Gran knew something about him anyway. It was in the way she avoided the subject—or became angry when he was mentioned. Why did she do that? What did she know that made her so uncomfortable? Maybe that was why Nest persisted in her questions about him, even silly ones like the one she had just asked. Her father couldn't be a forest creature. If he was, Nest would be a forest creature as well, wouldn't she?

"See you later, Gran," she said as she left the room.

She went down the hall to her room to shower and dress. There were all different kinds of forest creatures, Pick had told her once. Even if he hadn't told her exactly what they were. So did that mean there were some made of flesh and blood? Did it mean some were human, like her?

She stood naked in front of the bathroom mirror looking at herself for a long time before she got into the shower.

CHAPTER 3

Old Bob backed his weathered Ford pickup out of the garage, drove up the lane through the wide-boughed hardwoods, and turned onto Sinnissippi Road. In spite of the heat he had the windows rolled down and the air conditioner turned off because he liked to smell the woods. In his opinion, Sinnissippi Park was the most beautiful woods for miles—always had been, always would be. It was green and rolling where the cliffs rose above the Rock River, and the thick stands of shagbark hickory, white oak, red elm, and maple predated the coming of the white man into Indian territory. Nestled down within the spaces permitted by a thinning of the larger trees were walnut, cherry, birch, and a scattering of pine and blue spruce. There were wildflowers that bloomed in the spring and leaves that turned color in the fall that could make your heart ache. In Illinois, spring and fall were the seasons you waited for. Summer was just a bridge between the two, a three-to-four-month yearly preview of where you would end up if you were turned away from Heaven's gates, a ruinous time when Mother Nature cranked up the heat as high as it would go on the local thermostat and a million insects came out to feed. It wasn't like that every summer, and it wasn't like that every day of every summer, but it was like that enough that you didn't notice much of anything else. This summer was worse than usual, and today looked to be typical. The heat was intense already, even here in the woods, though not so bad beneath the canopy of the trees as it would be downtown. So Old Bob breathed in the scents of leaves and grasses and flowers and enjoyed the coolness of the shade as he drove the old truck toward the highway, reminding himself of what was good about his hometown on his way to his regular morning discussion of what wasn't.

The strike at Midwest Continental Steel had been going on for one hundred and seven days, and there was no relief in sight. This was bad news and not just for the company and the union. The mill employed twenty-five percent of the town's working population, and when twenty-five percent of a community's spending capital disappears, everyone suffers. MidCon was at one time the largest independently owned steel mill in the country, but after the son of the founder died and the heirs lost interest, it was sold to a consortium. That produced some bad feelings all by itself, even though one of the heirs stayed around as a nominal part of the company team. The bad feelings grew when the bottom fell out of the steel market in the late seventies and early eighties in the wake of the boom in foreign steel. The consortium underwent some management changes, the last member of the founding family was dismissed, the twenty-four-inch mill was shut down, and several hundred workers were laid off. Eventually some of the workers were hired back and the twenty-four-inch was started up again, but the bad feelings between management and union were by then so deep-seated and pervasive that neither side could bring itself ever again to trust the other.

The bad feelings had come to a head six months earlier, when the union had entered into negotiations for a new contract. A yearly cost-of-living increase in the hourly wage, better medical benefits, an expansion of what qualified as piecework, and a paid-holiday program were some of the demands on the union's agenda. A limited increase without escalators in the hourly wage over the next five years, a cutback in medical benefits, a narrowing down of the types of payments offered for piecework, and an elimination of paid holidays were high on the list of counter-demands made by the company. A deadlock was quickly reached. Arbitration was refused by both sides, each choosing to wait out the other. A strike deadline was set by the union. A back-to-work deadline was set by the company. As the deadlines neared and no movement was achieved in the bargaining process, both union and company went public with their grievances. Negotiators for each side kept popping up on television and radio to air out the particulars of the latest outrage perpetrated by the other. Soon both sides were talking to everyone but each other.

Then, one hundred and seven days ago, the union had struck the fourteen-inch and the wire mill. The strike soon escalated to include the twenty-four-inch and the twelve-inch, and then all of MidCon was shut down. At first no one worried much. There had been strikes before, and they had always resolved themselves. Besides, it was springtime, and with the passing of another bitterly cold Midwest winter, everyone was feeling hopeful and renewed. But a month went by and no progress was made. A mediator was called in at the behest of the mayor of Hopewell and the governor of the State of Illinois and with the blessing of both union and management, but he failed to make headway. A few ugly incidents on the picket line hardened feelings on both sides. By then, the effect of the strike was being felt by everyone—smaller companies who did business with the mill or used their products, retailers who relied on the money spent by the mill's employees, and professional people whose clientele was in large part composed of management and union alike. Everyone began to choose sides.

After two months, the company announced that it would no longer recognize the union and that it would accept back those workers who wished to return to their old jobs, but that if those workers failed to return in seven days, new people would be brought in to replace them. On June 1, it would start up the fourteen-inch mill using company supervisors as workers. The company called this action the first step in a valid decertification process; the union called it strikebreaking and union busting. The union warned against trying to use scabs in place of "real" workers, of trying to cross the picket line, of doing anything but continuing to negotiate with the union team. It warned that use of company people on the line was foolhardy and dangerous. Only trained personnel should attempt to operate the machinery. The company replied that it would provide whatever training was deemed necessary and suggested the union start bargaining in good faith.

From there, matters only got worse. The company started up the fourteen-inch several times, and each time shut it down again after only a few days. There were reports by the union of unnecessary injuries and by the company of sabotage. Replacement workers were bused in from surrounding cities, and fights took place on the picket line. The national guard was brought in on two occasions to restore order. Finally MidCon shut down again for good and declared that the workers were all fired and the company was for sale. All negotiations came to a halt. No one even bothered to pretend at making an effort anymore. Another month passed. The pickets continued, no one made any money, and the community of Hopewell and its citizens grew steadily more depressed.

Now, with the summer heat reaching record highs, spring's hopes were as dry as the dust that coated the roadways, and the bad feelings had burned down to white-hot embers.

Old Bob reached Lincoln Highway, turned on the lighted arrow off Sinnissippi Road, and headed for town. He passed the Kroger supermarket and the billboard put up six months ago by the Chamber of Commerce that read WELCOME TO HOPEWELL, ILLINOIS! WE'RE GROWING YOUR WAY! The billboard was faded and dust-covered in the dull shimmer of the late-morning heat, and the words seemed to mock the reality of things. Old Bob rolled up the windows and turned on the air. There weren't any smells from here on in that mattered to him.

He drove the combined four-lane to where it divided into a pair of one-ways, Fourth Street going west into town, Third Street coming east. He passed several fast-food joints, a liquor store, a pair of gas stations, Quik Dry Cleaners, Rock River Valley Printers, and an electrical shop. Traffic was light. The heat rose off the pavement in waves, and the leaves on the trees that lined the sidewalks hung limp in the windless air. The men and women of Hopewell were closeted in their homes and offices with the air conditioners turned on high, going about the business of their lives with weary determination. Unless summer school had claimed them, the kids were all out at the parks or swimming pools, trying to stay cool and keep from being bored. At night the temperature would drop ten to fifteen degrees and there might be a breeze, but still no one would be moving very fast. There was a somnolence to the community that suggested a long siesta in progress, a dullness of pace that whispered of despair.

Old Bob shook his head. Well, the Fourth of July was almost here, and the Fourth, with its fireworks and picnics and the dance in the park, might help take people's minds off their problems.

A few minutes later he pulled into a vacant parking space in front of Josie's and climbed out of the cab. The sun's brightness was so intense and the heat's swelter so thick that for a moment he felt light-headed. He gripped the parking mirror to steady himself, feeling old and foolish, trying desperately to pretend that nothing was wrong as he studied his feet. When he had regained his balance sufficiently to stand on his own, he walked to the parking meter, fed a few coins into the slot, moved to the front door of the coffee shop, and stepped inside.

Cold air washed over him, a welcome relief. Josie's occupied the corner of Second Avenue and Third Street across from the liquor store, the bank parking lot, and Hays Insurance. Windows running the length of both front walls gave a clear view of the intersection and those trudging to and from their air-conditioned offices and cars. Booths lined the windows, red leather fifties-era banquettes reupholstered and restitched. An L-shaped counter wrapped with stools was situated farther in, and a scattering of tables occupied the available floor space between. There were fresh-baked doughnuts, sweet rolls, and breads displayed in a glass case at the far end of the counter, and coffee, espresso, hot chocolate, tea, and soft drinks to wash those down. Josie's boasted black cows, green rivers, sarsaparillas, and the thickest shakes for miles. Breakfast was served anytime, and you could get lunch until three, when the kitchen closed. Takeout was available and frequently used. Josie's had the best daytime food in town, and almost everyone drifted in to sample it at least once or twice a week.

Old Bob and his union pals were there every day. Before the mill was shut down, only those who had retired came in on a regular basis, but now all of them showed up every morning without fail. Most were already there as Old Bob made his way to the back of the room and the clutch of tables those who had gotten there first had shoved together to accommodate late-comers. Old Bob waved, then detoured toward the service counter. Carol Blier intercepted him, asked how he was doing, and told him to stop by the office sometime for a chat. Old Bob nodded and moved on, feeling Carol's eyes following him, measuring his step. Carol sold life insurance.

"Well, there you are," Josie greeted from behind the counter, giving him her warmest smile. "Your buddies have been wondering if you were coming in."

Old Bob smiled back. "Have they now?"

"Sure. They can't spit and walk at the same time without you to show them how—you know that." Josie cocked one eyebrow playfully. "I swear you get better-looking every time I see you."

Old Bob laughed. Josie Jackson was somewhere in her thirties, a divorcée with a teenage daughter and a worthless ex-husband last seen heading south about half a dozen years ago. She was younger-looking than her years, certainly younger-acting, with big dark eyes and a ready smile, long blondish hair and a head-turning body, and most important of all a willingness to work that would put most people to shame. She had purchased Josie's with money loaned to her by her parents, who owned a carpet-and-tile business. Having worked much of her adult life as a waitress, Josie Jackson knew what she was doing, and in no time her business was the favorite breakfast and lunch spot in Hopewell. Josie ran it with charm and efficiency and a live-and-let-live attitude that made everyone feel welcome.

"How's Evelyn?" she asked him, leaning her elbows on the counter as she fixed him with her dark eyes.

He shrugged. "Same as always. Rock of ages."

"Yeah, she'll outlive us all, won't she?" Josie brushed at her tousled hair. "Well, go on back. You want your usual?"

Old Bob nodded, and Josie moved away. If he'd been younger and unattached, Old Bob would have given serious consideration to hooking up with Josie Jackson. But then that was the way all the old codgers felt, and most of the young bucks, too. That was Josie's gift.

He eased through the clustered tables, stopping for a brief word here and there, working his way back to where the union crowd was gathered. They glanced up as he approached, one after the other, giving him perfunctory nods or calling out words of greeting. Al Garcia, Mel Riorden, Derry Howe, Richie Stoudt, Penny Williamson, Mike Michaelson, Junior Elway, and one or two more. They made room for him at one end of the table, and he scooted a chair over and took a seat, sinking comfortably into place.

"So this guy, he works in a post office somewhere over in Iowa, right?" Mel Riorden was saying. He was a big, overweight crane operator with spiky red hair and a tendency to blink rapidly while he was speaking. He was doing so now. Like one of those ads showing how easy it is to open and close a set of blinds. Blink, blink,

blink. "He comes to work in a dress. No, this is the God's honest truth. It was right there in the paper. He comes to work in a dress."

"What color of dress?" Richie Stoudt interrupted, looking genuinely puzzled, not an unusual expression for Richie.

Riorden looked at him. "What the hell difference does that make? It's a dress, on a man who works in a post office, Richie! Think about it! Anyway, he comes to work, this guy, and his supervisor sees the dress and tells him he can't work like that, he has to go home and change. So he does. And he comes back wearing a different dress, a fur coat, and a gorilla mask. The supervisor tells him to go home again, but this time he won't leave. So they call the police and haul him away. Charge him with disturbing the peace or something. But this is the best part. Afterward, the supervisor tells a reporter—this is true, now, I swear—tells the reporter, with a straight face, that they are considering psychiatric evaluation for the guy. *Considering!*"

"You know, I read about a guy who took his monkey to the emergency room a few weeks back." Albert Garcia picked up the conversation. He was a small, solid man with thinning dark hair and close-set features, a relative newcomer to the group, having come up from Houston with his family to work at MidCon less than ten years ago. Before the strike, he set the rolls in the fourteen-inch. "The monkey was his pet, and it got sick or something. So he hauls it down to the emergency room. This was in Arkansas, I think. Tells the nurse it's his baby. Can you imagine? His baby!"

"Did it look anything like him?" Mel Riorden laughed.

"This isn't the same guy, is it?" Penny Williamson asked suddenly. He was a bulky, heavy-featured black man with skin that shone almost as blue as oiled steel. He was a foreman in the number-three plant, steady and reliable. He shifted his heavy frame slightly and winked knowingly at Old Bob. "You know, the postal-worker guy again?"

Al Garcia looked perplexed. "I don't think so. Do you think it could be?"

"So what happened?" Riorden asked as he bit into a fresh Danish. His eyes blinked like a camera shutter. He rearranged the sizable mound of sweet rolls he had piled on a plate in front of him, already choosing his next victim.

"Nothing." Al Garcia shrugged. "They fixed up the monkey and sent him home."

"That's it? That's the whole story?" Riorden shook his head.

Al Garcia shrugged again. "I just thought it was bizarre, that's all."

"I think you're bizarre." Riorden looked away dismissively. "Hey, Bob, what news from the east end this fine morning?"

Old Bob accepted with a nod the coffee and sweet roll Josie scooted in front of him. "Nothing you don't already know. It's hot at that end of town, too. Any news from the mill?"

"Same old, same old. The strike goes on. Life goes on. Everybody keeps on keeping on."

"I been getting some yard work out at Joe Preston's," Richie Stoudt offered, but everyone ignored him, because if brains were dynamite he didn't have enough to blow his nose.

"I'll give you some news," Junior Elway said suddenly. "There's some boys planning to cross the picket line if they can get their jobs back. It was just a few at first, but I think there's more of them now."

Old Bob considered him wordlessly for a moment. Junior was not the most reliable of sources. "That so, Junior? I don't think the company will allow it, after all that's happened."

"They'll allow it, all right," Derry Howe cut in. He was a tall, angular man with close-cropped hair and an intense, suspicious stare that made people wonder. He'd been a bit strange as a boy, and two tours in Vietnam hadn't improved things. Since Nam, he'd lost a wife, been arrested any number of times for drinking and driving, and spotted up his mill record until it looked like someone had sneezed into an inkwell. Old Bob couldn't understand why they hadn't fired him. He was erratic and error-prone, and those who knew him best thought he wasn't rowing with all his oars in the water. Junior Elway was the only friend he had, which was a dubious distinction. He was allowed to hang out with this group only because he was Mel Riorden's sister's boy.

"What do you mean?" Al Garcia asked quickly.

"I mean, they'll allow it because they're going to start up the fourteen-inch again over the weekend and have it up and running by Tuesday. Right after the Fourth. I got it from a friend on the inside." Howe's temple pulsed and his lips tightened. "They want to break the union, and this is their best chance. Get the company running again without us."

"Been tried already." Al Garcia sniffed.

"So now it's gonna get tried again. Think about it, Al. What have they got to lose?"

"No one from the union is going back to help them do it," Penrod Williamson declared, glowering at Howe. "That's foolish talk."

"You don't think there's enough men out there with wives and children to feed that this ain't become more important to them than the strike?" Howe snapped. He brushed at his close-cropped hair. "You ain't paying attention then, Penny. The bean counters have taken over, and guys like us, we're history! You think the national's going to bail us out of this? Hell! The company's going to break the union and we're sitting here letting them do it!"

"Well, it's not like there's a lot else we can do, Derry," Mel Riorden pointed out, easing his considerable weight back in his metal frame chair. "We've struck and picketed and that's all the law allows us. And the national's doing what it can. We just have to be patient. Sooner or later this thing will get settled."

"How's that gonna happen, Mel?" Howe pressed, flushed with anger. "Just how the hell's that gonna happen? You see any negotiating going on? I sure as hell don't! Striking and picketing is fine, but it ain't getting us anywhere. These people running the show, they ain't from here. They don't give a rat's ass what happens to us. If you think they do, well you're a damn fool!"

"He's got a point," Junior Elway agreed, leaning forward over his coffee, nodding solemnly, lank blond hair falling into his face. Old Bob pursed his lips. Junior always thought Derry Howe had a point.

"Damn right!" Howe was rolling now, his taut features shoved forward, dominating the table. "You think we're going to win this thing by sitting around bullshitting each other? Well, we ain't! And there ain't no one else gonna help us either. We have to do this ourselves, and we have to do it quick. We have to make them hurt more than we're hurting. We have to pick their pocket the way they're picking ours!"

"What're you talking about?" Penny Williamson growled. He had less use for Derry Howe than any of them; he'd once had Howe booted off his shift.

Howe glared at him. "You think about it, Mr. Penrod Williamson. You were in the Nam, too. Hurt them worse than they hurt you, that was how you survived. That's how you get anywhere in a war."

"We ain't in a war here," Penny Williamson observed, his finger pointed at Howe. "And the Nam's got nothing to do with this. What're you saying, man? That we ought to go down to the mill and blow up a few of the enemy? You want to shoot someone while you're at it?"

Derry Howe's fist crashed down on the table. "If that's what it takes, hell yes!"

There was sudden silence. A few heads turned. Howe was shaking with anger as he leaned back in his chair, refusing to look away. Al Garcia wiped at his spilled coffee with his napkin and shook his head. Mel Riorden checked his watch.

Penny Williamson folded his arms across his broad chest, regarding Derry Howe the way he might have regarded that postal worker in his dress, fur coat, and gorilla mask. "You better watch out who you say that to."

"Derry's just upset," said a man sitting next to him. Old Bob hadn't noticed the fellow before. He had blue eyes that were so pale they seemed washed of color. "His job's on the line, and the company doesn't even know he's alive. You can understand how he feels. No need for us to be angry with each other. We're all friends here."

"Yeah, Derry don't mean nothing," Junior Elway agreed.

"What do you think we ought to do?" Mike Michaelson asked Robert Roosevelt Freemark suddenly, trying to turn the conversation another way.

Old Bob was still looking at the man next to Howe, trying to place him. The bland, smooth features were as familiar to him as his own, but for some reason he couldn't think of his name. It was right on the tip of his tongue, but he couldn't get a handle on it. Nor could he remember exactly what it was the fellow did. He was a mill man, all right. Too young to be retired, so he must be one of the strikers. But where did he know him from? The others seemed to know him, so why couldn't he place him?

His gaze shifted to Michaelson, a tall, gaunt, even-tempered millwright who had retired about the same time Old Bob had. Old Bob had known Mike all his life, and he recognized at once that Mike was trying to give Derry Howe a chance to cool down.

"Well, I think we need a stronger presence from the national office," he said. "Derry's right about that much." He folded his big hands on the table before him and looked down at them. "I think we need some of the government people to do more—maybe a senator or two to intervene so we can get things back on track with the negotiations."

"More talk!" Derry Howe barely hid a sneer.

"Talk is the best way to go," Old Bob advised, giving him a look.

"Yeah? Well, it ain't like it was in your time, Bob Freemark. We ain't got local owners anymore, people with a stake in the community, people with families that live here like the rest of us. We got a bunch of New York bloodsuckers draining all the money out of Hopewell, and they don't care about us." Derry Howe slouched in his chair, eyes downcast. "We got to do something if we expect to survive this. We can't just sit around hoping for someone to help us. It ain't going to happen."

"There was a fellow out East somewhere, one of the major cities, Philadelphia, I think," said the man sitting next to him, his strange pale eyes quizzical, his mouth quirked slightly, as if his words amused him. "His wife died, leaving him with a five-year-old daughter who was mildly retarded. He kept her in a closet off the living room for almost three years before someone discovered what he was doing and called the police. When they questioned the man, he said he was just trying to protect the girl from a hostile world." The man cocked his head slightly. "When they asked the girl why she hadn't tried to escape, she said she was afraid to run, that all she could do was wait for someone to help her."

"Well, they ain't shutting me up in no closet!" Derry Howe snapped angrily. "I can help myself just fine!"

"Sometimes," the man said, looking at no one in particular, his voice low and compelling, "the locks get turned before you even realize that the door's been closed."

"I think Bob's right," Mike Michaelson said. "I think we have to give the negotiation process a fair chance. These things take time."

"Time that costs us money and gives them a better chance to break us!" Derry Howe shoved back his chair and came to his feet. "I'm outta here. I got better things to do than sit around here all day. I'm sick of talking and doing nothing. Maybe you don't care if the company takes away your job, but I ain't having none of it!"

He stalked away, weaving angrily through the crowded tables, and slammed the door behind him. At the counter, Josie Jackson grimaced. A moment later, Junior Elway left as well. The men still seated at the table shifted uncomfortably in their chairs.

"I swear, if that boy wasn't my sister's son, I wouldn't waste another moment on him," Melvin Riorden muttered.

"He's right about one thing," Old Bob sighed. "Things aren't the way they used to be. The world's changed from when we were his age, and a lot of it's gotten pretty ugly. People don't want to work things out anymore like they used to."

"People just want a pound of flesh," Al Garcia agreed. His blocky head pivoted on his bull neck. "It's all about money and getting your foot on the other guy's neck. That's why the company and the union can't settle anything. Makes you wonder if the government hasn't put something in the water after all."

"You see where that man went into a grocery store out on Long Island somewhere and walked up and down the aisles stabbing people?" asked Penny Williamson. "Had two carving knives with him, one in each hand. He never said a word, just walked in and began stabbing people. He stabbed ten of them before someone stopped him. Killed two. The police say he was angry and depressed. Well, hell, who ain't?"

"The world's full of angry, depressed people," said Mike Michaelson, rearranging his coffee cup and silver, staring down at his sun-browned, wrinkled hands fixedly. "Look what people are doing to each other. Parents beating and torturing their children. Young boys and girls killing each other. Teachers and priests taking advantage of their position to do awful things. Serial killers wandering the countryside. Churches and schools being vandalized and burned. It's a travesty."

"Some of those people you talk about live right here in Hopewell." Penny Williamson grunted. "That Topp kid who killed his common-law wife with a butcher knife and cut her up in pieces a few years back? I grew up with that kid. Old man Peters killed all those horses two weeks back, said they were the spawn of Satan. Tilda Mason, tried to kill herself three times over the past six months—twice in the mental hospital. Tried to kill a couple of the people working there as well. That fellow Riley Crisp, the one they call 'rabbit' lives down on Wallace? He stood out on the First Avenue Bridge and shot at people until the police came, then shot at them, and then jumped off the bridge and drowned himself. When was that? Last month?" He shook his head. "Where's it all going to end, I wonder?"

Old Bob smoothed back his white hair. None of them had the answer to that one. It made him wonder suddenly about Evelyn and her feeders. Might just as easily be feeders out there as something the government had put in the water.

He noticed suddenly that the man who had been sitting with Derry Howe was gone. His brow furrowed and his wide mouth tightened. When had the man left? He tried again to think of his name and failed.

"I got me some more work to do out at Preston's," Richie Stoudt advised solemnly. "You can laugh, but it keeps bread on the table."

The conversation returned to the strike and the intractable position of the company, and the stories started up again, and a moment later Old Bob had forgotten the man completely.

CHAPTER 4

The demon stepped out into the midday heat in front of Josie's and felt right at home. Perhaps it was his madness that made him so comfortable with the sun's brilliant white light and suffocating swelter, for it was true that it burned as implacably hot. Or perhaps it was his deep and abiding satisfaction at knowing that this community and its inhabitants were his to do with as he chose.

He followed Derry Howe and Junior Elway to the latter's Jeep Cherokee and climbed into the cab with them, sitting comfortably in the backseat, neither one of them quite aware that he was there. It was one of the skills he had acquired—to blend in so thoroughly with his surroundings that he seemed to be a part of them, to make himself appear so familiar that even those sitting right beside him felt no need to question his presence. He supposed there was still just enough of them in him that he was able to accomplish this. He had been human once himself, but that was long ago and all but forgotten. What remained of his humanity was just a shadow of a memory of what these creatures were, so that he could appear and act like them to the extent that his duplicity required it. His gradual transformation from human to demon had driven out the rest. He had found, after a time, that he did not miss it.

Junior turned over the Jeep's engine and switched on the air, blowing a thick wash of heat through the vents and into the closed interior. Junior and Derry rolled down their windows to let the heat escape as the Jeep pulled away from the curb, but the demon just breathed in contentedly and smiled. He had been in Hopewell a little more than a week, not wanting to come any sooner because John Ross still tracked him relentlessly and had displayed a disturbing ability to locate him even when there was no possible way he should have been able to do so. But a week had gone by, the Fourth of July approached, and it seemed possible that this time Ross might prove a step too slow. It was important that Ross not interfere, for the demon had sown his destructive seed deep and waited long for it to grow. Now the seed's harvest was at hand, and the demon did not want any interference. Everything was in place, everything that he had worked so long and hard to achieve—a clever subterfuge, an apocalyptic ruin, and an irreversible transformation that would hasten the coming of the Void and the banishment of the Word.

His mind spun with the possibilities as the Jeep turned off Second Avenue onto Fourth Street and headed west out of town. On his left the long, dark, corrugated-metal roofs of MidCon Steel could be glimpsed through gaps in the rows of the once-elegant old homes that ran the length of West Third coming in toward town from several blocks above Avenue G. The air-conditioning had kicked in, and with the windows rolled up again the demon took comfort instead from his inner heat.

His passion enveloped him, a cocoon into which he could retreat and from which he could feed, a red haze of intolerance and hate and greed for power.

"Those old boys don't know nothing," Derry Howe was saying, slouched back in his bucket seat, his bullet head shining in the sun. "I don't plan to listen to them no more. All they do is sit around and talk about sitting around some more. Old farts."

"Yeah, they ain't seeing it like it is," Junior agreed.

No, not like you, thought the demon contentedly. *Not with the bright, clear knowledge I have given to you.*

"We got to do something if we want to keep our jobs," Derry said. "We got to stop the company from breaking the union, and we got to stop them right now."

"Yeah, but how we gonna do that?" Junior asked, glancing over uncertainly, then gunning the Jeep through a yellow light turning red.

"Oh, there's ways. There's ways, buddy."

Yes, there are lots and lots of ways.

Derry Howe looked over at Junior, smiling. "You know what they say? Where there's a will, there's a way. Well, I've got me a will that won't quit. I just need me a way. I'm gonna find it, too, and you can take that to the bank! Old Bob and those others can go shove their patience where the sun don't shine."

They crossed Avenue G past the tire center, gas station, and west-end grocery and rode farther toward the cornfields. The buildings of the mill were still visible down the cross streets and between the old homes, plant three giving way to plant four, plant five still out ahead, back of the old speedway, the whole of MidCon spread out along the north bank of the Rock River. The demon studied the residences and the people they sped past, his for the taking, his to own, dismissing them almost as quickly as they were considered. This was a breeding ground for him and nothing more. On July fourth, all of it and all of them would pass into the hands of the feeders, and he would be on his way to another place. It was his world, too, but he felt no attachment to it. His work was what drove him, what gave him purpose, and his servitude to the dark, chaotic vision of the Void would allow for nothing else. There were in his life only need and compulsion, those to be satisfied through a venting of his madness, and nothing of his physical surroundings or of the creatures that inhabited them had any meaning for him.

The Jeep passed a junkyard of rusting automobile carcasses piled high behind a chain-link fence bordering a trailer park that looked to be the last stop of transients on their way to homelessness or the grave, and from behind the fence a pair of lean, black-faced Dobermans peered out with savage eyes. Bred to attack anything that intruded, the demon thought. Bred to destroy. He liked that.

His mind drifted in the haze of the midday summer heat, the voices of Derry and Junior a comfortable buzz that did not intrude. He had come to Hopewell afoot, walking out of the swelter of the cornfields and the blacktop roadways with the inexorable certainty of nightfall. He had chosen to appear in that manner, wanting to smell and taste the town, wanting it to give something of itself to him, something it could not give if he arrived by car or bus, if he were to be closed away. He had materialized in the manner of a mirage, given shape and form out of delusion and desperation, given life out of false hope. He had walked into a poor neighborhood on the fringe of the town, into a collection of dilapidated homes patched with tar paper and oilcloth, their painted wooden sides peeling, their shingled roofs cracked and blistered, their yards rutted and littered with ruined toys, discarded appliances, and rusting vehicles. Within the close, airless confines of the homes huddled the leavings of despair and endless disappointment. Children played beneath the shade of the trees, dust-covered, desultory, and joyless. Already they knew what the future would bring. Already their childhood was ending. The demon passed them with a smile.

At the corner of Avenue J and Twelfth Street, at a confluence of crumbling sheds, pastureland, and a few scattered residences, a boy had stood at the edge of the roadway with a massive dog. At well over a hundred pounds, all bristling hair and wicked dark markings, the dog was neither one identifiable breed nor another, but some freakish combination. It stood next to the boy, hooked on one end of a chain, the other end of which the boy held. Its eyes were deep-set and baleful, and its stance suggested a barely restrained fury. It disliked the demon instinctively, as all animals did, but it was frightened of him, too. The boy was in his early teens, wearing blue jeans, a T-shirt, and high-top tennis shoes, all of them worn and stained with dirt. The boy's stance, like the dog's, was at once strained and cocky. He was tall and heavyset, and there was no mistaking the bully in him. Most of what he had gotten in life he had acquired through intimidation or theft. When he smiled, as he did now, there was no warmth.

"Hey, you," the boy said.

The demon's bland face showed nothing. Just another stupid, worthless creature, the demon thought as he approached. Just another failed effort in somebody's failed life. He would leave his mark here, with this boy, to signal his coming, to lay claim to what was now his. He would do so in blood.

"You want to go through here, you got to pay me a dollar," the boy called out to the demon.

The demon stopped where he was, right in the middle of the road, the sun beating down on him. "A dollar?"

"Yeah, that's the toll. Else you got to go around the other way."

The demon looked up the street the way he had come, then back at the boy. "This is a public street."

"Not in front of my house it ain't. In front of my house, it's a toll road and it costs a dollar to pass."

"Only if you're traveling on foot, I guess. Not if you're in a car. I don't suppose that even a dog as mean as yours could stop a car." The boy stared at him, uncomprehending. The demon shrugged. "So, does the dog collect the dollar for you?"

"The dog collects a piece of your ass if you don't pay!" the boy snapped irritably. "You want to see what that feels like?"

The demon studied the boy silently for a moment. "What's the dog's name?"

"It don't matter what his name is! Just pay me the dollar!" The boy's face was flushed and angry.

"Well, if I don't know his name," said the demon softly, "how can I call him off if he attacks someone?"

The dog sensed the boy's anger, and his hackles rose along the back of his neck and he bared his teeth with a low growl. "You just better give me the dollar, buddy," said the boy, a thin smile twisting his lips as he looked down at the dog and jiggled the chain meaningfully.

"Oh, I don't think I could do that," said the demon. "I don't carry any money. I don't have any need for it. People just give me what I want. I don't even need a dog like this one to make them do it." He smiled, his bland features crinkling warmly, his strange eyes fixing the boy. "That's not very good news for you, is it?"

The boy was staring at him. "You better pay me fast, butthead, or I might just let go of this chain!"

The demon shook his head reprovingly. "I wouldn't do that, if I were you. I'd keep a tight hold on that chain until I'm well down the road from here." He slipped his hands in his pockets and cocked his head at the boy. "Tell you what. I'm a fair man. You just made a big mistake, but I'm willing to let it pass. I'll forget all about it if you apologize. Just say you're sorry and that will be the end of it."

The boy's mouth dropped. "What? What did you say?"

The demon smiled some more. "You heard me."

For an instant the boy froze, the disbelief on his face apparent. Then he mouthed a string of obscenities, dropped to his knee, and released the chain on the dog's collar. "Oops!" he snarled at the demon, flinging the chain away disdainfully, eyes hot and furious.

But the demon had already invoked his skill, a small, spare movement of one hand that looked something like the blessing of a minister at the close of a service. Outwardly, nothing seemed to change. The demon still stood there in the sweltering heat, head cocked in seeming contemplation, bland face expressionless. The boy lurched to his feet as he released the dog, urging him to the attack with an angry shout. But something profound had changed in the boy. His look and smell and movement had become those of a frightened rabbit, flushed from cover and desperately trying to scurry to safety. The dog reacted on instinct. It wheeled on the boy instantly, lunging for his throat. The boy gave a cry of shock and fear as the dog slammed into him, knocking him from his feet. The boy's hands came up as he tumbled into the dirt of his yard, and he tried desperately to shield his face. The dog tore at the boy, and the boy's cries turned to screams. Drops of blood flew through the air. Scarlet threads laced the dusty earth.

The demon stood watching for several moments more before turning away to continue down the road. He read later that if the boy's body hadn't been found in front of his house, the authorities would have needed dental records to identify him. His family couldn't recognize him from what was left of his face. The dog, which one of the neighbors described as the boy's best friend, was quarantined for the mandatory ten days to determine if it had rabies and then put down.

Junior Elway pulled the Jeep Cherokee against the curb in front of the dilapidated apartment complex situated on Avenue L and West Third where Derry Howe rented a small, one-bedroom unit. They talked for a moment while the demon listened, agreeing to meet at Scrubby's for pizza and beer that evening. Both were divorced, on the downside of forty, and convinced that a lot of women were missing a good bet. Derry Howe climbed out of the Jeep, and the demon climbed out with him. Together they went up the walk as Junior Elway drove off.

Inside the apartment, the window fan was rattling and buzzing as it fought to withstand the heat. It was not adequate to the task, and the air in the apartment was close and warm. Derry Howe walked to the refrigerator, pulled out a can of Bud, walked back to the living room, and flopped down on the sofa. He was supposed to be on picket duty at the number-three plant, but he had begged off the night before by claiming that his back was acting up. His union supervisor had probably known he was lying, but had chosen to let it slide. Derry was encouraged. Already he was wondering if he could pull the same scam for Sunday's shift.

The demon sat in the rocker that had belonged to Derry Howe's grandmother before she died, the one his mother had inherited and in turn passed on to him when he was married and she still had hopes for him. Now no one had any hopes for Derry Howe. Two tours in Vietnam followed by his failed marriage to a girl some thought would change him, a dozen arrests on various charges, some jail time served at the county lockup, and twenty years at MidCon with only one promotion and a jacket full of reprimands had pretty much settled the matter. The road that marked the course of his life had straightened and narrowed, and all that remained to be determined was how far it would run and how many more breakdowns he would suffer along the way.

It had not proved difficult for the demon to find Derry Howe. Really, there were so many like him that it scarcely took any effort at all. The demon had found him on the second day of his arrival in Hopewell, just by visiting the coffee shops and bars, just by listening to what the people of the town had to say. He had moved in with Howe right away, making himself an indispensable presence in the other's life, insinuating himself into the other's thoughts, twisting Derry's mind until he had begun to think and talk in the ways that were necessary. Hardly a challenge, but definitely a requirement if the demon's plans were to succeed. He was Derry Howe's shadow now, his conscience, his sounding board, his devil's advocate. His own, personal demon. And Derry Howe, in turn, was his creature.

The demon watched Howe finish his beer, struggle up in the stale air of the apartment, walk to the kitchen, and fish through the cluttered refrigerator for another. The demon waited patiently. The demon's life was wedded to his cause, and his cause required great patience. He had sacrificed everything to become what he was, but he knew from his transformation at the hands of the Void that sacrifice was required. After he had embraced the Void he had concealed himself until his conscience had rotted and fallen away and left him free. His name had been lost. His history had faded. His humanity had dissipated and turned to dust. All that he had been had disappeared with the change, so that now he was reborn into his present life and made over into his higher form. It had been hard in the beginning, and once, in a moment of great weakness and despair, he had even thought to reject what he had so readily embraced. But in the end reason had prevailed, and he had forsaken all.

Now it was the cause that drove him, that fed him, that gave him his purpose in life. The cause was everything, and the Void defined the cause as need required. For now, for this brief moment in time, the cause was the destruction of this town and its inhabitants. It was the release of the feeders that lurked in the caves beneath Sinnissippi Park. It was the subversion of Derry Howe. It was the infusion of chaos and madness into the sheltered world of Hopewell.

And it was one thing more, the thing that mattered most.

Derry Howe returned to the sofa and seated himself with a grunt, sipping at his beer. He looked at the demon, seeing him clearly for the first time because the demon was ready now to talk.

"We got to do something, bud," Derry Howe intoned solemnly, nodding to emphasize the importance of his pronouncement. "We got to stop those suckers before they break us."

The demon nodded in response. "If union men cross the picket line and return to work, the strike is finished."

"Can't let them do that." Howe worked his big hands around the beer bottle, twisting slowly. "Damn traitors, anyway! What the hell they think they're doing, selling out the rest of us!"

"What to do?" mused the demon.

"Shoot a few, by God! That'll show them we mean business!"

The demon considered the prospect. "But that might not stop the others from going back to work. And you would go to jail. You wouldn't be of any use then, would you?"

Derry Howe frowned. He took a long drink out of the bottle. "So what's the answer, bud? We have to do something."

"Think about it like this," suggested the demon, having already done so long ago. "The company plans to reopen the fourteen-inch using company men to fill the skill jobs and scabs to fill the gaps. If they can open one plant and bring back a few of the union men, they can work at opening the others as well. It will snowball on you, if they can just get one mill up and running."

Howe nodded, his face flushed and intense. "Yeah, so?"

The demon smiled, drawing him in. "So, what happens if the company can't open the number-three plant? What happens if they can't get the fourteen-inch up and running?"

Derry Howe stared at him wordlessly, thinking it through.

The demon gave him a hand. "What happens if it becomes clear to everyone that it's dangerous to cross the picket line and work in the mills? What happens, Derry?"

"Yeah, right." A light came on somewhere behind Derry Howe's flat eyes. "No one crosses the line and the strike continues and the company has to give in. Yeah, I get it. But why wouldn't they start up the fourteen-inch? All they need's the workers. Unless . . ."

The demon spoke the words for him, in his own voice, almost as if in his own mind. "Unless there is an accident."

"An accident," breathed Derry Howe. Excitement lit his rawboned features. "A really bad accident."

"It happens sometimes," said the demon.

"Yeah, it does, doesn't it? An accident. Maybe someone even gets killed. Yeah."

"Think about it," said the demon. "Something will come to you."

Derry Howe was smiling, his mind racing. He drank his beer and mulled over the possibilities the demon's words had suggested to him. It would take little effort from here. A few more nudges. One good push in the right direction. Howe had been a demolitions man in Vietnam. It wouldn't take much for him to figure out how to use that knowledge here. It wouldn't even take courage. It required stupidity and blind conviction, and Derry Howe had plenty of both. That was why the demon had picked him.

The demon leaned back in the rocker and looked away, suddenly bored. What happened with Derry Howe was of such little importance. He was just another match waiting to be struck. Perhaps he would catch fire. You never knew. The demon had learned a long time ago that an explosion resulted most often from an accumulation of sparks. It was a lesson that had served him well. Derry Howe was one of several sparks the demon would strike over the next three days. Some were bound to catch fire; some might even explode. But, in the final analysis, they were all just diversions intended to draw attention away from the demon's real purpose in coming to this tiny, insignificant Midwestern town. If things went the way he intended—and he had every reason to think they would—he would be gone before anyone had any idea at all of his interest in the girl.

And by then, of course, it would be too late to save her.

Chapter 5

Nest Freemark went down the back steps two at a time, letting the screen door slam shut behind her. She winced at the sound, belatedly remembering how much it irritated Gran. She always forgot to catch the door. She didn't know why, she just did. She skipped off the gravel walk and onto the lawn, heading across the yard for the park. Mr. Scratch lay stretched out in the shade beneath the closest oak, a white and orange tom, his fluffy sides rising and falling with each labored breath. He was thirteen or fourteen, and he slept most of the time now, dreaming his cat dreams. He didn't even look up at her as she passed, his eyes closed, his ragged ears and scarred face a worn mask of contentment. He had long ago forfeited his mouser duties to the younger and sprier Miss Minx, who, as usual, was nowhere to be seen. Nest smiled at the old cat as she passed. Not for him the trials and tribulations of dealing with the feeders of Sinnissippi Park.

Nest had always known about the feeders. Or at least for as long as she could remember. Even when she hadn't known what they were, she had known they were there. She would catch glimpses of them sometimes, small movements seen out of the corner of one eye, bits and pieces of shadow that didn't quite fit in with their surroundings. She was very small then and not allowed out of the house alone, so she would stand at the windows at twilight, when the feeders were most likely to reveal themselves, and keep watch.

Sometimes her grandmother would take her for walks in the stroller in the cool of the evening, following the dark ribbon of the roadway as it wound through the park, and she would see them then as well. She would point, her eyes shifting to find her grandmother, her child's face solemn and inquisitive, and her grandmother would nod and say, "Yes, I see them. But you don't have to worry, Nest. They won't bother you."

Nor had they, although Nest had never really worried about it much back then. Not knowing what the feeders were, she simply assumed they were like the other creatures that lived in the park—the birds, squirrels, mice, chipmunks, deer, and what have you. Her grandmother never said anything about the feeders, never offered any explanation for them, never even seemed to pay them much attention. When Nest would point, she would always say the same thing and then let the matter drop. Several times Nest mentioned the feeders to her grandfather, but he just stared at her, glanced at her grandmother, and then smiled his most indulgent smile.

"He can't see them," her grandmother told her finally. "There's no point talking about it with him, Nest. He just doesn't see them."

"Why doesn't he?" she had asked, mystified.

"Because most people don't. Most people don't even know they exist. Only a lucky few can see them." She leaned close and touched the tip of Nest's small nose.

"You and me, we can. But not Robert. Not your grandfather. He can't see them at all."

She hadn't said why that was. Her explanations were always like that, spare and laconic. She hadn't time for a lot of words, except when she was reading, which she did a lot. On her feet she was all movement and little talk, losing herself in her household tasks or her gardening or her walks in the park. That was then, of course. It wasn't the same anymore, because now Gran was older and drank more and didn't move around much at all. Small, gnarled, and gray, she sat at the kitchen table smoking her cigarettes and drinking her vodka and orange juice until noon and, afterward, her bourbon on the rocks until dusk. She still didn't say much, even when she could have, keeping what she knew to herself, keeping her explanations and her secrets carefully tucked away somewhere deep inside.

She told Nest early on not to talk about the feeders. She was quite emphatic about it. She did so about the same time she told the little girl that only the two of them could see the feeders, so there wasn't any point in discussing them with her grandfather. Or with anybody else, she amended soon after, apparently concerned that the increasingly talkative child might think to do so.

"It will just make people wonder about you," she declared. "It will make them think you are a bit strange. Because you can see the feeders and they can't. Think of the feeders as a secret that only you and I know about. Can you do that, Nest?"

Pretty much, she found she could. But the lack of a more thorough explanation on the matter was troubling and frustrating, and eventually Nest tested her grandmother's theory about other people's attitudes on a couple of her friends. The results were exactly as her grandmother had predicted. Her friends first teased her and then ran to their parents with the tale. Their parents called her grandmother, and her grandmother was forced to allay their concerns with an overly convoluted explanation centered around the effects of fairy tales and make-believe on a child's imagination. Nest was very thoroughly dressed down. She was made to go back to her friends and their parents and to apologize for scaring them. She was five years old when that happened. It was the last time she told anyone about the feeders.

Of course, that was just the first of a number of secrets she learned to conceal about the creatures who lived in the park. Don't talk about the feeders, her grandmother had warned, and in the end she did not. But there were a lot of other things she couldn't talk about either, and for a while it seemed there was something new every time she turned around.

"Do you think the feeders would ever hurt me, Gran?" she asked once, disturbed by something she had seen in one of her picture books that reminded her of the furtiveness of their movements in the shadows of summer twilight and the dismal gloom of midday winter. "If they had the chance, I mean?"

They were alone, sitting at the kitchen table playing dominoes on a cold midwinter Sunday, her grandfather ensconced in his den, listening to a debate over foreign aid.

Her grandmother looked up at her, her bright, darkly luminescent bird's eyes fixed and staring. "If they had the chance, yes. But that will never happen."

Nest frowned. "Why not?"

"Because you are my granddaughter."

Nest frowned some more. "What difference does that make?"

"All the difference" was the reply. "You and I have magic, Nest. Didn't you know?"

"Magic?" Nest had breathed the word in disbelief. "Why? Why do we have magic, Gran?"

Her grandmother smiled secretively. "We just do, child. But you can't tell anyone. You have to keep it to yourself."

"Why?"

"You know why. Now, go on, it's your turn, make your play. Don't talk about it anymore."

That was the end of the matter as far as her grandmother was concerned, and she didn't mention it again. Nest tried to bring it up once or twice, but her grandmother always made light of the matter, as if having magic was nothing, as if it were the same as being brown-eyed or right-handed. She never explained what she meant by it, and she never provided any evidence that it was so. Nest thought she was making it up, the same way she made up fairy tales now and then to amuse the little girl. She was doing it to keep Nest from worrying about the feeders. Magic, indeed, Nest would think, then point her fingers at the wall and try unsuccessfully to make something happen.

But then she discovered Wraith, and the subject of magic suddenly took on a whole new meaning. It was when she was still five, shortly after her attempt at telling her friends about the feeders and almost a year before she met Pick. She was playing in her backyard on the swing set, pretending at flying as she rose and fell at the end of the creaking chains, comfortably settled in the cradle of the broad canvas strap. It was a late-spring day, the air cool yet with winter's fading breath, the grass new and dappled with jack-in-the-pulpit and bleeding heart, the leaves on the oaks and elms beginning to bud. Heavy clouds scudded across the Midwest skies, bringing rain out of the western plains, and the sunlight was pale and thin. Her grandparents were busy inside, and since she was forbidden to leave the yard without them and had never done so before, there was no reason for them to believe she would do so now.

But she did. She got down out of the swing and walked to the end of the yard where the hedgerow was still thin with new growth, slipped through a gap in the intertwined limbs, and stepped onto forbidden ground. She didn't know exactly what it was that prompted her to do so. It had something to do with thinking about the feeders, with picturing them as they appeared and faded in shadowy patches along the fringes of her yard. She wondered about them constantly, and on this day she simply decided to have a look. Did they conceal themselves on the other side of the hedge, just beyond her view? Did they burrow into the ground like moles? What did they do back there where she couldn't see? Why, her inquisitive five-year-old mind demanded, shouldn't she try to find out?

So there she was, standing at the edge of the park, staring out across the broad, flat, grassy expanse of ball diamonds and picnic grounds to where the bluffs rose south and the wooded stretches began east, a pioneer set to explore a wondrous new world. Not that day, perhaps, for she knew she would not be going far on her first try. But soon, she promised herself. Soon.

Her eyes shifted then, and she became aware of the feeders. They were crouched within a copse of heavy brush that screened the Peterson backyard some fifty feet away, watching her. She saw them as you would a gathering of shadows on a gray day, indistinct and nebulous. She caught a glimpse of their flat, yellow eyes shining out of the darkness like a cat's. She stood where she was, looking back, trying to see them more clearly, trying to determine better what they were. She stared intently, losing track of time as she did so, forgetting where she was and what she was about, mesmerized.

Then a drop of rain fell squarely on her nose, cold and wet against her skin. She blinked in surprise, and suddenly the feeders were all around her, and she was so terrified that she could feel her fear writhing inside her like a living thing.

And, just as suddenly, they were gone again. It happened so fast that she wasn't sure if it was real or if she had imagined it. In the blink of an eye, they had appeared. In another blink, they had gone. How could they move so quickly? What would make them do so?

She saw Wraith then, standing a few feet away, a dark shape in the deepening gray, so still he might have been carved from stone. She didn't know his name then, or what he was, or where he had come from. She stared at him, unable to look away, riveted by the sight of him. She thought he was the biggest creature she had ever seen this close up, bigger even, it seemed to her at that moment, than the horses she had petted once on a visit to the Lehman farm. He appeared to be some sort of dog, immense and fierce-looking and as immovable as the massive shade trees that grew in her backyard. He was brindle in color; his muzzle and head bore tiger-stripe markings and his body hair bristled like a porcupine's quills. Oddly enough, she was not frightened by him. She would always remember that. She was awestruck, but she was not frightened. Not in the way she was of the feeders. He was there, she realized, without quite being sure why, to protect her from them.

Then he disappeared, and she was alone. He simply faded away, as if composed of smoke scattered by a sudden gust of wind. She stared into the space he had occupied, wondering at him. The park stretched away before her, silent and empty in the failing light. Then the rain began to fall in earnest, and she made a dash for the house.

She saw Wraith often after that, possibly because she was looking for him, possibly because he had decided to reveal himself. She still didn't know what he was, and neither did anyone else. Pick told her later that he was some sort of cross-breed, a mix of dog and wolf. But really, since he was created from and held together by magic, his genetic origins didn't make any difference. Whatever he was, he was probably the only one of his kind. Pick confirmed her impression that he was there to protect her. Matter of fact, he advised rather solemnly, Wraith had been shadowing her since the first time she had come into the park, still a baby in her stroller. She wondered at first how she could have missed seeing him, but then discovered that she had missed seeing a lot of other things as well, and it didn't seem so odd.

When she finally told her grandmother about Wraith, her grandmother's response was strange. She didn't question what Nest was telling her. She didn't suggest that Nest might be mistaken or confused. She went all still for a moment, her eyes assumed a distant look, and her thin, old hands tightened about the mittens she was knitting.

"Did you see anything else?" she asked softly.

"No," said Nest, wondering suddenly if there was something she should have seen.

"He just appeared, this dog did? The feeders came close to you, and the dog appeared?" Gran's eyes were sharp and bright.

"Yes. That first time. Now I just see him following me sometimes, watching me. He doesn't come too close. He always stays back. But the feeders are afraid of him. I can tell."

Her grandmother was silent.

"Do you know what he is?" Nest pressed anxiously.

Her grandmother held her gaze. "Perhaps."

"Is he there to protect me?"

"I think we have to find that out."

Nest frowned. "Who sent him, Gran?"

But her grandmother only shook her head and turned away. "I don't know," she answered, but the way she said it made Nest think that maybe she did.

For a long time, Nest was the only one who saw the dog. Sometimes her grandmother would come into the park with her, but the dog did not show himself on those occasions.

Then one day, for no reason that Nest could ever determine, he appeared out of a cluster of spruce at twilight while the old woman and her granddaughter walked through the west-end play area toward the cliffs. Her grandmother froze, holding on to the little girl's hand tightly.

"Gran?" Nest said uncertainly.

"Wait here for me, Nest," her grandmother replied. "Don't move."

The old woman walked up to the big animal and knelt before him. It was growing dark, and it was hard to see clearly, but it seemed to Nest as if her grandmother was speaking to the beast. It was very quiet, and she could almost hear the old woman's words. She remained standing for a while, but then she grew tired and sat down on the grass to wait. There was no one else around. Stars began to appear in the sky and shadows to swallow the last of the fading light. Her grandmother and the dog were staring at each other, locked in a strange, silent communication that went on for a very long time.

Finally her grandmother rose and came back to her. The strange dog watched for a moment, then slowly melted back into the shadows.

"It's all right, Nest," her grandmother whispered in a thin, weary voice, taking her hand once more. "His name is Wraith. He is here to protect you."

She never spoke of the meeting again.

As Nest wriggled her way through the hedgerow at the back of her yard, she paused for a moment at the edge of the rutted dirt service road that ran parallel to the south boundary of the lot and recalled anew how Sinnissippi Park had appeared to her that first time. So long ago, she thought, and smiled at the memory. The park had seemed much bigger then, a vast, sprawling, mysterious world of secrets waiting to be discovered and adventures begging to be lived. At night, sometimes, when she was abroad with Pick, she still felt as she had when she was five, and the park, with its dark woods and gloomy ravines, with its murky sloughs and massive cliffs, seemed as large and unfathomable as it had then.

But now, in the harsh light of the July midday, the sun blazing down out of another cloudless sky, the heat a faint shimmer rising off the burned-out flats, the park seemed small and constrained. The ball fields lay just beyond the service road, their parched diamonds turned dusty and hardened and dry, their grassy outfields gray-tipped and spiky. There were four altogether, two close and two across the way east. Farther on, a cluster of hardwoods and spruce shaded a play area for small children, replete with swings and monkey bars and teeter-totters and painted animals on heavy springs set in concrete that you could climb aboard and ride.

The entrance to the park was to Nest's immediate right, and the blacktop road leading into the park ran under the crossbar toward the river before splitting off in two directions. If you went right, you traveled to the turnaround and the cliffs, where the previous night she had rescued Bennett Scott. Beyond the turnaround, separated from the park by a high chain-link fence that any kid over the age of seven who was worth his salt could climb, was Riverside Cemetery, rolling, tree-shaded, and sublimely peaceful. The cemetery was where her mother was buried. If you turned left off the blacktop, you either looped down under a bridge to the riverbank at the bottom of the cliffs, where a few picnic tables were situated, or you continued on some distance to the east end of the park where a large, sheltered pavilion, a toboggan slide, a playground, and the deep woods waited. The toboggan slide ran all the way from the heights beyond the parking lot to the reedy depths of the bayou. A good run in deep winter would take you out across the ice all the way to the embankment that supported the railroad tracks running east to Chicago and west to the plains. Stretching a run to the embankment was every toboggan rider's goal. Nest had done it three times. There were large brick-chimney and smaller iron hibachi-style cooking stations and wooden picnic tables all over the park, so that any number of church outings or family reunions could be carried on at one time. Farther east, back in the deep woods, there were nature trails that ran from the Woodland Heights subdivision where Robert Heppler lived down to the banks of the Rock River. There were trees that were well over two hundred years old. Some of the oaks and elms and shagbark hickories rose over a hundred feet, and the park was filled with dark, mysterious places that whispered of things you couldn't see, but could only imagine and secretly wish for.

The park was old, Nest knew. It had never been anything but a park. Before it was officially titled and protected by state law, it had been an untamed stretch of virgin timber. No one had lived there since the time of the Indians. Except, of course, the feeders.

She took it all in for a moment, embracing it with her senses, reclaiming it for herself as she did each time she returned, familiar ground that belonged to her. She felt that about the park—that through her peculiar and endemic familiarity with its myriad creatures, its secretive places, its changeless look and feel, and its oddly compelling solitude, it was hers. She felt this way whenever she stepped into the park, as if she were fulfilling a purpose in her life, as if she knew that here, of all places in the world, she belonged.

Of course, Pick had more than a little to do with that, having enlisted her years ago as his human partner in the care and upkeep of the park's magic.

She walked across the service road, kicking idly at the dirt with her running shoes, moving onto the heat-crisped grasses of the ball diamond, intent on taking the shortcut across the park to Cass Minter's house on Spring Drive. The others were probably already there: Robert, Brianna, and Jared. She would be the last to arrive, late as usual. But it was summer, and it really didn't matter if she was late. The days stretched on, and time lost meaning. Today they were going fishing down by the old boat launch below the dam, just off the east end of the park. Bass, bluegill, perch, and sunfish, you could still catch them all, if not so easily as once. You didn't eat them, of course. Rock River wasn't clean enough for that, not the way it had been when her grandfather was a boy. But the fishing was fun, and it was as good a way as any to spend an afternoon.

She was skipping off behind the backstop of the closest ball field when she heard a voice call out.

"Nest! Wait up!"

Turning awkward and flushed the moment she realized who it was, she watched Jared Scott come loping up the service road from the park entry. She glanced down at her Grunge Lives T-shirt and her running shorts, at the stupid way they hung on her, at the flatness of her chest and the leanness of her legs and arms, and she wished for the thousandth time that she looked more like Brianna. She was angry at herself for thinking like that, then for feeling so bizarre over a boy, and then because there he was, right in front of her, smiling and waving and looking at her in that strange way of his.

"Hey, Nest," he greeted.

"Hey, Jared." She looked quickly away.

They fell into step beside each other, moving along the third-base line of the diamond, both of them looking at their feet. Jared wore old jeans, a faded gray T-shirt, and tennis shoes with no socks. Nothing fit quite right, but Nest thought he looked pretty cute anyway.

"You get any sleep last night?" he asked after a minute.

He was just about her height (oh, all right, he was an inch or so shorter, maybe), with dark blond hair cut short, eyes so blue they were startling, a stoic smile that suggested both familiarity and long-suffering indulgence with life's vicissitudes, and a penchant for clearing his throat before speaking that betrayed his nervousness at making conversation. She didn't know why she liked him. She hadn't felt this way about him a year ago. A year ago, she had thought he was weird. She still wasn't sure what had happened to change things.

She shrugged. "I slept a little."

He cleared his throat. "Well, no thanks to me, I guess. You saved my bacon, bringing Bennett home."

"No, I didn't."

"Big time. I didn't know what to do. I spaced, and the next thing I knew, she was outta there. I didn't know where she'd gone."

"Well, she's pretty little, so—"

"I messed up." He was having trouble getting the words out. "I should have locked the door or something, because the attacks can—"

"It wasn't your fault," she interrupted heatedly. Her eyes flicked to his, then away again. "Your mom shouldn't be leaving you alone to baby-sit those kids. She knows what can happen."

He was silent a moment. "She doesn't have any money for a sitter."

Oh, but she does have money to go out drinking at the bars, I suppose, Nest wanted to say, but didn't. "Your mom needs to get a life," she said instead.

"Yeah, I guess. George sure doesn't give her much of one."

"George Paulsen doesn't know how." Nest spit deliberately. "Do you know what he did with Bennett's kitten?"

Jared looked at her. "Spook? What do you mean? Bennett didn't say anything about it to me."

Nest nodded. "Well, she did to me. She said George took Spook away somewhere 'cause he doesn't like cats. You don't know anything about it?"

"No. Spook?"

"She was probably scared to tell you. I wouldn't put it past that creep to threaten her not to say anything." She looked off into the park. "I told her I'd help find Spook. But I don't know where to look."

Jared shoved his hands into his jeans pockets. "Me, either. But I'll look, too." He shook his head. "I can't believe this."

They crossed the park toward the woods that bordered the houses leading to Cass Minter's, lost in their separate thoughts, breathing in the heat and the dryness and watching the dust rise beneath their feet in small clouds.

"Maybe your mom will think twice before she goes out with him again, once she learns about Spook," Nest said after a minute.

"Maybe."

"Does she know about last night?"

He hesitated, then shook his head. "No. I didn't want to tell her. Bennett didn't say anything either."

They walked on in silence to the beginning of the woods and started through the trees toward the houses and the road. From somewhere ahead came the excited shriek of a child, followed by laughter. They could hear the sound of a sprinkler running. *Whisk, whisk, whisk.* It triggered memories of times already lost to them, gone with childhood's brief innocence.

Nest spoke to Jared Scott without looking at him. "I don't blame you. You know, for not telling your mom. I wouldn't have told her either."

Jared nodded. His hands slipped deeper into his pockets.

She gripped his arm impulsively. "Next time she leaves you alone to baby-sit, give me a call. I'll come over and help."

"Okay," he agreed, giving her a sideways smile.

But she knew just from the way he said it that he wouldn't.

Chapter 6

Nest and her friends spent the long, slow, lazy hours of the hot July afternoon fishing. They laughed and joked, swapped gossip and told lies, drank six-packs of pop kept cool at the end of a cord in the waters of the Rock River, and gnawed contentedly on twists of red licorice.

Beyond the shelter of the park, away from the breezes that wafted off the river, the temperature rose above one hundred and stayed there. The blue dome of the cloudless sky turned hazy with reflected light, and the heat seemed to press down upon the homes and businesses of Hopewell with the intention of flattening them. Downtown, the digital signboard on the exterior brick wall of the First National Bank read 103°, and the concrete of the streets and sidewalks baked and steamed in the white glare. Within their air-conditioned offices, men and women began planning their Friday-afternoon escapes, trying to think of ways they could cool down the blast-furnace interiors of their automobiles long enough to survive the drive home.

On the picket lines at the entrances to MidCon Steel's five shuttered plants, the union workers hunkered down in lawn chairs under makeshift canopies and drank iced tea and beer from large Styrofoam coolers, hot and weary and discouraged, angry at the intransigence of their collective fate, thinking dark thoughts and feeling the threads of their lives slip slowly away.

In the cool, dark confines of Scrubby's Bar, at the west edge of town just off Lincoln Highway, Derry Howe sat alone at one end of the serving counter, nursing a beer and mumbling unintelligibly of his plans for MidCon to a creature that no one else could see.

It was nearing five o'clock, the sun sinking west and the dinner hour approaching, when Nest and her friends gathered up their fishing gear and the last few cans of pop and made their way back through the park. They climbed from the old boat launch (abandoned now since Riverside had bought the land and closed the road leading in), gained the heights of the cemetery, and followed the fence line back along the bluff face to where the cliffs dropped away and the park began. They wormed their way through a gap in the chain-link, Jared and Robert spreading the jagged edges wide for the girls, followed the turnaround past the Indian mounds, and angled through the trees and the playgrounds toward the ball diamonds. The heat lingered even with the sun's slow westward descent, a sullen, brooding presence at the edges of the shade. In the darker stretches of the spruce and pine, where the boughs grew thick and the shadows never faded, amber eyes as flat and hard as stone peered out in cold appraisal. Nest, who alone could see them, was reminded of the increasing boldness of the feeders and was troubled anew by what it meant.

Robert Heppler took a deep drink from his can of Coke, then belched loudly at Brianna Brown and said with supreme insincerity, "Sorry."

Brianna pulled a face. She was small and pretty with delicate features and thick, wavy dark hair. "You're disgusting, Robert!"

"Hey, it's a natural function of the body." Robert tried his best to look put-upon. Short and wiry, with a mischievous face, a shock of unruly white-blond hair, Robert eventually aggravated everyone he came in contact with—particularly Brianna Brown.

"There is nothing natural about anything you do!" Brianna snapped irritably, although there wasn't quite enough force behind the retort to cause any of the others to be concerned. The feud between Robert and Brianna was long-standing. It had become a condition of their lives. No one thought much about it anymore, except where the occasional flare-up exacerbated feelings so thoroughly that no one could get any peace. That had happened only once of late, early in the summer, when Robert had managed to hide a red fizzie in the lining of Brianna's swimsuit just before she went into the pool at Lawrence Park. Mortified beyond any expression of outrage at the resulting red stain, Brianna would have killed Robert if she could have gotten her hands on him. As it was, she hadn't said a word to him for almost two weeks afterward, not until he apologized in front of everyone and admitted he had behaved in a stupid and childish manner—and even that seemed to please Robert in some bizarre way that probably not even he could fathom.

"No, listen, I read this in a report." Robert looked around to be sure they were all listening. "Belching and farting are necessary bodily functions. They release gases that would otherwise poison the body. You know about the exploding cows?"

"Oh, Robert!" Cass Minter rolled her eyes.

"No, cows can explode if enough gas builds up inside them. It's a medical condition. They produce all this methane gas when they digest grass. If they don't get rid of it, it can make them explode. There was this whole article on it. I guess it's like what happens to milk cows if you don't milk them." He took another drink of Coke and belched again. With Robert, you never knew if he was making it up. "Think about what could happen to us if we stopped belching."

"Maybe you should give up drinking Coke," Cass suggested dryly. She was a big, heavyset girl with a round, cheerful face and intelligent green eyes. She always wore jeans and loose-fitting shirts, an unspoken concession to her weight, and her lank brown hair looked as if no comb had passed through it any time in recent memory. Cass was Nest's oldest friend, from all the way back to when they were in second grade together. She winked at Nest now. "Maybe you should stick to tomato juice, Robert."

Robert Heppler hated tomato juice. He'd been forced to drink it once at camp, compelled to do so by a counselor in front of a dozen other campers, after which he had promptly vomited it up again. It was a point of honor with him that he would die before he ever did that again.

"Where did you read all this, anyway?" Jared Scott asked with benign interest.

Robert shrugged. "On the Internet."

"You know, you can't believe everything you read," Brianna declared, repeating something her mother frequently told her.

"Well, duh!" Robert sneered. "Anyway, this was a Dave Barry article."

"Dave Barry?" Cass was in stitches. "Now there's a reliable source. I suppose you get your world news from Liz Smith."

Robert stopped and slowly turned to face her. "Oh, I am cut to the quick!" He looked pointedly at Nest. "Like I can't tell the difference between what's reliable and what isn't, right?"

"Leave me out of this," Nest begged.

"Don't be so difficult, Robert!" Brianna chided, smoothing down her spotless white shorts. Only Brianna would wear white shorts to go fishing and somehow manage to keep them white.

"Difficult? I'm not difficult! Am I?" He threw up his hands. "Jared, am I?"

But Jared Scott was staring blankly at nothing, his face calm, his expression detached, as if he had removed himself entirely from everything that was happening around him and gone somewhere else. He was having another episode, Nest realized—his third that afternoon. The medicine he was taking didn't seem to be helping a whole lot. At least his epilepsy never did much more than it was doing now. It just took him away for a while and then brought him back again, snipping out small spaces in his life, like panels cut from a comic book.

"Well, anyway, I don't think I'm difficult." Robert turned back to Brianna. "I can't help it if I'm interested in learning about stuff. What am I supposed to do—stop reading?"

Brianna sighed impatiently. "You could at least stop being so dramatic!"

"Oh, now I'm too dramatic, am I? Gee, first I'm too difficult and then I'm too dramatic! How ever will I get on with my life?"

"We all ponder that dilemma on a daily basis," Cass observed archly.

"You spend too much time in front of your computer!" Brianna snapped.

"Well, you spend too much time in front of your mirror!" Robert snapped right back.

It was no secret that Brianna devoted an inordinate amount of time to looking good, in large part as the result of having a mother who was a hairdresser and who firmly believed that makeup and clothes made the difference in a young girl's lot in life. From the time her daughter was old enough to pay attention, Brianna's mother had instilled in her the need to "look the part," as she was fond of putting it, training her to style her hair and do her makeup and providing her with an extensive wardrobe of matching outfits that Brianna was required to wear whatever the occasion—even on an outing that centered around fishing. Lately Brianna had begun to chafe a bit under the constraints of her mother's rigid expectations, but Mom still held the parental reins with a firm grip and full-blown rebellion was a year or so away.

The mirror crack brought an angry flush to Brianna Brown's face, and she glared hotly at Robert.

Cass Minter was quick to intervene. "You both spend too much time in front of lighted screens, Robert"—she gave Nest another wink—"but in Brianna's case the results are more obviously successful."

Nest laughed softly in spite of herself. She envied Brianna's smooth curves, her flawless skin, and her soft, feminine look. She was beautiful in a way that Nest never would be. Her tiny, grade-school girl's body was developing curves on schedule while Nest's simply refused to budge. Boys looked at Brianna and were made hungry and awestruck. When they looked at Nest, they were left indifferent.

Robert started to say something and belched, and everyone laughed. Jared Scott cleared his throat, and his eyes refocused on his friends. "Are we going swimming tomorrow?" he asked, as if nothing had happened.

They walked through the center of the park, keeping to the shade of the big oaks that ran along the bluff up from the ball fields bordering Nest's backyard, then cut down toward Cass Minter's rambling two-story. A game was in progress on the fourth field, the one farthest into the park and closest to the toboggan run. They sauntered toward it, caught up in their conversation, which had turned now to the merits of learning a foreign language, and they were almost to the backstop when Nest realized belatedly that one of the players lounging on the benches, waiting his turn at bat, was Danny Abbott. She tried to veer away from him, pushing at Cass to get her to move back toward the roadway, but it was too late. He had already seen her and was on his feet.

"Hey, Nest!" he called out boldly. "Wait up!"

She slowed reluctantly as he started over, already angry with herself for letting this happen. "Oh, great!" Robert muttered under his breath. A scowl twisted his narrow lips.

"Go on," she told Cass, glancing at her shoes. "I'll be along in a minute."

Cass kept moving as if that had been her plan all along, and the other three dutifully followed. All of them drifted on for about twenty feet and stopped. Nest held her ground as Danny Abbott approached. He was big, strong, and good-looking, and for some reason he had a thing for her. A high-school junior in the fall, he was two years older than she was and convinced he was the coolest thing in jeans. A few months ago, at a Y dance, flattered by his interest, she had made the mistake of letting him kiss her. The kiss was all she wanted, and after she experienced it, she decided she wasn't that interested in Danny Abbott after all. But Danny couldn't let it go. He began to talk about her to his friends, and some of the stories got back to her. Danny was saying he had gotten a lot further with her than he had. Worse, he was saying she was anxious for more. She stopped having anything to do with him, but this just seemed to fuel his interest.

He strolled up to her with a confident smile, the big jock coming on to the impressionable little groupie. She felt her anger build. "So what's happening?" he asked, his voice slow and languid. "Catch anything?"

She shook her head. "Not much. What do you want?"

"Hey, don't be so prickly." He brushed at his dark hair and looked off into the distance, like he was seeing into the future and taking its measure. "I was just wondering why I hadn't seen you around."

She shifted her weight from one foot to the other, forcing herself to look at him, refusing to be intimidated. "You know why, Danny."

He pursed his lips and nodded, as if thinking it through. "Okay, I made a mistake. I said some stuff I shouldn't have. I'm sorry. Can we drop it now? I like you, Nest. I don't want you pissed off at me. Hey, why don't you stick around while I finish this game, and then we'll go out for a burger."

"I'm with my friends," she said.

"So? I'm with mine, too. They can go their way and we can go ours, right?"

He gave her his most dazzling smile, and it made her want to say yes in spite of herself. Stupid, stupid. She shook her head. "No, I've got to get home."

He nodded solemnly. "Okay. Maybe tomorrow night. You know what? There's a dance here at the park Sunday. The Jaycees are putting it on. Want to go with me?"

She shook her head a second time. "I don't think so."

"Why not?" A hint of irritation crept into his voice.

She bit her lip. "I'll probably come with my friends."

He gave a disgusted sigh. "You spend a lot of time with your friends, don't you?"

She didn't say anything.

He glanced past her and shook his head. "Why do you hang out with them, anyway? I don't get it." He was looking right at her now, facing her down. "It seems to me you're wasting your time."

Her lips tightened, but she still didn't say anything.

"I don't mean to be picking on them or anything, but just think about it. They're weird, Nest, in case you hadn't noticed. Barbie Doll, Big Bertha, Joe Space Cadet, and Bobby the Mouth. Weird, Nest. What are you doing with them?"

"Danny," she said quietly.

"Hey, I'm just trying to make a point. You've got a lot more going for you than they do, that's all I'm saying. You're one of the best runners in the state, and you're not even in high school! You're practically famous! Besides, you're a cool chick. You're nothing like them. I really don't get it."

She nodded slowly. "I know you don't. Maybe that's the point."

He sighed. "Okay, whatever. Anyway, why don't you stick around."

"Hey, Danny, you're up!" someone called.

"Yeah, in a minute!" he shouted back. He put his hands on her shoulders, resting them there casually. "C'mon, Nest. Tell me you'll stay until I finish my at bat."

She stepped back, trying to disengage herself. "I have to go."

"One at bat," he pressed. "Five minutes." He stepped forward, staying with her, keeping his hands in place. "What do you say?"

"Abbott, you're up!"

"Hey, Nest, take your shoulders out from under his hands!" shouted Robert Heppler suddenly. "You're making him nervous!"

Danny Abbott blinked, but kept his dark eyes fixed on Nest. His gaze was so intense, so filled with purpose, that it was all Nest Freemark could do to keep from wilting under its heat. But she was just angry enough by now that she refused to give him the satisfaction.

"I have to go," she repeated, keeping her eyes locked on his.

His hands tightened on her shoulders. "I won't let you," he said. He smiled, but the warmth was missing from his eyes.

"Take your hands away," she told him.

A couple of the boys who had been standing around the backstop started to drift over, curious to see what was happening.

"You're not so hot," he said quietly, so that only she could hear. "Not half as hot as you think."

She tried to twist away, but his grip was too strong.

"Hey, Danny, pick on someone your own size!" shouted Robert, coming forward a few steps.

One thing about Robert, he wasn't afraid of anyone. He'd been in so many fights in grade school that his parents had taken him to a psychiatrist. He'd been suspended more times than Nest could remember. His problem was that he wasn't very careful about choosing his opponents, and today was no exception. Danny Abbott looked over at him with undisguised contempt. Danny was bigger, stronger, quicker, and meaner than Robert, and he was looking for an excuse to slug someone.

"What did you say, Heppler?"

Robert held his ground and shrugged. "Nothing."

"That's what I thought, you little creep."

Robert threw up his hands in exaggerated dismay. "Oh, great! I'm being called a creep by a guy who wrestles with girls!"

Half-a-dozen ballplayers had congregated, and a few snickered at the remark. Danny Abbott dropped his hands from Nest's shoulders. His hands knotted into fists, and he turned toward Robert. Robert gave him a very deliberate smirk, but there was a shadow of doubt in his eyes now.

"Robert," Cass called in a low, warning voice.

"I'm going to wipe up the park with you," Danny Abbott said, and started forward.

Nest Freemark darted in front of him, bringing him to a stop. She stood there shaking, her arms at her sides. "Leave him alone, Danny. I'm the one you're angry at."

Danny shook his head. "Not anymore."

"You're twice his size!"

"Guess he should have thought of that before he opened his big mouth."

"Punch him out, Danny," one of his friends muttered, and a few others quickly echoed the sentiment.

Nest felt the late-afternoon heat scorch her throat as she breathed it in. "Look, forget about this, Danny," she insisted, still blocking his path to Robert. "I'll stay to watch you bat, okay?" She hated herself for saying the words, but she was frightened now. "Leave Robert alone."

He looked at her, and there was undisguised contempt in his eyes. He was enjoying this. "You should have thought about that before. You should have paid a little better attention to your mouth."

He started forward again, and she moved back quickly, still blocking his way. She could feel her control slipping, and her breath came more rapidly. She had promised herself! She had promised Gran! "Danny, don't do this!" she snapped at him.

"Danny, don't do this!" he sneered, mimicking her, and the boys with him laughed.

"Danny, please!"

"Get out of my way," he growled.

He reached for her, their eyes locked, and her magic slammed into him. In an instant he lay sprawled on the ground, his legs and arms tangled, a look of utter shock on his handsome face. The eager shouts of his friends turned to gasps, and Nest stepped quickly away, her face white, her eyes bright and intense with concentration. Danny struggled to his feet, glared at her in rage, not certain what had happened to him, but knowing that somehow she was to blame, and then lunged for her. Her eyes found his. Down he went again, crumpling like a rag doll, as if he could no longer manage to stand upright. He rolled over and over, shrieking unintelligibly, his voice unnaturally high and piercing, his words a jumble of unrecognizable sounds.

Everyone had gone completely still. They stood knotted into two groups, Nest's friends on one side, Danny's on the other, frozen in the swelter of heat and excitement, stunned by what they were witnessing, mesmerized by the spectacle of Danny Abbott's collapse. The park had become a vast arena, carpeted with grass, walled by trees, empty of sound. Magic raced through the air with savage grace and reckless need, but no one except Nest could sense its presence.

Danny came to his hands and knees and stayed there, his head hanging down between his shoulders, his chest heaving. He coughed violently and spit, then drew in several huge gulps of air. He tried to stand, then gave it up, mouthing a low obscenity at Nest that faded quickly into a whispered groan.

Nest turned away, feeling cold and empty and sick at heart. She did not look at Danny Abbott or his friends. She did not look at Cass or Robert or Brianna or Jared either. "Let's go," she whispered, barely able to speak the words, and without waiting to see if anyone would follow, she walked off into the park.

Nest had been eleven before she discovered she could work magic. She was never sure afterward if she had been able to do so all along and simply hadn't realized it or if her ability had matured with growth. Even Gran, when told about it, hadn't been able to say for sure. By then Nest had lived with the feeders and Wraith for close to six years and with Pick for almost that long and knew there was magic out there, so it wasn't all that weird to discover that a small piece of it was hers. Besides, Gran had been saying she had magic for so many years that, even without ever having been presented with any evidence of it, she had always half believed that it was so.

Her discovery that she really could do magic was due mainly to Lori Adami. As grade-school classmates, they had developed a deep and abiding dislike for each other. Each worked hard at snubbing the other and each made certain she told her friends what a creep the other was, and that was about the extent of it. But in the sixth grade the war between them suddenly escalated. Lori began to go out of her way to make cutting remarks about Nest, always in front of other kids and always just within earshot. Nest retaliated by acting as if she hadn't heard, all the while patiently waiting for Lori to tire of this latest game.

But Lori Adami was nothing if not persistent, and one day she said that Nest's mother was crazy and that was why she killed herself and that Nest was probably crazy, too. It was winter, and they were standing in the hall by their lockers before classes, stripping off their coats and boots. Nest heard the remark, and without even thinking about it, she dropped her coat and gloves on the floor, turned around, walked right up to Lori, and hit her in the face. Since Nest had never lifted a hand against her in all these years, Lori was caught completely by surprise. But Lori had been raised with three older brothers, and she knew how to defend herself. Hissing something awful at Nest, she went after her.

Then a funny thing happened. Nest, who didn't know much about fighting, was unsure what she should do. Anger and fear warred for control. Should she stand her ground or run for it? She stood her ground. Lori grabbed for her, their eyes locked, and Nest, raising her hands to defend herself, thought, *You better not touch me, you better quit right now, you better stop!* And down went Lori in a heap, legs tangled, arms askew, and mouth open in surprise. Lori scrambled up again, furious, but the moment their eyes met she began to stumble about helplessly. She tried to say something, but she couldn't seem to talk, the words all jumbled up and nonsensical. Some of the students thought she was having a fit, and they ran screaming for help. Nest was as shocked as they were, but for a different reason. She knew what had happened. She couldn't explain it, but she understood what it was. She had felt the magic's rush, like a gasp of breath as it left her body. She had felt it entangle Lori, its cords wrapping tightly and implacably about the other girl's ankles. She would never forget the horrified look on Lori Adami's face. She would never forget how it made her feel.

They were suspended from school for fighting. Nest had debated how much she should tell Gran, who was the one she had to answer to for any sort of misbehavior, but in the end, as she almost always did, she told her everything. She found she needed to talk to someone about what had happened, and Gran was the logical choice. After all, wasn't she the one who kept saying Nest had magic? Fine, then—let her explain this!

But Gran hadn't said anything at first on hearing Nest's tale. She merely asked if Nest was certain about what had happened and then let the matter drop. Only later had she taken Nest aside to speak with her, waiting until Old Bob was safely out of the house.

"It isn't as strange as you might think that you should be able to do magic, Nest," she told her. They were sitting at the kitchen table, Nest with a cup of hot chocolate in front of her, Gran with her bourbon and water. "Do you know why that is?"

Nest shook her head, anxious to hear her grandmother's explanation.

"Because you are your mother's daughter and my granddaughter, and the women of this family have always known something about magic. We aren't witches or anything, Nest. But we have always lived around magic, here by the park, by the feeders, and we've known about that magic, and if you live next to something long enough, and you know it's there, some of it will rub off on you."

Nest looked at her doubtfully. *Rub off on you?*

Her grandmother leaned forward. "Now, you listen to me carefully, young lady. Once upon a time, I warned you never to tell anyone about the feeders. You didn't pay attention to me then, did you? You told. And do you remember the sort of trouble it got you into?" Nest nodded. "All right. So you pay attention to me now. Using magic will get you into a whole lot worse trouble than talking about feeders. It will get you into so much trouble I might not be able to get you out. So I am telling you here and now that you are not to use your magic again. Do you hear me?"

Nest chewed her lip. "Yes."

"Good. This is important." Gran's face was scrunched up like a wadded paper sack. "When you are grown, you can decide for yourself when you want to use your magic. You can weigh the risks and the rewards. But you are not to use it while you are a child living in this house. Except," she paused, reminded of something, "if you are threatened, and your life is in danger, and you have no choice." She looked away suddenly, as if fleeing things she would rather not consider. "Then, you can use the magic. But only then."

Nest thought it over for a moment. "How am I supposed to be sure I've really got magic if I don't try it out?"

Her grandmother's gaze fixed on her anew. "You seemed sure enough about it when you were fighting with Lori Adami. Are you telling me that maybe you made it up?"

"No." Nest was immediately defensive. "I just don't know for sure. It all happened so fast."

Her grandmother took a long drink from her glass and lit a cigarette. "You know. Now you do as I say."

So Nest had, although it was very hard. Eventually, she broke her promise, but not for several months, when she used her magic on a boy who was trying to pull down her swimsuit at the pool. Then she used it again on a kid who was throwing rocks at a stray cat. She knew for sure then that the magic was real, and that she could use it on anyone she wished. But the odd thing was, using it didn't make her feel very good. It should have provided her with some measure of satisfaction, but all it did was make her feel sick inside, as if she had done something for which she should feel ashamed.

It was Pick who had straightened her out, telling her that what her grandmother meant was that she wasn't to use her magic against other people. Using it against other people would always make her feel bad, because it was like taking advantage of someone who couldn't fight back. Besides, it would attract a lot of unwanted attention. But the feeders were fair game. Why not use it against them?

Pick's idea had worked. Using her magic against the feeders satisfied her curiosity and gave her an opportunity to experiment. Eventually she told Gran. Gran, saying little in response, had approved. Then Pick had enlisted her aid in dealing with the nighttime activities of the feeders, and summoning the magic had suddenly become serious business. After that, she had been very careful not to use it again on people.

Until now, she thought wearily as she walked home through the park. She had split up with the others as soon as they were in the trees and out of sight of the ball field. See you tomorrow, she had told them, as if nothing had happened, as if everything were all right. See you tomorrow, they'd replied. Hardly a word had been spoken about the incident, but she knew they were all thinking about it, remembering anew some of the stories about her.

Only Robert had ventured a parting comment. "Jeez, it didn't even look like you touched him!" he'd said in his typically direct, unthinking, Robert way. She was so distressed she didn't even try to respond.

As she reached the edge of the service road, she thought suddenly she might vomit. Her stomach churned and her head ached. The inside of her mouth tasted coppery, and her breathing was quick and uneven. Using the magic on Danny Abbott had been a mistake, even though it had probably saved Robert a beating. She had promised Gran she wouldn't use it again. More important, she had promised herself. But something had happened to her this afternoon. She had been so angry she had forgotten her resolve. She had simply lost control of herself.

She angled through the trees and houses that paralleled the park, closing in now on her home, buoyed by the sight of its familiar white siding and its big stone chimney, her refuge from the world. She knew what troubled her most about what had happened. It was what Danny had said. Your friends are weird. What are you doing with them? But, really, she was the one who was weird, and using the magic as she had just pointed it up. Having magic made her different from everyone—but that was just part of it. How much stranger could you be than to know that you were the only one who could see feeders, the only one with some sort of monster dog for a protector, and the only one with a sylvan for a friend?

She was the one who didn't belong, she knew, tears running down her cheeks, and she wanted desperately not to feel that way.

Chapter 7

Nest went for a run before dinner, disdaining to wait for the heat to lessen, needing to escape. She asked Gran if it would be all right, and Gran, with those unerring instincts for evaluating the depth of her granddaughter's needs, told her to go ahead. It was after six, the sun still visible in the western sky, the glare of midday softened to a hazy gold. Colors deepened as the light paled, the green of the leaves and grasses turning damp emerald, the tree trunks taking on an inky cast, and the sky overhead becoming such a clear, depthless blue that it seemed that if gravity's hold could be broken you might swim it like an ocean. As Nest turned out of her drive and ran down Sinnissippi Road, she could feel the branches of the big hardwoods sigh with the faint passing of a momentary breeze, and the sigh seemed collective and all-encompassing. Friday was ending, the work week had come to a close, and now the long Fourth of July weekend could begin in earnest. She ran to the end of Sinnissippi, barely a block from her drive, and turned east onto Woodlawn. Ahead, the road stretched away, a wide, straight racetrack that narrowed between the houses with their lawns, hedgerows, and trees and faded into the horizon. She ran smoothly on its shoulder, feeling her blood hum, her heart pound, her breathing steady, and her thoughts scatter. The movement of her legs and the pounding of her feet absorbed her, enfolded her, and then swallowed her up. She was conscious of the world slipping past like a watercolor running on a canvas backdrop, and she felt herself melt into it. Neighbors worked in their gardens or sat on their porches sipping tea and lemonade and occasionally something stronger. Dogs and cats lay sleeping. Children played in their yards, and as she passed a few dashed toward her momentarily before stopping, as if they, too, were seeking an escape. Now and again someone waved or called out, making her feel welcome, a part of the world once more.

She ran the length of Woodlawn, then turned left to Moonlight Bay. She passed boats and trailers on their way to the launch and campers on their way to White Pines State Park sixty miles north. She ran the circle drive of the bay past the shorefront residences, then swung west again and ran back to her home. Slowly, surely, her trauma eased, left behind with her footprints in the dust. By the time she turned down her drive once more, she was feeling better about herself. Her shirt clung damply to her body and her skin was covered with a sheen of sweat. She felt drained and loose and renewed. As she came up to the back door, she permitted herself a quick glimpse into the park, looking backward in time to the events of the afternoon, better able now to face what she had done to Danny Abbott—or perhaps, more accurately, what she had done to herself. The ache that the memory generated in her heart was sharp, but momentary. She sighed wearily, telling herself what she sometimes did when things were bad—that she was just a kid—and knew as always that it wasn't so.

She showered quickly, dressed in fresh shorts and T-shirt (this one said Latte Lady), and came down for dinner. She sat at the kitchen table with her grandparents and ate tuna and noodle casserole with green beans and peaches off the everyday china. Gran nursed her bourbon and water and picked at her food, a voiceless presence. Old Bob asked Nest about her day, listened attentively as she told him about fishing with her friends, and didn't say a word about last night in the park. Through the open screen door came the sounds of the evening, distant and soft—the shouts of players and spectators as the night's softball games got under way in the park, the hiss of tires on hot asphalt from cars passing down Sinnissippi Road, the muted roar of a lawn mower cutting grass several houses down, and the faint, silvery laughter of children at play. There was no air-conditioning in the Freemark house, so the sounds were clearly audible. Nest's grandparents couldn't stomach the idea of shutting out the world. You can deal better with the heat if you live with it, they liked to say.

"Any news on the strike?" Nest asked her grandfather after they had finished talking about fishing, mostly in an effort to hold up her end of the conversation.

He shook his white head, swallowed the last bite of his dinner, and pushed his plate back. His big shoulders shrugged. "Naw, they can't even agree on what day of the week it is, Nest." He reached for his newspaper and scanned the headlines. "Won't be a resolution any time soon, I don't expect."

Nest glanced at Gran, but her grandmother was staring out the window with a blank expression, a lighted cigarette burning to ash between her fingers.

"Not my problem anymore," Old Bob declared firmly. "At least I got that to be thankful for. Someone else's problem now."

Nest finished her dinner and began thinking about Pick and the park. She glanced outside at the failing light.

"Look at this," Old Bob muttered, shaking out the paper as if it contained fleas. "Just look at this. Two boys dropped a five-year-old out a window in a Chicago apartment. Fifteen stories up, and they just dropped him out. No reason for it, they just decided to do it. The boys were ten and eleven. Ten and eleven! What in the hell is the world coming to?"

"Robert." Gran looked at him reprovingly over the rim of her glass.

"Well, you have to wonder." Old Bob lowered the paper and glanced at Nest. "Excuse my language." He was silent for a moment, reading. Then he opened the inside page. "Oh, my." He sighed and shook his head, eyes bright with anger. "Here's another, this one quite a bit closer to home. One of those Anderson girls used to live out on Route Thirty shot and killed her father last night. She claims he's been molesting all of the girls since they were little. Says she forgot about it until it came to her in a dream." He read on a bit, fuming. "Also says she has a history of mental problems and that the family hasn't had anything to do with her for some time."

He read for a little while longer, then tossed the paper aside. "The news isn't worth the paper it's printed on anymore." He studied the table a moment, then glanced at Gran, waiting for a response. Gran was silent, looking out the window once more. Her hand lowered in a mechanical motion to the ashtray to stub out the cigarette.

Old Bob's eyes turned sad and distant. He looked at Nest. "You going out to play again?" he asked quietly.

Nest nodded, already beginning to push back from the table.

"That's all right," her grandfather said. "But you be back by dark. No excuses."

The way he said it made it plain that, even though he hadn't brought the subject up at dinner, he hadn't forgotten about last night. Nest nodded again, letting him know she understood.

Her grandfather rose and left the table, taking the newspaper with him, retiring to the seclusion of his den. Nest sat for a moment staring after him, then started to get up as well.

"Nest," her grandmother said softly, looking directly at her now. She waited until she had the girl's attention. "What happened this afternoon?"

Nest hesitated, trying to decide what to say. She shrugged. "Nothing, Gran."

Her grandmother gave her a long, hard look. "Carry your dishes to the sink before you go," she said finally. "And remember what your grandfather told you."

Two minutes later, Nest was out the back door and down the porch steps. Mr. Scratch had disappeared and Miss Minx had taken his place. As designated mouser she had assumed a more alert position, crouched down by the toolshed, sniffing at the air and looking about warily. Nest walked over and scratched her white neck, then headed for the hedgerow and the park. Mosquitoes buzzed past her ears, and she swatted at them irritably. Magic didn't seem to do any good when it came to mosquitoes. Pick claimed once that he had a potion that would keep them at bay, but it turned out to be so evil-smelling that it kept everything else at bay as well. Nest grimaced at the memory. Even a hundred-and-fifty-year-old sylvan didn't know everything.

She was nearing the hedgerow, listening to the sounds of the softball games in progress on the other side, when she glanced left into the Peterson backyard and saw the feeders. There were two of them, hiding in the lilac bushes close by the compost heap that Annie Peterson used on her vegetable garden. They were watching Nest, staring out at her with their flat, expressionless eyes, all but invisible in the approaching twilight. Their boldness frightened her. It was as if they were lying in wait for her, hoping to catch her off-guard. They were implacable and relentless, and the certainty of what they would do to her if they had the chance was unnerving. Nest veered toward them, irritated anew by the feelings they aroused in her. It was getting so she couldn't go anywhere without seeing them.

The feeders blinked once as she neared, then simply faded away into the shadows.

Nest stared into the empty gloom and shivered. The feeders were like vultures, waiting to dispose of whatever leavings they could scavenge. Except that feeders were only interested in the living.

She thought back to what Pick had told her years ago when she had asked about the feeders. Her grandmother had avoided the subject for as long as Nest could remember, but Pick was more than willing to address it.

"Your grandmother won't talk about them? Won't say a single word about them? Not a single word? Well, now. Well, indeed!" He'd scrunched up his moss-bearded face and scratched at the side of his head as if to help free up thoughts trapped in his cranium. "All right, then, listen up. First off, you need to understand that feeders are an anomaly. You know what that word means, don't you?"

Since she'd been only eight at the time, she hadn't the slightest idea. "Not really," she'd said.

"Criminy, your education is a mess! Don't you ever read?"

"You don't read," she'd pointed out.

"That's different. I don't have to read. I don't need it in my line of work. But you, why, you should be reading volumes of . . ."

"What does anoma-whatever mean?" she'd pressed, unwilling to wait through the entirety of Pick's by-now-familiar lecture on the plight of today's undereducated youth.

He had stopped in midsentence, harrumphed disapprovingly at her impatience, and cleared his throat. "Anomaly. It means 'peculiar.' It means 'different.' It means feeders are hard to classify. You know that guessing game you used to play? The one where you start by asking, 'Animal, mineral, or vegetable?' Well, that's the kind of game you have to play when you try to figure out what feeders are. Except feeders aren't any of these things, and at the same time they're all of them, because what they are is determined to a large extent by what *you* are."

She'd stared at him blankly.

He'd frowned then, apparently deciding that his explanation was lacking. "Let's start at the beginning," he'd declared, scooting closer to her atop the picnic table in her backyard.

She'd leaned forward so that her chin was resting on her hands and her eyes were level with his. It was late on a spring afternoon, and the leaves of the trees were rustling with the wind's passing, and clouds were drifting across the sun like cottony caterpillars, casting dappled shadows that wriggled and squirmed.

"Feeders," he'd said, deepening his voice meaningfully, "don't come in different sizes and shapes and colors. They don't hardly have any faces at all. They're not like other creatures. They don't eat and sleep. They don't have parents or children or go to school or elect governments or read books or talk about the weather. The Word made feeders when he made everything else, and he made them as a part of the balance of things. You remember what I told you about everything being in balance, sort of like a teeter-totter, with some things on one end and some on the other, and both ends weighing the same. Feeders, they're part of that. Frankly, I don't know why. But, then, it's not my place to know. The Word made the decision to create feeders, and that's the end of it. But having said that, having said that it's not my place to know why these feeders were *made*, it is my place to know what they *do*. And that, young lady, is what's interesting. Feeders have only one purpose in this world, only one, single, solitary thing that they do."

He'd moved closer then, and his wizened face had furrowed with delight and his voice had lowered to a conspiratorial whisper. "Feeders, my young friend, devour people!"

Nest's eyes had gone wide, and Pick the sylvan had laughed like a cartoon maniac.

She still remembered him saying it. *Feeders devour people*. There was more to the explanation, of course, for the complexity of feeders could never be defined so simply. There was no mention of the feeders as a force of nature, as sudden, violent, and inexorable as a Midwest twister, or of their strange, symbiotic relationship with the humans they destroyed. Yet it was hard to get much closer to the heart of the matter. Pick's description, provocative and crude, was still the most accurate Nest had ever heard. Even now, six years later, his words resonated with truth.

The pungent smell of spruce filled her nostrils, borne on a momentary breeze, and the memories faded. She turned and jogged quickly to the end of her yard, slipping smoothly into the gap in the hedgerow. She was almost through when Pick appeared on her shoulder as if by magic, springing out of hiding from the leafy branches. At six inches of height and nine ounces of weight, he was as small and light as a bird. He was a wizened bit of wood with vaguely human features stamped above a mossy beard. Leaves grew out of his head in place of hair. His arms and legs were flexible twigs that narrowed to tiny fingers and stubby toes. He looked like a Disney animation that had been roughed up a bit. His fierce eyes were as hard and flat as ink dots on stone.

He settled himself firmly in place, taking hold of her collar. "What have I told you about provoking the feeders?" he snapped.

"Not to," she answered dutifully, swinging west down the service road toward the park entrance.

"Why don't you listen to me, then?"

"I do. But it makes me angry to see them nosing about when it's still light out." She darted a quick look at the ballplayers to make certain that Danny Abbott wasn't among them. "They didn't used to be like that. They never showed themselves when the sun was shining, not even where the shadows were deepest. Now I see them everywhere."

"Times change." Pick sounded disconsolate. "Something's happening, that much is sure, but I don't know what it is yet. Whatever it is, it's caused the balance of things to tip even further. There's been a lot of bad things happening around here lately. That's not good." He paused. "How's the little Scott girl?"

"Fine. But George Paulsen stole her cat, Spook." Nest slowed to a walk again. "I promised Bennett I'd try to find it. Can you help me?"

Even without being able to see him, she knew he was tugging on his mossy beard and shaking his leafy head. "Sure, sure, what else have I got to do but look for someone's lost cat? Criminy!" He was silent a moment as they passed behind the backstop. The spectators grouped at the edge of the ball field were drinking beer and pop and cheering on their favorite players. "Batter, batter, batter—swing!" someone chanted. No one paid any attention to Nest.

"I'll send Daniel out, see if he can find anything," Pick offered grudgingly.

Nest smiled. "Thanks."

"You can thank me by staying away from the feeders!" Pick was not about to be mollified. "You think your magic and that big dog are enough to protect you, but you don't know feeders the way I do. They aren't subject to the same laws as humans. They get to you when you're not expecting it!" She could feel him twisting about angrily on her shoulder. "Creepers! I don't know why I'm telling you this! You already know it, and I shouldn't have to say another word!"

Then please don't, she thought, hiding a grin. Wisely, she swallowed her words without speaking them. "I'll be careful, I promise," she assured him, turning up the blacktop road toward the cliffs.

"See that you do. Now, cut across the grass to the burial mounds. There's an Indian sitting up there at one of the picnic tables, and I want to know what he's up to."

She glanced sideways at him. "An Indian?"

"That's what I said, didn't I?"

"A real Indian?"

Pick sighed in exasperation. "If you do like I told you, you can decide for yourself!"

Curious now, wondering if there really was an Indian or if the sylvan was just making it up, she stepped off the roadway into the grass and began to jog steadily toward the cliffs.

Chapter 8

The Indian was sitting at a picnic table on the far side of the playground just across the roadway from the burial mounds. He was all alone, having chosen a spot well back in the tangle of pines and spruce that warded the park's northern boundary against the heavy winter storms that blew down from Canada. He sat with his back to the roadway and the broad expanse of the park, his gaze directed west toward the setting sun. Shadows dappled his still, solitary form, and if she had not known to look for him, Nest might have missed seeing him altogether.

He did not look up as she neared, and she slowed to a walk. His long, raven hair had been woven into a single braid that fell to the middle of his back, and his burnished skin shone with a copper glint where errant streaks of sunlight brushed against it. He was a big man, even hunched down at the table the way he was, and the fingers of his hands, clasped before him in a twisted knot, were gnarled and thick. He wore what appeared to be an army field jacket with the sleeves torn out, pants that were baggy and frayed, boots so scuffed they lacked any semblance of a shine, and a red bandanna tied loosely about his neck.

Somewhere in the distance a child squealed with delight. The Indian did not react.

Nest moved to a picnic table thirty feet away from the Indian and seated herself. She was off to one side, out of his direct line of sight, where she could study him at her leisure. Pick perched on her shoulder, whispering furiously in her ear. When she failed to respond, he began to jump up and down in irritation.

"What's the matter with you?" he hissed. "How can you learn anything from all the way back here? You've got to get closer! Must I tell you how to do everything!"

She reached up, lifted him off her shoulder, and placed him on the table, frowning in reproof. *Patience,* she mouthed.

In truth, she was trying to make up her mind about the man. He looked like he might be an Indian, but how could she be sure? Most of what she knew about Indians she'd learned from movies and a few reports she'd done in school—not what you'd call a definitive education. She couldn't see his face clearly, and he wasn't wearing anything that looked remotely Indian. No jewelry, no feathers, no buckskins, no buffalo robes. He looked more like a combat veteran. She wondered suddenly if he was homeless. A heavy knapsack and a bedroll were settled on the bench beside him, and he had the look of a man who had been out in the weather a lot.

"Who is he, do you think?" she asked softly, almost to herself. Then she glanced down at Pick. "Have you ever seen him before?"

The sylvan was apoplectic. "No, I haven't seen him before! And I don't have the foggiest notion who he is! What do you think we're doing out here? Haven't you heard anything I've said?"

"Shhhhh," she hushed him gently.

They sat there for a time without speaking (although Pick muttered incessantly) and watched the man. He did not seem aware of them. He did not turn their way. He did not move at all. The sun slipped below the treeline, and the shadows deepened. Nest glanced about guardedly, but she did not see the feeders. Behind her, back toward the center of the park, the baseball games were winding down and the first cars were beginning to pull out from the parking spaces behind the backstops and turn toward the highway.

Then suddenly the man rose, picked up his knapsack and bedroll, and came toward Nest. Nest was so surprised she did not even have the presence of mind to think of running away. She sat there, frozen in place as he approached. She could see his face clearly now, his heavy, prominent features—dark brows, flat nose, and wide cheekbones. He moved with the grace and ease of a younger man, but the lines at the corners of his eyes and mouth suggested he was much older.

He sat down across from her without a word, depositing his belongings on the bench beside him. She realized suddenly that Pick had disappeared.

"Why are you looking at me?" he said.

She tried to speak, but nothing came out. He didn't sound or look angry, but his face and voice were hard to read.

"Cat got your tongue?" he pressed.

She cleared her throat and swallowed. "I was wondering if you were an Indian."

He stared at her without expression. "You mean Native American, don't you?"

She bit her lower lip and blushed. "Sorry. Native American."

He smiled, a tight, thin compression of his lips. "I suppose it doesn't matter what you call me. Native American. Indian. Redskin. The words of themselves do not define me. No more so than your histories do my people." The dark eyes squinted at her. "Who are you?"

"Nest Freemark," she told him.

"Huh, little bird's Nest, crafted of twigs and bits of string. Do you live nearby?"

She nodded, then glanced over her shoulder. "At the edge of the park. Why did you call me 'bird's Nest' like that?"

The dark eyes bore into her. "Isn't that what you were called when you were little?"

"By my grandmother, a long time ago. Then by some of the kids in school, when they wanted to tease me." She held his gaze. "How did you know?"

"I do magic," he told her in a whisper. "Don't you?"

She stared at him, not knowing what to say. "Sometimes."

He nodded. "A girl named Nest is bound to be called 'bird's Nest' by someone. Doesn't take much to figure that out. But 'Nest'—that is a name that has power. It has a history in the world, a presence."

Nest nodded. "It is Welsh. The woman who bore it first was the wife and mother of Welsh and English kings." She was surprised at how freely she was talking with the man, almost as if she knew him already.

"You have a good name, Nest. My name is Two Bears. I was given my name by my father, who on seeing me, newly born and quite large, declared, 'He is as big as two bears!' So I was called afterward, although that is not my Indian name. In the language of my people, my name is O'olish Amaneh."

"O'olish Amaneh," Nest repeated carefully. "Where do you come from, Two Bears?"

"First we must shake hands to mark the beginning of our friendship, little bird's Nest," he declared. "Then we can speak freely."

He motioned for Nest to extend her hand, and then he clasped it firmly in his own. His hand was as hard and coarse as rusted iron.

"Good. Because of your age, we will skip the part that involves smoking a peace pipe." He did not smile or change expression. "You ask me where I come from. I come from everywhere. I have lived a lot of places. But this"—he gestured about him—"is my real home."

"You're from Hopewell?" Nest said dubiously.

"No. But my people are of this land, of the Rock River Valley, from before Hopewell. They have all been dead a long time, my people, but sometimes I come back to visit them. They are buried just over there." He pointed toward the Indian mounds. "I was born in Springfield. That was a long time ago, too. How old do you think I am?"

He waited, but she could only shake her head. "I don't know."

"Fifty-two," he said softly. "My life slips rapidly away. I fought in Vietnam. I walked and slept with death; I knew her as I would a lover. I was young before, but afterward I was very old. I died in the Nam so many times, I lost count. But I killed a lot of men, too. I was a LURP. Do you know what that means?"

Nest shook her head once more.

"It doesn't matter," he said, brushing at the air with his big hand. "I was there for six years, and when it was over, I was no longer young. I came home, and I no longer knew myself or my people or my country. I was an Indian, a Native American, and a Redskin all rolled into one, and I was none of these. I was dead, but I was still walking around."

He looked at her without speaking for a moment, his eyes impenetrable. "On the other hand, maybe it was all a dream." His flat features shifted in the failing light, almost as if they were changing shape. "The trouble with dreams is that sometimes they are as real as life, and you cannot tell the two apart. Do you have dreams, little bird's Nest?"

"Sometimes," she replied, fascinated by the way his voice rose and fell as he talked, rough and silky, soft and bold. "Are you really an Indian, Two Bears?"

He glanced down then for a moment, shifting his hard gaze away from her, placing the palms of his big hands flat against the top of the picnic table. "Why should I tell you?"

He kept his eyes lowered, not looking at her. Nest did not know what to say.

"I will tell you because we are friends," he offered. "And because there is no reason not to tell you." His eyes lifted again to find hers. "I am an Indian, little bird's Nest, but I am something more as well. I am something no one should ever be. I am the last of my kind."

He brought the index finger of his right hand to his nose. "I am Sinnissippi, the only one left, the only one in all the world. My grandparents died before I went to Nam. My father died of drink. My mother died of grief. My brother died of a fall from the steel towers he helped to build in New York City. My sister died of drugs and alcohol on the streets in Chicago. We were all that remained, and now there is only me. Of all those who were once Sinnissippi, who filled this valley for miles in all directions, who went out into the world to found other tribes, there is only me. Can you imagine what that is like?"

Nest shook her head, transfixed.

"Do you know anything of the Sinnissippi?" he asked her. "Do you study them in school? Do your parents speak of them? The answer is no, isn't it? Did you even know that we existed?"

"No," she said softly.

His smile was flat and tight. "Think on this a moment, little bird's Nest. We were a people, like you. We had traditions and a culture. We were hunters and fishermen for the most part, but some among us were farmers as well. We had homes; we were the keepers of this park and all the land that surrounds it. All of that is gone, and no record of us remains. Even our burial mounds are believed to belong to another tribe. It is as if we never were. We are a rumor. We are a myth. How is that possible? Nothing remains of us but a name. Sinnissippi. We are a park, a street, an apartment building. Our name is there, preserved after we are gone, and yet our name means nothing, says nothing, tells nothing of us. Even the historians do not know what our name means. I have studied on this, long ago. Some think the name is Sauk, and that it refers to the land. Some think the name is Fox, and that it refers to the river that runs through the land. But no one thinks it is the name of our people. No one believes that."

"Have you ever tried to tell them?" Nest asked when he fell silent.

He shook his head. "Why should I? Maybe they are right. Maybe we didn't exist. Maybe there were no Sinnissippi, and I am a crazy man. What difference does it make? The Sinnissippi, if they ever were, are gone now. There is only me, and I am fading, too."

His words trailed away in the growing silence of the park. The light was almost gone, the sun settled below the horizon so that its brilliant orange glare was only a faint smudge against the darkening skyline west. The buzzing of the locusts had begun, rising and falling in rough cadence to the distant sounds of cars and voices as the last of the ballplayers and spectators emptied out of the park.

"What happened to your people?" Nest asked finally. "Why don't we know anything about them?"

Two Bears' coppery face shifted away again. "They were an old people, and they have been gone a long time. The Sauk and the Fox came after them. Then white Europeans who became the new Americans. The Sinnissippi were swallowed up in time's passage, and no one who lived in my lifetime could tell me why. What they had been told by their ancestors was vague. The Sinnissippi did not adapt. They did not change when change was necessary. It is a familiar story. It is what happens to so many nations. Perhaps the Sinnissippi were particularly ill suited to make the change that was necessary to ensure their survival. Perhaps they were foolish or blind or inflexible or simply unprepared. I have never known." He paused. "But I have come back to find out."

His big hands clasped before his rugged face. "I was a long time deciding that I would do this. It seemed better to me in some ways not to know. But the question haunts me, so I am here. Tomorrow night, I will summon the spirits of the dead from where they lie within the earth. I have shaman powers, little bird's Nest, revealed to me in the madness of the war in Nam. I will use those powers to summon the spirits of the Sinnissippi to dance for me, and in their dance they will reveal the answers to my questions. I am the last of them, so they must speak to me."

Nest tried to picture it. The spirits of the Sinnissippi dancing at night in the park—in the same park where the feeders prowled, unfettered.

"Would you like to watch?" Two Bears asked quietly.

"Me?" She breathed the word as she would a prayer.

"Tomorrow, at midnight. Are you afraid?"

She was, but she refused to admit it.

"I am a stranger, a big man, a combat veteran who speaks of terrifying things. You should be afraid. But we are friends, Nest. Our friendship was sealed with our handshake. I will not hurt you."

The dark eyes reflected pinpricks of light from the rising moon. Darkness cloaked the park, the twilight almost gone. Nest remembered the promise she had made to her grandfather. She had to leave soon.

"If you come," said the big man softly, "you may learn something of your own people's fate. The spirits will speak of more than the Sinnissippi. The dance will reveal things that you should know."

Nest blinked. "What things?"

He shook his head slowly. "What happened to my people can happen to yours as well." He paused. "What if I were to tell you that it is happening now?"

Nest felt a tightening in her throat. She brushed at her short, curly hair with her hand. She could feel the sweat bead on her forehead. "What do you mean?"

Two Bears leaned back, and his face disappeared momentarily into shadow. "All peoples think they are forever," he growled softly. "They do not believe they will ever not be. The Sinnissippi were that way. They did not think they would be eradicated. But that is what happened. Your people, Nest, believe this of themselves. They will survive forever, they think. Nothing can destroy them, can wipe them so completely from the earth and from history that all that will remain is their name and not even that will be known with certainty. They have such faith in their invulnerability.

"Yet already their destruction begins. It comes upon them gradually, in little ways. Bit by bit their belief in themselves erodes. A growing cynicism pervades their lives. Small acts of kindness and charity are abandoned as pointless and somehow indicative of weakness. Little failures of behavior lead to bigger ones. It is not enough to ignore the discourtesies of others; discourtesies must be repaid in kind. Men are intolerant and judgmental. They are without grace. If one man proclaims that God has spoken to him, another quickly proclaims that his God is false. If the homeless cannot find shelter, then surely they are to blame for their condition. If the poor do not have jobs, then surely it is because they will not work. If sickness strikes down those whose lifestyle differs from our own, then surely they have brought it on themselves.

"Look at your people, Nest Freemark. They abandon their old. They shun their sick. They cast off their children. They decry any who are different. They commit acts of unfaithfulness, betrayal, and depravity every day. They foster lies that undermine beliefs. Each small darkness breeds another. Each small incident of anger, bitterness, pettiness, and greed breeds others. A sense of futility consumes them. They feel helpless to effect even the smallest change. Their madness is of their own making, and yet they are powerless against it because they refuse to acknowledge its source. They are at war with themselves, but they do not begin to understand the nature of the battle being fought."

He took a long, slow breath and released it. "Do even a handful among your people believe that life in this country is better now than it was twenty years ago? Do they believe that the dark things that inhabit it are less threatening? Do they feel safer in their homes and cities? Do they find honor and trust and compassion outweigh greed and deceit and disdain? Can you tell me that you do not fear for them?"

There was bleak appraisal in his dark eyes. "We do not always recognize the thing that comes to destroy us. That is the lesson of the Sinnissippi. It can appear in many different forms. Perhaps my people were destroyed by a world which demanded changes they could not make." He shook his head slowly, as if trying to see beyond his words. "But there is reason to think that your people destroy themselves."

He went silent then, staring at the girl, his eyes distant, his look impenetrable. Nest took a deep breath. "It is not that bad," she said, trying to keep the doubt from her voice.

Two Bears smiled. "It is worse. You know that it is. You can see it everywhere, even in this park." He glanced around, as if to find some evidence of it close at hand. Feeders were visible at the edges of the deeper shadows, but the Indian seemed oblivious of them. He looked back at Nest. "Your people risk the fate of the Sinnissippi. Come to the summoning tomorrow at midnight and judge for yourself. Perhaps the spirits of the dead will speak of it. If they do not, then perhaps I am just another Indian with too much firewater in his body."

"You're not that," Nest said quickly, not certain at the same time just exactly what he was.

"Will you come?" he pressed.

She nodded. "Okay."

Two Bears rose, a hulking figure amid the shadows. "The Fourth of July approaches," he said softly. "Independence Day. The birth of your nation, of the United States of America." He nodded. "My nation, too, though I am Sinnissippi. I was born to her. My dreams were nurtured by her. I fought for her in Vietnam. My people are buried in her soil. She is my home, whatever name she bears. So I suppose that I am right to be interested in her fate."

He picked up his knapsack and his bedroll and slung them over his shoulder. "Tomorrow night, little bird's Nest," he repeated.

She nodded in response. "At midnight, O'olish Amaneh."

He gave her a brief, tight-lipped smile. "Tell your little friend he can come out from under the picnic table now."

Then he turned into the darkness and strode silently away.

Saturday, July 2

CHAPTER 9

The Knight of the Word rode into Hopewell on the nine-fifteen out of Chicago and not one of the passengers who rode with him had any idea who he was. He wore no armor and carried no sword, and the only charger he could afford was this Greyhound bus. He looked to be an ordinary man save for the pronounced limp and the strange, haunted look that reflected in his pale green eyes. He was a bit stooped for thirty-eight years of age, a little weathered for being not yet forty. He was of average height and weight, rather lean, almost gaunt when seen from certain angles. His face was unremarkable. He was the kid who cut your lawn all through high school grown up and approaching middle age. His lank brown hair was combed straight back from his high forehead, cut shoulder-length and tied back with a rolled bandanna. He wore jeans, a blue denim work shirt, and high-top walking shoes that were scuffed and worn, the laces knotted in more than one place.

He had left his duffel bag for storage in the luggage compartment, and when the bus pulled to a stop in front of the Lincoln Hotel he moved to retrieve it. He leaned heavily on a gnarled black walnut staff for support as he made his way to the front of the bus, his knapsack slung loosely across one shoulder. He did not meet anyone's gaze. He appeared to those traveling with him, those whose journey would take them farther west to the Quad Cities and Des Moines, as if he might be drifting, and their assessment was not entirely wrong.

But for as much as he might appear otherwise, he was still a knight, the best that the people of the world were going to get and better perhaps than they deserved. For ten long years he had sought to protect them, a paladin in their cause. There were demons loose in the world, things of such evil that if they were not destroyed they would destroy mankind. Already the feeders were responding to them, coming out of their hiding places, daring to appear even in daylight, feeding on the dark emotions that the demons fostered in humans everywhere. The demons were skillful at their work, and the humans they preyed upon were all too eager to be made victims. The demons could be all things to all people just long enough to blacken their hearts, and by the time the people realized what had happened to them, it was too late. By then the feeders were devouring them.

The Knight of the Word had been sent to put an end to the demons. His quest had taken him from one end of the country to the other countless times over, and still he journeyed on. Sometimes, in his darker moments, he thought his quest would never end. Sometimes he wondered why he had accepted it at all. He had given up everything in its cause, his life irrevocably changed. The dangers it presented were more formidable than any faced by those who had ridden under Arthur's banner. Nor did he have a Round Table and fellow knights awaiting his return—no king to honor him or lady to comfort him. He was all alone, and when his quest was finished, he would still be so.

His name was John Ross.

He retrieved his duffel bag from the driver, thanked him for his trouble, then leaned on his staff and looked about as the bus door closed, the air brakes released, and his silver charger slowly pulled away. He was at the corner of Fourth Street and Avenue A, the hotel before him, a paint store across one street and a library across the other. Kitty-corner was a gas station and tire shop. All of the buildings were run-down and bleached by the sun, washed of every color but beige and sand, their bricks crumbling and dry, their painted wood sidings peeling and splintered with the heat. The concrete of the sidewalks and streets radiated with the sun's glare, and where the street had been patched with asphalt it reflected a damp, shimmering black.

He found himself staring down Fourth Street to its junction with First Avenue, remembering what he had seen in his dream. His eyes closed against the memory.

He picked up his duffel, limped up the steps to the front door of the hotel, and pushed his way inside. A blast of cool air from the air conditioner welcomed him, then quickly turned him cold. He checked himself in at the desk, taking the cheapest room they had, booking it for a week because the rate was less than for the three days he required. He was frugal with his money, for he lived mostly on the little his parents had left him when they died. Leaving his duffel and his knapsack with the desk clerk, who offered to carry them to his room, he picked up one of the slim pamphlets entitled "Hopewell—We're Growing Your Way" that were stacked next to the register, moved over to the tiny lobby sitting area, and lowered himself into one of the worn wing-back chairs.

The cover of the pamphlet was a collage of pictures—a cornfield, a park, a swimming pool, the downtown, and one of the plants at MidCon Steel. Inside was a rudimentary map. He read briefly that Hopewell had a population of fifteen thousand, was situated in the heart of Reagan country (both the town where Ronald Reagan was born and the one in which he grew up were within twenty miles), boasted more than seventy churches, offered easy freeway access to major cities in all directions, and was the home of Midwest Continental Steel, once the largest independently owned steel company in America. The pamphlet went on to say that while more than twenty percent of the working force of Hopewell was employed at MidCon Steel, the community was a source of employment for others as a result of a diverse and thriving agricultural and business economy.

The desk man returned with his room key. Not another soul had passed through the lobby in the time he had been gone. He seemed grateful when John Ross gave him a dollar for his trouble. Ross finished with the pamphlet and tucked it into the pocket of his jeans with his room key. He sat for a moment in the cool of the lobby, listening to the hum of the air-conditioning, looking down at his hands. He did not have much time to do what was needed. He knew enough from his dreams to make a start, but the dreams were sometimes deceptive and so could not be trusted completely. Nor were the dream memories of his future more than rudimentary. Nor were they stable; they tended to shift with the passing of events and the changing of circumstances. It was like trying to build with water and sand. Sometimes he could not tell which part of his life he was remembering or even at which point of time the events had occurred or would occur. Sometimes he thought it would drive him mad.

He hoisted himself out of the armchair, an abrupt, decisive movement. Leaning on his staff, he went out the front door into the heat and turned up Fourth Street toward the heart of the downtown. He walked slowly and methodically along the gauntlet of burning concrete, the sidewalks baking in the already near one-hundred-degree heat. The buildings had a flattened feel to them, as if weighted by the heat, as if compressed. The people he passed on the streets looked drained of energy, squinting into the glare from behind sunglasses, walking with their heads lowered and their shoulders hunched. He crossed Locust Street, the north-south thoroughfare that became State Route 88 beyond the town limits, continued on to Second Avenue, and turned down Second toward Third Street. Already he could see the red plastic sign on the building ahead that read JOSIE'S.

A church loomed over him, providing a momentary patch of shade. He slowed and looked up at it, studying its rust-colored stone, its stained glass, its arched wooden doors, and its open bell tower. A glass-enclosed sign situated on the patch of lawn at the corner said it was the First Congregational Church. Ralph Emery was the minister. Services were Sunday at 10:30 A.M. with Christian Education classes at 9:15. This Sunday's message was entitled, "Whither Thou Goest." John Ross knew it would be cool and silent inside, a haven from the heat and the world. It had been a long time since he had been in church. He found himself wanting to see how it would feel, wondering if he could still say his prayers in a slow, quiet way and not in a rush of desperation. He wondered if his God still believed in him.

He stood staring at the church for a moment more, then turned away. His relationship with God would have to wait. It was the demon he hunted who demanded his attention now, the one he had come to Hopewell to destroy. He limped on through the midmorning heat, thinking on the nature of his adversary. In a direct confrontation, he was certain he would prevail. But the demon was clever and elusive; it could conceal its identity utterly. It was careful never to permit itself to be fully engaged. Time and again John Ross had thought to trap it, to unmask it and force it to face him, and every time the demon had escaped. Like a sickness that passed itself from person to person, the demon first infected them with its madness, then gave them over to the feeders to devour. Until now Ross had searched in vain for a way to stop it. It had been difficult even to find it, virtually impossible to lay hands on it. But that was about to change. The dreams had finally revealed something useful to him, something beyond the haunting ruin of the future that awaited should he fail, something so crucial to the demon's survival that it might prove its undoing.

John Ross reached the corner of Second Avenue and Third Street and waited for the WALK sign. When it flashed on, he crossed over to Josie's, limped to the front door, and pushed his way inside.

The café was busy, the Saturday-morning crowd filling all but one of the tables and booths, the air pungent with the smell of coffee and doughnuts. Ross glanced about, taking in the faces of the customers, noting in particular the large table of men at the back, then moved to the counter. The stools were mostly vacant. He took one at the far end and lowered himself comfortably in place. The air-conditioning hummed, and the sweat dried on his face and hands. He leaned the black walking stick between the counter and his knee, bracing it there. Talk and laughter drifted about him in the mingling of voices. He did not look around. He did not need to. The man he had come to find was present.

The woman working the counter came over to him. She was pretty, with long, tousled blondish hair tied back in a ponytail, expressive dark eyes, and sun-browned skin. White cotton shorts and a collared blouse hugged the soft curves of her body. But it was her smile that captivated him. It was big and open and dazzling. It had been a long time since anyone had smiled at him like that.

"Good morning," she greeted. "Would you like some coffee?"

He stared at her without answering, feeling something stir inside that had lain dormant for a long time. Then he caught himself and shook his head quickly. "No, thank you, miss."

"Miss?" Her grin widened. "Been quite a while since anyone called me that. Do I know you?"

Ross shook his head a second time. "No. I'm not from around here."

"I didn't think so. I'm pretty good with faces, and I don't remember yours. Would you like some breakfast?"

He thought about it a moment, studying the menu board posted on the wall behind her. "You know, what I'd really like is a Cherry Coke."

She cocked an eyebrow at him. "I think we can fix you up."

She walked away, and he watched her go, wondering at the unexpected attraction he felt for her, trying to remember when he had last felt that way about anyone. He looked down at his hands where they rested on the counter. His hands were shaking. His life, he knew, was a shambles.

A man and a boy came into the coffee shop, approached the counter, glanced at the available seats, and then squeezed themselves in between two men farther down the way. Ross could feel their eyes on him. He did not react. It was always like this, as if somehow people could sense the truth of what he was.

The woman with the smile returned carrying his Cherry Coke. If she could sense the truth, she didn't show it. She set the Coke on a napkin in front of him and folded her arms under her breasts. She was probably somewhere in her thirties, but she looked younger than that.

"Sure you wouldn't like a Danish or maybe some coffee cake? You look hungry."

He smiled in spite of himself, forgetting for a moment his weariness. "I must be made of glass, the way you see right through me. As a matter of fact, I'm starved. I was just trying to decide what to order."

"Now we're getting somewhere," she declared, smiling back. "Since this is your first visit, let me make a suggestion. Order the hash. It's my own recipe. You won't be sorry."

"All right. Your own recipe, is it?"

"Yep. This is my place." She stuck out her hand. "I'm Josie Jackson."

"John Ross." He took her hand in his own and held it. Her hand was cool. "Nice to meet you."

"Nice to meet you, too. Nice to meet anyone who still calls me 'miss' and means it." She laughed and walked away.

He finished the Cherry Coke, and when the hash arrived he ordered a glass of milk to go with it. He ate the hash and drank the milk without looking up. Out of the corner of his eye, he caught Josie Jackson looking at him as she passed down the counter.

When he was finished, she came back and stood in front of him. There were freckles on her nose underneath the tan. Her arms were smooth and brown. He found himself wanting to touch her skin.

"You were right," he said. "The hash was good."

She beamed, her smile dazzling. "Do you want some more? I think the house can spare seconds."

"No, thank you anyway."

"Can I get you anything else?"

"No, that's fine." He glanced over one shoulder as if checking something, then looked back at her. "Can I ask you a question?"

Her mouth quirked at the corners. "That depends on the question."

He glanced over his shoulder again. "Is that Robert Freemark sitting back there with those men?"

She followed his gaze, then nodded. "You know Old Bob?"

Ross levered himself off the stool with the help of his walking stick. "No, but I was a friend of his daughter." The lie burned in his throat as he said it. "Will you hold my bill for a minute, Josie? I want to go say hello."

He limped from the counter toward the table in back, steeling himself against what he must do. The men sitting around it were telling stories and laughing, eating doughnuts and pastries, and drinking coffee. It looked like they felt at home here, as if they came often. Bob Freemark had his back turned and didn't see him until some of the others looked up at his approach. Then Old Bob looked around as well, his big, white head lifting, his piercing blue eyes fixing Ross with a thoughtful look.

"Are you Robert Freemark, sir?" John Ross asked him.

The big man nodded. "I am."

"My name is John Ross. We haven't met before, but your daughter and I were friends." The lie went down easier this time. "I just wanted to come over and say hello."

Old Bob stared at him. The table went silent. "Caitlin?" the other man asked softly.

"Yes, sir, a long time ago, when we were both in college. I knew her then." Ross kept his face expressionless.

Old Bob seemed to recover himself. "Sit down, Mr. Ross," he urged, pulling over an empty chair from one of the adjoining tables. Ross seated himself gingerly, extending his leg away from the table so that he was facing Robert Freemark but not the others. The conversations at the table resumed, but Ross could tell that the other men were listening in on them nevertheless.

"You knew Caitlin, you say?" Old Bob repeated.

"In Ohio, sir, when we were both in college. She was at Oberlin, so was I, a year ahead. We met at a social function, a mixer. We dated on and off, but it was nothing serious. We were mostly just friends. She talked about you and Mrs. Freemark often. She told me quite a lot about you. When she left school, I never saw her again. I understand she was killed. I'm sorry."

Old Bob nodded. "Almost fourteen years ago, Mr. Ross. It's all in the past."

He didn't sound as if that were so, Ross thought. "I promised myself that if I was ever out this way, I would try to stop by and say hello to you and Mrs. Freemark. I thought a lot of Caitlin."

The other man nodded, but didn't look as if he quite understood. "How did you find us here in Hopewell, Mr. Ross?"

"Please, sir, call me John." He eased his bad leg to a new position. The men at the table were losing interest in what he had to say. A fourteen-year-old friendship with a dead girl was not important to them. "I knew where Caitlin was from," he explained. "I took a chance that you and Mrs. Freemark were still living here. I asked about you at the hotel where I'm staying. Then I came here. Josie told me who you were."

"Well," Old Bob said softly. "Isn't that something?"

"Yes, sir."

"Where are you from, John?"

"New York City." He lied again.

"Is that so? New York City? What brings you out this way?"

"I'm traveling through by bus to see friends in Seattle. I don't have a schedule to keep to, so I took a small detour here. I suppose I decided it was time to keep my promise."

He paused, as if considering something he had almost forgotten. "I understand that Caitlin has a daughter."

"Yes, that would be Nest," Old Bob acknowledged, smiling. "She lives with us. She's quite a young lady."

John Ross nodded. "Well, that's good to hear." He tried not to think of the dreams. "Does she look at all like her mother?"

"Very much so." Old Bob's smile broadened. "Having Nest helps in some small way to make up for losing Caitlin."

Ross looked at the floor. "I expect it does. I wish I could see her. I think often of Caitlin." He went silent, as if unable to think of anything else to say. "Well, thank you, sir. I appreciate having had the opportunity of meeting you."

He started to rise, levering himself up with the aid of his staff. "Please give my regards to Mrs. Freemark and your granddaughter."

He was already moving away when Old Bob caught up with him. The big man's hand touched his arm. "Wait a minute, Mr. Ross. John. I don't think it's right that you've come all this way and don't get to talk about Caitlin more than this. Why don't you come to dinner tonight? You can meet Evelyn—Mrs. Freemark—and Nest as well. We'd like to hear more about what you remember. Would you like to come?"

John Ross took a long, deep breath. "Very much, sir."

"Good. That's good. Come about six, then." Old Bob brushed at his thick white hair with one hand. "Can you find a ride or shall I pick you up?"

"I'll manage to get there." Ross smiled.

Robert Freemark extended his hand and Ross took it. The old man's grip was powerful. "It was good of you to come, John. We'll be looking forward to seeing you this evening."

"Thank you, sir," Ross replied, meaning it.

He moved away then, back toward the counter, listening to the conversation of the other men at the table trail after him. *Knew Caitlin, did he? At college? What's his name again? You think he's one of those hippies? He looks a little frayed around the edges. What do you think he did to his leg?* Ross let the words wash off him and did not look around. He felt sad and old. He felt bereft of compassion. None of them mattered. No one mattered, in truth, besides Nest Freemark.

He came back to the counter and Josie Jackson. She handed him his bill and stood waiting while he pried loose several dollars from his jeans pocket.

"You knew Caitlin, did you?" she asked, studying him.

"A long time ago, yes." He held her gaze with his own, wanting to find a way to take something of her with him when he went.

"Is that what brought you to Hopewell? Because the fact of the matter is you don't look like a salesman or a truck driver or a bail bondsman or anything."

He gave her a quick, tight smile. "That's what brought me."

"So where are you off to now?" She took the money he handed her without looking at it. "If you don't mind my asking."

He shook his head. "I don't mind. To tell you the truth, I thought I'd go back to my room for a bit. I'm a little tired. I just came in on the bus, and I didn't sleep much." The word "sleep" sent an involuntary chill through his body.

"Are you staying at the Lincoln Hotel?" she asked.

"For a few days."

"So maybe we'll see some more of you while you're here?"

He smiled anew, liking the way she looked at him. "I don't see how you can avoid it if everything at Josie's is as good as the hash."

She smiled back. "Some things are even better." She kept her gaze level, unembarrassed. "See you later, John."

The Knight of the Word turned and walked out the door into the midday heat, riddled with shards of confusion and hope.

Seated at the table in the back of the café with Old Bob and the others, an invisible presence in their midst, the demon watched him go.

CHAPTER 10

It is night. The sky is clear, and the full moon hangs above the eastern horizon in brilliant opalescence. Stars fill the dark firmament with pinpricks of silver, and the breeze that wafts across his heated skin is cool and soft. He stands looking upward for a moment, thinking that nothing of the madness of the world in which he stands reflects in the heavens he views. He wishes he could find a way to smother the madness with the tranquillity and peace he finds there. He remembers for a moment the way things were.

Then he is moving again, jogging steadily down the concrete highway into the city, hearing already the screams and cries of the captives. The pens are two miles farther in, but the number of prisoners they contain is so vast that the sounds travel all the way to the farmlands. The city is not familiar to him. It lies in what was Kansas or perhaps Nebraska. The country about is flat and empty. Once it grew crops, but now it grows only dust. Nothing lives in the country. All of the fields have dried away. All of the animals have been killed. All of the people have been hunted down and herded into the pens by those who were once like them. In the silence of the night, there is only the buzzing and chirping of insects and the dry, papery whisper of old leaves being blown across stone.

Feeders peer out from the shadows as he passes, but they keep their distance. He is a Knight of the Word, and they have no power over him. They sense this, and they do not offer challenge. They are creatures of instinct and habit, and they react to what they find in humans in the way that predators react to the smell of blood. John Ross knows this about them. He understands what they are, a lesson imparted to him long ago when there was still hope, when there was still reason to believe he could make a difference. The feeders are a force of nature, and they respond to instinct rather than to reason. They do not think, because thinking is not required of them. They do not exist to think, but to react. The Word made them for reasons that John Ross does not understand. They are a part of the balance of life, but their particular place in the balance remains a mystery to him. They are attracted by the darker emotions that plague human beings. They appear when those emotions can no longer be contained. They feed on those emotions and in so doing drive mad the humans who are their victims. Given enough time and space and encouragement, they would destroy everything.

The Knight of the Word has tried hard to determine why this must be, but it requires a deeper understanding of human behavior than he possesses. So he has come to accept the feeders simply as a force of nature. He can see them, as most cannot, so he knows they are real. Few others understand this. Few have any idea at all that the feeders even exist. If they knew, they would be reminded of Biblical references and cautionary tales from childhood and be quick to describe the feed-

ers as Satan's creatures or the Devil's imps. But the feeders belong to the Word. They are neither good nor evil, and their purpose is far too complex to be explained away in such simplistic terms.

He passes through what was once an industrial storage area of the city, and the amber eyes follow him, flat and expressionless. The feeders feel nothing, reveal nothing. The feeders have no concern for him one way or the other. That is not their function. The Knight of the Word has to remind himself of this, for the glimmer of their eyes seems a challenge and a danger to him. But the feeders, as he has learned, are as impervious to emotion as fate is to prayers. They are like the wind and the rain; when conditions warrant, they will appear. Look for them as you would a change in the weather, for they respond in no less impersonal and arbitrary a way.

Nevertheless, it seems to him, as he passes their dark lair, that they know who he is and judge him accordingly. He cannot help himself, for they have been witness to his every failure. It feels as if they judge him now, remembering as he does the many opportunities he has squandered. Tonight provides another test for him. His successes of late might seem to offset his earlier failures, but it is the failures that matter most. If he had not failed in Hopewell with Nest Freemark, he thinks bitterly, there would be no need for successes now. He remembers her, a child of fourteen, how close he was to saving her, how badly he misjudged what was needed. He remembers the demon, prevailing even in the face of his fierce opposition. The memory will not leave. The memory will haunt him to the grave.

But he will not die tonight, he thinks. He carries in his hands the gleaming, rune-carved staff of magic that the Lady gave him all those years ago, wielding it as Arthur would Excalibur, believing there are no numbers great enough to stand against him or weapons strong enough to destroy him or evil dark enough to expunge the light of his magic. It is the legacy of his failure, the talisman bequeathed to him when nothing remained but the battle itself. He will fight on because fighting is all that is left. He is strong, pure, and fixed of purpose. He is a knight-errant adrift on a quest of his own making. He is Don Quixote tilting at windmills with no hope of finding peace.

He slows now to a walk, close enough to the pens to be able to see the smoky light of the torches that illuminate the compound. He has never been here before, but he knows what he will find. He has seen others of the same sort in other cities. They are all the same—makeshift enclosures into which humans have been herded and shut away. Men, women, and children run to ground and enslaved, there to be separated and processed, to be designated for a purpose, to be used and debilitated and ultimately destroyed. It is the way the world is now, the way it has been for more than seven years. All of the cities of America are either armed camps or ruins. Nuclear missiles and poison gas and defoliant were used early, when there were still governments and armies to wield them. Then the missiles and gas and defoliant were discarded in favor of more personal, rudimentary weapons as the governments and armies disintegrated and the level of savagery rose. Washington was obliterated. New York City tore itself apart. Atlanta, Houston, and Denver built walls and stockpiled weapons and began systematically to annihilate anyone who came close. Los Angeles and Chicago became killing grounds for the demons and their followers. Sides were chosen and battles fought at every turn. Reason gave way to bloodlust and was lost.

There are places somewhere, the Knight has heard, where the madness is still held at bay, but he has not found them. Some are in other countries, but he does not know where. Technology is fragmented and does not function in a dependable manner. Airplanes no longer fly, ships no longer sail, and trains no longer run. Knowledge dissipates with the passing of every day and the death of every man. The Void has no interest in technology because technology furthers progress. The demons multiply, and their purpose now is to break down what remains of human reason and to put an end to any resistance. Little stands in their way. The madness that marked the beginning of the end continues to grow.

But the Knight fights on, a solitary champion for the Word, shackled to his fate as punishment for his failure to prevent the madness from taking hold when he still had a chance to do so. He goes from city to city, from armed camp to armed camp, freeing those poor creatures imprisoned by the slave pens, hoping that some few will manage to escape to a better place, that one or two will somehow make a difference in the terrible battle being fought. He has no specific expectations. Hope of any sort is a luxury he cannot afford. He must carry on because he has pledged to do so. There is nothing else left for him. There is nothing else that matters.

John Ross slows to a steady walk, holding the staff crosswise before him with both hands. He remembers what it was like when the staff was his walking stick and gave support against his limp. But his dreams have ended and his future has become his present. Tomorrow's madness has become today's. The limp has disappeared, and he is transformed. The staff is now his sword and shield; he is infused with its power and made strong. The magic he had feared to use before is now used freely. It is a measure of his service that there are no longer any constraints placed on him, but it is also a mark of his failure.

Ahead, the torchlight grows brighter. The tools of living have become rudimentary once more. There is no electricity to power streetlamps, no fuel for turbines or generators, almost no coal or oil left to burn. There is no running water. There is no sewage or garbage disposal. There are few automobiles that run and few roads that will support them. The concrete of the streets is cracked and broken. Patches of grass and scrub push through. The earth slowly reclaims its own.

He slides to one side to keep within the shadows. He is not afraid, but there is an advantage in surprise. The feeders peering out at him draw back, wary. They sense that he can see them when most others cannot—even those who have fallen victim to the madness and serve the demons, even those the feeders rely upon to sustain them. Their numbers are huge now, grown so vast that there is not a darkened corner anywhere in which they do not lurk. They have bred in a frenzy as the madness consumed mankind, but of late their breeding has slowed. Some will begin to disappear soon, for the dwindling population of humans cannot continue to support them. With the passage of time the balance will shift back again, and the world will begin anew. But it is too late for civilization. Civilization is finished. Men are diminished, reduced to the level of animals. Rebirth, when it comes, will be a crapshoot.

He wonders momentarily how bad it is elsewhere in the world. He does not know for certain. He has heard it is not good, that what began in America spread more quickly elsewhere, that what took seed slowly here finds more fertile soil abroad. He believes that every country is under assault and that most are overrun. He believes that the destruction is widespread. He has not been visited by the Lady in a long time. He has seen no evidence that she still exists. He has heard nothing from the Word.

He approaches the pens now, a sprawling maze of wire mesh fences and gates behind which the humans are imprisoned. Torches smoke and blaze on tall stanchions, revealing the extent of the misery visited on the captives. Men, women, and children, all ages, races, and creeds—they have been flushed from their hiding places in the surrounding countryside, rounded up and herded like cattle into the pens, squeezed together with no thought for their comfort or their needs, provided with just enough of what they require to remain alive. They are used for work and breeding until they are no longer strong enough, and then they are exterminated. Their keepers are once-men, humans who have succumbed to the madness that the demons foster everywhere, the madness that was before isolated and is now rampant. Once it was accepted that all men were created equal, but that is no longer so. Humanity has evolved into two separate and distinct life-forms, strong and weak, hunter and hunted. The Void holds sway; the Word lies dormant. The once-men have given way completely to their darker impulses and now think only to survive, even at the cost of the lives of their fellow men, even at the peril of their souls. Given time, some few will evolve to become demons themselves. The feeders dine upon their victims, finding sustenance in the commission of atrocities so terrible that it is difficult even to contemplate them. It must have been like this in the concentration camps of old. But John Ross cannot imagine it.

He is close enough now that he can see the faces of the captives. They peer out at him from behind the wire, their eyes dull and empty. They are naked mostly, thrust up against the wire by those who push from behind, waiting for the night to end and the day to begin, waiting without hope or reason or purpose. They mewl and they cry and they curl up in fear. They scratch themselves endlessly. He can hardly bear to look on them, but he forces himself to do so, for they are the legacy of his failure. Once-men stand armed and ready in watchtowers all about the compound, holding automatic weapons. Weapons are still plentiful in this post-apocalyptic world, a paradox. Sentries patrol the perimeter of the compound. John Ross has come up on them so quickly that they are just now realizing he is there. Some turn to look, some swing their weapons about menacingly. But he is only one man, alone and unarmed. They are not alarmed. They are no better now at recognizing what will destroy them than they were when the first of the demons came among them all those years ago.

A few call out to him to halt, to stand where he is, but he comes on without slowing. A command rings out and shots are fired, a warning. He comes on. Shots ring out again, a flurry this time, meant to bring him down. But his magic is already in place. He calls it Black Ice—smooth, slippery, invisible. It coats him with its protective shield. The bullets slide off harmlessly. He pushes aside the closest of the once-men and strides to the wire mesh of the pens. Holding the staff firmly in both hands, he sweeps its tip across the diamond-shaped openings. Light flares, and the mesh falls apart like torn confetti. The occupants of the pens fall back in shock and fear, not certain what is happening, not knowing what to do. Ross ignores them, turning to face the once-men that rush to stop him. He scatters them with a single sweep of his staff. The guards in the watchtowers turn their weapons on him and begin to fire, but the bullets cannot harm him. He points his staff at the towers.

Light flares, incandescent and blinding, and one after another the towers collapse and burn.

The compound is in chaos now. The once-men are rushing about frantically, trying to regroup. The Knight of the Word is relentless. He tears at the wire mesh of the pens until it hangs in tatters. He yells at the cowering prisoners, urging them to get up, to run, to escape. At first no one moves. Then a few begin to creep out, the bolder ones, testing the waters of their newfound freedom. Then others follow, and soon the entire camp is rushing away into the night. Some few, those who still cling to some shred of their humanity, stop to help the children and the elderly. The once-men give chase, howling in frustration and rage, but they are swept aside by the tide and by the fire of the Knight's bright magic. John Ross strides through the camp unchallenged, flinging aside those who would stop him. The feeders have appeared by now, vast numbers of them, leaping and cavorting about him, seeing in him the prospect of fresh nourishment. He does not like serving as their catalyst, but he knows it cannot be helped. The feeders respond because it is in their nature to do so. The feeders are there because they are drawn by the misery and the pain of the humans. There is nothing he can do to change that.

He is making his way through the greater part of the camp, destroying the pens and freeing their occupants, when he sees the demon. It comes toward him almost casually, appearing out of the shadows. It still looks somewhat human, although grotesquely so, for most of its disguise has fallen away from lack of use. Once-men flank it, mirroring in their faces the hatred and fear that flares in the depths of its bright eyes. Although the demon has come to stop him, John Ross is not afraid. Others of its kind have tried to stop him before. All lie dead.

He swings to face the demon. Behind him, the captives of the pens stream through the empty streets of the ruined city for the flatlands beyond. Perhaps some will escape the pursuit that will follow. Perhaps they will find freedom in another place. The Knight has made what difference he can. It is all he can do.

All about him, the feeders cluster, anticipating that they will soon dine upon the leavings that a battle between the Knight and the demon will create. They creep like shadows in the smoky glow of the torches. Their fluid forms extend and recede like waves on a shore.

The Knight brings up his staff and starts for the demon. As he does so a net falls over him. It is heavy and thick, woven of steel threads and weighted on the ends. It bears him to his knees. Instantly the once-men are upon him, rushing from hiding, charging into the light. It is a trap, and the Knight has stumbled into it. The once-men are on him, seeking to tear the staff from his hands, to strip him of his only weapon. All about, the feeders leap and dart wildly, the frenzy drawing them like moths to a flame. In the background, the demon approaches, eyes intent, eager, and bright with hate.

Light flares along the length of the Knight's staff and surges into the midst of his attackers . . .

John Ross awoke with a cry, tearing at the enemies that were no longer there, thrashing beneath the light blanket he had thrown over himself when he succumbed to his need for sleep. He stifled his cry and ceased his struggle and lurched to a sitting position, the black walking staff clutched tightly in both hands. He sat staring into space, coming back from his dream, regaining his sense of place and time. The portable air conditioner thrummed steadily from its seating in the window, and the cool air washed over his sweating face. His breathing was quick and uneven, and his pulse pounded in his ears. He felt as if his heart would burst.

It was like this, sometimes. He would dream and then wake in the middle of his dream, his future revealed in tantalizing snippets, but with no resolution offered. Would he escape from the net and the once-men or would he be killed? Either was possible. Time was disjointed in his dreams, so he could not know. Sometimes the answers would be revealed in later dreams, but not always. He had learned to live with the uncertainty, but not to accept it.

He looked over at the bedside clock. It was midafternoon. He had only slept three hours. He closed his eyes against his bitterness. Three hours. He must sleep again tonight if he was to maintain his strength. He must go back again into the world of his dreams, into the future of his life, into the promise of what waited should he fail in the here and now, and there was no help for it. It was the price he paid for being what he was.

He lay back slowly on the bed and stared upward at the ceiling. He would not sleep again now, he knew. He could never sleep right after waking from the dreams, his adrenaline pumping through him, his nerve endings jagged and raw. It was just as well. He tried not to sleep at all anymore, or to sleep only in small stretches in an effort to lessen the impact of the dreams. But it was hard to live that way. Sometimes it was almost more than he could bear.

He let his thoughts drift. His memory of the times and places when he had felt at peace and there had been at least some small measure of comfort were distant and faded. His childhood was a blur, his boyhood a jumbled collection of disconnected faces and events. Even the years of his manhood, from before the coming of the Lady, were no longer clear in his mind. His entire life was lost to him. He had given it all away. Once it had seemed so right and necessary that he should do so. His passion and his beliefs had governed his reason, and the importance of the charge that had been offered him had outweighed any other consideration.

But that was a long time ago. He was no longer certain he had chosen rightly. He was no longer sure even of himself.

He called up a picture of Josie Jackson in an effort to distance himself from his thoughts. She materialized before him, tousled hair and sun-browned skin, freckles and bright smile. Thinking of her comforted him, but there was no reason for it. She had smiled at him, and they had talked. He knew nothing about her. He could not afford to think about knowing her better. In three days, he would be gone. What did it matter how she made him feel?

But if it did not matter, then why shouldn't he indulge himself for just a minute?

He stared at the ceiling, at the cracks in the plaster, at the lines the shadows threw across the paint, at worlds so far removed that they could only be found in dreams.

Or nightmares.

Josie Jackson disappeared. John Ross blinked. Tears formed at the corners of his eyes, and he was quick to wipe them away.

CHAPTER 11

Nest Freemark spent Saturday morning cleaning house with Gran. It didn't matter that it was the Fourth of July weekend or that Nest was particularly anxious to get outside. Nor did it matter how late you stayed up the night before. Saturday mornings were set aside for cleaning and that took precedence over everything. Gran was up at seven, breakfast was on the table at eight, and cleaning was under way by nine. The routine was set in stone. There was no sleeping in. Old Bob was already out of the house by the time Gran and Nest started work. There was a clear division of duties between Nest's grandparents, and the rough measure of it was whether the work took place inside or out. If it was inside, Gran was responsible. Cutting the grass, raking the leaves, plowing the snow, chopping wood, planting and tending the vegetable garden, fetching and hauling, and just about everything else that didn't involve the flower beds were Old Bob's responsibility. As long as he kept up the yard and the exterior of the house, he stayed on Gran's good side and was relieved of any work inside.

Nest, on the other hand, had responsibility for chores both inside and out, beginning with the Saturday-morning housecleaning. She rose with Gran at seven to shower and dress, then hurried downstairs for her breakfast of scrambled eggs, toast, and juice. The quicker she got started, she knew, the quicker she would get done. Gran was already chain-smoking and drinking vodka and orange juice, her breakfast untouched in front of her, Old Bob frowning at her in disapproval. Nest ate her eggs and toast and drank her juice in silence, trying not to look at either of them, consumed instead by thoughts of last night and of Two Bears.

"How did he know I was there?" Pick had demanded in exasperation as they made their way back across the park, the hot July darkness settled all about them like damp velvet. "I was invisible! He shouldn't have been able to see me! What kind of Indian is he, anyway?"

Nest had been wondering the same thing. The Indian part notwithstanding, Two Bears wasn't like anyone she had ever met. He was strangely reassuring, big, direct, and well reasoned, but he was kind of scary, too. Sort of like Wraith—a paradox she couldn't quite explain.

She pondered him now as she cleaned with Gran, dusting and polishing the furniture, vacuuming the carpet, sweeping and mopping the floors, wiping down the blinds and windowsills, scrubbing out the toilets and sinks, and washing out the tubs and showers. On a light cleaning day, they would stick to dusting and vacuuming, but on the first Saturday of the month they did it all. She helped Gran with the laundry and the dishes as well, and it was nearing noon when they finally finished. When Gran told her she could go, she wolfed down a peanut butter and jelly sandwich, drank a large glass of milk, and went out the back door in a rush, inadvertently letting the screen slam shut behind her once more. She cringed at the sound, but she didn't turn back.

"He said he was a shaman," Nest had remarked to Pick the previous night. "So maybe that means he sees things other people can't. Aren't Indian medicine men supposed to have special powers?"

"How am I supposed to know what medicine men can or can't do?" Pick had snapped irritably. "Do I look like an expert on Indians? I live in this park and I don't take vacations to parts of the country where there might be Indians like some people I could mention! Why don't you know what Indians do? Haven't you studied Indians in school? What kind of education are you getting, anyway? If I were you, I'd make certain I knew everything that was important about the history . . ."

And on and on he had gone, barely pausing for breath to say good night when she reached her house and left him to go in. Sometimes Pick was insufferable. A lot of times, really. But he was still her best friend.

Nest had met Pick at the beginning of the summer of her sixth year. She was sitting on the crossboard at the corner of her sandbox one evening after supper, staring out at the park, catching glimpses of it through gaps in the hedgerow, which was still filling in with new spring growth. She was humming to herself, picking idly at the sand as she scrutinized the park, when she saw the feeder. It was slipping through the shadows of the Petersons' backyard, hunkered down against the failing light as it made its way smoothly from concealment to concealment. She stared after it intently, wondering where it was going and what it was about.

"Weird, aren't they?" a voice said.

She looked around hurriedly, but there was no one to be seen.

"Down here," said the voice.

She looked down, and there, sitting on the crossboard at the opposite corner of the sandbox, was what looked like a tiny wooden man made out of twigs and leaves with a little old face carved into the wood and a beard made of moss. He was so small and so still that at first she thought he was a doll. Then he shifted his position slightly, causing her to start, and she knew he was alive.

"I don't scare you, do I?" he asked her with a smirk, wiggling his twiggy fingers at her.

She shook her head wordlessly.

"I didn't think so. I didn't think you would be scared of much. Not if you weren't scared of the feeders or that big dog. Nossir. You wouldn't be scared of a sylvan, I told myself."

She stared at him. "What's a sylvan?"

"Me. That's what I am. A sylvan. Have been all my life." He chuckled at his own humor, then cleared his throat officiously. "My name is Pick. What's yours?"

"Nest," she told him.

"Actually, I knew that. I've been watching you for quite a while, young lady."

"You have?"

"Watching is what sylvans do much of the time. We're pretty good at it. Better than cats, as a matter of fact. You don't know much about us, I don't expect."

She thought a moment. "Are you an elf?"

"An elf!" he exclaimed in horror. "An elf? I should guess not! An elf, indeed! Utter nonsense!" He drew himself up. "Sylvans are real, young lady. Sylvans are forest creatures—like tatterdemalions and riffs—but hardworking and industrious. Always have been, always will be. We have important responsibilities to exercise."

She nodded, not certain exactly what he was saying. "What do you do?"

"I look after the park," Pick declared triumphantly. "All by myself, I might add. That's a lot of work! I keep the magic in balance. You know about magic, don't you? Well, there's a little magic in everything and a lot in some things, and it all has to be kept in balance. There's lots of things that can upset that balance, so I have to keep a careful watch to prevent that from happening. Even so, I'm not always successful. Then I have to pick up the pieces and start over."

"Can you do magic?" she asked curiously.

"Some. More than most forest creatures, but then I'm older than most. I've been at this a long time."

She pursed her lips thoughtfully. "Are you like Rumpelstiltskin?"

Pick turned crimson. "Am I like Rumpelstiltskin? Criminy! What kind of question is that? What did I just get through telling you? That's the trouble with six-year-olds! They don't have any attention span! No, I am not like Rumpelstiltskin! That's a fairy tale! It isn't real! Sylvans don't go around spinning straw into gold, for goodness' sake! What kind of education are they giving you in school these days?"

Nest didn't say anything, frightened by the little man's outburst. The leaves that stuck out of the top of his head were rustling wildly, and his twiggy feet were stamping so hard she was afraid they would snap right off. She glanced nervously toward her house.

"Now, don't do that! Don't be looking for your grandmother, like you think you might need her to come out and shoo me away. I just got done telling you that I knew you weren't afraid of much. Don't make a liar out of me." Pick spread his arms wide in dismay. "I just get upset sometimes with all this fairy-tale bunk. I didn't mean to upset you. I know you're only six. Look, I'm over a hundred and fifty years old! What do I know about kids?"

Nest looked at him. "You're a hundred and fifty? You are not."

"Am so. I was here before this town was here. I was here when there were no houses anywhere!" Pick's brow furrowed. "Life was much easier then."

"How did you get to be so old?"

"So old? That's not old for a sylvan! No, sir! Two hundred and fifty is old for a sylvan, but not one hundred and fifty." Pick cocked his head. "You believe me, don't you?"

Nest nodded solemnly, not sure yet if she did or not.

"It's important that you do. Because you and I are going to be good friends, Nest Freemark. That's why I'm here. To tell you that." Pick straightened. "Now, what do you think? Can we be friends, even though I shout at you once in a while?"

Nest smiled. "Sure."

"Friends help each other, you know," the sylvan went on. "I might need your help sometime." He gave her a conspiratorial look. "I might need your help keeping the magic in balance. Here, in the park. I could teach you what I know. Some of it, anyway. What do you think? Would you like that?"

"I'm not supposed to go into the park," Nest advised him solemnly, and glanced furtively over her shoulder at the house again. "Gran says I can only go into the park with her."

"Hmmm. Well, yes, I suppose that makes sense." Pick rubbed at his beard and grimaced. "Parental rules. Don't want to transgress." He brightened. "But that's just for another year or so, not forever. Just until you're a little older. Your lessons could begin then. You'd be just about the right age, matter of fact. Meanwhile, I've got an idea. A little magic is all we need. Here, pick me up and put me in your hand. Gently, now. You're not one of those clumsy children who drop things, are you?"

Nest reached down with her hands cupped together, and Pick stepped into them. Seating himself comfortably, he ordered her to lift him up in front of her face.

"There, hold me just like that." His hands wove in feathery patterns before her eyes, and he began to mutter strange words. "Now close your eyes," he told her. "Good, good. Keep them closed. Think about the park. Think about how it looks from your yard. Try to picture it in your mind. Don't move . . ."

A warm, syrupy feeling slipped through Nest's body, beginning from somewhere behind her eyes and flowing downward through her arms and legs. Time slowed.

Then abruptly she was flying, soaring through the twilight high over Sinnissippi Park, the wind rushing past her ears and across her face, the lights of Hopewell distant yellow pinpricks far below. She was seated astride an owl, the bird's great brown-and-white feathered wings spread wide. Pick was seated in front of her, and she had her arms about his waist for support. Amazingly, they were the same size. Nest's heart lodged in her throat as the owl banked and soared with the wind currents. What if she were to fall? But she quickly came to realize that the motion would not dislodge her, that her perch astride the bird was secure, and her fear turned to exhilaration.

"This is Daniel," Pick called back to her over his shoulder. In spite of the rush of the wind, she could hear him clearly. "Daniel is a barn owl. He carries me from place to place in the park. It's much quicker than trying to get about on my own. Owls and sylvans have a good working relationship in most places. Truth is, I'd never get anything done without Daniel."

The owl responded to a nudge of Pick's knees and dropped earthward. "What do you think of this, Nest Freemark?" Pick asked her, indicating with a sweep of his hand the park below.

Nest grinned broadly and clutched the sylvan tightly about the waist. "I think it's wonderful!"

They flew on through the twilight, crossing the playgrounds and the ballparks, the pavilions and the roadways. They soared west over the rows of granite and marble tombstones that dotted the verdant carpet of Riverside Cemetery, east to the tree-shaded houses of Mineral Springs, south to the precipitous cliffs and narrow banks of the sprawling Rock River, and north to the shabby, paint-worn town houses that fronted the entry to the park. They flew the broad expanse of the Sinnissippi to the wooded sections farther in, skimming the tops of the old growth, of the oaks, elms, hickories, and maples that towered out of the growing darkness as if seeking to sweep the starry skies with their leafy branches. They found the long slide of the toboggan run, its lower section removed and stored beneath, waiting for winter and snow and ice. They discovered a doe and her fawn at the edge of the reedy waters of the bayou, back where no one else could see. Deep within the darkest part of the forest they tracked the furtive movement of shadows that, cloaked in twilight's gray mystery, might have been something alive.

They swept past a massive old white oak, one much larger than its fellows, its trunk gnarled by age and weather, its limbs crooked and twisted in a way that suggested immense fury and desperation captured in midstride, as if a giant had been frozen in place and transformed one bare instant before it had fallen upon the world it now shadowed.

Then a flash of lamplight struck Nest full in the eyes as they crossed back toward Woodlawn, and she blinked in surprise, momentarily blinded.

"Nest!"

It was Gran calling. She blinked again.

"Nest! It's time to come inside!"

She was sitting once more on the crossboard of her sandbox, staring out into the darkening stretch of her yard toward the park. Her hands were cupped before her, but they were empty. Pick was gone.

She didn't tell Gran about him that night, wary by now of telling anyone anything about the park and its magic, even Gran. She waited instead to see if Pick would return. Two days later he did, appearing at midday while she poked along the hedgerow, sitting on a limb above her head, waving a skinny stick limb in greeting, telling her they had to hurry, there were things to do, places to go, and people to see. Then, when she did tell Gran about him, that very night, the old woman simply nodded, as if the sylvan's appearance was the most natural thing in the world, and told her to pay close attention to what Pick had to say.

Pick was her closest friend after that, closer to her than her school friends, even those she had known all her life. She couldn't explain why that was. After all, he was a forest creature, and for most people such creatures didn't exist. On the surface of things, they had nothing in common. Besides being a sylvan, he was a hundred and fifty years old and a big grouch. He was fastidious and temperamental. He had no interest in the playthings she tried to share with him or in the games she favored.

What drew them together, she decided when she was older, what bonded them in a way nothing else could, was the park. The park with its feeders and its magic, its secrets and its history, was their special place, their private world, and even though it was public and open and everyone could come visit, it belonged only to them because no one else could appreciate it the way they could. Pick was its caretaker, and she became his apprentice. He taught her the importance of looking for damage to the woods and injury to the creatures that inhabited them. He explained to her the nature of the world's magic, how it inhabited everything, why there was a balance to it, and what could be done on a small scale to help keep it in place. He instructed her on how to deal with the feeders when they threatened the safety of those who could not protect themselves. He enlisted her aid against them. He gave her an insight into the coexisting worlds of humans and forest creatures that changed her life.

He told her, eventually, that Gran and her mother and three generations of her mother's side of the family before Gran had helped him care for the park.

She was thinking of this as she crossed the backyard that Saturday morning. She paused to give a sleeping Mr. Scratch a rub behind his grizzled ears and glanced about in vain for Miss Minx. The day was hot and slow, and the air was damp and close. Her friends wanted to go swimming, but she hadn't made up her mind whether to join them. She was still preoccupied with Two Bears and not yet ready to think of anything else. She squinted up at the sun, full and brilliant in a cloudless sky, brushed at a fly that flew into her face, and moved to the hedgerow and the park. The grass beneath her feet was brittle and dry and crunched softly. Questions pressed in about her. Would the spirits of the Sinnissippi appear tonight as Two Bears believed? Would they reveal to her something of the future? Only to her? What would they say? How would she respond?

She brushed at her curly hair, ungluing a handful of strands from her forehead. Sweat was dampening her skin already, and a fresh mosquito bite had appeared on her forearm. She scratched at it ruefully. She had asked Pick repeatedly why it was that she was the only one who could see the feeders, or see him, or know about the magic in the park. Pick had told her the first time she asked that she wasn't the only one, her grandmother could see the forest creatures and the feeders and knew more about the magic than Nest did, and there were others like her in other places. After that, when she narrowed the scope of the question so that it excluded Gran and people in other places, Pick brushed the matter aside by saying that she was lucky, was all, and she ought to be grateful and let it go at that. But Nest couldn't let it go, not even now, after all these years of living with it. It was what set her apart from everyone else. It was what defined her. She would not be satisfied until she understood the reasons behind it.

A few weeks ago she had pressed Pick so hard about it that he had finally revealed something new.

"It has to do with who you are, Nest!" he snapped, facing her squarely. His brow furrowed, his eyes steadied, and his rigid stance marked his determination to lay the matter to rest for good. "You think about it. I'm a sylvan, so I was born to the magic. For you to have knowledge of the magic and me, you must have been born to it as well. Or, in the alternative, share a close affinity with it. You know the word, don't you? 'Affinity'? I don't have time to be teaching you everything."

"Are you saying I have forest-creature blood?" she exclaimed softly. "Is that what you're saying? That I'm like you?"

"Oh, for cat's sake, pay attention!" Pick had turned purple. "Why do I bother trying to tell you anything?"

"But you said . . ."

"You're nothing like me! I'm six inches high and a hundred and fifty years old! I'm a sylvan! You're a little girl! Forest creatures and humans are different species!"

"All right, all right, settle down. I'm not like you. Thank goodness, I might add. Crabpuss." When he tried to object, she hurried on. "So there's an affinity we share, a bond of the sort that makes us both so much at home in the park . . ."

But Pick had waved his hands dismissively and cut her off. "Go ask your grandmother. She's the one who said you could do magic. She's the one who should tell you why."

That was the end of the matter as far as Pick was concerned, and he had refused to say another word about it since. Nest had thought about asking Gran, but Gran never wanted to discuss the origins of her magic, only what the consequences would be if she were careless. If she wanted a straight answer from Gran, she would have to approach the matter in the right way at the right time and place. As of now, Nest didn't know how to do that.

Pick jumped down onto her shoulder from a low-hanging branch as she neared the gap in the hedgerow. It used to frighten her when he appeared unexpectedly like that, like having a large bug land on you, but she had gotten used to it. She glanced down at him and saw the impatience and distress mirrored in his eyes.

"That confounded Indian has disappeared!" he snapped, forgoing any greeting.

"Two Bears?" She slowed.

"Keep moving. You can spit and whistle at the same time, can't you?" He straddled her shoulder, kicking at her with his heels as you might a recalcitrant horse. "Disappeared, gone up in a puff of smoke. Not literally, of course, but he might as well have. I've looked for him everywhere. I was sure I'd find him back at that table, looking off into the sunrise with that blank stare of his. But I can't even find his tracks!"

"Did he sleep in the park?" Nest nudged her way through the hedgerow, being careful not to knock Pick from his perch.

"Beats me. I scouted the whole of the park from atop Daniel early this morning. Flew end to end. The Indian's gone. There's no sign of him." Pick pulled and tugged mercilessly at his beard. "It's aggravating, but it's the least of our troubles."

She stepped into the park and crossed the service road toward the ball diamonds. "It is?"

"Trust me." He gave her a worried glance. "Take a walk up into the deep woods and I'll show you."

Never one to walk when she could run, Nest broke into a steady jog that carried her across the open expanse of the central park toward the woods east. She passed the ball fields, the playgrounds, and the toboggan run. She rounded the east pavilion and skirted a group of picnickers gathered at one of the tables. Heads turned to look, then turned away again. She could smell hot dogs, potato salad, and sweet pickles. Sweat beaded on her forehead, and her breath felt hot and dry in her throat. The sunlight sprinkled her with squiggly lines and irregular spots as she ran beneath the broken canopy of the hardwoods, moving downhill off the high ground toward the bayou and the deep woods beyond. She passed a couple hiking one of the trails, smiled briefly in greeting, and hurried on. Pick whispered in her ear, giving her directions interspersed with unneeded advice about running between trees.

She crossed the wooden bridge at the stream that emptied out of the woods into the bayou and turned uphill again. The woods ahead were thick with shadows and scrub. There were no picnic tables or cooking stations back here, only hiking trails. The trees were silent sentinels all around her, aged dark hulks undisturbed since their inception, witnesses to the passing of generations of life. They towered over everything, a massive and implacable presence. Sunlight was an intruder here, barely able to penetrate the forest canopy, appearing in a scattering of hazy streaks amid the gloom. Feeders skulked at the edges of her peripheral vision, small movements gone as quickly as they were glimpsed.

"Straight ahead," Pick directed as they crested the rise, and she knew at once where they were going.

They plunged deep into the old growth, the trails narrowing and coiling like snakes. Thorny branches of scrub poked in from the undergrowth and sometimes threatened to cut off passage entirely. Itchweed grew in large patches, and mounds of thistles bristled from amid the saw grass. It was silent here, so still you could hear the voices of the picnickers from back across the stream almost a quarter of a mile away. Nest navigated her way forward carefully, choosing her path from experience, no longer relying on Pick to tell her where to go. Sweat coated her skin and left her clothing feeling damp and itchy. Mosquitoes and flies buzzed past her ears and flew at her nose and eyes. She brushed at them futilely, wishing suddenly she had something cold to drink.

She emerged finally in the heart of the deep woods in a clearing dominated by a single, monstrous oak. The other trees seemed to shy away from it, their trunks and limbs twisted and bent, grown so in an effort to reach the nourishing light denied them by the big oak's sprawling canopy. The clearing in which the old tree grew was barren of everything but a few small patches of saw grass and weeds. No birds flitted through the oak's ancient branches. No squirrels built their nests within the crook of its limbs. No movement was visible or sound audible from any part of its gloomy heights. All about, the air was heavy and still with heat and shadows.

Nest stared upward into the old tree, tracing the line of its limbs to the thick umbrella of leaves that shut away the sky. She had not come here for a long time. She did not like being here now. The tree made her feel small and vulnerable. She was chilled by the knowledge of the dark purpose it served and the monstrous evil it contained.

For this was the prison of a maentwrog.

Pick had told her the maentwrog's story shortly after their first meeting. She remembered the aged tree from her flight into the park atop Daniel. She had seen it in the hazy gloom of the deepening twilight, and she had marked it well. Even at six, she knew when something was dangerous. Pick confirmed her suspicions. Maentwrogs were, to use the sylvan's own words, "half predator, half raver, and all bad." Thousands of years ago they had preyed upon forest creatures and humans alike, devouring members of both species in sudden, cataclysmic, frenzied bursts triggered by a need that only they understood. They would tear the souls out of their victims while they still lived, leaving them hollow and consumed by madness. They fed in the manner of the feeders, but did not rely on dark emotions for their response. They were thinking creatures. They were hunters. This one had been imprisoned in the tree a thousand years ago, locked away by Indian magic when it became so destructive that it could no longer be tolerated. Now and again, it threatened to escape, but the magic of the park's warders, human and sylvan, had always been strong enough to contain it.

Until now, Nest thought in horror, realizing why Pick had brought her here. The massive trunk of the ancient oak was split wide in three places, the bark fissured so that the wood beneath was exposed in dark, ragged cuts that oozed a foul, greenish sap.

"It's breaking free," the sylvan said quietly.

Nest stared wordlessly at the jagged rifts in the old tree's skin, unable to look away. The ground about the oak was dry and cracked, and there were roots exposed, the wood mottled and diseased.

"Why is this happening?" she asked in a whisper.

Pick shrugged. "Something is attacking the magic. Maybe the shift in the balance of things has weakened it. Maybe the feeders have changed their diet. I don't know. I only know we have to find a way to stop it."

"Can we do that?"

"Maybe. The fissures are recent. But the damage is far more extensive than I have ever seen before." He shook his head, then glanced left and right into the trees about them. "The feeders sense it. Look at them."

Nest followed his gaze. Feeders lurked everywhere in the shadows, hanging back in the gloom so that only their eyes were visible. There was an unmistakable eagerness in their gaze and in their furtive movements, an expectancy that was unsettling.

"What happens if the maentwrog breaks free?" she asked Pick softly, shivering with the feel of those eyes watching.

Pick cocked an eyebrow and frowned. "I don't know. It's been a prisoner of the tree for so long that I don't think anyone knows. I also don't think anyone wants to find out."

Nest was inclined to agree. "So we have to make sure that doesn't happen. What can I do to help?"

Pick jumped down from her shoulder to her arm, then scooted down her leg to the ground. "Bring me some salt. One of those big bags of the stuff they use in the water conditioners. Rock salt, if that's all you can find. I'll need a bag of compost, too. A wheelbarrow full. A bag of fertilizer or manure is okay. Pitch or tar, too. To fill in those splits." He looked at her. "Do the best you can. I'll stay here and work on strengthening the magic."

Nest shook her head in dismay, looking back again at the tree. "Pick, what's going on?"

The sylvan understood what she was asking. He tugged up his shirtsleeves angrily. "Some sort of war, I'd guess. What does it look like to you? Now get going."

She took a deep breath and darted away through the trees. She raced down the narrow trail, heedless of the brambles and the stinging nettles that swiped at her. Even without hearing him speak the words, she could feel Pick urging her to hurry.

Chapter 12

Ten minutes later, she was racing up the gravel drive to Robert Heppler's house. Cass Minter was closer, and Nest might have gone to her instead, but Robert was more likely to have what she needed. The Hepplers lived at the end of a private road off Spring Drive on three acres of woodland that bordered the park at its farthest point east, just up from the shores of the Rock River. It was an idyllic setting, a miniature park with great old hardwoods and a lawn that Robert's dad, a chemical engineer by trade but a gardener by avocation, kept immaculate. Robert found his father's devotion to yard work embarrassing. He was fond of saying his father was in long-term therapy to cure his morbid fascination with grass. One day he would wake up and discover he really wasn't Mr. Green Jeans after all.

Nest reached the Heppler property by climbing a split-rail fence on the north boundary and sprinting across the yard to intercept the gravel drive on its way to the house. The house sat large and quiet in front of her, a two-story Cape Cod rambler with weathered shingle-shake sides and white trim. Patterned curtains hung in the windows, and flowers sprouted in an array of colors from wooden window boxes and planters. The bushes were neatly trimmed and the flower beds edged. The wicker porch furniture gleamed. All the gardening and yard tools were put away in the toolshed. Everything was in its place. Robert's house looked just like a Norman Rockwell painting. Robert insisted that one day he would burn it to the ground.

But Nest spared little thought for the Heppler house today, Pick's words and looks weighing heavily on her mind. She had seen Pick worried before, but never like this. She tried not to dwell on how sick the big oak looked, the rugged bark of its trunk split apart and oozing, its roots exposed in the dry, cracked earth, but the image was vivid and gritty in her mind. She raced up the Heppler drive, her shoes churning up the gravel in puffs of dust that hung suspended in the summer heat. Robert's parents would be at work, both of them employed at Allied Industrial, but Robert should be home.

She jumped onto the neatly swept porch, trailing dust and gravel in her wake, rang the doorbell with no perceptible effect, and then banged on the screen impatiently. "Robert!"

She knew he was there; the front door was open to the screen. She heard him finally, a rapid thudding of footsteps on the stairs as he dashed down from his room.

"All right already, I'm coming!" His blond head bobbed into view through the screen. He was wearing a T-shirt that said Microsoft Rules and a pair of jeans. He saw Nest. "What are you doing, banging on the door like that? You think I'm deaf or something?"

"Open the door, Robert!"

He moved to unfasten the lock. "This better be important. I'm right in the middle of downloading a fractal coding system it took me weeks to find on the Net. I just left it sitting there, unprotected. If I lose it, so help me . . ." His fingers fumbled with the catch. "What are you doing here? I thought you were going swimming with Cass and Brianna. Matter of fact, I think they're waiting for you. Didn't Cass call you at your house? What am I, some sort of messenger service? Why does everything always depend on . . . Hey!"

She had the screen door open now, and she dragged him outside by his arm. "I need a bag of compost and a bag of softener salt."

He jerked his arm free irritably. "What?"

"Compost and softener salt!"

"What are you talking about? What do you want with those?"

"Do you have them? Can we go look? This is important!"

Robert shook his head and rolled his eyes. "Everything is important to you. That's your problem. Chill out. Be cool. It's summer, in case you hadn't noticed, so you don't have to . . ."

Nest reached out and took hold of his ears. Her grip was strong and Robert gasped. "Look, Robert, I don't have time for this! I need a bag of compost and a bag of softener salt! Don't make me say it again!"

"All right, all right!" Robert was twisting wildly from the neck down, trying not to move his head or put further pressure on his pinioned ears. His narrow face scrunched up with pain. "Leggo!"

Nest released him and stepped back. "This is important, Robert," she repeated carefully.

Robert rubbed at his injured ears and gave her a rueful look. "You didn't have to do that."

"I'm sorry. But you have a way of bringing out the worst in me."

"You're weird, Nest, you know that?"

"I need some pitch, too."

Robert gave her a look. "How about a partridge in a pear tree while we're at it?"

"Robert."

Robert stepped back guardedly. "Okay, let me go take a look out in the toolshed. I think there's a couple bags of compost stored there. And there's some salt for the conditioner in the basement. Jeez."

They trotted out to the storage shed and found the compost, then returned to the house and went down into the basement, where they found the softener salt. The bags weighed fifty pounds, and it took both of them to haul each one out to the front porch. They were sweating freely when they finished, and Robert was still griping about his ears.

They dropped the compost on top of the softener salt, and Robert kicked at the bags angrily. "You better not grab me like that again, Nest. If you weren't a girl, I'd have decked you."

"Do you have any pitch, Robert?"

Robert put his hands on his narrow hips and glared at her. "What do you think this is, a general store? My dad counts all this stuff, you know. Maybe not the salt, since that doesn't have anything to do with his precious yard, but the compost for sure. What am I supposed to tell him when he asks me why he's missing a bag?"

"Tell him I borrowed it and I'll replace it." Nest glanced anxiously towards the park. "How about the pitch?"

Robert threw up his hands. "Pitch? What's that for? You mean like for patching roads? Tar? You want tar? Where am I supposed to find that?"

"No, Robert, not tar. Pitch, the kind you use to patch trees."

"Is that what we're doing here? Patching up trees?" Robert looked incredulous. "Are you nuts?"

"Do you have a wagon?" she asked. "You know, an old one from when you were little?"

"No, but I think it might be a good idea to call one for you! You know, the padded kind?" Robert was apoplectic. "Look, I found the compost and the salt, and that's all I . . ."

"Maybe Cass has one," Nest interrupted. "I'll call her. You go back out to the shed and look for the pitch."

Without waiting for his response, she darted into the house and through the hall and living room to the kitchen phone, the screen door banging shut behind her. She felt trapped. It was hard knowing what she did of the park and of its creatures and their magic and never being able to speak of it to her friends. But what if they knew? What would happen if the maentwrog were to break free of its prison? Something that terrible would be too obvious to miss, wouldn't it? Not like the feeders or Pick or even Wraith. What would that do to the barrier of secrecy that separated the human and forest-creature worlds?

She dialed the phone, chewing nervously on her lower lip. This was all taking too much time. Cass picked up on the second ring. Nest told her friend what she needed, and Cass said she would be right down. Good old Cass, Nest thought as she hung up the phone. No questions, no arguments—just do it.

She went back outside and sat on the porch waiting for Robert. He reappeared a few moments later with a bucket of something labeled Tree Seal that he said he thought would do the trick. He'd found an old stirring stick and a worn brush to apply the contents. He dumped them on the ground and sat down beside her on the steps. Neither of them said anything, staring out into the shaded yard and the heat. Somewhere down the way, off toward Woodlawn, they could hear the music of an ice-cream truck.

"You know, I would have been all right yesterday," Robert said finally, his voice stubborn. "I'm not afraid of Danny Abbott. I'm not afraid to fight him." He scuffed at the porch step with his shoe. "But thanks, anyway, for doing whatever it was you did."

"I didn't do anything," she told him.

"Yeah, sure." Robert smirked.

"Well, I didn't."

"I was there, Nest. Remember?"

"He tripped over himself." She smoothed the skin on her knees with the palms of her hands, looking down at her feet. "I didn't touch him. You saw."

Robert didn't say anything. He hunched forward and buried his face in his knees. "All I know is I'd rather have you for a friend than an enemy." He peeked up at her and rubbed his reddened ears gingerly. "So we're off to patch up a tree, are we? Jeez. What a treat. Good thing I like you, Nest."

A few minutes later Cass arrived with Brianna, pulling a small, red metal wagon.

They loaded the softener salt, compost, and bucket of Tree Seal into the bed and headed back down the drive, Nest and Robert pulling the wagon, Cass and Brianna helping to balance its load. They followed the road out to Spring, then turned down Spring until they reached Mrs. Eberhardt's blacktop drive, which ran back through her lot to her garage at the edge of the park. They were halfway down the drive when Alice Eberhardt appeared, yelling at them for trespassing on private property. This was nothing new. Mrs. Eberhardt yelled at every kid who cut through her yard, and there were a lot of them. Robert said it was Mrs. Eberhardt's fault for providing them with a shortcut in the first place. He assured her now, giving her his "don't mess with me" look, that this was an emergency, so the law was on their side. Mrs. Eberhardt, who was a retired insurance adjuster and convinced that all kids were looking to get into trouble, but especially the ones in her yard, shouted back that she knew who Robert was and she was going to speak to his parents. Robert said she should call the house before seven, because his father was still doing nights in jail until the end of the month and his mother would probably go off to visit him after dinner.

They reached the end of the driveway, detoured around the garage to the back of the lot, and set off into the park. The woods began immediately, so they moved to the nearest trail and followed it in.

"You are really asking for it, Robert," Brianna observed, but there was a hint of admiration in her voice.

"Hey, this is how I look at it." Robert cocked his head, a savvy bantam rooster. "Each day is a new chance to get into trouble. I don't ever pass up those kinds of chances. You know why? Because even when I don't go out of the house, I get into trouble. Don't ask me why. It's a gift. So what's the difference if I get into trouble at Mrs. Eberhardt's or at home? It's all relative." He gave Brianna a smirk. "Besides, getting into trouble is fun. You should try it sometime."

They worked their way deeper into the woods, the heat and the silence growing. The sounds of the neighborhood faded. Gnats flew at them in clouds.

"Yuck." Brianna grimaced.

"Just a little additional protein for your diet," Robert cracked, licking at the air with his tongue.

"What are we doing out here?" Cass asked Nest, plodding along dutifully, one hand balancing the sacks of salt and compost in the swaying wagon.

Nest spit out a bug. "There's a big oak that's not looking too good. I'm going to see what I can do to help it."

"With salt and compost?" Robert was incredulous. "Tree Seal, I can see. But salt and compost? Anyway, why are you doing this? Don't they have people who work for the parks who are supposed to patch up sick trees?"

The trail narrowed and the ground roughened. The wagon began to bounce and creak. Nest steered around a large hole. "I tried getting hold of someone, but they're all off for the Fourth of July weekend," she improvised.

"But how do you know what to do?" Cass pressed, looking doubtful as well.

"Yeah, have you nursed other sick trees back to health?" Robert asked with his trademark smirk.

"I watched Grandpa once. He showed me." Nest shrugged dismissively and pushed on.

Fortunately, no one asked her for details. They worked their way along the trail through the weeds and scrub, swatting at bugs and brushing aside nettles, hot and miserable in the damp heat. Nest began to feel guilty for forcing her friends to come. She could probably handle this alone, now that she had the wagon and the supplies. Robert could go back to his computer and Cass and Brianna could go swimming. Besides, what would she do about Pick?

"You don't have to come any farther," she said finally, glancing over her shoulder at them, tugging on the wagon handle. "You can head back. I can manage."

"Forget it!" Robert snapped. "I want to see this sick tree."

Cass nodded in agreement. "Me, too. Anyway, this is more fun than doing hair." She gave Brianna a wry glance.

"Is it much farther?" Brianna asked, stepping gingerly around a huge thistle.

Five minutes later, they reached their destination. They pulled the wagon into the clearing and stood looking at the tree in awe. Nest wasn't sure if any of them had ever seen it before. She hadn't brought them herself, so maybe they hadn't. Whatever the case, she was certain from the looks on their faces that they would never forget it.

"Wow," whispered Robert. Uncharacteristically, he was otherwise at a loss for words.

"That is the biggest oak tree I have ever seen," Cass said, gazing up into its darkened branches. "The biggest."

"You know what?" Robert said. "When they made that tree, they threw away the mold."

"Mother Nature, you mean," Cass said.

"God," Brianna said.

"Whoever," Robert said.

Nest was already moving away from them, ostensibly to take a closer look at the oak, but really to find Pick. There was no sign of him anywhere.

"Look at the way the bark is split," said Cass. "Nest was right. This tree is really sick."

"Something bad has gotten inside of it," Brianna declared, taking a tentative step forward. "See that stuff oozing out of the sores?"

"Maybe it's only sap," said Robert.

"Maybe pigs fly at night." Cass gave him a look.

Nest rounded the tree on its far side, listening to the silence, to the murmur of her friends' voices, to the rustle of the feeders lurking in the shadows back where they couldn't be seen. She glanced left and right, seeing the feeders, but not Pick. Irritation shifted to concern. What if something had happened to him? She glanced at the tree, afraid suddenly that the damage was more extensive than they had believed, that somehow the creature trapped within was already loose. Heat and fear closed about her.

"Hey, Nest!" Robert called out. "What are we supposed to do, now that we're here?"

She was searching for an answer when Pick dropped from the tree's branches onto her shoulder, causing her to start in spite of herself. "Pick!" she gasped, exhaling sharply.

"Took you long enough," he huffed, ignoring her. "Now listen up, and I'll tell you what to do."

He gave Nest a quick explanation, then disappeared again. Nest walked back around the tree, gathered her friends together, and told them what was needed. For the next half hour they worked to carry out her instructions. Robert was given the Tree Seal to apply to the splits in the trunk, and he used the stirring stick and brush to slap the pitchlike material into place in thick gobs. Cass and Brianna spread the compost over the exposed roots and cracks, dumping it in piles and raking it in with their hands. Nest took the conditioner salt and poured it on the ground in a thin line that encircled the tree some twenty-five feet out from its base. When Robert asked what she was doing, she told him she was using the salt to protect the tree from a particularly deadly form of wood bore that was causing the sickness. The pitch would heal the sores, the compost would feed the roots, and the salt would keep other wood bores from finding their way back to the tree. It wasn't true, of course, but it sounded good.

When they were done, they stood together for a time surveying their handiwork. Robert gave his theory on tree bores, some wild concoction he said he had picked up on the Internet, and Brianna gave her theory on Robert. Then Cass allowed as how standing there looking at the tree was like watching grass grow, Brianna complained about being hot and thirsty, and Robert remembered the program he was downloading on his computer. It was not yet midafternoon, so there was still time to go swimming. But Nest told them she was tired and thought she would go home instead. Robert snorted derisively and called her a wimp and Cass and Brianna suggested they could just hang out. But Nest persisted, needing to be alone with Pick, distracted by thoughts of the maentwrog and tonight's meeting with Two Bears. The lie felt awkward, and she added to her discomfort by saying that Gran had asked her to do some additional chores around the house. She promised to meet them the following day in the park by the Indian mounds after church services and lunch.

"Hey, whatever." Robert shrugged, failing to hide his irritation and resentment.

"Call you tonight," Cass promised.

She picked up the handle of the wagon and trudged off, with Brianna and Robert trailing after. More than once her friends glanced back at her. She could read the questions in their eyes. She stared after them, unable to look away, feeling selfish and deceitful.

When they were out of sight, she called softly for Pick. The sylvan appeared at her feet, and she reached down, picked him up, and set him on her shoulder.

"Will any of this help?" she asked, gesturing vaguely at the tree, struggling to submerge her feelings.

"Might," he answered. "But it's a temporary cure at best. The problem lies with a shifting in the balance. The magic that wards the tree is being shredded. I have to find out why."

They stood without speaking for a time, studying the big oak, as if by doing so they might heal it by strength of will alone. Nest felt hot and itchy from the heat and exertion, but there was a deeper discomfort working inside her. Her eyes traced the outline of the tree against the sky. It was so massive and old, a great, crooked-arm giant frozen in time. How many years had it been alive? she wondered. How much of the land's history had it witnessed? If it could speak, what would it tell her?

"Do you think the Word made this tree?" she asked Pick suddenly.

The sylvan shrugged. "I suppose so."

"Because the Word made everything, right?" She paused. "What does the Word look like?"

Pick looked at her.

"Is the Word the same as God, do you think?"

Pick looked at her some more.

"Well, you don't think there's more than one God, do you?" Nest began to rush her words. "I mean, you don't think that the Word and God and Mother Nature are all different beings? You don't think they're all running around making different things—like God makes humans and the Word makes forest creatures and Mother Nature makes trees? Or that Allah is responsible for one race and one part of the world and Buddha is responsible for some others? You don't think that, do you?"

Pick stared.

"Because all these different countries and all these different races have their own version of God. Their religions teach them who their God is and what He believes. Sometimes the different versions even hold similar beliefs. But no one can agree on whose God is the real God. Everyone insists that everyone else is wrong. But unless there is more than one God, what difference does it make? If there's only one God and He made everything, then what is the point of arguing over whether to call Him God or the Word or whatever? It's like arguing over who owns the park. The park is for everyone."

"Are you having some sort of identity crisis?" Pick asked solemnly.

"No. I just want to know what you believe."

Pick sighed. "I believe creatures like me are thoroughly misunderstood and grossly underappreciated. I also believe it doesn't matter what I believe."

"It matters to me."

Pick shrugged.

Nest stared at her feet. "I think you are being unreasonable."

"What is the point of this conversation?" Pick demanded irritably.

"The point is, I want to know who made me." Nest took a deep breath to steady herself. "I want to know just that one thing. Because I'm sick and tired of being different and not knowing why. The tree and I are alike in a way. The tree is not what it seems. It might have grown from a seedling a long, long time ago, but it's been infused with magic that imprisons the maentwrog. Who made it that way? Who decided? The Word or God or Mother Nature? So then I think, What about me? Who made me? I'm not like anyone else, am I? I'm a human, but I can do magic. I can see the feeders when no one else can. I know about this other world, this world that you come from, that no one else knows about. Don't you get it? I'm just like that tree, a part of two worlds and two lives—but I don't feel like I really belong in either one."

She took him off her shoulder and held him in the palm of her hand, close to her face. "Look at me, Pick. I don't like being confused like this. I don't like feeling like I don't belong. People look at me funny; even if they don't know for sure, they sense I'm not like them. Even my friends. I try not to let it bother me, but it does sometimes. Like right now." She felt the tears start, and she forced them down. "So, you know, it might help if I knew something about myself, even if it was just that I was right about God and the Word being the same. Even if it was only that, so I could know that I'm not parts of different things slapped together, not something totally weird, but that I was made whole and complete to be just the way I am!"

Pick looked uncomfortable. "Criminy, Nest, I don't have any special insight into how people get made. You don't seem weird to me, but I'm a sylvan, so maybe my opinion doesn't count."

She tightened her mouth. "Maybe it counts for more than you think."

He gave an elaborate sigh, tugged momentarily on his mossy beard, and fixed her with his fierce gaze. "I don't like these kinds of conversations, so let's dispense with the niceties. You pay attention to me. You asked if I believe God and the Word are the same. I do. You can call the Word by any name you choose—God, Mohammed, Buddha, Mother Nature, or Daniel the Owl; it doesn't change anything. They're all one, and that one made everything, you included. So I wouldn't give much credence to the possibility that you were slapped together and modified along the way by a handful of dissatisfied deities. I don't know why you turned out the way you did, but I'm pretty sure it was done for a reason and that you were made all of a piece."

His brows knit. "If you want to worry about something, I don't think it should be about whether you owe your existence to God or the Word or whoever. I think you should worry about what's expected of you now that you're here and how you're going to keep from being a major disappointment."

She shook her head in confusion. "What do you mean?"

"Just this. Everything that exists has a counterpart. The Word is only half of the equation, Nest. The Void is the other half. The Word and the Void—one a creator, one a destroyer, one good, one evil. They're engaged in a war and they've been fighting it since the beginning of time. One seeks to maintain life's balance; the other seeks to upset it. We're all a part of that struggle because what's at risk is our own lives. The balance isn't just out there in the world around us; it's inside us as well. And the good that's the Word and the evil that's the Void is inside us, too. Inside us, each working to gain the upper hand over the other, each working to find a way to overcome the other."

He paused, studying her. "You already understand that you aren't like most people. You're special. You have one foot firmly planted in each of two worlds, forest creature and human. There're not many like you. Like I've said, there's a reason for this, just like there's a reason for everything. Don't you think for a minute that the Void doesn't realize this. You have a presence and a power. You have a purpose. The Void would like to see all that turned to his use. You may think you are a good person and that nothing could change that. But you haven't been tested yet. Not really. You haven't been exposed to the things in life that might change you into something you wouldn't even recognize. Sooner or later, that's going to happen. Maybe sooner, given the amount of unrest among the feeders. Something is going on, Nest. You better concentrate your concerns on that. You better be on your guard."

There was a long silence when he finished as she digested the implications of his admonition. He stood rigid in her hand, arms folded across his wooden chest, mouth set in a tight line, eyes bright with challenge. He was trying to tell her something, she realized suddenly. His words had more than one meaning; his warning was about something else. A sense of uneasiness crept through her, a shadow of deep uncertainty. She found herself thinking back on the past few days, on Bennett

Scott's rescue from the cliffs, on the maentwrog's emergence from its prison, and on the increased presence and boldness of the feeders. Did it have to do with these?

What was Pick trying to say?

She knew she would not find out today. She had seen that look on his face before, stubborn and irascible. He was done talking.

She felt suddenly drained and worn. She lowered Pick to the ground, waited impatiently for him to step out of her hand, and then stood up again. "I'm going home after all," she told him. "I'll see you tonight."

Without waiting for his reply, she turned and walked off into the trees.

She didn't go home, however. Instead, she walked through the park, angling down off the heights to the bayou's edge and following the riverbank west. She took her time, letting her emotions settle, giving herself a chance to think through the things that were bothering her. She could put a voice to some of them, but not yet to all. What troubled her was a combination of what had already come about and what she sensed was yet to happen. The latter was not a premonition exactly—more an unpleasant whisper of possibility. The day was hot and still, and the sun beat down out of the cloudless sky on its slow passage west. The park was silent and empty-feeling, and even the voices of the picnickers seemed distant and subdued. As if everyone was waiting for what she anticipated. As if everyone knew it was coming.

She passed below the toboggan slide and above a pair of young boys fishing off the bank by the skating shelter. She glanced up the long, straight, wooden sluice to the tower where the sledders began their runs in winter, remembering the feeling of shooting down toward the frozen river, gathering speed for the launch onto the ice. Inside she felt as if it were happening to her now in another way, as if she were racing toward something vast and broad and slick, and that once she reached it she would be out of control.

The afternoon wore on. She looked for feeders, but did not see any. She looked for Daniel and did not see him either. She remembered that she had forgotten to ask Pick if he was making any progress in the search for Bennett Scott's cat, Spook. Leaves threw dappled shadows on the ground she walked across, and she imagined faces and shapes in their patterns. She found herself wondering about her father and her mother, both such mysterious figures in her life, so removed in time, almost mythical. She thought of Gran and her stubborn refusal to speak of them in any concrete way. A cold, hard determination grew inside her. She would make Gran tell her, she promised herself. She would force her to speak.

She walked to the base of the cliffs, staying back from where the caves tunneled into the rock. Pick had told her never to go there. He had made her promise. It wasn't safe for her, he insisted. It didn't matter that other kids explored the caves regularly and no harm came to them. Other kids couldn't see the feeders. Other kids didn't have use of the magic. She was at risk, and she must keep away.

She shook her head as she turned and began to walk up the roadway that led to the bluff. There it was again, she thought. The realization that she was different. Always different.

She reached the heights and turned toward the cemetery. She thought she might visit her mother's grave. She had a sudden need to do so, a need to connect in some small way with her lost past. She crossed the road in front of the Indian mounds and turned in to the trees. The sun burned white-hot in the afternoon sky, its glare blinding her as she walked into it. She squinted and shaded her eyes with her hand.

Ahead, someone moved in the blaze of light.

She slowed in a patch of shade and tried to see who it was. At first she thought it was Two Bears, returned early for tonight's visit. But then she saw it was a man in forest green coveralls, a maintenance employee of the park. He was picking up trash with a metal-tipped stick and depositing it into a canvas bag. She hesitated, then continued on. As she approached, he turned and looked at her.

"Hot one, isn't it?" His bland face was smooth and expressionless, and his blue eyes were so pale they seemed almost devoid of color.

She nodded and smiled uncertainly.

"Off for a visit to the cemetery?" he asked.

"My mother is buried there," she told him, stopping now.

The man placed the sharp tip of the stick against the ground and rested his hands on the butt. "Hard thing to lose a mother. She been gone a long time?"

"Since I was a baby."

"Yeah, that's a long time, all right. You know, I hardly remember mine anymore."

Nest thought momentarily to tell him about the big oak, but then decided there was nothing he could do in any case, that it was better off in Pick's capable hands.

"You still got your father?" the man asked suddenly.

Nest shook her head. "I live with my grandparents."

The man looked sad. "Not the same as having a father, is it? Old folks like that aren't likely to be around for too much longer, so you got to start learning to depend pretty much on yourself. But then you start to wonder if you're up to the job. Think about one of these trees. It's old and rugged. It hasn't really ever had to depend on anyone. But then along comes a logger and cuts it down in minutes. What can it do? You catch my drift?"

She looked at him, confused.

The man glanced at the sky. "The weather's not going to change for a while yet. Are you coming out for the fireworks Monday?"

She nodded.

"Good. Should be something. Fourth of July is always something." His smile was vaguely mocking. "Maybe I'll see you there."

She was suddenly uneasy. Something about the man upset her. She wanted to move away from him. She was thinking that it was getting close to dinnertime anyway and she should be getting home. She would visit her mother's grave that evening instead, when it was cool and quiet.

"I've got to be going," she said perfunctorily.

The man looked at her some more, saying nothing. She forced herself to smile at him and turned away. Already the shadows of the big trees were lengthening. She went quickly, impelled by her discomfort.

She did not look back, and so she did not see the man's strange eyes turn hard and cold and fixed of purpose as he watched her go.

When Nest Freemark was safely out of sight, the demon hoisted the canvas sack and stick over his shoulder and began walking. He crossed the roadway to the Indian mounds and angled down toward the river, whistling softly to himself. Keeping within the shelter of the trees, he worked his way steadily east through the park. The light was pale and gray where the hillside blocked the sun, the shadows deep and pooled. Afternoon ball games were winding down and picnickers were heading home. The demon smiled and continued on.

Richie Stoudt was waiting at the toboggan slide, seated at one of the picnic tables, staring out at the river. The demon was almost on top of him before Richie realized he was there. Richie leaped up then, grinning foolishly, shaking his head.

"Hey, how's it going?" he sputtered. "Didn't hear you come up. Been waiting though, just like you said to do. Got your message all right. Finished up at the Prestons' and came right over."

The demon nodded, smiled, and kept walking. "Let's get started then."

"Sure, sure." Richie was right on his heels. He was small and wiry, and his thin face peeked out from under a mop of unruly dark hair. He was wearing coveralls over a blue denim shirt and high-top work boots, everything looking ragged and worn. "Didn't know you worked for the park, I guess," he said, trying to make conversation. "Pretty steady hours and all, I suppose. You sure this is all right, this late in the day and all? What is it we're doing, anyway?"

The demon didn't answer. Instead, he led Richie east into the big trees beyond the pavilion toward the slope that ran down to the little creek. The air was hot and still beneath the canopy of branches, and the mosquitoes were beginning to come out in swarms. Richie slapped at them irritably.

"Hate these things," he muttered. When the demon failed to respond, he said, "You said this would pay pretty well and I might have a chance to catch on with the city? That right?"

"Right as rain," the demon replied, not bothering to look at him.

"Well, all right, that's great, just great!" Richie sounded enthused. "I mean, I don't know if that damn strike is ever gonna get settled, and I need me something secure."

They descended the slope to the creek, crossed the wooden bridge, and began to climb the opposite embankment toward the deep woods. In the distance, the bayou was as flat and gray as hammered tin. Richie continued to mutter about the mosquitoes and the heat, and the demon continued to ignore him. They crested the rise, following the path that Nest and Pick had taken earlier, and moments later they were standing in front of the big oak. The demon glanced about cautiously, but there was no sign of anyone except the feeders, who had followed them every step of the way and crouched now at the edge of the clearing, their eyes glimmering watchfully.

"Whoa, will you look at that!" Richie exclaimed, staring up at the sickened tree. "That guy looks like a goner!"

"That's what we're here to determine," the demon explained, his bland face expressionless.

Richie nodded eagerly. "All right. Just tell me what to do."

The demon dropped the canvas sack and took a new grip on the metal-tipped stick. He put his free hand on Richie's shoulder. "Just walk over here to the trunk with me for a moment," he said softly.

The shadows were deep and pervasive as they moved forward, the demon keeping his hand on Richie Stoudt's shoulder. When they were right next to the massive trunk, the demon took his hand away.

"Look up into the branches," he said.

Richie did so, peering intently into the shadows. "I can't see anything. Not in this light."

"Step a little closer. Put your face right up against the trunk."

Richie glanced at him uncertainly, then did as he was told, pressing his cheek against the rough bark, staring up into the branches. "I still can't . . ."

The demon drove the pointed end of his stick through Richie's neck with a furious lunge. Richie gasped in shock and pain as his windpipe and larynx shattered. He tried to cry out, but his voice box was gone and the blood pouring down his throat was choking him. His fingers clawed at the tree as if to tear the bark away, and his eyes bulged. He thrashed wildly, trying to break free, but the demon pressed firmly on the wooden shaft, keeping Richie pinned, watching the dark blood spurt from his ruptured throat.

Feeders raced from among the trees and began throwing themselves on Richie, tearing at his convulsed body, beating past his futile efforts to protect himself, anxious to taste his pain and fear.

Then the bark of the tree, wet with Richie's blood, began to split apart in long, ragged fissures, and parts of Richie were drawn into the cracks. His hands and knees went first, pressing into the trunk as if into soft mud as he struggled to escape. His scream of horror came out a strangled cough, and then more of him was sucked slowly, relentlessly from view. When his head was swallowed, all sound ceased. The demon yanked free his pointed stick and stood watching as Richie's back bucked and heaved in a last futile effort to break free.

A moment later, Richie Stoudt was gone completely. The feeders melted back into the night.

The demon waited for a time, watching as the tree began to ooze what it didn't want of Richie, the bark splitting further and deeper as the blood offering did its work. Within its prison, the maentwrog was feasting, gaining the strength it needed to break free, readying itself for the demon's summons.

The demon looked down. One of Richie's work boots lay on the ground. The demon reached down and picked it up. He would carry it to the riverbank where the water turned rough above the dam and leave it where it could be found. Let people draw their own conclusions.

Humming, he collected his canvas sack and disappeared back into the trees.

Chapter 13

Nest pushed open the screen door off the porch just in time to hear the big grandfather clock in the den strike the half hour between five and six. As she paused in the silence that followed, Gran materialized out of the shadows of the kitchen, a thin, gray apparition gripping a pot holder.

"Dinner's in an hour, Nest. Go wash up. We've got company coming."

Nest caught the screen door as it started to swing back on its springs and eased it quietly into place. She could feel the sweat, warm and sticky on her skin beneath her clothes. "Who is it?" she asked.

"Someone your grandfather invited. You'll have to ask him." Gran looked less than pleased. She gestured with the pot holder. "Go clean up first, though. You look like something the cat dragged in."

She disappeared back into the kitchen. Nest could smell pot roast cooking, rich and savory, and she realized suddenly how hungry she was. She went down the hallway past Gran and the good smells and glanced into the den in search of her grandfather, but he was not there. She took a moment longer to listen for him; then, hearing nothing, she continued on to her room, closed the door, popped Nirvana into her CD player, stripped off her clothes, and headed for the shower. She tried not to look at herself in the mirror, but ended up doing so anyway. The girl looking back at her was skinny and flat-chested. She had bony arms and legs and looked as if she would disappear altogether if she turned sideways. She might have been half-pretty if her face hadn't been breaking out so badly. As usual, Nest didn't much care for her.

She spent a long time in the shower washing and soaking. Then she dried, dressed, and stared out the window into the park. She thought about Pick and the big oak tree, about her friends and the magic she hid from them, about the maintenance man and Wraith, and about the feeders. She thought about Two Bears and the dance of the spirits of the Indian dead, now less than six hours away. She wondered if Two Bears could see the feeders. He had seen Pick clearly enough, so shouldn't he be able to see the feeders as well? She had never met anyone who could see the feeders besides herself and Gran. Pick said there were others, but not many and they all lived elsewhere. Pick said only a handful of people could see the feeders, and that was because you had to have some connection with magic. Maybe Two Bears could do magic, she thought. Wouldn't he have to be able to do magic in order to summon spirits?

She left the window and went down the hall toward the living room, wrapped in her speculations. Her hair was still damp and loose. The curls tickled her ears. She brushed at them self-consciously, wishing suddenly that they weren't having company for dinner, thinking about how boring it was likely to be, already planning how she would excuse herself as soon as the meal was consumed . . .

"Hello."

She stopped in surprise. A man was standing just inside the front door looking at her. She had been so preoccupied with her musings she had missed seeing him.

"Hello," she replied.

"Sorry if I startled you."

"No, that's all right. I was thinking about something."

The words sounded stupid, and she colored slightly. The man didn't seem to notice. His green eyes stayed fixed on her, his gaze so intense that she blinked in spite of herself.

"You must be Nest." He smiled as if pleased by this. "My name is John Ross."

He extended his hand, and she took it in her own. His grip was strong, and she thought he must be used to hard work. He seemed to her to be constructed all of bones and muscle, but his clothes hung on him as they would have hung on a scarecrow. He looked strange with his shoulder-length hair tied back in that bandanna, but kind of cool, too. She thought it made him look like a little boy. She wondered suddenly what he was doing there. Was he their dinner company or just someone looking to do yard work?

She realized she was still holding his hand and quickly released it. "Sorry."

He smiled and looked around. His eyes settled on the portraits of the Freemark women, grouped to one side of the entry door. "Your family?" he asked.

She nodded. "Six generations of us."

"Handsome women. This house has a good feel to it. Have you lived here all your life?"

She was pondering whether to answer his question or ask one of her own when her grandfather appeared from the den. "Sorry to take so long. I was just looking for her yearbook, senior year, when she was president of the student council. Nest, have you met Mr. Ross?"

Nest nodded, watching her grandfather closely. It was her mother's yearbook he was holding.

"Mr. Ross knew your mother in school, Nest. In college, in Ohio." He seemed fascinated by the idea. "He came down to visit us, to say hello. I ran into him at Josie's this morning and invited him to join us for dinner. Look here, John, this is Caitlin's picture from her senior year."

He opened the yearbook and held it out for John Ross to see. Ross limped gingerly over for a look, and for the first time Nest noticed the polished black staff leaning against the wall next to the umbrella stand. The staff was covered with strange symbols carved into wood black and depthless beneath the staff's worn sheen. Nest stared at the markings for a long moment as John Ross and her grandfather studied her mother's yearbook. There was something familiar about the markings. She had seen them somewhere before. She was certain of it.

She looked at John Ross anew and wondered how that could be.

Moments later, Gran called them in to dinner. She seated them at the big dining-room table, Nest next to John Ross across from Robert and herself. She placed the food on the table, then finished off her bourbon and made herself another before taking her seat. She picked up her fork and began to eat with barely a glance at her company. Very unlike Gran, who was a stickler for good manners. Nest thought something was clearly troubling her.

"Did you know my mother a long time?" Nest asked, curious now to know more about this stranger.

Ross shook his head. He took small, careful bites as he ate. His green eyes were distant as he spoke. "No, I'm afraid I didn't. I didn't meet her until her second year, and she went home at the end of it. We only had a few months together. I wish I had known her better."

"She was pretty, wasn't she?"

John Ross nodded. "She was."

"You were a year ahead of her at Oberlin, you said," Old Bob encouraged. "Did you stay on and graduate?"

"Caitlin could have graduated, too, if she'd wanted," Gran said quietly, giving him a sharp glance.

"I think Caitlin was one of the smartest people I've ever known, Mrs. Freemark," John Ross offered, looking now at Gran. She looked back at him very deliberately. "But she was fragile, too. Very sensitive. She could be hurt more easily than most. I admired that about her."

Gran put down her fork and sipped at her bourbon. "I don't know that I understand what you're saying, Mr. Ross."

Ross nodded. "It's just that most of us are so hardened to life that we've forgotten how to respond to pain. Caitlin wasn't like that. She understood the importance of recognizing the little hurts that other people ignore. She was always concerned with healing. Not physical injuries, you understand. Emotional hurts, the kind that inflict damage on your soul. She could identify and heal them with a few well chosen words. She was better at it than anyone. It was a genuine gift."

"You said you dated? You and Caitlin?" Old Bob helped himself to more of the roast, ignoring the look Gran shot him. Nest watched the interplay with fascination. Something about John Ross being here had Gran very upset. Nest had never seen her so on edge.

"On and off for some of that year." John Ross smiled, but kept his eyes fixed on his plate. "Mostly we were just friends. We went places together. We talked a lot. Caitlin talked about you all the time. And about her home. She loved the park."

"I have to tell you that she never mentioned you, Mr. Ross," Gran observed pointedly, watching his face.

John Ross nodded. "I'm sorry to hear that. But she kept a lot to herself. I don't suppose I was very important to her in the larger scheme of things. But I admired her greatly."

"Well, she may have mentioned you, and we've just forgotten," Old Bob soothed, giving Gran a warning glance. Gran sniffed and sipped some more of her drink.

"She had a lot of friends while she was at Oberlin," Ross added suddenly, glancing around at their faces as if to confirm that what he was saying was true. He looked at Gran. "This roast is delicious, Mrs. Freemark. I haven't tasted anything this good in a long time. I'm very grateful you included me."

"Well," Gran said, her sharp face softening slightly.

"She did have a lot of friends," Old Bob declared. "Caitlin had a lot of friends, all through school. She had a good heart. People saw that in her."

"Did you know my father?" Nest asked suddenly.

The table went silent. Nest knew at once that she had asked something she should not have. Gran was glaring at her. Her grandfather was staring at his plate, absorbed in his food. John Ross took a drink of his water and set the glass carefully back in place on the table.

"No," he said quietly. "I'm sorry, but I never met him."

The dinner conversation resumed after a few moments and continued throughout in fits and starts, with Nest's grandfather asking questions of John Ross, Ross offering brief replies, and Gran sitting angry and still throughout. Nest finished her meal, asked to be excused, and left almost before permission was given. She walked out onto the porch and down the steps to the backyard. Mr. Scratch was sprawled on the lawn sleeping and Miss Minx was watching him with studied suspicion. Nest moved to the rope swing, seated herself in its weathered old tire, and rocked gently in the evening heat. She felt embarrassed and frustrated by her grandparents' reaction to her question and wondered anew why no one ever wanted to say anything about her father. It was more than the fact that he got her mother pregnant and never married her. That was no big deal; that happened all the time. It was more than the fact that he disappeared afterward, too. Lots of kids grew up in one-parent households. Or with their grandparents, like she was doing. No, it was something more, and she wasn't even sure that it was something anyone could actually explain. It was more like something they suspected, but could not put words to. It was like something that was possible, but they were refusing to look too closely at it for fear that it might be so.

A few minutes later John Ross came out the back door leaning on his cane, carefully negotiated the worn steps, and limped over to where she twisted and bobbed in the swing. Nest steadied herself as he came up, grounding her feet so that she could watch him.

"I guess that question about your father touched a sore spot," he said, his smile faint and pained, his eyes squinting as he looked off toward the approaching sunset. The sky to the west was colored bright red and laced with low-hanging clouds that scraped across the trees of the park.

Nest nodded without replying.

"I was wondering if you would walk me to your mother's grave," Ross continued, still looking west. "Your grandfather said it would be all right for you to do so. Your grandmother gave him one of those looks, but then she agreed, too." He turned back to her, his brow furrowed. "Maybe I'm misreading her, but I have the uncomfortable feeling she thinks she's giving me just enough rope to hang myself."

Nest smiled in response, thinking of Wraith.

Ross ran his hand slowly down the length of his staff. "To tell you the truth, I don't think your grandmother trusts me. She's a very careful woman where you are concerned."

Nest supposed that was so. Gran was fierce about her sometimes, so consumed with watching out for her that Nest would find herself wondering if there was a danger to her that she did not realize.

"So, would that be all right with you?" Ross pressed. "Would you be willing to walk me over to the cemetery?"

Nest nodded, climbed out of the swing, and pointed to the gap in the hedgerow. She led the way wordlessly, setting a slow pace so that he could follow, glancing back to make certain he was able to keep up. In point of fact, he seemed stronger and more agile than she had expected. She wondered what had happened to his leg, if there was a way she could ask him without being rude.

They crossed the yard, pushed through the gap in the hedgerow, and entered the park. The evening ball games were already under way, the diamonds all in use, the benches and grassy areas behind the backstops crowded with families and fans. She led Ross down the service road behind the nearest backstop to the crossing gate at the park entrance, then along the roadway toward the burial mounds and the cliffs. Neither of them spoke. The day's heat hung thick and heavy in the evening air, and there was little indication that the temperature would change with night's coming. The insects buzzed and hummed in dull cacophony in the shade of the trees, and the sounds of the ballplayers rose sharp and sudden with the ebb and flow of the games' action.

After a moment, she dropped back a step to walk beside him. "How long are you visiting?" she asked, wanting to know something more about him, about his involvement with her mother.

"Just a few days." His movements were steady and unhurried. "I think I'll stay for the fireworks. I hear they're pretty spectacular."

"You can sit with us, if you'd like," she offered. "That way you'll be with someone you know. You don't know anyone else in Hopewell, do you?"

He shook his head.

"This is your first visit?"

"This is my first visit."

They crossed the road at the divide and turned west toward the turnaround and the entry to Riverside. John Ross was looking off toward the cliffs, out to where the Rock River flowed west on both sides of the levy and the railroad tracks. Nest watched him out of the corner of her eye. He seemed to be seeing something beyond what he was looking at, his gaze distant and distracted, his expression riddled with pain. He looked almost young to her for an instant, as if the years had dropped away. She thought she could see the boy in him, the way he was maybe twenty years ago, the way he had been before his life had taken him down whatever rough road it was he had traveled.

"Were you in love with my mother?" she asked him suddenly.

He looked at her in surprise, his lean face intense, his green eyes startled. He shook his head. " I think I could have been if I had gotten to know her better, but I didn't get the chance." He smiled. "Isn't that tragic?"

They walked up through the spring-mounted children's toys toward the spruce groves. "You look like her," Ross said after a moment.

Nest glanced over at him, watching him limp alongside her, leaning on his staff, his gaze directed ahead to where they were going. " I don't think I do," she said. "I don't think I look like anybody. Which is just as well, because I don't much like the way I look, just at the moment."

Ross nodded. "We're our own worst critics, sometimes." Then he cocked an eyebrow at her. "But I like the way you look, even if you don't. So sue me."

She smiled in spite of herself. They passed through the spruce trees to the turnaround and the cliffs. There were two cars parked at the cliff edge and a family on the swings nearby. She thought back to Bennett Scott and the feeders, picturing it in her mind, remembering the night and the heat and the fear. She thought about Two Bears and wondered suddenly if he was there in the park again. She glanced about to see if she could spy him, but he was nowhere in sight. She let her thoughts of Two Bears and the spirits of the dead Sinnissippi drift away.

She led Ross to the gap in the fence line and through to the cemetery beyond. They walked along the edge of the blacktop roadway, through the rows of marble and granite tombstones, across the immaculate grass carpet, and under the stately, silent old hardwoods. The mingled scents of pine and new-mown grass filled the air, rich and pungent. Nest found herself strangely at ease. John Ross made her feel that way. The longer she was with him, the more comfortable she felt—as if she had known him a long time rather than for only a few hours. It was in the way he talked to her, neither as a child nor as an adult, but simply as a person; in the way he moved, neither self-conscious nor protective of his damaged body, not favoring it in an obvious, discomforting way, accepting it as it was; and mostly in the way he was at peace with the moment, as if only the here and now mattered, as if taking this walk with her were enough and what had gone before or what would come after had no place in his thoughts.

They walked through the rolling green of the cemetery and down its tree-shaded rows of markers to where her mother lay, out on a bluff overlooking the river and the land beyond. Her mother's headstone was gray with black lettering and bore the words BELOVED DAUGHTER & MOTHER just beneath her name, Caitlin Anne Freemark. Nest stared at the grave without speaking, immutable and remote, borne to other times and places on the wings of her thoughts.

"I don't remember her at all," she said finally, tears springing to her eyes with her admission.

John Ross looked off into the trees. "She was small and gentle, with sandy hair and blue-gray eyes you couldn't look away from. She was pretty, almost elfin. She was very smart, intuitive about things others would miss entirely. When she laughed, she could transport you to a better time and place in your life if you were sad or make you glad you were there with her if you were happy. She was daring and unafraid. She was never satisfied with just being told how something was; she always wanted to experience it for herself."

He stopped, went silent suddenly, as if he'd come up against something he did not care to explore any further. Nest did not try to look at him. She brushed at her eyes and bit her lip to steady herself. It was always like this when she came to visit. No matter how much time had passed, it was always the same.

Afterward, they walked back through the cemetery to the fence line in the waning light, listening to the dying sounds of a distant mower and the occasional honk of a car horn out on the highway. There was no one in the cemetery this night; its tree-sheltered, rolling green expanse was cradled in silence and empty of movement. The Midwest evening was sultry, the air tasted of sweat, and it felt as if time had slowed its inexorable march to a crawl. There was a sense of something slipping away, gone like chances at love or hopes for understanding.

"Thank you for telling me about her," Nest said quietly as they walked down the blacktop roadway toward the park fence. Her eyes were dry again and her mind was clear.

"Well, you remind me of her," John Ross replied after a moment. "That helps me in telling you what she was like."

"I have pictures," said Nest. "But it isn't the same."

"Not if you don't have the memories of the times those pictures capture, no."

Ross limped steadily forward, his staff clicking softly against the blacktop with each step.

"I like your staff," Nest ventured. "Have you had it a long time?"

Ross glanced over at her and smiled. "Sometimes it seems like I have had it all my life. Sometimes it seems like I was born with it. I think maybe, in a sense, I was."

He didn't say anything more. They reached the fence and slipped through the gap and into the park once more. They were back at the turnaround, close by the cliffs. The twilight was deepening, the sun gone down behind the horizon, leaving only its crimson wake to light the world. The family on the swings and the two cars that had been parked at the turnaround were gone. In the distance, the baseball games were winding down.

In the shadows of the trees that bracketed the cliff edge, feeders were gathering, their squat, dark bodies shifting soundlessly, their yellow eyes winking like fireflies. As John Ross and Nest passed down the roadway, their numbers grew. And grew still more. Nest glanced left and right nervously, finding eyes everywhere, watching intently, implacably. Why were there so many? The chilling possibility crossed her mind that they intended to attack, all of them, too many to defend against. They had never done anything like that before, but there was nothing to say they wouldn't do so now. Feeders were nothing if not unpredictable. She tensed expectantly, wondering what she should do. Her heart beat fast and her breathing quickened.

"Don't let them bother you," John Ross told her quietly, his voice soft and calm. "They're not here because of you. They're here because of me."

He said it so matter-of-factly that for a moment the words didn't register. Then she looked at him in surprise and whispered, "You can see them?"

He nodded without looking at her, without appearing to look at anything. "As clearly as you can. It's why I'm here. It's why I've come. To help, if I can. I'm in service to the Word."

Nest was stunned. They continued to walk down the darkening roadway through the masses of feeders as if taking a garden stroll, and Nest fought to collect her thoughts.

"You know about the feeders, don't you?" he asked conversationally. "You know what draws them?" She nodded dully. "They are attracted to me because of the staff." She glanced over immediately, eyes fastening on its black, rune-scrolled walnut length. "The staff is a talisman, and its magic is very powerful. It was given to me when I entered into service to the Word. It is the weapon I carry into battle each and every day. It is also the ball and chain that binds me to my fate."

His words were muted and harsh, but strangely poetic as well, and Nest found herself looking at his face, seeing him anew. He did not look back, but continued to keep his gaze directed forward, away from her, away from the feeders.

"Are you a caretaker?" he asked after a moment. "Are you partnered with a sylvan to look after this park?"

The number of her questions doubled instantly, and she was confused all over again. "Yes. His name is Pick."

"I am a Knight of the Word," he said. "Has Pick told you of the Knights?"

She shook her head no. "Pick doesn't say much about anything that goes on outside of the park."

Ross nodded. They were even with the burial mounds now and turning in to the playground, stepping carefully over the low chain dividers. They moved across the twig-strewn grass beneath the hardwoods, solitary ghosts. Ahead, the baseball diamonds were filling with shadows and emptying of people. Nest could see lights beginning to come on in the houses of the subdivisions bordering the park and in the Sinnissippi Townhomes. Stars were beginning to appear in the darkening sky east, and a crescent moon hung suspended north across the river.

"Did you really know my mother?" Nest asked him, a twinge of doubt nudging at her, suspicious now of everything he had said.

He seemed not to have heard her. He said nothing for a moment, then slowed and looked over at her. "Why don't we sit somewhere and talk, and I'll tell you what I'm doing here."

She studied him carefully while he waited for her answer. "All right," she agreed finally.

They moved out of the hardwoods and away from the playground. The feeders that had been shadowing them fell away as they moved into the open again, unwilling to follow. They stayed on the west side of the road leading out of the park, away from the ball games that were ending and the players and fans packing up their blankets and gear, and moved to a picnic table just at the edge of a solitary spruce close by the crossbar.

They sat across from each other in the failing light, the girl and the man, and they might have been either confidants or combatants from the set of their shoulders and the positioning of their hands, and in the vast, empty space of night and sky that closed about them, their words could not be heard.

"This is how I became a Knight of the Word," John Ross said softly, his green eyes steady and calm as they fixed on her.

And he told Nest Freemark his story.

Chapter 14

He was still a young man when he began his odyssey, not yet turned thirty. He was drifting again, as he had been drifting for most of his life. He had earned an undergraduate degree in English literature (he had done his senior thesis on William Faulkner), and his graduation had marked the conclusion of any recognizable focus in his life. Afterward, he had migrated to a series of different schools and graduate programs, twice coming close to completing his masters, each time stepping back when he got too close. He was a classic case of an academic unready and unwilling to confront the world beyond the classroom. He was intelligent and intuitive; he was capable of finding his way. The problem with John Ross was always the same. The way never seemed important enough for him to undertake the journey.

He had always been like that. He had excelled in school from an early age, easily gaining honors recognition, effortlessly garnering high praise and enthusiastic recommendations. While he was attending school full-time, while he was *required* to be there, it was never necessary that he consider doing anything more. It was a comfortable, regimented, encapsulated existence, and he was happy. But with his graduation it became apparent that he must point toward something specific. He might have become a teacher, and thus remained within the classroom, kept himself safe within an academic confinement, but teaching did not interest him. It was the discovery that mattered, the uncovering of truths, the deciphering of life's mysteries that drew him into his studies. And so he moved from college to university, from graduate studies in American literature to funded research in Greek history, all the while waiting for the light to shine down the road his life must necessarily take.

It did not happen, though, and as he approached the age of thirty, he began to think that it never would. His parents, always supportive of him, were beginning to despair of his life. An only child, he had always been the sole focus of their expectations and hopes. They did not say so, but he could read their concerns for him in their studied silence. They no longer supported him—he had long since learned the art of securing scholarships and grants—so money was not an issue. But his options for continued study were drawing to a close, and he was still nowhere close to choosing a career. What could he do with his English degree and his raft of almost completed esoteric studies? If he didn't choose to teach, what could he do? Sell insurance or cars or vacuum cleaners? Go into business? Work for the government? When none of it mattered, when nothing seemed important enough, what could he do?

He chose to go to England. He had saved some money, and he thought that perhaps a trip abroad might give him fresh insight. He had never been outside the

United States, save for a brief trip into Canada in his teens and a second into Mexico in his early twenties. He had no experience as a tourist, barely any experience in life beyond the classroom, but he was persuaded to take the plunge by his growing desperation. He would be going to an English-speaking country (well, of course), and he would be discovering (he hoped) something about his substantially English heritage. His one extracurricular activity throughout school had been hiking and camping, so he was strong and able to look after himself. He had some contacts at a few of the universities, and he would find help with lodging and shelter. Perhaps he would even find a smidgen of guest-lecturer work, although that was not important to him. What mattered was removing himself from his present existence in an effort to find his future.

So he applied for and was granted a passport, booked his airline reservation, said good-bye to his parents, and began his journey. He had no timetable for his visit, no date in mind on which he would return, no particular expectation for what he would do. He drifted anew and with careless disregard for his plans to discover himself, traveling through England and Scotland, through London and Edinburgh, south to north and back again. He renewed old acquaintances from his American university days, visited briefly at the places he had marked off on his list of must-see items, and moved on. He walked when he could, finding it the best and most thorough way to see the countryside, saving his money in the not quite acknowledged but inescapable recognition that his travels seemed to be bringing him no closer to his goals.

In the late spring of the year following his summer arrival, the first twelve months of his visit coming to a rapid close, he traveled for the first time into Wales. His decision to go there was oddly precipitated. He was reading on the history of the Welsh and English kings, on Edward I and the iron ring of fortresses he had built to contain the Welsh in Snowdonia, and a friend to whom John Ross had mentioned his reading told him of a cottage her parents owned outside of Betws-y-Coed where he could stay for the asking. Having no better plan for the spending of his time and intrigued by the history he had been reading, he accepted his friend's offer.

So he traveled into Gwynedd, Wales, found the cottage, and began to explore the country surrounding Betws-y-Coed. The village sat in the heart of the Gwydir Forest at the juncture of the Conwy, Llugwy and Lledr valleys within the vast, sprawling wilderness of Snowdonia National Park. Snowdonia, which occupied much of Gwynedd, was mountainous and thickly forested, and his hikes into her wilderness proved long and arduous. But what he found was breathtaking and mysterious, a secretive world that had offered shelter and hiding, but little on which to subsist, to the Welsh during the siege of Edward Longshanks in the late 1200s. He took day trips to the castles, to Harlech, Caernarfon, Beaumaris, and Conwy and all the others that Edward had built, rebuilt, and garrisoned in the forging of his ring of iron. He visited the towns and villages scattered about, poking into their folklore as much as into their history, and he was surprised to discover that some whisper of purpose was drawing him on, that in indulging his curiosity about the past he was embracing an unspoken promise that a form of revelation on the future of his own life might somehow be possible. It was an irrational, unfounded hope, but one that was compelling in its hold over him. He passed that spring and summer in Betws-y-Coed, and he did not think of leaving. He wondered now and again if he was overstaying his welcome, but neither his friend nor her parents contacted him and he was content to leave well enough alone.

Then, on a summer day filled with sunshine and the smell of grasses and wildflowers, he came out of a hike south beyond the Conwy Falls to a sign that said FAIRY GLEN. It was just a weathered board, painted white with black letters, situated at the entrance to a rutted dirt and gravel lane leading off the blacktop through trees and fences, over a rise and into shadow. There was a small parking lot for cars and a box for donations. There was nothing else. He stared at the sign, amused, then intrigued. Why would it be called Fairy Glen? Because it was magical, of course. Because it had a supposed connection to a fairy world. He smiled and turned down the lane. What could it hurt to see? He left a pound in the box and hiked back along the fence line, over the rise, and through a corridor of big trees to a barely recognizable opening in the fence that led toward the sound of rushing water. He stepped through the opening, went down a winding pathway through trees and rocks to the source of the rushing water, and found himself in the glen.

For a long time he just stood there looking about, not moving, not thinking of anything. The glen was deep and shadowed, but streaked with bright sunlight and roofed by a cloudless blue sky. Massive rocks, broken and cracked, littered the slopes and floor of the glen, as if in ancient, forgotten times a volcanic upheaval had ruptured and split the earth. The water spilled from a series of falls to his left, the rush of their passage a low thunder against the silence. The stream broadened and narrowed by turns as it worked its way through channels formed by the positioning of the boulders. In some places it ran fast and wild and in others it formed pools so calm and still you could see the riverbed as clearly as if it were covered over with glass. Colored rocks littered the bottom of the stream, visible through the crystalline waters, and wildflowers grew in clusters all along the banks and slopes. The Fairy Glen formed a cathedral of jumbled rocks and trees that closed in the sounds of the twisting waters and shut out the intrusions of the world. Within its sanctuary, you were alone with whatever god you embraced and whatever beliefs you held.

John Ross stepped forward to the water's edge after a moment, squatted, and touched the stream. The water was ice cold, as he had expected. He stared down into its rush for a moment, losing himself in time's passage and the memories of his life. He looked at himself in the water's shimmering reflection, sun-browned from his year of hiking through England, strong and fit, his gaze steady and assured. He did not look like himself, he thought suddenly. What had changed? He had spent another year drifting, accomplishing nothing, arriving at no decision on his life. What was different?

He rose and walked along the jagged rock banks of the glen, working his way over the massive boulders, finding footholds amid the eddies and pools that filled the gaps between. He squinted when he passed through patches of bright sunlight, enjoying the warmth on his face, pausing in the shadows to look more closely at what might be hidden, wondering idly where the fairies were. He hadn't seen any so far. Maybe they were all on vacation.

"If it's magic you're looking for," a deep voice said, "you should come here at night."

John Ross nearly jumped out of his skin, teetering momentarily in midstep on the rocks, then righting himself and looking about quickly for the voice's source.

"It's more a fairy glen when the sun's down, the moon's up, and the stars lend their radiance."

He saw the man then, hunkered down just ahead in a heavy patch of shade, wrapped in a greatcoat and shadowed by a broad-brimmed hat pulled low over his face. He held a fishing pole loosely before him, the line dangling in a deep, still pool. His hands were brown and rough, crosshatched by tiny white scars, but steady and calm as they gently shifted the pole and line.

"You would like to see the fairies, wouldn't you?" he asked, tilting the brim of his hat up slightly.

John Ross shrugged uncomfortably. "I suppose so. At night, you say? You've seen them, have you?" He was trying to find something in their conversation that made sense, to frame a reply that fit.

The man's chuckle was low and deep. "Maybe I have. Maybe I've seen them come out of the falls, tumbling down the waters like tiny bright lights, as if they were stars spilling out of the heavens. Maybe I've seen them come out of the shadows where they hide by day, back there atop the falls, within the rocks and the earth—there, where the sun breaks through the trees."

He pointed, and John Ross looked in spite of himself, peering through a glaze of sunlight across the jumble of rocks to where the falls fell in a dazzling silver sweep. Bits of light danced atop the surface of the water, and behind the shimmering curtain shadows seemed to move . . .

Ross turned back suddenly to the man, anxious to know more. But the man was gone. Ross stared for a moment in disbelief, then glanced hurriedly from one bank to the other, from one place to the next. He searched the shadows and the sunny patches with equal care, but the man was nowhere to be found.

Shaken, he left the glen and walked back up the dirt and gravel lane to the blacktop, and from there back to the village. That night he pondered what he had seen, hunched over his dinner in an alehouse close to his lodgings, nursing a pint of Welsh beer and trying to make sense of it all. There was no way the fisherman could have disappeared so swiftly, so utterly. There was no place for him to go. But if he hadn't disappeared, then he wasn't there in the first place, and Ross wasn't prepared to deal with that.

For several days he refused to return to the glen, even though he wanted to. He thought about going at night, as the fisherman had urged, but he was afraid. Something was waiting for him, he believed. What if it was something he was not prepared to face?

Finally, three days later, he went back during the day. It was gray and overcast, the clouds threatening more of the rain that had already fallen intermittently since dawn. Again, the parking lot was deserted as he made his way off the blacktop and down the rutted lane. Cows looked at him from the pasture on his left, placid, disinterested, and remote. He tightened his rain slicker against the damp and chill, passed through the opening in the fence, and started down the trail. He was thinking that it was a mistake to do this. He was thinking that it was something he would come to regret.

He continued on anyway, stubbornly committed. Almost immediately he saw the fisherman. It was the same man; there was no mistaking him. He wore his broad-brimmed hat and greatcoat and was fishing with the same pole and line. He sat somewhat farther away from the falls than he had the previous day, as if thinking to find better fishing farther downstream. Ross walked carefully across the rocks to reach him, keeping close watch as he approached, making sure that what he was seeing was real.

The fisherman looked up. "Here you are again. Good day to you. Have you done as I suggested? Have you come at night?"

Ross stopped a dozen yards away from him. The man was sitting on a flat rock on the opposite bank, and there was no place close at hand to cross over. "No, not yet."

"Well, you should, you know. I can see in your eyes that you want to. The fairies mean something to you, something beyond what they might mean to an average man. Can you feel that about yourself?"

Ross nodded, surprised to find that he could. "I just . . ." He stopped, not knowing where to go. "I find it hard . . ."

"To believe," the other finished softly.

"Yes."

"But you believe in God, don't you?"

Ross felt a drop of rain nick the tip of his nose. "I don't know. I guess so."

The man adjusted the pole and line slightly. "Hard to believe in fairies if you don't believe in God. Do you see?"

Ross didn't, but he shook his head yes. Overhead, the clouds were darkening, closing in, screening out the light. "Who are you?" he asked impulsively.

The man didn't move. "Owain. And you?"

"John Ross. I'm, uh, traveling about, seeing a little of the world. I was in graduate studies for a number of years, English and Ancient Civilizations, but I, uh . . . I needed . . ."

"To come here," the man said quickly. "To come to the Fairy Glen. To see if the fairies were real. That was what you needed. Still need, for that matter. So will you come, then? As I suggested? Come at night and see them for yourself?"

Ross stared at him, groping for an answer. "Yes," he said finally, the word spoken before he could think better of it.

The man nodded. "Come in two nights, when the moon is new. Then's the best time for catching them at play; there's only the starlight to reveal them and they are less wary." His face lifted slightly, just enough so that Ross could catch a glimpse of his rough, square features. "It will be a clear night for viewing. A clear night for seeing truths and making choices."

Rain was spattering on the rocks and earth, on the surface of the stream. Shadows were deepening within the glen, and there was a rumble of thunder. "Better take shelter now," the man said to John Ross.

Then the skies opened and the rain poured down. Instinctively Ross lowered his head and pulled up the hood to his slicker, covering himself. When he looked back again, the fisherman was gone.

The rain continued all the rest of that day and into the next. John Ross was paralyzed with indecision. He told himself that he would not go back to the Fairy Glen, that he would not put himself at such obvious risk, that what was at stake was not simply his life but possibly his soul. It felt that way to him. He stayed within his rooms reading, trying not to think, and when thinking became inescapable, he went to the pubs and drank until he slept. He would have run if there had been any place left to run to, but he had exhausted his possibilities for running long ago. He knew that he had come as far as he could go that way, and that all that was left to him was to stand. But did standing entail going to the glen or staying clear? He drifted in increasingly smaller circles as the hours passed and the time of his summoning drew closer, and he despaired of his life. What had he done to bring himself to this end, to a strange and unfamiliar land, to a ghost who drew him as a flame did a moth, to a fairy glen in which magic might be possible, to the brink of madness?

After a time, he came to believe that whatever waited in the Fairy Glen was inextricably bound to him, a fate that could not be avoided and therefore must be embraced. With acceptance of this came a sort of peace, and he found himself wondering on the day of his appointed summoning if what had drawn him here and made him feel that self-discovery was at hand was linked in some way to what would happen that night in the glen.

When it was dark and he had eaten his dinner, he put on his warm clothing, his hiking boots, and his slicker, pocketed a flashlight, and went out the door of his cottage. He hitched a ride for part of the distance, then walked the rest. It was nearing midnight when he turned up the dirt and gravel lane past the sign that read FAIRY GLEN. The night was still and empty-feeling, but the skies were clear of clouds and filled with stars, just as the fisherman had foreseen. Ross breathed in the night air and tried to stay calm. His eyes adjusted to the darkness as he moved along the road, through the fence, and down the trail into the glen.

It was darker here, the starlight failing to penetrate much beyond the overhanging branches of the trees. The glen was a world apart, a rush of tumbling water and a jumble of broken rocks. Ross made his way over the massive boulders and along the stream banks to where he had twice seen the fisherman. There was no sign of him now. Within the moss and vine-grown walls of the glen, there was no movement. Belatedly, Ross thought of his failure to advise anyone of his plans. If he should disappear, no one would know where to look for him. No one would know where he might be found.

He reached an open space on the near bank between two huge boulders, a place where the starlit sky was clearly visible overhead. He glanced back at the falls, but he could not see them, could only hear the sound of the water spilling off the rocks. He stood there waiting, not knowing what he should look for, not certain yet if he should stay or run.

The minutes slipped past. He glanced about expectantly, emboldened by the fact that nothing had happened. Perhaps nothing was going to happen. Perhaps the fisherman had played a joke on him, on a gullible American, leading him on about magic and fairies . . .

"John Ross."

The sound of his name was a silvery whisper in the silence, spoken so softly that it might have come from inside him. He stood perfectly still, afraid even to breathe.

"John Ross, I am here."

He turned then, and he saw her standing at the water's edge across from him, not quite in the stream and not quite out of it either. She seemed to be balanced between water and earth, on the brink of falling either way. She was young and beautiful and so ethereal in the bright starlight that she was almost not there. He stared at her, at her long hair, at her gown, at her slender arms raised toward him.

"John Ross, I have need of you," she said.

She moved slightly, and the light shifted about her. He saw then that she was not real, not solid, but made of the starlight and the shadows, made of the night. She was the ghost he had thought the fisherman to be—still thought he might be now. He swallowed hard against the tightness in his throat and could not speak.

"You were summoned to me by Owain Glyndwr, my brave Owain, as he in his time was summoned by another in my service. I am the Lady. I am the Light. I am the voice of the Word. I have need of you. Will you embrace me?"

Her voice whispered in the deep night silence, low and compelling, vast and unalterable, the sum of all that could ever be. He knew her for what she was instantly, knew her for her power and her purpose. He went to his knees before her on the crushed rock bed of the glen's damp floor, his eyes fixed on her, his arms clutching his body in despair. Behind her, where the waterfall tumbled away in the darkness, lights began to twinkle and shimmer against the black. One by one they blinked on, then soared outward on the cool air, on gossamer wings that glimmered faintly with color, like fireflies. He knew they were the fairies he had come to find, and tears sprang to his eyes.

"I'm sorry," he whispered finally. "I'm sorry I didn't believe."

"You do not believe yet," the Lady sang, as if the words were cotton and the air a net in which they were to be caught and held up for admiration. "You lack reason to believe, John Ross. But that will change when you enter into my service. All will change. Your life and your soul will be transformed. You will become for me, as Owain Glyndwr once was, as others have been, a Knight of the Word. Stand now."

He rose and tried to gather up his scattered thoughts. *Owain Glyndwr*. The fisherman? Was he *that* Owain Glyndwr, the Welsh patriot and warrior? He had read of him. Owain Glyndwr had fought the English Bolingbroke, Henry IV, in the early 1400s. For a time he had prevailed over Henry, and the Welsh were made free again. No one could stand against him, not even the vaunted Prince of Wales, who in time would be Henry V, and the Welsh armies under Glyndwr's command marched into England itself. Then he simply disappeared—vanished so completely that there was no record of what had become of him. And the English marched back into Wales once more.

"It is so," said the Lady, who, though he had not given voice to his thoughts, seemed to have heard them anyway.

"He was in your service?" John Ross whispered. "Owain Glyndwr?"

"For many years." The Lady shimmered with movement as she passed to another point, closer to where the fairies spilled down off the waterfall in a shower of light. "He chose service to me over service to his country, a new life and commitment in exchange for an old. My need for him was greater. He understood that. He understood that only he would do. He sacrificed himself. He was valiant and strong in the face of terrible danger. He was one of the brave. And more. Look closely on his face, John Ross."

One arm gestured, and the fisherman reappeared, standing close beside her. His cloak and broad-brimmed hat were gone, replaced by chain mail and armor plate. His fishing pole was gone as well, and he held instead a broadsword. He looked on John Ross, his face fully revealed by the starlight, and in that face Ross saw himself.

"You carry his blood in your veins." The Lady's voice floated on a whisper of night breeze. "That is why you are summoned to me. What was best in him six hundred years ago reflects anew in you, born of the time and the need, by my will and my command."

The Fairy Glen echoed with her words, the sounds reverberating off the rush of the water, off the shimmer of the light from stars and fairies. John Ross was frozen with fear and disbelief, so petrified he could not move. A part of him thought to run, a part to stand, and a part to scream, to give voice to what roiled within. This was all wrong; it was madness. Why him? Why, even if he was Owain Glyndwr's kin? He was no warrior, no fighter, no leader, no man of courage or strength. He was a failed scholar and a drifter with no purpose or conviction. He might have thought to find himself by coming here, but not in this way, and surely not in whatever cause it was the Lady championed.

"I cannot be like him," he blurted out in despair. "Look at me!"

"Watch," she whispered in reply, and brushed at the air before him with a feathery touch.

What he witnessed next was unspeakable. A black hole opened, and suddenly he stood in a world of such bleak landscape and dark despair that he knew instinctively it lacked even the faintest semblance of hope. What moved through it was unrecognizable—things that looked vaguely human, but walked on all fours, creatures dark and scaled, shadows with blunted, scarred features and eyes that reflected with a flat, harsh light. They moved through the debris of a ruined civilization, through remnants of buildings and roads, the consequences of a catastrophe of monumental proportions. The creatures seemed part of that landscape, wedded to it in the way that ash is to fire, and were one with the shadows that cloaked everything.

The setting shifted. John Ross stood within the camps in which the survivors of the holocaust were penned, imprisoned to live out their lives in servitude to those who had been like them, but had embraced the madness that had destroyed their world. Both showed themselves, victors and victims, born of the same flesh and blood; both had been transformed into something barely recognizable and impossibly sad.

There was more, scene after scene of the destruction, of its aftermath, of the madness that had consumed everything. Ross felt something shift inside him, a lurching recognition, and even before she spoke the words that came next, he knew what they would be.

"It is the future," she said softly, her words as delicate as flower petals. "It approaches."

The vision disappeared. The black hole closed. Ross stood again before her, surrounded by the fairies and the night. Once more, he found his voice. "No," he said. "No, it will never be like that. We would never allow ourselves to become like that. Never."

She floated on the surface of the stream now, balanced on the night air. "Would you change the future, John Ross? Would you be one of those who would forbid it? Then do as Owain Glyndwr once did, as all the others did who entered into my service. Embrace me."

She approached him slowly, a wraith in the starlight, advancing without apparent motion. "This is what is required of you. You must become one of my champions, my paladins, my knights-errant. You must go forth into the world and do battle with those who champion the Void. The war between us is as old as time and as endless. You know of it, for it is revealed by every tongue and written in every language. It is the confrontation between good and evil, between creation and destruction, between life and death. There are warriors that serve each of us, but only a handful like you. You have long sought after yourself, John Ross, searching for the way that you were meant to travel in your life. You have come to me for that reason. Your way lies through me. I am the road that you must take."

Ross shook his head anew. "I can't do this. I haven't the . . . I'm not strong enough, not . . ."

"Give me your hand."

She held forth her own, shimmering like quicksilver in the starlight. Ross flinched away, unwilling to do as she asked. His eyes lowered, and he tried to hide. The Lady waited, her hand held forth, her body still. She had approached to within a yard of him now, so close that he could feel the heat of her, an invisible fire that burned somewhere deep within. Although he tried not to, he could not help himself. He looked at her.

"Oh, my God, my God," he whispered in awe and fear.

"Give me your hand," she repeated.

He did so then, compelled by the force of her voice and the recognition that he could not escape what was about to happen. He placed his hand of flesh and blood within her own of heat and light, and the shock of the contact dropped him instantly to his knees. He threw back his head and tried to scream what he was feeling, but no sound would come from his mouth. He closed his eyes and waited to die, but found instead that it was not death that had come to claim him, but life. Strength filled him, drawn from the well of his heart. Visions flooded his mind, and he saw himself as he could be, as he must be, a man become new again, a man reborn. He saw his future in the Lady's service, saw the roads he would travel down and the journeys he would make, saw the people whose lives he would change and those he might save. In the mix of passion and heat that twisted and built within the core of his being, he found the belief the Lady had foreseen.

She released him then, and he sagged forward, gasping for air, feeling the cool dampness of the earth against his knees and palms, feeling the power of her touch rush through him.

"Rise," she whispered, and he did, surprised to find that he could do so, that there was within him, sparking like flint on stone, the promise that he could do anything.

"Embrace me," she whispered, and he did that as well, without hesitation or deliberation, casting off his doubt and fear and taking on the mantle of his newfound certainty and belief, reaching for her, committing himself irrevocably and forever to her service.

CHAPTER 15

With twilight deepening to night and the park emptying of its last visitors, John Ross walked Nest Freemark home again. He had finished his tale, or as much of it as he wished to confide in her, and they were speaking now of what had brought him to Hopewell. Pick had joined them, come out of nowhere to sit all fidgety and wide-eyed on the girl's shoulder, trying his best not to appear awestruck in the presence of a vaunted Knight of the Word, but failing miserably. Pick knew of the Word's champions—knew as well what having one come to Hopewell meant. It was vindication, of a sort, for his frequently expressed suspicions.

"I told you so!" he declared triumphantly, over and over again, tugging at his mossy beard as if to rid himself of fleas. "I knew it all along! A shift in the balance this extreme could only be the work of something purposefully evil and deliberately ill-intentioned! A demon in the park! Criminy!"

He was the guardian of Sinnissippi Park, and therefore entitled to a certain amount of respect, even from a Knight of the Word, so John Ross indulged his incessant chatter while struggling to complete his explanation to Nest. He had been tracking this particular demon for months, he continued, momentarily silencing Pick. He had sought to bring him to bay on countless occasions, had thought he had done so more than once, but each time had failed. Now he had tracked him here, to Hopewell, where the demon meant to precipitate an event of such far-reaching consequence that it would affect the entire country for years to come. The event itself would not necessarily be dramatic or spectacular enough to draw national attention; that was not how things worked. The event would be the culmination of many other events, all leading to the proverbial last straw that would tip the scales in the demon's favor. Of small events are great catastrophes constructed, and it would be so here.

"The demon will attempt something this weekend that will shift the balance in a way that will make it difficult, if not impossible, to right." John Ross kept his voice calm and detached, taking care not to reveal the rest of what he knew. "What we must do is discover what he intends and put a stop to it."

"How are we supposed to do that?" Pick interrupted for the twentieth time. "Demons can disguise themselves so thoroughly that even a forest creature can't recognize them! If we don't know who he is, how are we supposed to disrupt his plans?"

John Ross was silent for a moment. They were passing down the service road now, the lights of the Freemark house shining ahead through the trees. He had not told them of his dreams. He had not told them of the future he had seen, the future that had revealed to him the truth about what the demon intended to accomplish by coming to Hopewell. He could not tell them that, of course. He could never tell them that.

"The demon is not perfect," he said, choosing his words carefully. "He makes mistakes, just like humans. He was human once; he cannot free himself of his mortal coil completely. If we keep close watch, we will find him out. He will do something to reveal himself. One of us will learn something that will help."

"How much time do we have?" Nest asked quickly.

Ross took a deep breath. "Until Monday. July fourth."

"July fourth?" She looked over at him curiously. "How do you know that?"

Ross slowed and stopped, leaning heavily on his staff, suddenly weary. He had slipped up. "Sometimes the Lady tells me things," he said quietly. "She confides in me."

The lie burned in his mouth, but there was no help for it. He had told her as much as he could, as much as he dared. He would tell her more tomorrow, after she had been given time to consider what she had already learned. He must be careful about this. He must not give away too much too soon.

He said good night to her in her backyard, out by the tire swing, where she said she would remain to talk a bit with Pick. He told her he would see her again tomorrow and they would talk some more. He asked her to keep her eyes open and be careful. Pick was quick to declare that he would keep his eyes open for both of them and if the demon was out there he would find him quickly enough. It was bold talk, but it felt reassuring to hear.

John Ross went inside the house then to thank Nest's grandparents once more for the dinner, moving slowly through the shadows, the staff providing him support and guidance where the light was dimmest. He was conscious of the girl's eyes following after him, aware that already her doubts about him were starting to surface. She was too smart to be fooled easily. He could not expect to do much more than delay giving out the truths she would all too soon demand to know.

He felt the weight of his task settle over him like lead. He wished he had known sooner and been given more time. But his dreams did not work like that. Time was not a luxury permitted him, but a quixotic variable that seemed to thwart him at every turn. He thought again of all the things he had not told her. Of the secret of the staff he bore. Of the reason for his limp. Of the price he paid for the magic he had been given.

Of what would become of Nest Freemark if the future were not changed by his coming.

Nest sat in the tire swing with Pick on her shoulder and told him all of what she had learned about John Ross. As she repeated the tale, she found herself beset by questions she had not thought to ask earlier. She was surprised at how many things Ross had failed to address, and she wished now that she could call him back again. He had come to Hopewell to see her grandparents, to visit her mother's grave, to keep a promise to himself, and to revive old memories. But he had come to stand against the demon as well. It seemed a rather large coincidence that he was there to do both. Were the two connected in some way? What was the demon doing here in the first place, in this tiny town, in the middle of Reagan country? Wasn't there some other, larger place where his efforts might have a more far-reaching result? What was so special about Hopewell?

There was something even more disturbing to her, something that had not been addressed at all. Apparently John Ross had known nothing of her before coming to Hopewell, for he had not seen or spoken with her mother since college. If that was so, then why did she feel that he knew so much about her? He hadn't said anything specific, but the feeling was inescapable. He had recognized her ability to see the feeders. He had known about her relationship with Pick without ever having met the sylvan. He had opened up to her about himself as if this was necessary, as if she was already his ally. Yet what exactly did he expect from her? Was it only that he needed another pair of eyes to help look for the demon? Was it just that if Pick were to know of his coming, so necessarily must she? Or was there something more?

"What do you think?" she asked Pick impulsively.

The sylvan scowled. "What do I think about what?"

"About him. About John Ross."

"I think we are fortunate he is here! What else would I think?" The sylvan looked indignant. "He's a Knight of the Word, Nest—one of the Word's anointed champions! He's come because there's a demon on the loose and that means we're in a lot of trouble! You don't know about demons; I do. A demon is the worst sort of creature. If this one accomplishes whatever it is he's set out to do, the result will be something that none of us wants even to consider! Criminy!"

Nest found herself thinking about Two Bears and his warning of the previous night. *There is reason to think that your people will destroy themselves.* Perhaps, she surmised, they would do so a little more quickly with the help of a demon.

"How do you know he is a Knight of the Word?" she pressed.

"John Ross? Because he is!" Pick snapped irritably. "Why are you being so difficult, Nest?"

She shrugged. "I'm just asking, that's all."

The sylvan sighed laboriously. "I know because of the staff. A staff like that is given only to a Knight of the Word. Been so for centuries. No one else can carry them; no one else is allowed. Every sylvan knows what they look like, how they're marked. The runes—did you notice them? Do they seem familiar to you?"

They did, of course, and now she realized why. Pick had drawn those same runes in the park's earth on several occasions when working his healing magic. That was where she had seen them before.

"He seems very tired," she observed, still musing on what he had revealed about himself, still working it through in her mind.

"You would be tired, too," he sniffed, "if you spent all your time tracking demons. Maybe if you and I do what he's asked of us and spot the demon, then he can get some rest!"

Unperturbed by the rebuke, she looked off into the trees. The shadows had melted into a black wall, and only the faint, silvery streamers of light from moon and stars and the harsher yellow glare of house lamps penetrated the darkness. Mosquitoes buzzed at her, but she ignored them, swinging idly, lazily in the tire, still thinking about John Ross. Something wasn't right. Something about him was different from what he wanted her to believe. What was it?

"Drat!" exclaimed Pick suddenly, springing to his feet on her shoulder. "I forgot to tell him about the maentwrog! Criminy sakes! I'll bet the demon has something to do with weakening the magic that imprisons it! Maybe that's what the demon has come here to do—to set the maentwrog free!"

"He said he was here to see about the feeders," Nest replied thoughtfully.

"Well, of course! But the feeders respond to human behavior, and certainly setting free the maentwrog would stir up a few emotions in the good citizens of Hopewell, don't you think?"

Maybe, maybe not, Nest thought, but she kept her opinion to herself. Why, she wondered once again, were there suddenly so many feeders in Sinnissippi Park? If they were attracted by human emotion, if they responded to what was dark and scary and terrible, why were so many gathered here? What had drawn them to this time and place? Was it whatever John Ross had come to prevent? If so, if it was that, then what were they doing here already, clustered thick as fall leaves even before whatever it was that was going to happen had happened?

She leaned back in the swing, letting her head and shoulders hang down and her legs tilt up. Dislodged from his perch, Pick gave a sharp exclamation, jumped down, and was gone. Nest let him go, weary of talking. She swung slowly in the humid night air, looking up at the stars, wishing suddenly that she could go fishing or hiking or maybe run far out on the roadways that led through the surrounding farmland, wishing that she could be someplace else or maybe even be some other person. She felt a sudden need to escape her present and flee back into her past. She could feel her childhood slipping away, and she despaired suddenly of losing it. She did not want to grow up, even after having struggled so hard to do so. She wanted to go back, just for a little while, just long enough to remember what it was like to have the world be no bigger than your backyard. Then she would be all right. If she could just have one more chance to see things the way they were, she would be all right.

Behind her, Miss Minx strolled out of the shadows, eyes gleaming, paused for a long look, and disappeared back into the dark. Nest watched her go, hanging upside down in the swing, and wondered where she went at night and what she did.

Then her ruminations drifted once more to John Ross, to the mystery that surrounded his coming, and she had a strange, unsettling thought.

Was it possible that he . . . ?

That he was . . . ?

She could not finish the thought, could not put it into words. She held it before her, suspended, a fragile piece of glass. She felt her heart stop and her stomach go cold. No, it was silly. It was foolish and impossible. No.

She closed her eyes and breathed the night air. Then she opened them again and let the thought complete itself.

Could John Ross be her father?

Robert Heppler was sitting alone in his room at his computer, pecking idly at the keys while he talked on the phone with Brianna Brown. "So, what do you think?"

"I think you're making something out of nothing as usual, Robert."

"Well, what does Cass think?"

"Ask her yourself."

He heard the phone being handed off to Cass Minter. He had called Cass first, thinking her the better choice for this conversation, but Mrs. Minter had said she was staying overnight at Brianna's. Now he was stuck with talking to both of them.

"Ask me what?" Cass growled into his ear.

"About Nest. Don't you think she's acting weird? I mean, weirder than usual?"

"Weirder than you, you mean?"

"Sure. Weirder than me. If it makes you happy."

Cass thought it over. "I don't like the word 'weird.' She's got something on her mind, that's all."

Robert sighed heavily. "Look. She comes to my house and practically drags me through the door, collects a bunch of dirt and salt, commandeers you and Brianna and your sister's red wagon, then hauls the bunch of us out to the park to do some voodoo magic stuff on a sick tree. Then, when we're done, she tells us to go on home, she's too tired to go swimming. Just like that. Miss Aqua-Lung, who's never turned down a chance to go swimming in her life. You don't think that's weird?"

"Look, Robert. People do things that other people find strange. That's the way it is. Look at Cher. Look at Madonna. Look at you. Don't be so judgmental!"

"I'm not being judgmental!" Robert was growing exasperated. "I'm worried, that's all. There's a difference, you know. I just wonder if there's something wrong that she's not telling us about. I just wonder if there's something we ought to be doing! We're supposed to be her friends, aren't we?"

Cass paused again. In the background, Robert could hear Brianna arguing with her mother. It had something to do with spending too much time on the phone. Robert rolled his eyes. "Someone ought to tell that woman to get a life," he muttered.

"What?" Cass asked, confused.

"Nothing. So what do you think? Should one of us call her up and ask her if she's all right?"

"One of us?"

"Okay, you. You're her best friend. She'd talk with you. She probably wouldn't tell me if her socks were on fire."

"She might, though, if yours were."

"Big yuck."

He heard the phone being passed again. "Hello? Who is this, please?"

It was Brianna's mother talking. Robert recognized the nasal whine laced with suspicion. "Hello, Mrs. Brown," he answered, trying to sound cheerful. "It's Robert Heppler."

"Robert, don't you have something better to do than call up girls?"

Matter of fact, yes, Robert thought. But he would never admit it to her. "Hmmm, well, I had a question and I was hoping Brianna or Cass could help me with it."

"What sort of question?" Mrs. Brown snapped. "Something a mother shouldn't hear?"

"Mother!" Robert heard Brianna gasp in the background, which gave him a certain sense of satisfaction.

A huge fight broke out, with shouting and screaming, and even the muffling of the receiver by someone's hand couldn't hide what was happening. Robert took the phone away from his ear and looked at it with helpless resignation.

Then Cass came back on the line. "Time to say good night, Robert. We'll see you at the park tomorrow."

Robert sighed. "Okay. Tell Brianna I'm sorry."

"I will."

"Parents are a load sometimes."

"Keep that in mind for when you're one. I'll have a talk with Nest, okay?"

"Okay." Robert hesitated. "Tell her I went back out this evening to see how her tree was coming along. Tell her it looks worse than before. Maybe she should call someone."

There was renewed shrieking. "Good-bye, Robert."

The phone went dead.

Jared Scott came down from his room for a snack to find his mother and George Paulsen drinking beer in front of the television. The other kids were asleep, all of them crammed into a tiny pair of hot, airless bedrooms. Jared had been reading about Stanley and Livingstone, using a tiny night-light that his mother had given him for Christmas. He liked reading stories about exploring faraway places. He thought that this was something he would like to do one day, visit strange lands, see who lived there. He saw the light from the television as he made the bend in the stairs and knew his mother and George were still up, so he crept the rest of the way on cat's paws and was turning in to the kitchen when George called to him.

"Hey, kid, what are you doing?"

He turned back reluctantly, trying not to look at either of them. His mother had been dozing, a Bud Light gripped in her hand. She looked around in a daze at the sound of George's voice. At thirty-two, she was slender still, but beginning to thicken about the waist. Her long dark hair was lank and uncombed, her skin pale, and her eyes dull and lifeless. She had been pretty once, but she looked old and worn-out now, even to Jared. She had five children, all of them by different men. Most of the fathers had long since moved on; Enid was only sure of two of them.

"Jared, why aren't you asleep?" she asked, blinking doubtfully.

"I asked you a question," George pressed him. He was a short, thickset man with dark features and a balding head. He worked part-time at a garage as a mechanic and there was always grease on his hands and clothing.

"I was getting something to eat," Jared answered, keeping his tone of voice neutral. George had hit him several times just for sounding smart-mouthed. George liked hitting him.

"You get what you need, sweetie," his mother said. "Let him be, George."

George belched loudly. "That's your trouble, Enid—you baby him." Jared hurried into the kitchen, George's voice trailing after him. "He needs a firm hand, don't you see? My father would have beat me black and blue if I'd come down from my room after hours. Not to mention thinking about getting something else to eat. You ate your dinner at the table and that was it until breakfast."

His voice was rough-edged and belligerent; it was the same voice he always used around Enid Scott and her children. Jared rummaged through the refrigerator for an apple, then headed back toward the stairs.

"Hey!" George's voice stopped him cold. "Just hold on a minute. What do you have there?"

"An apple." Jared held it up for him to see.

"That all?"

Jared nodded.

"I don't want to catch you drinking any beer around here, kid. You want to do that with your friends, away from home, fine. But not here. You got that?"

Jared felt a flush creep into his cheeks. "I don't drink beer."

George Paulsen's chin jerked up. "Don't get smart with me!"

"George, he can't!" His mother glanced hurriedly at Jared. "He can't drink alcohol of any kind. You know that. His medication doesn't mix with alcohol."

"Hell, you think for one minute that would stop him, Enid? You think it would stop any kid?" George drank from his own can, draining the last of its contents. "Medication, hell! Just another word for drugs. Kids do drugs and drink beer everywhere. Always have, always will. And you think your kid won't? Where'd you check your brain at, anyway? Christ almighty! You better let me do the thinking around here, okay? You just stick to cooking the meals and doing the laundry." He gave her a long look and shook his head. "Change the channel; I want to watch Leno. You can do that, can't you?"

Enid Scott looked down at her hands and didn't say anything. After a moment she picked up the remote and began to flick through the channels. Jared stared at her, stone-faced. He wanted her to tell George to get out of their house and stay out, but he knew she would never do that, that she couldn't make herself. He stood there feeling foolish, watching his mother be humiliated.

"Get on upstairs and stay there," George told him finally, waving him off with one hand. "Take your goddamn apple and get out of here. And don't be coming down here and bothering us again!"

Jared turned away, biting at his lip. Why did his mother stay with him? Sure, he gave her money and bought her stuff, and sometimes he was even halfway nice. But mostly he was bad-tempered and mean-spirited. Mostly he just hung out and mooched off them and found ways to make their lives miserable.

"You remember one thing, buster!" George called after him. "You don't ever get smart with me. You hear? Not ever!"

He kept going, not looking back, until he reached the top of the stairs, then stood breathing heavily in the hallway outside his room, rage and frustration boiling through him. He listened to the guttural sound of George Paulsen's voice, then to the silence that followed. His fists clenched. After a moment, tears flooded his eyes, and he stood crying silently in the dark.

Saturday night at Scrubby's was wild and raucous, the crowd standing three-deep at the bar, all the booths and tables filled, the dance floor packed, and the jukebox blaring. Boots were stomping, hands clapping, and voices lifting in song with Garth Brooks, Shania Twain, Travis Tritt, Wynonna Judd, and several dozen more of country-and-western's favorite sons and daughters. The mingled smells of sweat and cologne and beer permeated the air and smoke hung over everything in a hazy shroud, but at least the air-conditioning was keeping the heat at bay and no one seemed to mind. The workweek was done, the long awaited Fourth of July weekend was under way, and all was right with the world.

Seated in the small, two-person booth crammed into a niche between the storeroom door and the back wall, Derry Howe sat talking to Junior Elway, oblivious of all of it. He was telling Junior what he was going to do, how he had worked it all out the night before. He was explaining to Junior why it would take two of them, that Junior had to be a part of it. He was burning with the heat of his conviction; he was on fire with the certainty that when it was all said and done, the union could dictate its own terms to high-and-mighty MidCon. But his patience with Junior, who had the attention span of a gnat, was wearing thin. He hunched forward over the narrow table, trying to keep his voice down in case anyone should think to listen in, trying as well to keep Junior's mind on the business at hand instead of on Wanda Applegate, seated up at the bar, whom he'd been looking to hit on for the past two hours. Over and over he kept drawing Junior's eyes away from Wanda and back to him. Each time the eyes stayed focused for, oh, maybe thirty seconds before they wandered off again like cats in heat.

Finally he seized the front of Junior's shirt and dragged him halfway across the table, spilling beer and sending ashtrays and napkins flying. "You listen to me, goddamn it!" he screamed. "You listen to me when I talk to you!"

A few people turned to see what was happening, but when they saw the look on Derry Howe's face, they quickly went back to their own conversations. The music boomed out, the dancers yelled and clapped, and the confrontation in the tiny corner booth went mostly unnoticed.

"Okay, okay, I'm listening!" Junior snapped, jerking free. He was twenty pounds heavier and two inches taller, but there was fear in his eyes as he spoke the words. Damn well ought to be, Derry Howe thought with satisfaction.

"You heard anything I said so far, porkypine?" he sneered. "Anything at all?"

Junior ran his hand over his head, feeling the soft bristles of hair that were the product of this afternoon's visit to the Clip Joint, where he'd impulsively decided on a brush cut. He'd thought it would make him look tougher, he'd told Derry afterward. He'd thought it would make him look like a lean, mean cat. What it did was make him look like a jerk. Derry had begun ragging on him right away, calling him names. Porkypine. Cactus head. Nazi brain. Like that.

"I heard every damn thing you said!" Junior snapped furiously, sick and tired of Derry's attitude. "You want me to repeat it, smartass? Want to hear me stand up and shout it out loud maybe?"

If Derry Howe had been angry before, he was positively livid now. His expression changed, his eyes went flat and cold, and all the color drained out of his face. He looked at Junior as if a line had been crossed and Junior were no longer among the living.

Junior's mouth worked against the sudden dryness in his throat. "Look, I just meant . . ."

"Shut up," Derry Howe said softly. Even in the din, Junior heard the words plainly. "You just shut your mouth and listen. I ever hear you say something like that again, and you're history, bub. You believe me? Do you?"

Junior nodded, sitting there as still as stone, staring into the eyes of the man across from him, the man who had been his best friend until just a moment ago and who now was someone else entirely.

"This is too important for me to let you screw it up, you understand?" Derry Howe's voice was a soft hiss. "There's too much at stake for you to be making stupid statements or wiseass remarks. You with me on this or not? Answer me, damn it!"

Junior nodded. He'd never seen Derry like this. "Yeah, sure, course I am."

Derry Howe gave him a long, hard look. "All right, then. Here's the rest of it. Don't say nothing till I'm finished. Just listen. This is for keeps, Junior. We can't go pussyfooting about and hope the company will just come to their senses all on their own. My uncle and those other old farts might think that'll work, but they're whistling down a rat hole. They're old and they're worn-out and the company knows it. The company ain't about to negotiate. Never was. There's just you and me, bub. It's up to us. We have to bring them to the table, kicking and screaming if that's what it takes, but with them understanding they got to reopen the mill. Right? Okay. So we've got to have some leverage."

He leaned so close to Junior that his friend could smell the beer on his breath. "When this thing happens, it's got to be big enough that it will bring the national in. It ain't enough if it looks like an accident. It ain't enough, even if it looks like it's the company's fault. That won't do it. There's got to be casualties. Someone's got to be hurt, maybe even killed."

Junior stared openmouthed, then quickly shook his head. "Man, this is crazy . . ."

"Crazy because it gets the job done?" Derry snapped. "Crazy because it just might work? Hell, because it *will* work? Every war has its sacrifices, Junior. And this is a war, don't kid yourself. It's a war we're going to win. But that won't happen if the company isn't held accountable for something they can't talk their way out of. It won't happen if it don't draw the national's attention."

"But you can't just . . . You can't . . ."

"Go on, say it, Junior," Derry hissed derisively.

"Kill someone, damn it!"

"No? Why not? Why the hell not?"

He could, of course. He'd already decided it, in fact. He would do it because it was necessary. He would do it because it was a war, just like he'd said, and in a war, people got killed. He'd talked it over with himself the day before, after he'd come up with the accident idea. It was almost like having someone sitting there with him, having a conversation with a trusted friend, talking it through, reasoning it out. It all made perfect sense. He was certain of it. He was positive.

Junior kept shaking his head. "Damn it, Derry, you're talking about murder!"

"No, I ain't. Don't use that word. It ain't murder if it's a war. This is just—what do you call it?—a sacrifice for the greater good. For the community, for you and me and all the rest. You can see that, can't you?"

Junior nodded doubtfully, still trying to come to terms with the idea. "All right, okay, it's a war. So that's different. And it's gonna be an accident, right? Just part of something else that happens?" He wiped his mouth with the back of his hand, then looked carefully at Derry once more. "But it's not gonna be deliberate, is it?"

Derry Howe's expression did not change. Junior was such a dork. He forced himself to smile. "Course not. It's gonna be an accident. When there's an accident, people get hurt. It will be a real tragedy when it happens. It will make everyone feel bad, but particularly the company, because it will be the company's fault."

He reached out, fastened his hand around the back of Junior's neck, and pulled his friend's tensed face right up against his own. "Just you remember that, Junior," he whispered. "It won't be our fault. It will be the company's fault. High-and-mighty MidCon's fault." He squeezed Junior's neck roughly. "They'll crawl over broken glass to get back to the bargaining table then. They'll beg to get back. Hide and watch, Junior. Hide and watch."

Junior Elway reached for what was left of his beer.

Nest stayed in the swing another few minutes, lost in her thoughts of John Ross, then climbed out and stood looking off into the blackness of the park. She wondered if the demon he hunted was hiding there. She wondered if it preferred the dark, twisting caves where the feeders concealed themselves to the lighted houses of the humans it preyed upon. Miss Minx crept by, stalking something Nest could not see. She watched the cat move soundlessly through the dark, silken and deadly in its pursuit, and she had a sudden sense of what it would be like to be hunted like that.

She moved toward the house, thinking to go in, knowing she would have only an hour or two of sleep before it was time to meet Two Bears at the Sinnissippi burial mounds. She wondered what Two Bears knew about all this. Did he know of the demon and John Ross and of the war they fought? Did he know of the Word and the Void? Was he aware of the existence of this other world, of its proximity to the human world, and of the ties that bound the two? She felt certain he knew a great deal he wasn't telling her, much like John Ross. She wondered if they shared a common purpose in coming to Hopewell, perhaps a purpose no one else recognized, one tied to both the spirits of the Sinnissippi and the coming of the demon. She sighed and shook her head. It was all speculation, but speculation was all she had.

She moved up to the screen door, then slowed when she heard voices coming from the kitchen. Her grandparents were arguing. She hesitated, then moved down the side of the house to the window that opened above the sink to eavesdrop. It wasn't something she normally did, but she'd heard John Ross's name, and she was curious to know if he was the cause of the argument. She stood silent and unmoving in the shadows, listening.

"He seems like a fine young man to me," her grandfather was saying. He was leaning against the counter at the sink, his back to the window. Nest could see his shadow in a pool of light thrown on the ground. "He was pleasant and straightforward when he came up to speak to me at Josie's. He didn't ask for a thing. It was my idea to invite him to dinner."

"You're too trusting, Robert," her grandmother replied. "You always have been."

"He's given us no reason to be anything else."

"Don't you think it's a bit odd, him showing up like this, unannounced, uninvited, just to see us, to talk about a girl he hasn't seen in over fifteen, sixteen years? A girl who's been dead all that time and never a word from him? Do you remember Caitlin ever saying anything about him, ever even mentioning his name?"

Old Bob sipped from his coffee cup, thinking. "No, but that doesn't mean she didn't know him."

"It doesn't mean he was a friend, either." Nest could picture Gran sitting at the kitchen table, bourbon and water in hand, smoking her cigarette. "I didn't like the way hc took to Nest."

"Oh, for God's sake, Evelyn."

"Don't invoke God for my sake, Robert!" Gran shot back. "Use the brain he gave you instead! Suppose, for a minute, John Ross is not who he claims. Suppose he's someone else altogether."

"Someone else? Who?"

"Him, that's who."

There was the sound of ice cubes tinkling in an empty glass and of a fresh cigarette being lit, then silence. Nest watched her grandfather place his coffee cup on the counter, saw his leonine head lower, heard him sigh.

"He's gone, Evelyn. He's not coming back. Ever."

Her grandmother pushed back her chair and rose. Nest could hear her move to the counter and pour herself a drink. "Oh, he's coming, all right, Robert. He's coming. I've known it from the first, from the moment Caitlin died and he disappeared. I've always known it."

"Why would he do that?" Old Bob's voice sounded uneasy. "Evelyn, you can't be serious."

Nest stood transfixed in the heat and the dark, unable to turn away. They were talking about her father.

"He wants Nest," Gran said quietly. She drew on the cigarette and took a long swallow of the drink. Nest heard each sound clearly in the pause between her grandmother's words. "He's always wanted her."

"Nest? Why would he want Nest? Especially after all this time?"

"Because she's his, Robert. Because she belongs to him, and he doesn't give anything up this side of the grave. Don't you know that by now? After Caitlin, don't you know that?"

There was another pause, and then some sounds that Nest could not identify, muttered words perhaps, grumbling. Her grandfather straightened at the window.

"It's been fifteen years, but I remember him well enough." Old Bob spoke softly, but distinctly. "John Ross doesn't look anything like him, Evelyn. They're not the same man."

Gran gave a quick, harsh laugh. "Really, Robert. Sometimes you appall me. Doesn't look like him? You think for a minute that man couldn't change his looks if there was reason enough to do so? You think he couldn't look like anyone he wanted to? Don't you realize what he is?"

"Evelyn, don't start."

"Sometimes you're a fool, Robert," Gran declared sharply. "If you want to go on pretending that I'm a crazy old woman who imagines things that aren't there, that's fine. If you want to pretend there's no feeders in the park, that's fine, too. But there's some things you can't wish away, and he's one of them. You saw what he was. You saw what he did to Caitlin. I wouldn't put anything past him. He's coming here, coming for Nest, and when he does he won't be stupid enough to look the same as he did when he left. You do what you want, Robert, but I plan to be ready for him."

The kitchen was silent again. Nest waited, straining to hear.

"I notice you didn't worry about letting him take her into the park," Old Bob said finally.

Gran didn't say anything. Nest could hear the sound of her glass being raised and lowered.

"So maybe there's not as much to be afraid of as you'd like me to believe. Maybe you're not sure who John Ross is either."

"Maybe," Gran said softly.

"I invited him to come to church tomorrow morning," Old Bob went on deliberately. "I asked him to sit with us. Will you be coming?"

There was a pause. "I don't expect so," Gran replied.

Nest took a long, slow breath. Her grandfather moved away from the window.

"I invited him to picnic with us in the park afterward, too. So we could talk some more." Her grandfather cleared his throat. "I like him, Evelyn. I think Nest likes him. I don't think there's any reason to be scared of him."

"You will pardon me if I reserve my opinion on that?" Gran replied after a moment. "That way, we won't all be caught by surprise." She laughed softly. "Spare me that look. And don't ask me if I plan to have another drink either, because I do. You go on to bed, Robert. I'll be just fine by myself. Have been for a long time. Go on."

Nest heard her grandfather move away wordlessly. She stayed where she was for a moment longer, staring up at the empty, lighted kitchen window, listening to the silence. Then she slipped back through the shadows like the ghost of the child she had grown out of being.

Chapter 16

Nest did not sleep when she finally reached her bedroom, but lay awake in the dark staring up at the ceiling and listening to the raucous hum of the locusts through the screen window. The air felt thick and damp with the July heat, and even the whirling blades of the big floor fan did little to give relief. She lay atop her covers in her running shorts and T-shirt, waiting for midnight and her rendezvous with Two Bears. The bedroom door stood open; the hallway beyond was silent and dark. Gran might have gone to bed, but Nest could not be certain. She imagined her grandmother sitting alone at the kitchen table in the soft, tree-filtered light of moon and stars, smoking her cigarettes, drinking her bourbon, and reflecting on the secrets she hid.

Nest watched those secrets dance as shadows on her ceiling.

Was John Ross her father? If he was, why had he abandoned her?

The questions repeated themselves over and over in her mind, suspended in time and wrapped in chilly, imperious solitude. They whispered to her, haunting and insidious.

If John Ross was her father, why was Gran so bitter toward him? Why was she so mistrustful of his motives? What was it that her father had done?

She closed her eyes, as if the answers might better be found in darkness. She stilled herself against the beating of her heart, against the pulse of her blood as it raced through her veins, but she could find no peace.

Why was her father such an enigmatic figure, a shadow barely recognizable as being a part of her life? Why did she know so little about him?

Outside an owl hooted softly, and Nest wondered if Daniel was calling to her. He did that sometimes, reaching out to her from the dark, a gesture she did not fully understand. But she did not rise to look this night, locked in her struggle to understand the doubts and confusion that beset her at every turn. Like a Midwest thunderstorm building out on the plains and working its way east, dark and forbidding and filled with power, a revelation approached. She could feel it, could taste it like rain and smell it like electricity in the air. The increasing boldness of the feeders, the deterioration of the maentwrog's prison, and the coming of John Ross and the demon signaled a shift in the balance of things. In a way Nest did not yet understand, it was all tied to her. She could sense that much from the time she had spent with John Ross. It was in the words he had used and the secrets he had shared. He had taken her into his confidence because she was directly involved. The challenge she faced now, on thinking it through, was in persuading him to tell her why.

When it was nearing midnight, the time reflected by the luminous green numbers on her digital clock, she rose and walked to her open bedroom door and stood listening. The house was dark save for the single lamp that Gran always left burning in the front entry. Nest moved back across the room to turn down the bed and place the extra pillows under the sheet to make it look like she was sleeping. Then she removed the window screen from its fastenings and slipped through, put the screen back in place, and turned toward the park.

In the distance a dog barked, the sound piercing and clear in the deep night silence, and Nest was reminded suddenly of Riley. Riley was the last dog they had owned. A black lab with big feet, sad eyes, and a gentle disposition, he came to her as a puppy, given to her by her grandfather on her third birthday. She had loved Riley from the moment he had bounded into her arms, all rough pads and wet tongue, big ears and squirming body. She had named him Riley because she thought he just looked like a Riley, even though she had never actually known one. Riley had been her dog all through growing up, there for her when she left for school, waiting for her when she came home, with her when she went down the road to visit her friends, at her side when she slipped into the park. He was there when she saw the feeders, Pick, and even Wraith, although he did not seem to see any of them as she did. She was almost twelve when he developed a tumor in his lungs. Inoperable, she was told. She went with her grandfather to have her faithful friend and companion put down. She stood watching, dry-eyed and stoic, as the vet injected Riley and his sleek body stiffened and his soft eyes fixed. She did not cry until later, but then she did not think she would ever stop.

What she remembered most, however, was Gran's reaction. Gran had stayed behind and cried alone; Nest could tell she had cried from her red eyes and the wrinkled Kleenex wads in the waste basket next to the kitchen table where she had begun to take up permanent residence with her bourbon and her cigarettes. Gran said nothing on their return, but at dinner that night she announced in a tone of voice that brooked no argument that they had acquired their last dog. Cats were sufficient. Cats could look after themselves. Dogs were too dependent, required too much, and stole away your heart. Ostensibly, she was speaking of Riley, but Nest had been pretty certain that in an odd way she was speaking of Caitlin as well.

She stood now for a moment in the darkness of the summer night, remembering. She missed Riley more than she could say. She had never told Gran this. She knew it was something Gran did not want to hear, that it would only suggest to her how much she, in turn, missed Caitlin.

Nest glanced at the silent house, thinking Gran might appear, that she might somehow know what Nest was about. But there was no movement and no sound from within. Nest turned away once more and crept through the shadows of the backyard, eyes searching. Miss Minx slunk from beneath a big oak, low to the ground and furtive. Another cat, a strange striped one, followed. Out in the park, beyond the wall of the hedge, moonlight bathed the open ball fields and play areas with silver brightness. It was her secret world, Nest thought, smiling at the idea. Her secret world, belonging only to her. No one knew it as she did, not even Gran, for whom it was now distant and foreign. Nest wondered if it would become that way for her someday, if by growing she would lose her child's world as she would lose her childhood, that this was the price you paid for becoming an adult. There was that gap between adults and children that reserved to each secrets that were hidden from the other. When you were old enough, you became privy to the secrets that belonged only to adults and lost in turn those that belonged only to children. You did not ever gain all of one or lose all of the other; of each, some you kept and some you never gained. That was the way it worked. Gran had told her that almost a year ago, when Nest had felt her child's body first begin its slow change to a woman's. Gran had told her that life never gave you everything or took everything away.

She slipped through the gap in the hedgerow, and Pick dropped onto her shoulder with an irritated grunt.

"It's about time! What took you so long? Midnight's the appointed time, in case you've forgotten! Criminy!"

She kept her eyes directed forward. "Why are you so angry?"

"Angry? I'm not angry! What makes you think I'm angry?"

"You sound angry."

"I sound the way I always do!"

"Well, you always sound angry. Tonight, especially." She felt him squirming on her shoulder, leaves and twigs rustling, settling into place. "Tell me something about my father."

He spit like a cat. "Your father? What are you talking about?"

"I want to know something about my father."

"Well, I don't know anything about your father! I've told you that! Go ask your grandmother!"

She glanced down at him, riding her shoulder in sullen defiance. "Why is it that no one ever wants to talk about my father? Why is it that no one ever wants to tell me anything about him?"

Pick kicked at her shoulder, exasperated. "It's rather hard to talk about someone you don't know, so that might explain my problem with talking to you about your father! Are you having a problem with your hearing, too?"

She didn't answer. Instead, she broke into a fast trot, jogging swiftly down the service road and past the nearest backstop, then cutting across the ball diamond toward the cliffs and the river. The humid night air whipped past her face as her feet flew across the newly mowed grass. She ran as if she were being chased, arms and legs churning, chest expanding and contracting with deep, regular breaths, blood racing through her in a hot pulse. Pick gave a surprised gasp and hung on to her T-shirt to keep from falling off. Nest could hear him muttering as she ran, his voice swept away by the rush of the air whipping past her ears. She disappeared into herself, into the motion of her arms and legs, into the pounding of her heart. She covered the open ground of the ball fields and the playgrounds, crossed the main roadway, hurdled the chain dividers, and darted into the trees that fronted the burial mounds. She ran with fury and discontent, thinking suddenly that she might not stop, that she might just keep on going, running through the park and beyond, running until there was nowhere left to go.

But she didn't. She reached the picnic benches across the road from the burial mounds and slowed, winded and shot through with the heat of her exertion, but calm again as well, distanced momentarily from her frustration and doubt. Pick was yapping at her like a small, angry dog, but she ignored him, looking about for Two Bears and the spirits of the dead Sinnissippi. She glanced down at her wristwatch. It was almost midnight, and he was nowhere in sight. The burial mounds were dark and silent against the starry backdrop of the southern horizon where moonlight spilled from the heavens. The park was empty-feeling and still. Nothing moved or showed itself. Even the feeders were nowhere to be seen.

A trace of wood smoke wafted on the still air, pungent and invisible.

"Where is he?" she asked softly, turning slowly in the humid dark, eyes flicking left and right, heart pounding.

"Here, little bird's Nest," his familiar voice answered, and she jumped at the sound of it.

He was standing right in front of her, so close she might have reached out to touch him if she had wished to do so. He had materialized out of nowhere, out of the heat and the night, out of the ether. He was stripped to the waist, to his baggy pants and worn army boots, and he had painted his face, arms, and chest in a series of intricate black stripes. His long hair was still braided, but now a series of feathers hung from it. If he had seemed big to her before, he looked huge now, the coppery skin of his massive chest and arms gleaming behind the bars of paint, his blunt features chiseled by shadows and light.

"So you've come," he said softly, looking down at her with curious eyes. "And you've brought your shy little friend."

"This is Pick." She introduced the sylvan, who was sitting up straight on her shoulder, eyeing the big man.

"Charmed," Pick snapped, sounding anything but. "How come you can see me when no one else can?"

The smile flashed briefly on Two Bears' face. "Indian magic." He looked at Nest. "Are you ready?"

She took a deep breath. "I don't know. What's going to happen?"

"What I have told you will happen. I will summon the spirits of the Sinnissippi and they will appear. Maybe they will speak with us. Maybe not."

She nodded. "Is that why you're dressed like that?"

He looked down at himself. "Like this? Oh, I see. You're afraid I might be wearing war paint, that I might be preparing to ride out into the night and collect a few paleface scalps."

She gave him a reproving frown. "I was just asking."

"I dress like this because I will dance with the spirits if they let me. I will become for a few brief moments one with them." He paused. "Would you like to join me?"

She considered the possibility of dancing with the dead Sinnissippi. "I don't know. Can I ask you something, O'olish Amaneh?"

He smiled anew on hearing his Indian name. "You can ask me anything."

"Do you think the spirits would tell me who my father is if I asked them? Do you think they would tell me something like that?"

He shook his head. "You cannot ask them anything. They do not respond to questions or even to voices. They respond to what is in your heart. They might tell you of your father, but it would have to be their choice. Do you understand?"

She nodded, suddenly nervous at the prospect of discovering the answer to this dark secret. "Do I have to do anything?"

He shook his head once more. "Nothing. Just come with me."

They crossed to a small iron hibachi that sat next to a picnic table. A gathering of embers, the source of the wood smoke, glowed red within. Two Bears removed a long, intricately carved pipe from the top of the picnic table, checked to see that the contents within its charred bowl were tightly packed, then dipped the bowl to the embers, put the other end of the pipe in his mouth, and puffed slowly to light it. The contents of the bowl ignited and gleamed, and smoke curled into the air.

"Peace pipe," he declared, removing it from his lips and winking at her. He puffed on it some more, drawing the smoke deep into his lungs. Then he passed the pipe to her. "Now you. Just a few puffs."

She took the pipe reluctantly. "What's in it?" she asked.

"Herbs and grasses. They won't harm you. Smoking the pipe is ritual, nothing more. It eases the passage of the spirits from their resting place into our world. It makes us more accessible."

She sniffed at the contents of the bowl and grimaced. The night around her was deep and still, and it felt as if she were all alone in it with the Indian. "I don't know."

"Just take a few puffs. You don't have to draw it into your lungs." He paused. "Don't be frightened. You have Mr. Pick to watch over you."

She considered the pipe a moment longer, then put it to her lips and drew in the smoke. She took several quick puffs, wrinkled her nose, and passed the pipe back to Two Bears. "Yuck."

Two Bears nodded. "It's an acquired taste." He inhaled the pungent smoke, then carefully placed the pipe across the rim of the hibachi. "There."

Then he moved out onto the open grass and seated himself cross-legged facing the burial mounds. Nest joined him, sitting cross-legged as well, positioning herself next to him in the dark. Pick still rode her shoulder, but he had gone strangely silent. She glanced down at him, but he was staring out into the night, oblivious of her. She let him be. Overhead, the sky was crosshatched by the limbs of the trees, their dappled shadows cast earthward in a tangled net by the bright moonlight. Nest waited patiently, saying nothing, losing herself in the silence.

Two Bears began to chant, the words coming in a soft, steady cadence. The words were foreign to Nest, and she thought they must be Indian, probably Sinnissippi. She did not look at Two Bears, but looked instead where he looked, out over the roadway to the burial mounds, out into the night. Pick sat frozen on her shoulder, become momentarily a part of her, as quiet as she had ever seen him. She felt a twinge of fear, wondering suddenly if what she was doing was somehow more than she believed, if it would lead to a darker result than she anticipated.

Two Bears continued to chant, his deep voice steady and toneless. Nest felt the first stirrings of doubt mingle with her uneasiness. Nothing was happening; maybe nothing would.

Then a wind blew off the river, cool and unexpected, carrying with it the smell of things forgotten since childhood—of her grandmother's kitchen, of her sandbox, of Riley, of her cedar toy chest, of Wisconsin's lakes in summer. Nest started in surprise. The wind brushed past her and was gone. In the stillness that followed, she felt the hair on the back of her neck prickle.

Small glimmerings of light appeared at the edges of the burial mounds, rising up into the night, flickering and fading again, moving with rhythmic grace against the darkness. At first they were nothing, simply bright movements that lacked definition. Slowly they began to take shape. Arms and legs appeared, then bodies and heads. Nest felt her throat tighten and her mouth grow dry. She leaned forward, peering expectantly, trying to make certain of what she was seeing. On her shoulder, she heard Pick utter a faint, surprised exclamation.

Then up from the darkness rose the Sinnissippi, their spirits taking form, coming back into a shadowy semblance of their lost bodies. They lifted free of the earth to hang upon the air, twisting and turning in small arcs. They were dancing, Nest could see, but not in the fashion she had expected, not as Indians did in the television shows and movies she had seen, rising and falling in that familiar choppy motion, but in another way altogether. Their movements were more balletic, more sinuous, and they danced free of one another, as if each had a story to tell, each a different tale. Nest watched, awed by the beauty of it. After a time, she felt the dance begin to draw her in. She thought she could sense something of what the dancers were trying to convey. She felt herself swaying with them, heard the sounds of their breathing, smelled the sweat of their bodies. They were ghosts, she knew, but they were real, too. She wanted to call out to them, to make them turn and look at her, to acknowledge her presence. But she stayed silent.

Suddenly Two Bears was on his feet and striding forward. He reached the dancers and joined in their dance, his big, powerful body swaying and weaving as smoothly as their own. Nest marveled at the ease with which he moved, smiled at his grace. She felt the heat of his body fill her own, as if his pulse had mingled with hers. She watched in shock, then with a glimmer of terror, as his flesh-and-blood body began to fade into the darkness and turn as ghostly as the spirits of the dead Sinnissippi. There were drums now, their booming rising out of the night—or maybe the sounds were only in her mind, the rhythm of her heartbeat. She watched Two Bears become one with the dead, watched him become as they were, translucent and ephemeral, ghostly and unreal. She stared transfixed as he danced on, the sound of the drums heightening, the movements of the dancers quickening. She felt the summer's heat flood through her, causing her to blink against sudden flashes of crimson and gold.

Then she was on her feet as well, dancing with Two Bears, moving through the ghosts of the Sinnissippi. She did not feel herself rise or walk to him, did not know how it came to pass, but suddenly she was there among the Indian spirits. She floated as they did, not touching the earth, suspended on the night air, caught between life and death. She heard herself cry out with joy and hope. She danced with wild abandon and frantic need, whirling and twisting, reaching for something beyond what she could see, reaching past memories, past her own life, past all she knew . . .

Like a fever dream, the vision appears to her then. It comes out of nowhere, filling her mind with bright colors and movement. She is in another part of the park, a part she does not recognize. It is night, black and clouded, empty of moon and stars, a devil's night filled with pitch. Dark figures run through the trees, hunched over, lithe and supple. Feeders, she sees, dozens of them, their yellow eyes gleaming in the black. She feels her stomach knot with the realization that they are certain to see her. Across the grassy stretches and along the pathways they bound, swift and certain. A woman leads them, young and strong, her shadowed face smiling and wild-eyed, her long, dark hair streaming out behind her. Nest blinks against the sight—a human at play with feeders, running with them, unafraid. The woman spins and wheels, and everywhere she goes, the feeders chase after her. She teases and taunts them, and it is clear that they are infatuated by her. Nest stands spellbound within the darkened park, staring in disbelief as the woman rushes toward her, all wicked smiles and laughter. She looks into the woman's eyes, and sees there the lines that have been crossed and the taboos that have been broken. She sees the woman's life laid bare, sees her soul unfettered and her heart unafraid. She will dare anything, this woman, and has. She will not be cowed or chastened; she will not be made ashamed.

She dashes into Nest's arms, draws her close, and holds her tight. Nest recoils, then stares in shock. She knows this woman. She recognizes her face. She has seen her face, just as it is now, in a collection of framed photographs that sits upon the mantel over the fireplace in the living room. It is Caitlin Anne Freemark. It is her mother.

And yet it isn't. Not quite. Something is amiss. It is almost her mother, but it is someone else, too. Nest gasps in shock, not quite certain what she is seeing. The woman breaks free, her face suddenly filled with regret and despair. Behind her, barely visible in the darkness, a man appears. He materializes suddenly, and the feeders, who are clustered all about the woman, give way instantly at his approach. Nest tries to see his face, but cannot. The woman sees him and hisses in anger and frustration. Then she flees into the night, racing away shadow-quick with the feeders bounding in pursuit, and is gone.

Nest blinked anew against the darkness and the sudden bright pain that stabbed her eyes. Images whirled and faded, and her vision cleared. She was sitting once more on the grass, cross-legged in the darkness, her hands clasped before her as if in prayer. Two Bears was seated next to her, his eyes closed, his chiseled body still. In the distance, the burial mounds rose silent and empty of life. No lights moved across the grassy slopes; no warriors danced on the air above. The ghosts of the Sinnissippi had gone.

Two Bears opened his eyes and stared out into the darkness, calm and distanced. Nest seized his arm.

"Did you see her?" she asked, unable to keep the anguish from her voice.

The big man shook his head. His painted copper face was bathed in sweat, and his brow was furrowed. "I did not share your vision, little bird's Nest. Can you tell me of it?"

She tried to speak, to say the words, and found she could not. She shook her head slowly, feeling paralyzed, her skin hot and prickly, her face flushed with shame and confusion.

He nodded. "Sometimes it is better not to speak of what we see in our dreams." He took her hand in his own and held it. "Sometimes our dreams belong only to us."

"Did it really happen?" she asked softly. "Did the Sinnissippi come? Did we dance with them?"

He smiled faintly. "Ask your little friend when you find him again."

Pick. Nest had forgotten him. She glanced down at her shoulder, but the sylvan was gone.

"I learned many things tonight, little bird's Nest," Two Bears told her quietly, regaining her attention. "I was told of the fate of the Sinnissippi, my people. I was shown their story." He shook his head. "But it is much more complicated than I thought, and I cannot yet find the words to explain it, even to myself. I have the images safely stored"—he touched his forehead—"but they are jumbled and vague, and they need time to reveal themselves." His brow furrowed. "This much I know. The destruction of a people does not come easily or directly, but from a complex scheme of events and circumstances, and that, in part, is why it can happen. Because we lack the foresight to prevent it. Because we do not guard sufficiently against it. Because we do not truly understand it. Because we are, in some part, at least, the enemy we fear."

She squeezed his hand. "I don't think I learned anything. Nothing of what might destroy us. Nothing of what threatens. Nothing of Hopewell or anywhere else. Just . . ." She shook her head.

Two Bears rose, pulling her up with him, lifting her from the ground as if she were as light as a feather. The black paint gleamed on his face. "Maybe you were shown more than you realize. Maybe you need to give it more time, like me."

She nodded. "Maybe."

They stood facing each other in awkward silence, contemplating what they knew and what they didn't. Finally, Nest said, "Will you come back tomorrow night and summon the spirits of the Sinnissippi again?"

Two Bears shook his head. "No. I am leaving now."

"But maybe the spirits . . ."

"The spirits appeared, and I danced with them. They told me what they wished. There is nothing more for me to do."

Nest took a deep breath. She wanted him to stay for her. She found comfort in his presence, in his voice, in the strength of his convictions. "Maybe you could stay until after the Fourth. Just another few days."

He shook his head. "There is no reason. This is not my home, and I do not belong here."

He walked to the hibachi and retrieved his pipe. He knocked the contents of the bowl into the hibachi, then stuck the pipe in his belt. He took a cloth and carefully wiped the black paint from his face and arms and chest, then slipped into his torn army field jacket. He retrieved his backpack and bedroll from the darkness and strapped them on. Nest stood watching, unable to think of anything to say, watching as he transformed back into the man he had been when she had first encountered him, ragged and worn and shabby, another nomad come off the nation's highways.

"This could be your home," she said finally, her voice taking on an urgency she could not conceal.

He walked over to her and stared into her eyes. "Speak my name," he commanded softly.

"O'olish Amaneh."

"And your own."

"Nest Freemark."

He nodded. "Names of power. But yours is the stronger, little bird's Nest. Yours is the one with true magic. There is nothing more that I can do for you. What remains to be done, you must do for yourself. I came to speak with the dead of my people, and I have done so. I saw that it would help you to be there with me, and so I asked you to attend. What there was that I could offer, I have given. Now you must take what you have gained and put it to good use. You do not need me for that."

She stood staring at him in the humid dark, at his strong, blunt features, at the implacable certainty mirrored in his eyes. "I'm afraid," she said.

"Yes," he agreed. "But fear is a fire to temper courage and resolve. Use it so. Speak my name once more."

She swallowed. "O'olish Amaneh."

"Yes. Say it often when I am gone, so that I will not be forgotten."

She nodded.

"Good-bye, little bird's Nest," he whispered.

Then he turned and walked away.

Nest stood watching after him until he was out of sight. She could see him until he reached the edge of the park, and then he seemed to fade into the darkness. She thought more than once to call him back or to run after him, but she knew he would not want that. She felt drained and worn, emptied of emotion and strength alike, and she found herself wondering if she would ever see Two Bears again.

"O'olish Amaneh," she whispered.

She started back across the park, wondering anew what had become of Pick. One moment he had been sitting on her shoulder, all quiet and absorbed in the spirit dance, and the next he had been gone. What had happened? She trudged through the dark, moving toward home and bed, starting to be sleepy now in spite of all that had happened. She tried to make sense of the vision she had seen of the young woman and the feeders and the shadowy figure who accompanied them, but failed. She tried to draw something useful from what Two Bears had told her and failed there, as well. Everything seemed to confuse her, one question leading to another, none of them leading to the answers she sought.

In the shadows about her, a handful of feeders kept pace, as if predators waiting for their prey to falter. They watched her with their steady, implacable gaze, and she could feel the weight of their hunger. They did not stalk her, she knew; they simply watched. Usually, their presence didn't bother her. Tonight she felt unnerved.

She was out of the park and walking through her backyard toward the house when she realized suddenly what was amiss about the young woman in her vision. She stopped where she was and stared wide-eyed into the darkness, feeling the crawl of her skin turn to dryness in her throat. She knew the woman, of course. She had been right about that. And she had seen the woman's photograph on the fireplace mantel, too. But the photograph wasn't of her mother. It was of another woman, one who had been young a long time ago, before Nest or her mother were even born.

The photograph was of Gran.

Sunday, July 3

CHAPTER 17

It was approaching seven when Nest awoke the following morning, and the sun had already been up for an hour and a half. She had slept poorly for most of the night, haunted by the vision of Gran, plagued by questions and suspicions and doubts, and she did not sleep soundly until almost sunrise. Bright sunlight and bird-song woke her, and she could tell at once that it was going to be another hot, steamy July day. The air from the fan was warm and stale, and through her open window she could see the leaves of the big oaks hanging limp and unmoving. She lay motionless beneath the sheet for a time, staring up at the ceiling, trying to pretend that last night hadn't happened. She had been so eager to watch the dance of the spirits of the Sinnissippi, so anxious to learn what the spirits would tell her of the future. But she had been shown nothing of the future. Instead, she had been given a strange, almost frightening glimpse of the past. She felt cheated and angry. She felt betrayed. She told herself she would have been better off if she had never met Two Bears.

O'olish Amaneh.

But after a while her anger cooled, and she began to consider the possibility that what she had been shown was more important than she realized. Two Bears had hinted that she would need time to understand the vision, to come to grips with what it meant in her own life. She stared at the ceiling some more, trying to make sense of the shadows cast there by the sun, superimposing her own images, willing them to come to life so that they might speak to her.

Finally she rose and went into the bathroom, stopping at the mirror to look at herself, to see if she had changed in some way. But she saw only the face she always saw when she looked at herself, and nothing of secrets revealed. She sighed disconsolately, stripped off her sleep shirt, and stepped into the shower. She let cold water wash over her hot skin, let it cool her until she was chilled, then stepped out and dried. She dressed for church, knowing her grandfather would be expecting her to go, slipping into a simple print dress and her favorite low heels, and went down to breakfast. She passed through the living room long enough to check the pictures on the mantel. Sure enough, there was Gran, looking just as she had in the vision last night, her face young, her eyes reckless and challenging as they peered out from the scrolled iron frame.

She ate her breakfast without saying much, feeling awkward and uncomfortable in her grandmother's presence. She should speak to Gran of the vision, but she didn't know how. What could she say? Should she tell Gran what the vision had revealed or take a more circumspect approach and ask about her youth, about whether she had ever run with the feeders? And what did that mean, anyway? What did it mean when you ran with the feeders as Gran had done in the vision? Feeders were to be avoided; that was what Nest had been taught from the time she was little. Pick had warned her. Gran had warned her. So what did it mean that she was forbidden from doing something Gran had done?

And what, she wondered suddenly, had her mother done when she was a child? What did any of this have to do with her?

"You should eat something, Evelyn," her grandfather said quietly, breaking the momentary silence.

Gran was drinking her vodka and orange juice and smoking her cigarettes. There was no food in front of her. "I ate some toast earlier," the old woman responded distantly. Her eyes were directed out the window again, toward the park. "Just eat your own; don't worry about me."

Nest watched her grandfather shake his head and finish the last of his coffee. "Ready, Nest?"

She nodded and rose, gathering her dishes to carry to the sink. "Leave them," Gran called after her. "I'll clean up while you're gone."

"Sure you don't want to come?" Old Bob pressed gently. "It would be good for you."

Gran gave him a sideways look. "It would be good for the church gossips, maybe. You go on. I'll work on the picnic lunch." She paused long enough to take a hard drag on her cigarette. "You might want to give some more thought to inviting that boy, Robert. He's not what you think."

Her meaning was plain. Nest placed her dishes in the sink and waited for someone to speak. When no one did, she left the room and went down the hall to brush her teeth and give her hair a final comb. In the kitchen, she could hear her grandparents' voices, low and deliberate, arguing over John Ross.

She rode downtown in the pickup with her grandfather, neither of them saying anything, the windows rolled down so that Old Bob could smell the trees and flowers. It was just after ten o'clock, so the Illinois heat was not yet unbearable and there was still a hint of night's cool. Traffic on Lincoln Highway was light, and the parking lot at the supermarket as they turned off Sinnissippi Road was mostly empty. Nest breathed the summer air and looked down at her hands. She felt oddly disconnected from everything, as if she had been taken away from the home and the people she had always known and relocated to another part of the country. She felt she should be doing something—she had already been enlisted in the fight against the demon—but she had no idea where she ought to begin.

She looked at her reflection in the windshield and wondered if she really was only fourteen or if she was in fact much older and had missed some crucial part of her life while she slept.

Old Bob parked the pickup on Second Avenue in front of Kelly's Furniture directly opposite the First Congregational Church. They got out and crossed the street, stopping momentarily on the sidewalk to say hello to a handful of others on their way inside. Effusive compliments were extended to Nest on her achievements in running, sprinkled with comments concerning the depth of her competition, the state of her health, and the nature of the town's expectations for her. Nest smiled and nodded dutifully, suffering it all as graciously as she could, all the while looking around without success for John Ross.

Then they were inside the church, passing through wide, double doors into a vestibule that wrapped the sanctuary on two sides. It was cool and dark, the intense heat kept at bay by central air, the burning sunlight filtered by ribbons of stained glass. Greeters stood at each door, waiting to shake hands with those entering, and to pin flowers on the men's coats and the women's dresses. An elderly couple welcomed Nest and her grandfather, and the woman asked after Evelyn. An usher took them to a pew about halfway down on the left side of the sanctuary. The church was filling rapidly, and more than half the pews were occupied already. Nest and her grandfather sat on the aisle, holding their programs and glancing around in the hushed, cool gloom. The cathedral ceiling arched darkly overhead, its wooden beams gleaming. Organ music played softly, and the candles on the altar had already been lit by the acolytes. Nest looked again for John Ross, but he was nowhere to be seen. He wasn't coming, she thought, disappointed. But, after all, why would he?

Robert Heppler was sitting with his parents on the other side of the sanctuary near the back. The Hepplers liked the Congregational Church because it wasn't mired in dogma (this from Robert, purportedly quoting his father) and it embraced a larger span of life choices and secular attitudes. Robert said this was very different from being Catholic. Robert gave Nest a brief wave, and she gave him one back. She saw one of her grandfather's steel-mill friends, Mr. Michaelson, sitting with his wife several rows in front of the Hepplers.

The choir filed in and took their seats in the loft beside the pulpit, and everyone opened their programs and began studying the order of events and their hymnals.

Then John Ross appeared at the far side of the chamber, limping through the doorway with the aid of his black staff. He wore a fresh shirt, slacks, and a tie, and his long hair was carefully combed and tied back. He looked ill at ease and unsure of himself. Nest tried and failed to get his attention. Ross followed the usher down the aisle to a mostly empty row behind the Michaelsons and eased himself gingerly into place.

Now the choir rose, and the organist played a brief introduction. The minister appeared through a side door on the dais and walked to the pulpit. Ralph Emery was round and short and sort of strange-looking, with large ears and heavy jowls, but he was kind and funny and he was well known for giving thought-provoking sermons. He stood now in his black robes looking out over the congregation as if trying to decide whether to proceed. Then he asked the congregation to bow their heads, and he gave a brief invocation. When he was finished, he asked everyone to rise and turn to hymn number 236. The congregation stood, opened their hymnals, and began to sing "Morning Has Broken."

They had just reached the second verse when the feeders began to appear, dozens of them, materializing out of the gloom like ghosts. They crept from behind the empty pews down front where no one liked to sit and from under the offertory and sacrament tables at the chamber's rear. They rose out of the choir loft, from behind the blue velvet drapes that flanked the altar, and from under the cantilevered pulpit. They seemed to be everywhere. Nest was so stunned that she stopped singing. She had never seen feeders in the church. She had never imagined they could enter here. She stared at the closest in disbelief, a pair that slithered beneath the pew in front of her between the legs of the Robinson sisters. She fought down the revulsion she felt at seeing them here, in this place where God was worshipped and from which dark things were banished. She glanced around in horror, finding them hanging from the ceiling rafters, curled around the chandeliers, and propped up within the frescoes and bays. Yellow eyes stared at her from every quarter. Her heart quickened and her pulse began to race. No one could see the feeders but her. But even that didn't help. She could not tolerate having them here. She could not abide their presence. What were they doing in a church? In *her* church! What had drawn them? Despite the cool air of the sanctuary, she began to sweat. She glanced at her grandfather, but he was oblivious of what was happening, his gaze focused on his hymnal.

Then she turned in desperation to find John Ross.

John Ross had seen the feeders at the same moment as Nest. But unlike the girl, Ross knew what was happening. Only the demon's coming could have caused so many feeders to gather—the demon's coming coupled with his own, he amended, which now, in hindsight, seemed painfully ill advised. He should not have done this, come into this holy place, given in to his own desperate need to ease in some small measure the loneliness that consumed his life. He should have rejected Robert Freemark's offer and remained in his hotel room. He should not have been influenced by the attraction he had felt for this church while on his way to Josie's. He should have done what he knew was best for everyone and stayed away.

He willed himself to remain calm, not to give away what he was feeling, not to do anything to startle those around him. His staff was propped against the seat beside him, and his first impulse was to seize it and ready himself for battle. But he could not find his enemy, could not identify him even though he knew he was there, hiding in plain sight.

An elderly lady several seats away glanced at him and smiled. He realized he had stopped singing. He forced himself to smile back, to begin singing anew, first reaching down for the staff, planting it squarely before him, and leaning on it as if he were suddenly in need of its support.

It was then that he glanced across the heads of the congregation and saw Nest Freemark looking at him. He met her gaze squarely, letting her know he understood what she was seeing and that he was seeing it, too. He saw the fear and horror in her eyes, saw how deep it tunneled, and he understood far better than she what it was that motivated it. He fixed her with his gaze and slowly shook his head. Do nothing, he was warning her. Stay where you are. Keep your head.

He saw in her eyes that she understood. He saw as well that she did not know if she could do what he was asking. He thought to go to her, but there was no way to do that without drawing attention to himself. The hymn was finished, and the congregation was sitting down again. He cast a quick eye over the assemblage on the off chance he might find the demon. The minister was giving the Scripture lesson. The feeders crawled over the dais at his feet, dark shadows that made the scarlet carpet of the sanctuary appear as if it had been stained by ink. The minister finished the Scripture reading and went on to give the church announcements. John Ross felt his skin turn hot as he sat nailed in place in the pew, unable to act. I should not be here, he kept thinking. I should leave now.

The choir rose to sing, and John Ross looked back at Nest Freemark. Nest was sitting right on the edge of her seat beside her grandfather, her face pale and drawn, her body rigid. Her eyes were shifting right and left, following the movements of the feeders closest to her. Several were almost on top of her, slithering between the legs of the parishioners like snakes. One drew itself right up in front of her, as if taunting her, as if daring her to do something about it. Ross saw the desperation mirrored in her face. She was on the verge of panic, ready to bolt. He knew he had to do something. The choir finished, and the congregation rose to join the minister in a responsive prayer.

When that happened, something caused Nest Freemark to glance suddenly toward the back of the sanctuary, and Ross saw her expression mirror her shock.

Then he saw it, too.

Wraith stood in the doorway, thick fur bristling, tiger-striped face lowered, ears laid back, green eyes narrowed and glittering. He was so massive that he filled the entire opening, a monstrous apparition stalking out of the gloom. His big head swung left and right with slow deliberation, and his muzzle drew back, revealing all of his considerable teeth. He made no sound as he stood there, surveying the unwary assemblage, but his intent was unmistakable. Nest's fear had drawn him, summoned him to a place he had never been, brought him out of the deep woods and into this unfamiliar setting. His deliberate stare was filled with hunger.

Nest felt her stomach lurch. *No, Wraith, no, go away, go away!* Feeders scattered everywhere, crawling under pews, skittering down the aisles, and climbing the wood-paneled walls, their dark forms bleeding into the shadows. Their scrambling was so frantic that it stirred the air in the chamber, and among the congregation several heads lifted in surprise.

Wraith took a moment to consider his options, then started forward in that familiar, stiff-legged walk.

Nest was out of her seat and striding up the aisle to intercept him instantly. She did not stop to think about what she was doing. She did not stop to consider that she had never even thought to approach him before, that she had no idea whether she could control him. She did not say anything to her grandfather as she wheeled out of the pew; she did not even look at him. All she could think about was what would happen if Wraith managed to get hold of one of the feeders—here, in her church, among her family and friends and neighbors. She did not know what it would do to the fabric that separated the human and nonhuman worlds, and she did not want to find out.

The responsive reading concluded, and the congregation reseated itself. Heads turned to look at her as she closed on Wraith—on the ghost wolf they could not see—but she ignored them. Wraith seemed to grow even larger as she approached him, and his predatory gaze fixed on her. She felt small and vulnerable in his presence, a fragile bit of life that he could snuff out with barely a thought. But still she came on, fixed of purpose, steeled by her determination to turn him back.

And as she reached him, as it seemed she must come right up against him, right onto the tips of those gleaming teeth and that bristling fur, he simply faded away and was gone.

She continued without slowing through the space he had occupied, eyes closing against the rush of cold that washed over her, until she passed through the doorway and into the hall beyond. She stood there shaking, taking deep breaths to steady herself, leaning against the Christian-literature table, out of sight of those gathered within.

She jumped as a hand touched her shoulder. "Nest?"

John Ross was standing next to her, leaning on his black, rune-scrolled staff, his pale green eyes intense. He must have followed her out, she realized, and done so quickly.

"Are you all right?" he asked.

She nodded. "Did you see?"

He glanced about the deserted hall as if someone might be listening. Within the sanctuary, Reverend Emery was beginning his sermon, "Whither Thou Goest."

"I saw," he answered. He bent close. "What was that creature? How does it know you?"

She swallowed against the dryness in her throat. "That was Wraith." She shook her head, refusing to offer any further explanation. "Where did all these feeders come from? What's happening?"

Ross shifted uneasily. "I think the demon is here. I think that's what's drawing them."

"Here? Why?"

Ross shook his head. "Because of me." He looked suddenly tired. "I don't know. I'm only guessing."

She felt a deep cold settle in the pit of her stomach. "What should we do?"

"Go back inside. Stay with your grandfather. I'll wait out here until after the service. Maybe the demon will show himself. Maybe I'll catch sight of him." His green eyes fixed on her.

She nodded uncertainly. "I have to go to the bathroom first. I'll be right back."

She hurried off down the hall to the Christian Education wing, Reverend Emery's deep, compelling voice trailing after her, floating over the hush of the congregation. She did not feel very good; her stomach was rolling and her head pounding. She glanced through the open doors into the cavernous gloom of the sanctuary; the feeders had disappeared. She frowned in surprise, then shook her head and went on. It didn't matter why they were gone, she told herself, only that they were. Her footsteps echoed softly on the wooden floor as she crossed the lower foyer. She pushed through the doors leading into the reception room, feeling worn and harried. Mrs. Browning, who had been her fifth-grade teacher, was arranging cups and napkins on several long tables in preparation for the fellowship to be held after the service. The bathrooms lay beyond. Nest slipped past Mrs. Browning without being noticed, went into the kitchen, and disappeared into the women's bathroom.

When she came out, a man was standing there, surveying rows of cookies and cakes arranged on serving trays. He looked up expectantly as she entered.

"Ah, there you are," he greeted, smiling. "Good morning."

"Good morning," she replied automatically, and then stopped in surprise. It was the maintenance man who had spoken with her the previous day when she had wandered through the park after working on the injured tree. She recognized his strange, pale eyes. He was wearing a suit now, rather than his working clothes, but she was certain it was the same man.

"Not feeling so good?" he asked.

She shook her head.

He nodded. "Well, that's too bad. You don't want to miss out on all these treats. Missing out on the sermon is one thing, but missing out on these cookies and brownies and cakes? No, sir!"

She started past him.

"Say, you know," he said suddenly, stepping in front of her, blocking her way, "there's a little something I want to share with you. A private fellowship, you might say. It's this. I remember when sermons meant something. It's been a while, but the old-time evangelists had a way of communicating that made you sit up and take notice. Now there's the televangelists with their high-profile ministries, their colleges and their retreats, but they don't talk about what matters. None of them do. Because they're afraid. You know why? Because what matters is how the world will end."

Nest stared at him, openmouthed.

"Sure, that's what really matters. Because we might all be here to see it happen, you know. There's every reason to think so. Just take a look around you. What do you see? The seeds of destruction, that's what." A comfortable smile creased his bland features. "But you know something? The destruction of the world isn't going to happen in the way people think. Nope. It isn't going to happen in a flood or a fire. It isn't going to happen all at once, brought about by some unexpected catastrophe. It won't be any one thing you can point to. That's not how it works. The Bible had it wrong. It will happen because of a lot of little things, an accumulation of seemingly insignificant events. Like dominoes tipped over, one against the other—that's how it will happen. One thing here, another there, next thing you know it all comes tumbling down." He paused. "Of course, someone has to topple that first domino. It all has to start with someone, doesn't it? Tell me. Does any of this sound familiar to you?"

Nest stood speechless before him, her mind screaming at her to run, her body paralyzed.

"Sure it does," he continued, inclining his head conspiratorially. His strange eyes narrowed, burning with a fire she could not bear to look upon. "Tell you something else. The destruction of the world depends on the willingness of the people in it to harm each other in any way necessary to achieve their own ends and to further their own causes. And we got that part down pat, don't we? We know how to hurt each other and how to think up whatever excuses we need to justify it. We're victims and executioners both. We're just like those dominoes I mentioned, arranged in a line, ready to tip. All of us. Even you."

"No," she whispered.

His smile had turned chilly. "You think you know yourself pretty well, don't you? But you don't. Not yet."

She took a step backward, trying to gauge whether or not she could reach the door before he grabbed her. As she did so, the door swung inward, and Mrs. Browning pushed through.

"Oh, hello, Nest," she greeted. "How are you, dear?" She seemed surprised to see the man standing there, but she smiled at him cheerfully and moved to pick up another tray of brownies.

As she did so, the man said to Nest, "No, I'm afraid you don't know yourself at all."

He gestured swiftly toward Mrs. Browning, who gasped as if she had been struck by a fist. She dropped the tray of brownies and clutched at her chest, sinking toward the floor. Her eyes went wide in horror, and her mouth gaped open. Nest cried out and started toward her, but the man with the strange eyes intervened, moving swiftly to block her way. Nest cringed from him, riddled with fear. He held her gaze, making sure she understood how helpless she was.

Mrs. Browning was on her knees, her head lowered, her face white, her throat working rapidly as she tried to swallow. Blood spurted from her nose and mouth. Nest's scream froze in her throat, locked away by the man's hard eyes.

Then Mrs. Browning slid forward onto her face and lay still, her eyes open and staring.

The man turned to Nest and cocked one eyebrow quizzically. "You see what I mean? There wasn't a thing you could do, was there?" Then he laughed. "Maybe I won't stay for the fellowship after all. Like I said, church isn't what it used to be. Ministers are all just voices in the wind, and congregations are just marking time." He walked to the back door, stopped with his hand on the knob, and glanced over his shoulder at her. "Be good."

He opened the door and closed it softly behind him. Nest stood alone in the kitchen, looking down at Mrs. Browning, waiting for the shaking to stop.

Chapter 18

When she could make herself do so, Nest left the kitchen and walked back through the reception room. She was still shaking, the image of Mrs. Browning's final moments burned into her mind. She found one of the ushers and told him to call for an ambulance right away. Then she continued on. She found John Ross standing in the deserted narthex outside the sanctuary. She drew him down the long corridor to where they could not be seen or heard and related what had happened. Was it the demon? He nodded solemnly, asked if she was all right, and did not look or sound nearly as surprised as she thought he should. After all, if the demon had come looking for him, and that was what had drawn all those feeders into the church, what was it doing talking to her, threatening her, and making an object lesson of poor Mrs. Browning? Why was it talking to her about people destroying themselves, parroting in part, at least, much of what she had heard from Two Bears? What in the world was going on?

"What did the demon want with me?" she blurted out.

"I don't know," John Ross answered, giving her a steady, reassuring look, and she knew at once that he was lying.

But Reverend Emery had finished his sermon and the congregation had risen to sing the closing hymn, so her chance to ask anything further came and went. Ross sent her back inside to be with her grandfather, telling her they would talk later. She did as she was told, dissatisfied with his evasiveness, suspicious of his motives, but thinking at the same time she must tread carefully if she was to learn the truth of things. She slipped back down the aisle and into the pew beside her grandfather, giving him a rueful smile as the voices of the congregation rose all around her. She was starting the third verse of the hymn when it struck her that the demon might be trying to get to John Ross through her, and that was why he had cornered her in the church kitchen. That, in turn, would explain why Ross claimed he didn't know what was going on. It made sense if he was her father, she thought. It made perfect sense.

Mrs. Browning had been taken away by the time the fellowship began, but all the talk was of her sudden, unexpected demise. Nest thought she would be able to speak further with John Ross, but she could not manage to get him alone. First there was her grandfather, greeting Ross in a solemn, subdued voice, telling him how sorry he was that he had been introduced to the church under such tragic circumstances, pleased nevertheless that Ross had come to the worship service, reminding him of the afternoon's picnic and eliciting his promise that he would be there. Then there was Reverend Emery, greeting Ross with a sad face, a firm handshake, and a cautious inquiry into his needs while visiting in Hopewell. Then there was Robert Heppler, who latched on to Nest with such persistence that she finally told him they were breathing the same air and to back off. Robert seemed convinced she was suffering from some hidden malady, and while he was not entirely mistaken, he was annoying enough in his determination to uncover the source of her discontent that she wouldn't have told him the truth if her life had depended on it.

When she finally managed to get free of Robert and all the parishioners who stopped to remark on how awful it was about Mrs. Browning and to inquire after Gran's health, John Ross was gone.

She rode home with her grandfather in a dark mood, staring out the window at nothing, mulling over the events of the past few days and particularly the past few hours, struggling to untangle the web of confusion and contradiction that surrounded her. When her grandfather asked why she had run out of the sanctuary, she told him that she had felt sick and gone to the bathroom. When he asked if she was all right now, she said she was still upset about Mrs. Browning and didn't want to talk about it. It was close enough to the truth that he left her alone. She was getting good at making people believe things that weren't true, but she had an unpleasant feeling that she was nowhere near as good as John Ross.

He knew something about her that he was keeping to himself, she thought darkly. He knew something important, and it had much to do with his coming to Hopewell. It was tied to the demon and tied to her mother. It was at the heart of everything that was happening, and she was determined to find out what it was.

She believed, though she refused as yet to let herself accept it fully and unconditionally, that it had to do with the fact that he was her father.

By the time her grandfather pulled the old pickup down the drive and next to the house, she had made up her mind to confront Gran. She stepped out into the heat, the midday temperature already approaching one hundred, the air thick with dampness and the pungent smell of scorched grasses and weeds, the wide-spread limbs of the big shade trees languid and motionless beneath the sun's relentless assault. Nest walked to the porch, stooped to give Mr. Scratch an ear rub, then went inside. Gran was sitting at the kitchen table in a flowered housedress and slippers, sipping a bourbon and water and smoking a cigarette. She looked up as Nest passed by on her way to her bedroom, but didn't say anything. Nest went into her room, slipped off the dress, slip, shoes, and stockings, and put on her running shorts, a T-shirt that said Never Grow Up, and tennis shoes and socks. She could hear her grandparents talking down the hall. Gran was asking about John Ross, and she didn't seem happy with what she was hearing. Old Bob was telling her to keep her voice down. Nest took a moment to brush her hair while they finished the hottest portion of their conversation, then went back down the hall to the kitchen.

They stopped talking as she entered, but she pretended she didn't notice. She walked to the refrigerator and looked inside. The smell of fried chicken still lingered in the air, so she wasn't surprised to find a container of it sitting on the top shelf. There was also a container of potato salad, one of raw vegetables soaking in water, and a bowl of Jell-O. When had Gran done all this? Had she done it while they were in church?

She glanced over her shoulder at the old woman. "I'm amazed," she said, smiling. "It looks great."

Gran nodded. "I had help from the wood fairies." She shot Old Bob a pointed look.

Old Bob responded with a strangely sweet, lopsided grin. "You've never needed any help from wood fairies, Evelyn. Why, you could teach them a thing or two."

Gran actually blushed. "Old man," she muttered, smiling back at him. Then the smile fell away, and she reached down for her drink. "Nest, I'm sorry about Mrs. Browning. She was a good woman."

Nest nodded. "Thanks, Gran."

"Are you feeling all right now?"

"I'm fine."

"Good. You both had phone calls while you were in church. Cass Minter called for you, Nest. And Mel Riorden wants you to call him right away, Robert. He said it was urgent."

Old Bob watched wordlessly as she took a long pull on her drink. He was still wearing his suit coat, and he took time now to slip it off. He looked suddenly rumpled and tired. "All right. I'll take care of it. Excuse me, please."

He turned and disappeared down the hallway. Nest took a deep breath, walked over to the kitchen table, and sat down across from her grandmother. Sunlight spilled through the south window and streaked the tabletop, its brightness diffused by the limbs of the shade trees and the lace curtains so that intricate patterns formed on the laminated surface. It fell across Gran's hands as they lay resting beside her ashtray and drink and made them look mottled and scaly. The tabletop felt warm, and Nest pressed her palms against it, edging her fingers into one of the more decorative markings of shadows and light, disrupting its symmetry.

"Gran," she said, then waited for the old woman to look at her. "I was in the park last night."

Gran nodded. "I know. I was up and looked in on you. You weren't there, so I knew where you'd gone. What were you doing?"

Nest told her. "I know it sounds a little weird, but it wasn't. It was interesting." She paused. "Actually, it was scary, too. At least, part of it was. I saw something I don't understand. I had this . . . vision, I guess. A sort of daydream—except it was night, of course. It was about you."

She watched her grandmother's eyes turn cloudy and unfocused. Gran reached for her cigarette and drew the smoke deep into her lungs. "About me?"

Nest held her gaze. "You were much younger, and you were in the park at night, just like me. But you weren't alone. You were surrounded by feeders. You were running with them. You were part of them."

The silence that followed was palpable.

Old Bob closed the door to his den and stood looking into space. His den was on the north side of the house and shaded by a massive old shagbark hickory, but the July heat penetrated even here. Old Bob didn't notice. He laid his suit coat on his leather easy chair and put his hands on his hips. He loved Evelyn, but he was losing her. It was the drinking and the cigarettes, but it was mostly Caitlin and all the things the two of them had shared and kept from him. There was a secret history between them, one that went all the way back to the time of Caitlin's birth—maybe even further than that. It involved this nonsense about feeders and magic. It involved Nest's father. It went way beyond anything reasonable, and it imprisoned Evelyn behind a wall he could not scale, a wall that had become impenetrable since Caitlin had killed herself.

There. He had said the words. *Since Caitlin had killed herself.*

He closed his eyes to stop the tears from coming. It might have been an accident, of course. She might have gone into the park that night, just as she had done as a child, and slipped and fallen from the cliffs. But he didn't believe it for a minute. Caitlin knew the park like she knew the back of her hand. Like Nest did. Like Evelyn. It had always been a part of their lives. Even Evelyn had grown up in a house that adjoined the park. They were a part of it in the same way as the trees and the burial mounds and the squirrels and birds and all the rest. No, Caitlin didn't slip and fall. She killed herself.

And he still didn't know why.

He stared out the window at the drive leading up to Sinnissippi Road. It was hard losing Caitlin, but he thought it would be unbearable if he lost Evelyn. Their time together spanned almost fifty years; he couldn't remember what his life had been like before her. There really wasn't anything without her. He hated the drinking and the smoking, hated the way she had retired to the kitchen table and taken up residence, and hated the hard way she had come to view her life. But he would rather have her that way than not have her at all.

But what was he going to do to keep her? She was slipping away from him, one day at a time, as if she were sitting in a raft with the mooring lines slipped, drifting slowly out to sea while he stood helplessly on the shore and watched. He clasped his big hands before him and shrugged his shoulders. He was strong and smart and his life was marked by his accomplishments, but he did not know what to do to save her.

He reached up and loosened his tie. What could he do, after all, that would make a difference? Was there anyone who could tell him? He had spoken with Ralph Emery, but the minister had told him that Evelyn had to want to be helped before anyone could reach her. He had come out to the house to talk with her once or twice, but Evelyn had shown no interest in reaching out. Nest was the only one she cared about, and he thought sometimes that maybe Nest made a small difference in Evelyn just by being there. But Nest was still a child, and there was only so much a child could do.

Besides, he thought uneasily, Nest was too much like her grandmother for comfort.

He pulled off his tie, draped it over the easy chair with his coat, and walked to the phone to call Mel Riorden. He dialed, and the phone rang only once before Mel picked up.

"Riorden."

"Mel? It's Bob Freemark."

"Yeah, thanks for calling back. I appreciate it."

Old Bob smiled to himself. "What were you doing, standing by the phone waiting for me?"

"Something like that. This isn't funny. I've got a problem." Mel Riorden's tone of voice made that abundantly apparent, but Old Bob said nothing, waiting Mel out. "You have to keep this to yourself, Bob, if I tell you. You have to promise me that. I wouldn't involve you if I didn't have to, but I can't let this thing slide and I don't know how to deal with it. I've already tried and been told to go to hell."

Old Bob pulled back the desk chair and seated himself. "Well, this doesn't have to go beyond you and me if you don't want it to, Mel. Why don't you just tell me what it is?"

Mel Riorden gave a worried sigh. "It's Derry. The kid's more trouble than a dozen alligators in the laundry chute and stupid to boot. If he wasn't my sister's kid . . ." He trailed off. "Well, you've heard it all before. Anyway, I'm in church for the early mass with Carol and a couple of the grandkids. Al Garcia's there, too. With Angie and their kids. So afterward, I go in for a coffee and a cookie like everyone else. I say hello to Al and Angie, to a couple of others. Everyone's having a nice visit. I'm standing there, munching my cookie, sipping my coffee, Carol's off with the grandkids, all's right with the world, and up comes my sister. She looks really bad, worried as can be, all bent out of shape. First off, I think she's been drinking. But then I see it's something else. She says to me, 'Mel, you got to talk to him. You got to find out what's going on and put a stop to it.' "

"Put a stop to what?"

"I'm coming to that." Mel Riorden paused, arranging his thoughts in the silence. "See, I keep thinking of those newspaper stories we joke about over coffee at Josie's. The ones about the people who suddenly go berserk. Their minds snap and they go crazy, insane, for no real reason. You wonder how it could happen, how the people who know them could let it. It's like that. Like that schoolteacher walking in and killing all those kindergarten kids in Mississippi because he'd lost his job. You read about that in today's paper?"

Old Bob shook his head at the phone. "I haven't read the paper yet. I just got back from church myself."

"Yeah, well, that's one good reason for being Catholic. You get church out of the way early and have the rest of the day to yourself. Al and I talked it over once, the advantages of being Catholic over being Protestant . . ."

"Mel." Old Bob stopped him midsentence. "What about Derry? Are you saying he's planning to kill someone?"

"No, not exactly." Mel Riorden paused. "Hold on a minute, will you? I want to make sure Carol's not back from the store yet." He put down the phone and was gone for a minute before picking it up again. "I don't want her to hear any of this. I don't want anyone to hear."

"You want to meet me someplace private and talk about this?" Old Bob asked him.

"No, I want to get it out of the way right now. Besides, I don't know how much time we've got if we're going to do anything."

"Do anything? What are we going to do, Mel?"

"Bear with me." Mel Riorden cleared his throat. "My sister tells me, when I get her calmed down a bit and off to the side, that someone called her, some friend, and said they'd heard that Derry was out at Scrubby's last night drinking with Junior Elway and talking about some plan to shut down MidCon. The conversation wasn't all that clear, but there was some mention of an accident, maybe someone getting killed."

Old Bob shook his head slowly. "Maybe they heard it wrong."

"Well, with anyone else, you might shrug it off to talk and booze. But Derry's been short-circuited since Vietnam, and he knows a lot about weapons and explosives. My sister begs me to talk to him. I don't want to do that, because I know Derry thinks I'm an old fart, but I tell her I'll give it a try. So when I get home, I give him a call. He's sleeping, and I wake him. He's not pleased. I decide it's best to get right to the point. I tell him about the conversation with my sister and ask him if there's anything to it. He tells me, hell, yes, there's a lot to it, but it's got nothing to do with me. I tell him he'd better think twice about whatever it is. First off, people already know that if something happens, it's because of him; he made sure of that at the tavern. Second, anything he does outside the union will just get him in trouble with us. He says he doesn't care who knows and that the only way anything will ever get done is outside the union."

"What do you think he's got in mind?" Old Bob pressed.

"I don't know. He wouldn't tell me. But he might tell you. He's still got some respect for you, which is something he doesn't have for me. And I think maybe he's a little afraid of you. Not physically, but . . . you know, of your reputation. If you were to ask him what he's planning, he might open up." There was a long pause. "Bob, I don't know who else to turn to."

Old Bob nodded, thinking it over. Derry Howe was full of himself and his wild ideas, but he was mostly talk. The danger came from his army training and his inability to adjust to any kind of normal life since his return from Vietnam. Mel was right about that; you couldn't just dismiss his talk out of hand.

"Bob, are you still there?"

"I'm here," he answered. He didn't want any part of this. He wasn't sure at all that Derry Howe thought anything about him one way or the other. He wasn't sure at all that Derry would give him the time of day. Mel had more faith in him than he had in himself. Besides, he had problems of his own that needed his attention, and the biggest was sitting just down the hall in the kitchen. This whole business with Derry sounded like trouble he didn't need. "I don't know, Mel," he said.

"You and Evelyn going to the park today? For a picnic and the dance? Didn't you say you were?"

"We're going."

"Well, Derry will be there, too. He's going to enter the horseshoe tournament with Junior and some others. All I'm asking is that you take five minutes of your time and talk with him. Just ask him what's up, that's all. If he won't tell you, fine. But maybe he will. Maybe, if it's you."

Old Bob shook his head. He didn't want to get involved in this. He closed his eyes and rubbed them with his free hand. "All right, Mel," he said finally. "I'll give it a try."

There was an audible sigh of relief. "Thanks, Bob. I'll see you there. Thanks."

Old Bob placed the receiver gently back on the cradle. After a moment, he stood up and went over to open the door again.

"Nest, I want you to listen to me," Gran said quietly.

They were seated at the kitchen table, facing each other in the hazy sunlight, eyes locked. Gran's hands were shaking, and she put one on top of the other to keep them still. Nest saw disappointment and anger and sadness in her eyes all at the same time, and she was suddenly afraid.

"I won't lie to you," Gran said. "I have tried never to lie to you. There are things I haven't told you. Some you don't need to know. Some I can't tell you. We all have secrets in our lives. We are entitled to that. Not everything about us should be known. I expect you understand that, being who you are. Secrets allow us space in which to grow and change as we must. Secrets give us privacy where privacy is necessary if we are to survive."

She started to reach for her drink and stopped. At her elbow, her cigarette was burned to ash. She glanced at it, then away. She sighed wearily, her eyes flicking back to Nest.

"Was it you, Gran?" Nest asked gently. "In the park, with the feeders?"

Gran nodded. "Yes, Nest, it was." She was silent a moment, a bundle of old sticks inside the housecoat. "I have never told anyone. Not my parents, not your grandfather, not even Caitlin—and God knows, I should at least have told her. But I didn't. I kept that part of my life secret, kept it to myself."

She reached across the table for Nest's hand and took it in her own. Her hands were fragile and warm. "I was young and headstrong and foolish. I was proud. I was different, Nest, and I knew it—different like you are, gifted with use of the magic and able to see the forest creatures. No one else could see what I saw. Not my parents, not my friends, not anyone. It set me apart from everyone, and I liked that. My aunt, Opal Anders, my mother's sister, was the last to have the magic before me, and she had died when I was still quite young. So for a time, there was only me. I lived by the park, and I escaped into it whenever I could. It was my own private world. There was nothing in my other life that was anywhere near as intriguing as what waited for me in the park. I came at night, as you do. I found the feeders waiting for me—curious, responsive, eager. They wanted me there with them, I could tell. They were anxious to see what I would do. So I came whenever I could, mingling with them, trailing after them, always watching, wondering what they were, waiting to see what they would do next. I was never afraid. They never threatened me. There didn't seem to be any reason not to be there."

She shook her head slowly, her lips tightening. "As time passed, I became more comfortable with feeders than with humans. I was as wild as they were; I was as uninhibited. I ran with them because that was what made me feel good. I was self-indulgent and vain. I think I knew there was danger in what I was doing, but it lacked an identity, and in the absence of knowing there was something bad about what I was doing, I just kept doing it. My parents could not control me. They tried keeping me in my room, tried reasoning with me, tried everything. But the park was mine, and I was not about to give it up."

A car backfired somewhere out on Woodlawn, and Gran stopped talking for a moment, staring out the window, squinting into the hot sun. Nest felt the old woman's hand tighten about her own, and she squeezed back to let Gran know it was all right.

"The Indian had no right to tell you," Gran said finally. "No right."

Nest shook her head. "I don't think it was Two Bears, Gran. I don't think he was the one."

Gran didn't seem to hear. "Why would he do such a thing? Whatever possessed him? He doesn't even know me."

Nest sighed, picturing Two Bears dancing with the spirits of the Sinnissippi, seeing anew the vision of Gran, wild-eyed and young, at one with the feeders. "When did you stop, Gran?" she asked softly. "When did you quit going into the park?"

Gran's head jerked up, and there was a flash of fear in her narrowed eyes. "I don't want to talk about it anymore."

"Gran," Nest pressed, refusing to look away. "I have to know. Why did I have this vision of you and the feeders, do you think? I still don't know. You have to help me."

"I don't have to help you do another thing, Nest. I've said everything I have to say."

"Tell me about the other—the shadowy figure whose face I couldn't see. Tell me about him."

"No!"

"Gran, please!"

The door to the library opened and Old Bob shambled down the hall. He stopped in the kitchen doorway, his coat and tie draped over one arm, his big frame stooped and weary-looking. He stared at them, his eyes questioning. Gran took her hand from Nest's and picked up her drink. Nest lowered her gaze to the table and went still.

"Robert, I want you to change into your old clothes and then go out and haul that brush out to the roadway for Monday pickup," Gran said quietly.

Old Bob hesitated. "Tomorrow's a holiday, Evelyn. There's no pickup until Tuesday. We've got plenty of . . ."

"Just do it, Robert!" she snapped, cutting him off. "Nest and I need a little time to ourselves, if you please."

Nest's grandfather flushed, then turned wordlessly and went back down the hallway. Nest and her grandmother listened to his footsteps recede.

"All right, Nest," Gran said, her voice deadly calm. "I'll tell you this one last thing, and then I'm done. Don't ask me anything more." She tossed back the last of her drink and lit a cigarette. Her gray hair was loose and spidery about her face. "I quit going to the park because I met someone else who could see the feeders, who was possessed of the magic. Someone who loved me, who wanted me so badly he would have done anything to get me." She took a long pull on the cigarette and blew out a thick stream of smoke. "Hard to imagine now, someone wanting this old woman. Just look at me."

She gave Nest a sad, ironic smile. "Anyway, that's what happened. At first, I was attracted to him. We both ran the park with the feeders and used the magic. We dared anything. We dared things I can't even talk about, can't even make myself think about anymore. It was wrong to be like that, to do the things we did. But I couldn't seem to help myself. What I didn't realize at first was that he was evil, and he wanted me to be like him. But I saw what was happening in time, thank God, and I put a stop to it."

"You quit going into the park?"

Gran shook her head. "I couldn't do that. I couldn't give up the park."

Nest hesitated. "Then what did you do?"

For a minute she thought her grandmother was going to say something awful. She had that look. Then Gran picked up her cigarette, ground it out in the ashtray, and gave a brittle laugh.

"I found a way to keep him from ever coming near me again," she said. Her jaw muscles tightened and her lips compressed. Her words were fierce and rushed. "I had to. He wasn't what he seemed."

It was the way she said it. Nest gave her a hard look. "What do you mean, 'He wasn't what he seemed'?"

"Let it be, Nest."

But Nest shook her head stubbornly. "I want to know."

Gran's frail hands knotted. "Oh, Nest! He wasn't human!"

They stared at each other, eyes locked. Gran's face was contorted with anger and frustration. The pulse at her temples throbbed, and her mouth worked, as if she were chewing on the words she could not make herself speak. But Nest would not look away. She would not give it up.

"He wasn't human?" she repeated softly, the words digging and insistent. "If he wasn't human, what was he?"

Gran shook her head as if to rid herself of all responsibility and exhaled sharply. "He was a demon, Nest!"

Nest felt all the strength drain from her body in a strangled rush. She sat frozen and empty in her chair, her grandmother's words a harsh whisper of warning in her ears. *A demon. A demon. A demon.*

Gran bent forward and placed her dry, papery hands over Nest's. "I'm sorry to have disappointed you, child," she whispered.

Nest shook her head quickly, insistently. "No, Gran, it's all right."

But it wasn't, of course, and she knew in the darkest corners of her heart that it might never be again.

Chapter 19

Gran did a strange thing then. She rose without another word, went down the hall to her bedroom, and closed the door behind her. Nest sat at the kitchen table and waited. The minutes ticked by, but Gran did not return. She had left her drink and her cigarettes behind. Nest could not remember the last time Gran had left the kitchen table in the middle of the day like this. She kept thinking the old woman would reappear. She sat alone in the kitchen, bathed in the hot July sunlight. Gran stayed in her bedroom.

Finally Nest stood up and walked to the doorway and looked down the hall. The corridor was silent and empty. Nest nudged the wooden floor with the tip of her tennis shoe. *A demon, a demon, a demon!* Her mind spun with the possibilities. Was the demon Gran had known the same demon that was here now? She remembered John Ross saying he didn't know why the demon was interested in her, and she wondered if it was because of Gran. Perhaps the demon was trying to get to Gran through her, rather than to John Ross. Maybe that was its intention.

She looked down at her feet, down her tanned legs and narrow body, and she wished that someone would just tell her the truth and be done with it. Because she was pretty certain no one was doing that now.

After a few more moments of waiting unsuccessfully for Gran to emerge, she went back into the kitchen and picked up the phone to call Cass. The house felt oppressive and secretive to her, even in the brightness of midday. She listened to its silence over the ringing of the telephone. Cass Minter's mother picked up on the third ring and advised Nest that Cass and Brianna had already left and would meet her in the park by the toboggan slide. Nest thanked Mrs. Minter and hung up. She looked around the kitchen as if she might find someone watching, haunted by what Gran had told her. *A demon.* She closed her eyes, but the demon was there waiting for her, bland features smiling, pale eyes steady.

She glanced at the clock and went down the hall and out the back door. The picnic with John Ross was not until three. She had a little less than two hours to spend with Cass and the others before getting back. She stepped out into the heat and squinted up at the brilliant, sunlit sky. The air was thick with the rich smells of dry earth and grasses and leaves. Robins sang in the trees and cars drove down Sinnissippi Road, their tires whining on the hot asphalt. She wet her lips and looked around. Her grandfather came up the drive, returning from carrying up the yard waste. He slowed as he approached, and an uncertain smile creased his weathered face.

"Everything all right?" he asked. His big hands hung limp at his sides, and there was sweat on his brow.

Nest nodded. "Sure. I'm on my way to meet Cass and the others in the park."

Her grandfather glanced toward the house hesitantly, then back at her. "John will be here at three for the picnic."

"Don't worry, I'll be back." She gave him a reassuring smile. How much did he know about Gran and the feeders? "Bye, Grandpa."

She stepped around a sleeping Mr. Scratch and crossed the yard quickly, eyes determinedly forward so she would not look back. She felt as if her grandfather had read everything she was thinking in her eyes, and she did not want that. She felt as if everything was kept secret from her, while she had no secrets of her own. But there was John Ross, of course. She was the only one who knew the truth about him. Well, some of the truth, anyway. Maybe. She sighed helplessly.

She was pushing her way through the gap in the bushes when Pick dropped onto her shoulder.

" 'Bout time," he grumbled, settling himself into place. "Some of us have been up since daybreak, you know."

She gave him an angry look. "Good for you. Some of us have been trying to figure out why others of us aren't a little more truthful about things."

The wooden brow furrowed and the black-pool eyes crinkled. "What's that supposed to mean?"

She stopped abruptly beside the service road and looked off into the park. There were families laying out blankets and picnic baskets on the grassy lawn farther east where the shade trees began. There were baseball games under way, softball pickup contests. Two boys were throwing a Frisbee back and forth and a dog was running hopefully between them, giving chase. It was all familiar to her, but it felt quite alien, too.

"It means you were awfully quick to disappear last night after the spirits of the Sinnissippi appeared." She glared at him. "Why was that?"

The sylvan glared back. "Bunch of mumbo jumbo, that's why. I got bored."

"Don't you lie to me!" she hissed. She snatched him off her shoulder by the nape of his twiggy neck and held him kicking and squirming before her. "You saw the vision, too, didn't you? You saw the same thing I did, and you don't want to admit it! Well, it's too late for that, Pick!"

"Put me down!" he raged.

"Or what? What will you do?" She felt like tossing him out on the grass and leaving him there. "I know who it was! It was Gran! I knew it from a picture on the fireplace mantel! I thought it was Mom at first, but it was Gran! You knew, didn't you? Didn't you?"

"Yes!" He lashed out.

He stopped squirming and stared balefully at her. Nest stared back. After a moment, she placed him in the palm of her hand and squatted down in the grass next to the service road, holding him up to her face. Pick righted himself indignantly, brushing at his arms and legs as if he had been dumped in a pile of dirt.

"Don't you ever do that again!" he warned, so furious he refused even to look at her.

"You stop lying to me and maybe I won't!" she snapped back, just as angry as he was.

His mouth worked inside his mossy beard. "I haven't lied to you. But it isn't my place to tell you things about your family! It isn't right for me to do that!"

"Well, what kind of a friend are you, then?" she demanded. "A real friend doesn't keep secrets!"

Pick snorted. "Everyone keeps secrets. That's part of life. None of us tells the other everything. We can't. Then there wouldn't be any part of us that didn't belong to someone else!" He tugged on his beard in frustration. "All right, so I didn't tell you about your grandmother and the feeders. But she didn't tell you either, did she? So maybe there's a reason for that, and maybe it's up to her to decide if she wants you to know that reason and maybe it's not up to me!"

"Maybe this, maybe that! Maybe it doesn't matter, now! She told me when I asked her, even though she didn't want to! She told me, but it would have been easier if it had come from you!" Nest shook her head, and her voice quieted. "She told me about the demon, too. Is it the same one that's here now?"

Pick threw up his hands. "How am I supposed to answer that when I haven't even seen him?"

Nest studied him doubtfully for a moment. "He probably wouldn't look the same anyway, would he?"

"Hard to say. Demons don't change much once they're demons." He blinked. "Wait a minute. You haven't seen him, have you?"

Nest told him then about the encounter in church, about the appearance of the feeders and Wraith, about poor Mrs. Browning, and about John Ross. When she was done, Pick sat down heavily in her palm and shook his head.

"What's going on here?" he asked softly, not so much of her as of himself.

She looked off into the park again, thinking it over, searching for an answer that refused to be found. Then she stood up, put him back on her shoulder, and began to walk once more along the edge of the service road toward the east end of the park. "Tell me about my grandmother," she asked him after a moment.

Pick looked at her. "Don't start with me. I've said all I have to say about that."

"Just tell me what she was doing with the feeders, running with them, being part of them." Nest felt her voice catch as the ugly vision played itself through again in her mind.

Pick shrugged. "I don't know what she was doing. She was young and wild, your grandmother, and she did a lot of things I didn't much agree with. Running with the feeders was one of them. She did it because she felt like it, I guess. She was different from you."

Nest looked at him. "Different how?"

"She was the first to have the magic in your family when there was no one to guide her in its use," he replied. "She didn't know what to do with it. There wasn't any balance in her life like there is in yours. Not then, at least. She's given you that balance, you know. She's been there to warn you about the magic right from the first. No one was there for her. Opal, the last before her, was dead by the time she was eight. So there was only me, and she didn't want to listen to me. She thought I was out for myself, that what I said didn't mean anything." He pursed his lips. "Like I said, she was headstrong."

"She said she was in love with the demon."

"She was, for a time."

"Until she found out the truth about him."

"Yep, until then."

"What did she do to keep him away from her?"

Pick looked at her. "Didn't she tell you?"

Nest shook her head. "Will you?"

Pick sighed. "Here we go again."

"All right, forget it."

They walked on in silence, passing the east ball diamond and turning up toward the parking lot that fronted the toboggan slide. Ahead, the trees shimmered hotly in the midday sun and the river reflected silver and gold. In the backyards of the houses bordering the park, people were working in their flower beds and mowing the grass. The smell of hamburgers cooking on an open grill wafted heavily on the humid air.

"I shouldn't tell you," Pick insisted quietly.

"Then don't."

"I shouldn't."

"All right."

Pick hunched his shoulders. "Your grandmother," he said wearily, staring straight ahead. For a minute he didn't say anything else. "The demon underestimated her, too bad for him. See, she understood him better than he thought. She'd learned a few things running with him, being part of his life, those nights in the park. She knew it was her magic that attracted him to her. She knew the magic was everything to him. He wanted her because she had it. She was very powerful in those days, Nest. Maybe as powerful as he was. So she told him that if he stayed in the park, if he kept after her, she'd use it against him. She'd use it up, every last bit of it. She'd kill him or herself or both of them. She didn't care which."

He paused. "She would have done it, too. She was very determined, very tough-minded, your grandmother." He scratched his mossy beard. "Anyway, the demon was convinced. He backed down from her. He hated her for that afterward. Hated himself, too. By the time she was finished with him, he didn't want anything to do with her anymore."

Nest tried to imagine Gran confronting the demon, threatening to kill him if he refused to leave her alone. Frail, weary old Gran.

"Now, that's all I'm saying on the subject," Pick interjected heatedly. "If you want to know anything more, ask your grandmother. But I'd think twice about it, if I were you. Just my opinion. Some things are better left alone, and this is one of them. Take my word for it. Let it be."

"The Beatles, 1969?"

"What?"

"Never mind." Nest was sick of the whole subject. Nothing she had heard was making her feel any better. Pick was just irritating her with his refusal to talk about it, but she guessed that he was right, that it should come from Gran. Maybe it was time to ask about her father, too. Maybe it was time to insist on an answer. There were too many secrets in her family, and some of them needed revealing. Didn't she have a right to know?

"I have to be going," Pick announced, rising to his knees on her shoulder. She stopped and looked at his narrow face. His fierce eyes stared back at her. "Just make sure you bring John Ross to the maentwrog's tree so he can have a look for himself at what's happening."

Nest nodded. "I'll bring him up after the picnic."

She lowered Pick to the ground, and he disappeared without a word, vanishing into the grass as if he were an ant. " 'Bye," she murmured at the space he left behind.

She walked on across the grass into the parking lot that fronted the toboggan slide, kicking at rocks and staring at the ground as it passed beneath her feet. Her skin was hot and sticky already. She brushed at her curly damp hair, moving it off her forehead and away from her eyes. She felt awkward and stupid. She hated who she was. She wondered what she could do to change things.

Someone yelled at her from the ball field, and she glanced over. A group of boys was standing by home plate looking at her; she thought it was one of them who had called to her. Worse, she thought it was Danny Abbott. She looked away and kept on walking.

She crossed the parking lot to the toboggan slide and saw Cass and the others grouped at a picnic table under one of the big oaks. Behind them, down the hill, the river flowed with sluggish indifference beyond the levy. A few boats bobbed gently on its surface, their occupants hunched over fishing poles and cans of bait. She strolled over to her friends, trying to appear casual, trying to make herself believe that nothing was different. They were all there—Cass, Brianna, Robert, and Jared. They looked up as she approached, and she had the feeling they had been talking about her.

"Hey," she said.

"Pete and Repeat are out walking," said Robert, straight-faced. "Pete goes home. Who's left?"

"Elvis?" she asked, squeezing in between Cass and Brianna.

"Nice try. Two guys walk into a bar. One's got a Doberman, the other a terrier. Bartender says . . ."

"Robert!" snapped Brianna, cutting him short. "Geez!"

"Enough with the jokes," Cass agreed. "They weren't funny the first time, back when Washington was president."

"Oh, big yuck." Robert looked annoyed. "All right, so what are we going to do, then? And don't tell me we're going to spend the day trying to heal any more sick trees." He gave Nest a pointed look. "Especially since we didn't do so well with the last one."

"What do you mean?" she asked.

"I mean, it looks terrible." He pushed up his glasses on his nose and brushed back his blond hair. "We walked by it on the way over, and it looks like it's a goner. Whatever we did, it didn't help."

"We could go swimming," Brianna suggested brightly, ignoring him.

Nest shook her head. "I can't. I have to be back by two. How bad is it, Robert?"

"The bark's all split open and oozing something green and there's dead leaves everywhere." He saw the look on Nest's face and stopped. "What's going on? What's this sick-tree business all about?"

Nest took a deep breath and bit her lower lip. "Someone is poisoning the trees in the park," she said, giving a slight edge of truth to what was otherwise an outright lie.

They stared at her. "Why would anyone do that?" Cass asked.

"Because . . ." She shrugged. "Because they're nuts, I guess."

Robert frowned. "How do you know this?"

"Grandpa told me. He heard it from the park people. I guess it's happened in some other places, too." She was rolling now, sounding very sure of herself. "It's one guy that's doing it. He was seen in another park, so they got a description. Everyone's been looking for him."

Robert frowned some more. "This is the first I've heard of it. My dad never said anything about anyone poisoning trees in the parks. You sure about this?"

Nest gave him a disgusted look. "Of course I'm sure. Why would I say it if I wasn't?"

"So they know what this guy looks like?" Jared asked quietly. He looked tired, as if he hadn't been sleeping well.

"Yep." She glanced at them conspiratorially. "I'll tell you something else, too. Grandpa thinks he might be in the park this weekend. See, sometimes he dresses like a park maintenance man in order not to be noticed. That's how he gets away with poisoning the trees."

"He might be in the park this weekend?" Brianna parroted, her porcelain features horror-struck.

"Maybe," Nest advised. "So we have to watch for him, keep an eye out. This is what he looks like." She provided a careful description of the demon, from his pale eyes to his bland face. "But if you see him, don't try to go near him. And don't let him know he's been seen. Just come get me."

"Come get you?" Robert repeated suspiciously.

"So I can tell Grandpa, because he knows what to do."

Everyone nodded soberly. Nest held her breath and waited for more questions, but there weren't any. Way to go, she thought, not knowing whether to laugh or cry at her subterfuge. You can lie with the best of them, can't you? You can lie even to your friends.

They walked through the park for a while afterward, killing time. Nest watched her friends surreptitiously checking faces as if they might really find the tree poisoner, and she pondered if she had done the right thing. She needed any help she could get, and this would give her friends something to do besides wonder why she was acting odd, but it made her feel ashamed of herself anyway. She didn't believe any of them would find the demon. She thought only John Ross could do that, and she wasn't sure of him. What persuaded her that she should even try to do something was her memory of the morning's encounter in the church kitchen, of the murder, of the pale eyes studying her, of the calm, even voice talking to her about the way the world would end. She could rationalize what had happened from now until Christmas, but she still felt desperate, almost hopeless.

The park was beginning to fill with families come to picnic and participate in the games the Jaycees were running prior to this evening's community dance. There would be softball, badminton, horseshoes, and footraces of various sorts for adults and children both. Members of the club were already preparing for the events. Food and drink stands were being set up. The smells of hot dogs and hamburgers wafted in the thick July air, and smoke curled lazily from the brick chimneys of the cook centers in the pavilion. Bushy-tailed red squirrels scampered along the limbs of the big oaks, and a few dogs chased after balls. Laughter and shouts rose from all about.

A slight breeze wafted off the river, causing Nest to glance skyward. A thin lacework of clouds drifted across the blue. She had heard her grandfather say there was a chance of rain for the Fourth.

She left the others then, promising to meet up with them later on in the afternoon when family obligations were satisfied. Robert was having a cookout in his backyard with his parents and some cousins. Cass and Brianna were going to a church picnic. Jared had to go home to watch the younger kids while his mother and George Paulsen came over to the park so that George could compete in the horseshoe tournament.

Jared and Nest walked back across the park, neither of them saying anything. Jared seemed preoccupied, but she liked being with him no matter what his mood. She liked the way he was always thinking things over, giving careful consideration to what he was going to say.

"You going to the dance tonight, Nest?" he asked suddenly, not looking at her.

She glanced over in surprise. "Sure. Are you?"

"Mom says I can go for a while. The kids are staying at Mrs. Pinkley's for the night, except Bennett is going to Alice Workman's. You know, the social worker. George and Mom are going out somewhere, then coming back to watch TV."

They walked on, the silence awkward. "You want to go to the dance with me?" he asked after a minute.

Nest felt a warm flush run down her neck. "Sure."

"Cool. I'll meet you about seven." He was so serious. He cleared his throat and shoved his hands in his jeans pockets. "You don't think this is weird or anything, do you?"

She smiled in spite of herself. "Why would I think that?"

"Because it would be you and me, and not all of us. Robert and Cass and Brianna might think it's weird, us not including them."

She glanced quickly at him. "I don't care what they think."

He thought about it a moment, then nodded solemnly. "Good. Neither do I."

She left him on the service road and slipped through the gap in the bushes at the edge of her backyard, feeling light-headed from more than just the heat.

CHAPTER 20

John Ross rode out to Sinnissippi Park with the desk clerk from the Lincoln Hotel, who was having Sunday dinner with his brother and sister-in-law just to the north. The man dropped him at the corner of Third Street and Sixteenth Avenue, and Ross walked the rest of the way. The man would have driven him to the Freemarks' doorstep—offered to do so, in fact—but it was not yet two o'clock and Ross was not expected until three and did not want to arrive too early. So instead he limped up Third to Riverside Cemetery, leaning heavily on his black staff, moving slowly in the heat, and found his way to Caitlin Freemark's grave. The day was still and humid, but it was cool and shady where he walked beneath the hardwood trees. There were people in the cemetery, but no one paid any attention to him. He was wearing fresh jeans, a pale blue collared shirt, and his old walking shoes. He had washed his long hair and tied it back with a clean bandanna. He looked halfway respectable, which was as good as it got.

He stood in front of Caitlin Freemark's grave and looked down at the marble stone, read the inscription several times, studied the rough, dark shadow of the letters and numbers against the bright glassy surface. CAITLIN ANNE FREEMARK, BELOVED DAUGHTER & MOTHER. He felt something tug at him, a sudden urge to recant his lies and abandon his subterfuge, to lay bare to the Freemarks the truth of who he was and what he was doing. He looked off toward their house, not able to see it through the trees, visualizing it instead in his mind. He pictured their faces looking back at him. He could not tell them the truth, of course. Gran knew most of it anyway, he suspected. She must. And Robert Freemark? Old Bob? Ross shook his head, not wanting to hazard a guess. In any case, Nest was the only one who really mattered, and he could not tell her. Perhaps she did not ever need to know. If he was quick enough, if he found the demon and destroyed it, if he put an end to its plans before it revealed them fully . . .

He blinked into the heat, and the image of the Freemarks faded from his mind.

Forgive me.

He walked on from there into the park, skirting its edges, following the cemetery fence to Sinnissippi Road, then the road past the townhomes to the park entrance and beyond through the big shade trees to the Freemark residence. Old Bob greeted him at the door, ebullient and welcoming. They stood within the entry making small talk until Gran and Nest joined them, then gathered up the picnic supplies from the kitchen. Ross insisted on helping, on at least being allowed to carry the blanket they would sit on. Nest picked up the white wicker basket that contained the food, Old Bob took the cooler with the drinks and condiments, and with Gran leading the way they went out the back door, down the steps past a sleeping Mr. Scratch, across the backyard to the gap in the bushes, and into the park.

The park was filled with cars and people. Picnickers already occupied most of the tables and cooking stations. Blankets were spread under trees and along the bluff, softball games were under way on all the diamonds, and across from the pavilion the Jaycee-sponsored games were being organized. There was a ring toss and a baseball throw. The horseshoe tournament was about to start. Carts dispensing cotton candy and popcorn had been brought in, and the Jaycees were selling pop, iced tea, and lemonade from school-cafeteria folding tables. Balloons filled with helium floated at the ends of long cords. Red, white, and blue bunting hung from the pavilion's rafters and eaves. A band was playing under a striped tent, facing out onto the pavilion's smooth concrete floor. Parents and children crowded forward, anxious to see what was going on.

"Looks like the whole town is here," Old Bob observed with a satisfied grin.

Ross glanced around. It seemed as if all the good places had been taken, but Gran led them forward determinedly, past the diamonds, the pavilion, the games, the cotton candy and popcorn, the band, and even the toboggan slide, past all of it and down the hill toward the bayou, to a grassy knoll tucked back behind a heavy stand of brush and evergreens that was shaded by an aging oak and commanded a clear view of the river. Remarkably, no one else was there, save for a couple of teenagers snuggling on a blanket. Gran ignored them and directed Ross to place the blanket in the center of the knoll. The teens watched tentatively as the Freemarks arranged their picnic, then rose and disappeared. Gran never looked at them. Ross shook his head. Old Bob caught his eye and winked.

The heat was suffocating on the flats, but here it was eased by the cool air off the water and by the shade of the big oak. It was quieter as well, the sounds of the crowd muffled and distant. Gran emptied the contents of the picnic basket, arranged the dishes, and invited them to sit. They formed a circle about the food, eating fried chicken, potato salad, Jell-O, raw sticks of carrot and celery, deviled eggs, and chocolate cupcakes off paper plates, and washing it all down with cold lemonade poured from a thermos into paper cups. Ross found himself thinking of his childhood, of the picnics he had enjoyed with his own family. It was a long time ago. He visited the memories quietly while he ate, glancing now and again at the Freemarks.

Should I tell them? What should I tell them? How do I do what is needed to help this girl? How do I keep from failing them?

"Did you enjoy the service, John?" Old Bob asked him suddenly, chewing on a chicken leg.

Ross glanced at Nest, but she did not look at him. "Very much, sir. I appreciate being included."

"You say you're on your way to Seattle, but maybe you could postpone leaving and stay on with us for a few more days." Old Bob looked at Gran. "We have plenty of extra room at the house. You would be welcome."

Gran's face was tight and fixed. "Robert, don't be pushy. Mr. Ross has his own life. He doesn't need ours."

Ross forced a quick smile. "I can't stay beyond tomorrow or the day after, thanks anyway, Mr. Freemark, Mrs. Freemark. You've done plenty for me as it is."

"Well, hardly." Old Bob cleared his throat, regarded the leg bone in his hand. "Darn good chicken, Evelyn. Your best yet, I think."

They finished the meal, Old Bob talking of Caitlin as a girl now, recalling stories about how she had been, what she had done. Ross listened and nodded appreciatively. He thought it might have been a while since the old man had spoken of his daughter like this. Gran seemed distracted and distant, and Ross did not think she was paying much attention. But Nest was watching raptly, studying her grandfather's face as he related the stories, listening carefully to his every word. Her concentration was so complete that she did not seem aware of anything else. Ross watched her, wondered what she was thinking, wished suddenly that he knew.

I should tell her. I should take the chance. She's stronger than she looks. She is older than her fourteen years. She can accept it.

But he said nothing. Old Bob finished, sighed, glanced out across the bayou as if seeing into the past, then reached over impulsively to pat his wife's hand. "You're awfully quiet, Dark Eyes."

For just an instant all the hardness went out of Evelyn Freemark's face, all the lines and age spots vanished, and she was young again. A smile flickered at the corners of her mouth, and her eyes lifted to find his.

Ross stood up, leaning on his staff for support. "Nest, how about taking a walk with me. My leg stiffens up if I sit for too long. Maybe you can keep me from getting lost."

Nest put down her plate and looked at her grandmother. "Gran, do you want me to help clean up?"

Her grandmother shook her head, said nothing. Nest waited a moment, then rose. "Let's go this way," she said to Ross. She glanced at her grandparents. "We'll be back in a little while."

They climbed the hill at an angle that took them away from the crowds, east toward the park's far end, where the deep woods lay. They walked in silence, Nest pacing herself so that Ross could keep up with her, limping along with the aid of his staff. They worked their way slowly through the shady oaks and hickories, passing families seated on blankets and at tables eating their picnic lunches, following the curve of the slope as it wound back around the rise and away from the river. Soon Gran and Old Bob were out of sight.

When they were safely alone, Ross said to her, "I'm sorry about what happened at church. I know it was scary."

"I have to show you something," she said, ignoring his apology. "I promised Pick."

They walked on for a ways in silence, and then she asked sharply, accusingly, "Are you an angel? You know, in the Biblical sense? Is that what you are?"

He stared over at her, but she wasn't looking at him, she was looking at the ground. "No, I don't think so. I'm just a man."

"But if God is real, there must be angels."

"I suppose so. I don't know."

Her voice was clipped, surly. "Which? Which don't you know? If there are angels or if God is real?"

He slowed and then stopped altogether, forcing her to do the same. He waited until she was looking at him. "What I told you was the truth—about the Fairy Glen, and the Lady, and the voice, and the way I became a Knight of the Word. What are you asking me, Nest?"

Her eyes were hot. "If there really is a God, why would He allow all those feeders in His church? Why would He allow the demon in? Why would He allow Mrs. Browning to die? Why didn't He stop it from happening?"

Ross took a long, slow breath. "Maybe that isn't the way it works. Isn't the church supposed to be open to everyone?"

"Not to demons and feeders! Not to things like that! What are they doing here, anyway? Why aren't they somewhere else?" Her voice was hard-edged and shaking now, and her hands were gesturing wildly. "If you really are a Knight of the Word, why don't you do something about them? Don't you have some kind of power? You must! Can't you use it on them? Why is this so hard?"

Ross looked off into the trees. *Tell her*. His hands tightened on the staff. "If I destroy the feeders, I reveal myself." He looked back at her. "I let people know what I am. When that happens, I am compromised. Worse, I weaken myself. I don't have unlimited power. I have . . . only so much. Every time I use it, I leave myself exposed. If the demon finds me like that, he will destroy me. I have to be patient, to wait, to choose my time. Ideally, I will only have to use my power once—when I have the demon before me."

He felt trapped by his words. "Pick must have told you about the feeders. The feeders are only here because of us. They react to us, to us as humans. They feed on our emotions, on our behavior. They grow stronger or weaker depending on how we behave. The Word made them to be a reflection of us. If we behave well, we diminish them. If we behave badly, we strengthen them. Give them too much to feed on and they devour us. But they're not subject to the same laws as we are. They don't have life in the same way we do; they don't have substance. They creep around in the shadows and come out with any release of the dark that's inside us. I can burn them all to ash, but they will just come back again, born out of new emotions, new behavior. Do you understand?"

The girl nodded dubiously. "Are they everywhere, everywhere in the world?"

"Yes."

"But aren't there more in places where things are worse? In places where the people are killing each other, killing their children?"

"Yes."

"Then why aren't you there? What are you doing here, in this little, insignificant Midwestern town? No one is dying here. Nothing is happening here!" Her voice rose. "What is so important about Hopewell?"

Ross did not look away, dared not. "I can't answer that. I go where I'm sent. Right now, I'm tracking the demon. I'm here because of him. I know that something pivotal is going to take place, something that will affect the future, and I have to stop it. I know it seems incredible that anything occurring in a tiny place like Hopewell could have such an impact. But we know how history works. Cataclysms are set in motion by small events in out-of-the-way places. Maybe that's what's happening."

She studied him fixedly. "It has something to do with me, doesn't it?"

Tell her! "It looks that way," he hedged.

She waited a moment, then said, "I had a . . . dream about Gran last night. She was a girl, the way she looks in one of the pictures on the mantel. She was running in the park with the feeders. She was one of them. I asked her about it, and she admitted that she had done that when she was a girl." She paused. "There was a demon with her. She admitted that, too. She said she didn't know at first what it was, and that when she found out, she sent it away. Pick said that was true." She paused. "What I wonder is if this might be the same demon, if it might have come back to hurt Gran through me."

Ross nodded slowly. "It's possible."

She glared at him, needing more, wanting a better answer. "But how would that change anything about the future? What difference would that make to anyone but us?"

Ross started walking again, forcing her to follow. "I don't know. What was it you were going to show me?"

She caught up to him easily, kept her hot gaze turned on him. "If you're hiding something, I'll find out what it is." Her voice was hard-edged and determined, challenging him to respond. When he failed to do so, she moved ahead of him as if to push the matter aside, dismissive and contemptuous. "This way, over there, in those trees."

They descended a gentle slope to a small stream and an old wooden bridge. They crossed the bridge and started up the other side into the deep woods. It was silent here, empty of people, of sound, of movement. The heat was trapped in the undergrowth, and none of the river's coolness penetrated to ease the swelter. Insects buzzed annoyingly in their faces, attracted by their sweat.

"Actually, it wasn't a dream," she said suddenly. "About Gran, I mean. It was a vision. An Indian named Two Bears showed it to me. He took me to see the spirits of the Sinnissippi dance in the park last night after you left. He says he is the last of them." She paused. "What do you think?"

A chill passed over John Ross in spite of the heat. O'olish Amaneh. "Was he a big man, a Vietnam vet?"

She looked over at him quickly. "Do you know him?"

"Maybe. There are stories about an Indian shaman, a seer. He uses different names. I've come across people who've met him once or twice, heard about some others." He could not tell her of this, either. He could barely stand to think on it. O'olish Amaneh. "I think maybe he is in service to the Word."

Nest looked away again. "He didn't say so."

"No, he wouldn't. He never does. He just shows up and talks about the future, how it is linked to the past, how everything is tied together; then he disappears again. It's always the same. But I think, from what I've heard, that maybe he is one of us."

They pushed through a tangle of brush that had overgrown the narrow trail, spitting out gnats that flew into their mouths, lowering their heads against the shards of sunlight that penetrated the shadows.

"Tell me something about Wraith," John Ross asked, trying to change the subject.

The girl shrugged. "You saw. I don't know what he is. He's been there ever since I was very little. He protects me from the feeders, but I don't know why. Even Gran and Pick don't seem to know. I don't see him much. He mostly comes out when the feeders threaten me."

She told him about her night forays into the park to rescue the strayed children, and how Wraith would always appear when the feeders tried to stop her. Ross mulled the matter over in his mind. He had never heard of anything like it, and he couldn't be certain from what Nest told him if Wraith was a creature of the Word or the Void. Certainly Wraith's behavior suggested his purpose was good, but Ross knew that where Nest Freemark was concerned things were not as simple as they might seem.

"Where are we going?" Ross asked her as they crested the rise and moved into the shadow of the deep woods.

"Just a little farther," she advised, easing ahead on the narrow path to lead the way.

The ground leveled and the trees closed about, leaving them draped in heavy shadow. The air was fetid and damp with humidity, and insects were everywhere. Ross brushed at them futilely. The trail twisted and wound through thick patches of scrub and brambles. Several times it branched, but Nest did not hesitate in choosing the way. Ross marveled at the ease with which she navigated the tangle, thinking on how much at home she was here, on how much she seemed to belong. She had the confidence of youth, of a young girl who knew well the ground she had already covered, even if she did not begin to realize how much still lay ahead.

They passed from the thicket into a clearing, and there, before them, was a giant oak. The oak towered overhead, clearly the biggest tree in the park, one of the biggest that Ross had ever seen. But the tree was sick, its leaves curling and turning black at the tips, its bark split and ragged and oozing discolored fluid that stained the earth at its roots. Ross stared at the tree for a moment, stunned both by its size and the degree of its decay, then looked questioningly at the girl.

"This is what I wanted you to see," she confirmed.

"What's wrong with it?"

"Exactly the question!" declared Pick, who materialized out of nowhere on Nest Freemark's shoulder. "I thought that you might know."

The sylvan was covered with dust and bits of leaves. He straightened himself on the girl's shoulder, looking decidedly out of sorts.

"Spent all morning foraging about for roots and herbs that might be used to make a medicine, but nothing seems to help. I've tried everything, magic included, and I cannot stop the decay. It spreads all through the tree now, infecting every limb and every root. I'm at my wits' end."

"Pick thinks it's the demon's work," Nest advised pointedly.

Ross looked at the tree anew, still perplexed. "Why would the demon do this?"

"Well, because this tree is the prison of a maentwrog!" Pick declared heatedly. Quickly, he told John Ross the tale of the maentwrog's entrapment, of how it had remained imprisoned all these years, safe beyond the walls of magic and nature that combined to shut it away. "But no more," the sylvan concluded with dire gloom. "At the rate the decay is spreading, it will be free before you know it!"

Ross walked forward and stood silently before the great oak. He knew something of the creatures that served the Void and particularly of those called maentwrogs. There were only a handful, but they were terrible things. Ross had never faced one, but he had been told of what they could do, consumed by their need to destroy, unresponsive to anything but their hunger. None had been loose in the world for centuries. He did not like thinking of what it would mean if one were to get loose now.

In his hand, the black staff pulsed faintly in response to the nearness of the beast, a warning of the danger. He stared upward into the branches of the ancient tree, trying to see something that would help him decide what to do.

"I lack any magic that would help," he said quietly. "I'm not skilled in that way."

"It's the demon's work, isn't it?" Pick demanded heatedly.

Ross nodded. "I expect it is."

The sylvan's narrow face screwed into a knot. "I knew it, I just knew it! That's why none of our efforts have been successful! He's counteracting them!"

Ross looked away. It made sense. The maentwrog would be another distraction, another source of confusion. It was the way the demon liked to work, throwing up smoke and mirrors to mask what he was really about.

Nest was telling Pick about the encounter with the demon in church that morning, and the sylvan was jumping up and down on her shoulder and telling her he'd warned her, he'd told her. Nest looked appalled. They began to argue. Ross glanced over at them, then walked forward alone and stood directly before the tree. The staff was throbbing in his hand, alive with the magic, hot with anticipation for what waited. *Not yet.* He reached forward with his free hand and touched the damaged bark gently. The tree felt slick and cold beneath his fingers, as if its sickness had come to the surface, coated its rough skin. A maentwrog, he thought grimly. A raver.

Ross studied the ground about him, and everywhere the earth was damp and pitted, revealing long stretches of the tree's exposed roots. No ants or beetles crawled upon its surface. There was no movement anywhere. The tree and its soil had become anathema to living things.

Ross sighed deeply. His inadequacy appalled him. He should be able to do something. He should have magic to employ. But he was a knight, and the magic he had been given to use could only destroy.

He turned back again. Nest and Pick had stopped arguing and were watching him silently. He could read the question in their eyes. What should they do now? They were waiting on him to provide them with an answer.

There was only one answer he could give. They would have to find the demon.

Which was, of course, like so many things, much easier said than done.

Chapter 21

After John Ross and Nest departed, Old Bob helped Evelyn clean up the remains of the picnic lunch. While his wife packed away the dishes and leftovers, he gathered together the used paper plates, cups, and napkins and carried them to a trash bin over by one of the cook stations. When they were done, they sat together on the blanket and looked out through the heat to where the sunlight sparkled off the blue waters of the Rock River in brilliant, diamond bursts.

She liked it when I called her Dark Eyes, he thought as he sat with his hand covering hers, remembering the sudden, warm look she had given him. It took him back to when they were much younger, when Caitlin was still a baby, before the booze and the cigarettes and all the hurt. He remembered how funny she had been, how bright and gay and filled with life. He glanced over at her, seeing the young girl locked deep inside her aging body. His throat tightened. If she would just let me get close again.

On the river, boats were drifting with the current, slow and aimless. Some carried fishermen, poles extended over the water, bodies hunched forward on wooden seats in silent meditation. Some carried sunbathers and swimmers on their way to the smattering of scrub islands that dotted the waters where they widened just west of the park and the bayou. There were a few large cruisers, their motors throbbing faint and distant like aimless bumblebees. Flags and pennants flew from their masts. A single sailboat struggled to catch a breeze with its limp triangular sail. In the sunlight, birds soared from tree to tree, out over the waters and back again, small flickers of light and shadow.

After a time, he said, "I'm going to take a walk up to the horseshoe tournament, talk to a couple of the boys. Would you like to come along?"

She surprised him. "Matter of fact, Robert, I would."

They rose and began the walk up the hill, leaving the blanket, the picnic basket, and the cooler behind. No one would steal them; this was Hopewell. Old Bob was already thinking ahead to what he was about to do. He had promised Mel Riorden he would speak with Derry Howe, and he tried hard to keep the promises he made. He had no idea what he was going to say to the boy. This wasn't his business, after all. He no longer worked at MidCon; he was not an active member of the union. His connection with the mill and those who worked there was rooted mainly in the past, a part of a history that was forever behind him. What happened now would probably not affect him directly, not in the time he had left in this life. It might affect Nest, of course, but he thought she would leave when she was grown, move on to some other life. She was too talented to stay in Hopewell. He might argue that he had a lot of himself invested in the mill, but the truth was he had never been a man in search of a legacy, and he didn't believe much in carrying the past forward.

Still, there were other people to be considered, and it was not in his nature to disregard their needs. If Derry was planning something foolish, something that would affect unfavorably those who had been his friends and neighbors, he owed it to them to try to do something about it.

But what should he say? What, that would make any difference to a boy like Derry, who had little respect for anyone, who had no reason to listen to him, to give him so much as the time of day?

But Mel thought the boy would listen to him, had respect for him. So he would try.

Evelyn's arm linked with his, and he felt her lean into him. There was nothing to her anymore—bird bones held together by old skin and iron determination. He drew her along easily, liking the feel of her against him, the closeness of her. He loved her still, wished he could bring her back to the way she had been, but knew he never could. He smiled down at her, and the sharp, old eyes glanced briefly at him, then away. *Love you forever*, he thought.

They crested the rise and were back among the crowds. Children ran everywhere, trailing balloons and crepe-paper streamers, laughing and shrieking. People stood three and four deep in front of the refreshments, loading up on cans of pop, bags of popcorn, and cones of cotton candy. Old Bob steered a path behind them and veered toward the horseshoe tournament, which was set up out in the flats south of the pavilion. He could see Derry Howe already, standing easily in a crowd of other young men, tall and angular in his jeans, T-shirt, and old tennis shoes, a can of beer in his hand.

Old Bob caught sight of Mike Michaelson and his wife, waved hello, and led Evelyn over to talk to them. Mike wanted to know if Old Bob had heard anything from Richie Stoudt. Richie's landlord had called, said Richie was supposed to do some work for him and hadn't shown up. There was no answer at his apartment either. Old Bob shook his head. Al Garcia wandered over, eager to show his latest pictures of the new grandbaby. After a few minutes, Mel Riorden appeared, touting the lemonade they were selling, giving Old Bob a meaningful glance. His wife Carol joined him, a warm and embracing woman, cooing over the grandbaby and joshing Al Garcia about his camera work. Laughter and warm feelings laced the conversation, but Old Bob felt locked away from it, distanced by the task he had agreed to undertake and the implications it bore. His mind struggled with the problem of how to approach Derry Howe. Was it really necessary? Maybe Mel was mistaken. Wouldn't be the first time. Sure wouldn't be the last.

Penny Williamson strode up, his black skin glistening with sweat, his massive arms streaked with dust. Wasn't anyone going to beat him this year in the horseshoe tournament, he announced. He was on, baby, he was dead on. Four ringers already. He clapped Old Bob on the back and bent to look at the pictures, asking Al Garcia whose grandbaby that was, wasn't Al's for sure, didn't look ugly like Al, must be a ringer. There was more laughter, kidding.

Old Bob took a deep breath, whispered to Evelyn, asking her to wait for him a moment, excused himself, and moved away. He eased through the knots of people, tasting dust and sweat in the air, smelling the popcorn and cotton candy. People said hello, greeted him as he passed. He moved toward Derry Howe, thinking he should probably just let it go. Howe saw him coming, watched him, took a long swig of his beer, shook his head. In his eyes, Old Bob saw suspicion, wariness, and a wealth of impatience.

He walked up to Derry, nodded, said, "Got a moment?"

Howe looked at him, debating whether to give him the moment or not. Then he smiled, the soul of equanimity, sauntered forward to join him, said, "Sure, Robert. What's up?"

Old Bob swung into step with him and they walked slowly past the participants in the horseshoe tournament. He nodded toward the field. "Having any luck?"

Derry Howe shrugged, looked at him, waiting.

"Heard a rumor that you were planning something special for the Fourth."

Derry's expression did not change. "Where'd you hear that?"

"Heard you were planning an accident, maybe." Old Bob ignored him, did not look at him. "Something to persuade the MidCon people they ought to work a little harder at settling this strike."

"Man, the things you hear." Derry tossed the beer can into a metal trash bin and shoved his hands in his jeans pockets. He was smiling, being cool. "You planning on coming out for the fireworks, Robert? Celebrating our independence?"

Old Bob stopped now, faced him, eyes hard. "Listen to me. If I know about it, others know about it, too. You're not being very smart, son."

Derry Howe's smile froze, disappeared. "Maybe certain people ought to mind their own business."

Old Bob nodded. "I'll assume you're not talking about me, because we've both got the same business interests where MidCon is concerned."

There was a long pause as Derry studied him. He had misread the comment. "You saying you want in on this?"

"No."

"Then what are you saying?"

Old Bob sighed. "I'm saying that maybe you ought to think this through a little further before you act on it. I'm saying it doesn't sound like a very good idea. If you do something to the company, something that gets people hurt, it might rebound on you. You might get hurt, too."

Derry Howe sneered. "I ain't afraid of taking a chance. Not like Mel and the rest of you, sitting around talking all day while your lives go right down the toilet. I said it before, I'll say it again. This ain't going to get settled unless we do something to help it along. The company's just going to wait us out. They're starting up the fourteen-inch—hell, already started it up, I expect. They'll have it up and running Tuesday morning, bright and early. They're bringing in scabs and company men to run it. Some of the strikers are talking about going back, giving in because they're scared. You know how it goes. When that happens, we're done, Robert Roosevelt Freemark. And you know it."

"Maybe. But blowing things up isn't the answer either."

Derry pulled a face. "Who said anything about blowing something up? Did I say anything like that? That what you heard?"

"You were a demolitions man in Vietnam. I can put two and two together."

Howe laughed. "Yeah? Well, your addition stinks. That explosives stuff is all ancient history. I barely remember any of that. Time marches on, right?"

Old Bob nodded, patient the way you were with a child. "So it wouldn't be your fault if there was an accident, would it?"

"Not hardly."

"An accident that would make MidCon look like a bunch of clowns, trying to reopen the mill without the union?"

"Sort of like kids playing with matches in a pile of fireworks?"

"Like that."

Derry nodded thoughtfully. "You know, Robert, the thing about fireworks is that they're touchy, unpredictable. Sometimes they don't behave like you think they should. That's how all those accidents happen, people getting their hands blown off and such. They play with explosives they aren't trained to handle. They take foolish chances."

Old Bob shook his head. "We're not talking about fireworks here. We're talking about MidCon and people getting killed!"

Derry Howe's eyes were bright and hard. "You got that right."

Old Bob looked off into the trees, into the cool shade. "I don't like what I'm hearing."

"Then don't listen." Derry smiled disdainfully. "Do yourself a favor, Robert. Sit this one out. It ain't right for you anyway. You or Mel or any of the others. You had your day. Time to step aside. Stay home on the Fourth. Watch a movie or something. Keep away from the fireworks—all of them."

He paused, and a dark, wild look came into his eyes. "It's settled with me, Robert Roosevelt. I know what I'm about. I'm going to put an end to this strike. I'm going to give MidCon a Fourth of July to remember, and when it's over they won't be able to get to the bargaining table quick enough. That's the way it's going to be, and there ain't nothing they can do about it." He ran his fingers through his short-cropped hair, a quick, dismissive movement. "Or you either. You stay out of my way. Be better for you if you did."

He gave Old Bob a wink and walked back to his friends.

Robert Freemark stood watching after him angrily for a moment, then turned away. He moved back through the crowds toward Evelyn, his anger turning to disappointment. He supposed he hadn't really expected to change Derry Howe's mind. He supposed he hadn't really expected to accomplish much of anything. Maybe he was hoping it would turn out Mel Riorden was mistaken, that Derry wasn't really planning something foolish. Whatever the case, his failure to achieve anything left him feeling empty and disgruntled. He should have made a stronger argument, been more persuasive. He should have found a way to get through.

He worked his way back to Evelyn, burdened by both the weight of the July heat and his anger. Somewhere deep inside, where he hid the things he didn't want other people to see, he felt a darkness rise up and begin to take shape. Something bad was going to happen. Maybe Derry intended to damage the machinery at the mill. Maybe he intended to put a serious dent in the company's pocketbook or its image. But for some reason Old Bob felt like it might be even worse than that. He felt it might be catastrophic.

He moved up to Mel and Carol Riorden, Al Garcia, Penny Williamson, and Evelyn, smiling easily, comfortably to hide his concerns. They were still talking about the new grandbaby. Mel gave him a questioning look. He frowned and shook his head slowly. He could see the disappointment in his friend's face.

Evelyn took him by the arm and pulled him away. "Come with me," she directed, steering him through the crowd. "I have a little business of my own to take care of."

He let himself be led back toward the horseshoe tournament, back toward Derry Howe. Old Bob glanced quickly at her, thinking, No, it can't be about Derry, can it? Evelyn did not return the glance, her gaze directed forward, intense and immutable. He had seen that look before, and he knew that whatever she had set herself to do, she would not be dissuaded. He kept his mouth shut.

The crowd observing the horseshoe contest parted before them. Evelyn veered left, taking Old Bob with her, striding down the line of spectators toward the participants at the far end.

"Just stand next to me, Robert," she said quietly. "You don't have to say anything. I'll do the talking."

She released his arm and stepped in front of him, taking the lead. He caught sight of George Paulsen staring at them from among the competitors, but Evelyn seemed oblivious of him. She moved, instead, toward Enid Scott, who was standing with her youngest, Bennett, to one side.

Enid saw Evelyn coming and turned to face her, surprise reflecting in her pale, tired eyes. She was dressed in matching shorts and halter top that had fit better when she was twenty pounds lighter. She brushed back a few loose strands of her lank, tousled hair and dragged out an uncertain smile.

"Hello, Mrs. Freemark," she greeted, her voice breaking slightly as she caught the look in Evelyn's dark eyes.

Evelyn came to a stop directly before her. "Enid, I'll come right to the point," she said softly. They were alone except for Bennett and Old Bob; no one else could hear what was being said. "I know you've had some rough times, and that raising five children all alone is no picnic. I think you've done better than a lot of women would have in your circumstances, and I admire you for it. You've kept your family together the best you could. You've got five children you can be proud of."

"Thank you," Enid stammered, surprised.

"I'm not finished. The flip side of this particular coin is that you've made a whole bunch of decisions in your life that testify to the distinct possibility that you have the common sense of a woodchuck. Sooner or later, some of those decisions are going to come back to haunt you. Your choice in men, for example, is abominable. You've got five fatherless children as proof of that, and I don't see much improvement of late. Your frequent visits to the bars and nightspots of this community suggest that alcohol is becoming a problem for you. And it is no shame to be unemployed and on welfare, but it is a shame not to want to do anything about it!"

Robert blinked in disbelief, hearing the fire in his wife's voice, seeing the stiff set of her back rigid within her flowered dress. Little Bennett was staring at Evelyn, her mouth open.

"Well, I don't think you have the right to tell me . . ." Enid Scott began, flustered and angry now.

"Understand something, Enid. I'm not standing here as an example of how a woman ought to live her life." Evelyn cut her short, brushing aside her attempt at defending herself. "Matter of fact, I've made some of the same mistakes you're making, and I've made them worse. I'm closer to you than you realize. That gives me not only the right to talk to you this way, but the obligation as well. I can see where you're headed, and I can't let you walk off the end of the pier without shouting out a warning of some sort. So this is that warning. You can make a lot of mistakes in this life and get away with it. We both know that. But there's one mistake you can't make—not ever, if you want to live with yourself afterward. And that's not being there for your children when they need you. It's happened several times already. Don't say anything, Enid. Don't say it isn't so, because that would be a terrible lie, and you don't want to add that to your catalogue of sins. Point is, nothing bad has happened yet. But sooner or later, it will. If it does, that will be the end of you."

Evelyn held the other woman's gaze, took a quick breath, and stepped forward. Enid Scott flinched, and Bennett jumped. But all Evelyn did was reach down and take Enid's hand in her own, hold it, and then pat it gently.

"If you ever need anyone, you call me," she said quietly. "Any time, for any reason. You call me. I'll be there. That's a promise."

A few people were looking over now, sensing that something was going on, not sure exactly what it was. George Paulsen detached himself from the horseshoe competitors and sauntered over, mean eyes narrowing. "What's going on here?" he snapped.

Evelyn ignored him. "Are you all right, Enid? I didn't speak too harshly, did I?"

"Well," whispered Enid Scott uncertainly.

"I did, I expect." Evelyn continued to pat her hand, to hold it between her own, her voice soothing and calm. "I speak the way I do because I believe it is best to be direct. But I would like to be your friend, if you would let me. I know you have no family here, and I don't want you to think that you are alone."

"She ain't alone, she's got me!" George Paulsen declared, coming up to them.

Gran fixed him with a withering gaze. "Having you for company is not something I would think she would be anxious to brag on!" she snapped.

Paulsen flushed angrily. "Listen here, old woman . . ."

Old Bob started forward protectively, but Evelyn was too quick for him. She moved right up against George Paulsen, the index fingers of both hands aimed at him like the barrels of guns.

"Don't you mess with me, George," she hissed. "Don't you even think about it. You haven't the iron. Now, you listen to me. You can stay with Enid or not—that's between you and her. But if I hear one more story about you striking that woman or any of her children, if I see one bruise on any of them that I don't like the looks of, if I so much as see you raise a threatening hand against them, you will think that God must have reached down out of heaven and squashed you like a bug. Do you understand me, sir?"

George Paulsen flinched as her fingers slowly extended to touch his chest.

"And don't you believe for one minute that you can hide anything from me, George," she continued softly. "Even if you think I won't find out, I will. I'll come after you, no matter how fast or how far you try to run from me." She lifted her fingers away. "You remember that."

For a moment Old Bob thought George Paulsen would strike Evelyn. But he must have seen something in her face or found something in his own heart that told him it would be a mistake. He tried to speak, failed, shot a venomous look at Enid, and stalked away.

There were a lot of people staring now. Evelyn ignored them, was oblivious of them. She turned back to Enid Scott and Bennett, gave Enid a reassuring nod and

Bennett a smile. "You come by for ice cream, little one," she invited. "Nest and I would love to have you any time. Bring your mother with you when you do."

"Mrs. Freemark," Enid Scott tried, but was unable to continue.

Evelyn met her gaze, her own steady and fixed. "My name is Evelyn. That's what all my friends call me. You think on what I've said, Enid. I'll be looking in on you."

She walked back to Old Bob then, took his arm in hers, and turned him back toward the river. "Shame to waste a nice day like this standing about in the heat. Why don't we go sit out by the river and wait for Nest."

He stared at her. "You amaze me, Evelyn," he told her, not bothering to hide the astonishment in his voice. "You really do."

A faint smile played at the corners of her mouth, a hint of mischievousness that appeared and faded all at once. "Now and then, Robert," she replied softly. "Now and then."

CHAPTER 22

Though he had not admitted it to Nest Freemark, John Ross had met O'olish Amaneh before. It was O'olish Amaneh who had given him his limp.

"Your old life is finished, my brave knight-errant," the Lady had whispered that night in the Fairy Glen as she held him to her, accepting the pledge of his faith, taking the measure of his strength. All about them, the fairies darted in the blackness of the water and the cool of the shadows, rippling with the sound of her voice in his ear. "Now, for as long as I deem it necessary, you belong to me. You will care for and be faithful to no other. You will forsake your home. You will forsake your family and your friends. Do you understand?"

"Yes," he had said.

"You will be asked to sacrifice, of your body and your soul, of your heart and your mind, in this world and the world to come. Your sacrifice will be great, but it will be necessary. Do you understand?"

"Yes," he had said once more.

"I brought you to me, John Ross. Now I send you back again. Leave this country and return to your home. It is there that you are needed to do battle in my service. I am the light and the way, the road you must travel and the life you must lead. Go now, and be at peace."

He did as he was told. He went from the Fairy Glen to his cottage in Betws-y-Coed, packed his bags, traveled east into England, and caught a standby flight to the States. He did so in the firm belief that his life had been changed in the way he had always anticipated it one day would and with the hope that here, at last, was the purpose he had sought. He did not know yet what he was supposed to do. He had become a Knight of the Word, but he did not know what was expected of him. He carried inside him the blood of Owain Glyndwr, and he would be the Word's champion and do battle with the Void as his ancestor had before him. He did not know what that meant. He was terrified and exhilarated and filled with passion. The visions of the future that the Lady had shown him were burned into his mind forever, and when he recalled them they brought tears to his eyes. He was just a man, just one man, but he knew that he must do whatever was asked of him—even if it meant giving up his life.

But it was not real to him yet. It was still a dream, and as he traveled farther away from the Fairy Glen and that night, it became steadily more so. He went home to his parents, who were still alive then, to let them know he was well, but would not be staying. He was purposefully vague, and he told them nothing of what had befallen him. He had not been forbidden to do so, but he knew that it would be foolish to speak of it. His parents, whether they believed him or not, would be needlessly worried. Better that they thought him a wanderer still when he left them. Better that they lived without knowing.

So he waited, frozen in time. He tried to envision what his life would be like in service to the Lady. He tried to resolve his doubts and his fears, to settle within himself the feelings of inadequacy that had begun to surface. What could he do, that would make a difference? What would be required of him, that he would be able to respond? Was he strong enough to do what was needed? Was he anything of what the Lady believed?

He waited for her to speak to him, to reveal her purpose for him. She did not. He visited with friends and acquaintances from his past, marking time against an uncertain future. Weeks went by. Still the Lady did not appear. Doubts set in. Had he dreamed it all? Had he imagined her? Or worse, had he mistaken her intent? What if the great purpose he had envisioned, the purpose for which he had searched so long, was a lie? Doubts turned to mistrust. What if he had been deceived? He was beset by nightmares that woke him shaking and chilled on the hottest nights, sweating and fiery in the coldest of rooms. Something had gone wrong. Perhaps he was not the champion she had been looking for, and she had realized it and abandoned him. Perhaps she had forsaken him entirely.

Strong belief turned slowly to fragile hope, the Lady's whispered promise echoing through the empty corridors of his mind.

Your way lies through me. I am the road that you must take.

Then the Indian came to him. He was sitting on the bed in his room, alone in the house, his parents gone for the afternoon. He was staring at words on a paper before him, words that he had written in an effort to find reason in what had happened to him, when the door opened and the Indian was standing there.

"I am O'olish Amaneh," he said quietly.

He was a big man, his skin copper-colored, his hair braided and black, his eyes intense and probing. He wore old army clothes and moccasins and carried a backpack and bedroll. In one massive hand, he gripped a long black staff.

He came into the room and shut the door behind him. "I have come to give you this," he said, and held out the staff.

Ross stared, saw the sheen of the wood, the rune marks cut into the shiny surface, and the way the light played over both. He sat there on the bed, frozen in place.

"You are John Ross?" O'olish Amaneh asked him.

Ross nodded, unable to speak.

"You are a Knight of the Word?"

Ross blinked rapidly and swallowed against the dryness in his throat. "Do you come from her?" he managed.

The Indian did not answer.

"Are you in service to the Lady?" he pressed.

"The staff belongs to you," O'olish Amaneh insisted quietly, ignoring him. "Take it."

Ross could not do so. He knew with sudden, terrifying certainty that if he did, there would be no turning back. The clarity of his knowledge was appalling. It was the staff, something in the way it gleamed, in its blackness, in the intricacy of its carvings. It was in the implacable way the Indian urged him to take hold of it. If he did so, he was finished. If he did so, it was the end of him. He was not ready for this after all, he saw. He no longer wanted to be a part of what had happened in the Fairy Glen, in Wales, in the realm of the Lady's magic.

The Indian was a rock, standing before him unmoved. "Your faith must be stronger than this," he advised in a whisper. "Your faith must sustain you. You swore to serve. You cannot recant. It is forbidden."

"Forbidden?" Ross repeated in disbelief. He was nearly in tears, filled with contempt for himself, for his weakness, for his failing resolve. "Don't you understand?" he breathed.

The Indian gave no sign as to whether he did or not. "You are a Knight of the Word. You have been chosen. You have need of the staff. Take it."

Ross shook his head slowly. "I can't."

"Stand up," O'olish Amaneh ordered.

There was no change of expression in the big man's face, no sign of disappointment, of anger, of anything. The eyes fixed on John Ross, calm and steady, as dark and deep as night pools, bottomless pits within the shadow of the great brow. Ross could not look away. Slowly he rose to his feet. The Indian came forward and held the staff out to him, before his terrified face, the carved markings, the polished wood, the gnarled length.

"Take the staff," he said quietly.

John Ross tried to step away, struggled to break free of the eyes that held him bound.

"Take the staff," O'olish Amaneh repeated.

Ross brought his hands up obediently, and his fingers closed about the polished wood. Instantly, fire ripped through his body. *Oh, God!* His left foot began to cramp, pain seizing and locking about it, working its way down to the bone. Ross tried to scream, but found he could make no sound. The pain intensified, growing worse than anything he had ever experienced, than anything he had imagined possible. His hands fastened so tightly about the staff that his knuckles turned white. He felt as if his fingers were imprinting the wood. He could not make himself let go. His foot jerked and twisted, and the pain climbed up his leg, cramping his muscles, tearing his ligaments, setting fire to his nerves. It bore into his knee, and now his mouth was open wide and his head thrown back in agony.

Then, just as quickly as it had appeared, the pain was gone. John Ross gasped in shock and relief, his head sagging on his chest. He leaned heavily on the black staff, letting it support him, relying on its strength to hold him erect. *My God, my God!*

Slowly O'olish Amaneh stepped away. "Now it belongs to you," the Indian repeated. "You are bound to it. You are joined as one. You cannot give it up until you are released from your service. Remember that. Do not try to put it from you. Do not try to cast it away. Ever."

Then O'olish Amaneh was gone, out the door and down the hall, as silent as a ghost. Ross waited half a breath, then took a quick step toward the door to close it. He collapsed instantly, his foot turning in, his leg unable to bear the weight of his body. He struggled back to his feet, leaning on the staff for support, and fell again. He sprawled on the floor, staring down at his leg. Once more he climbed to his feet, gritting his teeth, squeezing shut his eyes, so fearful of what had been done to him that he could barely breathe.

He was finally able to stand, but only with the aid of the staff. He was going to have to learn to walk all over again. He leaned against the wall and cried with rage and frustration.

Why has this been done to me?

He would have his answer that night when he dreamed for the first time of the future that was his to prevent.

"Penny for your thoughts, John Ross."

It was evening, the daylight gone hazy and dim with twilight's slow descent, the heat lingering in a thick blanket across the broad stretch of the park. Ross was sitting alone on the grass beneath an old hickory just back from where the band was setting up for the dance in the pavilion. People were milling about, watching the proceedings, eating popcorn, ice cream, and cotton candy and drinking pop, lemonade, and iced tea. Ball games were still under way on the diamonds, but the last of the organized races and the horseshoe tournament had come to a close. Ross had been lost momentarily in the past, in the days before he understood what the Lady required of him and what it meant to be a Knight of the Word.

The familiar voice brought him out of his reverie. He looked up and smiled at Josie Jackson. "A penny? I expect that's more than they're worth. How are you?"

"I'm fine, thank you." She stood looking at him for a moment, openly appraising him. She was wearing a flower-print blouse with a scoop neck and a full, knee-length skirt cinched about her narrow waist. She had tied back her blond hair with a ribbon, and wore sandals and a gold bracelet. She looked fresh and cool, even in the stifling heat. "I missed you at breakfast this morning. You didn't come in."

He smiled ruefully. "My loss. I overslept, then went straight to church. The Freemarks invited me." He drew up his good leg and clasped his hands about his knee. "I don't get to church as much as I should, I'm afraid."

She laughed. "So how was it?"

He hesitated, picturing in his mind the dark shapes of the feeders prowling through the sanctuary, Wraith stalking out of the gloom of the foyer, and the demon hiding somewhere farther back in the shadows. *How was it?* "It wasn't quite what I remember," he replied without a trace of irony.

"Nothing ever is." She came forward a step. "Are you alone this evening?"

The expressive dark eyes held him frozen in place. He looked away to free himself, then quickly back again. Nest had gone off with her friends. Old Bob had taken Evelyn home. He was marking time now, waiting on the demon. "Looks that way," he said.

"Do you want some company?" she asked, her voice smooth and relaxed.

He felt his throat tighten. He was tired of being alone. What harm could it do to spend a little time with her, to give a little of himself to a pretty woman? "Sure," he told her.

"Good." She sat down next to him, a graceful movement that put her right up against him. He could feel the softness of her shoulder and hip. She sat without speaking for a moment, looking at the people gathered about the pavilion, her gaze steady and distant. He studied the freckles on her nose out of the corner of his eye, trying to think of something to say.

"I'm not much of a dancer," he confessed finally, struggling to read her thoughts.

She looked at him as if amazed that he would admit such a thing, then gave him a quirky smile. "Why don't we just talk, then?"

He nodded and said nothing for a moment. He looked off toward the pavilion. "Would you like an ice cream or something to drink?"

She was still looking at him, still smiling. "Yes."

"Which?"

"Surprise me."

He levered himself to his feet using the staff, limped over to the food stand, bought two chocolate ice-cream cones, and limped back again, squinting against the sharp glare of the setting sun. It was just for a little while, he told himself. Just so that he could remember what it was like to feel good about himself. He sat down beside her again and handed her a cone.

"My favorite," she said, sounding like she meant it. She took a small bite. Her freckled nose wrinkled. "Hmmmm, really good." She took another bite and looked at him. "So tell me something about yourself."

He thought a moment, staring off into the crowds, then told her about traveling through Great Britain. She listened intently as he recounted his visits to the castles and cathedrals, to the gardens and the moors, to the hamlets and the cities. He liked talking about England, and he took time to give her a clear picture of what it was like there—of the colors and the smells when it rained, which was often; of the countryside with its farms and postage-stamp fields, walled by stone; of the mist and the wildflowers in the spring, when there was color everywhere, diffused and made brilliant in turn by the changes in the light.

She smiled when he was done and said she wanted to go someday. She talked about what it was like to run a coffee shop, her own business, built from scratch. She told him what it was like growing up in Hopewell, sometimes good, sometimes bad. She talked about her family, which was large and mostly elsewhere. She did not ask him what he did for a living or about his family, and he did not volunteer. He told her he had been a graduate student for many years, and perhaps she thought he still was one. She joked with him as if she had known him all his life, and he liked that. She made him feel comfortable. He thought she was pretty and funny and smart, and he wanted to know her better. He was attracted to her as he had not been attracted to a woman in a very long time. It was a dangerous way for him to feel.

At one point she said to him, "I suppose you think I'm pretty forward, inviting myself to spend the evening with you."

He shook his head at once. "I don't think that at all."

"Do you think I might be easy?" She paused. "You know."

He stared at her, astonished by the question, unable to reply.

"Good Heavens, you're blushing, John!" She laughed and poked him gently in the ribs. "Relax, I'm teasing. I'm not like that." She grinned. "But I'm curious, and I'm not shy. I don't know you, but I think I'd like to. So I'm taking a chance. I believe in taking chances. I think that if you don't take chances, you miss out."

He thought of his own life, and he nodded slowly. "I guess I agree with that."

The sun had dropped below the horizon, and darkness had fallen over the park. The band had begun playing, easing into a slow, sweet waltz that brought the older couples out onto the dance floor beneath the colored lamps that had been strung about the pavilion. Out in the grass, small children danced with each other, mimicking the adults, taking large, deliberate steps. John Ross and Josie Jackson watched them in silence, smiling, letting their thoughts drift on the music's soft swell.

After a time, he asked her if she would like to take a walk. They climbed to their feet and strolled off into the darkened trees. Josie took his free arm, and moved close to him, matching his halting pace. They walked from the pavilion toward the toboggan slide, then down through the trees toward the river. The music trailed after them, soft and inviting. The night was brilliant with stars, but thick with summer heat, the air compressed and heavy beneath the pinpricked sky. It was dark and silent within the old hardwoods, and the river was a gleaming, silver-tipped ribbon below them.

They stopped on a rise within a stand of elm to stare down at it, still listening to the strains of the distant music, to the jumbled sounds of conversation and laughter, to the buzz of the locusts far back in the woods. On the river, a scattering of boats bobbed at anchor, and from farther out in the dark, over on the far bank of the Rock River, car lights crawled down private drives like the eyes of nocturnal hunters.

"I like being with you, John," Josie told him quietly. She squeezed his arm for emphasis.

He closed his eyes against the ache her words generated within him. "I like being with you, too."

There was a long silence, and then she leaned over and kissed him softly on the cheek. When he turned to look at her, she kissed him on the mouth. He put caution aside and kissed her back.

She broke the embrace, and he saw the bright wonder in her eyes. "Maybe, just this once," she whispered, "I'm going to be a little more forward than I thought."

It took a moment for the import of the words to register, and then another for the familiar chill to run through him as the memories began to scream in the silence of his mind.

When he sleeps the night after O'olish Amaneh has given him the black walnut staff with its strange rune markings and terrible secret, he dreams for the first time of the future the Lady had prophesied. It is not a dream of the sort that he has experienced before. The dream is not fragmented and surreal as dreams usually are. It is not composed of people and places from his life, not formed of events turned upside down by the workings of his subconscious. The dream is filled with the sounds, tastes, smells, sights, and feelings of life, and he knows in a strange and frightening way that what he is experiencing is real.

He is not simply dreaming of the future; he is living in it.

He closes his eyes momentarily against the feelings this revelation generates within him. Then he opens them quickly to look about. The world in which he finds himself is nightmarish. It is dark and misted and filled with destruction. He is on a hillside overlooking the remains of a city. The city was once large and heavily populated; now it lies in ruins, empty of life. It does not smolder or steam or glow with fading embers; it has been dead a long time. It sits lifeless and still, its stones and timbers and steel jutting out of the flattened earth like ravaged bones.

After a time, he begins to see the feeders. There are only a few, prowling the ruins, dark shapes barely visible in the gloom, eyes yellow and gleaming. He knows instinctively what they are. They are far away, down within the rubble, and they do not seem aware of him. He feels a twinge in his right hand, and looks down to find that he holds the black staff. Where he grips it, light pulses softly. The light signals the readiness of the staff's magic to respond to his summons. The magic is his to wield in his service to the Word. It is vast and formidable. It enables him to withstand almost anything. It gives him the power to destroy and to defend. It is the Word's magic, drawn from deep within the earth. It whispers to him in seductive tones and makes him promises it cannot always keep. His immediate response is to want to cast the staff away, but something rooted deep within forbids him from doing so.

He feels exposed on the hillside, and starts to move tentatively toward the shelter of some trees. When he does so, he finds that he no longer limps, that his leg is healed. He is not surprised; he knew it would be so.

When he reaches the trees, the Lady is waiting for him. She is a small, faint whiteness within the dark, as ethereal as gossamer. She looks at him, smiles, and then fades. She is not real after all, he realizes; she is not even there. She is a memory. He has been to this place before, in another, earlier time, before the destruction, and coming here again has triggered the memory.

He begins to understand now. He is living in the future, but only in his sleep. It is the cost of the magic he wields, the title he bears, and the responsibility he shoulders. He will live his life henceforth in two worlds—the present when awake, the future when asleep. The images come in a rush, like the waters of a river overflowing its banks in a flood. He is a Knight of the Word, and he must prevent the future in which he stands. But he needs the knowledge the future can give him in order to do so. He must learn from the future of the mistakes and missed opportunities of the past. If he can discover them, perhaps he can correct them. Each time he sleeps, he has another chance to learn. Each time he sleeps, the future whispers secrets of the past. But the future is never the same because the past advances and alters it. Nor does his sleep lend order, coherence, or chronology to what he witnesses. The future comes to him as it will and reveals itself as it chooses. He cannot control it; he must simply abide it.

And survive. For he is hunted by the demons and their allies, by the once-men who serve them, and by the things that are given over to the Void. Few remain who can resist them. He is one. They hunt him every night of his life. They have caught him more than once. They have killed him, he thinks, but he does not know for sure. The future changes each night. Perhaps it changes his fate as well.

He recalls all of it now. He has his memories of the past to fill in the gaps, so that even though it is his first night, he is a veteran of his dreams already. The truths rise up and confront him. He is crippled so that he will not ever give up the staff. Without the staff, he has no magic. Without the staff, he is helpless. If he cannot walk without the staff to aid him, he is far less likely to be careless with it. After all, it is his only protection. He is crippled so that he will remember.

So it has been settled on him. His past is linked to his future. If he fails in his mission of service to the Word, the future he resides in each night will come to pass. He will be whole again, but he will inherit the destruction and ruin he surveys. And he will pay a further price. Magic summoned in the present will be lost to him in the future. Each time he uses the magic in his former life, he is deprived of it in the latter for an indeterminate amount of time. He must use the magic wisely and ef-

fectively when he invokes it, or one day, at a time or place not of his choosing, in a situation when he needs it most, he may find himself weaponless.

He stands alone within the trees on the hillside above the ruined city and ponders what it means for him to sleep and why he must always keep solitary and apart . . .

"Josie," he said softly, searching for the right words.

There was sudden movement in the shadows, the sound of rushing footsteps and heavy breathing. Ross turned as the shadows closed on him, swift and menacing. He stepped away from Josie, trying to place her behind him. He heard her gasp in surprise, saw the masked faces of the men who reached for him. He struggled to comprehend their muttered threats, and then they were upon him.

They bore him backward toward the crest of the rise, reaching for his arms and shoulders, trying to tear the staff from his hands. He cried out to them, *No, wait, what are you doing?* He fought to free himself, wrenching the staff away, shielding it. One took a swing at him, trying to hit him in the face, but he ducked aside. He could not move quickly, could not run with his bad leg. He was forced to stand. He heard one of them call him names, ugly and crude, heard another call him "spy" and "company pig." *I'm not!* he tried to explain. Josie shouted at them, furious, *What are you doing? Stop it! Get away from him!* He was in danger of going down. He braced himself against the rush and swung the high end of the staff sharply at the nearest attacker. He felt the wood connect with bone, and the man grunted and staggered back. He used the lower end to hammer the shins of another man, and that one howled openly in pain.

Then they were all over him, bearing him to the ground. Fists struck at him as he slammed into the earth. Someone was kicking at his ribs. He heard Josie scream, saw her rush forward to try to protect him, arms flailing. A boot slammed into his head, bringing pain and bright light. He tried to throw off the ones who held him down, tried to regain his feet. The staff had been pushed aside so that he could no longer bring it to bear. They were still trying to wrench it from his hands, to take away his only protection. He felt the blows rain down on him, felt blood fill his mouth. It was getting harder to breathe. Josie was still screaming, but her voice was hoarse, and it sounded as if a hand had been clamped over her mouth.

A boot pinned his left wrist to the earth. *Don't do this!* he wanted to scream at them, but could not make himself. He fought in silent, futile desperation to break free. They were wrenching at the staff, tearing at his fingers, leaving him no choice . . .

Stop, please!

The runes carved into the polished black surface began to pulse with light. A fiery heat burned its gnarled length.

No!

The magic exploded from the staff in a rush of white brilliance, detonating with such fury that it seemed to consume the air itself, a whirlwind of power unleashed. It was not summoned, but came alive on its own, reacting to its master's need. With a single incendiary burst, it flung John Ross's attackers into the night. They flew from him as if they were paper cutouts, weightless in a high wind, and he was free once more. He lay gasping for breath in the aftermath, the magic gone as swiftly as it had appeared. In the darkness, his attackers climbed dazedly to their feet and stumbled away, their resolve shattered, their purpose forgotten, their confusion profound.

Too late for me, John Ross thought in despair, knowing the price he would now be forced to pay for having required use of the magic. *Way too late.*

As he closed his eyes against his body's and spirit's pain, he heard Josie call his name, and in the ensuing silence he reached out his hand to find her.

Chapter 23

Nest Freemark sat with her friends on the grass at the edge of the pavilion and watched the dancers sway and glide to the strains of the music. All about them, families and couples sat visiting on blankets and lawn chairs, their faces reflecting the colors of the lanterns strung from the pavilion's eaves. The sun's heat lingered, but a faint breeze wafted off the river now and cooled those gathered just enough that they could put the salty aftertaste of the daylight's swelter behind them. The breeze and the music wove together, soothing nerves and easing discomfort. Smiles came out of hiding, and people remembered the importance of using kind words. The night was as soft as velvet, and it cradled them in its arms and eased them toward sleep.

Robert was explaining something about computers to Jared. Brianna and Cass were talking about school clothes and makeup. Nest was wondering how she had let this happen.

It could have been so wonderful, she thought wistfully.

Things weren't working out the way she had planned. Jared had found her easily enough in the twilight hour before sunset when the band was setting up and the floor of the pavilion was being swept clean. For a few brief moments, while they were standing alone beneath one of the old hardwoods, she had thought that now, at last, she would have her chance to talk with him, to really talk with him, just the two of them. She had thought he might confide in her, that he might tell her something he had never told anyone—and that perhaps she would tell him something wonderful or startling in turn. She had come out of the day worn and dejected from her battle to discover the truth behind John Ross and her family, and she had reached a point where she just wanted to let go of everything for a little while. No demon, no maentwrog, no Pick, no magic. Just a boy she liked and wanted to be with. It didn't seem too much to ask. She had looked forward to it all day. She had imagined what it would be like, how good it would make her feel. She would talk with him, dance with him and, if things worked out just right, let him kiss her. She would look at him and feel good about herself for just a few moments.

They were easing in that direction when Robert, Cass, and Brianna joined them. One, two, three, there they were, her friends, all smiles, clueless that she wanted to be alone with Jared, wanted them to get lost, to just disappear. Why she hadn't seen that this might happen, she didn't know. But now that it had, she felt oddly betrayed. It was selfish and small of her to feel that way, but she couldn't help herself. She was feeling trapped at every turn, so hemmed in by the events of her life that she was finding it difficult to breathe. She had thought she might gain a small respite from her troubles at this dance. It didn't look like that was going to happen.

She shifted uncomfortably on the grass, trying to decide what to do. Maybe she should go home. Maybe she should just give it up. She glanced at Jared, her eyes hot and angry, willing him to say something, to do something. Anything. She kept thinking he would, but he just sat there. Maybe she should be the one to say or do something, she fumed, but that didn't seem right either.

So she sat there with her momentarily inconvenient friends, listening to the music, watching the dancers, and wishing for a minor miracle.

She got her miracle when Jared finally stood up and in a breathless rush of words asked her to dance. With a hasty apology to the other three, she scrambled to her feet and followed him out onto the dance floor, a surge of adrenaline sending her pulse racing and her spirits soaring. She took his left hand in her right and moved awkwardly into his embrace. His arm went about her waist and his hand rested on the small of her back. She could feel the heat of his skin. They began to dance, slowly, cautiously, gradually adjusting to each other's movements. Jared led tentatively, but determinedly, easing her between the other dancers, moving with the rhythm of the slow, soft music. Nest was as tall as he was, and she ducked her chin toward his shoulder to make herself smaller. She liked the way he held her. She liked how he smelled and how he glanced at her every so often to see if she was all right. His shy smile made her want to weep.

She closed her eyes and eased closer to him, feeling his arms tighten about her. She had her escape. She buried her face in his shoulder. She did not try to look for Cass or Brianna or Robert. She did not try to look for anyone. She kept her eyes closed and moved with Jared Scott, letting him take her wherever he would, giving herself over to him.

They danced that dance and several more. When the music quickened, they continued to dance slow. Nest felt her weariness, doubt, and fear slip away, fading into the background of movement and sound. She felt wonderfully at peace; she felt loving and hopeful. She held Jared close, pressing herself to him, her face buried in his neck, in the rough tangle of his hair. They did not speak, not a word the entire time. There was nothing to say that needed saying, and any attempt at words would spoil what was happening.

So good, Nest thought, her breathing soft and slow. So sweet.

Then she let her eyes slip open for just a moment, and she saw the demon.

He was walking past the dance floor, weaving through the families clustered on the grass, a solitary, shadowy figure. He was still in his human guise as the park maintenance man, though he did not wear coveralls or work clothes this night, but plain slacks and a collared shirt. He was not looking at her, or at anyone, but at some point in the distance beyond what she could see, his gaze bright and intense. Nest stopped dancing at once, staring after him as he moved away. Where was John Ross? She hadn't seen him since her grandparents had gone home after the picnic. She had to find him at once.

But the demon was already disappearing into the darkness, withdrawing from the light. She was going to lose him.

"What's the matter?" Jared asked, his hands releasing her as she backed away. She could tell from the sound of his voice that he was afraid he might have done something wrong. His face was pained and uncertain as he stared at her.

Her eyes locked instantly on his. "That's the man I've been searching for, the one I told you about, the one who's poisoning the trees." Her words came in a rush. "Go get the others, Jared, then go find John Ross. You know John, you saw him earlier with my grandparents. Find him and tell him where I've gone—that way." She pointed in the direction of the demon, who was already almost out of sight. "Hurry, I'll be out there waiting!"

She was moving quickly now, leaving Jared and his futile protests behind, darting through the crowd in an effort to keep up with the demon. She would not approach him, of course. She knew how dangerous that would be. But she would keep him in sight and try to find out where he was going.

She hustled past the people gathered about the pavilion and hurried into the dark. She could still see the demon, just at the edge of her vision as he crossed the grass toward the toboggan slide and turned down along the edge of the roadway leading to the west end of the park. She slowed a bit, not wanting to get too close, relying on the darkness to conceal her. She wished she had Pick or Daniel with her to help track the demon, but she hadn't seen either one in several hours. She would have to make do without them. Her eyes swept the darkness of the trees about her. Was Wraith anywhere close? If the demon should turn on her, would she have any protection at all? She pushed the question aside and went on.

The sounds of the music and the dance faded behind her, giving way to the steady buzz of the locusts and the more distant, intermittent sounds of traffic from the highway. She slipped silently through the park trees, shadowy and invisible in the night. She could move without making any sound; Pick had taught her how to do that. She had good night vision as well. The demon wouldn't lose her easily. Not that it appeared as if he would try. It didn't seem that he was worried about being followed. He walked without looking back, his eyes straight ahead, his pace steady. Nest crept along in his wake.

She followed the demon through the trees above the river from the east end of the park to the west, closing on the bridge that spanned the road where it looped back on itself and descended from the heights to the base of the cliffs. She kept looking over her shoulder, hoping to discover John Ross following, come to her aid, but there was no sign of him. She wondered more than once if she ought to turn back, but each time she told herself she would go on just a little farther. The sky was bright with stars, but the heavy canopy of the trees masked much of their light and left the woods in heavy darkness. There was no one out this far, she knew. Anyone in the park tonight was at the dance. If the demon kept going, he would soon be in the cemetery. Nest wondered suddenly if that was his destination. She thought suddenly of her mother, buried there. She thought next of Two Bears.

Then abruptly the demon stopped beneath a streetlamp just before the bridge span and stood looking off into the distance. Was he expecting someone? Nest crept closer. Careful, she warned herself. This was as close as she needed to be.

She hunched down beside a stand of fir, waiting for something to happen. Then a familiar voice hissed at her from behind. "Hey, Nest, whatcha doing?"

She jumped to her feet and whirled about. Danny Abbott stood six feet away, hands on his hips, grinning broadly. "Who're you spying on?"

"Danny, get out of here!" she hissed furiously.

His grin widened. "That guy over there?" he asked, and pointed behind her.

When she turned to see if the demon was still there, if he had been warned, a rush of shadows closed on her. She cried out and fought to escape, but she was knocked from her feet and slammed to the ground. The air went out of her lungs, and bright lights exploded behind her eyes as her head struck the exposed root of a tree. She could hear Danny Abbott laughing. Someone was sitting astride her, forcing her face into the dirt. A strip of electrician's tape was slapped over her mouth. Her arms were pinned behind her, and more tape was wound about her wrists. Then she was yanked to her feet and a burlap feed sack was pulled over her head and body and more tape was wound about her ankles, securing the open end of the sack below her knees.

When she was thoroughly bagged and trussed, she was slung over a burly shoulder. For a second everything went quiet except for the breathing of her attackers and her own stifled sobs.

"You crying?" Danny Abbott said, his mouth right next to her ear. She heard the pleasure in his voice and went still instantly. "You think you're so tough, don't you? Well, let's just see how tough you really are. Let's put it to the test. We're gonna take you down where the sun don't shine, little girl, and see how you like it. Let you spend a night in the dark. Know what I'm talking about, Nest? Sure, you do. The caves, sweet stuff. That's where you're going. Way down in the deep, dark caves."

They carried her like a sack of grain down the road that wound under the bridge to the base of the cliffs. She was cocooned in hot blackness inside the feed sack and jostled against the bony back and shoulders of the boy carrying her. She screamed against the tape that bound her mouth, but her cries were muffled and futile. She was furious with Danny Abbott and however many of his friends were responsible for this idiotic stunt, but she was mostly afraid. She had been warned over and over again by Pick never to go down into the caves. The caves were where the feeders lived, where they hid themselves from humans. It was not safe for her in the caves. And now she was being taken there.

She was afraid, too, because there was nothing she could do to help herself. She was bound so tightly by the tape that she could not free her arms and legs. The tape over her mouth kept her from crying out. Because she was inside the feed sack, she could not even see what was happening to her. She could not use the magic because the magic relied on sight contact and she was cloaked in blackness. John Ross would come looking for her, but how would he ever find her? Pick and Daniel were nowhere in sight. Her grandparents had gone home. Her friends were only kids like her.

What about Wraith? Her spirits jumped a notch. Surely he would be able to find her, to do something to help.

She could feel her kidnappers picking their way over uneven ground, their steps growing slow and uncertain. They were leaving the paved road. She heard the click of a flashlight, and Danny Abbott said something about taking it easy. She felt the air grow cooler about her exposed ankles, and then just a bit inside the stifling feed sack. They were entering the caves.

"Set her down over there," Danny Abbott said.

She fought to contain her growing desperation and tried to reason through what had happened. How had Danny and his friends crept up on her like that without her knowing? They couldn't have. They must have been waiting. But for them to have been waiting, they must have known she would be coming. A cold, sinking feeling invaded the pit of her stomach. The demon had arranged it all. He had let her see him at the dance, enticed her to follow, and led her to where the boys were waiting to snatch her up and carry her down into the caves. It had to have happened that way.

But why would the demon do that? She closed her eyes inside the blackness of the sack and swallowed against the dryness in her throat. She wasn't sure she wanted to know the answer to that question.

She was lowered from the shoulder of the boy carrying her onto a cold, flat slab of rock. She lay there without moving, listening to the sounds of shuffling feet and low voices.

She heard the rustle of clothing as someone bent over her. "Guess we'll be going home now," Danny Abbott said, his voice sounding mean and smug. "You have a nice night, Nest. Think about what a bitch you are, okay? If you think about it hard enough, maybe I'll decide to come back in the morning and set you free. Maybe."

They moved away then, laughing and joking about ghosts and spiders, offering up unsavory images of what could happen to someone left alone in the caves. She gritted her teeth and thought with disdain that they didn't know the half of it.

Then it was quiet, the silence profound. All the night sounds had disappeared—from the woods, the river, the park, the homes, the streets, the entire city. It was as if she had been deposited in one of those sensory-deprivation tanks she had read about. Except, of course, that she could feel the chill of the cave rock working its way through the feed sack and into her body. And she could feel herself trying not to scream.

Water was dripping nearby. She mustered her strength, made a tentative effort at moving, and found she could do so. She worked her way onto her side and managed to sit up. She might be able to get to her feet, she thought suddenly. But then what would she do? She stayed where she was, thinking. Someone would come. Her friends, even if they didn't find John Ross. They would not abandon her—even though earlier she had wished they would. Tears came to her eyes as she remembered. She was ashamed and embarrassed about the way she had felt. She wished she could take it back.

She pushed her face against the weave of the feed sack so that she could see out. But it was so black inside the caves that even after giving her eyes time to adjust to whatever light there might be, she still couldn't see a thing. She worked for a long time on freeing her hands, but the tape was strong and pliable, and the adhesive kept it firmly glued to her skin. She was sweating freely within the sack, but even her sweat did not provide sufficient lubrication for her to work her way loose.

She wondered again where Wraith was. Couldn't he find her here? Was it possible that he couldn't come into the caves?

Time passed, and despair began to erode her resolve. Maybe no one could find her. It wasn't as if she had left tracks that anyone could follow. All anyone knew was that she had left the dance at the pavilion and gone west into the park. She could be anywhere. It might take them all night to find her. It might take them more than that. She could easily be here when Danny Abbott and his low-life friends returned in the morning. If they returned at all.

Why had this happened?

She heard voices then. Someone on the road outside! She tried to call out to them, tried to shout through the tape. She thrashed inside the feed sack, kicking out at anything she could reach to signal them. But the voices passed and receded into silence. No one came. She sat trembling in the dark from her exertion, the sweat drying on her skin.

When she had calmed herself, she began rethinking the possibility of rescue. Whatever else happened, her grandparents would not leave her out here all night. When she didn't come home from the dance, they would begin searching. Lots of people would help. She would be found. Of course she would be found. Danny Abbott would be sorry then. Her glee at the prospect wavered into uncertainty. Didn't he know how this would turn out? Didn't he know what kind of trouble he would be in?

Or was there some reason he wasn't worried about it?

Time dragged on. After a while, she became aware that she wasn't alone. It didn't happen all at once; the feeling crept over her gradually as she pondered her fate. She couldn't hear or see anyone, but she could sense that someone was there with her. She went quiet, a slow sense of dread growing inside. Of course there was someone else in the caves, she reproached herself with a mix of fear and anger.

There were the feeders.

They moved almost soundlessly as they surrounded her. She could feel them looking at her, studying her, maybe wondering what she was doing there. She fought down her revulsion, willed herself to stay calm against the sea of despair that threatened to drown her. She felt their hands brush against her, small pricklings that raised goose bumps on her skin. *Touching her!* She could not identify the feeling—like old paper sacks, maybe, or clothes stiffened with sweat and oil. They had never touched her before, had never had this opportunity, and the thought that they could do so now made her crazy. She fought against the urge to thrash and scream. She forced herself to breathe normally. She tried to pray. Please, God, come for me. Please, don't let me be hurt.

"It's scary to be down here all alone, isn't it?" a voice whispered.

Nest jumped inside her burlap prison. The demon. She swallowed and exhaled quickly, noisily.

"All alone, down in the dark, in a black pit where your greatest enemies dwell. Helpless to prevent them from doing whatever they choose. You hate being helpless, don't you?"

The demon's voice was soft and silky. It rippled through the silence like bat wings. Nest closed her eyes against its insidious sound and gritted her teeth.

"Will someone come for you, you must be wondering? How long before they do? How much more of this must you endure?" The demon paused as if to consider. "Well, John Ross won't be coming. And your grandparents won't be coming. I've seen to that. So who else is there? Oh, I forgot. The sylvan. No, I don't think so. Have I missed anyone?"

Wraith!

The demon chuckled in a self-satisfied way. "The fact is, you have only yourself to blame for this. You should never have tried to follow me. Of course, I knew you would. You couldn't help yourself, could you? It was all so simple, making the suggestion to young Danny Abbott. He's so angry at you, Nest. He hates you. It was easy to persuade him that he could get even with you if he just did what I told him. He was so eager, he didn't even bother to consider the consequences of his act. None of them did. They are such foolish, malleable boys."

The demon's voice had shifted, moving to another part of the cave. But Nest could not hear the demon himself move, could not pick up a single footfall.

"So, here you are, alone with me. Why, you might have asked yourself? Why am I bothering to do this? Why don't I just . . . drop you into a hole and cover you up?" The demon's voice trailed off in a hiss. "I could, you know."

He waited a moment, as if anticipating her response, then sighed anew. "But I don't want to hurt you. I want to teach you. That's why I brought you here. I want you to understand how helpless you are against me. I want you to realize that I can do whatever I like with you. You can't prevent it. Your friends and family can't prevent it. No one can. You need to accept that. I brought you here so that you could discover firsthand what I was talking about yesterday, about the importance of learning to be alone, of learning to depend only on yourself. Because you can't depend on other people, can you? I mean, who's going to save you from this? Your mother is gone, your grandparents are old, your friends are feckless, and no one else really gives a damn. When it comes right down to it, you have only yourself."

Nest was awash with rage and humiliation. She would have killed the demon gladly if she had been free to do so and been offered a way. She hated the demon as she had never hated anyone in her life.

"I have to be going now," he said, the location of his voice shifting again, moving away. "I have things to do while the night is still young. I have enemies to eliminate. Then I'll be back for you. Danny Abbott won't, of course. By morning, he will have forgotten you are even here. So you have to depend on me. Keep that in mind."

Then the voice dropped into a rough whisper that scraped at her nerve endings like sandpaper. "Maybe it would be wise if you were to use your time among the feeders to consider what's important to you. Because your life is about to change, Nest. It is going to change in a way you would never have dreamed possible. I'm going to see to it. It's what I've come here to do."

The silence returned, slow and thick within the dark. Nest waited for the demon to say something more, to reveal some further insight. But no sound came. She sat wrapped within the hot blackness of the burlap, embittered, frightened, and alone.

Then the feeders returned. When the touching began anew, her resolve gave way completely and she screamed soundlessly into the tape.

CHAPTER 24

Old Bob was finishing up the Sunday edition of the *Chicago Tribune* when the doorbell rang. He'd begun the paper early that morning before church and spent his free time during the course of the day working his way through its various sections. It was part of his Sunday ritual, an unhurried review of the events of the world with time enough to give some measured consideration to what they meant. He was sitting in his easy chair in the den, his feet up on the settee, and he glanced immediately at the wall clock.

Ten-forty. Late, for someone to be visiting.

He climbed to his feet and walked out into the hall, the first stirrings of anxiety roiling his stomach. Evelyn was already standing in the foyer, rooted in place six feet from the front door, as if this was as close as she dared to come. She held her cigarette in one hand, its smooth, white length burning slowly to ash, a silent measure of the promptness of his response. The look his wife gave him was unreadable. They had come home together at dusk, bidding John Ross good night and leaving Nest with her friends. They had unpacked the leftover food and eating utensils from the picnic basket, unloaded the cooler, and put away the blanket. Evelyn had barely spoken as they worked, and Old Bob had not asked what she was thinking.

"Open it, Robert," she said to him now as he came down the hall, as if he might have been considering something else.

He released the latch and swung the door wide. Four youngsters were huddled together in the halo of the porch light, staring back at him through the screen. Nest's friends. He recognized their faces and one or two of their names. Enid Scott's oldest boy. Cass Minter. John and Alice Heppler's son. That pretty little girl who always looked like she was on her way to a photo shoot.

The Heppler boy was the one who spoke. "Mr. Freemark, can you come help us find Nest, please? We've looked everywhere, and it's like she dropped into a hole or something. And we tried to find John Ross, like she asked, but he's disappeared, too. I think Danny Abbott knows what's happened to her, but he just laughs at us."

Robert Heppler, Old Bob remembered suddenly. That was the boy's name. What had he said? "What do you mean, Nest has dropped into a hole?"

"Well, she's been gone for close to two hours," Robert continued, his concern reflected in his narrow face. He pushed his glasses up on his nose and ran a hand through his unruly blond hair. "She went off after this guy, the one who's been poisoning the trees? The one you warned her about? She thought she saw him, so she . . ." He bit off whatever it was he was going to say and looked at the Scott boy. "Jared, you were there; you tell it."

Jared Scott looked pale and anxious as he spoke. His words were slow and measured. "We were dancing, me and Nest, and she saw this guy, like Robert says. She gets this funny look on her face and tells me he's the one who's been poisoning the trees, and I have to find Robert and Cass and Brianna and then we have to find John Ross and tell him to go after her. Then she runs off after this guy. So we all go looking for Mr. Ross, but we can't find him."

Old Bob frowned, thinking. Someone's poisoning trees?

"So, anyway, we can't find Mr. Ross," Robert interrupted Jared impatiently, "so we start looking around for Nest on our own. We try to find where she went, going off in the same direction, and that's when we run into Danny Abbott and his friends coming toward us. They're laughing and joking about something, and when they see us, they go quiet, then really start breaking up. I ask them if they've seen Nest, and they get all cute about it, saying, 'Oh, yeah, Nest Freemark, remember her?' and stuff like that. See, we had this run-in with them just the other day, and they're still pissed off. 'Scuse me. Upset. Anyway, I tell them this isn't funny, that there's a guy out there poisoning trees, and he might hurt Nest. Danny says something like 'What guy?' and I can tell he knows. Then he and his Neanderthal pals push me and Jared down and go right past us and back to the dance. That's when we decided to come get you."

Old Bob stood there, trying to sort the story through, trying to make some sense of it, still stuck on the part about someone poisoning trees in the park. It was Evelyn who spoke first.

"Robert," she said, coming forward now to stand in front of him, her eyes bright and hard in the porch light. There was no hesitation in her voice. "You get out there right away and find that girl and bring her home."

Old Bob responded with a quick nod, saying, "I will, Evelyn," then turned to Nest's friends and said, "You wait here," and went into the kitchen to find a flashlight. He was back in seconds, carrying a four-cell Eveready, his walk quick and certain. He touched his wife on the shoulder as he brushed past, said, "Don't worry, I'll find her," and went out the door and into the night.

When John Ross was able to stand again, Josie Jackson helped him walk back up the hill, bypass the crowded pavilion, and maneuver his way to her car. She wanted to drive him to the hospital, but he told her it wasn't necessary, that nothing was broken, which he believed, from experience, to be so. She wanted him to file a police report, but he declined that offer as well, pointing out that neither of them had the faintest idea who had attacked him (beyond the fact that they were probably MidCon union men) and that he was a stranger in the community, which usually didn't give you much leverage with the police in a complaint against locals.

"John, damn it, we have to do something about this!" she exclaimed as she eased him into the passenger seat of her Chevy, dabbing at his bloodied face with a handkerchief. She had stopped crying by now and was flushed with anger. "We can't just pretend that nothing happened! Look what they did to you!"

"Well, it was all a mistake," he alibied, forcing a smile through his swollen lips, trying to ease her concern and indignation, knowing it was the demon who was responsible and there was nothing to be done about it now. "Just take me back to the hotel, Josie, and I'll be fine."

But she wouldn't hear of it. It was bad enough that he wouldn't go to the emergency room or file a complaint with the police, but to expect her to take him back to the hotel and leave him was unthinkable. He was going to her house and spending the night so that she could keep an eye on him. He protested that he was fine, that he just needed to wash up and get a good night's sleep (ignoring the pain in his ribs, a clear indication one or more were cracked, and the throbbing in his head from what was, in all likelihood, a concussion), but she was having none of it. She could see the deep gash in his forehead, the cuts and bruises on his face, and the blood seeping through his torn clothing, and she was determined that someone would be there for him if he needed help. Her own face and clothing were streaked with blood and dirt, and her tousled hair was full of twigs and leaves, but she seemed oblivious of that.

"If I ever find out who did this . . ." she swore softly, leaving the threat unfinished.

He put his head back on the seat and closed his eyes as she pulled out of the parking lot and headed toward the highway. He was upset that he had been caught off guard by the attack and forced to use his magic to defend himself, but he was encouraged as well, because it implied that the demon was worried about him. Planting a suggestion in the minds of a bunch of MidCon strikers that he was a company spy was a desperate ploy by any measure. Perhaps his chances at stopping the demon were better than he believed. He wondered if he had missed something in his analysis of the situation, in the content of the dream that had brought him here. Josie told him to open his eyes, not to go to sleep yet, because concussions were nothing to fool with. He did as she advised, turning his head so that he could look at her face. She gave him a quick, sideways smile, warming him inside where thoughts of the demon had left a chill.

She drove him to her home, an aging, two-story wood frame house overlooking the Rock River at the bottom of a dead-end street. She parked in the driveway and came around to help him out. She walked him up the steps, her arm around his waist as he leaned on his staff to support his crippled leg, then guided him through the door and down a hall to the kitchen. She seated him at the wooden breakfast table, gathered up clean cloths, hot water, antiseptic, and bandages, and went to work on his injuries. She was quiet as she repaired his damaged face, her dark eyes intense, her hands gentle and steady. The house was silent about them. Her daughter was staying at a friend's, she explained, then quickly changed the subject.

"You really should have stitches for this," she said, fitting the butterfly bandages in place over the gash in his forehead, closing the wound as best she could. Her eyes left the injury and found his. "What happened out there? That white flash—it looked like something exploded."

He gave her his best sheepish grin. "Fireworks. I had them in my pocket. They spilled out on the ground during the fight, and I guess something caused them to ignite."

Her eyes moved away, back to his damaged face, but not before he caught a glimpse of the doubt mirrored there. "I'm sorry this happened," he said, trying to ease past the moment. "I was enjoying myself."

"Me, too. Hold still."

She finished with his face and moved down to his body. She insisted he remove his shirt, against his protests, and her brow furrowed with worry when she saw the deep bruises flowering over his ribs. "This is not good, John," she said softly.

She cleaned his scrapes and cuts, noting the way he winced when she put pressure on his ribs, then applied a series of cold compresses to the more severely damaged areas. She made him hot tea, then excused herself to go wash up. He heard her climb the stairs, then heard a shower running. He sipped at the tea and looked around the kitchen. It was filled with little touches that marked it as Josie's—a series of painted teakettles set along the top of the cupboards; pictures of her daughter, tacked to a bulletin board; drawings taped to the refrigerator that she must have done at different ages, some beginning to fray about the edges; fresh flowers in a vase at the window above the sink; and a small dish with cat food in it sitting by the back door. He studied the bright print curtains and wallpaper, the mix of soft yellows, blues, and pinks that trimmed out the basic white of the plaster and woodwork. He liked it here, he decided. He felt at home.

He was beginning to grow sleepy, so he refilled his teacup and drank deeply, trying to wake himself up with the caffeine. If he went to sleep now, he would dream. If he dreamed, he would be back in the future—only this time, because he had used the staff's magic to save himself in the present, he would be bereft of any protection until he woke. He knew what that would feel like. It had happened before. It would happen again. It was the price he paid for serving as a Knight of the Word. It was the cost of staying alive.

Josie came back downstairs in fuzzy slippers and a white bathrobe, her long, light hair shiny with dampness. She gave him her best smile, radiant and embracing, and asked how he was feeling. He told her he was better, admiring the fresh-scrubbed glow of her skin and the high curve of her cheekbones. She asked him if he was hungry, laughed when he told her no, made him some toast anyway, put out butter and jam, and sat down across from him to watch him eat. She sipped at her tea, telling him about the way her grandmother always made her toast and tea late at night when neither of them could sleep. Ross listened without saying much, finding he was hungry after all. He glanced once at the clock. It was after eleven, later than he had thought.

"Are you tired, John?" she asked when he was finished eating. "You must be. I think it's safe for you to sleep now."

He smiled at the thought. "I should be going, Josie."

She shook her head vehemently. "Not a chance, buster. You're staying here tonight. I've got too much invested in you to let you wander off to that hotel room alone." She paused, realizing the implication of what she had said. She recovered with a shrug. "I thought I made it pretty clear that I would feel better if you slept here tonight. Do you mind?"

He shook his head. "No, I just don't want to be underfoot. I feel bad enough about what's happened."

She stood up, tossing back her hair. "In more ways than one, I bet. You come with me."

She put her arm around his waist to help him to his feet, then kept it there as she guided him down the hall and up the stairs. The house was mostly dark; the light from the kitchen stretched only as far as the first half-dozen steps. After that, they were left in starlit gloom. Beneath their feet, the old wooden stairs creaked softly. Ahead, from farther down the hallway that connected the second-story rooms, lamplight glimmered softly. Ross felt his way up the stairs with his staff and Josie's surefooted guidance, taking his time, leaning on her even when it wasn't necessary, liking the feel of her body against his and the smell of her hair against his face.

"Careful, John," she cautioned as they made their way, her arm tightening about his waist, trying to stay below his injured ribs.

He winced silently. "I'm fine."

At the top of the stairs they paused for a moment, still locked together. "Okay?" she asked, and he nodded. She lifted her face and kissed him on the mouth. His lips were bruised and swollen, and her kiss was gentle. "Does that hurt?" she asked, and he shook his head wordlessly.

She eased him down the hall and into a darkened bedroom, a guest room, he decided, the large bed neatly made, the cushion of the love seat smooth and undisturbed, the dresser top bare. She left him just inside the doorway, moved to the bed, and pulled back the spread and covers. Then she came back for him and walked him over. He could hear the soft throbbing of an air conditioner in the window and feel the cool air on his bare arms and torso. The room was dark and the only light came from down the hallway and from the stars that shone faintly through the curtained window. She eased him onto the bed, bending close to kiss him on the forehead.

"Wait here," she said.

She left the room and disappeared down the hall. A moment later, the hallway light went out. She reappeared soundlessly, a shadowy figure in the gloom. She crossed to the bed and stood next to him, looking down. He could just make out the sheen of her tousled hair and the curve of her hip.

"Can you take the rest of your clothes off by yourself?" she asked.

He slipped off his walking shoes, socks, and jeans, then eased himself into the cool sheets, letting his head sink into the softness of the pillows. A profound weariness settled over him, and he knew that sleep would claim him soon. There was nothing he could do about it; he would sleep and then he would dream. But perhaps the dream would not be as bad as he feared.

"John?" Josie spoke his name softly in the dark.

He took a deep breath and let it out again slowly. "Yeah, I'm still here. I'll be all right, Josie. You go on to bed. Thanks again for . . ."

He felt her weight settle on the bed, and then she was lying next to him, pressing close, her cool arms enfolding him, her bathrobe gone. "I think I better stay with you," she whispered, kissing his cheek.

He closed his eyes against the smooth, soft feel of her body, against the soap scent of her skin and hair. "Josie . . ."

"John, do me a big favor," she interrupted him, her lips brushing his cheek. The fingers of one hand stroked his arm like threads of silk. "Don't say anything for a little while. I made it this far on raw courage and faith in my instincts. If you say the wrong thing, I'll fall to pieces. I don't want anything from you that you don't want to give me. I just want you to hold me for a while. And to let me hold you. That's all I want. Okay?"

Her touch made the pain in his body ease and his fear of sleep's approach lessen. He knew the risk of what he was doing, but he couldn't help himself. "Okay."

"Put your arms around me, please."

He did as she asked, drawing her close, and all the space between them disappeared.

Old Bob crossed the grassy expanse of Sinnissippi Park, heading straight for the pavilion and the crowd, his shoulders squared, his big face intense. Nest's friends struggled to keep up with him, whispering among themselves as they marked the determination in his long strides. Someone was gonna get it now, he heard the Heppler boy declare gleefully. He ignored the remark, his brow furrowed, his eyes troubled. Something wasn't right about all this. That Nest was missing was reason enough all by itself for concern, but this business about poisoning trees suggested a depth to the matter that he knew he didn't begin to understand. Nor did he like the fact that a bunch of older boys were involved. But mostly there was the look in Evelyn's eyes. Behind the worry and fear for the safety of their granddaughter, Old Bob had seen something else. Evelyn knew something about this, something that transcended the boundaries of his own knowledge. Another secret perhaps, or maybe just a suspicion. But the look was unmistakable.

He crossed the parking lot fronting the pavilion and slowed as he approached the crowd. The band was still playing and couples still danced beneath the colored lanterns and bunting. The humid night air was filled with the bright, clear sounds of laughter and conversation. He glanced over his shoulder for Nest's friends, then waited for them to catch up.

"Which one is Danny Abbott?" he asked.

They glanced about without answering. His heart tightened in his chest. If the boy had gone home, he was in trouble.

Then Brianna Brown said, "There he is."

She was pointing at a good-looking boy with dark hair and big shoulders standing in the shadows just beyond the tables where the soft drinks and lemonade were served. Some other boys were with him, and all of them were talking and joking with a pair of young girls dressed in cutoffs and halter tops.

Old Bob took a deep breath. "Stay here," he said, and started forward.

He was right on top of Danny Abbott before the boy saw him. He smiled when Danny turned and put a friendly arm about his shoulder, drawing him close, holding him fast. "Danny, I'm Robert Freemark, Nest's grandfather." He saw frightened recognition flood the boy's eyes. "Now, I don't want to waste any time on this, so I would appreciate a quick answer. Where is my granddaughter?"

Danny Abbott tried to back away, but Old Bob kept a tight hold on him, taking a quick measure of his friends to see if any of them meant trouble. No one looked anxious to get involved. The girls were already moving away. The boys looked eager to follow. "You gentlemen stick around a minute, please," he ordered, freezing them in their tracks.

"Mr. Freemark, I don't know what . . ." Danny Abbott began.

Old Bob moved his hand to the back of Danny's neck and squeezed hard enough to make the boy wince. "That's a bad beginning, son," he said quietly. "I know your father, Ed. Know your mother, too. They're good people. They wouldn't appreciate finding out that their son is a liar. Not to mention a few other things. So let's get this over with before I lose my temper. Where is Nest?"

"It was just a joke," one of the other boys mumbled, hands digging in his jeans pockets, eyes shifting away.

"Shut up, Pete!" Danny Abbott hissed furiously, the words out of his mouth before he could think better of them. Then he saw the look on Old Bob's face and went pale.

"One more chance, Danny," Old Bob told him softly. "Give me a straight answer and we'll put this behind us. No calls to your parents, nothing more between you and me. Otherwise, the next stop for both of us is the police station. And I will press charges. Are we clear on this?"

Danny Abbott nodded quickly, and his eyes dropped. "She's in the caves, taped up inside a gunnysack." His voice was sullen and afraid. "Pete's right, it was just a joke."

Old Bob studied him a moment, weighing the depth of the truth in the boy's words, then let him go. "If she's come to any harm," he said to all of them, looking deliberately from one face to the next, "you'll answer for it."

He walked back to where Nest's friends waited in a tight knot at the edge of the parking lot, their eyes bright with excitement. He surveyed the crowd, looking to see if there was anyone he could call upon to help. But none of the faces were familiar enough that he felt comfortable involving the few he recognized. He would have to do this alone.

He came up to Nest's friends and gave them a reassuring smile. "You young people go on home now," he told them. "I believe I know what's happened, and it's nothing serious. Nest is all right. You go on. I'll have her call you when she gets home."

He moved away from them without waiting for an answer, not wanting to waste any more time. He followed the edge of the paved road toward the west end of the park and the caves. He went swiftly and deliberately, and he did not look over his shoulder until he was well away from the crowd and deep into the darkness of the trees. No one followed him. He carried the flashlight loosely in his right hand, ready to use it for any purpose it required. He didn't think he would be attacked, but he wasn't discounting the possibility. He glanced around once more, saw nothing, no one, and turned his attention to the darkness ahead.

He followed the roadway to where it looped back on itself under the bridge and turned down. The streetlamps provided sufficient light that he was able to find his way without difficulty, keeping in the open where he could see any movement about him. He was sweating now from his exertion, the armpits and collar of his shirt damp, his forehead beaded. The park was silent about him, the big trees still, their limbs and leaves hanging limp and motionless in the heavy air, their shadows webbing the ground in strange, intricate patterns. A car's headlights flared momentarily behind him, then swung away, following the road leading out of the park. He passed beneath the shadow of the bridge and emerged in muted starlight.

"Hang on, Nest," he whispered quietly.

He moved quickly down the road toward the black mouth of the caves. The river was a silver-tipped satin sheet on his left and the cliffs towered blackly above him on his right. His shoes crunched softly on gravel. In his mind, he saw again the look in Evelyn's eyes, and a cold feeling reached down into his stomach. What did she know that she was hiding from him? He thought suddenly of Caitlin, falling from these same cliffs more than a dozen years earlier to land on the rocks below, broken and lifeless. The image brought a bloodred heat to his eyes and the back of his throat. He could not stand it if he were to lose Nest, too. It would be the end of him—the end of Evelyn as well. It would be the end of everything.

He reached the entrance to the caves and flicked on the flashlight. The four-cell beam cut a bright swath through the darkness, reaching deep into the confines of the rock. He worked his way carefully forward, pausing to listen, hearing something almost immediately—a muffled sound, a movement. He scrambled ahead, plunging inside the caves now, swinging the flashlight's beam left and right with frantic movements, searching the jagged terrain.

Then abruptly the light found her. He knew at once it was Nest, even though she was trussed up inside a gunnysack with only her ankles and feet showing. He scrambled forward, calling out to her, stumbling several times on the loose rock before he reached her.

"Nest, it's me, Grandpa," he said, breathing heavily, thinking, *Thank God, thank God!* He reached into his pants and brought out his pocketknife to cut away the tape and burlap from her ankles. When that was done and the sack was removed, he cut the tape from her hands as well. Then, as gently as he could, he pulled the last strip off her mouth.

Her arms came around him at once. "Grandpa, Grandpa," she sobbed, shaking all over, tears running down her cheeks.

"It's all right, Nest," he whispered softly, stroking her hair the way he had when she was a little girl. "It's all right, kiddo. You're all right."

Then he picked her up, cradling her in his big arms as he would a baby, and carried her back out into the night.

Jared Scott raced across the front lawn of his apartment building, dark hair flying, T-shirt laced with sweat. He caught a glimpse of the television screen through the curtained windows of his living room and knew his mother and George were inside. He picked up his pace, anxious to tell them what had happened, all about Nest and Danny Abbott and Mr. Freemark. He burst through the screen door already yelling.

"Mom, some guys kidnapped Nest and took her down to the caves, and we told Mr. Freemark to come help us . . ."

He drew up short at the living-room entrance, the words freezing in his throat. His mother lay on the couch with George Paulsen next to her. Most of their clothes were on the floor. There were beer cans everywhere.

His mother tried to cover herself with her arms, smiling weakly, ashen-faced as he stared at her.

"Jared, sweetie . . ."

Jared backed away, averting his eyes. "Sorry, Mom, I just . . ."

"What the hell do you think you're doing, you little bastard!" George roared, scrambling up from the couch, lurching toward him in fury.

"George, he didn't mean anything!" His mother was trying to slip back into her blouse, her movements cumbersome and slow.

Jared tried to run, but he caught his foot on the carpet and slipped. George was on top of him instantly, hauling him back to his feet by his shirtfront, yelling at him, screaming at him. Jared tried to say he was sorry, tried to say something in his defense, but George was shaking him so hard he couldn't get the words out. His mother was yelling, too, her face flushed and her eyes bright as she stumbled across the littered floor.

Then George struck him across the face with his hand, and without thinking twice, Jared struck him back. He caught George flush on the nose, and blood spurted out. George released him and stumbled back in surprise, both hands going to his face. In that instant, something raw surged through Jared Scott. He remembered the way Old Bob Freemark had walked up to Danny Abbott and his friends and confronted them. He remembered the set of the old man's shoulders and the determination in his eyes.

"You get out of here!" he shouted at George, bracing himself in a fighter's stance, raising his fists threateningly. "This isn't your home! It's mine and my brothers' and my sisters' and my mom's!"

For a moment George Paulsen just stood there, blood running down his mouth and chin, shock registering on his face. Then a wild look came into his eyes, and he threw himself on Jared, catching him by the throat and bearing him to the floor. Jared twisted and squirmed, trying to get away, but George held him down, screaming obscenities. George rose over him and began to hit him with his fists, striking him in the face with solid, vicious blows that rocked his head and brought bright lights to his eyes. He tried to cover up, but George just knocked his hands aside and kept hitting him. Then dark shapes swarmed out of the shadows, things Jared had never seen before, eyes cat-bright and wild. They fell on George with the raw hunger of predators, their supple, invasive limbs twisting about him, ensnaring him, molding to his body. Their presence seemed to drive George to an even greater frenzy. The blows quickened, and Jared's defenses began to collapse. His mother began screaming, begging George to stop. There was the sound of bones snapping, and a warm rush of blood flooded Jared's mouth and throat.

Then the pain froze him, and all sound and movement ceased, disappearing like a movie's final scene into slow, hazy blackness.

At the beginning of the roadway leading up under the bridge to the cliffs. Nest asked her grandfather to set her on her feet again. She had stopped crying, and her legs were steady enough to support her. Once righted, she stared out across the river for long moments, collecting herself, trying to blot the memory of what had happened from her mind. Her grandfather stood next to her and waited in silence.

"I'm all right," she said finally, repeating his words back to him.

They walked up the road side by side, the old man and the girl, no longer touching, saying nothing, eyes lowered to the pavement. They passed under the bridge and came out of the darkness onto the park's grassy flats. Nest glanced about surreptitiously for the feeders, for their eyes, for some small movement that would signal their presence, but found nothing. She could still feel their hands on her, feel them worming their way beneath her skin, into her blood and her bones, past all her defenses, deep inside where her fear and rage roiled and they might feed.

She felt violated and ashamed, as if she had been stripped naked and left soiled and debased.

"How did you find me?" she asked, keeping her eyes lowered so he could not see what was reflected there.

"Your friends," her grandfather replied, not looking at her. "They came to the house, brought me out to look for you."

She nodded, thinking now of Danny Abbott and the demon, and she was about to say something more when they heard the heavy boom of a shotgun. Her grandfather's white head lifted. Both stopped where they were, staring out into the darkness. The shotgun fired again. And again. Six times, it roared.

"Evelyn," Nest heard her grandfather whisper hoarsely.

And then he was running through the park for the house.

Chapter 25

Evelyn Freemark walked out onto the big veranda porch and watched Robert and the children disappear around the corner of the house, headed for the park in search of Nest. Even when they were no longer in sight, swallowed up by the night's blackness, she stared after them, standing in the yellow halo of the light cast by the porch lamp, motionless as her thoughts drifted back through the years to Nest and Caitlin and her own childhood. She had lived a long life, and she was always surprised on looking back at how quickly the time had passed and how close together the years had grown.

The screen door started to swing shut behind her, and she reached back automatically to catch it and ease it carefully into place. In the deep night silence, she could hear the creak of its hinges and springs like ghost laughter.

After a moment, she began to look around, searching the shadows where the lawn lengthened in a darkening carpet to the shagbark hickories fronting the walk leading in from Woodlawn Road and to the mix of blue spruce and walnut that bracketed the corners of their two-acre lot. She knew already what she would find, but the porch light was blinding her. She reached inside the doorway and shut it off, leaving her in darkness. Better, she thought. She could see them clearly now, the gleaming yellow eyes, dozens strong, too many to be coincidental, too many to persuade her she had guessed wrong about what was going to happen.

She smiled tightly. If you understood them well enough, the feeders could tell you things even without speaking.

Her eyes were fully adjusted to the darkness now, able to trace the angular shapes of the trees, the smooth spread of the lawn, the flat, broad stretch of the roadway, and the low, sprawling roofs of the houses farther down the way. She gave the landscape a moment's consideration, then turned her attention to the porch on which she stood—to its eaves and railings, its fitted ceiling boards, and its worn, tongue-and-groove wooden flooring. Finally her eyes settled on the old peg oak rocker that had been with her from the time of her marriage to Robert. She could trace the events of her life by such things. This house had borne mute witness to the whole of her married life—to the joy and wonder she had been privileged to experience, to the tragedy and loss she had been forced to suffer. These walls had given her peace when it was needed. They had lent her strength. They were part of her, rooted deep within her heart and soul. She smiled. She could do worse than end her life here.

She gave the feeders another quick study, then slipped through the screen door and walked to the back of the house. She would have to hurry. If the demon was coming for her, as she was certain now he was, he would not waste any time. With Robert out of the way, he would hasten to put an end to matters quickly. He would be confident that he could do so. She was old and worn, and no longer a match for him. She laughed to herself. He was predictable in ways he did not begin to recognize, and in the end they would prove his undoing.

She went past her own bedroom and into Robert's. She no longer slept there, but she cleaned for him, and she knew where he kept his things. She clicked on the bedside lamp and went into his closet, the light spilling after her in a bright sliver through the cracked door. In the rear of his closet was a smaller door that opened into a storage area. She found the key on the shelf above, where she knew he kept it, fitted the key in place, and released the lock.

Inside was the twelve-gauge pump-action shotgun he had once used for hunting and now kept mostly out of habit. She removed it from its leather slipcase and brought it into the light. The polished wooden stock and smooth metal barrel gleamed softly. She knew he cleaned it regularly, that it would fire if needed. There were boxes of shells in a cardboard box at the back of the storage area. She brought the box into the closet and opened it, bypassing the birdshot for the heavier double-ought shells that could blow a hole through you the size of a fist if the range was close and your aim true. Her hands were steady as she slid six shells through the loading slot into the magazine and dumped another six in a pocket of her housedress.

She stood motionless then, looking down at the shotgun, thinking that it had been almost ten years since she had fired it. She had been a good shot once, had hunted alongside Robert in the crisp fall days when duck season opened and the air smelled musky and the wind had a raw edge. It was a long time ago. She wondered if she could still fire this weapon. It felt familiar and comfortable in her hands, but she was old and not so steady. What if her strength failed her?

She chambered a shell with a quick, practiced movement of her hands, checked to make certain the safety was on, and smiled wryly. That would be the day.

Shotgun in hand, she exited the closet and moved back through the house. She stopped off in Nest's room long enough to scribble a few words on a piece of notebook paper, which she then tucked under her granddaughter's favorite down pillow. Satisfied that she had done what she could, she advanced down the hallway on mouse paws, listening to the silence, feeling the tension within her beginning to mount. It would happen quickly now. She was glad Robert was not there, that she did not have to worry about him. By the time he returned with Nest, it would be over. She wasn't really worried about the girl, despite the urgency of her admonition to Robert to find her. Nest was better protected than any of them; she had seen to that. The monster that had appeared to threaten her didn't know the half of it.

She emerged from the house with the shotgun pressed against her side where it could not be clearly seen, and she stopped just beyond the screen door to survey the darkness beyond, her senses alert. Nothing had changed. He was not there yet. Only the feeders had gathered. She moved down the porch to where her rocker was situated, leaned the gun up against the wall in the deep shadows, and settled herself comfortably in place.

Yea, though I walk through the valley of the shadow of death, I shall fear no evil . . .

The demon would come for her. It would come for her because it hated her for what she had done to it all those years ago and because she was the one human it feared. Odd, that it should still feel this way, now that she was old and frail and virtually powerless. She wondered at the symmetry of life, at the ways the good and the bad of what you did came back to repay you, to reveal you. She had made so many mistakes, but she had made good choices, too. Robert, for openers. He had loved her through everything, even when Caitlin's death had shattered her and her drinking and smoking had left her dissipated and hollowed out and bereft of peace. And Nest, linked to her by blood and magic, the image of herself as a girl, but stronger and more controlled. She closed her eyes momentarily, thinking of her granddaughter. Nest, sweet child, who stood unseeing at the center of the maelstrom that was about to commence.

"Good evening, Evelyn."

Her eyes snapped open, raking the dark. She recognized his voice instantly, the smooth, insinuating lilt rising softly out of the heat. He was standing just off the walk, not quite close enough that she could see him clearly.

She tried to still the shaking inside, rocking slowly to settle her fear. "You took your time," she said.

"Well, time has never been of much concern to me." She could feel as much as see his smile. "It's too bad you can't say the same, Evelyn. You have grown quite old."

She was briefly angry, but she kept her voice calm. "Well, I don't pretend to be something I'm not, either. I'm pretty well content with being who I am. I've learned to live with myself. I doubt that you can say the same."

The demon chuckled, crossing his arms on his chest. "Oh, that's a terrible lie, Evelyn! Shame on you! You hate yourself! You hate your life!" The laugh died away. "That's why you drink and smoke and hide out in your house, isn't it? It wasn't like that before. You should have embraced the magic in the same way I did, years ago, when you were still young and pretty and talented. You had that chance, and you gave it up. You gave me up as well. Look at what it's cost you. So, please. I think I can live with myself better than you can." He paused. "Which is what matters have to come down to, haven't they?"

She nodded. "I suppose they have."

The demon studied her. "You knew I'd come back to finish things, didn't you? You didn't think you could escape me?"

"Not for a moment. But I'm surprised you thought you needed help."

He stared at her, a hint of confusion in his bland face. "I'm afraid you've lost me."

"John Ross."

The demon snorted. "Oh, Evelyn, don't be obtuse. Ross is a creature of the Word. He's been tracking me for some time. Without much success, I might add."

Well, well, it seems I was wrong about Mr. Ross, she thought in surprise.

The demon was watching her closely. "Don't get your hopes up, dear heart. John Ross is not going to change the outcome of things. I've already seen to that."

"I expect you have," she replied quietly.

He made a point of glancing around then, a slow, casual survey of the shadows. His smile was empty and cold. "Look who's come to say good-bye to you."

She had already seen them. Feeders by the dozens, slinking out of the darkness to gather at the edges of the light, crowding forward in anticipation, eyes unblinking and expressionless, dark bodies coiled. Some had already advanced to the far ends of the porch, their heads pressed up against the railing like grotesque children in search of a treat.

She gave him a flat, hard stare. "Perhaps they've come to say good-bye to you, instead." She beckoned casually. "Step closer so I can see you better."

The demon did so, moving just out of the shadows, his arms loose, his pale, washed-out blue eyes looking almost sleepy.

"Oh, you've changed considerably," she told him. "If you think I've aged, you ought to take a close look at yourself. Is that the best you can do? Did you sell your soul for so little? How sad."

There was a long silence between them. Then the demon whispered, "This is the end of the line for you, Evelyn."

She rose to her feet and stood looking at him, feeling small and vulnerable in the presence of his strength. But she was buttressed by her anger and by her certainty that he was not half so clever as he thought. She moved slowly around to the back of her rocker and leaned on it, giving him a broad, sardonic smile.

"Why don't you come up on the porch so we can discuss it?" she said.

He smiled in return. "What are you up to, Evelyn?" He cocked his head to one side as if reflecting on the possibilities.

She waited patiently, saying nothing, and after a moment he started toward her, accepting her challenge. The feeders trailed after him, skittish with anticipation. She had not seen so many in one place in years. Not since she had played with them at night in the park as a young girl. Not since the demon and she were lovers. The memories roiled within her, a bitter stirring of emotions that turned the night's heat and darkness suffocating.

When he was almost to the steps, she reached behind her for the shotgun and brought it up in a single, smooth movement so that the long barrel was leveled directly at his chest. She flipped off the safety and placed her finger over the trigger. He was less than fifteen feet away, a clear target. He stopped instantly, genuine surprise showing on his face.

"You can't hurt me with that," he said.

"I can blow that disguise you're hiding behind to smithereens," she declared calmly. "And it will take you a while to put together another, won't it? A little extra time might be all I need and more than you can afford."

He laughed softly in response, his hands clasping before him as if in childish admiration. "Evelyn, you are astonishing! I missed it completely! How could I have been so stupid? You've lost your use of the magic, haven't you? That's why you have the shotgun! Your magic doesn't work anymore!" He grinned, excited by his discovery. "And to think I was worried that you might prove troublesome. Tell me. What happened? Did you use it all up? No, you wouldn't have done that. You were saving it to use against me. Or against yourself. Remember how you threatened to do that when you found out what I was? That was a long time ago. Oh, I hated you so for that! I've waited patiently to make you pay for what you did to me. But there was always your magic to consider, wasn't there?" He paused. "Ah-ha! That's it! You lost it because you *didn't* use it! You worked so hard at hoarding it, you grew old and tired and lost it completely! That's why you haven't come after me. That's why you've waited for me to come to you. Oh, dear! Poor Evelyn!"

"Poor you," she replied, snapped the gun stock to her shoulder, and blew a hole right through his chest. The whole front of his shirt exploded in a gruesome red shower and the demon was knocked backward onto the shadow-streaked lawn.

Except that a moment later, he wasn't there at all. He simply disappeared, fading away into the ether. Then abruptly he reappeared six feet farther to the right, unharmed, standing there looking at her, laughing softly.

"Your aim was a little off." He smirked.

Feeders raced back and forth, darting toward her with lightning-quick rushes, frantic with hunger. She realized at once what had happened. It wasn't the demon she had fired at. It was an illusion he had created to fool her.

"Good-bye, Evelyn," he whispered.

His hand lifted in a casual gesture, drawing her eyes to his, and she felt a crushing force close about her chest. She wrenched her eyes away, brought up the shotgun, and fired a second time. Again, the demon's chest blew apart and he was flung away. The feeders ran in all directions, clawing their way onto the porch only to leap off again, lantern eyes wild with expectation. Evelyn was already swinging the barrel of the shotgun about, searching for him, firing both left and right of where he had been, the heavy shot ripping the air, lead pellets hammering into the fence posts at the gate and into the trunks of the old shagbarks and the graceful limbs of the spruce. Lights started to come on in the houses closest to hers.

"Damn you!" she hissed.

She racked the slide a fifth time, chambering a fresh shell, swung the barrel to her right, where the feeders were massed thickest, and fired into their midst, the shotgun booming. Her arms and shoulders throbbed with weariness and pain, and her rage burned in her throat and chest like fire. One shell left. She saw him climbing over the railing at the other end of the porch, pumped the final shell into the firing chamber, swung the shotgun left, and fired down the length of the house.

Reload!

She backed against the screen door and fumbled for the shells in her dress pocket, kicking at the empties underfoot. He was right in front of her then, reaching out his hand. She felt his fingers on her chest, pressing. The shotgun fell away as she sought to claw his face.

Then the feeders swarmed over her, and everything disappeared in a bright red haze.

George Paulsen ran from the Sinnissippi Townhomes and the screams of Enid Scott, his hands covering his face. He burst through the screen door of the Scott apartment with such force that he ripped it from its hinges and tore the skin from his hands. There was blood on him everywhere, and the stink of it was in his nostrils. But it was not from the screams or the blood or even the ragged, broken form he had left crumpled on the living-room floor that he fled.

It was from Evelyn Freemark.

She was right in front of him, a shimmering image come out of the ether, dark and spectral. No matter which way he turned, there she was. She whispered at him, repeating the words she had spoken earlier that day in the park, her dark warning of what would happen if he laid a hand on Enid Scott or her children. He screamed against the persistent sound of it, tearing at the air and at his own face. He ran mindlessly across the barren dirt yard into the roadway, desperate to escape.

The dark things bounded after him, the creatures that had appeared as he beat aside Jared Scott's futile defenses. They had encouraged him to hurt the boy; they had wanted the boy to suffer.

But now they were coming after him as well.

He could feel their hunger in the ragged sound of their breathing.

Oh, God! Oh, God! He screamed the words over and over into the silence and the dark.

Staggering blindly up the roadway, he crested the rise that led out to Lincoln Highway, and a car came out of the lights of the buildings ahead. George Paulsen lurched aside as the car raced past, its horn blaring angrily. The dark things caught him then, bore him back against the cemetery fence, and began to rip him apart. His insides were being shredded beneath their claws and teeth; he could hear himself shriek. With the dark things clinging to him, he turned toward the cemetery fence and scrambled up the chain links. He reached the top, lost his footing, and slid back heavily. He grabbed for something to slow his fall, hooked his fingers into the mesh, and caught his neck on the exposed edges of a gap near the fence top.

Jagged steel sliced through soft flesh and exposed arteries, and George Paulsen's blood gushed forth. He sagged weakly, pain flooding through him. The dark things slowed their attack, closing on him more deliberately, taking their time. He wouldn't escape them now, he knew. He closed his eyes against his fear and desperation. They were touching him, their fingers dipping experimentally in his blood. *Oh, God!*

A moment later, the life went out of him.

Chicago is afire. Everywhere the Knight of the Word looks the flames rise up against the darkening skyline, bleeding their red glare into the smoky twilight. It is an exceptionally hot, dry summer, and the parched grasses that fill the empty parks and push through the cracks in the concrete burn readily. The homes closest to the hollowed-out steel-and-glass monoliths of the abandoned downtown wait their turn, helpless victims of the destruction that approaches. Down along the piers and shipyards, old storage tanks and fuel wells blaze brightly, the residue of their contents exploding like cannon shots.

John Ross jogs quickly along the walkway bordering the Chicago River, moving south from the breach in the fortress walls. He carries his staff before him, but he has temporarily lost the use of its magic, the consequence of another of those times in the past when he was forced to call upon it—before the Armageddon, before the fall. Thus he must flee and hide as common men. Already, his enemies look for him. They have tracked him here, as they track him everywhere, and they know that somewhere in the conflagration he will be found. A Knight of the Word is a great prize, and those who find him will be well rewarded. But they know, too, that he will not be taken easily, and their caution gives him an edge.

He has come late to the city's fall. The attack has been in progress for months, the once-men and their demon masters laying siege to the makeshift walls and reinforced gates that keep the people within protected. Chicago is one of the strongest bastions remaining, a military camp run with discipline and skill, its people armed and trained. But no bastion is impregnable, and the attackers have finally found a way in. He is told they gain entry through the sewers, that there is no longer any way of keeping them out. Now the end is at hand, and there is nothing anyone can do but flee or die.

Bodies line the streets, flung casually aside by those who leave them lifeless. Men, women, and children—no exceptions are made. Slaves are plentiful and food is scarce. Besides, a lesson is needed. Feeders slink through the shadows, working their way from corpse to corpse, seeking a shred of fading life, of pain, of horror, of helpless rage, of shock and anguish on which to feed. But the battle moves on to other places, and so the feeders follow after. Ross works his way along a brick wall fronting the postage-stamp yards of a line of abandoned brick homes, searching for a way out, listening to the screams and cries of those who have failed to do so. The attack shifts to a point ahead of him, and he recognizes the danger. He must turn back. He must find another way. But his options are running out, and without the magic to protect him he is less certain of what he should do.

Finally he begins to retrace his steps, angling west toward the outskirts of the city, away from Lake Michigan and the downtown. It will be nightfall soon, and the hunters will not find him so easily. If he can reach the freeways, he can follow them into the suburbs and be gone before they realize he has escaped. His throat is dry, and his muscles ache, for he has not slept in days. His coming to the city was in response to a dream that foretold of its destruction. But he is mistrusted everywhere, a Cassandra crying out in the wilderness of a crumbling Troy, and his warnings are ignored. Some would imprison him as a spy. Some would throw him from the walls. If they did not fear his magic, he would already be dead. It is a pointless, debilitating life he leads, but it is all he has left.

He comes up against a firefight at an intersection in the streets and spins quickly back into a shadowed niche to hide from the combatants. Automatic weapons riddle wooden doors and pock brick walls and take the lives of everyone caught in their field of fire. The feeders frolic through the carnage, leaping and twisting with unrestrained glee, feeding on the rage and fear of the combatants. Killing is the most powerful form of madness and therefore the feeders' strongest source of food, and they are drawn to it as flies to blood. No sounds come from them, nor is any form of recognition accorded them, for they are a silent, invisible presence. But in their lantern eyes Ross sees the pleasure they derive from the dark emotions the killing releases, and he is reminded of the Furies in the old Greek myths, driving insane those who had committed unconscionable crimes. If there were Furies in real life, he thinks, they would be mothers to these feeders.

When the fighting dies away, he moves on, running swiftly toward the confluence of freeways that lead into the city from the west, anxious to find his way clear. Night slips down about him like window shades drawn against the smoky, fiery light of the city's destruction. The smells that assail his nostrils are acrid and rank—charred flesh and blackened blood. Disease will follow, and many of those who do not die in the fighting will die in the aftermath. Thousands are driven from this city into the wilderness. How many will survive to take refuge somewhere else?

He reaches the arterials winding into the main east/west freeway, but the attackers throng from all quarters before him, lining the four-lane, gathering for an unknown reason. He edges back cautiously and works his way down the backyards of houses and the shattered glass fronts of businesses to where those who celebrate do not mass so thickly. He finds a rise on which an abandoned housing development is settled, and he enters a house that gives him a clear view of the freeway leading in. From an upstairs window, he looks out on a grand procession approaching from the west. He uses his binoculars to get a clearer look, a cold suspicion beginning to surface.

There, on the buckled, cracked ribbon of concrete that spreads like a length of worn pewter into the horizon, he sees the first lines of captured humans, shackled and bent as they shuffle forward in long trains, their lives spared so that they may serve as slaves. Cages on wheels contain those who will be accorded a special death. Heads strung on ropes and mounted on poles attest to the number who have found death already.

Then he sees her. She rides on a flatbed wagon pulled by several dozen of those she has subjugated. She sits amid the demons who are her favorites, tall, regal, and as cold as death, queen of the destruction she surveys. Her history is legend. She was a world-class athlete who medaled twice in the Olympics. She became an activist, first for reform, later for revolution, gifted with charismatic speaking powers. She was revered and trusted by everyone, and she betrayed them all. Along the freeway, the once-men who serve her go quiet and bow their heads in obeisance. John Ross feels his stomach knot. Even from where he hides he can see the emptiness in her eyes. She is devoid of emotion, as dead inside as the creatures she has crushed in her passing. She is a pivotal figure in the Void's implacable war against the Word. She is John Ross's greatest failure.

He knew her when she was different, many years ago, when there was still time to save her.

He knew her as Nest Freemark.

Monday, July 4

CHAPTER 26

Nest Freemark woke to the sound of voices, hushed and cautious outside her bedroom door. The big floor fan had been turned off and shoved to one side and the door closed, so she could not see who was there. She tried to pick up on what was being said, but the words were indistinct. She lay facing the door, staring at its familiar paneled frame, the bed-sheet pulled up to her chin, her fists clenched about the wrinkled border. She did not know when she had finally fallen asleep or how long she had slept. The room's light was gray and muted, and the temperature cool, so she thought it might only be dawn. But when she looked at her bedside clock, she saw it was almost noon.

She took a deep breath and exhaled slowly, then turned over to look out the window. A small section of the sky was visible through the curtains. Clouds drifted slowly across the blue expanse, and the sun cast their shadows on the earth and marked their passing with changes in the light. The breeze that wafted through her open window smelled damp and fetid.

Had it rained during the night? Her thoughts drifted. Gran had always loved the sound of falling rain.

Her eyes teared, and she brushed at them quickly. She would not cry again—not right away. She had cried enough. She felt something scratchy against her bare elbow, and she reached beneath the covers to extract Gran's crumpled note. She had found it beneath her pillow when her grandfather had finally gotten her to bed—after they had taken Gran away, after all the policemen, medics, firemen, and neighbors had gone, after she had refused over and over again to go somewhere else for the night. Alone in the darkness of her room, trapped in the downward spiral of her sadness and rage, she had curled into a ball atop her sheets, the fan blowing cool air over her heated skin, her eyes scrunched tight against her horror and misery, and clutched her pillow to her face. That was when her fingers had come upon the note. She had pulled it out, opened it, and stared at it in disbelief. The note was from Gran. She had read it so many times since that she knew the words by heart.

When he comes for you,
use your magic.
Trust Wraith.

Love you.
Gran

She looked at the writing again now, trying to gain some new insight, to find hidden meaning behind the words. But the note was straightforward and the warning it contained unmistakable. Gran had written the note in the moments before she died. She had written it, in all probability, knowing she was going to die. Nest had thought it all through carefully, looking it over from every conceivable viewpoint, and argued the possibilities with herself until she was certain. The police and the firemen and the medics and the neighbors might agree among themselves that Gran was an old drunk who saw things that weren't there and finally drank so much she took out a shotgun to blow away her phantoms and brought on the heart attack that killed her. They might dismiss her with a shrug, a few words of sympathy, and an unspoken conviction that anyone crazy enough to go around shooting holes in trees and fences was just asking for trouble. They might sleep a whole lot better living with that explanation than with the truth. But the fact remained that the truth was something else entirely. Gran wasn't dead because she drank or she was crazy. She was dead because the demon had killed her.

I have enemies to eliminate.

Nest could still hear his words, spoken to her in the blackness of the caves, disembodied and remote and rife with malice. The demon had gone about the business of eliminating Gran quite deliberately. He had taken great pains to sidetrack everyone who might protect her, and then he had come for her. Nest knew it was so. She had never been so certain of anything in her life.

Now Gran was warning her, in the crumpled note she held in her hands, that the demon was coming for her as well.

Why?

Nest had pondered the question all night and she still didn't have an answer. She had assumed all along that the demon's interest in her was strictly secondary to his interest in Gran or John Ross, that he was using her to get to them. But Gran's note suggested that his intentions were more personal. Gran obviously believed the demon was after Nest as well. *Use your magic. Trust Wraith.* Gran could have written anything in those last few moments, but she had chosen to write this.

Why?

Because Gran had thought it more important than anything else. Because she knew what was going to happen.

Which was more than Nest could say.

What did the demon want with her?

She rolled onto her back and stared at the flat surface of the ceiling. *Use your magic. Trust Wraith.* As if the magic had done Gran any good. And where was Wraith last night when she was fighting to keep her sanity as the feeders crawled all over her? Why should she believe either one would be of any use against the demon? Questions buzzed in her mind like gnats, and she closed her eyes against their persistent whine. The answers that would silence them were nowhere to be found. God, she was going to miss Gran. Her eyes filled with tears immediately. She still couldn't believe her grandmother was gone, that she wasn't sitting there at the kitchen table with her orange juice and vodka and her cigarette and ashtray, that she wouldn't be asking Nest what time she planned to be home from the fireworks that night, that she wouldn't be there to talk about the feeders and the forest creatures and the magic in the park.

Nest sobbed quietly. She could still see the look on Gran's face as she lay lifeless on the porch, the shotgun clutched in her hands. She would always see that look, a cold haunting at the fringes of her warmer memories. She had known the truth about how Gran died the instant she had seen her face. The note only confirmed it.

She turned on her side again, staring at the curtained window and the clouded sky beyond. The back of her throat ached with what she was feeling. She would never get over this, she thought. She would never be the same again.

Footsteps approached along the hallway beyond her room and stopped outside her door. A moment later the door opened, and someone stepped inside. She lay without moving, listening to the silence. She hoped that whoever was there would go away.

"Nest?" her grandfather called softly.

She did not respond, but he crossed to the bed anyway and sat down next to her.

"Did you sleep at all?" he asked.

She closed her eyes against the sound of his voice. "Yes."

"That's good. I know it wasn't easy. But you needed to get some rest." He was quiet for a few moments, and she could feel his eyes on her. She remained motionless beneath the sheet, curled into herself. "Are you hungry?"

"No."

"There's a lot of food out there. People have been stopping by all morning, bringing casseroles and tins filled with everything you can imagine." He chuckled softly. "Looks like some of them emptied out their entire kitchens. We've got enough food to feed an army. I don't know what we're going to do with all of it."

His hand rested on her shoulder. "Why don't you get up and come out and keep me company?"

She was silent a moment, thinking it over. "I heard voices."

"Friends. Neighbors. Everyone's gone now. It's just you and me." He shifted on the bed, and she could hear him sigh. "They say she didn't suffer, Nest. She was gone almost right away. Massive heart attack. I spoke with the doctor a little while ago. He was very kind. I've got to go down to the funeral home and pick out a casket this afternoon. A notice has already been sent to the paper. Reverend Emery helped prepare it. He's agreed to speak at the funeral on Thursday."

He trailed off, as if he didn't quite know where to go next. In the silence, Nest could hear the old clock ticking down the hall.

After a moment, her grandfather said quietly, his voice filled with sadness, "I just don't understand."

She nodded without offering a reply, thinking that she understood better than he did, but didn't know how to explain it to him.

His hand tightened on her shoulder. "You might have heard some comments last night, loose talk about your grandmother. You'll probably hear more. I don't want you to pay any attention to it. Your grandmother was a special person. A lot of people didn't understand that. They thought she was peculiar. I guess she was, but she was good-hearted and caring and she knew how to look after people. You know that. And I don't care what anyone says, she wasn't out there shooting that shotgun at nothing. Your grandmother wasn't like that."

"I know," Nest said quickly, hearing the despair build in his voice.

She twisted about so that she could see his face. It looked careworn and tired, the age lines more deeply etched, the thick white hair mussed and badly combed. When she looked into his eyes she could tell he had been crying.

His voice shook. "She was fine when I left her, Nest. She was worried about you, of course, but she was fine. I just don't know what happened. I don't think she would have brought out the shotgun if she wasn't in danger. She hasn't even looked at it in years."

He paused, his eyes searching her face. He was waiting for her to speak, to respond to his comments. When she stayed silent, he cleared his throat, and his voice steadied again.

"Your young friends said something strange when they came by the house to ask me to help look for you last night. They said you were chasing after someone who was poisoning trees in the park, someone I'd told you about. But I don't know anything about this." He looked away a moment. "The thing of it is, Nest, I get the feeling I don't know anything about a lot of what's going on. It wasn't so important before." His eyes shifted back to her. "But after what happened last night, I guess now it is."

His eyes stayed locked on hers. Nest felt like a deer caught in the headlights. She didn't know what to say. She didn't even know where to begin.

"Can we talk about this a little later, Grandpa?" she said finally. "I just can't do it right now."

He considered her request a moment, and then nodded. "All right, Nest. That seems fair." He rose, his eyes traveling about the room as if seeking something. "Will you come out and eat?"

She raised herself to a sitting position and forced a smile. "Sure. Just give me a minute, okay?"

He went back through the door and closed it softly behind him. Nest sat in the bed without moving, staring into space. What could she say to him? She got up finally and went into the bathroom and took a shower. She let the water wash over her for a long time, her eyes closed, her thoughts wandering off to other times and places, then returning to focus on what lay ahead. She dried off and began to dress. She had just finished pulling on shorts and a T-shirt and was bending down to tie her tennis shoes when she heard a scrabbling sound at the window.

"Nest!" Pick called urgently.

"Pick!" she exclaimed in relief, and rushed over to push aside the curtains.

The sylvan was standing on the sill looking disheveled and grimy, as if he had been rolled in dirt. His leafy head was soiled and his twiggy feet were caked with mud. "I'm sorry to be late, girl. I've had a dreadful night! If I don't get some help, I don't know what I'm going to do! The balance of things is upset in a way I've never seen! The feeders are all over the place!" He caught his breath, and his face softened. "I heard from Daniel about your grandmother. I'm sorry, Nest. I can't believe it happened."

"Was it the demon?" she asked quickly.

"Of course it was the demon!" He was so matter-of-fact about it, so unshakably certain, so *Pick*, that she smiled in spite of herself. Pick scowled. "The stink of his magic is all over your front yard! He must have come right up to the front door! How did he do that? Where were you and your grandfather?"

Quickly she filled him in on what had happened—how she had been lured away from the dance by the demon, how Danny Abbott and his friends had stuffed her in a burlap bag and hauled her down to the caves, how the demon had come to her there and taunted her, how her grandfather had been summoned by her friends to find her, and how Gran had ended up being left alone.

"Oh, that's a nasty piece of work!" Pick spit indignantly. "Your grandmother would have been a match for him once. More than a match for him, fact of the matter is. I told you as much. Would have split him up the middle if he'd tried something like this!"

Nest knelt at the windowsill, her face even with his. "So why didn't she, Pick?" she asked. "She always said she had magic, that we both did. Why didn't she use it?"

Pick scrunched up his seamed face, his sharp blue eyes narrowing, his mouth disappearing into his beard. "I don't know. She wouldn't have needed a shotgun if she'd had the magic. She was powerful, Nest—strong-minded and able. She'd studied on her magic; she'd learned how to use it. She might not have been as strong as he was, but he would have come out of a fight with her with a whole lot less skin! And there wasn't a sign of her magic amid the leavings of his!" He rubbed his beard. "Truth is, I haven't seen her use it in a long time—not in a very long time, girl. Not since your mother . . ."

He trailed off, staring at her as if seeing her in a new light.

"What?" she asked quickly.

"Well, I don't know," he answered vaguely. "I was just wondering."

She let the matter drop, choosing instead to tell him about the note. She took it out of her pocket and unfolded it so that he could see that it was Gran's writing, and then she read it to him. When he heard the words, his face underwent a strange transformation. "Criminy," he whispered.

"What is it?" she demanded. "Stop making me guess what you're thinking, Pick!"

"Well, it's just that . . ." He shook his head slowly, his lips still moving, but no sound coming out.

"Why would the demon be coming after me?" she pressed, poking at him insistently with her finger.

Then the bedroom door opened, and her grandfather looked in. Pick disappeared instantly. Nest stood up, smoothing down the front of her T-shirt, composing her face.

"Your friends are at the back door," her grandfather said. "I think you ought to see them."

Reluctantly Nest came out of the bedroom and followed him down the hall. The old grandfather clock marked the cadence of their steps. As they passed the living room, she glanced in at the pictures of her mother and Gran resting on the fireplace mantel. Gran's cross-stitch project rested on the arm of the old easy chair, unfinished. Her crosswords sat in a pile on the floor beside the chair. There were small pieces of her everywhere. Dull slants of gray light wedged their way through the drawn curtains and window shades, but the room felt musty and empty of life.

In the kitchen, dozens of containers of food sat unattended on the table and counters like forgotten guests. Her grandfather slowed and looked vaguely at the array of dishes. "I better see to this. You go on outside. It might be more private for you in the backyard."

She went the rest of the way down the hall to the screen door and opened it. Robert, Cass, and Brianna stood waiting for her. Cass held a bouquet of daisies, mums, and marigolds.

"Hey," she said by way of greeting.

"Hey," they replied in jumbled unison.

Cass passed her the flowers, dark eyes bright with tears. "Sorry about Gran, Nest. We'll all miss her."

"She was the best," Brianna agreed, wiping at her nose.

Robert shoved his hands into his pockets and looked at his shoes in a way that suggested he had never seen them before.

"Thanks for coming by." Nest sniffed at the flowers automatically. "These are really pretty."

"Well, daisies were always her favorite," Cass said.

"You remember when she laid into me for cutting down that stand out back?" Robert asked suddenly. He seemed surprised he had said something and gave Nest a quick, hopeful look. "Man, she was upset. But when you told her I was taking them home to my mom, she said right away that it was all right, and she took us inside and gave us milk and cookies. Remember?"

"I remember when she helped me make that Cinderella costume for Halloween when I was six," Brianna said, smiling. "She did most of the work, but she told my mom we did it together."

"I still can't believe she's gone," Cass said.

They were silent a moment, and then Robert said, "What happened to her anyway, Nest? There's all kinds of stories floating around."

Nest crossed her arms defensively. "She had a heart attack." She tried to think what else she could say. Her gaze shifted away from Robert and back again. "I suppose you heard about the shotgun."

Robert shrugged. "Everybody's talking about that part, and you can guess what some of them are saying. But my dad says people will talk no matter who you are or what you do, so you might as well get used to it."

"People are mean," Brianna said to no one in particular.

No one spoke, eyes shifting uneasily in the silence.

"Thanks for not leaving me last night." Nest tried to change the subject. "You know, for getting Grandpa to come back over and find me."

She told them what had happened to her, only leaving out the part about the demon, then adding at the end that she was all right, no harm had been done, and they should all forget about it.

"What about the man who's poisoning the trees?" Brianna said, her brow knit anxiously.

Nest shook her head. "I don't know. He's still out there."

"Danny Abbott is a butt-face." Robert muttered angrily. "You should have let me punch him out when I had the chance, Nest."

Hearing him say it made her smile. She came through the doorway, and the four of them walked out into the shady backyard and sat down at the old picnic table. Thick, gray clouds floated overhead, drifting out of the west where the sky was already darkening. Rain was on the way, sure enough. In the park, the first of the softball games had started up. Families were arriving by the carloads to set up their picnic lunches and to settle in for the day's events and the evening's fireworks. Nest watched a line of cars crawl down Sinnissippi Road past the townhomes.

"Where's Jared?" she asked, wondering for the first time why he was missing. No one said anything. Nest saw the discomfort mirrored in their faces. "What's wrong? Where is he?"

"He's in the hospital, Nest," Cass said, her eyes lifting. "That's what we came to tell you. It was on the news this morning, but we thought maybe you hadn't heard."

"George Paulsen beat him up real bad," Brianna said softly.

"He beat him within an inch of his life!" growled Robert, shoving back his shock of blond hair aggressively. "The jerk."

Nest felt her stomach go cold and her throat tighten. She shook her head slowly, awash in disbelief.

"I guess it happened right after your grandpa sent us home," Cass explained. Her round face was filled with pain, and her dark eyes blinked rapidly. "Jared came in the door, and George got mad at him for something and hit him. Jared hit him back, and then George really unloaded."

"Yeah, and then he runs off before the police arrive." Robert's face was flushed with anger. "But it didn't do him much good. He fell trying to climb the cemetery fence and tore his throat open on the exposed ends. Bled to death before anyone could reach him. My dad says it's the best thing that could have happened to him."

Nest felt a vast, empty place open inside. "How's Jared?"

Cass shook her head. "He's in a coma. It's pretty bad."

"Mom says he might die," Brianna said.

Nest swallowed and fought to keep the tears from coming. "He can't die."

"That's what I said," Robert agreed quickly. "Not Jared. He's just gone away, like he does sometimes. He'll be back when he's feeling better." He looked away quickly, as if embarrassed by what he had said.

Nest brushed at her eyes, remembering the shy way Jared always looked at her. She struggled to bring herself under control. "Why would George Paulsen do something like that?"

"You know," Robert snorted. "Old Enid and he were drinking and fooling around." Cass gave him a sharp look. "Well, they were! My dad says they were."

"Your dad doesn't know everything, Robert," Cass said evenly.

"Tell him that."

"Mom says they tried to lie about it at first," Brianna interrupted, "but then Mrs. Scott broke down and told them everything. They didn't arrest her, but they took her kids away and put them in foster care. I guess she's in big trouble."

Everyone in that family is in trouble, Nest thought sadly. But it's Jared who's paying the price. Someone should have done something to help him a long time ago. Maybe it should have been her. She'd helped Bennett when she was lost; why hadn't she found a way to help Jared? Why hadn't she seen he might need her help? She could picture George Paulsen hitting him, could see the feeders rising up out of the shadows to spur George on. She could see Gran as well, standing on the porch with the shotgun pointed at the demon as hundreds of lantern eyes stared hungrily from the shadows.

"It just isn't fair," said Brianna.

They talked a while longer, sitting out under the oak trees in the seclusion of the backyard while beyond the hedgerow the park continued to fill with picnickers. Finally Nest told them she had to go in and get something to eat. Robert wanted to know if she was coming over to the park later for the fireworks, and Cass gave him a look and told him he was an idiot. But Nest said she might, that she had been thinking about it and there was no reason to just sit around the house. Gran would have wanted her to go. She would ask her grandfather.

She waited until they disappeared through the hedgerow into the park, then rose and walked slowly back toward the house. She had a curious, unpleasant feeling that everything was slipping away from her. She had always felt secure about her life, able to face whatever changes might come. But now she felt her grip loosening, as if she might no longer be able to count on anything. It was not just losing Gran and maybe Jared; it was the dark way the world beyond the park had suddenly intruded on her life. It was John Ross and O'olish Amaneh appearing. It was the coming of the demon. It was the danger the maentwrog posed, threatening to break free of its centuries-old prison. It was the sudden emergence of so many feeders in places they had never been seen before and Pick's warning of a shift in the balance. It was the revival of the mystery surrounding her mother and father. It was Wraith's failure to protect her last night.

But mostly, she thought, it was the fear and uncertainty she felt at the prospect of having to rely on her magic to stay alive—her magic, which she mistrusted and disliked, a genetic gift come out of her own flesh and blood that she had never fully understood. Gran had left her with a single admonition. *When he comes for you, use your magic.* Not "if he comes" or "should he come." There was no room for debate on what was going to happen or what was required of her, and Nest Freemark, at fourteen years of age, isolated by loss and doubt and secrets kept hidden from her, did not feel ready to deal with it.

She was still wrestling with her sense of vulnerability, standing alone not ten feet from her back door, when the demon appeared.

Chapter 27

The demon stepped from behind the garage where it opened onto the driveway leading down the lane, emerging from a patch of shadows cast by one of the old shagbark hickories. Nest froze on seeing him, the thoughts that cluttered her mind disappearing with the quickness of fireflies in daylight. She was so surprised by his appearance that she didn't even think to call out. She just stood there, staring at him in shock. His bland face was expressionless, as if coming upon her like this was quite natural. He studied her with his washed-out blue eyes, and his gaze was almost tender. He seemed to be seeing something about her that she herself could not, measuring it, weighing it, giving it full and deliberate consideration. She could hear Gran's words screaming in her ear. *When he comes for you. When he comes for you.* The words faded into a high-pitched ringing that deafened her. She tried to break free of him, to bolt for the safety of the house, but his gaze held her fast. No matter how hard she struggled, she could not escape. She felt tears come to her eyes. Rage and frustration boiled up within her, but even these were not powerful enough to release her.

Then the demon cocked his head, as if his attention had been drawn away. He smiled at her, a quick, empty gesture, a reflection of some private amusement. He lifted his fingers to his lips and blew her a kiss off the tips. A moment later, he was gone, stepping back into the shadows in the lee of the garage and fading away.

Nest stood rooted in place, her hands shaking. She waited for him to reappear, to come for her as Gran had said he would. But nothing happened. The ringing in her ears faded, and she began to hear the sounds of the people in the park again, the robins singing in the trees in her yard, and the cars passing down Woodlawn Road. She took a deep breath and held it, trying to still herself.

"Nest!"

John Ross limped slowly into view through the gap in the hedgerow from off the service road. A surge of relief flooded through her. She ran to him without thinking, racing across the backyard, barely able to contain the cry of gratitude that rose in her throat. Her legs churned and her arms pumped, and she threw off the last links of her immobilizing chains. She ran to outstrip her fear and revulsion, to leave them stymied and powerless in the wake of her quickness.

When she reached John Ross, she threw herself into his arms and clung to him.

"Hey, hey, it's all right," he said quickly, bracing himself with his staff, his free arm coming about her shoulders reassuringly. "What's wrong, Nest? Hey, stop crying."

She shook her head against his chest, fighting the tears, gasping for breath as she tried to speak. Everything washed out of her in a hot flush, all the rage and fear and horror and sadness of last night, evaporating like rainwater on hot concrete in the aftermath of a summer storm.

"I heard about your grandmother, and I came right out," he said quietly. "I'm sorry, Nest. I wish I had known he would do this. I would have tried to prevent it. I know how you must feel. I know how hard it must be."

"I hurt so bad," she said finally, the words coming from her mouth in little gulps.

"It can't be any other way," he replied. "Not when you lose someone you love so much."

She shook her head slowly, rubbing her face against his shirt, still pressing against him. "Why did this happen? Why did he do it? Was he just trying to get back at her for what happened when she was a girl? Is that it?" The pitch of her voice began to rise and the words to come faster. "John, he was just here, standing down by the garage, staring at me. I couldn't move! If you hadn't come . . ."

"Nest, slow down, it's all right." He patted her back in an effort to calm her.

She clutched him more tightly. "Gran left a note, John. Just before she died. She knew what was going to happen. The note says the demon is coming for me, too. For me! Why?"

The words hung sharp-edged and immobile in the silence that followed. John Ross said nothing, but in doing so said everything. Nest felt the precipice she had sought to escape drawing near once more. Ross knew, but would not tell her. Like Gran, he had secrets to hide. Her resolve began to falter. She heard the screen door open and saw her grandfather emerge, looking for her. She felt besieged on all sides, boxed in by her ignorance and confusion. She had to know what was happening. She had to know before it was too late.

A surge of wild determination and reckless courage flooded through her. "John," she said quickly, lifting her face away from his chest to look at him. Her heart pounded. "Are you my father?"

The pain that filled his eyes when she spoke the words was palpable. He stared at her with such intensity that if felt to her as if he was unable to convey with words what he was feeling.

"It's just that Gran seemed so suspicious and resentful of you," Nest hurried on, trying to make the answer easier for him, to let him tell her what she already knew was so. "I heard her talking to Grandpa. She was saying things that made it pretty clear . . . I'm not angry or anything, you know. I just . . . I just . . ."

He brought his hand to her face, resting the palm against her cheek. "Nest," he said softly. "I wish to God I were your father. I would be proud to be your father." He shook his head sadly. "But I'm not."

She stared at him in disbelief, feeling her expectation crumple inside and turn to despair. She had been so sure. She had known he was her father, known it from the way that Gran reacted to him, from the way he spoke of her mother, from his history, from his voice and eyes, from everything he was. How could he not be? How could he not?

Her grandfather came up behind them, and Nest turned toward him. He saw the stricken look in her face, and his jaw tightened. His eyes locked at once on John Ross.

"Morning, John," he said, a decided edge to his voice. He placed a reassuring hand on Nest's shoulder.

"Good morning, sir," Ross answered, taking his own hand away.

"Is something wrong here?"

"No, sir. I just came by to offer my condolences. I'm very sorry about Mrs. Freemark. I believe she was a remarkable woman."

"Thank you for the kind words and for your concern." The old man paused. "Mind telling me what happened to your face?"

Nest, who had been staring at nothing, still stunned from learning that Ross was not her father, glanced up at him quickly and for the first time noticed the cuts and bruises.

"I was attacked by some men from MidCon at the dance last night," Ross said, giving a barely perceptible shrug. "It was a case of mistaken identity. They thought I was a company spy."

"A company spy?" Nest's grandfather looked incredulous. "The company doesn't have any spies. Who would they be spying on? For what reason?"

Ross shrugged again. "It's over now. I'm fine. I just wish I had been here for you and Nest."

Nest's grandfather looked at her. "You've been crying, Nest. Are you all right now?"

Nest nodded, saying nothing, feeling dead inside. She looked at her grandfather, then looked quickly away.

Robert Freemark straightened and turned back to John Ross. "John, I have to tell you something. Evelyn wasn't all that warm toward you, I know. She thought that maybe you were someone other than who you claimed. She was suspicious of your motives. I told her she was being silly, that I thought you were a good man."

He shook his head slowly. "But I have to admit that a lot of strange things have happened since you arrived. Nest hasn't been herself for several days. Maybe she doesn't think I've noticed, but I have. Last night's events have made me think. A lot of things don't add up. I guess I need to ask you to explain some of them."

Ross met his frank gaze with a weary, distant look. He seemed to weigh the matter a moment before answering. "I think you deserve that much, Mr. Freemark."

Nest's grandfather nodded. Nest stepped back so that she could see them both, sensing the start of something that was not going to end pleasantly.

"Well, there's this business of the man who's been poisoning trees in the park." Robert Freemark cleared his throat. "Nest's friends told me about him when they came by to ask for my help in finding her." Quickly, he told John Ross what had happened. "They said she sent them first in search of you, making it pretty clear, I think, that you know about this man, too."

He paused, waiting. John Ross glanced at Nest. "I know about him. I came to Hopewell because I was tracking him."

"Tracking him?"

"It's what I do."

"You track people? Are you with the police? Are you a law-enforcement officer?"

Ross shook his head. "I work on my own."

Nest's grandfather stared. "Are you telling me, John, that you are a private detective? Or a bounty hunter?"

"Something else."

There was a long pause as Nest's grandfather studied the other man, hands resting loosely on his hips. "Did you know my daughter Caitlin at all, John? Was any of that true?"

"I knew of her, but I didn't know her personally. I didn't go to school with her. We weren't classmates. I'm sorry, I made that up. I needed to meet you. More to the point, I needed to meet Nest."

Another pause, longer this time. "Why, John?"

"Because while I didn't know Nest's mother, I do know her father."

Now Nest was staring hard at him, too, a look of horror spreading over her face. She swallowed against the sudden ache in her throat and looked quickly at her grandfather. Old Bob's face was pale. "Maybe you better just spit it out," he said.

John Ross nodded, bringing the black staff around in front of him so that he could lean on it, as if the talk was wearing on him in unseen ways. He looked down at his shoes momentarily, then directly at Nest.

"I'm sorry, Nest, this is going to hurt a lot. I wish I didn't have to tell you, but I do. I hope you'll understand." He looked back at her grandfather. "There's a lot of talk about how your wife died, sir. Some people are saying she was a crazy old woman who died shooting at ghosts. I don't think that's true. I think she was shooting at the man I've been tracking, the man I came here to find. She was trying to defend herself. But he is a very resourceful and dangerous adversary, and she wasn't strong enough to stop him. He's caused a lot of trouble and pain, and he's not finished. He came to Hopewell for a very specific purpose. He doesn't realize it yet, but I know what that purpose is."

Nest took a deep breath as his green eyes shifted back to hers. "He's come for you. Your grandmother knew. That made her a threat to him, so he got rid of her."

His gaze was steady. "He's your father, Nest."

In his dream, the Knight of the Word stands with a ragged band of survivors atop a wooded rise south of the burning city. Men have devoted such enormous time and energy to destroying themselves that they are exhausted from their efforts, and now the demons and the once-men have picked up the slack. At first it was the tented camps and nomads who were prey, but of late the attacks have shifted to the walled cities. The weakest have begun to fall and the nature of the adversary to make itself known. The Knight has battled the demons all through the destruction of the old world, confronting them at every opportunity, trying to slow the erosion of civilization. But the tide is inexorable and undiminished, and a new dark age has descended.

The Knight looks around to be certain that the women and children are being led to safety while he acts as sentry. Most have already disappeared into the night, and the rest are fading with the swiftness of ghosts. Only a few remain behind to stand with him, a handful of those who have discovered too late that he is not the enemy. Below, the city burns with an angry crackle. Hordes of captives are being led away, those who did not flee when there was time, who did not heed his warning. The Knight closes his eyes against the sadness and despair that wells within him. It does not change. He cannot make them listen. He cannot make them believe.

Look! says a weathered man next to him, his voice a low hiss of fear and rage. It's her!

He sees the woman then, striding forward out of the darkness and into the light, surrounded by men who are careful not to come too near. She is tall and regal, and her features are cold. He has never seen her before, but there is something familiar about her nevertheless. He is immediately intrigued. She radiates power and is an immutable presence. She is clearly the leader of those about her, and they hasten to do her bidding. A captive is brought before her and forced to kneel. He will not look at her, his head lowered stubbornly between his shoulders. She reaches for his hair and jerks savagely on it. When their eyes meet, he undergoes a terrible transformation. He twists and shakes, an animal trapped within a snare, enraged and terrified. He says things, screams them actually, the words indistinct, but the sounds clear. Then she is finished with him and he arches as if skewered on the point of a spear and dies writhing in the dirt.

The woman steps around him without a second glance and continues on, the flames of the city catching in their orange glow the empty look upon her face.

Do you know her? the Knight asks the man who has spoken.

Oh, yes, I know her. The man whispers, as if the night breeze might carry his words to her. His face is scarred and worn. She was a girl once. Before she became what she is. Her name was Nest Freemark. She lived in a little town called Hopewell, Illinois. Her father came for her on the Fourth of July when she was just fourteen and changed her forever. Her father, a demon himself, made her one, too. I heard him say so to a man he knew, just before he killed him. It was in a prison. Her father would have killed me as well, had he known I was listening.

Tell me about her, the Knight says quietly.

He turns the man in to the trees so that they can follow the others to safety, and in the course of their furtive withdrawal from the horror taking place on the plains below, the man does.

When John Ross awoke that morning in Josie Jackson's bed, he was in such pain that he could barely move. All of his muscles and joints had stiffened during the night, and the bruises from his beating had flowered into brilliantly colored splotches on his chest and ribs. He lay next to Josie and tried shifting various parts of himself without waking her. Everything ached, and he knew it would be days before he could function in a normal way again.

Last night's dream hung with veiled menace in the dark seclusion of his mind, a horror he could not dispel, and he was reminded anew of the older dream, the one that had given him his first glimpse of the monster Nest Freemark would become.

Should I tell her? he wondered anew. Now, while there is still time? Will it help her to know?

When they rose, Josie drew a hot bath for him and left him to soak while she made breakfast. He was dressing when she came in with the news of Evelyn Freemark's death. The details were on the radio, and several of Josie's friends had called as well. Ross walked in silence to the kitchen to eat, the momentary joy he had found during the night already beginning to fade. He tried not to show what he was feeling. The demon had outsmarted him. The demon had provoked last night's attack on him not because he was a threat to its plans, but to get him out of the way so he could not help Evelyn Freemark. He had spent so much time worrying about Nest that he had forgotten to consider the people closest to her. The demon was breaking Nest down by stripping away the people and defenses she relied upon. Ross had missed it completely.

He finished his breakfast and told Josie he was going out to see Old Bob, and she offered to come with him. He thanked her, but said he thought he should do this alone. She said that was fine, looking away quickly, the hurt showing in her dark eyes. She walked to the counter and stood there, looking out the kitchen window.

"Is this good-bye, John?" she asked after a minute. "You can tell me."

He studied the soft curve of her shoulders against the robe. "I'm not sure."

She nodded, saying nothing. She ran a hand through her tousled hair and continued to stare out the window.

He groped for something more to say, but it was too late for explanations. He had violated his own rules last night by letting himself get close to her. Involvement with anyone was forbidden for a Knight of the Word. It was one thing to risk his own life; it was something else again to risk the life of another.

"I'll be leaving Hopewell soon, maybe even sometime today. I don't know when I'll be back." His eyes met hers as she turned to look at him. "I wish it could be different."

She studied him a moment. "I'd like to believe that. Can I write you?"

He shook his head slowly. "I don't have an address."

Her smile was wan and fragile. "All right. Will you write me sometimes?"

He told her he would try. He could tell she wanted to say more, to ask him why he was being so difficult, so secretive. But she did not. She just kept looking at him, as if knowing somewhere deep inside that it was useless, that she would never see him again.

She drove him back to the hotel so that he could change his clothes, then drove him out to the Freemarks' and dropped him off at the entrance to the park. She barely spoke the entire time. But when he started to get out of the car, she reached over and put her arms around his neck and kissed him hard on the mouth.

"Don't forget me," she whispered, and gave him a hint of the smile that had drawn him to her that first day.

Then she straightened herself behind the steering wheel while he closed the car door and drove away without looking back.

He had made up his mind in that instant to tell Nest Freemark about her father.

Now, as he stood looking at Nest's shattered face, he wondered if he had made the right decision. The mix of shock and horror that flooded her eyes was staggering. She blinked rapidly, and he could tell that she wanted to look away from him, to hide from his terrible revelation, but she could not. She tried to speak, but no words would come. Old Bob was stunned as well, but his exposure to the truth wasn't as complete. He didn't know what Nest did. He didn't know that her father was a demon.

"My father?" she whispered finally. "Are you sure?"

The words hung between them in the ensuing silence, a poisonous and forbidding accusation.

"Nest," her grandfather began, reaching for her.

"No, don't say anything," she said quickly, silencing him, stepping back. She tore her gaze from Ross and looked out into the park. "I need to . . . I just have to . . ."

She broke off in despair, tears streaming down her face, and bolted from the yard through the hedgerow and into the park. She ran past the ball diamond behind the house, down the service road toward the park entrance, and off toward the cemetery. John Ross and her grandfather stood looking after her helplessly, watching her angular figure diminish and disappear into the trees.

Old Bob looked at Ross then, a flat, expressionless gaze. "Are you certain about this?"

Ross nodded, feeling the grayness of the day descend over him like a pall. "Yes, sir."

"I don't know that you should have told her like that."

"I don't know that I should have waited this long."

"You've tracked him here, her father, to Hopewell?"

"Yes, sir."

"And he's come for Nest?"

Ross sighed. "Yes, sir, he has. He means to take her with him."

Old Bob shook his head in disbelief. "To kidnap her? Can't you arrest him?"

Ross shook his head. "I haven't the authority. Besides, I can't even find him. If I do, I can't prove any of what I've told you. All I can do is try to stop him."

Old Bob slipped his big hands into his pockets. "How did you find all this out?"

"I can't tell you that."

Old Bob looked away, then back again, his face growing flushed and angry. "You come to Hopewell with a story about your college days with Caitlin that's all a lie. You manage to get yourself invited to our home and then you keep from us the truth of what you are really doing here. You do not warn us about Nest's father. You may think you have good reasons for everything you've done, John, but I have to tell you that I've put up with as much of this as I'm going to. You are no longer welcome here. I want you off my property and out of our lives."

John Ross stood firm against the old man's withering stare. "I don't blame you, sir. I would feel the same. I'm sorry for everything." He paused. "But none of what you've said changes the fact that Nest is still in danger and I'm the best one to help her."

"Somehow I doubt that, John. You've done a damn poor job of protecting any of us, it seems to me."

Ross nodded. "I expect I have. But the danger to Nest is something I understand better than you."

Old Bob took his hands out of his pockets. "I don't think you understand the first thing about that girl. Now you get moving, John. Go find Nest's father, if that's what you want to do. But don't come back here."

John Ross stood where he was a moment longer, looking at the old man, trying in vain to think of something else to say. Then he turned without a word and limped away.

CHAPTER 28

Nest fled into the park in mindless shock, her thoughts scattered, her reason destroyed. Had she known a way to do so, she would have run out of her skin, out of her body, out of her life. The face of the demon would not leave her, the image burned so deeply into her mind that she could not dispel it, his features bland and unremarkable, his blue eyes pale and empty.

Your father . . .

Your father . . .

She flew into a dark stand of pine and spruce, flinging herself into the concealing shadows, desperate to hide from everything, frantic to escape. The leathery branches whipped at her face and arms, bringing tears, but the pain was solid and definable and slowed her flight. She staggered to a halt, grounded anew, lacking a reason to run farther or a better place to go. She moved aimlessly within the tangle of the grove, tears welling in her eyes, fists clenching at her sides. This wasn't happening, she thought. It couldn't be happening. She walked through the conifers to a massive old oak, put her arms about the gnarled trunk, and hugged it to her. She felt the rough bark bite into her arms and legs, into her cheeks and forehead, and still she pressed harder.

Your father . . .

She could not say the words, could not complete the thought. She pressed and pressed, willing her body to melt into the tree. She would become one with it. She would disappear into it and never be seen again. She was crying hard now, tears running down her face, her body shaking. She squeezed her eyes tight. Had her father really killed Gran? Had he killed her mother as well? Would he now try to kill her?

Do something!

She forced herself to go still inside and the tears to stop. Her sobs died away in small gulps as the cold realization settled over her that the crying wasn't doing any good, wasn't helping anything. She pushed away from the tree and stared out into the park through gaps in the conifers, rebuilding her composure from tiny, scattered fragments. She caught glimpses between the needled branches of other lives being led, all of them distant and removed. It was the Fourth of July, America's day of independence. What freedom should she celebrate? She looked down at her arms, at how the oak's bark had left angry red marks that made her skin look mottled and scaly.

A shudder overtook her. Could she ever look at herself again in the same way? How much of her was human and how much something else? She remembered asking Gran only a few days earlier, weary of the years of secrecy, if her father might be a forest creature. She remembered wondering afterward what that would feel like.

Now she could wonder about this.

She shifted her gaze inward, staring at nothing, still unable to believe it was true. Maybe John Ross was mistaken. Why couldn't he be? But she knew there was no mistake. That was why Gran had been so anxious to avoid any discussion of her father all those years. She felt sick inside thinking of it, of the lies and half truths, of the rampant deception. Awash with misery and fear, she felt bereft of anything and anyone she could depend upon, mired in a life history that had compromised and abandoned her.

She moved back to the oak and sat down, leaning against the rugged trunk, suddenly worn out. She was still sitting there, staring at the trees around her, trying to decide what to do next, when Pick dropped out of the tree across the way and hurried over.

"Criminy, I thought I'd never catch up with you!" he gasped, collapsing to his knees in front of her. "If it wasn't for Daniel, I'd never get anywhere in this confounded park!"

She closed her eyes wearily. "What are you doing here?"

"What am I doing here? What do you *think* I'm doing here? Is this some sort of trick question?"

"Go away." Her voice was a flat, hollow whisper.

Pick went silent and stayed that way until she opened her eyes to see what he was doing. He was sitting up straight, his eyes locked on hers. "I'm going to pretend I didn't hear that," he said quietly, "because I know how upset you are about your father."

She started to say something flip, then saw the look in his eyes and caught herself just in time. She felt her throat tighten. "You heard?"

Pick nodded.

"Everything?"

"Everything." Pick folded his wooden arms defensively. "Do me a favor. Don't tell me I should have told you about him before this. Don't make me remind you of something you already know."

She compressed her lips into a tight line to keep the tears in check. "Like what?"

"Like how it's not my place to tell you secrets about your family." Pick shook his head admonishingly. "I'm sorry you had to find out, but not sorry it didn't come from me. In any case, it's no reason for you to leap up and run off. It's not the end of the world."

"Not yours, anyway."

"Not yours, either!" The words snapped at her. "You've had a nasty shock, and you have a right to be upset, but you can't afford to go to pieces over it. I don't know how John Ross found out about it, and I don't know why he decided to tell you. But I do know that it isn't going to help matters if you crawl off into a hole and wait for it all to go away! You have to *do* something about it!"

Nest almost laughed. "Like what, Pick? What should I do? Go back to the house and get the shotgun? A lot of good that did Gran! He's a demon! Didn't you hear? A demon! My father's a demon! Jeez! It sounds like a bad joke!" She brushed away fresh tears. "Anyway, I'm not talking about this with you until you tell me the truth about him. You know the truth, don't you? You've always known. You didn't tell me while Gran was alive because you didn't feel you should. Okay. I understand that. But she's dead now, and somebody better tell me the truth right now or I'm probably going to end up dead, too!"

She was gulping against the sobs that welled up in her throat, angry and afraid and miserable.

"Oh, for goodness' sake!" Pick threw up his hands in disgust and began tugging on his beard. "Exactly what is it you think I should tell you, Nest? What part of the truth haven't you figured out, bright girl that you are? Your grandmother was a wild thing, a young girl who bent a lot of rules and broke a few more. That Indian showed you most of it, with his dancing and his visions. She ran with the feeders in Sinnissippi Park, daring anything, and that led to her involvement with the demon. The demon wanted her, whether for herself or her magic, I don't know. He was furious when she found out what he was and told him she didn't want anything more to do with him. He threatened her, told her the choice wasn't hers to make. But she was tough and hard and not afraid of him, and she wouldn't back down. She told him what she would do if he didn't leave her alone, and he knew she meant business."

The sylvan stamped his foot. "Are you with me so far? Good. Here's the rest of it. He waited for his chance to get even, the way demons do. He was mostly smoke and dark magic, so aging wasn't a problem for him. He could afford to be patient. He waited until your grandmother married and your mother came along. He waited for your mother to grow up. I think your grandmother believed she'd seen the last of him by then, but she was wrong. All that time, he was waiting to get back at her. He did it through your mother. He deceived her with his magic and his lies, and then he seduced her. Not out of love or even infatuation. Out of hate. Out of a desire to hurt your grandmother. Deliberately, maliciously, callously. You were the result. Your grandmother didn't know he was responsible at first, and even if she had, she wouldn't have told your mother. But the demon waited until you were a few months old and then told them both. Together."

Nest stared at him, horrified.

His face knotted. "Told them why, too. Took great delight in it. I was there. Your mother went off the cliffs shortly afterward. I think maybe she did it on purpose, but nobody saw it happen, so I can't be sure."

His frustration with her attitude seemed to dissipate. His voice softened. "The thing that concerns me is that the demon wanted to hurt your grandmother, to get even with her for what she'd done to him, and that was why he destroyed your mother, but I think he's after you for a different reason. I think he believes you belong to him, that you're his child, his flesh and blood, and that's why he's come back—to claim what's his."

Nest hugged her knees to her chest, listening to the soft rustle of spruce and pine boughs as a breeze passed through the shadowed grove. "Why does he think I would go with him? Or stay with him if he took me? I'm nothing like him."

But even as she said it, she wondered if it was so. She looked and talked and acted like a human being, but so did the demon, in his human guise, when it suited him. Underneath was that core of magic that defined them both. She did not know its source in her. But if she had inherited it from her father, then perhaps there was more of him in her than she wished.

Pick pointed a finger at her. "Don't be doubting yourself, Nest. Having him for your father is an accident of birth, nothing more. Having his magic doesn't mean anything. Whatever human part of him went into the making of you is long since dead and gone, swallowed up by the thing he's become. Don't look for something that isn't there."

She tightened her lips stubbornly. "I'm not."

"Then what are you thinking, girl?"

"That I'm not going with him. That I hate him for what he's done."

Pick looked doubtful. "He must know that, don't you expect? And it mustn't matter to him. He must think he can make you come, whether you want to go with him or not. Think it through. You have to be very careful. You have to be smart."

He put his chin in his hands and rested his elbows on his knees. "This whole business is very confusing, if you ask me. I keep wondering what John Ross is doing in Hopewell, of all places. Why would a Knight of the Word choose to fight this particular battle? To save you? Why, when there's dozens of others being lost everywhere you turn? You're my best friend, Nest, and I'd do anything to help you. But John Ross doesn't have that connection. There's a war being waged out there between the Word and the Void, and what's going on here in Sinnissippi Park seems like an awfully small skirmish, the presence of your father notwithstanding. I think there must be something more to all this, something we don't know about."

"Do you think Gran knew?" she asked hesitantly.

"Maybe. Maybe that's why the demon killed her. But I don't think so. I think he killed your grandmother because he was afraid of her, afraid that she would get in his way and spoil his plans. And because he wanted to get even with her. No, I think John Ross is the one who knows. I think that's what he's doing here. Maybe it was your grandmother's death that prompted him to tell you about your father—because of what he knows that we don't."

Nest shook her head doubtfully. "Why wouldn't he just tell me what it is?"

"I don't know." Pick tugged hard on his beard. "I wish I did."

She gave him a wry, sad grin. "That's not very comforting."

They were silent for a moment, staring at each other through the growing shadows, the sounds of the park distant and muffled. A few stray raindrops fell on Nest's face, and she reached up to brush them away. A dark cloud was passing overhead, but the sky behind it showed patches of brightness. Perhaps there wouldn't be a thunderstorm after all.

"That note your grandmother left you reminds me of something," Pick said suddenly, straightening. "Remember that story you told me about your grandmother seeing Wraith for the very first time? You were in the park, just the two of you, and she went right up to him. Remember that? He was standing just within the shadows, you said, not moving, and they stared at each other for a long time, like they were communicating somehow. Then she came back and told you he was there to protect you." He paused. "Doesn't it make you wonder just exactly where Wraith came from?"

Nest stared at him, her mind racing as she considered where he was going with this. "You think it was Gran?"

"Your grandmother had magic of her own, Nest, and she learned some things from your father before she found out who he was and quit having anything to do with him. Wraith appeared after your mother died, after your father revealed himself, after it was clear that you could be in danger. More to the point, maybe, he appeared about the same time your grandmother quit using her magic, the magic she no longer had to defend herself with when your father came for her last night."

"You think Gran made Wraith?"

"I think it's possible. Hasn't Wraith been there to protect you from the time you were old enough to walk?" Pick's brow furrowed deeply. "He's a creature of magic, not of flesh and blood. Who else could have put him there?"

Disbelief and confusion reflected on Nest's face. "But why wouldn't Gran tell me? Why would she pretend she wasn't sure?"

Pick shrugged. "I don't know the answer to that any more than I know why John Ross won't tell you what he's really doing here. But if I'm right, and Wraith was made to protect you, then that would explain the note, wouldn't it?"

"And if you're wrong?"

Pick didn't answer; he just stared at her, his eyes fierce. He didn't think for a moment he was wrong, she realized. He was absolutely certain he was right. Good old Pick.

"Think about this, while you're at it," he continued, leaning forward. "Say John Ross is right. Say your father has come back for you. Look at how he's going about it. He didn't just snatch you up and cart you off. He's taking his time, playing games with you, wearing you down. He found you in the park and teased you about not being able to rely on anyone. He came to your church and confronted you. He used his magic on that poor woman to demonstrate what could happen to you. He had that Abbott boy kidnap you and take you down into the caves, then teased you some more, telling you how helpless you were. He killed your grandmother, and sidetracked John Ross and your grandfather and me as well. Where do you think I was all night? I was out trying to keep the maentwrog locked up in that tree, and it took everything I had to get the job done. But you see, don't you? Your father's gone to an awful lot of trouble to make you think that he can do anything he wants, hasn't he?"

She nodded, studying his wizened face intently. "And you think you know why?"

"I do. I think he's afraid of you."

He let the words hang in the silence, his sharp eyes fixed on her, waiting for her response. "That doesn't make any sense," she said finally.

"Doesn't it?" Pick cocked one bushy eyebrow. "I know you're scared about what's happened and you think you don't have any way of protecting yourself, but maybe you do. Your grandmother told you what to do. She told you to use your magic and trust Wraith. Maybe you ought to listen to her."

Nest thought it over without saying anything, sitting face-to-face with the sylvan, alone in the shadows of the grove. Beyond her momentary shelter, the world went about its business without concern for her absence. But it would not let her forget where she belonged. Its sounds beckoned to her, reminding her that she must go back. She thought of how much had changed in a single day. Gran was dead. Jared might die. Her father had come back into her life with a vengeance. Her magic had become the sword and shield she must rely upon.

"I guess I have to do something, don't I?" she said quietly. "Something besides running away and hiding." She tightened her jaw. "I guess I don't have much choice."

Pick shrugged. "Well, whatever you decide to do, I'll be right there with you.

Daniel and me. Maybe John Ross, too. Whatever his reasons, I think he intends to see this through."

She gave him a skeptical look. "I hope that's good news."

The little man nodded soberly. "Me, too."

Derry Howe was standing at the window of his tiny apartment in a T-shirt and jeans, looking out at the clouded sky and wondering if the weather would interfere with the night's fireworks, when Junior Elway pulled up in his Jeep Cherokee. Junior drove over the curb trying to parallel park and then straightened the wheels awkwardly as the Jeep bumped back down into the street. Derry took a long pull on his Bud and shook his head in disgust. The guy couldn't drive for spit.

The window fan squeaked and rattled in front of him, blowing a thin wash of lukewarm air on his stomach and chest. The apartment felt hot and close. Derry tried to ignore his discomfort, but his tolerance level was shot. A headache that four Excedrin hadn't eased one bit throbbed steadily behind his temples. His hand ached from where he had cut himself the day before splicing wires with a kitchen knife. Worst of all, there was a persistent buzzing in his ears that had been there on waking and refused to fade. He thought at first that he was losing his hearing, then changed his mind and wrote it off to drinking too much the night before and got out a fresh Bud to take the edge off. Three beers later, the buzzing was undiminished. Like a million bees inside his head. Like dozens of those weed eaters.

He closed his eyes momentarily and worked his jaws from side to side, trying to gain a little relief. Damn, but the noise was aggravating!

Seated comfortably in the rocker that had belonged to Derry's mother, the demon, an invisible presence, cranked up the volume another notch and smiled.

Derry finished off his Bud and walked to the front door. He kept watch through the peephole until Junior was on the steps, then swung open the door and popped out at him like a jack-in-the-box.

Junior jumped a foot. "Damn you, don't do that!" he snapped angrily, pushing his way inside.

Derry laughed, an edgy chuckle. "What, you nervous or something?"

Junior ignored him, looked quickly about to see that they were alone, decided they were, glanced at Derry's beer, and went into the kitchen to get one of his own. "I'm here, ain't I?"

Derry rolled his eyes. "Nothing gets by you, does it?" He lifted his voice a notch. "Bring me a cold one, too, long as you're helping yourself!"

He waited impatiently for Junior to reappear, took the beer out of his hands without asking, and motioned him over to the couch. They sat down together, hands cupped about the chilled cans, and stared at the remains of a pizza that sat congealing in an open cardboard box on the battered coffee table.

"You hungry?" Derry asked, not caring one way or the other, anxious to get on with it.

Junior shook his head and took a long drink of his beer, refusing to be hurried. "So. Everything set?"

"You tell me. Are you scheduled for tonight's shift?"

Junior nodded. "Like we planned. I went in yesterday, told them I was sick of the strike, that I wanted back on the line, asked to be put on the schedule soon as possible. You should have seen them. They were grinning fools. Said I could start right away. I did like you told me, said I'd like the four to midnight shift. I go on in . . ." He checked his watch. "Little over an hour. All dressed and ready. See?"

He pointed down to his steel-toed work boots. Derry gave him a grudging nod of approval. "We got 'em by the short hairs, and they don't even know it."

"Yeah, well, let's hope." Junior didn't look convinced.

Derry tried to keep the irritation out of his voice. "Hope ain't got nothing to do with it. We got us a plan, bub, and the plan is what's gonna get this particular job done." He gave Junior a look. "You wait here."

He got up and left the room. The demon watched Junior fidget on the couch, playing with his beer, taking a cold piece of sausage off the top of the pizza and popping it in his mouth, staring at the ancient window fan as if he'd never seen anything like it.

Derry came back carrying a metal lunch box with clips and a handle. He passed it to Junior, who took it gingerly and held it at arm's length.

"Relax," Derry sneered, reseating himself, taking another pull on his Bud. "Ain't nothing gonna happen until you set the switch. You can drop it, kick it around, do almost anything, it's safe until you set it. See the metal slide on the back, underneath the hinge? That's the switch. Move it off the green button and over the red and you got five minutes—plenty of time. Take it in with you, leave it in your locker when you start your shift, carry it out on your break like you're having a snack, then slip it under the main gear housing and walk away. When it goes off, it'll look like the roller motors overheated and blew. Got it?"

Junior nodded. "Got it."

"Just remember. Five minutes. It's preprogrammed."

Junior set the lunch box back on the coffee table next to the pizza. "Where's yours?"

Derry shrugged. "Back in the bedroom. Want to see it?"

They got up and went through the bedroom door, finishing off their beers, relaxed now, joking about what it was going to be like come tomorrow. The demon watched them leave the room, then rose from the rocker, walked over to the coffee table, and opened the lid to the lunch box. Sandwiches, a chip bag, a cookie pack, and a thermos hid what was underneath. The demon lifted them away. Derry was exactly right; he had set the clock to trigger the explosives five minutes after the slide was pushed.

The demon shook his head in disapproval and reset it from five minutes to five seconds.

Derry and Junior came back out, sat on the couch, drank another beer, and went over the plan one more time, Derry making sure his buddy had it all down straight. Then Junior picked up the lunch box and left, heading for the steel mill. When he was gone, Derry massaged his temples, then went into the bathroom to get a couple more Excedrin, which he washed down with a fresh beer.

Better go easy on this stuff, he admonished himself, and set the can aside. Want to be sharp for tonight. Want to be cool.

He dumped the pizza in the trash and brought out the second device, this one fashioned a little differently than the other to accomplish its intended purpose, and finished wiring it. When he was done, he placed it inside a plastic picnic cooler, fastened it in place, and closed the lid. He leaned back and studied it with pride. This baby will do the job and then some, he thought.

The demon came over and sat down next to him. Derry couldn't see him, didn't know he was there. "Better take your gun," the demon whispered, a voice inside Derry's head.

Derry looked at the rattling old window fan, matching its tired cadence to the buzzing in his head. "Better take my gun," he repeated absently.

"In case anyone tries to stop you."

"Ain't no one gonna stop me."

The demon laughed softly. "Robert Freemark might."

Derry Howe stared off into space. "Might try, anyway." His jaw was slack. "Be too bad for him if he did."

When he got up to go into his bedroom to collect his forty-five from the back of his closet, the demon opened the picnic cooler and reset that clock, too.

Nest walked back through the park to her home, Pick riding on her shoulder, both of them quiet. It was nearing four o'clock, and the park was filled with people. She skirted the families occupying picnic tables and blankets in the open areas and followed the line of trees that bordered Sinnissippi Road on the north. It wasn't that she was trying to hide now; it was just that she didn't feel like talking to anyone. Even Pick understood that much and was leaving her alone.

Feeders shadowed her, flashes of dark movement at the corners of her eyes, and she struggled unsuccessfully to ignore them.

She passed the park entrance and started down the service road behind her house. Overhead, clouds drifted in thick clusters, and the sun played hide-and-seek through the rifts. Bright, sunny streamers mixed with gray shadows, dappling the earth, and to the west, dark thunderheads massed. Rain was on the way for sure. She glanced skyward and away again without interest, thinking about what she had to do to protect herself. She had assumed right up until last night that the demon and John Ross and the madness they had brought to Hopewell had nothing to do with her personally, that she stood on the periphery of what was happening, more observer than participant. Now she understood that she was not just a participant, but the central player, and she had decided she would be better off not counting on anyone's help but her own. Maybe Pick and Daniel would be able to do something. Maybe John Ross would be there for her. Maybe Wraith would defend her when it mattered. But maybe, too, she would be on her own. There was good reason to think so. The demon had managed to isolate her every time he had appeared, and she had to assume he would manage it again.

Her father.

But she could not think of him that way, she knew. He was a demon, and he was her enemy.

She pondered Gran's note. Should she rely on it? Was Pick right in his assumption that Gran had made Wraith and given up her magic to do so? Was that why she was defenseless against the demon? *Trust Wraith.* She remembered Gran telling her over and over again that the feeders would never hurt her, that she was special, that she was protected. She had never questioned it, never doubted it. But the demon was not a feeder, and perhaps this time Gran was wrong. Why hadn't Gran told her more when she'd had the chance? Why hadn't she given Nest something she could rely upon?

I'm so afraid, she thought.

She pushed through the gap in the hedgerow and entered her backyard. The house loomed dark and gloomy before her, and she was reluctant to enter it. Pick had disappeared from her shoulder, gone back into the trees. She hesitated a moment, then walked up to the back door, half expecting the demon to jump out at her.

But it was her grandfather who appeared, stepping from the shadow of the porch entry. "Are you all right, Nest?" he asked quietly, standing there on the steps, his big hands hanging awkwardly at his sides. He looked gaunt and tired.

She nodded. "I'm okay."

"It was a terrible shock, hearing something like that about your father," he said, testing her with the words. He shook his head. "I'm still not sure I believe it."

She felt suddenly sad for him, this strong man who had lost so much. She gave him a faint smile and a look that said, *Me either.*

"I sent John away," he said. "I told him I didn't appreciate him coming to my house under false pretenses, whatever his reason for it, and I felt it would be better if he didn't come back. I'm sorry if that upsets you."

Nest stared, uncomprehending. She wanted to ask him if he had lost his mind, but she held her tongue. Her grandfather didn't know what she did about John Ross, so it wasn't fair for her to judge him. It was clear he had acted out of concern for her. Would she have acted any differently in his place?

"I'm going to lie down for a little while, Grandpa," she said, and went past him up the steps and into the house.

She went down the hall to her room and closed the door behind her. Shadows dappled the walls and ceiling, and the air was still and close. She felt suddenly trapped and alone.

Would John Ross abandon her? Would he give up on her in the face of her grandfather's antagonism? Even worse, was it possible there was nothing more he could do?

As she lay down on her bed, she found herself praying fervently, desperately that when the demon appeared next, she would not have to face him alone.

Chapter 29

Afternoon passed into evening, a gradual fading away of minutes and hours measured by changes in the light and a lengthening of shadows. The rain did not come, but the clouds continued to build in the west. Old Bob wandered through the house like a restless ghost, looking at things he hadn't looked at in years, remembering old friends from other times, and conjuring up memories of his distant past. Visitors came and went, bringing casseroles and condolences. Fresh-cut flowers and potted plants arrived, small white cards tucked carefully inside their plain white envelopes, words of regret neatly penned. The news of Evelyn Freemark's death had spread by radio and word of mouth; the newspaper article would not appear until tomorrow. Phone calls asked for details, and Old Bob dutifully provided them. Arrangements for the funeral, memorial service, and burial were completed. A fund that would accept monetary donations was established in Evelyn's name by the local Heart Association. Old Bob went through the motions with resigned determination, taking care of the details because it was necessary, trying to come to grips with the fact that she was really gone.

Nest stayed in her room with the door closed and did not reappear until Old Bob called her to dinner. They ate at the kitchen table without speaking. Afterward, as the light began to fail and the dusk to descend, her friends called and asked if she wanted to meet them in the park to watch the fireworks. She asked him if she could, and while he was inclined to say no, to keep her safe in the house and close to him, he realized the foolishness of taking that particular course of action. He might shelter her for a day or even a week, but then what? At some point he would have to let her go off on her own, and there was no reason that he could see to postpone the inevitable. Nest was smart and careful; she would not take chances, especially after last night. In any case, was her father really out there? No one besides John Ross had actually seen him, and he was not sure he trusted Ross anymore. Gran had worried that Nest's father might return, but she had never actually said he was back. Old Bob had thought at first that he should call the police and warn them of his concerns, but on reflection he realized he didn't have anything concrete to offer, only a bunch of vague suspicions, most of them based on John Ross' word.

In the end, he let the matter slide, giving Nest his permission to go, extracting in exchange her firm promise that she would sit with her friends in a crowded place and would not go off alone. The park was safe for her, he believed. She had lived in it all her life, wandered it from end to end, played her childhood games in it, adopted it as her own backyard. He could not see forbidding her to go into it now, especially while she was still dealing with the shock of her grandmother's death.

After she was gone, he began cleaning up the kitchen by putting away the food gifts. The refrigerator and the freezer were soon filled to capacity, and there were still dozens of containers sitting out. He picked up the phone and called Ralph Emery's house, and when the minister answered he asked him if he would mind sending someone around first thing in the morning to take all this food down to the church for distribution to those who could make better use of it. The minister said he would take care of it, thanked him for his generosity, spoke with him about Evelyn for a few minutes, and said good night.

The shadows in the house had melted together in a black mass, and Old Bob walked through the empty rooms and turned on the lights before coming back into the kitchen to finish up. The shotgun was gone, taken by the police for reasons he failed to comprehend, part of their investigation, they told him, and he felt strangely uneasy in its absence. You'd think it would be the other way around, he kept telling himself. He washed some dishes by hand, something he hadn't done in a long time, finding that it helped him relax. He thought always of Evelyn. He glanced over at the kitchen table more than once, picturing her there, her bourbon and water in front of her, her cigarette in hand, her face turned away from the light, her eyes distant. What had she been thinking, all those times she'd sat there? Had she been remembering her childhood in the little cottage several houses down? Had she been thinking of Nest? Of Caitlin? Of him? Had she been wishing that her life had turned out differently, that she had done more with it? Had she been thinking of missed chances and lost dreams? His smile was sad. He regretted now that he had never asked.

He finished the dishes, dried them, and put them away. He glanced around, suddenly lost. The house was alive with memories of his life with Evelyn. He walked into the living room and stood looking at the fireplace, at the pictures on the mantel, at the place in the corner by the bowed window where the Christmas tree always sat. The memories swirled around him, some distant and faded, some as new and sharp as the grief from her loss. He moved to the couch and sat down. Tomorrow his friends would gather at Josie's for coffee and doughnuts, and in his absence they would talk of Evelyn in the same way they had talked of that postal worker in the gorilla suit or the fellow who killed all those children. They would not do so maliciously, but because they had thought her curious and now found her death somehow threatening. After all, she had died here, in Hopewell—not in some other town in some other state. She had died here, where they lived, and she was someone they knew. Yes, she was odd, and it wasn't really any surprise that she had died of a heart attack blasting away at shadows with a shotgun, because Evelyn Freemark had done stranger things. But in the back of their minds was the conviction that she really wasn't so different than they were, and that if it could happen to her, it could happen to them. Truth was, you shared an uneasy sense of kinship with even the most unfortunate, disaffected souls; you felt you had known at least a few of them during your life. You had all been children together, with children's hopes and dreams. The dark future that had claimed those few was never more than an arm's length away from everyone else. You knew that. You knew that a single misfortune could change your life forever, that you were vulnerable, and to protect yourself you wanted to know everything you could about why it had touched another and passed you by.

Old Bob listened to the silence and let the parade of memories march away into the darkness. My God, he was going to miss her.

After a time his thoughts wandered to the call he had received earlier from Mel

Riorden. Mel and Carol had been by that morning to offer condolences, promising they would have him over for dinner after the funeral, when he was feeling up to it. Old Bob had taken their hands, an awkward ritual between long-standing friends where something profound had changed their lives and left them insufficient words to convey their understanding of what it meant. Later Mel had called on the phone, keeping his voice down, telling Old Bob that there was something he ought to know. Seemed that Derry had called him up out of the blue and apologized for scaring him with his talk about MidCon. Said he really hadn't meant anything by it. Said he was just blowing off steam, and that whatever the union decided was good enough for him. Said he wanted to know if he could go to the fireworks with Mel and Carol and some of the others and sit with them. Mel paused every so often to make sure Old Bob was still listening, his voice sounding hopeful. Maybe he was mistaken about his nephew, he concluded tentatively. Maybe the boy was showing some common sense after all. He just wanted Old Bob to know.

When Mel hung up, Old Bob stood looking at the phone, wondering if he believed any of it and if it made any difference if he did. Then he dropped the matter, going about the business of his own life, of finishing the funeral preparations and worrying about Nest. But now the matter surfaced anew in his thoughts, and he found himself taking a fresh look at it. Truth was, it just didn't feel right. It didn't sound like Derry Howe. He didn't think that boy would change in a million years, let alone in twenty-four hours. But maybe he was being unfair. People did change—even people you didn't think would ever be any different from what they'd been all their lives. It happened.

He drummed his fingers on the arm of the couch, staring off into space. Going to the fireworks with Mel and Carol, was he? That was a first. Where was his buddy, Junior Elway, that he'd opted for an evening out with the old folks?

He got up from the sofa and went into the kitchen to fish around in the packed-out refrigerator for a can of root beer. When he found it, he popped the top and carried it back into the living room and sat down again.

Fireworks. The word kept digging at him, suggesting something different from the obvious, something he couldn't quite grasp. Hadn't he and Derry talked about fireworks yesterday, when he had approached the boy about what sort of mischief he might be planning? Derry Howe, the Vietnam vet, the demolitions expert, talking about playing with matches in a pile of fireworks, about how fireworks were touchy if you didn't know what you were doing, that they could cause accidents . . .

He sat up straight. What was it Derry had said? *I'm going to give MidCon a Fourth of July to remember.* But more, something else, something personal. A warning. *Stay home on the Fourth. Keep away from the fireworks.*

Old Bob set the can of root beer down on the coffee table, barely aware of what he was doing, his mind racing. What he was thinking was ridiculous. It didn't make any sense. What would Derry Howe gain by sabotaging the Fourth of July fireworks? How would that have any effect on MidCon Steel? He looked the possibilities over without finding anything new. There didn't seem to be any connection.

Then something occurred to him, and he got to his feet quickly and walked out onto the screened porch where he kept the old newspapers. He bent down and began to go through them. Most were old *Chicago Tribunes*, but there were a few *Hopewell Gazettes* among them. Friday's had gone out with the trash, he remembered, used to wrap the garbage. He found the one from Thursday, pulled it out, and went through it quickly, searching. There was nothing on the Fourth of July. But he seemed to remember seeing something, a big ad of some kind. He wished he had paid better attention, but it had been years since he had concerned himself with what went on in the park over the Fourth. The fireworks were all Evelyn and he had ever cared about, and you knew without having to ask when to be there for them.

He tossed the Thursday paper aside, wondering what had become of the Saturday-morning edition. He went down the hall to his den and looked for it there, but couldn't find it. He stood motionless for a moment, trying to think what he had done with it. Then he walked back to the kitchen. He found the Saturday paper sitting on the counter under several of the casseroles he had set aside for the church. He extracted it gingerly, spread it out on the table, and began to scan its pages.

He found what he was looking for right away. The Jaycees had inserted a flyer for the Sunday-Monday events in Sinnissippi Park, admission free, everyone welcome. Games, food, and fun. The events culminated on Monday, the Fourth, with fireworks at sunset. This year, the flyer proclaimed in bold letters, the fireworks were being sponsored and paid for by MidCon Steel.

For long moments, Old Bob just stared at the flyer, not quite trusting himself. He must be wrong about this, he kept thinking. But it was the way a guy like Derry Howe thought, wasn't it? Sabotage the fireworks sponsored by MidCon, maybe blow up a few people watching, cause a lot of hard feelings. But then what? Everybody blames MidCon? MidCon has to do something to regain favor, so it settles the strike? It was such a stretch that for a few seconds he dismissed his reasoning altogether. It was ludicrous! But Derry Howe wouldn't think so, would he? Old Bob felt a cold spot settling deep in his chest. No, not Derry.

He looked at his watch. After nine o'clock. He glanced out the window. It was growing dark. They would start the fireworks soon now. He thought suddenly of Nest. She would be sitting with everyone else, at risk. He could hear Evelyn saying to him, as she had on the last night of her life, "Robert, you get right out there and find that girl and bring her home."

He grabbed his flashlight off the counter and went out the door in a rush.

By now, the largest part of the Fourth of July crowd had abandoned the playgrounds, ball diamonds, and picnic tables to gather on the grassy slopes that flanked the toboggan slide and ran down to the river's edge. The fireworks would be set off over the bayou from a staging area located on a flat, open stretch of the riverbank below. A line had been strung midway up the slope to cordon off the crowd from the danger zone. Strips of fluorescent tape dangled from the line, and volunteers with flashlights patrolled the perimeter. The spectators were bunched forward on the hillside to the line's edge, settled on blankets and in lawn chairs, laughing and talking as the darkness descended. Children ran everywhere, sparklers leaving bright comet tails in the wake of their passing. Now and again a forbidden firecracker would explode off in the trees to either side, causing old people to jump and parents to frown. Shadows deepened and the outlines of the park and its occupants grew fuzzy. By the blackness of the river, a trio of flashlights wove erratic patterns as the staging crew completed their preparations for the big event.

Nest Freemark sat with her friends on a blanket, eating watermelon slices and drinking pop. They were situated high on the slope to the west of the slide where the darkness was deepest and the park lights didn't penetrate. There were families around them, but Nest couldn't see their faces or recognize their voices. The gloom made everyone anonymous, and Nest felt comfortable in that environment. Aside from her friends, she was anxious to avoid everyone.

She had come into the park late, when dusk had begun to edge toward nightfall and it was already getting hard to see. She had crossed her backyard with a watchful eye, half expecting the demon to leap out at her from the shadows. When Pick had dropped onto her shoulder as she pushed her way through the bushes, she had jumped in spite of herself. He was there to escort her into the park, he had informed her in his best no-nonsense voice. He had been patrolling the park since sunset, riding the windless heat atop Daniel, crisscrossing the woods and ballparks and playgrounds in search of trouble. As soon as Nest was safely settled with her friends, he would resume his vigil. For the moment, everything was peaceful. There was no sign of the demon. There was no sign of John Ross. The maentwrog, still imprisoned in its ravaged tree, was quiet. Even the feeders were staying out of sight. Pick shrugged. Maybe nothing was going to happen after all.

Nest gave him a look.

When Pick left her on nearing the crowded pavilion with its cotton-candy, popcorn, hot-dog, and soft-drink stands, she moved quickly toward the rendezvous point she had settled on with her friends. One or two people glanced her way, but no one called out to her. She was stopped only once, by Gran's friend Mildred Walker, who happened to be standing right in front of her as she passed and couldn't be avoided. Mrs. Walker told her she was sorry about Gran and about her young friend Jared Scott, and that she wasn't to worry, that the Social Services people were going to see to it that nothing further happened to any of those children. She said it with such feeling and such obvious concern that it made Nest want to cry.

Later, Brianna confided to all of them that her mother had told her the Social Services people were already looking for temporary homes for the Scott kids. Her mother also told her that Jared was still in a coma and that wasn't good.

Now Nest sat in the darkness sipping at her can of pop and reflecting on how unfair life could be. Out on the river, in a sea of blackness, the running lights of powerboats shone red and green, motionless on the becalmed waters. There was no wind; the air had gone back to being hot and sticky, and the taste of dust and old leaves had returned. But the sky was thick with clouds, which screened away the moon and stars, and rain was on the way. Nest wished it would hurry up and get here. Maybe it would help cool things down, clean stuff up, and give everyone a fresh attitude. Maybe it would help wash away some of the madness.

A stray firefly blinked momentarily in front of her face and disappeared in the darkness. Somebody in a lawn chair sneezed, and the sneeze sounded like a dog's bark. A ripple of laughter rose. Robert made a comment about the nature of germs in people's mouths, and Brianna told him he was gross and disgusting. Robert stood up and announced he was off to buy some popcorn and would anybody like some? Nobody would, he was informed, and Brianna said he should take his time coming back, maybe even think about going home and checking his mouth in the mirror. Robert walked off whistling.

Nest smiled, at ease with herself. She was thinking how comfortable she felt, sitting here in the darkness, surrounded by all these people. She felt sheltered and safe, as if nothing could touch her here, nothing could threaten. How deceptive that was. She wished she could disappear into the gloom and become one with the night, invisible and substanceless, impervious to harm. She wondered if Pick was having any luck. She tried to picture what the sylvan would do to defend her if the need arose, and couldn't. She wondered if the demon was out there, waiting for her. She wondered if John Ross was waiting, too.

After a time, she began to think of Two Bears, wishing that he was still there and could help her. There was such strength in him, a strength she didn't feel in herself, even though he had told her it was there. They had names of power, he said. But hers was the stronger, the one with true magic. He had given her what he could; the rest must come from her.

But what was it he had given her? That brief vision of her grandmother as a young girl, running wild in the park with the feeders and the demon? An insight into her convoluted and tragic family history? She didn't know. Something more, she believed. Something deeper, more personal. *Think.* It was his desire to commune with the spirits of his people, the Sinnissippi, that had brought him to Hopewell, but it was her ties to the magic that had drawn him to her. Your people risk the fate of mine, he had warned, wanting her to know, to understand. No one knows who my people were. No one knows how they perished. It can happen to your people, too. It is happening now, without their knowledge and with their considerable help. Your people are destroying themselves.

We do not always recognize the thing that comes to destroy us. That is the lesson of the Sinnissippi.

But he might have been speaking of her father as well.

She stared into the darkness, lost in thought. It was all tied together. She could feel it in her bones. The fate of her friends and family and neighbors and of people she didn't even know. Her own fate. The fates of the demon and John Ross. Of O'olish Amaneh, too, perhaps. They were all bound up by a single cord.

I am not strong enough for this.

I am afraid.

She stared at nothing, the words frozen in her mind, immutable. Then she heard Two Bears' clear response, the one he had given her two nights earlier.

Fear is a fire to temper courage and resolve. Use it so.

She sat alone in the darkness, no longer comfortable with pretending at invisibility, and tried to determine if she could do as Two Bears expected.

Twenty feet away, a shadowy figure in the deepening gloom, John Ross kept watch over her.

After Old Bob had dismissed him, he had walked into the park in search of the demon, determined to hunt him down. He went to the caves where the feeders made their lair, followed the riverbank east toward the toboggan slide and the deep woods beyond, and climbed to the prison of the maentwrog, that aging, ravaged oak that held the monster bound, but the demon was nowhere to be found.

He debated returning to Nest Freemark then, but did not. What could he say to her that he hadn't already said—or decided against saying? It was sufficient that he had told her the truth about her father. Telling her more would risk undermining what courage and resolve she could still muster. The best he could do was to watch over her, to wait for the demon to come to her, to be there when it appeared, and to do what he could to save her then.

He left the park and walked out to Lincoln Highway to have dinner at a McDonald's, then walked back again. Sitting in a crowd of spectators on the bleachers at the ball diamond closest to the Freemark house, he watched the sun move west toward the horizon. When dusk approached and the game began to break up, he walked to a stand of pine bordering the service road. Using magic to make certain they could not see him, he stood for a time in the shelter of the trees, watching Pick and Daniel as they wheeled overhead. When Nest went into the park, he followed.

Now he stood waiting, close enough to make certain he could act when the demon appeared, close enough to go to her aid if the need arose. All about him, the Fourth of July spectators were shrouded in gloom, vague and featureless in the night. Shouts and laughter rose from the crowded hillside amid the bang of firecrackers and the whistle of small rockets. The air was humid and still, filled with the erratic buzzing of insects and the raw smell of pine needles and wood smoke. He gripped his staff tightly in his hand, feeling anxious and uncertain. He needed only one chance at the demon, but would he get even that? How strong would Nest Freemark be then? He edged his way east toward the woods behind the pavilion, changing his location yet again, trying to avoid notice from the people gathered, concentrating on Nest. He could just make her out, sitting with her friends near the back of the crowd.

Then he caught sight of a familiar face and turned his head aside quickly as Robert Heppler walked past on his way back from the popcorn stand.

"So, did I miss anything?" Robert asked the girls as he plopped back down comfortably on the blanket, his bag of popcorn firmly in hand. "Want some?" he asked Brianna Brown. "I only breathed on it a little. Or did you pig out on the rest of the watermelon while I was gone?"

Brianna grimaced. "I leave the pigging out in life to you, Robert. You're so good at it."

Nest was staring off into space, barely aware of the conversation. Robert glanced over. "Hey, Nest, guess who I just saw standing . . ."

A child flew out of the darkness and into their midst, a little boy running blindly through the night, sparklers waving in both hands. He saw them too late, veering aside when he was already on top of them, nearly losing his balance and toppling onto Robert. Robert yelled angrily at him, and sparks showered everywhere. Cass and Brianna leaped to their feet, stamping at the embers that had tumbled onto the blanket.

Nest rose with them, stepping back, distracted, and as she did so she heard Pick scream. He was screaming inside her head, throwing his voice so that only she could hear, throwing it from somewhere far away so that it was faint and fragmented. But it was terror-stricken, too.

Nest, Nest . . . quick, run . . . here, the oak collapsing . . . demon . . . knows you are . . . the maentwrog breaking . . .

Then the screaming stopped, abruptly, completely, leaving an echo that rang in her ears as she stood shocked and frozen amid the crowd and her friends.

"Pick?" she whispered into the silence he had left behind. Her hand groped blindly at the air before her. "Pick?"

Her friends were staring at her, eyes filled with uncertainty. “Nest, what’s wrong?” Cass asked urgently.

But Nest was already turning from her, beginning to run. “I have to go,” she shouted over her shoulder, and raced away into the night.

CHAPTER 30

It was an act of instinct rather than of reason, a response to an overwhelming, terrifying fear that another life precious to her was about to be lost. Nest did not hesitate as she bolted through the crowd. Of course the demon was drawing her out. Of course it was a trap. She didn't have to think twice about it to know it was true. If she stayed where she was, safe within the crowd gathered on the slopes of Sinnissippi Park, he could not reach her so easily. But it was Pick who was at risk, her best friend in the whole world, and she would not abandon him even to save her own life.

She darted through the crowd as if become one of the wild children who waved their sparklers, dodging lawn chairs and coolers, avoiding blankets filled with people, seeking the open blackness of the woods beyond. She knew where to go, where the demon would be waiting, where Pick could be found; the sylvan's frantic words had told her that much. The deep woods. The maentwrog's prison. The aging oak from which, it seemed, the monster was threatening to break free. She thought she heard shouts trailing after her, calling her name, but she ignored them, burying them in her determination not to be slowed. She vaulted the last of the coolers that obstructed her passage and broke for the trees.

In the open, beyond the scattering of flashlights and sparklers, she slowed just enough to let her vision adjust to the change of light. Ahead, the trees rose in dark, vertical lines against the softer black of the night. She angled past picnic tables and cook stations, running toward the rolling hills that fronted the deep woods. The sounds of the crowd faded behind her, receding into the distance, leaving her alone with the huff of her breathing and the beat of her heart. She heard her name called clearly then, but she forced herself to go on, trying to ignore the unwelcome summons, trying to outdistance it. When it continued, and she determined with certainty its source, she slowed reluctantly and turned to face a hard-charging Robert Heppler.

"Wait up, Nest!" he shouted as he rushed up to her from out of the darkness, blond hair swept back from his angular face.

She shook her head in disbelief. "Robert, what are you doing? Go back!"

"Not a chance." He came to a ragged halt before her, breathing hard. "I'm going with you."

"You don't even know what I'm doing!"

"Doesn't matter. You're not doing it alone."

"Robert . . ."

"The last time I let you wander off by yourself," he interrupted heatedly, "you ended up in the caves and I had to get your grandfather to come find you! I'm not going through that again!"

He brushed at his tousled hair, his mouth set, his eyes determined. He looked pugnacious and challenging. "You're going out to that big oak, aren't you? This has something to do with that tree, doesn't it? What's going on?"

"Robert!" she snapped at him, suddenly angry. "Get out of here!"

He stared back at her defiantly. "No way. I'm going with you. You're stuck with me."

"Robert, don't argue with me! This is too dangerous! You don't know what you're . . ." She stopped in exasperation. "Turn around, Robert! Right now!"

But he refused to budge. She came toward him menacingly. "I'm not afraid of you, Nest," he said quickly, clenching his fists. "I'm not Danny Abbott, either. You can't make me do anything I don't want to do. I don't know what's going on, but I . . ."

She locked his eyes with hers and struck out at him with her magic in a swift, hard attack. Robert Heppler went down like a stone, his muscles turned to jelly and his words became mush. He jerked once where he lay in the thinning forest grass, gave a long sigh, and blacked out.

She blocked the feelings of guilt that immediately assailed her and turned away, racing on. It was better this way. She knew Robert; he would not turn back. She would attempt an explanation later. If there was a later. Desperation and anger swept aside her attempts at forming an apology. She had done what she had to do. It didn't matter that she had promised not to use the magic, that she hated to use it, that it left her feeling sullied and drained. Gran was gone, and in moments she would face her killer, and all she had to rely on was the magic she had just used on Robert.

A fierce glee rocked her, a strange sense of chains being cast aside and freedom being gained. The defiance she felt at having done something forbidden lent her a certain satisfaction. The magic was a part of her. Why should it ever be wrong to use it?

She charged down the slope into the ravine that separated the picnic grounds from the deep woods, feeling her feet beginning to slide on the loose earth and long grasses. She caught herself with her hands to keep from falling, straightened up again as she reached the base of the ravine, and ran on. The bridge that spanned the little creek appeared through the gloom, and she thundered onto it, tennis shoes pounding as she crossed to the far side and began to climb the slope into the woods.

When she reached the top of the rise, she slowed again. Ahead, a wicked green light pulsed faintly within the trees, like the heartbeat of something alive. She pushed the thought aside and went on, jogging now, her breathing slowing, her eyes flicking from side to side watchfully, trying to penetrate the wall of shadows. The trail had narrowed, choked with brush and hemmed by the trees, a twisting serpent's spine. It was black there, so dark that only the greenish light gave any illumination against the night. She was being drawn to it; she could not pretend otherwise. She repeated the words of Gran's note over and over in her mind, a litany to lend her courage. She brushed at the insects that buzzed at her, thick clouds of them that flew at her eyes and mouth. Her fear returned in a sudden wave as she pictured what waited ahead. But she did not turn back. She could not. It was no different now than it had been when she had gone to save Bennett Scott from the feeders. No different at all.

Please, Pick, don't give up. I'm coming.

Moments later, she stepped from the woods into the clearing where the big oak stood. The tree was a vast, crooked monster within the darkness, its bark wet-looking and ravaged, as if skin split from the bones and muscles of a corpse. The wicked green light emanated from here, given off by the trunk of the old tree, pulsing slowly, steadily against the darkness. Nest stared in dismay. The tree was still intact, but it had the look of a dying creature. It reminded her of pictures she had seen of animals caught in steel traps, their limbs snared, their eyes glazed with fear and pain.

The demon stood next to the tree, his calm eyes fixed on her. He seemed to think nothing was out of place, nothing awry. It was all she could do to make herself meet his gaze.

"Where is Pick?" she demanded.

Her voice sounded impossibly childish and small, and she saw herself as the demon must see her, a young girl, weaponless and desperate in the face of power she could not even begin to comprehend.

The demon smiled at her. "He's right over there," he replied, and pointed.

Five feet or so off the ground, a small metal cage hung from the branches of a cherry. Within its shadowed interior, Nest could just make out a crumpled form.

"Safely tucked away," the demon said. "To keep him from meddling where he shouldn't. He was flying about on that owl, trying to see what I was up to, but he wasn't very smart about it." He paused. "A cage wasn't necessary for the owl."

A feathered heap lay at the edge of the trees, wings splayed wide. Daniel. "He came right at me when I knocked the sylvan off his back," the demon mused. "Can you imagine?"

He motioned vaguely at the cage. "You do know about sylvans and cages, don't you? Well, perhaps not. Sylvans can't stand being caged. It drains away their spirit. Happens rather swiftly, as a matter of fact. A few hours, and that's it. That will be the fate of your friend if someone doesn't release him."

Nest! Pick gasped in a frantic attempt to signal her. Then he went silent again, his voice choked off.

"Your little friend would like to say something to you about his condition, I'm sure," the demon breathed softly, "but I think it best he save his strength. Don't you?"

Nest felt alone and vulnerable, felt as if everything was being stripped from her. But that was the plan, wasn't it? "Let him go!" she ordered, staring at the demon as if to melt him with the heat of her anger.

The demon nodded. "After you do what I tell you." He paused. "Child of mine."

Her skin crawled at the sound of his words, and a new wave of rage swept through her. "Don't call me that!"

The demon smiled, satisfaction reflecting in his eyes. "You know then, don't you? Who told you? Evelyn, before she died? The sylvan?" He shrugged. "I guess it doesn't matter. That you know is what matters. That you appreciate the special nature of our relationship. Who you are will determine what you become, and that is what we are here to decide."

He looked past her, suddenly startled. A hint of irritation flashed across his strange empty features. "Ah, it's the bad penny. He's turned up after all."

John Ross emerged from the trees, sweat-streaked and hard-eyed. He seemed taller and broader than she remembered, and the black staff gleamed and shimmered with silver light. "Get behind me," he said at once, his green eyes fixed on the demon.

"Oh, she doesn't want to do that!" the demon sneered, and threw something dark and glittering at the ravaged oak.

Instantly the tree exploded in a shower of bark and wood splinters, and the green light trapped within burst forth.

Old Bob crossed to the fireworks from his home as the crow flies, not bothering with the service road or any of the pathways, the beam of his flashlight scanning the darkness before him as he went. The weariness he had felt earlier fell away in the face of his fear, and a rush of adrenaline surged through him, infusing him with new strength. The sounds of laughter and conversation and the momentary flare of sparklers guided him through the broad expanse of the grassy flats, and in moments he had reached the rear edge of the crowd.

He began to ask at once if anyone had seen Mel Riorden. He knew most of the people gathered, and once he got close enough to make out their faces, he simply offered a perfunctory greeting and inquired about Mel. He was a big man with a no-nonsense way about him, a man who had just suffered a terrible loss, and those he spoke with were quick to reply. He moved swiftly in response, easing forward through the crowd toward the cordoned perimeter west of the slide. He was sweating freely, his underarms and back damp, his face flushed from his efforts. He did not have a definite plan. He was not even certain that he needed one. He might be mistaken about Derry Howe. He might be overreacting. If he was, fine. He would feel foolish, but relieved. He could live with that. He would find Derry, talk to him, possibly confront him with his suspicions, and deal with his feelings later.

He wove his way through knots of people sprawled on blankets and seated in lawn chairs, through darting children and ambling teens. The viewing area was packed. Some looked at him with recognition, and a few spoke. Some he stopped to talk with took time to offer condolences on his loss, but most simply answered his questions about Mel and let him go his way. His eyes flicked left and right as he proceeded, searching the darkness. He could no longer see the riverbank clearly, and the trees had faded into a black wall. The fireworks would begin any moment.

Finally, he found Mel and Carol seated together on a blanket at the very edge of the crowd with a handful of family and friends. Mel's sister was among them, but not her son. Old Bob said hello to everyone, then drew Mel aside where they could talk privately.

"Did Derry come to the fireworks with you?" he asked quietly, trying to keep his voice calm, to keep his fear hidden.

"Sure, you just missed him," his friend answered. "Been here with us all evening. Something wrong?"

"No, no, I just wanted to talk with him a moment. Where is he?"

"He took some drinks down to the guys shooting off the fireworks. Guess he knows one of them." Mel glanced over his shoulder. "I told him I didn't know if they'd let him go down there, but he seemed to think they would."

Old Bob nodded patiently. "He took them some drinks?"

"Yeah, beer and pop, like that. He had this cooler he brought with him. Hey, what's this about, Robert?"

Old Bob felt the calm drain away in a sudden rush, and the fears that had been teasing and whispering at him from the shadows suddenly emerged like predators. "Nothing," he said. He looked toward the river and the movement of flashlights. "He's still down there?"

"Yeah, he just left." Mel cocked his head and his eyes blinked rapidly. "What's the matter?"

Old Bob shook his head and began to move away. "I'll tell you when I get back."

He moved more quickly now, following the line that cordoned off the staging area as it looped down toward the river's edge. He passed several of the Jaycees responsible for patrolling it, younger men he did not know well or at all, and he asked each of them in turn if he had seen Derry Howe. The third man he passed told him Derry had just gone inside the line, that he had been permitted inside only after identifying a member of the staging crew who he claimed was a friend. Old Bob nodded, told him that this was a violation of the agreement the Jaycees had signed with the park district in order to be allowed to sponsor this event, but that he would forget about reporting it if he could go down there right now and bring Derry back before anything happened. He gave the impression without saying so that he was with the park service, and the younger man was intimidated sufficiently by his words and the look on his face to stand aside and let him pass.

Seconds later, Old Bob was inside the line and working his way down the slope toward the moving flashlights of the men preparing to set off the fireworks. He had to hurry now. The fireworks were scheduled to begin at ten o'clock sharp, and it was almost nine-fifty. He turned off his own flashlight, letting his eyes adjust to the darkness. As he neared, he could make out the figures of the staging crew moving through the firing platforms to make their last-minute preparations.

He saw Derry Howe then, his tall, lank figure unmistakable, even in the darkness, standing with one of the crew, talking. As Old Bob swerved toward them, the crewman started to move away. Old Bob waited a few heartbeats, then flicked on the flashlight.

"Derry!" he called out boldly. Derry Howe turned into the light, squinting. Old Bob slowed. "Been looking all over for you."

Derry's eyes flicked right and left. He was holding a small cooler in his left hand. His grin was weak and forced. "What are you doing down here, Robert? You're not supposed to be here."

"Neither are you." Old Bob gave him an indulgent smile. He was less than fifteen feet away now and closing. "You done here? Give everyone a drink yet? Got one left for me?"

Derry held up his hand quickly. "Stop right there. Right there, Bob Freemark."

Old Bob stopped, and gave him a calm, steady look. "What's in the cooler, Derry?"

Derry Howe's face flushed and tightened with sudden anger. "Get out of here!" he spat angrily. "Get away from me!"

Old Bob shook his head. "I can't do that. Not unless you come with me."

Derry took a quick step back from him. "I'm not going anywhere with you! Get the hell out of my face!"

"What are you doing down here, Derry?" Old Bob pressed, starting forward again.

He could see the desperation in the younger man's eyes as they fixed on him. He looked trapped, frustrated. Suddenly, he laughed. "You want to know what I'm doing?" He was backing off as he spoke, edging down the line of platforms and scaffolding, away from the flashlight's steady beam. Abruptly he stopped. "All right, I'll show you."

He turned away a moment, his movements concealed by the darkness. When he turned back again, he was holding a gun.

The buzzing inside Derry's head had become a dull roar, a Niagara Falls of pounding white noise. He leveled the gun at Robert Freemark and his finger tightened on the trigger.

"Turn off the flashlight, old man."

Old Bob glanced to his left where the staging crew was gathered around the framework that supported the flag display. But they were too far away to see what was happening. No help was coming from there. Old Bob looked back at Derry and the flashlight went dark.

Derry nodded. "First smart thing you've done yet." He licked at his dry lips. "Walk toward me. Stop, that's far enough. You want to know what I'm up to? Fine, I'll tell you. Tell you everything. You know why? No, don't say anything, damn you, just listen! I'll tell you because you got a right to know. See, I knew you were coming. I knew it. Even though I told you to stay away, I knew you'd be here. Big mistake, old man."

"Derry, listen—" Old Bob began.

"Shut up!" Derry's face contorted with rage. "I told you not to say anything, and I damn well mean it! You listen to me! While you and those other old farts have been sitting around waiting for a miracle to end this damn strike, I've found a way to make the miracle happen!"

He edged back toward a grouping of rocket launchers, the cooler dangling from his hand, his eyes on Old Bob, ten feet away. He held the gun level on the old man, making sure it didn't waver, not wanting Old Bob to do something stupid, force him to fire the gun now, before he was ready, ruin everything. Oh, sure, he was going to shoot Mr. Robert Freemark, no question about that. But not quite yet. Not until he was somewhere no one could hear or see. He glanced over to where the staging crew shone their flashlights on the flag display, making sure they were still busy with their work. He grinned. Everything was working out just right.

He knelt in the shadows and set the cooler behind him, close to the launching platform. "Don't you move," he told Old Bob softly. "Just stand there. You ain't carrying a gun, are you?"

Old Bob shook his head. His big hands hung limply at his sides, and his body slumped. "Don't do this, Derry. There are women and children up there. They could be hurt."

"Ain't nobody going to be hurt, old man. What do you think I am, stupid?"

He kept the gun leveled as he lifted the cooler onto the platform and shoved it back into the shadows between the fireworks cases where it couldn't be seen if you weren't looking. Well, okay, maybe a few people would end up getting hurt, hit by debris or something. After all, that was part of the plan, wasn't it? Someone gets hurt, MidCon looks even worse. Derry gave a mental shrug. Point is, the strike will be over and in the long run everyone'll be happy.

He reached behind the cooler to where he had placed the timer switch and activated it. He had five minutes. He stood up, feeling good. "See, easy as pie. Now you turn around and walk down along the riverbank, Robert Freemark, nice and slow. I'll be right behind . . ."

Then everything flared white hot about him, and it felt as if a giant fist had slammed into his back.

The force of the bomb's blast blew Derry Howe forward into Old Bob and carried both of them fifteen feet through the air before it dumped them in a tangled heap. Old Bob lay crumpled in the grass, one arm twisted awkwardly, Derry sprawled half on top of him. His ears rang and his head throbbed, and after a minute he felt the pain begin. I'm dying, he thought. Fireworks were exploding all around him, rockets going off in their launcher tubes or spinning wildly off into the darkness or streaming fire into the trees and sky and out over the river. The launching platform was in flames, and the frameworks for the flag display and others hung in ragged, half-burned tatters. The spectators were running and screaming in all directions, blankets scattered, lawn chairs dumped, coolers abandoned. Deep booms and ear-piercing whistles marked the detonation of explosive after explosive from within the white-hot inferno below. Old Bob felt blood on his chest and face and could not tell if it was his or Derry's. He could feel blood leaking inside his mouth and down his throat. When he tried to free himself from Derry, he found he could not move.

He closed his eyes against his pain and weariness.

Well, that's it, that's all she wrote.

He had just enough time left to wonder about Nest, and then everything went black.

CHAPTER 31

The creature that emerged from the shattered remnants of the old oak was so loathsome that it defied comparison with anything John Ross had ever seen. It slouched out of the smoke and ruin, materializing as the pulsating green light fragmented, a nightmare come to life. It walked upright on two legs, but it was hunched over and crook-backed, as if its huge shoulders would not permit it to straighten. Tufts of coarse, black hair dotted its scaly surface, and it had a snake's hooded yellow eyes and wicked tongue. Toes and fingers split in tripods from its feet and hands, ending in claws that seemed better suited to a great cat. Its face was long and narrow and featureless except for the slits that served as its eyes and mouth, and its head was a smooth, sinuous extension of its corded neck. It was big, fully ten feet in height, even stooped as it was, and its mass suggested that it weighed well over five hundred pounds. It swung around guardedly as it stepped forward into the clearing, casting its flat, empty gaze left and right, looking over the unfamiliar world into which it had emerged.

After centuries of being locked away, the maentwrog was free once more.

John Ross stared at the monster. It looked too huge to have been contained by the old tree, and he wondered how it could ever have been imprisoned. Not that it mattered now. All that mattered now was whether he was going to do anything about the fact that it was loose. His purpose in coming to Hopewell had nothing to do with the maentwrog. The maentwrog was an unneeded and dangerous distraction. He knew what he should do, what he had been sent to do. He should let the monster go its way, let it do what it would, let someone else deal with it. But there was no one else, of course. There was only him. By the time sufficient force was brought to bear, the maentwrog would have killed half the people of the town. It was a berserker, a killing machine that lacked any other purpose in life. It did not kill out of hunger or in self-defense, but out of primal need. It was not his responsibility, but he knew he could not let it pass.

And that was what the demon was counting on—the reason he had set the maentwrog free. John Ross was being given a choice, and the fact that he was human and not a forest creature made the outcome of his choosing a foregone conclusion.

He turned to Nest Freemark, who stood transfixed behind him, her eyes wide and staring, her curly hair wild and damp against her heated face. "Move back from me," he told her softly.

"John, no, it's too big," she whispered, her eyes filled with fear and terror.

"Move back, Nest."

She did so reluctantly, slowly withdrawing toward the wall of the trees. The clearing was lit by the remnants of the oak, a scattering of shards which were still infused with the green light and clung to the limbs and tall grasses. Overhead, the sky was dark and choked with clouds, the moon and stars hidden. In the distance, he heard the slow rumble of thunder. A sad, wistful resignation filled him. There was no way out of this. In his hands, the black walnut staff pulsed with light.

Ignoring the demon, who backed to the tree line, bland features lit with expectation, Ross stepped forward. He kept his eyes on the maentwrog, who was watching him now, seeing him for the first time, realizing that a confrontation was at hand. The creature dropped down on all fours, muscles bunching, tongue flicking out experimentally. Its mouth parted to reveal multiple rows of sharpened teeth, and it gave a deep, slow hiss of warning.

Ross summoned the magic from his staff, and it flowed over him like liquid light, encasing him in its armor, giving him protection for the battle ahead. The maentwrog cringed in revulsion as Ross slowly transformed, becoming less himself, less the human he had been, turning bright and hard within the magic's armor. His features melted, smoothing out within the light, and when he advanced in a slow, almost sensual glide, his limp had disappeared completely.

Within the shadows of the clearing, time seemed to slow and sound to cease.

Then the maentwrog threw itself at its adversary in a stunningly swift attack, claws ripping. But the Knight of the Word sidestepped with ease, and the gleaming black staff hammered into the monster as it hurtled past. Fire flared like molten steel, and the creature howled, a high-pitched, ragged snarl, its neck arching, its body writhing. It spun about as it was struck, one arm whipping at the Knight, who was not quite quick enough to avoid it. The blow sent him sprawling backward across the clearing, and he felt the impact even through the shield of his magic.

He scrambled to his feet as the creature launched itself at him a second time. Again he avoided the attack, using the staff to block the deadly claws. The staff's magic flared and burned, stripping off ragged lengths of reptilian skin, and the maentwrog spun away.

The Knight of the Word righted himself and moved to the center of the clearing, close to the remains of the maentwrog's shattered prison. From the corner of his eye, he saw Nest crouched down at the fringe of the trees, ready to bolt. But she would not run. She would not leave Pick. Or him, he believed. Whatever happened, she would stand her ground. She might be only a young girl, but she had the heart and soul of a warrior. He knew that much about her. He wished anew that he had been able to tell her more, to give her something else with which to defend herself. But it was a pointless exercise; whether he lived or died, he had done everything for her that he could.

He edged left toward the demon. There was his real enemy. If the maentwrog gave him even a moment's respite, he could . . . But no, it was too late for that, too late for anything but letting events unfold as they would. He felt a great despair at his limitations, at the narrowness of the charge he had been given, at the hard truths that belonged to him alone.

The maentwrog crept toward him once more, body lowered to the earth, eyes bright and gleaming. It would not stop until one of them was dead. The Knight understood the nature of his adversary, and he knew there would be no quarter. The beast had killed stronger creatures in its time, and it was not afraid. Fueled by savagery and rage, it knew only one way.

It attacked, feinting several times in an effort to distract the Knight, then launched itself across the clearing, an unstoppable juggernaut of muscle, claws, and teeth. The Knight of the Word stood his ground and delivered a powerful blow, lashing out with such force that the magic's fire engulfed the maentwrog. But the monster's rush carried it past his defenses and right into him. The Knight was slammed against the earth, the armored light that protected him crushed downward like plastic. He rolled aside as the maentwrog thrashed within the cloak of fire, trying to reach him but tearing only the earth. He struck it repeatedly, slamming his staff against the massive body, fire bursting from its polished length. The maentwrog screamed and struggled to pin him to the ground, twisting and arching in fury. Twice the Knight was felled, the breath knocked from his lungs, pain filling his body, his strength momentarily leaving him. Both times he rallied, refusing to back away. He could no longer see either the demon or Nest. He could barely make out where he was, the clearing filled with smoke and soot, the shards of light from the devastated tree obscured. He moved in a world of sound and sudden movement, of responses born of instinct and swift reaction, where an instant's hesitation would mean his death.

He broke from the maentwrog momentarily, sliding away through the murky gloom like a ghost, knowing he must wait for an opening. His strength was beginning to fail, and his magic was tiring. If he did not bring this battle to a swift conclusion, he would lose it. He was so battered already that he could no longer move without pain, his legs cramped, his arms leaden and weak. He had not been much of a fighter in the time before he had become a Knight of the Word, and so fighting did not come instinctively to him. He had learned what little he knew from his dreams of the future and his confrontations in the present, and he was a novice compared with the thing he battled. His magic had made the difference so far, but his magic was not without limits and it was tailored to a different end.

Then the maentwrog swiped at him from out of the smoke and dust, knocking him from his feet. In an instant, the creature was on top of him, bearing down with its forelegs, pinning him fast. Its jaws snapped at his head, scraping against the magic's armored light, ripping at the fabric. The Knight drove his feet into the monster's chest, fire exploding at the contact, but could not break free.

In that instant, Nest Freemark rushed out of the smoke and darkness, screaming in fury, no longer able simply to stand by and watch. Wielding a six-foot piece of deadwood, she swung it at the maentwrog in an effort to distract it, desperate to do something to help. The Knight cried out at her to go back, but she ignored him. Surprised, the maentwrog swiped at her with one massive foreleg, and sent her cartwheeling back into the night.

One arm suddenly free, the Knight thrust the black staff deep into the monster's maw and sent the magic forth. Fire lanced into the monster's throat, burning and consuming, and the maentwrog reared backward in pain, trying to break free. But the Knight clung to it stubbornly as the maentwrog beat at him with its arms and tore at him with its claws, shrieking. The Knight felt as if everything was breaking apart inside his body, but the staff remained buried in the beast's throat, the fire exploding out of it.

The maentwrog stumbled and fell, then lay writhing on the earth, frantically trying to rise, to rid itself of the fire within. The Knight yanked the staff from its throat and drove it into one baleful eye, feeling the maentwrog's head shudder beneath the blow. He struck a second time, then a third, as fire flared in brilliant spurts and smoke billowed into the night.

When he could no longer lift his staff to strike, he tried to disengage himself from the shapeless mass at his feet, but his legs refused to respond.

Don't leave Nest alone! he screamed in silent desperation, and then his strength gave out completely and he collapsed.

In the smoky aftermath, the clearing went still.

Raindrops fell on Nest Freemark's face, soft, cool splashes against her heated skin. They fell out of the blackness in a ragged scattering, and then began to quicken. Nest brushed at them absently as she lay sprawled on the earth at the edge of the clearing, her eyes locked on the mix of smoke and gloom that roiled before her. She could not see what was happening. In the last desperate moments of the struggle between John Ross and the monster, everything had disappeared. Fire belched and inhuman shrieks rent the air, and then suddenly there was only silence.

"John," she said softly, his name a whisper that only she was meant to hear.

A sudden breeze rose off the waters of the Rock River, gusted through the deep woods, and began to sweep away the haze. As the night air cleared, she could see both combatants, sprawled on the ground, motionless. She climbed slowly to her feet. Steam was rising off the maentwrog, and as she watched, it began to disintegrate, collapsing on itself as if a shell in which air had been trapped and released. The massive body broke apart and fell earthward in a cloud of dust and ash, and in seconds only an outline remained, a dark shadow against the torn and bloodied earth.

John Ross remained where he was, motionless and crumpled. The black staff no longer gleamed. Nest moved to where he lay and stared down at him in horror.

A sudden, violent explosion shattered the silence, and the force of the explosion was so powerful that the shock wave rocked her as it passed. The explosion had come from some distance off. She turned to look for its source, and she saw fireworks exploding everywhere. But they were not going off in any pattern, and the flashes of color that identified their location were not only overhead, but at ground level as well.

She swung back to find the demon standing only a dozen feet away, come forward out of the gloom to confront her. Shock and surprise jolted her.

"It's only you and me now," he said quietly, a serene look on his face, his hands folded comfortably before him. "I suspected that Mr. Ross might try to intervene in this, so I arranged a minor distraction. It looks to me as if it did the job. Care to check for yourself?"

She straightened, forcing herself to stand fast, closing away her emotions so that he would not see them. "What do you want from me?" she asked, keeping her tone of voice flat and expressionless.

"I want you, child. My daughter. I want you with me, where you belong."

She choked back the urge to scream in rage. "I told you not to call me that. I am not your daughter. I am nothing like you. I have no intention of going with you anywhere. Not now, not ever. If you make me go, I will run away from you the first chance I get."

He shook his head admonishingly. "You are in deep denial, Nest. Do you know what that means? You can pretend all you want, but when all is said and done, I am still your father. You can't change that. Nothing can. I made you. I gave you life. You can't just dismiss the fact of my existence."

Nest laughed. A surge of adrenaline rushed through her. "You gave me life out of hate for my mother and my grandmother. You gave me life for all the wrong reasons. My mother is dead because of you. I don't know if you killed her or if she killed herself, but you are responsible in either case."

"She killed herself," the demon interjected with a shrug. "She was weak and foolish."

Nest felt her face turn hot. "But my grandmother didn't kill herself, did she?"

"She was dangerous. If I had let her live, she might have killed me."

"And so now I belong with you?" Nest was openly incredulous. "Why would you think I would even consider such a thing?"

The demon's bland features tightened. "There is no one else to look after you."

"What are you talking about? What about Grandpa?" She pointed at him threateningly, aggressively. "Get out of here! Leave me alone!"

"You have no one. Your grandfather is dead. Or if not, he will be soon."

"You're lying!"

The demon shrugged again. "Am I? In any case, none of them matter. Only me."

Nest was shaking with fury. "Why you would think, after all you've done, that I would do *anything* you wanted, is beyond me. I hate you. I hate what you are. I hate it that I am any part of you. You don't matter to me. You matter less than nothing!"

"Nest." He spoke her name calmly and evenly. "You can say or do anything you like, but it won't change what's going to happen."

She took a deep breath to steady herself. "Nothing's going to happen."

"You are my flesh and blood, Nest. We are the same."

"We are not the same. We will never be the same."

"No?" The demon smiled. "You want to believe that, I expect. But you're not certain, are you? How can you be? Don't you wonder how much of me is inside you?" He paused. "Don't you owe it to yourself to find out?"

He started forward. "Don't touch me!" Nest snapped, clenching her fists at her sides.

The demon stopped, laughing. "But I must. I must touch you if I am to help you see who you can become, who you really are. I must, if I am to help you free the part of me you keep buried."

She shook her head rapidly from side to side. "Keep away from me."

He looked skyward, as if discovering the rain for the first time. It was falling more rapidly now, a slow, steady patter against the leaves of the trees, its dampness spreading darkly across the bare ground. Nest glanced down at John Ross, but he still wasn't moving. She looked over at Pick, slumped on the floor of his iron cage.

You have to help them.

Then, for the first time that night, she saw the feeders. They had ringed the clearing, hundreds—perhaps thousands—of them, bodies scrunched together within the shadows cast by the trees, eyes bright with expectation as they gleamed catlike in the darkness. She had never seen so many gathered in one place, never in numbers like this. It seemed, on looking about, as if all the feeders in the world had come together in these woods.

"You belong to me," the demon repeated, watching her closely. "Child of mine."

She closed her eyes momentarily, blinking rapidly against the tears that were threatening to form. She was all alone, she knew. He had seen to that. He had done that to her. She stared balefully at him, daring him to come closer, hating him as she had never hated anyone. Her father. *A demon. A demon. A demon.*

"Step away from Mr. Ross, please," he ordered softly.

She stood her ground in challenge. "No."

The demon smiled coldly. "No?"

He gestured at her almost casually, and she was assailed with such fear that her legs buckled and her breath caught in her throat. She staggered under the weight of the attack, and as she did so the feeders came at her from every side. She whirled to meet their assault, her eyes locking quickly on those of her attackers, her magic turning them to mush. One by one they crumpled before her, falling to the sodden earth and melting away. But for each one she destroyed, two more took its place. She hissed at them like a cat, enraged and terrified by their closeness and numbers. They were touching her now, grappling for her, too many to fend off completely, and she was back once more in the darkness of the caves beneath the park, wrapped in electrician's tape and unable to help herself. She fought on, striking out wildly, destroying any feeder who would look at her, forcing some to cringe away as she wheeled on them, thrashing against those who tried to crawl over her.

But there were so many. *Too many! Too many!*

She clasped her head between her arms and closed her eyes, screaming defiantly.

Then suddenly the feeders were gone back into the night, and she was alone again. She lifted her head and found the demon watching her, amusement reflected in his pale eyes.

He started toward her again, a slow advance through the empty gloom and soft rain.

"Wraith!" she cried out desperately.

Abruptly, the big ghost wolf appeared. He emerged from the trees behind the demon and stalked into the ravaged clearing with his massive head lowered and his hackles raised. Nest felt her heart leap as her giant protector advanced on the demon.

The demon stopped and looked casually over his shoulder. Wraith stopped as well.

The demon turned back to Nest, smiling. "I have a confession to make," he said. "I have been keeping something from you. Would you like to know what it is? It's rather important." Nest said nothing, suddenly terrified. He was enjoying the moment. "It's about this creature. Your protector. It's an elemental, a thing created of magic and the elements, a sort of familiar. You probably think your grandmother made it; maybe she even told you she did. But she didn't. I did."

His words spun through the silence like chips of jagged metal, cutting apart what remained of Nest's courage and resolve. She stared at him in disbelief. "You're lying."

He shook his head. "Think about it. I left you behind after you were born. Why would I do that if I thought any harm would come to you? You were my child; quite possibly you would have magic at your command. The feeders would be drawn to you. At times, you would be in danger." He shrugged. "So I created a protector to watch over you, to keep you from harm."

She shook her head slowly. "I don't believe you."

"No?" He laughed softly. "Watch."

He turned back to Wraith and made a quick gesture. Wraith sat back on his haunches obediently. The demon smiled at Nest. He made another gesture, and Wraith lay down and put his head between his paws, docile and responsive.

The demon faced Nest once more. "See?" He gave her a wink.

Nest felt the last of her hope fade, watched her last chance for survival drift off into the night. *Use your magic. Trust Wraith.* But Wraith was his creature. *His.* The truth burned in her throat and left her dizzy and sick inside.

Oh, my God, my God! What am I supposed to do now?

The demon spread his arms in a gesture intended to convey his sympathy. "You're all alone, Nest. There isn't anyone left for you to turn to except me. But maybe that isn't as bad as you think. Let me take your hands in mine. Just for a few moments. Let me touch you. I can make you see things in different ways. I can give you an understanding of who you really are. What harm can come from that? If you don't like what you see, I'll leave."

But he wouldn't, she knew. He would never leave. And if she let him touch her as he wanted, she would be destroyed forever. She would be subverted in ways she could not begin to imagine. Her father was anathema to her. To any human. He was a demon, and there was nothing good that could come from embracing any part of what he offered.

"Stay away from me," she told him for the second time that night.

But he came toward her anyway, certain of himself now, confident that he held her fate in his hands, that there was nothing she could do to stop him. Nest was shaking with fear and helpless anger, but she stood her ground. There was nowhere to run and no reason to try. Sooner or later, he would find her. The feeders began to edge out from the shadows again, their eyes brightening. She felt the rain fall steadily on her face, and she realized her clothing was soaked. Behind, through the trees of the deep woods, the fireworks were still exploding in a series of ragged bangs and whumps.

I will not become like him, she told herself then. *I will never let that happen. I will die first.*

She waited until he was so close she could make out the lines of his face in the gloom, and then she attacked him with her magic. She struck out with ferocious determination, using every bit of power she could summon. She met his gaze squarely, locked his eyes with hers, and went after him. He was not expecting it. The force of her assault jolted him back a step, shook him from head to foot. His mouth opened in surprise, and his eyes went wide. But he did not collapse as Danny Abbott and Robert Heppler had. He kept his feet. His face underwent a frightening transformation, and for a moment she could see clearly the depth of his evil.

"You foolish little girl!" he hissed in undisguised fury.

He came at her again, stronger this time, breaking past her defenses, brushing aside her attack. She retreated from him, trying to bring more power to bear, to slow him, to keep him at bay. The feeders were scrambling and leaping wildly, closing about, tightening their circle. She felt their anticipation, sensed their readiness. They would feed soon. They would feed on her.

Then she saw Wraith. He left the ground as if catapulted, his huge, rippling body uncoiling, his muscles stretching. He crossed the open space between them in a handful of heartbeats, paws tearing at the earth, jaws spread wide. A high-pitched snarl broke from his throat, so dark and terrible that for a second everything seemed to freeze with its sound.

In that second, Nest was certain he was coming for her and she was about to die. She brought her arms up quickly to shield herself and dropped to one knee.

But it was the demon Wraith had targeted, and he flew through the air in a blur of black and gray tiger stripes, crashing into his creator and bearing him to the earth in a bright flash of white teeth. The demon disappeared under the beast, body twisting, arms flailing in an effort to find purchase. Nest staggered back from them, nearly falling, not understanding what had happened. Why was Wraith attacking the demon? The demon screamed in rage and pain as the ghost wolf tore at him. It seemed as if the beast had gone insane, attacking with such ferocity that there was no stopping him. Feeders broke over them both, writhing and twisting jubilantly in response to the battle, frenzied in their eagerness to dine. They scattered momentarily as the demon threw off Wraith with a superhuman effort and struggled to his feet, torn and bloodied and battered. But Wraith was on top of him again in an instant, jaws snapping.

The demon screamed something then, just one time, a name that Nest heard clearly. *"Evelyn!"* There was recognition in the cry; there was rage and terror. *Evelyn!*

Then Wraith was all over him, dragging him down and ripping him apart. Blood and flesh flew in ragged gouts, and the demon's screams turned to muffled gasps. Arms and legs flopped wide in limp surrender, and the demon began to come apart, throat and chest gaping, insides spilling out. Feeders tore at him hungrily, swarming out of the night. The demon's savaged body lurched upward as if jolted by electricity, and something dark and winged and unspeakable tried to break free from the gore. But Wraith caught it as it emerged, and his jaws snapped down with an audible crunch. Nest heard a single, horrifying shriek, and then silence.

Wraith moved away from the demon's body then, head lowered, jaws dark and wet with blood. The demon lay crumpled and motionless before her, no longer recognizable as anything human, reduced to something foul and wretched. She stared at it a moment, watching it collapse on itself as the maentwrog had done, watching it sink into the earth and fade to an outline and then disappear.

The rain was falling in a steady downpour now, and thunder rumbled through the darkness, approaching from the west. The feeders faded back into the night, reduced to a scattering of lantern eyes that winked out one by one like searchlights being extinguished. Wraith shook himself, a gesture that seemed almost dismissive. His huge, tiger-striped face lifted into the darkness and his gleaming eyes fixed on Nest. For just an instant, and Nest was never certain afterward if she had actually seen it or just imagined it, she thought she saw Gran's sharp old eyes peering out of the ghost wolf's head.

Then Wraith turned and walked back into the trees, melting away into the darkness, becoming one with the air.

Nest went to Pick first, breaking off the pin that secured the cage door and gently lifting the sylvan into the open air. Pick sat dazed and shaking in her palm for a few moments, holding his head in his hands as he collected himself. Then he smoothed back the leaves that were clustered atop his head, brushed at his wooden arms and legs, and without looking at her, asked about Daniel. When she told him, fighting back her tears, he shook his head sadly and told her in a calm voice not to cry, but to remember that Daniel had been a good friend and never to forget him.

Then he looked directly at her, his narrow face composed, his button eyes steady. His voice was sandpaper rough. "Do you understand what's happened here, Nest? Do you know what your grandmother did for you?"

Nest shook her head slowly. "I'm not sure. I know I heard the demon call her name. And I think I saw her eyes in Wraith's, there at the end." She sank down on her knees in the darkness and rain. "I think she was there with him in some way."

The sylvan nodded. "She was there, all right. But not the way I had it figured. I had it wrong, I admit that. I thought that she had created Wraith to be your protector. But it was the demon who made Wraith. What your grandmother did was to stir up the magic a bit. She must have realized where Wraith came from when you first told her about seeing him. She must have understood right away that it meant the demon planned to return for you someday. And she knew when he did she might not be strong enough to stop him! Sharp as a tack, your grandmother. So she used her magic, all of it, to turn his own creation against him. On the outside, Wraith looked the same. But inside, he was something different. If the demon ever came back for you, Wraith was waiting to have at him. That was the secret ingredient your grandmother's magic added to the mix. The demon never figured it out, but that's why your grandmother didn't have any magic to protect herself when he came for her. She used it all to change Wraith."

"But why did Wraith protect me this time when he didn't protect me before?" Nest demanded quickly. "Why didn't he attack the demon in the park or down in the caves or even in church?"

Pick lifted one forefinger in front of his grainy face and shook it slowly. "Use your brain. Your grandmother wanted to be certain that Wraith didn't intervene unless it was absolutely necessary. She didn't want any mistakes, any mix-ups. Wraith wasn't supposed to protect you unless you tried to protect yourself! Do I need to draw you a picture? It was your magic, Nest! Your grandmother reasoned that you would only use it if you were in the worst kind of danger. Remember how she cautioned you against using it foolishly? Reminded you over and over again, didn't she? That was because she wanted you to save it for when you really needed it. Think about it! That was the reason for your grandmother's note! She was admonishing you to stand and fight! If the demon came after you and you summoned up even the littlest part of your magic to save yourself, Wraith would have to help!"

He was animated now, infused with the passion of his certainty. "Oh, I know you would have done so anyway. Sure, I know that. But your grandmother wasn't taking any chances. It was a clever trap, Nest. Criminy, yes! When Wraith came to your defense, the demon was facing a combination of both his own magic and your grandmother's. It was too much for him." He took a deep breath and exhaled slowly. "That was the sacrifice your grandmother made for you."

Nest stayed silent, stunned. It was difficult for her to imagine her grandmother doing what Pick had described. But Gran had been her fearless champion, and Nest knew the sylvan was right. Gran had given up her magic and thereby her life for her granddaughter.

She set Pick upon the ground then and bent over John Ross. He was stirring at last, trying to right himself. His pale green eyes fixed on her, and for an instant she saw a mix of despair and resolve that frightened her. He asked what had happened, and she told him. When she was finished, he reached for his staff and levered himself slowly and gingerly to his feet.

"You saved us, Nest," he said. He brushed at his clothing, a muddied and rumpled scarecrow in the rain-drenched gloom.

"I was worried about you," she replied softly. "I thought the maentwrog might have . . ."

She trailed off, unable to finish, and he put his arm around her and held her against him. "I'm sorry this had to happen to you, Nest. I wish it could have been otherwise. But life chooses for us sometimes, and all we can do is accept what happens and try to get through it the best way we can."

She nodded into his shirt. "It never felt as if he was my father," she whispered. "It never felt as if he was any part of me."

"He was part of what's bad about the world, but a part that happened to be closer to you than most." Ross stroked her damp hair. "Put it behind you, Nest. It won't happen all at once, but if you give it a chance, it will go away."

"I know. I'll try." She hugged him gratefully. "I'm just glad you were here to help me."

There was an uneasy pause. His hand stopped moving in her hair.

"What's wrong?" she asked.

He seemed to be thinking it over. "What do you think would have happened, Nest, if your father had touched you?"

She was quiet for a moment. "I don't know."

She heard him sigh. "I'm going to tell you something I've kept secret until now. I'm going to tell you because you need to know. Because someday the knowledge might save your life."

His face lowered into her hair. "I dream about the future, Nest. I dream about it every night of my life. I dream about the way things will be if everything breaks down and the feeders consume us. I dream about the end of civilization, the end of the world. The dreams are real, not pretend. It is the price I pay for being a Knight of the Word. It is a reminder of what will happen if I fail. More importantly, it is a window into time that lets me discover exactly what it is I must try to prevent."

He stepped away from her, keeping his hands on her shoulders. Rain glistened on his lean face and in his mud-streaked hair. "I found out about you through my dreams. I found out that the demon was your father. But most important of all, I saw what you became because he touched you here tonight, in this place, in this park. I came to Hopewell to stop that from happening."

"What did I become?" she asked, her voice shaking.

He shook his head. "It doesn't matter. It can't happen now. The window of opportunity is past. The demon is gone. The events can't re-create themselves. You won't become what I saw in my dream. You will become what you make of yourself, but it won't be a bad thing. Not after what you did tonight. Not after you've heard what I have to say."

His smile was tight and bitter. "Some of what I do as a Knight of the Word is difficult for me to live with. I can't always change the future with words and knowledge. The demons I hunt are elusive and clever, and I don't always find them. Sometimes they accomplish what they intend, and I am left to deal with the results. Because I know from my dreams what those results signify, I must change them any way I can."

His brow furrowed with hidden pain. "It was necessary for you to face your father and reject him. I came to Hopewell to see if you could do that. I would have destroyed him beforehand if I could, but I knew from the beginning that my chances were poor. I knew it would probably be left up to you. I gave you what help I could, but in my heart. Nest, in my soul, I knew it would come down to you."

He stood tall in front of her, suddenly unapproachable, become as impenetrable as the darkness that shrouded them both.

"Do you understand?" he asked softly. "If you had failed in what was required of you, if the demon had touched you and you had become what he intended, if you had been unable to withstand him and your magic had darkened to his use . . ."

He took his hands from her shoulders, his voice trailing off. Their eyes locked. "My purpose in coming here, Nest, was to stop you from becoming the creature I saw in my dreams." He paused, letting the full import of his words sink in. "I would have done whatever was needed to accomplish that."

Recognition of his meaning ran through her like shards of ice, and she stared at him in horror and disbelief. *Whatever was needed.* She tried to say something in response, to let him know what she was feeling, but she could not find the words. The chasm he had opened between them was so vast that she could not find a way to bridge it.

"Good-bye, Nest," he said finally, stepping back from her, his mouth crooked in a tight, sad smile. "I wish I could have been your father."

He stood there a moment longer, a lean, hunched figure in the rain-drenched night. Her savior. Her executioner. She felt her heart break with the realization.

Then he turned away, his black staff gleaming, and disappeared into the night.

Tuesday, July 5

Chapter 32

By morning, news services from as far away as Chicago were reporting the story. Variations in word usage and presentation aside, it read pretty much the same everywhere. A disgruntled union worker at MidCon Steel in Hopewell, Illinois, had attempted to sabotage a fireworks display sponsored by the company. Derry Howe, age thirty-eight, of Hopewell, was killed when the bomb he was attempting to plant within the staging area exploded prematurely. Also injured were Robert Freemark, aged sixty-five, of Hopewell, a retired member of the same union; two members of the staging crew; and several spectators. In a related incident, a second man, Junior Elway, aged thirty-seven, of Hopewell, was killed attempting to plant a bomb in the fourteen-inch mill at MidCon during a break in his work shift. It was thought that the dead men, longtime friends and union activists, were acting in concert, and that the bombs were intended to halt efforts by MidCon to reopen the company in defiance of a strike order and to initiate a new round of settlement talks. Police were continuing with their investigation.

In a second, much smaller news item, the weather service reported extensive damage to parts of Sinnissippi Park in the wake of a thunderstorm that passed through Hopewell sometime around midnight. High winds and lightning had toppled a white oak thought to be well over two hundred years old as well as several smaller trees within a heavily wooded section of the park. The storm had moved out of the area by early morning, but phone and electrical lines were still down in parts of the city.

Nest heard most of it from television reports as she wandered back and forth between the Community General Hospital lounge and the lunchroom waiting for her grandfather to wake up. It had been almost midnight when she walked home through the driving rain, the park deserted save for a cluster of patrol cars parked in front of the pavilion and toboggan slide, their red and blue lights flashing. Police officers in yellow slickers were stringing tape and examining the grounds, but she didn't attach any particular significance to the matter until she got home and found another cruiser parked in her driveway and more officers searching her home. She was told then that her grandfather had been taken to the hospital with a broken shoulder, cracked ribs, and possible internal injuries following a bombing attempt in the park, and that she had been reported missing and possibly kidnapped.

After determining that she was all right, they had driven her to the hospital to be with her grandfather. Old Bob had been treated and sedated, and she was told by the nurses on duty that he would probably sleep until morning. She had sufficient presence of mind to call Cass Minter to let her know she was all right and to tell her where she was. Even though it was almost one in the morning, Cass was still awake. Brianna was there with her, spending the night, and Robert was at home waiting to hear something as well. It was Robert who had called the police, telling them about the man poisoning trees in the park and insisting he might have gotten hold of Nest. He had even suggested, rather bizarrely, that the man might be using a stun gun.

Nest dozed on and off all night while her grandfather slept. Cass came up with her mother to check on her the following morning, and when Mrs. Minter discovered what state she was in, they took her home to shower and change, made her a hot meal, and then drove her back again.

When they left around midafternoon, she called the Lincoln Hotel and asked for John Ross, but was told he had checked out early that morning and taken a bus west to the Quad Cities. He had left no forwarding address.

Her grandfather was still sleeping, so she parked herself in a quiet corner of the lounge to wait. As she read magazines and stared into space, her thoughts constantly strayed to the events of the past few days. Faces and voices recalled themselves in random visits, like ghosts appearing from the shadows. The demon. John Ross. Wraith. Two Bears. Pick. She tried to listen to them, to understand what they were telling her, to fit together the pieces of jagged memory that lay scattered in her mind. She tried to make sense of what she had experienced. She thought often of Gran, and doing so left her sad and philosophical. It seemed, in the wake of last night's events, as if Gran had been gone a long time already. The news of her death, so fresh yesterday morning, was already stale and fading from the public consciousness. Today's news was all of Derry Howe and Junior Elway and the bombings. Tomorrow's news would be about something else. It diminished the importance of what had happened, she thought. It was the nature of things, of course. Life went on. The best you could do was to hold on to the memories that were important to you, so that even if everyone else forgot, you would remember. She could do that much for Gran.

She was dozing in the lounge, listening with half an ear to a television report that said authorities were dragging Rock River above Sinnissippi Park for a missing Hopewell man, when one of the nurses came to tell her that her grandfather was awake and asking for her. She rose and walked quickly to his room. He was sitting up in bed now, a cast on his arm and shoulder, bandages wrapped about his ribs, and tubes running out of his arm. His white hair was rumpled and spiky as he turned his head to look at her. She smiled back bravely.

"Hi, Grandpa," she said.

"Rough night, wasn't it?" he replied, seeing the concern in her eyes. "Are you all right, Nest?"

"I'm fine." She sat next to him on the bed. "How about you?"

"Stiff and sore, but I'll live. You heard what happened, I suppose?"

She nodded. "This guy was trying to blow up the fireworks and you stopped him." She took his hand in hers. "My grandpa, the hero."

"Well, I didn't stop him, matter of fact. He stopped himself. All I did, come right down to it, was to make sure people knew the truth about what he was trying to do. Maybe it will help ease tensions a little." He paused. "They tell you how long I'm going to be here?"

She shook her head. "They haven't told me anything."

"Well, there's not much to tell. I'll be fine in a day or two, but they might keep me here a week. I guess they plan to let me out for your grandmother's funeral.

Doctor says so, anyway." He paused. "Will you be all right without me? Do you want me to call someone? Maybe you could go stay with the Minters."

"Grandpa, don't worry, I'm fine," she said quickly. "I can take care of myself."

He studied her a moment. "I know that." He glanced at his nightstand. "Would you hand me a cup of water, please?"

She did, and he took a long drink, lifting his head only slightly from the pillows. The room was white and still, and she could hear the murmur of voices from the hall outside. Through cracks in the window blinds, she could see blue sky and sunlight.

When her grandfather was finished with the water, he looked at her again, his eyes uneasy. "Did you run into your father out there last night?"

Her throat tightened. She nodded.

"Did he hurt you?"

She shook her head. "He tried to persuade me to come with him, like John Ross said he would. He threatened me. But I told him I wasn't coming and he couldn't make me." Her brow furrowed. "So he gave up and went away."

Her grandfather studied her. "Just like that? Off he went, back to poisoning trees in the park?"

"Well, no." She realized how ridiculous it sounded. She looked out the window, thinking. "He didn't just go off. It's kind of hard to explain, actually." She hesitated, not sure where to go. "I had some help."

Her grandfather kept staring at her, but she had nothing left to say. Finally, he nodded. "Maybe you'll fill me in on the details sometime. When you think I'm up to it."

She looked back at him. "I forgot something. He told me about Gran. He said he tried to come after me, and she chased him off with the shotgun." She watched her grandfather's eyes. "So she wasn't just shooting at nothing."

He nodded again, solemn, introspective. "That's good to know, Nest. I appreciate you telling me. I thought it must be something like that. I was pretty sure."

He closed his eyes momentarily, and Nest exhaled slowly. No one spoke for a moment. Then Nest said, "Grandpa, I was wondering." She waited until he opened his eyes again. "You know about Jared Scott?" Her grandfather nodded. "They took his brothers and sisters away afterward. Mrs. Walker says they're going to be put in foster care. I was wondering if, maybe after you're home again, we could see if Bennett Scott could come stay with us."

She bit her lip against the sudden dampness in her eyes. "She's pretty little to be with strangers, Grandpa."

Her grandfather nodded, and his hand tightened about hers. "I think that would be fine, Nest," he said quietly. "We'll look into it."

She went home again when her grandfather fell back asleep, walking the entire way from the hospital, needing the time alone. The sun shone brightly out of a cloudless sky, and the temperature had fallen just enough that the air was warm without being humid. She wondered if it was anything like this where John Ross had gone.

The house was quiet and empty when she arrived home. The casseroles and tins were gone from the kitchen, picked up by Reverend Emery, who had left a nice note for her on the counter saying he would stop by the hospital to visit her grandfather that night. She drank a can of root beer, sitting on the back porch steps with

Mr. Scratch, who lay sprawled out at her feet, oblivious of everything. She looked off into the park frequently, but made no move to go into it. Pick would be at work there, healing the scarred landscape of the deep woods. Maybe she would look for him tomorrow.

When it began to grow dark, she made herself a sandwich and sat eating alone at the kitchen table where she had sat so often with Gran. She was midway through her meal when she heard a kitten cry. She sat where she was a moment, then got up and went to the back door. There was Spook. Bennett Scott's kitten was ragged and scrawny, but all in one piece. Nest slipped outside and picked up the kitten, holding it against her breast. Where had he come from? There was no sign of Pick. But Spook couldn't have found his way here all alone.

She put milk in a bowl and set the bowl on the porch for Spook to drink. The kitten lapped hungrily, a loud purr building in its furry chest. Nest watched in silence, thinking.

After a while, she picked up the phone and called Robert.

"Hey," she said.

"Nest?"

"Want to go for a bike ride and visit Jared?"

There was a long pause. "What did you do to me last night?"

"Nothing. Want to go with me or not?"

"You can't visit Jared. He's off limits. They've got him in intensive care."

Nest looked at the shadows lengthening in the park. "Let's go see him anyway."

She hung up and when the phone rang, she left it alone. With Robert, it was best not to argue or explain.

Twenty minutes later he wheeled into her drive, dropped his bike in the grass, and walked up to her where she was back sitting out on the porch steps. He brushed at his unruly blond hair as he strode up, bouncing defiantly on the balls of his feet.

"Why'd you hang up on me?" he demanded.

"I'm a girl," she said, shrugging. "Girls do things like that. Want a root beer?"

"Geez. Bribery, yet." He followed her into the kitchen. "How's your grandpa?"

"Good. He won't be able to come home for a while, maybe a week. But he's okay."

"Good for him. Wish I could say the same."

She cocked one eyebrow speculatively. "What's the matter? Did I hurt you last night?"

"Ah-hah! You admit it!" Robert was ecstatic. "I knew you did something! I knew it! What was it? C'mon, tell me!"

She reached into the refrigerator, brought out a can of root beer, and handed it to him. "I used a stun gun."

He stared at her, openmouthed. Then he flushed. "No, you didn't! You're just saying that because that was what I told the cops! Where would you get a stun gun, anyway? Come on! What did you do?"

She cocked her head. "You mean you lied to the police?"

He continued to stare at her, frustration mirrored in his narrow, bunched features. Then he crooked his finger. "C'mere."

He led her back outside, down the steps and into the yard. Then he shook the can of root beer as hard as he could, pointed it at her, and popped the top. Cold fizz sprayed all over her. He waited until she was glaring openly at him, then took a long drink from the can and said, "Okay, now we're even."

She went inside to wash and change her T-shirt, then came back out to find him dangling a length of string in front of Spook, who was watching with a mix of curiosity and mistrust. "Are you ready?" she asked, picking the kitten up and depositing him inside the house.

He shrugged. "Why are we doing this, anyway?" He dropped the string and walked over to retrieve his bike.

She kicked at his tire as she walked past. "Because I'm afraid Jared might not come back from wherever he's gone if one of us doesn't go get him."

They wheeled their bikes to the top of the drive, climbed onto the seats, and began to pedal into the twilight. They rode down Sinnissippi Road and across Lincoln Highway to the back streets that led to the hospital. They rode in silence, watching the city darken around them, its people settling in behind lighted windows in front of lighted screens. Children played in yards, and lawn mowers roared. Starlings sang raucously, and elderly couples walked in slow motion down the concrete sidewalks that had become the measure of their lives.

When they reached the hospital, Nest and Robert chained their bikes to the rack by the front entry and went inside. It was after nine o'clock, and the waiting room was quiet, most of the visitors gone home for the night. Side by side, they walked up to look in on Nest's grandfather, but he was sleeping again, so they didn't stay. Instead, they found a stairwell that connected the six floors of the hospital and stood just outside, glancing around surreptitiously.

"So, what's the plan, Stan?" Robert asked, lifting one eyebrow.

"He's in five fourteen," Nest answered. "Just off the stairway. You go up the elevator and talk to whoever's working the nursing station. Ask about Jared or something. I'll go up the stairs and slip into his room while they're busy with you."

Robert smirked. "That's your whole plan?"

"Assuming you intend to help."

He stared at her. "Tell you what. I'll help if you'll tell me what you did to me last night. The truth, this time."

She stared back at him without answering, thinking it over. Then she said, "I used magic on you."

He hesitated, and she could tell that for just half a second he believed her. Then he smirked dismissively. "You're weirder than I am, Nest. You know that? Okay, let's go."

She waited until she saw him stop in front of the elevator; then she entered the stairwell and began to climb. She reached the fifth floor, inched the door open, and peered out into the hall. It was virtually deserted. She could see room 514 almost directly across from her. When Robert stepped out of the elevator a moment later and walked over to the nursing station, she slipped from her hiding place.

A moment later, she was inside Jared's room.

Jared Scott lay motionless in a hospital bed, looking small and lost amid an array of equipment, eyes staring at nothing behind half-closed lids, arms and legs laid out straight beneath the covers, face pale and drawn. The room was dark except for the lights from the monitors and a small night-light near the door. The blinds to the street were closed, and the air conditioner hummed softly. Nest glanced around the room, then back at Jared. A bandage covered the top half of his head, and there were raw, savage marks on his face and arms from the beating he had received. She stared at him in despair, her eyes shifting from his face to the blinking green lights of the monitoring equipment and back again.

She had been thinking about coming to see him all afternoon, ever since leaving her grandfather. Spook had decided her. She would use her magic to help Jared. She didn't know for certain that she could, of course. She had never used the magic this way. But she understood its potential to affect the human body, and there was a chance she could do some good. She needed to try, perhaps as much for herself as for him. She needed to step out from her father's shadow, from the dark legacy of his life, something she would never be able to do until she embraced what he had given her and turned it to a use he would never have considered. She would start here.

She walked over to Jared's bed and lowered the railing so that she could sit next to him. "Hey, Jared," she said softly.

She touched his hand, held it in her own as she had held her grandfather's that afternoon, and reached up to stroke his face. His skin felt warm and soft. She waited to see if he would respond, but he didn't. He just lay there, staring. She fought to hold back her tears.

This would be dangerous, she knew. It would be risky. If the magic failed her, she might kill Jared. But she knew as well, somewhere deep inside, that if she failed to act, she would lose him anyway. He was not coming back alone from wherever he had gone. He was waiting there for her to come get him.

She leaned over him, still holding his hand, and stared down into his unseeing eyes. "Jared, it's me, Nest," she whispered.

She moved until she was directly in his line of sight, her face only inches from his own. The room was still except for the slight hiss and blip of the machines, cloaked in darkness and solitude.

"Look at me, Jared," she whispered.

She reached out to him with her magic, spidery tendrils of sound and movement that passed through his staring eyes and probed inward. "Where are you, Jared?" she asked softly. "We miss you. Me, Cass, Robert, Brianna. We miss you."

She nudged him gently, tried to reach deeper. She could feel something inside him resisting her, could feel it draw back, a curtain that tightened. She waited patiently for the curtain to loosen. If she pushed too hard, she could damage him. She experienced a sudden rush of uncertainty. She was taking an enormous chance, using the magic like this, experimenting. Perhaps she was making a mistake, thinking she could help, that the magic could do what she expected. Perhaps she should stop now and let nature take its intended course, unhindered by her interference.

She felt him relax then, and she probed anew, stroking him, brushing lightly against his fragile consciousness, the part he had locked deep inside where it was dark and safe.

Within her body, the magic hummed and vibrated, a living thing. She had never gotten this close to it for this long. She could feel its power building, working its way through her, heat and sound and motion. It was like trying to direct the movements of a cat; you felt it could spring away at any moment.

"Jared, look at me," she whispered.

Careful, careful. The magic prodded gently, insistently. Sweat beaded on Nest's forehead, and her chest and throat tightened with her efforts.

"I'm here, Jared. Can you hear me?"

Time slipped away. She lost track of how much, her concentration focused on making contact with him, on breaking through the shell into which he had retreated. Once, she heard someone approach, but the steps turned away before they reached Jared's room. Her concentration tightened. She forgot about Robert, about the nurses, about everything. She stayed where she was, not looking up, not shifting her gaze away from Jared, not even for a moment. She refused to give up. She kept talking to him, saying his name, using her magic to bump him gently, to open the door to his safehold just a crack.

"Jared," she said over and over. "It's me, Nest."

Until finally his eyes shifted to find hers, and he replied in a hoarse whisper, "Hey, Nest," and she knew he was going to be all right.

On a Greyhound traveling west between Denver and Salt Lake City, John Ross sat staring out into the night, watching the lights of ranches and towns hunkered down in the empty flats below the Rockies flash by in the darkness. He sat alone at the rear of the bus, his staff propped up against the seat beside him, the roar of the engine and the whine of the wheels drowning out the snoring of his fellow passengers. It was nearing midnight, and he was the only one awake.

He sighed wearily. Soon he would sleep, too. Because he would have to. Because the demands of his body would give him no choice.

Almost two days had passed since he had left Nest Freemark standing in the rain in Sinnissippi Park. He had gone back to the hotel, gathered up his things, and waited in the lobby for the early-morning bus. When it arrived, he had climbed aboard without a backward glance and ridden away. Already his memory of Hopewell and her people was beginning to fade, the larger picture shrinking to small, bright moments that he could tuck away and carry with him. Old Bob; greeting him that first day at Josie's, believing him Caitlin's friend. Gran, her sharp old eyes raking across him as she sought to see through the façade he had created. Josie Jackson, sleepy-eyed and warm, lying next to him on their last day. Pick, the sylvan, the keeper of Sinnissippi Park. Daniel. Wraith. The demon.

But mostly there was Nest Freemark, a fourteen-year-old girl who could work magic and by doing so come to terms with the truth about her family, when anything less would have destroyed her. He could see her face clearly, her freckles and quirky smile and curly dark hair. He would remember the long, smooth strides she took when she ran and the way she stood her ground when it mattered. In a world in which so much of what he encountered only served to reinforce his fears that the future of his dreams was an inevitability, Nest gave him hope. When so many others might have succumbed to their fear and despair, Nest had not. She represented a little victory when measured against the enormity of the battle being fought by the Word and the Void, but sometimes little victories made the difference. Little victories, like the small events that tipped the scales in the balance of life, really could change the world.

I wish I could have been your father, he had said, and he had meant it.

He wondered if he would ever see her again.

He straightened in his seat, looking down the aisle past the slouched forms of the sleepers to where the driver hunched over the steering wheel, eyes on the road. In the bright glare of the headlights, the highway was an endless concrete ribbon unrolling out of the black. Morning was still far away; it was time to sleep. He had not slept since he had left Hopewell, and he could not put it off any longer. He shivered involuntarily at the prospect. It would be bad, he knew. It would be horrendous. He would be bereft of his magic, a night's payment for his expenditure in his battle with the maentwrog. He would be forced to run and to hide while his enemies hunted him; he would be alone and defenseless against them. Maybe they would find him this night. Maybe they would kill him. In the world of his dreams, all things were possible.

Weary and resigned, he eased his bad leg onto the padded bench and propped his body between the seat back and the bus wall. He was afraid, but he would not allow his fear to master him. He was a Knight of the Word, and he would find a way to survive.

John Ross closed his eyes, a warrior traveling through time, and drifted away to dream of a future he hoped would never be.

A KNIGHT OF THE WORD

TO JIM SIMONSON, LAURIE JAEGER, LARRY GRELLA, &
MOLLIE TREMAINE

Good friends and the best of neighbors.

Prologue

He stands on a hillside south of the city looking back at the carnage. A long, gray ribbon of broken highway winds through the green expanse of woods and scrub to where the ruin begins. Fires burn among the steel and glass skeletons of the abandoned skyscrapers, flames bright and angry against the washed-out haze of the deeply clouded horizon. Smoke rises in long, greasy spirals that stain the air with ash and soot. He can hear the crackling of the fires and smell their acrid stench even here.

That buildings of concrete and iron will burn so fiercely puzzles him. It seems they should not burn at all, that nothing short of jackhammers and wrecking balls should be able to bring them down. It seems that in this postapocalyptic world of broken lives and fading hopes the buildings should be as enduring as mountains. And yet already he can see sections of walls beginning to collapse as the fires spread and consume.

Rain falls in a steady drizzle, streaking his face. He blinks against the dampness in order to see better what is happening. He remembers Seattle as being beautiful. But that was in another life, when there was still a chance to change the future and he was still a Knight of the Word.

John Ross closes his eyes momentarily as the screams of the wounded and dying reach out to him. The slaughter has been going on for more than six hours, ever since the collapse of the outer defenses just after dawn. The demons and the oncemen have broken through and another of the dwindling bastions still left to free men has fallen. On the broad span of the high bridge linking the east and west sections of the city, the combatants surge up against one another in dark knots. Small figures tumble from the heights, pinwheeling madly against the glare of the flames as their lives are snuffed out. Automatic weapons—fire ebbs and flows. The armies will fight on through the remainder of the day, but the outcome is already decided. By tomorrow the victors will be building slave pens. By the day after, the conquered will be discovering how life can sometimes be worse than death.

At the edges of the city, down where the highway snakes between the first of the buildings that flank the Duwamish River, the feeders are beginning to appear. They mushroom as if by magic amid the carnage that consumes the city. Refugees flee and hunters pursue, and wherever the conflict spreads, the feeders are drawn. They are mankind's vultures, picking clean the bones of human emotion, of shattered lives. They are the Word's creation, an enigmatic part of the equation that defines the balance in all things and requires accountability for human behavior. No one is exempt; no one is spared. When madness prevails over reason, when what is darkest and most terrible surfaces, the feeders are there.

As they are now, he thinks, watching. Unseen and unknown, inexplicable in their single-mindedness, they are always there. He sees them tearing at the combatants closest to the city's edges, feeding on the strong emotions generated by the individual struggles of life and death taking place at every quarter, responding instinctively to the impulses that motivate their behavior. They are a force of nature and, as such, a part of nature's law. He hates them for what they are, but he understands the need for what they do.

Something explodes in the center of the burning city, and a building collapses in a low rumble of stone walls and iron girders. He could turn away and look south and see only the green of the hills and the silver glint of the lakes and the sound spread out beneath the snowy majesty of Mount Rainier, but he will not do that. He will watch until it is finished.

He notices suddenly the people who surround him. There are perhaps several dozen, ragged and hollow-eyed figures slumped down in the midday gloom, faces streaked with rain and ash. They stare at him as if expecting something. He does not know what it is. He is no longer a Knight of the Word. He is just an ordinary man. He leans on the rune-carved black staff that was once the symbol of his office and the source of his power. What do they expect of him?

An old man approaches, shambling out of the gloom, stick-thin and haggard. An arm as brittle as dry wood lifts and points accusingly.

I know you, he whispers hoarsely.

Ross shakes his head in denial, confused.

I know you, the old man repeats. Bald and white-bearded, his face is lined with age and by weather and his eyes are a strange milky color, their focus blurred. I was there when you killed him, all those years ago.

Killed who? Ross cannot make himself speak the words, only mouth them, aware of the eyes of the others who are gathered fixing on him as the old man's words are heard.

The old man cocks his head and lets his jaw drop, laughing softly, the sound high and eerie, and with this simple gesture he reveals himself. He is unbalanced—neither altogether mad nor completely sane, but something in between. He lives in a river that flows between two worlds, shifting from one to the other, a leaf caught by the current's inexorable tug, his destiny beyond his control.

The Wizard! The old man spits, his voice rising brokenly in the hissing sound of the rain. The Wizard of Oz! You are the one who killed him! I saw you! There, in the palace he visited, in the shadow of the Tin Woodman, in the Emerald City! You killed the Wizard! You killed him! You!

The worn face crumples and the light in the milky eyes dims. Tears flood the old man's eyes and trickle down his weathered cheeks. He whispers, Oh, God, it was the end of everything!

And Ross remembers then, a jagged-edged, poisonous memory he had thought forever buried, and he knows with a chilling certainty that what the old man tells him is true.

John Ross opened his eyes to the streetlit darkness and let his memory of the dream fade away. Where had the old man been standing, that he could have seen it all? He shook his head. The time for memories and the questions they invoked had come and gone.

He stood in the shadows of a building backed up on Occidental Park in the heart of Pioneer Square, his breath coming in quick, ragged gasps as he fought to draw the cool, autumn night air into his burning lungs. He had walked all the way from the Seattle Art Museum, all the way from the center of downtown Seattle some dozen blocks away. Limped, really, since he could not run as normal men could and relied upon a black walnut staff to keep upright when he moved. Anger and despair had driven him when muscles had failed. Crippled of mind and body and soul, reduced to an empty shell, he had come home to die because dying was all that was left.

The shade trees of the park loomed in dark formation before him, rising out of cobblestones and concrete, out of bricks and curbing, shadowing the sprawl of benches and trash receptacles and the scattering of homeless and disenfranchised that roamed the city night. Some few looked at him as he pushed off the brick wall and came toward them. One or two even hesitated before moving away. His face was terrible to look upon, all bloodied and scraped, and the clothes that draped his lean body were in tatters. Blood leaked from deep rents in the skin of his shoulder and chest, and several of his ribs felt cracked or broken. He had the appearance of a man who had risen straight out of Hell, but in truth he was just on his way down.

Feeders gathered at the edges of his vision, hunchbacked and beacon-eyed, ready to show him the way.

It was Halloween night, All Hallows' Eve, and he was about to come face-to-face with the most personal of his demons.

His mind spun with the implications of this acknowledgment. He crossed the stone and concrete open space thinking of greener places and times, of the smell of grass and forest air, lost to him here, gone out of his life as surely as the hopes he had harbored once that he might become a normal man again. He had traded what was possible for lies and half truths and convinced himself that what he was doing was right. He had failed to listen to the voices that mattered. He had failed to heed the warnings that counted. He had been betrayed at every turn.

He stopped momentarily in a pool of streetlight and looked off into the darkened spires of the city. The faces and voices came back to him in a rush of sounds and images. Simon Lawrence. Andrew Wren. O'olish Amaneh. The Lady and Owain Glyndwr.

Nest Freemark.

Stefanie.

His hands tightened on the staff, and he could feel the power of the magic coursing through the wood beneath his palms. Power to preserve. Power to destroy. The distinction had always seemed a large one, but he thought now that it was impossibly small.

Was he still, in the ways that mattered, a Knight of the Word? Did he possess courage and strength of will in sufficient measure that they would sustain him in the battle that lay ahead? He could not tell, could not know without putting it to the test. By placing himself in harm's way he would discover how much remained to him of the power that was once his. He did not think that it would be enough to save his life, but he hoped that it might be enough to destroy the enemy who had undone him.

It did not seem too much to ask.

In truth, it did not seem half enough.

Somewhere in the distance a siren sounded, shrill and lingering amid the hard-edged noises that rang down the stone and glass corridors of the city's canyons.

He took a deep breath and gritted his teeth against the pain that racked his body. With slow, measured steps, he started forward once more.

Death followed in his shadow.

Sunday, October 28

Chapter 1

It was dawn when she woke, the sky just beginning to brighten in the east, night's shadows still draping the trunks and limbs of the big shade trees in inky layers. She lay quietly for a time, looking through her curtained window as the day advanced, aware of a gradual change in the light that warmed the cool darkness of her bedroom. From beneath the covers she listened to the sounds of the morning. She could hear birdsong in counterpoint to the fading hum of tires as a car sped down Woodlawn's blacktop toward the highway. She could hear small creaks and mutterings from the old house, some of them so familiar that she remembered them from her childhood. She could hear the sound of voices, of Gran and Old Bob, whispering to each other in the kitchen as they drank their morning coffee and waited for her to come out for breakfast.

But the voices were only in her mind, of course. Old Bob and Gran were gone.

Nest Freemark rose to a sitting position, drew up her long legs to her chest, rested her forehead against her knees, and closed her eyes. Gone. Both of them. Gran for five years and Old Bob since May. It was hard to believe, even now. She wished every day that she could have them back again. Even for five minutes. Even for five seconds.

The sounds of the house wrapped her, small and comforting, all part of her nineteen years of life. She had always lived in this house, right up to the day she had left for college in September of last year, a freshman on a full ride at one of the most prestigious schools in the country. Northwestern University. Her grandfather had been so proud, telling her she should remember she had earned the right to attend this school, but the school, in turn, had merited her interest, so both of them should get something out of the bargain. He had laughed, his voice low and deep, his strong hands coming about her shoulders to hold her, and she had known instinctively that he was holding her for Gran, as well.

Now he was gone, dead of a heart attack three days before the end of her first year, gone in a moment, the doctor said afterward—no pain, no suffering, the way it should be. She had come to accept the doctor's reassurance, but it didn't make her miss her grandfather any the less. With both Gran and Old Bob gone, and her parents gone longer still, she had only herself to rely upon.

But, then, she supposed in a way that had always been so.

She lifted her head and smiled. It was how she had grown up, wasn't it? Learning to be alone, to be independent, to accept that she would never be like any other child?

She ticked off the ways in which she was different, running through them in a familiar litany that helped define and settle the borders of her life.

She could do magic—had been able to do magic for a long time. It had frightened her at first, confused and troubled her, but she had learned to adapt to the magic's demands, taught first by Gran, who had once had use of the magic herself, and later by Pick. She had learned to control and nurture it, to find a place for it in her life without letting it consume her. She had discovered how to maintain the balance within herself in the same way that Pick was always working to maintain the balance in the park.

Pick, her best friend, was a six-inch-high sylvan, a forest creature who looked for the most part like something a child had made of the discards of a bird's nest, with body and limbs of twigs and hair and beard of moss. Pick was the guardian of Sinnissippi Park, sent to keep in balance the magic that permeated all things and to hold in check the feeders that worked to upset that balance. It was a big job for a lone sylvan, as he was fond of saying, and over the years various generations of the Freemark women had helped him. Nest was the latest. Perhaps she would be the last.

There was her family, of course. Gran had possessed the magic, as had others of the Freemark women before her. Not Old Bob, who had struggled all his life to accept that the magic even existed. Maybe not her mother, who had died three months after Nest was born and whose life remained an enigma. But her father . . . She shook her head at the walls. Her father. She didn't like to think of him, but he was a fact of her life, and there was enough time and distance between them now that she could accept what he had been. A demon. A monster. A seducer. The killer of both her mother and her grandmother. Dead now, destroyed by his own ambition and hate, by Gran's magic and his own, by Nest's determination, and by Wraith.

Wraith. She looked out the window in the diminishing shadows and shivered. The ways in which she had been different from other children began and ended with Wraith.

She sighed and shook her head mockingly. Enough of that sort of rumination.

She rose and walked into the bathroom, turned on the shower, let it run hot, and stepped in. She stood with her eyes closed and the water streaming over her, lost in the heat and the damp. She was nineteen and stood just under five feet ten inches. Her honey-colored hair was still short and curly, but most of her freckles were gone. Her green eyes dominated her smooth, round face. Her body was lean and fit. She was the best middle-distance runner ever to come out of the state of Illinois and one of the best in history. She didn't think about her talent much, but it was always there, in much the same way as her magic. She wondered often if her running ability was tied in some way to her use of the magic. There was no obvious connection and even Pick tended to brush the suggestion aside, but she wondered anyway. She had been admitted to Northwestern on a full track-and-field scholarship. Her grades were good, but it was her athletic skills that got her in. She had won several middle-distance events at last spring's NCAA track-and-field championships. She had already broken several college records and one world. In two years the summer Olympics would be held in Melbourne, Australia. Nest Freemark was expected to contend for a medal in multiple running events. She was expected to win at least one gold.

She turned off the shower, stepped out onto the mat, grabbed a towel, and dried herself off. She tried not to think about the Olympics too often. It was too distant in time and too mind-boggling to consider. She had learned a hard lesson when she was fourteen and her father had revealed himself for what he was. Never take anything in your life for granted; always be prepared for radical change.

Besides, there were more pressing problems just now. There was school; she had to earn grades high enough to allow her to continue to train and to compete. There was Pick, who was persistent and unending in his demand that she give more of her time and effort to helping him with the park—which seemed silly until she listened to his reasoning.

And, right at the moment, there was the matter of the house.

She dressed slowly, thinking of the house, which was the reason she was home this weekend when her time would have been better spent at school, studying. With her grandfather's death, the house and all of its possessions had passed to her. She had spent the summer going through it, room by room, closet by closet, cataloguing, boxing, packing, and sorting what would stay and go. It was her home, but she was barely there enough to look after it properly and, Pick's entreaties notwithstanding, she had no real expectation of coming back after graduation to live. The Realtors, sensing this, had already begun to descend. The house and lot were in a prime location. She could get a good price if she was to sell. The money could be put to good use helping defray her training and competition expenses. The real estate market was strong just now, a seller's market. Wasn't this the right time to act?

She had received several offers over the summer, and this past week Allen Kruppert had called from ERA Realty to tender one so ridiculously high that she had agreed to consider it. She had come after classes on Friday, skipping track-and-field practice, so that she could meet with Allen on Saturday morning and look over the papers. Allen was a rotund, jovial young man, whom she had met on several occasions at church picnics, and he impressed her because he never tried to pressure her into anything where the house was concerned but seemed content just to present his offers and step back. The house was not listed, but if she was to make the decision to sell, she knew, she would almost certainly list it with him. The papers he had provided on this latest offer sat on the kitchen table where she had left them last night. The prospective buyer had already signed. The financing was in place. All that was needed was her signature and the deal was done.

She put the papers aside and sat down to eat a bowl of cereal with her orange juice and coffee, her curly hair still damp against her face as golden light spread through the curtained windows and the sun rose over the trees.

If she signed, her financial concerns for the immediate future would be over.

Pick, of course, would have a heart attack. Which was not a good thing if you were already a hundred and fifty years old.

She was just finishing the cereal when she heard a knock at the back door. She frowned; it was only eight o'clock in the morning, not the time people usually came calling. Besides, no one ever used the back door, except . . .

She walked from the kitchen down the hall to the porch. A shadowy figure stood leaning into the screen, trying to peer inside. Couldn't be, could it? But, as she stepped down to unlatch the screen door, she could already see it was.

"Hey, Nest," Robert Heppler said.

He stood with his hands shoved deep into the pockets of his jeans and one tennis shoe bumping nervously against the worn threshold. "You going to invite me in or what?" He gave her one of his patented cocky grins and tossed back the shoulder-length blond hair from his angular face.

She shook her head. "I don't know. What are you doing here, anyway?"

"You mean like, 'here at eight o'clock in the morning,' or like, 'here in Hopewell as opposed to Palo Alto'? You're wondering if I was tossed out of school, right?"

"Were you?"

"Naw. Stanford needs me to keep its grade point average high enough to attract similarly brilliant students. I was just in the neighborhood and decided to stop by, share a few laughs, maybe see if you're in the market for a boyfriend." He was talking fast and loose to keep up his confidence. He glanced past her toward the kitchen. "Do I smell coffee? You're alone, aren't you? I mean, I'm not interrupting anything, am I?"

"Jeez, Robert, you are such a load." She sighed and stepped back. "Come on in."

She beckoned him to follow and led him down the hall. The screen door banged shut behind them and she winced, remembering how Gran had hated it when she did that.

"So what are you really doing here?" she pressed him, gesturing vaguely in the direction of the kitchen table as she reached for the coffeepot and a cup. The coffee steamed in the morning air as she poured it.

He shrugged, giving her a furtive look. "I saw your car, knew you were home, thought I should say hello. I know it's early, but I was afraid I might miss you."

She handed him the coffee and motioned for him to sit down, but he remained standing. "I've been waiting to hear from you," she said pointedly.

"You know me, I don't like to rush things." He looked away quickly, unable to meet her steady gaze. He sipped gingerly from his cup, then made a face. "What is this stuff?"

Nest lost her patience. "Look, did you come here to insult me, or do you need something, or are you just lonely again?"

He gave her his hurt puppy look. "None of the above." He glanced down at the real estate papers, which were sitting on the counter next to him, then looked up at her again. "I just wanted to see you. I didn't see you all summer, what with you off running over hill and dale and cinder track."

"Robert, don't start . . ."

"Okay, I know, I know. But it's true. I haven't seen you since your grandfather's funeral."

"And whose fault is that, do you think?"

He pushed his glasses further up on his nose and screwed up his mouth. "Okay, all right. It's my fault. I haven't seen you because I knew how badly I messed up."

"You were a jerk, Robert."

He flinched as if struck. "I didn't mean anything."

"You didn't?" A slow flush worked its way up her neck and into her cheeks. "My grandfather's funeral service was barely finished and there you were, making a serious effort to grope me. I don't know what that was all about, but I didn't appreciate it one bit."

He shook his head rapidly. "I wasn't trying to grope you exactly."

"Yes, you were. Exactly. You might have done yourself some good, you know, if you'd stuck around to apologize afterward instead of running off."

His laugh was forced. "I was running for my life. You just about took my head off."

She stared at him, waiting. She knew how he felt about her, how he had always felt about her. She knew this was difficult for him and she wasn't making it any easier. But his misguided attempt at an intimate relationship was strictly one-sided and she had to put a stop to it now or whatever was left of their friendship would go right out the window.

He took a deep breath. "I made a big mistake, and I'm sorry. I guess I just thought you needed . . . that you wanted someone to . . . Well, I just wasn't thinking, that's all." He pushed back his long hair nervously. "I'm not so good at stuff like that, and you, well, you know how I feel . . ." He stopped and looked down at his feet. "It was stupid. I'm really sorry."

She didn't say anything, letting him dangle in the wind a little longer, letting him wonder. He looked up at her after a minute, meeting her gaze squarely for the first time. "I don't know what else to say, Nest. I'm sorry. Are we still friends?"

Even though he had grown taller and gotten broader through the shoulders, she still saw him as being fourteen. There was a little-boy look and sound to him that she thought he might never entirely escape.

"Are we?" he pressed.

She gave him a considering look. "Yes, Robert, we are. We always will be, I hope. But we're just friends, okay? Don't try to make it into anything else. If you do, you're just going to make me mad all over again."

He looked doubtful, but nodded anyway. "Okay." He glanced down again at the real estate papers. "Are you going to sell the house?"

"Robert!"

"Well, that's what it looks like."

"I don't care what it looks like, it's none of your business!" Irritated at herself for being so abrupt, she added, "Look, I haven't decided anything yet."

He put his coffee cup in the exact center of the papers, making a ring. "I don't think you should sell."

She snatched the cup away. "Robert . . ."

"Well, I don't. I think you should let some time pass before you do anything." He held up his hands in a placating gesture. "Wait, let me finish. My dad says you should never make any big changes right after someone you love dies. You should wait at least a year. You should give yourself time to grieve, to let everything settle so you know what you really want. I don't think he's right about much, but I think he might be right about this."

She pictured Robert's father in her mind, a spectacled, gentle man who was employed as a chemical engineer but spent all his free time engaged in gardening and lawn care. Robert used to call him Mr. Green Jeans and swore that his father would have been happier if his son had been born a plant.

"Robert," she said gently, "that's very good advice."

He stared at her in surprise.

"I mean it. I'll give it some thought."

She put the coffee cups aside. Robert was annoying, but she liked him anyway. He was funny and smart and fearless. Maybe more to the point, she could depend on him. He had stood up for her five years earlier when her father had come back into her life. If not for Robert, her grandfather would never have found her trussed up in the caves below the Sinnissippi Park cliffs. It was Robert who had come after her on the night she had confronted her father, when it seemed she was all alone.

She had knocked the pins out from under him for his trouble, leaving him senseless on the ground while she went on alone. But he had cared enough to follow.

She felt a momentary pang at the memory. Robert was the only real friend she had left from those days.

"I have to go back to school tonight," she said. "How long do you have?"

He shrugged. "Day after tomorrow."

"You came all the way home from California for the weekend?"

He looked uncomfortable. "Well . . ."

"To visit your parents?"

"Nest . . ."

"You can't say it, can you?"

He shook his head and blushed. "No."

She nodded. "Just so you don't think I can't see through you like glass. You just watch yourself, buster."

He looked down at his feet, embarrassed. She liked him like this—sweet and vulnerable. "You want to walk over to Gran and Grandpa's graves with me, put some flowers in their urns?"

He brightened at once. "Sure."

She was already heading for the hall closet. "Let me get my coat, Mr. Smooth."

"Jeez," he said.

CHAPTER 2

They went out the porch door, down the steps, across the yard, and through the hedgerow that marked the back end of the Freemark property, then struck out into Sinnissippi Park. Nest carried a large bundle of flowers she had purchased the night before and left sitting overnight in a bucket of water on the porch. It was not yet nine, and the air was still cool and the grass slick with damp in the pale morning light. The park stretched away before them, broad expanses of lush, new-mown grass fading into distant, shadowy woods and ragged curtains of mist that rose off the Rock River. The bare earth of the base paths, pitcher's mounds, and batting boxes of the ball diamonds cornering the central open space were dark and hard with moisture and the night's chill. The big shade trees had shed most of their leaves, the fall colors carpeting the areas beneath them in a patchwork mix of red, gold, orange, and brown. Park toys dotted the landscape like weird sculpture, and the wooden trestle and chute for the toboggan slide glimmered with a thin coating of frost. The crossbar at the entrance was lowered, the fall hours in effect so that there was no vehicle access to the park until after ten. In the distance, a solitary walker was towed in the wake of a hard-charging Irish setter that bounded through the haze of soft light and mist in a brilliant flash of rust.

The cemetery lay at the west end of the park on the other side of a chain-link fence. Having grown up in the park, they had been climbing that fence since they were kids—Robert and Cass Minter and Brianna Brown and Jared Scott and herself. Best friends for years, they had shared adventures and discoveries and hopes and dreams. Everything but the truth about who Nest was.

Robert shoved his bare hands in his pockets and exhaled a plume of white moisture. "We should have driven," he declared.

He was striding out ahead of her, taking the lead in typical Robert fashion, not in the least intimidated by the fact that she was taller and stronger and far more familiar with where she was going than he was.

She smiled in spite of herself. Robert would lead even if he were blindfolded.

She remembered telling him her deepest secret once, long ago, on the day after she had eluded him on her way to the deadly confrontation with her father. She had done something to him, he insisted, and he wanted to know what it was. That was the price he was demanding for his help in getting into the hospital to see Jared. She told him the truth, that she had used magic. She told him in a way that was meant to leave him in doubt. He could not quite believe her, but not quite ignore her, either. He had never been able to resolve his confusion, and that was a part of what attracted him to her, she supposed.

But there were distances between them that Robert could not even begin to understand. Between her and everyone she knew, now that Gran was gone, because

Nest was the only one who could do magic, the only one who would ever be able to do magic, the only one who would probably ever even know that magic was out there. She was the one who had been born to it, a legacy passed down through generations of the Freemark women, but through her demon father, as well. Magic that could come to her in the blink of an eye, could come unbidden at times. Magic that lived within her heart and mind, a part of her life that she must forever keep secret, because the danger that came from others knowing far outweighed the burden of clandestine management. Magic to heal and magic to destroy. She was still struggling to understand it. She could still feel it developing within her.

She looked off into the shadows of the woods that flanked the cliffs and cemetery ahead, where the night still lingered in dark patches and the feeders lurked. She did not see them, but she could sense that they were there. As she had always been able to when others could not. Unseen and unknown, the feeders existed on the fringes of human consciousness. Sylvans like Pick helped to keep them in check by working to maintain a balance in the magic that was invested in and determinative of the behavior of all living things. But humans were prone to adversely affect that balance, tilting it mostly without even knowing, changing it with their behavior and their feelings, altering it in the careless, unseeing way that mudslides altered landscapes.

This was the other world, the one to which Nest alone had access. Since she was very small, she had worked to understand it, to help Pick maintain it, and to find a way to reconcile it with the world that everyone else inhabited and believed fully defined. There, in no-man's-land between the known and the secret, she was an anomaly, never entirely like her friends, never just another child.

"You've lived in your grandparents' house all your life," Robert said suddenly, eyes determinedly fixed in a forward direction. They were crossing the entrance road and moving into the scattering of shade trees and spruce that bordered the picnic grounds leading to the chain-link fence and the cemetery. "That house is your home, Nest. If you sell it, you won't have a home anymore."

She scuffed at the damp grass with her tennis shoes. "I know that, Robert."

"Do you need the money?"

"I could use it. Training and competition is expensive. The school doesn't pay for everything."

"Why don't you take out a mortgage, then? Why sell, if you don't have to?"

She couldn't explain it to him, not if she tried all day. It had to do with being who she was, and that wasn't something Robert could know about without having lived her life. She didn't even want to talk about it with him because it was personal and private.

"Maybe I want a new home," she said enigmatically, giving sudden, unexpected voice to the feelings that churned inside her. It was hard to keep from crying as she thought back upon their genesis.

Her friends were gone, all but Robert. She could still see their faces, but she saw them not as they were at the end, but as they were when they were still fourteen and it seemed as if nothing in their lives would ever change. She saw them as they were during that last summer they were all together, on that last weekend before everything changed—when they were close and tight and believed they could stand up to anything.

Brianna Brown and Jared Scott moved away within a year of that summer. Brianna wrote Nest at first, but the time between letters steadily lengthened, and finally the letters ceased altogether. Nest heard later that Brianna was married and had a child.

She never heard from Jared at all.

Cass Minter remained her oldest and closest friend all through high school. Different from each other in so many ways, they continued to find common ground in a lifetime of shared experiences and mutual trust. Cass planned to go to the University of Illinois and study genetics, but two weeks before graduation, she died in her sleep. The doctor said it was an aneurysm. No one had suspected it was there.

Jared, Brianna, and Cass—all gone. Of her old friends, that left only Robert, and by the end of her freshman year at Northwestern, Nest could already feel herself beginning to drift. Her parents were gone. Her grandparents were gone. Her friends were gone. Even the cats, Mr. Scratch and Miss Minx, were gone, the former dead of old age two years earlier, the latter moved to a neighbor's home with her grandfather's passing. Her future, she thought, lay somewhere else. Her life was going in a different direction, and she could feel Hopewell receding steadily into her past.

They reached the chain-link fence and, without pausing to debate the matter, scrambled over. Holding the flowers for Nest while she completed the climb, Robert gave them a cursory sniff before handing them back. Side by side, the two made their way down the paved road that wound through the rows of tombstones and markers, feeling the October sun grow warmer against their skin as it lifted into a clear autumn sky. Summer might be behind them and winter closing fast, but there was nothing wrong with this day.

She felt her thoughts drift like clouds, returning to the past. She had acquired new friends in high school but they lacked the history she shared with the old, and she couldn't seem to get past that.

Of course, the Petersons still lived next door and Mildred Walker still lived down the street. Reverend Emery still conducted services at the First Congregational Church, and a few of her grandfather's old cronies still gathered for coffee at Josie's each morning to share gossip and memories. Once in a while, she even saw Josie, but she could sense the other's discomfort, and understanding its source, kept her distance. In any event, these were people of a different generation, and their real friendships had been with her grandparents rather than with her.

There was always Pick, though. And, until a year or so ago, there had been Wraith . . .

Robert left the roadway to cut through the rows of markers, bearing directly for the gravesites of her grandparents. Isn't it odd, she thought, trailing distractedly in his wake, that Hopewell should feel so alien to her? Small towns were supposed to be stable and unchanging. It was part of their charm, one of their virtues, that while larger communities would almost certainly undergo some form of upheaval, they would remain the same. But Hopewell didn't feel like that to her. It felt altered in ways that transcended expectation, ways that did not involve population growth or economic peaks. Those were substantially the same as they had been five years earlier. It was something else, an intangible that she believed might have influenced only her.

Perhaps it *was* her, she pondered. Perhaps it was she who had changed and not the town at all.

They walked up to her grandparents' graves and stopped below the markers, looking down at the mounds that fronted them. Gran's was thick and smooth with autumn grass; the grass on Old Bob's was still sparse and the earth less settled. Identical tombstones marked their resting places. Nest read her grandmother's. EVELYN OPAL FREEMARK. BELOVED WIFE OF ROBERT. SLEEP WITH ANGELS. WAKE WITH GOD. Old Bob had chosen the wording for Gran's marker, and Nest had simply copied it for his.

Her mother's gravestone stood just to the left. CAITLIN ANNE FREEMARK. BELOVED DAUGHTER & MOTHER.

A fourth plot, just a grassy space now, was reserved for her.

She studied it thoughtfully for a moment, then set about dividing up the flowers she had brought, arranging them carefully in each of the three metal vases that stood on tripods before the headstones. Robert watched her as she worked, saying nothing.

"Bring some water," she said, pointing toward the spigot and watering can that sat in a small concrete well several dozen yards off.

Robert did, then poured water into each vase, being careful not to disturb Nest's arrangements.

Together, they stood looking down at the plots, the sun streaming through the branches of the old shade trees that surrounded them in curtains of dappled brightness.

"I remember all the times your grandmother baked us cookies," Robert said after a minute. "She would sit us down at the picnic table out back and bring us a plate heaped with them and glasses of cold milk. She was always saying a child couldn't grow up right without cookies and milk. I could never get that across to my mother. She thought you couldn't grow up right without vegetables."

Nest grinned. "Gran was big on vegetables, too. You just weren't there for that particular lecture."

"Every Christmas we had that cookie bake in your kitchen. Balls of dough and cookie sheets and cutters and frosting and little bottles of sprinkles and whatnot everywhere. We trashed her kitchen, and she never blinked an eye."

"I remember making cookies for bake sales." Nest shook her head. "For the church, for mission aid or something. It seemed for a while that I was doing it every other weekend. Gran never objected once, even after she stopped going to church altogether."

Robert nodded. "Your grandmother never needed to go to church. I think God probably told her she didn't have to go, that he would come to see her instead."

Nest looked at him. "That's a very nice thing to say, Robert."

He pursed his lips and shrugged. "Yeah, well, I'm just trying to get back into your good graces. Anyway, I liked your grandmother. I always thought, when things got a little rough at home, that if they got real bad I could move in with you if I really wanted to. Sure, you and your grandfather might object, but your grandmother would have me in an instant. That's what I thought."

Nest nodded. "She probably would have, too."

Robert folded his arms across his chest. "You can't sell your house, Nest. You know why? Because your grandmother's still there."

Nest was silent for a moment. "I don't think so."

"Yes, she is. She's in every room and closet, in every corner, and under every carpet, down in the basement and up in the attic. That's where she is, Nest. Where else would she be?"

Nest didn't answer.

"Up in Heaven playing a harp? I wouldn't think so. Too boring. Not floating around on a cloud either. Not your grandmother. She's in that house, and I don't think you should move out on her."

Nest wondered what Robert would say if he knew the truth of things. She wondered what he would say if he knew that Gran's transgressions years earlier had doomed her family in ways that would horrify him, that Gran had roamed the park at night like a wild thing, that she had run with the feeders and cast her magic in dangerous ways, that her encounter with a demon had brought about both her own death and the death of Nest's mother. Would he think that she belonged in an afterlife of peace and light or that perhaps she should be consigned to a place where penance might be better served?

She regretted the thought immediately, a rumination both uncharitable and harsh, but she found she could not dispel it entirely.

Still, was Robert's truth any less valid in determining the worth of Gran's life than her own?

Robert cleared his throat to regain her attention. She looked at him. "I'll think about it," she said.

"Good. 'Cause there are a lot of memories in that house, Nest."

Yes, there are, she thought, looking off into the sun-streaked trees to where the river was a blue glint through the dark limbs. But not all the memories were ones she wanted to keep, and perhaps memories alone were not enough in any case. There was a lack of substance in memories and a danger in embracing them. You did not want to be tied too closely to something you could never recapture.

"I wouldn't sell if it was me, you know," Robert persisted. "I wouldn't sell unless I didn't have a choice."

He was pushing his luck, irritating her with his insistence on making the decision for her, on assuming she couldn't think it through as carefully as he could and needed his advice. It was typical Robert.

She gave him a look and dared him to speak. To his credit, he didn't. "Let's go," she said.

They walked back through the cemetery in silence, climbed the fence a second time, and crossed the park. The crossbar was raised now, and a few cars had driven in. One or two families were playing on the swing sets, and a picnic was being spread in a sunny spot across from the Sinnissippi burial mounds. Nest thought suddenly of Two Bears, of O'olish Amaneh, the last of the Sinnissippi. She hadn't thought of him in a long time. She hadn't seen him in five years. Now and then she wondered what had become of him. As she wondered what had become of John Ross, the Knight of the Word.

The memories flooded through her.

At the hedgerow bordering her yard, she leaned over impulsively and gave Robert a kiss on the cheek. "Thanks for coming by. It was sweet of you."

Robert looked flustered. He was being dismissed, and he wasn't ready for that. "Uh, are you, do you have any plans for the rest of the day? Or anything?"

"Or anything?" she repeated.

"Well, lunch, maybe. You know what I mean."

She knew exactly. She knew better than he did. Robert would never change. The best thing she could do for them both was not to encourage him.

"I'll call you if I get some time later, okay?"

It had to be okay, of course, so Robert shrugged and nodded. "If it doesn't work out, I'll see you at Thanksgiving. Or Christmas."

She nodded. "I'll drop you a note at school. Study hard, Robert. I need to know you're out there setting an example for the rest of us."

He grinned, regaining a bit of his lost composure. "It's a heck of a burden, but I try." He began to move away into the park. "See you, Nest." He tossed back his long blond hair and gave her a jaunty wave.

She watched him walk down the service road that ran behind her backyard, then cut across the park toward his home, which lay beyond the woods at the east end. He grew smaller and less distinct as he went, receding slowly into the distance. It was like watching her past fade before her eyes. Even when she saw him again, it would not be the same. She knew it instinctively. They would be different people leading different lives, and there would be no going back to the lives they had lived as children.

Her throat tightened, and she took a deep breath. *Oh, Robert!*

She waited a moment longer, letting the memories flood through her one final time, then turned away.

Chapter 3

As Nest pushed through the hedgerow into her backyard, Pick dropped from the branches onto her shoulder with a pronounced grunt.

"That boy is sweet on you. Sweet, sweet, sweet."

Pick's voice was harried and thin, and when he spoke he sounded like one of those fuzzy creatures on *Sesame Street*. Nest thought he wouldn't be so smug if he could hear himself on tape sometime.

"They're all sweet on me," she said, deflecting his dig, moving toward the picnic table. "Didn't you know?"

"No, I didn't. But if that one were any sweeter, he could be bottled for syrup." Pick sniffed. "Classic case of youthful hormonal imbalance."

She laughed. "Since when did you know anything about 'youthful hormonal imbalance'? Didn't you tell me once that you were born in a pod?"

"That doesn't mean I don't know about humans. I suppose you don't think I've learned anything in my life, is that it? Since I'm roughly ten times your age, it's probably safe to assume I've learned a great deal more than you have!"

She straddled one of the picnic bench seats, and Pick slid down her arm and jumped onto the table in front of her, hands on hips, eyes defiant. At first glance, he looked like a lot of different things. A quick glimpse suggested he was some sort of weird forest flotsam and jetsam, shed by a big fir or blown off an aging cedar. A second look suggested he was a poorly designed child's doll made out of tree parts. A thick layer of bark encrusted him from head to foot, and tiny leaves blossomed out of various nooks and crannies where his joints were formed. He was a sylvan, in fact, six inches high and so full of himself Nest was sometimes surprised he didn't just float away on the wind. He never stopped talking and, in the many years she had known him, had seldom stopped moving. He was full of energy and advice, and he had a tendency to overwhelm her with both.

"Where have you been?" he demanded, clearly agitated that he had been forced to wait on her return.

She brushed back her cinnamon-colored hair and shook her head at him. "We walked over to the cemetery and put flowers on my grandparents' and mother's graves. What is your problem, anyway?"

"*My* problem?" Pick huffed. "Well, since you asked, *my* problem is that I have this entire park to look after, all two-hundred-odd acres of it, and I have to do it *by myself*! Now, you might say, 'But that's your job, Pick, so what are you complaining about?' Well, that's true enough, isn't it? But time was I had a little help from a certain young lady who lived in this house. Now what was her name again? I forget, it's been so long since I've seen her."

"Oh, please!" Nest moaned.

"Sure, it's easy for you to go off to your big school and your other life, but words like 'commitment' and 'responsibility' mean something to some of us." He stamped hard on the picnic table. "I thought the least you could do was to spend *some* time with me this weekend, this *one* solitary weekend in the *whole* of this autumn that you've chosen to come home! But no, I haven't seen you for five minutes, have I? And now, today, what do you do? Go off with that Heppler boy instead of looking for me! I could have gone to the graves with you, you know. I would have liked to go, as a matter of fact. Your grandmother was my friend, too, and I don't forget my friends . . ." He trailed off meaningfully.

"Unlike some people," she finished for him.

"I wasn't going to say that."

"Oh, not for a minute." She sighed. "Robert came by to apologize for his behavior last spring at the funeral."

"Oh, that. Criminy." Pick knew right away. They might fight like cats and dogs, but they confided in each other anyway.

"So I had to spend a little time with him, and I didn't think it would hurt if we walked over to the cemetery. I was saving the rest of the day to work with you, all right? Now stop complaining."

He held up his twiggy hands. "Too late. Way too late."

"To stop complaining?"

"No! To do any work!"

She hunched down so that her face was close to his. It was a little like facing down a beetle. "What are you talking about? It isn't even noon. I don't have to go back until tonight. Why is it too late?"

He folded his stick arms across his narrow chest, scrunched up his face, and looked off into the park. She always wondered how he could make his features move like that when they were made out of wood, but since he had a tendency to regard such questions as some sort of invasion of his personal life, she'd never had the courage to ask. She waited patiently as he sighed and fussed and jittered about.

"There's someone here to see you," he announced finally.

"Who?"

"Well, I think you had better see for yourself."

She studied him a moment. He refused to meet her eyes, and a cold feeling seeped through her. "Someone from before?" she asked quietly. "From when my father . . . ?"

"No, no!" He held up his hands quickly to calm her fears. "No one you've met before. No one from then. But . . ." He stopped. "I can't tell you who it is without getting myself in deeper than I care to go. I've thought about it, and it will be better if you just come with me and ask your questions there."

She nodded. "Ask my questions where?"

"Down by the bayou below the deep woods. She's waiting there."

She. Nest frowned. "Well, when did *she* get here?"

"Early this morning." Pick sighed. "I just wish these things wouldn't happen so suddenly, that's all. I just wish I'd be given a little notice beforehand. It's hard enough doing my job without these constant interruptions."

"Well, maybe it won't take long," she offered, trying to ease his obvious distress. "If it doesn't, we can still get some work done in the park before I have to go back."

He didn't even argue the point. His anger was deflated, his fire burned to ash. He just stared off at nothing and nodded.

Nest straightened. "Pick, it's a beautiful October morning, filled with sunshine. The park has never looked better. I haven't seen a single feeder, so the magic is in some sort of balance. You've done your job well, even without my help. Enjoy yourself for five minutes."

She reached over, plucked him off the tabletop, and set him on her shoulder. "Come on, let's take a walk over to the deep woods."

Without waiting for an answer, she rose and headed for the hedgerow, pushing through the thin branches into the park. Sunshine streamed down out of a cloudless sky, filling the morning air with the pale, washed-out light peculiar to late autumn. There was a nip in the air, a hint of winter on the rise, but there was also the scent of dried leaves and cut grass mingling with the pungent smells of cooking that wafted out of barbecue grills and kitchen vents from the houses bordering the park. Cars dotted the parking lots and turnoffs beneath the trees, and families were setting out picnic lunches and running with dogs and throwing Frisbees across the grassy play areas ahead.

On such days, she thought to herself with a smile, she could almost imagine she would never leave.

"Pick, if we don't get back to it today, I'll come home again next weekend," she announced impulsively. "I know I haven't been as good about working with you as I should. I've let other things get in the way, and I shouldn't do that. This is more important."

He rode her shoulder in silence, apparently not ready to be mollified. She glanced down at him covertly. He didn't seem angry. He just seemed distant, as if he were looking beyond her words to something else.

She traversed the central open space to the parking lot serving the ball diamonds and play areas at the far end of the park, crossed the road, and entered the woods. The toboggan slide stood waiting for winter, the last sections of the wooden chute and the ladder that allowed access to the loading platform still in storage, removed and locked away as a safeguard against kids' climbing on and falling off before the snows came. It never seemed to help much, of course. Kids climbed anything that had footholds whether it was intended for that purpose or not, and the absence of stairs just made the challenge that much more attractive. Nest smiled faintly. She had done it herself more times than she could count. But she supposed that one day some kid would fall off and the parents would sue and that would be the end of it; the slide would come down.

She walked through the hilly woods that marked the beginning of the eastern end of the park, alone now with Pick, wrapped in the silence of the big hardwoods. The trees rose bare-limbed and skeletal against the autumn sky, stripped of their leaves, waiting for winter's approach. Their colors not yet completely faded, the fallen leaves formed a thick carpet on the ground, still damp and soft with morning dew. She peered ahead into the tangled clutter of limbs and scrub and shadow. The forest had a bristling, hostile appearance. Everything looked as if it were wrapped in barbed wire.

Her long strides covered the ground rapidly as she descended to the creek that wound out of the woods and emptied into the bayou. How much bigger the park had seemed when she was a child growing up in it. Sometimes her home felt the same way—too small for her now. She supposed it was true of her child's world entirely, that she had outgrown it, that she needed more room.

"How much farther?" she asked as she crossed the wooden bridge that spanned the creek bed, and started up the slope toward the deep woods.

"Bear right," he grunted.

She angled toward the bayou, following the tree line. She glanced involuntarily toward the deep woods, just as she always did, any time she came here, remembering what had taken place there five years earlier. Sometimes she could see it all quite clearly, could see her father and John Ross and the maentwrog. Sometimes she could even see Wraith.

"Has there been any sign of him?" she asked suddenly, the words escaping from her mouth before she could think better of them.

Pick understood what she was talking about. "Nothing. Not since . . ."

Not since she turned eighteen two summers ago, she finished as he trailed off. That was the last time either of them had seen Wraith. After so many years of having him around, it seemed impossible that he could be gone. Her father had created the giant ghost wolf out of his dark magic to serve as a protector for the daughter he intended one day to return for. Wraith was to keep her safe while she grew. All the time she had worked with Pick to keep the magic in balance and the feeders from luring children into the park, Wraith had warded her. But Gran had discerned Wraith's true purpose and altered his makeup with her own magic in such a way that when her father returned to claim her, Wraith destroyed him.

She could see it happening all over again through the dark huddle of the trees. Night cloaked the deep woods, and on the slopes of the park, over by the toboggan slide, Fourth of July fireworks were exploding in a shower of bright colors and deep booms. The white oak that had imprisoned the maentwrog was in shreds, and the maentwrog itself was turned to ash. John Ross lay motionless upon the charred earth, damaged and exhausted. Nest faced her father, who approached with hand outstretched and soothing, persuasive words. *You belong to me. You are my blood. You are my life.*

And Wraith, come out of the night like an express train exploding free of a mountain tunnel . . .

She was fourteen when she learned the truth about her father. And her family. And herself. Wraith had stayed as her protector afterward, a shadowy presence in the park, showing himself only occasionally as the next few years passed, but always when the feeders came too close. Now and then she would think that he seemed less substantive than she remembered, less solid when he loomed out of the darkness. But that seemed silly.

However, as she neared her eighteenth birthday, Wraith turned pale and then ethereal and finally disappeared completely. It happened quickly. One day he was just as he had always been, his thick body massive and bristling, his gray and black tiger-stripe facial markings wicked and menacing, and the next he was fading away. Like the ghost he had always seemed, but finally become.

The last time she saw him, she was walking the park at sunset, and he had appeared unexpectedly from the shadows. He was already so insubstantial she could see right through him. She stopped, and he walked right up to her, passing so close that she felt his rough coat brush against her. She blinked in surprise at the unexpected contact, and when she turned to follow him, he was already gone.

She hadn't seen him since. Neither had Pick. That was almost a year and a half ago.

"Where do you think he's gone?" she asked quietly.

Pick, riding her shoulder in silence, shrugged. "Can't say."

"He was disappearing though, there at the end, wasn't he?"

"It looked that way, sure enough."

"So maybe he was all used up."

"Maybe."

"Except you told me magic never gets used up. You told me it works like energy; it becomes transformed. So if Wraith was transformed, what was he transformed into?"

"Criminy, Nest!"

"Have you noticed anything different about the park?"

The sylvan tugged at his beard. "No, nothing."

"So where did he go then?"

Pick wheeled on her. "You know what? If you spent a little more time helping me out around here, maybe you could answer the question for yourself instead of pestering me! Now turn down here and head for the riverbank and stop asking me stuff!"

She did as he asked, still pondering the mystery of Wraith, thinking that maybe because she was grown up and Wraith had served his purpose, he had reverted to whatever form he had occupied before he was created to be her protector. Yes, maybe that was it.

But her doubts lingered.

She reached the riverbank and stopped. The bayou spread out before her, a body of water dammed up behind the levy on which the railroad tracks had been built to carry the freight trains west out of Chicago. Reeds and cattails grew in thick clumps along the edges of the water, and shallow inlets that eroded the riverbank were filmed with stagnation and debris. There was little movement in the water, the swift current of the Rock River absent here.

She looked down at Pick. "Now what?"

He gestured to her right without speaking.

She turned and found herself staring right at the tatterdemalion. She had seen only a handful in her life, and then just for a few seconds each time, but she knew this one for what it was right away. It stood less than a dozen yards away, slight and ephemeral in the pale autumn light. Diaphanous clothing and silky hair trailed from its body and limbs in wispy strands, as if on the verge of being carried off by the wind. The tatterdemalion's features were childlike and haunted. This one was a girl. Her eyes were depthless in dark-ringed sockets and her rosebud mouth pinched against her sunken face. Her skin was the color and texture of parchment. She might have been a runaway who had not eaten in days and was still terrified of what she had left behind. She had that look. But tatterdemalions were nothing of the sort. They weren't really children at all, let alone runaways. They weren't even human.

"Are you Nest Freemark?" this one asked in her soft, lilting childlike voice.

"I am," Nest answered, risking a quick glance down at Pick. The sylvan was mired in the deepest frown she had ever seen on him and was hunched forward on her shoulder in a combative stance. She had a sudden, inescapable premonition he was trying to protect her.

"My name is Ariel," said the tatterdemalion. "I have a message for you from the Lady."

Nest's throat went dry. She knew who the Lady was. The Lady was the Voice of the Word.

"I have been sent to tell you of John Ross," Ariel said.

Of course. John Ross. She had thought of him earlier that morning for the first time in weeks. She pictured him anew, enigmatic and resourceful, a mix of light and dark, gone from Hopewell five years earlier in the wake of her father's destruction, gone out of her life. Maybe she had inadvertently wished him back into it. Maybe that was why the mention of him seemed somehow inevitable.

"John Ross," she repeated, as if the words would make of his memory something more substantial.

Ariel stood motionless in a mix of shadow and sunlight, as if pinned like a butterfly to a board. When she spoke, her voice was reed-thin and faintly musical, filled with the sound of the wind rising off trees heavy with new leaves.

"He has fallen from grace," she said to Nest Freemark, and the dark eyes bore into her. "Listen, and I will tell you what has become of him."

CHAPTER 4

As with almost everything since John Ross had become a Knight of the Word, this disintegration began with a dream.

His dreams were always of the future, a future grim and horrific, one where the balance of magic had shifted so dramatically that civilization was on the verge of extinction. The Void had gained ascendancy over the Word, good had lost the eternal struggle against evil, and humanity had become a pathetic shadow of the brilliant ideal it had once approached. Men were reduced to hunters and hunted, the former led by demons and driven by feeders, the latter banded together in fortress cities and scattered outposts in a landscape fallen into ruin and neglect. Once-men and their prey, they were born of the same flesh, but changed by the separate and divisive moral codes they had embraced and by the indelible patterns of their lives. It had taken more than a decade, but in the end governments had toppled, nations had collapsed, armies had broken into pieces, and peoples worldwide had reverted to a savagery that had not been in evidence since well before the birth of Christ.

The dreams were given to John Ross for a purpose. It was the mission of a Knight of the Word to change the course of history. The dreams were a reminder of what the future would be like if he failed. The dreams were also a means of discovering pivotal events that might be altered by the Knight on waking. John Ross had learned something of the dreams over time. The dreams always revealed events that would occur, usually within a matter of months. The events were always instigated by men and women who had fallen under the sway of the demons who served the Void. And the men and women who would perpetrate the monstrous acts that would alter in varying, cumulative ways the direction in which humanity drifted could always be tracked down.

But even then there was a limit to what a Knight of the Word could do, and John Ross discovered the full truth of this at San Sobel.

In his dream, he was traveling through the nightmare landscape of civilization's collapse on his way to an armed camp in San Francisco. He had come from Chicago, where another camp had fallen to an onslaught of demons and once-men, where he had fought to save the city and failed, where he had seen yet another small light smothered, snuffed out in an ever-growing darkness. Thousands had died, and thousands more had been taken to the slave pens for work and breeding. He had come to San Francisco to prevent this happening again, knowing that a new army was massing and moving west to assault the Bay Area fortress, to reduce humanity's tenuous handhold on survival by yet another digit. He would plead with those in charge once again, knowing that they would probably refuse to listen, distrustful of him, fearful of his motives, knowing only that their past was lost and their future had become an encroaching nightmare. Now and again, someone would pay heed. Now and again, a city would be saved. But the number of his successes was dwindling rapidly as the strength of the Void's forces grew. The outcome was inevitable; it had been foreordained since he had become a Knight of the Word years ago. His failure then had writ in stone what the future must be. Even in his determined effort to chip away the hateful letters, he was only prolonging the inevitable. Yet he went on, because that was all that was left for him to do.

The dream began in the town of San Sobel, west and south of the Mission Peak Preserve below San Francisco. It was just another town, just one more collection of empty shops and houses, of concrete streets buckling with wear and disuse, of yards and parks turned to weeds and bare earth amid a jumble of debris and abandoned cars. Wild dogs roamed in packs and feral cats slunk like shadows through the midday heat. He walked past windows and doors that gaped broken and dark like sightless eyes and voiceless mouths. Roofs had sagged and walls had collapsed; the earth was reclaiming its own. Now and again he would spy a furtive figure making its way through the rubble, a stray human in search of food and shelter, another refugee from the past. They never approached him. They saw something in him that frightened them, something he could not identify. It was in his bearing or his gaze or perhaps in the black, rune-scrolled staff that was the source of his power. He would stride down the center of a boulevard, made whole now with the fulfillment of the Word's dark prophecy, his ruined leg healed because his failure had brought that prophecy to pass, and no one would come near him. He was empowered to help them, and they shunned him as anathema. It was the final irony of his existence.

In San Sobel, no one approached him either. He saw them, the strays, hiding in the shadows, skittering from one bolt-hole to the next, but they would not come near. He walked alone through the town's ruin, his eyes set on the horizon, his mind fixed on his mission, and he came upon the woman quite unexpectedly. She did not see him. She was not even aware of him. She stood at the edge of a weed-grown lot and stared fixedly at the remains of what had once been a school. The name was still visible in the crumbling stone of an arch that bridged a drive leading up to the school's entry. SAN SOBEL PREPARATORY ACADEMY. Her gaze was unwavering as she stood there, arms folded, body swaying slightly. As he approached, he could hear small, unidentifiable sounds coming from her lips. She was worn and haggard, her hair hung limp and unwashed, and she looked as if she had not eaten in a while. There were sores on her arms and face, and he recognized the markings of one of the cluster of new diseases that were going untreated and killing with increasing regularity.

He spoke to her softly, and she did not reply. He came right up behind her and spoke again, and she did not turn.

When finally he touched her, she still did not turn, but she began to speak. It was as if he had turned on a tape recorder. Her voice was a dull, empty monotone, and her story was one that quite obviously she had told before. She related it to him without caring whether he heard her or not, giving vent to a need that was self-contained and personal and without meaningful connection to him. He was her audience, but his presence served only to trigger a release of words she would have spoken to anyone.

He was my youngest child, she said. *My boy, Teddy. He was six years old. We had enrolled him in kindergarten the year before, and now he was finishing first grade. He was so sweet. He had blond hair and blue eyes, and he was always smiling. He could change the light in a room just by walking into it. I loved him so much. Bert and I both worked, and we made pretty good money, but it was still a stretch to send him here. But it was such a good school, and we wanted him to have the best. He was very bright. He could have been anything, if he had lived.*

There was another boy in the school who was a little older, Aaron Pilkington. His father was very successful, very wealthy. Some men decided to kidnap him and make his father pay them money to get him back. They were stupid men, not even bright enough to know the best way to kidnap someone. They tried to take him out of the school. They just walked right in and tried to take him. On April Fools' Day, can you imagine that? I wonder if they knew. They just walked in and tried to take him. But they couldn't find him. They weren't even sure which room he was in, which class he attended, who his teacher was, anything. They had a picture, and they thought that would be enough. But a picture doesn't always help. Children in a picture often tend to look alike. So they couldn't find him, and the police were called, and they surrounded the school, and the men took a teacher and her class hostage because they were afraid and they didn't know what else to do, I suppose.

My son was a student in that class.

The police tried to get the men to release the teacher and the children, but the men wouldn't agree to the terms the police offered and the police wouldn't agree to the terms the men offered, and the whole thing just fell to pieces. The men grew desperate and erratic. One of them kept talking to someone who wasn't there, asking, What should he do, what should he do? They killed the teacher. The police decided they couldn't wait any longer, that the children were in too much danger. The men had moved the children to the auditorium where they held their assemblies and performed their plays. They had them all seated in the first two rows, all in a line facing the stage. When the police broke in, they started shooting. They just . . . started shooting. Everywhere. The children . . .

She never looked at him as she spoke. She never acknowledged his presence. She was inaccessible to him, lost in the past, reliving the horror of those moments. She kept her gaze fixed on the school, unwavering.

I was there, she said, her voice unchanging, toneless and empty. *I was a room mother helping out that day. There was going to be a birthday party at the end of recess. When the shooting began, I tried to reach him. I threw myself . . . His name was Teddy. Theodore, but we called him Teddy, because he was just a little boy. Teddy . . .*

Then she went silent, stared at the school a moment longer, turned, and walked off down the broken sidewalk. She seemed to know where she was going, but he could not discern her purpose. He watched after her a moment, then looked at the school.

In his mind, he could hear the sounds of gunfire and children screaming.

When he woke, he knew at once what he would do. The woman had said that one of the men spoke to someone who wasn't there. He knew from experience that it would be a demon, a creature no one but the man could see. He knew that a demon would have inspired this event, that it would have used it to rip apart the fabric of the community, to steal away San Sobel's sense of safety and tranquillity, to erode its belief that what happened in other places could not happen there. Once such seeds of doubt and fear were planted, it grew easier to undermine the foundations of human behavior and reason that kept animal madness at bay.

It was late winter, and time was already short when he left for California. He reached San Sobel more than a week before April 1, and he felt confident that he had sufficient time to prevent the impending tragedy. There had been no further dreams of this event, but that was not unusual. Often the dreams came only once, and he was forced to act on what he was given. Sometimes he did not know where the event would happen, or even when. This time he was lucky; he knew both. The demon would have set things in motion already, but Ross had come up against demons time and again since he had taken up the cause of the Word, and he was not intimidated. Demons were powerful and elusive adversaries, relentless in their hatred of humans and their determination to see them subjugated, but they were no match for him. It was the vagaries of the humans they used as their tools that more often proved troubling.

There were the feeders to be concerned about, too. The feeders were the dark things that drove humans to madness and then consumed them, creatures of the mind and soul that lived mostly in the imagination until venal behavior made them real. The feeders devoured the dark emotions of the humans they preyed upon and were sustained and given life by. Few could see them. Few had any reason to. They appeared as shadows at the corner of the eye or small movements in a hazy distance. The demons stirred them into the human population as they would a poison. If they could infect a few, the poison might spread to the many. History had proved that this was so.

The feeders would delight in a slaughter of innocents, of children who could barely understand what was wanted of them by the men John Ross would confront. He could not search out these men; he had no way to do so. Nor could he trace the demon. Demons were changelings and hid themselves with false identities. He must wait for the men and the demons who manipulated them to reveal themselves, which meant that he must be waiting at the place he expected them to strike.

So he went to San Sobel Preparatory Academy to speak with the headmaster. He did not tell the headmaster of his dream, or of the demon, or of the men the demon would send, or of the horror that waited barely a week away. There was no point in doing that because he had no way to convince the headmaster he was not insane. He told the headmaster instead that he was the parent of a child who would be eligible for admission to the academy in the fall and that he would like some information on the school. He apologized for his appearance—he was wearing jeans and a blue denim shirt under his corduroy jacket with the patches on the elbows and a pair of worn walking shoes—but he was a nature writer on assignment, and he was taking half a day off to make this visit. The headmaster took note of his odd walking staff and his limp, and his clear blue eyes and warm smile gave evidence of the fact that he was both sympathetic and understanding of his visitor's needs.

He talked to John Ross of the school's history and of its mission. He gave Ross materials to read. Finally, he took Ross on a tour of the buildings—which was what Ross had been waiting for. They passed down the shadowed corridors from one classroom to the next and at last to the auditorium where the tragedy of the dream would occur. Ross lingered, asking questions so that he would have time to study the room, to memorize its layout, its entries and exits and hiding places. A quick study was all it took. When he was satisfied, he thanked the headmaster for his time and consideration and left.

He found out later in the day that a boy named Aaron Pilkington attended the academy, that he was enrolled in the third grade, and that his parents had been made enormously wealthy through his father's work with microchips.

That night, he devised a plan. It was not complicated. He had learned that by keeping his plans simple, his chances of successfully implementing them improved. There were small lives at stake, and he did not want to expose them to any greater risk than necessary.

It seemed to him, thinking the matter through in his motel room that night, that he had everything under control.

He waited patiently for the days to pass. On the morning of April 1, he arrived at the school just before sunrise. He had visited the school late in the afternoon of the day before and left a wedge of paper in the lock of one of the classroom windows at the back of the main building so the lock would not close all the way. He slipped through the window in the darkness, listening for the movement of other people as he did so. But the maintenance staff didn't arrive for another half hour, and he was alone. He worked his way down the hallway to the auditorium, found one of the storage rooms where the play props were kept at the rear and side of the stage, and concealed himself inside.

Then he waited.

He did not know when the attack would come, but he did know that until the moment of his intervention, history would repeat itself and the events of the dream would transpire exactly as related by Teddy's mother. It was up to him to choose just when he would try to alter the outcome.

He crouched in the darkness of his hiding place and listened to the sounds of the school about him as the day began. The storage room had sufficient space that he was able to change positions and move around so his leg didn't stiffen up. He had brought food. Time slipped away. No one came to the auditorium. Nothing unusual occurred.

Then the doors burst open, and Ross could hear the screams and cries of children, the pleas of several women, and the angry, rough voices of men fill the room. Ross waited patiently, the storage door cracked open just far enough that he could see what was happening. A hooded figure bounded onto the stage between the half-closed curtains, glanced around hurriedly, and began barking orders. A second figure joined him. The women and children filed hurriedly into the front rows of the theater in response to the men's directions.

Still Ross waited.

One of the men had a cell phone. It rang, and he began talking into it, growing increasingly angry. He jumped down off the stage, screaming obscenities into the mouthpiece. Ross slipped out of the storage room, the black staff gleaming with the magic's light. He moved slowly, steadily through the shadows, closing on the lone man who stood at the front of the stage. The man held a handgun, but he was looking at his captives. Ross could see a third man now, one standing at the far side of the room, looking out the door into the hallway.

Ross came up to the man standing on the stage and leveled him with a single blow of the staff. He caught a glimpse of the other two, the one on the phone still yelling and screaming with his back turned, the other wheeling in surprise as he caught sight of Ross. The children's eyes went wide as Ross appeared, and with a sweep of his staff Ross threw a heavy blanket of magic over the children, a weighted net that forced them to lower their heads and shield their eyes. The man at the door was swinging his AK-47 around to fire as Ross hit him with a bolt of bright magic and knocked him senseless.

The third man dropped the phone, still screaming, and brought up a second AK-47. But Ross was waiting for him as well, and again the magic lanced from the staff. A burst from the man's weapon sprayed the ceiling harmlessly as he went down in a heap.

Ross scanned the room swiftly for other kidnappers. There were none. Just the three. The children and their teacher and two other women were still crouched in their seats, weighted down by the magic. Ross lifted it away, setting them free. No one was hurt. Everything was all right . . .

Then he saw the feeders, dozens of them, oozing through cracks in the windows and doors, sliding out of corners and alcoves, dark shadows gathering to feast, sensing something that was hidden from him.

Ross wheeled about in desperation, searching everywhere at once, his heart pounding, his mind racing . . .

And police burst through the doors and windows, shattering wood and glass. Someone was yelling, Throw down your weapons! Now, now, now! The women and children were screaming anew, scrambling out of their seats in terror, and someone was yelling, He's got a gun! Shoot him, shoot him! Ross was trying to tell them, No, no, it's all right, it's okay now! But no one was listening, and everything was chaotic and out of control, and the feeders were leaping about in a frenzy, climbing over everything, and there were weapons firing everywhere, catching the kidnapper who was just coming to his knees in front of the stage, still too stunned to know what was happening, lifting him in a red spatter and dropping him back again in a crumpled heap, and small bodies were being struck by the bullets as well, hammered sideways and sent flying as screams of fear turned to shrieks of pain, and still the voice was yelling, He's got a gun, he's got a gun! Even though Ross still couldn't see any gun, couldn't understand what the voice was yelling about, the police kept firing, over and over and over into the children . . .

He read about it in the newspapers in the days that followed. Fourteen children were killed. Two of the kidnappers died. There was considerable debate over who fired the shots, but informed speculation had it that several of the children had been caught in a crossfire.

There was only brief mention of Ross. In the confusion that followed the shooting, Ross had backed away into the shadows and slipped out through the rear of the auditorium into a crowd of parents and bystanders and disappeared before anyone could stop him. The teacher who had been held hostage told of a mysterious man who had helped free them, but the police insisted that the man was one of the kidnappers and that the teacher was mistaken about what she had seen. Descriptions of what he looked like varied dramatically, and after a time the search to find him waned and died.

But John Ross was left devastated. How had this terrible thing happened? What had gone wrong? He had done exactly as he intended to do. The men had been subdued. The danger was past. And still the children had died, the police misreading the situation, hearing screams over the kidnapper's dropped cell phone, hearing the AK-47 go off, bursting in with weapons ready, firing impulsively, foolishly . . .

Fourteen children dead. Ross couldn't accept it. He could tell himself rationally that it wasn't his fault. He could explain away everything that had happened, could argue persuasively and passionately to himself that he had done everything he could, but it still didn't help. Fourteen children were dead.

One of them, he discovered, was a blond, blue-eyed little boy named Teddy.

He saw all of their pictures in magazines, and he read their stories in papers for weeks afterward. The horror of what had happened enveloped and consumed him. It haunted his sleep and destroyed his peace of mind. He could not function. He sat paralyzed in motel rooms in small towns far away from San Sobel, trying to regain his sense of purpose. He had experienced failures before, but nothing with consequences that were so dramatic and so personal. He had thought he could handle anything, but he wasn't prepared for this. Fourteen lives were on his conscience, and he could hardly bear it. He cried often, and he ached deep inside. He replayed the events over and over in his mind, trying to decide what it was he had done wrong.

It was weeks before he realized his mistake. He had assumed that the demon who sought to inspire the killings had relied on the kidnappers alone. But it was the police who had killed the children. Someone had yelled at them to shoot, had prompted them to fire, had put them on edge. It took only one additional man, one further intent, one other weapon. The demon had seduced one of the police officers as well. Ross had missed it. He hadn't even thought of it.

After a time, he began to question everything he was doing in his service to the Word. What was the point of it all if so many small lives could be lost so easily? He was a poor choice to serve as a Knight of the Word if he couldn't do any better than this. And what sort of supreme being would permit such a thing to happen in the first place? Was this the best the Word could do? Was it necessary for those fourteen children to die? Was that the message? John Ross began to wonder, then to grow certain, that the difference between the Word and the Void was small indeed. It was all so pointless, so ridiculous. He began to doubt and then to despair. He was servant to a master who lacked compassion and reason, whose poor efforts seemed unable to accomplish anything of worth. John Ross looked back over the past twelve years and was appalled. Where was the proof that anything he had done had served a purpose? What sort of battle was it he fought? Time after time he had stood against the forces of the Void, and what was there to show for it?

There was a limit to what he could endure, he decided finally. There was a limit to what he could demand of himself. He was broken by what had happened in San Sobel, and he could not put himself back together again. He no longer cared who he was or what he had pledged himself to do. He was finished with everything.

Let someone else take up the Word's cause.

Let someone else carry the burden of all those lives.

Let someone else, because he was done.

CHAPTER 5

Ariel paused, and Nest found that she couldn't keep quiet any longer. "You mean he quit?" she demanded incredulously. "He just quit?"

The tatterdemalion seemed to consider. "He no longer thinks of himself as a Knight of the Word, so he has stopped acting like one. But he can never quit. The choice isn't his to make."

Her words carried a dark implication that Nest did not miss. "What do you mean?"

Ariel's childlike face seemed to shimmer in the midday sun as she shifted her stance slightly. It was the first time she had moved, and it almost caused her to disappear.

"Only the Lady can create a Knight of the Word, and only the Lady can set one free." Ariel's voice was so soft that Nest could barely hear her. "John Ross is bound to his charge. When he took up the staff that gives him his power, he bound himself forever. He cannot free himself of the staff or of the charge. Even if he no longer thinks of himself as a Knight of the Word, he remains one."

Nest shook her head in confusion. "But he isn't doing anything to be a Knight of the Word. He's given it all up, you said. So what difference does it make whether or not he really is a Knight of the Word? If he's not only stopped thinking of himself as a Knight, but he's stopped functioning as one, he might as well be a bricklayer."

Ariel nodded. "This is what John Ross believes, as well. This is why he is in so much danger."

Nest hesitated. How much of this did she really want to know? The Lady hadn't sent Ariel just to bring her up to date on what was happening to John Ross. The Lady wanted something from her, and where Ross was concerned, she wasn't at all sure it would be something she wanted to give. She hadn't seen or heard from Ross in five years, and they hadn't parted under the best of circumstances. John Ross had come to Hopewell to accomplish one of two things—to help thwart her father's intentions for her or to make certain she would never carry them out. He had seen her future, and while he would not describe it to her, he made it clear that it was dark and horrific. So she would live to change it or she would die. That was his mission in coming to Hopewell. He had admitted it at the end, just before he left. She had never quite gotten over it. This was a man she had grown to like and respect and trust. This was a man she had believed for a short time to be her father—a man she would have liked to have had for a father.

And he had come to kill her if he couldn't save her. The truth was shattering. He was not a demon, as her real father had been, but he was close enough that she was still unable to come to terms with how she felt about him.

"The difficulty for John Ross is that he cannot stop being a Knight of the Word just because he chooses to," Ariel said suddenly.

She had moved to within six feet of Nest. Nest hadn't seen her do that, preoccupied with her thoughts of Ross. The tatterdemalion was close enough that Nest could see the shadowy things that moved inside her semitransparent form like scraps of stray paper stirred by the wind. Pick had told her that tatterdemalions were made up mostly of dead children's memories and dreams, and that they were born fully grown and did not age afterward but lived only a short time. All of them took on the aspects of the children who had formed them, becoming something of the children themselves while never achieving real substance. Magic shaped and bound them for the time they existed, and when the magic could no longer hold them together, the children's memories and dreams simply scattered into the wind and the tatterdemalion was gone.

"But the magic John Ross was given binds him forever," Ariel said. "He cannot disown it, even if he chooses not to use it. It is a part of him. It marks him. He cannot be anything other than what he is, even if he pretends otherwise. Those who serve the Word will always know him. More importantly, those who serve the Void will know him as well."

"Oh, oh," muttered Pick, sitting up a little straighter.

"He is in great danger," Ariel repeated. "Neither the Word nor the Void will accept that he is no longer a Knight. Both seek to bind him to their cause, each in a different way. The Word has already tried reason and persuasion and has failed. The Void will try another approach. A Knight who has lost his faith is susceptible to the Void's treachery and deceit. The Void will seek to turn John Ross through subterfuge. He will have begun to do so already. John Ross will not know that it is happening. He will not see the truth of things until it is too late. It does not happen all at once; it does not happen in a recognizable way. It will begin with a single misstep. But once that first step is taken, the second becomes much easier. The path is a familiar one. Knights have been lost to the Void before."

Nest brushed at a few stray strands of hair that had blown into her eyes. Clouds were moving in from the west. She had read that rain was expected later in the day. "Does he know this will happen?" she asked sharply, almost accusatorily. She was suddenly angry. "How many years of his life has he given to the Word? Doesn't he at least deserve a warning?"

Ariel's body shimmered, and her eyes blinked slowly, flower petals opening to the sun. "He has been warned. But the warning was ignored. John Ross no longer trusts us. He no longer listens. He believes himself free to do as he chooses. He is a prisoner of his self-deception."

Nest thought about John Ross, picturing him in her mind. She saw a lean, rawboned, careworn man with haunted eyes and a rootless existence. But she saw a fiercely determined man as well, hardened of purpose and principle, a man who would not be easily swayed. She could not imagine how the Void would turn him. She remembered the strength of his commitment; he would die before he would betray it.

Yet he had already given it up, hadn't he? By shedding his identity as a Knight of the Word, he had given it up. She knew the truth of things. People changed. Lives took strange turns.

"The Lady sent me to ask you to go to John Ross and warn him one final time."

Ariel's words jarred her. Nest stared in disbelief. "Me? Why would he listen to me?"

"The Lady says you hold a special place in his heart." Ariel said it in a matter-of-fact way, as if Nest ought to know what this would mean. "She believes that John Ross will listen to you, that he trusts and respects you, and that you have the best chance of persuading him of the danger he faces."

Nest shook her head stubbornly. "I wouldn't know what to say. I'm not the right choice for this." She hesitated. "Look, the truth is, I'm not even sure how I feel about John Ross. Where is he, anyway?"

"Seattle."

"Seattle? You want me to go all the way out to Seattle?" Nest was aghast. "I'm in school! I've got classes tomorrow!"

Ariel stared at her in silence, and suddenly Nest was aware of how foolish she sounded. The tatterdemalion was telling her John Ross was in danger, his life was at risk, she might have a chance to help him, and she was busy worrying about missing a few classes. It was more than that, of course, but it hadn't come out sounding that way.

"This is a lot of nonsense!" Pick stormed suddenly, leaping to his feet on her shoulder. "Nest Freemark is needed here, with me! Who knows what could happen to her out there! After what she went through with her father, she shouldn't have to go anywhere!"

"Pick, relax," Nest soothed.

"Criminy!" Pick was not about to relax. "Why can't the Lady go herself? Why can't she speak to Ross? She's the one who recruited him, isn't she? Why can't she send one of her other people, another Knight, maybe?"

"She has already done what she could," Ariel answered, her strange voice calm and distant, her slight form ephemeral in the changing light. "She has sent others to speak for her. He ignores them all. He is lost to himself, locked away by his choice to abandon his charge, and given over to his doom." Her childlike hand gestured. "There is only Nest."

"Well, she's not going!" Pick declared firmly. "So that's it for John Ross, I guess. Thanks for coming, but I think you'd better be on your way."

"Pick!" Nest admonished, surprised at his vehemence. "Be nice, will you?" She looked at Ariel. "What happens if I don't go?" she asked.

Ariel's strange eyes, clear as stream water, locked on her own. "John Ross has had a dream. The events of the dream will occur in three days. On the last day of October. On Halloween. Ross will be a part of these events. To the extent that he is, there is a very great chance he will become ensnared by the Void and will begin to turn. The Lady cannot know this for certain, but she suspects it. She will not let that happen. She has already sent someone to see that it doesn't."

Nest felt a chill sweep through her. *Like she sent Ross to me, five years ago. If Ross is subverted, he will be killed. Someone has been sent to see to it.*

"You are his last chance," Ariel said again. "Will you go to him? Will you speak to him? Will you try to save him?"

Her thin voice drifted on the autumn breeze and was lost in a rustle of dry leaves.

Nest walked back through the park, lost in thought. Pick rode her shoulder in silence. The afternoon was lengthening out from midday, and the park was busy with fall picnickers, hikers, a few stray pickup ballplayers, and parents with kids and dogs. The blue skies were still bright with sunshine, but the sun was easing steadily west toward a large bank of storm clouds that were rolling out of the plains. Nest could smell the coming rain in the soft, cool air.

"What are you going to do?" Pick asked finally.

She shook her head. "I don't know."

"You're seriously thinking about going, aren't you?"

"I'm thinking about it."

"Well, you should forget about it right here and now."

"Why do you feel so strongly about this?" She slowed in the shadow of a large oak and looked down at him. "What do you know that you're not telling me?"

Pick's wooden face twisted in an expression of distaste, and his twiggy body contorted into a knot. His eyes looked straight ahead. "Nothing."

She waited, knowing from experience that there would be more.

"You remember what happened five years ago," Pick said finally, still not looking at her. "You remember what that was like—with John Ross and your grandparents and your . . . You remember?" He shook his head. "It wasn't any of it what it seemed to be at first glance. It wasn't any of it what you thought it was. There were things you didn't know. Things I didn't know, for that matter. Secrets. It was over before you found out everything."

He paused. "It will be like that with this business, too. It always is. The Word doesn't reveal everything. It isn't His nature to do so."

Something was being hidden from her; Pick could sense it, even if he couldn't identify what it was. Maybe so. Maybe it was even something that could hurt her. But it didn't change what was happening to John Ross. It didn't change what was being asked of her. Did she have the right to use it as a reason for not going?

She tried a different tack. "Ariel says she will go with me, that she will help me."

Pick snorted. "Ariel is a tatterdemalion. How much help can she be? She's made out of air and lost memories. She's only alive for a heartbeat. She doesn't know anything about humans and their problems. Tatterdemalions come together mostly by chance, wander about like ghosts, and then disappear again. She's a messenger, nothing more."

"She says she can serve as a guide for me. She says that the Lady has sent her for that purpose."

"The blind leading the blind, as your grandmother used to say." Pick was having none of it.

Nest angled through the trees, bypassing the picnickers and ballplayers, turning up the service road that ran along the backside of the residences bordering the park. Her mind spun in a jumble of concerns and considerations. This was not going to be an easy decision to make.

"Would you come with me?" she asked suddenly.

Pick went still, stiffening. He didn't say anything for a moment, then muttered in a barely audible voice, "Well, the fact of the matter is, I've never been out of the park."

She was surprised, although she shouldn't have been. Why would Pick ever have gone anywhere else? What would have taken him away? The park was his home, his work, his life. He was telling her, without quite speaking the words, that the idea of leaving was frightening to him.

She had embarrassed him, she realized.

"Well, I'm being selfish asking you to go," she said quickly, as if brushing her suggestion aside. "Who would look after the park if you weren't here? It's bad enough that I'm gone so much of the time. But if you left, there wouldn't be anyone to keep an eye on things, would there?"

Pick shook his head quickly. "True enough. No one at all. It's a big responsibility."

She nodded. "Just forget I said anything."

She turned down the service road toward home. Shadows were already beginning to lengthen, the days growing shorter with winter's approach. They spread in black pools from the trees and houses, staining the lawns and roadways and walks. A Sunday type of silence cloaked the park, sleepy and restful. Sounds carried a long way. She could hear voices discussing dinner from one of the houses to her right. She could hear laughter and shouts from off toward the river, down below the bluff where children were playing. She could hear the deep bark of a dog in the woods east.

"I could do this trip in a day and be back," she said, trying out the idea on him. "I could fly out, talk to him, and fly right back."

Pick did not respond. She walked down the roadway with him in silence.

She sat inside by herself afterward, staring out through the curtains, thinking the matter over. Clouds masked the sky beyond, and rain was starting to fall in scattered drops. The people in the park had gone home. Lights were beginning to come on in the windows of the houses across Woodlawn Road.

What should I do?

John Ross had always been an enigma. Now he was a dilemma as well, a responsibility she did not want. He had been living in Seattle for over a year, working for a man named Simon Lawrence at a place called Fresh Start. She remembered both the man and the place from a report someone had done in one of her classes last year. Fresh Start was a shelter for battered and homeless women, founded several years ago by Lawrence. He had also founded Pass/Go, a transitional school for homeless children. The success of both had been something of a celebrity cause for a time, and Simon Lawrence had been labeled the Wizard of Oz. Oz, because Seattle was commonly known as the Emerald City. Now John Ross was there, working at the shelter. So Ariel had informed her.

Nest scuffed at the floor idly with her tennis shoe and tried to picture Ross as a Munchkin in the employ of the great and mighty Oz.

Oh, God. What should I do?

She had told Ariel she would think about it, that she would decide by evening. Ariel would return for her answer then.

She got up and walked into the kitchen to make herself a cup of hot tea. As she stood by the stove waiting for the kettle to boil, she glanced over at the real estate papers for the sale of the house. She had forgotten about them. She stared at them, but made no move to pick them up. They didn't seem very important in light of the John Ross matter, and she didn't want to think about them right now. Allen Kruppert and ERA Realty would just have to wait.

Standing at the living room picture window, holding her steaming cup of tea in front of her, she watched the rain begin to fall in earnest, streaking the glass, turning the old shade trees and the grass dark and shiny. The feeders would come out to prowl in this weather, bolder when the light was poor and the shadows thick. They preferred the night, but a gloomy day would do just as well. She still watched for them, not so much afraid anymore as curious, always thinking she would solve their mystery somehow, that she would discover what they were. She knew what they did, of course; she understood their place in nature's scheme. No one else even knew they were out there. But there was so much more—how they procreated, what they were composed of, how they could inflict madness, how they could appear as shadows and still affect things of substance. She remembered them touching her when her father had made her a prisoner in the caves below the park. She remembered the horror and disgust that blossomed within her. She remembered how badly she had wanted to scream.

But her friends and her grandparents had been there to save her, and now only the memory remained.

Maybe it was her turn to be there for John Ross.

Her brow furrowed. No matter how many ways she looked at the problem, she kept coming back to the same thing. If something happened to John Ross and she hadn't tried to prevent it, how could she live with herself? She would always wonder if she might have changed things. She would always live in doubt. If she tried and failed, well, at least she would have tried. But if she did nothing . . .

She sipped at her tea and stared out the window fixedly. John Ross, the Knight of the Word. She could not imagine him ever being different from what he had been five years ago. She could not imagine him being anything other than what he was. How had he fallen so far away from his fierce commitment to saving the world? It sounded overblown when she said it, but that was what he was doing. Saving the world, saving humanity from itself. O'olish Amaneh had made it plain to her that such a war was taking place, even before Ross had appeared to confirm it. We are destroying ourselves, Two Bears had told her; we are risking the fate of the Sinnissippi—that we shall disappear completely and no one will know who we were.

Are we still destroying ourselves? she wondered. *Are we still traveling the road of the Sinnissippi?* She hadn't thought about it for a long time, wrapped up in her own life, the events of five years earlier behind her, buried in a past she would rather forget. She had been only a girl of fourteen. Her world had been saved, and at the time she had been grateful enough to let it go at that.

But her world was expanding now, reaching out to places and people beyond Hopewell. What was happening in that larger world, the world into which her future would take her? What would become of it without John Ross?

Rain coated the windows in glistening sheets that turned everything beyond into a shimmering haze. The park and her backyard disappeared. The world beyond vanished.

She walked to the phone and dialed Robert Heppler. He answered on the fourth ring, sounding distracted. "Yeah, hello?"

"Back on the computer, Robert?" she asked teasingly.

"Nest?"

"Want to go out for a pizza later?"

"Well, yeah, of course." He was alert and eager now, if surprised. "When?"

"In an hour. I'll pick you up. But there's a small price for this."

"What is it?"

"You have to drive me to O'Hare tomorrow morning. I can go whenever you want, and you can use my car. Just bring it back when you're done and park it in the drive."

She didn't know how Ariel would get to Seattle, but she didn't think it was something she needed to worry about. The Lady's creatures seemed able to get around just fine without any help from humans.

She waited for Robert to say something. There was a long pause before he did. "O'Hare? Where are you going?"

"Seattle."

"Seattle?"

"The Emerald City, Robert."

"Yeah, I know what it's called. Why are you going there?"

She sighed and stared off through the window into the rainy gloom. "I guess you could say I'm off to see the Wizard." She paused for effect. "Bye, Robert."

Then she hung up.

Monday, October 29

CHAPTER 6

John Ross finished the closing paragraph of Simon's Seattle Art Museum speech, read it through a final time to make certain it all hung together, dropped his pen, and leaned back in his chair with a satisfied sigh. Not bad. He was getting pretty good at this speech-writing business. It wasn't what Simon had hired him for, but it looked like it was a permanent part of his job description now. All those years he had spent knocking around in graduate English programs were serving a useful purpose after all. He grinned and glanced out the window of his tiny office. Morning rain was giving way to afternoon sun. Overhead, the drifting clouds were beginning to reveal small patches of blue. Just another typical Seattle day.

He glanced at the clock on his desk and saw that it was nearing three. He had been at this since late morning. Time for a break.

He pushed back his chair and levered himself to his feet. He was three years beyond forty, but when rested he could easily pass for ten years less. Lean and fit, he had the sun-browned, rawboned look of an outdoorsman, his face weathered, yet still boyish. His long brown hair was tied back with a rolled bandanna, giving him the look of a man who might not be altogether comfortable with the idea of growing up. Pale green eyes looked out at the world as if still trying to decide what to make of it.

And, indeed, John Ross had been working on deciphering the meaning of life for a long time.

He stood with his hand gripping the polished walnut staff that served as his crutch, wondering again what would happen if he simply cast it away, if he defied the warning that had accompanied its bestowal and cut loose his final tie to the Word. He had considered it often in the last few months, thinking there was no reason for further delay and he should simply make the decision and act on it. But he could never quite bring himself to carry through, even though he was no longer a Knight of the Word and the staff's power was no longer a part of his life.

He ran his fingers slowly up and down the smooth wood, trying to detect whether he was still bound to it. But the staff revealed nothing. He did not even know if the magic it contained was still his to command; he no longer felt its warmth or saw its gleam in the wood's dark surface. He no longer sensed its presence.

He closed his eyes momentarily. He had wanted his old life back, the one he had given up to become a Knight of the Word. He had been willing to risk everything to regain it. And perhaps, he thought darkly, he had done exactly that. The Word, after all, was the Creator. What did the Creator feel when you told Him you wanted to back out of an agreement? Maybe Ross would never know. What he did know was that his life was his own again, and he would not let go of it easily. The staff, he reasoned, looking warily at it, was a reminder of what it would mean for him if he did.

Raised voices, high-pitched and tearful, chased Della Jenkins down the hall. Della swept past his doorway, muttering to herself, giving him a frustrated shake of her head. She was back a moment later, returning the way she had come, a clutch of papers in one hand. Curious, he trailed after her up the hallway to the lobby at the front of the old building, taking his time, leaning on his staff for support. Della was working the reception desk today, and Mondays were always tough. More things seemed to happen over the weekend than during the week—confrontations of all sorts, exploding out of pressure cookers that had been on low boil for weeks or months or even years. He could never understand it. Why such things were so often done on a weekend was a mystery to him. He always thought a Friday would do just as well, but maybe weekends for the battered and abused were bridges to the new beginnings that Mondays finally required.

By the time Ross reached the lobby, the voices had died away. He paused in the doorway and peeked out guardedly. Della was bent close to a teenage girl who had collapsed in a chair to one side of the reception desk and begun to cry. A younger girl was clinging tightly to one arm, tears streaking her face. Della's hand was resting lightly on the older girl's shoulder, and she was speaking softly in her ear. Della was a large woman with big hair, skin the color of milk chocolate, and a series of dresses that seemed to come only in primary colors. She had both a low, gentle voice and a formidable glare, and she was adept at bringing either to bear as the situation demanded. In this instance, she seemed to have abandoned the latter in favor of the former, and already the older girl's sobs were fading. A handful of women and children occupied chairs in other parts of the room. A few were looking over with a mix of curiosity and sympathy. New arrivals, applying for a bed. When they saw Ross, the women went back to work on their application forms and the children shifted their attention to him. He gave them a smile, and one little girl smiled back.

"There, now, you take your time, look it all over, fill out what you can, I'll help you with the rest," Della finished, straightening, taking her hand from the older girl's shoulder. "That's right. I'll be right over here, you just come on up when you're ready."

She moved back behind the desk, giving Ross a glance and a shrug and settling herself into place with a sigh. Like all the front-desk people, she was a trained professional with experience working intake. Della had been at Fresh Start for something like five years, almost from its inception, according to Ray Hapgood, so she had pretty much seen and heard it all.

Ross moved over to stand beside her, and she gave him a suspicious frown for his trouble. "You at loose ends, Mr. Speechwriter? Need something more to do, maybe?"

"I'm depressed, and I need one of your smiles," he answered with a wink.

"Shoo, what office you running for?" She gave him a look, then gestured with her head. "Little lady over there, she's seventeen, says she's pregnant, says the father doesn't want her or the baby, doesn't want nothing to do with none of it. Gangbanger or some such, just eighteen himself. Other girl is her sister. Been living wherever, the both of them. Runaways, street kids, babies making babies. Told her we could get them a bed, but she had to see a doctor and if there were parents, they had to be notified. Course, she doesn't want that, doesn't trust doctors, hates her parents, such as they are. Good Lord Almighty!"

Ross nodded. "You explain the reason for all this?"

Della gave him the glare. "Course I explained it! What you think I'm doing here, anyway—just taking up space? Who's been here longer, you or me?"

Ross winced. "Sorry I asked."

She punched him lightly on the arm. "No, you ain't."

He glanced around the room. "How many new beds have come in today?"

"Seven. Not counting these." Della shook her head ruefully. "This keeps up, we're going to have to start putting them up in your office, having them sleep on your floor. You mind stepping over a few babies and mothers while you work—assuming you actually do any work while you're sitting back there?"

He shrugged. "Wall-to-wall homeless. Maybe I can put some of them to work writing for me. They probably have better ideas about all this than I do."

"They probably do." Della was not going to cut him any slack. "You on your way to somewhere or did you just come out here to get underfoot?"

"I'm on my way to get some coffee. Do you want some?"

"No, I don't. I got too much work to do. Unlike some I know." She returned to the paperwork on her desk, dismissing him. Then she added, "Course, if you brought me some—cream and sugar, please—I guess I'd drink it all right."

He went back down the hall to the elevator and pressed the button. The staff's coffee room was in the basement along with a kitchen, storage rooms for food and supplies, maintenance equipment, and the water heaters and furnace. Space was at a premium. Fresh Start sheltered anywhere from a hundred and fifty to two hundred women and children at any given time, all of them homeless, most of them abused. Administrative offices and a first-aid room occupied the ground floor of the six-story building, and the top five floors had been converted into a mix of dormitories and bedrooms. The second floor also housed a dining hall that could seat up to a hundred people, which worked fine if everyone ate in shifts. Just next door, in the adjacent building, was Pass/Go, the alternative school for the children housed at Fresh Start. The school served upward of sixty or seventy children most of the time. The Pass/Go staff numbered twelve, the Fresh Start staff fifteen. Volunteers filled in the gaps.

No signs marked the location of the buildings or gave evidence of the nature of the work conducted within. The buildings were drab and unremarkable and occupied space just east of Occidental Park in the Pioneer Square district of Seattle. The International District lay just to the south above the Kingdome. Downtown, with its hotels and skyscrapers and shopping, lay a dozen blocks north. Elliott Bay and the waterfront lay west. Clients were plentiful; you could find them on the streets nearby, if you took the time to look.

Fresh Start and Pass/Go were nonprofit corporations funded by Seattle Public Schools, various charitable foundations, and private donations. Both organizations were the brainchild of one man—Simon Lawrence.

John Ross looked down at his feet. Simon Lawrence. The Wizard of Oz. The man he was supposed to kill in exactly two days, according to his dreams.

The elevator doors opened and he stepped in. There were stairs, but he still walked with difficulty, his resignation from the Word's service notwithstanding. He supposed he always would. It didn't seem fair he should remain crippled after terminating his position, given that he had become crippled by accepting it, but he guessed the Word didn't see matters that way. Life, after all, wasn't especially fair.

He smiled. He could joke about it now. His new life allowed for joking. He wasn't at the forefront of the war against the creatures of the Void, wasn't striving any longer to prevent the destruction of humanity. That was in the past, in a time when there was little to smile about and a great deal to fear. He had served the Word for the better part of fifteen years, a warrior who had been both hunter and hunted, a man always just one step ahead of Death. He had spent each day of the first twelve years trying to change the horror revealed in his dreams of the night before. San Sobel had been the breaking point, and for a while he thought he might never recover from it. Then Stef had come along, and everything had changed. Now he had his life back, and his future was no longer determined by his dreams.

His dreams? His nightmares. He seldom had them now, their frequency and intensity diminishing steadily from the time he had walked away from being a Knight of the Word. That much, at least, suggested his escape had been successful. The dreams had come every night when he was a Knight of the Word, because the dreams were all he had to work with. But now they almost never came, and when they did, they were vague and indistinct, shadows rather than pictures, and they no longer suggested or revealed or threatened.

Except for his dream about Simon Lawrence, the one in which the old man recognized him from the past, the one in which he recognized that the old man's words were true and he had indeed killed the Wizard of Oz. He'd had that same dream three times now, and each time it had revealed a little bit more of what he would do. He had never had a dream three times, even when he was a Knight of the Word; he had never had a dream more than once. It had frightened him at first, unnerved him so that even though he was already living in Seattle and working for Simon he had thought to leave at once, to go far, far away from even the possibility of the dream coming to pass.

It was Stef who had convinced him that the way you banish the things you fear is to stand up to them. He had decided to stay finally, and it had been the right choice. He wasn't afraid of the dream anymore. He knew it wasn't going to happen, that he wasn't going to kill Simon. Simon Lawrence and his incredible work at Fresh Start and Pass/Go was the future John Ross had chosen to embrace.

Ross stepped out of the elevator into the coffee room. The room was large but bare, save for a couple of multipurpose tables with folding chairs clustered about, the coffee machine and cups sitting on a cabinet filled with coffee-making materials, a small refrigerator, a microwave, and a set of old shelves containing an odd assortment of everyday china pieces, silverware, and glasses.

Ray Hapgood was sitting at one of the tables as Ross appeared, reading the *Post-Intelligencer*. "My man, John!" he greeted, glancing up. "How goes the speech-writing effort? We gonna make the Wiz sound like the Second Coming?"

Ross laughed. "He doesn't need that kind of help from me. Most people already think he *is* the Second Coming."

Hapgood chuckled and shook his head. Ray was the director of education at Pass/Go, a graduate of the University of Washington with an undergraduate degree in English literature and years of teaching experience in the Seattle public school system, where he had worked before coming to Simon. He was a tall, lean black man with short-cropped hair receding dramatically toward the crown of his head, his eyes bright and welcoming, his smile ready. He was a "black" man because that was what he called himself. None of that "African American" stuff for him. Black American was okay, but black was good enough. He had little time or patience for that political-correctness nonsense. What you called him wasn't going to make any difference as to whether or not he liked you or were his friend. He was that kind of guy—blunt, open, hardworking, right to the point. Ross liked him a lot.

"Della sends you her love," Ross said, tongue firmly in cheek, and moved over to the coffee machine. He would have preferred a latte, but that meant a two-block hike. He wasn't up to it.

"Yeah, Della's in love with me, sure enough," Ray agreed solemnly. "Can't blame the woman, can you?"

Ross shook his head, pouring himself a cup and stirring in a little cream. "But it isn't right for you to string her along like you do. You have to fish or cut bait, Ray."

"Fish or cut bait?" Ray stared at him. "What's that, some sort of midwestern saying, something you Ohio homeboys tell each other?"

"Yep." Ross moved over and sat down across from him, leaning the black staff against his chair. He took a sip. "What do you Seattle homeboys say?"

"We say, 'Shit or get off the pot,' but I expect that sort of talk offends your senses, so I don't use it around you." Ray shrugged and went back to his paper. After a minute, he said, "Damn, why do I bother reading this rag? It just depresses me."

Carole Price walked in, smiled at Ross, and moved over to the coffee machine. "What depresses you, Ray?"

"This damn newspaper! People! Life in general!" Ray Hapgood leaned back and shook the paper as if to rid it of spiders. "Listen to this. There's three stories in here, all of them the same story really. Story one. Woman living in Renton is depressed—lost her job, ex-husband's not paying support for the one kid that's admittedly his, boyfriend beats her regularly and with enough disregard for the neighbors that they've called the police a dozen times, and then he drinks and totals her car. End result? She goes home and puts a gun to her head and kills herself. But she takes time first to kill all three children because—as she says in the note she so thoughtfully leaves—she can't imagine them wanting to live without her."

Carole nodded. Blond, fit, middle-aged, a veteran of the war against the abuse of women and children, she was the director of Fresh Start. "I read about that."

"Story two." Hapgood plowed ahead with a nod of satisfaction. "Estranged husband decides he's had enough of life. Goes home to visit the wife and children, two of them his from a former marriage, two of them hers from same. Kills her, 'cause she's his wife, and kills *his* children, 'cause they're *his*, see. Lets *her* children live, 'cause they aren't his and he doesn't see them as his responsibility."

Carole shook her head and sighed.

"Story three." Hapgood rolled his eyes dramatically before continuing. "Ex-husband can't stand the thought of his former wife with another man. Goes over to their trailer with a gun, shoots them both, then shoots himself. Leaves three small children orphaned and homeless in the process. Too bad for them."

He threw down the newspaper. "We could have helped all these people, damn it! We could have helped if we could have gotten to them! If they'd just come to us, these women, just come to us and told us they felt threatened and . . ." He threw up his hands. "I don't know, it's all such a waste!"

"It's that, all right," agreed Carole. Ross sipped his coffee and nodded, but didn't say anything.

"Then, right on the same page, like they can't see the irony of it, is an article about the fuss being created over the Pirates of the Caribbean exhibit in Disney World!" Ray looked furious. "See, these pirates are chasing these serving wenches around a table and then auctioning them off, all on this ride, and some people are offended. Okay, I can understand that. But this story, and all the fuss over it, earns the same amount of space, and a whole lot more public interest, than what's happened to these women and children. And I'll bet Disney gives the pirates more time and money than they give the homeless. I mean, who cares about the homeless, right? Long as it isn't you or me, who cares?"

"You're obsessing, Ray," said Jip Wing, a young volunteer who had wandered in during the exchange. Hapgood shot him a look.

"How about the article on the next page about the kid who won't compete in judo competition anymore if she's required to bow to the mat?" Carole grinned wolfishly. "She says bowing to the mat has religious connotations, so she shouldn't have to do it. Mat worship or something. Her mother backs her up, of course. That story gets half a page, more than the killings or the pirates."

"Well, the priorities are all skewed, that's the point." Ray shook his head. "When the newspapers start thinking that what goes on at Disney World or at a judo competition deserves as much attention as what goes on with homeless women and children, we are in big trouble."

"That doesn't even begin to address the amount of coverage given to sports," Jip Wing interjected with a shrug.

"Well, politically incorrect pirates and mat worship, not to mention sports, are easier to deal with than the homeless, aren't they?" Carole snapped. "Way of the world, Ray. People deal with what they can handle. What's too hard or doesn't offer an easy solution gets shoved aside. Too much for me, they think. Too big for one man or woman. We need committees, experts, organizations, entire governments to solve this one. But, hey, mat worship? Pirates chasing wenches? I can handle those."

Ross stayed quiet. He was thinking about his own choices in life. He had given up the pressures of trying to serve on a far larger and more violent battlefield than anything that was being talked about here. He had abandoned a fight that had become overwhelming and not a little incomprehensible. He had walked away from demons and feeders and maentwrogs, beings of magic and darkness, creatures of the Void. Because after San Sobel he felt that he wasn't getting anywhere with his efforts to destroy them, that he couldn't control the results anymore, that it was dumb luck if he ended up killing the monsters instead of the humans. He felt adrift and ineffective and dangerously inadequate. Children had died because of him. He couldn't bear the thought of that happening again.

Even so, it seemed as if Ray were speaking directly to him, and in the other man's anger and frustration with humanity's lack of an adequate response to the problem of homeless and abused women and children, he felt the sharp sting of a personal reprimand.

He took a deep breath, listening as Ray and Carole continued their discussion.

How much good do you think we're doing? he wanted to ask them. *With the homeless. With the people you're talking about. Through all our programs and hard work. How much good are we really doing?*

But he didn't say anything. He couldn't. He sat there in silence, contemplating his own failures and shortcomings, his own questionable choices in life. The fact remained that he liked what he was doing here and he did think he was doing some good—more good than he had done as a Knight of the Word. Here, he could see the results on a case-by-case basis. Not all of his efforts—their efforts—were successful, but the failures were easier to live with and less costly. If change for the better was achieved one step at a time, then surely the people involved with Fresh Start and Pass/Go were headed in the right direction.

He took a fresh grip on his commitment. The past was behind him and he should keep it there. He was not meant to be a Knight of the Word. He had never been more than adequate to the undertaking, never more than satisfactory. It required someone stronger and more fit, someone whose dedication and determination eclipsed his own. He had done the best he could, but he had done as much as he could, as well. It was finished after San Sobel. It was ended.

"Time to get back to work," he said to no one in particular.

The talk still swirled about him as he rose. A couple of other staffers had wandered in, and everyone was trying to get a word in edgewise. With a nod to Ray, who glanced up as he moved toward the elevator, he crossed the room, pressed the button, stepped inside the empty cubicle when it arrived, and watched the break room and its occupants disappear as the doors closed.

He rode up to the main floor in silence, closing his eyes to the past and its memories, sealing himself in a momentary blackness.

When the elevator stopped and he stepped out, Stefanie Winslow was passing by carrying two latte containers, napkins, straws, and plastic spoons nestled in a small cardboard tray.

"Coffee, tea, or me?" she asked brightly, tossing back her curly black hair, looking curiously girlish with the gesture.

"Guess." He pursed his lips to keep from smiling. "Whacha got there?"

"Two double-tall, low-fat, vanilla lattes, fella."

"One of those for me?"

She smirked. "You wish. How's the speech coming?"

"Done, except for a final polish. The Wiz will amaze this Halloween." He gestured at the tray. "So who gets those?"

"Simon is in his office giving an interview to Andrew Wren of *The New York Times*. That's Andrew Wren, the *investigative* reporter."

"Oh? What's he investigating?"

"Well, sweetie, that's the sixty-four-thousand-dollar question, isn't it?" She motioned with her head. "Out of my way, I have places to go."

He stepped obediently aside, letting her pass. She glanced back at him over her shoulder. "I booked dinner at Umberto's for six. Meet you in your office at five-thirty sharp." She gave him a wink.

He watched her walk down the hall toward Simon's office. He was no longer thinking about the homeless and abused, about Ray and Carole, about his past and its memories, about anything but her. It was like that with Stef. It had been like that from the moment they met. She was the best thing that had ever happened to him.

He loved her so much it hurt. But the hurt was pleasurable. The hurt was sweet. The way she made him feel was a mystery he did not ever want to solve.

"I'll be there," he said softly.

He had to admit, his new life was pretty good. He went back to his office smiling.

CHAPTER 7

Andrew Wren stood looking out the window of the Wiz's corner office at the derelicts occupying space in Occidental Park across the way. They slouched on benches, slept curled up in old blankets in tree wells, and huddled on the low steps and curbing that differentiated the various concrete and flagstone levels of the open space. They drank from bottles concealed in paper sacks, exchanged tokens and pennies, and stared into space. Tourists and shoppers gave them a wide berth. Almost no one looked at them. A pair of cops on bicycles surveyed the scene with wary eyes, then moved over to speak to a man staggering out of a doorway leading to a card shop. Pale afternoon sunlight peeked through masses of cumulous clouds on their way to distant places.

Wren turned away. Simon Lawrence was seated at his desk, talking on the phone to the mayor about Wednesday evening's festivities at the Seattle Art Museum. The mayor was making the official announcement of the dedication on behalf of the city. An abandoned apartment building just across the street had been purchased by the city and was being donated to Fresh Start to provide additional housing for homeless women and children. Donations had been pledged that would cover needed renovations to the interior. The money would bring the building up to code and provide sleeping rooms, a kitchen, dining room, and administrative offices for staff and volunteers. Persuading the city to dedicate the building and land had taken the better part of two years. Raising the money necessary to make the dedication meaningful had taken almost as long. It was, all in all, a terrific coup.

Andrew Wren looked down at his shoes. The Wizard of Oz had done it again. But at what cost to himself and the organizations he had founded? That was the truth Wren had come all the way from New York to discover.

He was a burly, slow-moving man with a thatch of unruly, grizzled brown hair that refused to be tamed and stuck out every which way no matter what was done to it. The clothes he wore were rumpled and well used, the kind that let him be comfortable while he worked, that gave him an unintimidating, slightly shabby look. He carried a worn leather briefcase in which he kept his notepads, source logs, and whatever book he was currently reading, together with a secret stash of bagged nuts and candy that he used to sustain himself when meals were missed or forgotten in the heat of his work. He had a round, kindly face with bushy eyebrows, heavy cheeks, and he wore glasses that tended to slide down his nose when he bent forward to listen to compensate for his failing hearing. He was almost fifty, but he looked as if he could just as easily be sixty. He could have been a college professor or a favorite uncle or a writer of charming anecdotes and pithy sayings that stayed with you and made you smile when you thought back on them.

But he wasn't any of these things. His worn, familiar teddy-bear look was what made him so effective at what he did. He looked harmless and mildly confused, but how he looked was dangerously deceptive. Andrew Wren was a bulldog when it came to ferreting out the truth. He was relentless in getting to the bottom of things. Investigative reporting was a tough racket, and you had to be both lucky and good. Wren had always been both. He had a knack for being in the right place at the right time, for sensing when there was a story worth following up. His instincts were uncanny, and behind those kindly eyes and rumpled look was a razor-sharp mind that could peel away layers of deception and dig down to that tiny nugget of truth buried under a mound of bullshit. More than one overconfident jackass had been undone by underestimating Andrew Wren.

Simon Lawrence was not likely to turn into one of these unfortunates, however. Wren knew him well enough to appreciate the fact that the Wiz hadn't gotten where he was by underestimating anyone.

Simon hung up the phone and leaned back in his chair. "Sorry about that, Andrew, but you don't keep the mayor waiting."

Wren nodded benignly, shrugging. "I understand. Wednesday's event means a lot to you."

"Yes, but more to the point, it means a lot to the mayor. He went out on a limb for us, persuading the council to pass a resolution dedicating the building, then selling the idea to the voters. I want to be certain that he comes out of this experience feeling good about things."

Wren walked over to the easy chair that fronted Simon's desk and sat down. Even though they had met only once before, and that was two years ago, Simon Lawrence felt comfortable enough with Wren to call him by his first name. Wren wouldn't do anything to discourage that just yet.

"I should think just about everyone is feeling pretty good about this one, Simon," he complimented. "It's quite an accomplishment."

Simon leaned forward and put his elbows on his desk and his chin in his hands, giving Wren a thoughtful look. He was handsome in a rugged sort of way, with nicely chiseled features, thick dark hair, and startling blue eyes. When he walked, he looked like a big cat, sort of gliding from place to place, slow and graceful, never hurried, with an air of confidence about him that suggested he would not be easily surprised. Wren placed him at a little over six feet and maybe two hundred pounds. His birth certificate, which Wren had ferreted out by searching the records in a suburb of St. Louis two years earlier in an unsuccessful attempt to learn something about his childhood, put him at forty-five years of age. He was unmarried, had no children, had no living relatives that anyone could identify, lived alone, and was the most important voice of his generation in the fight against homelessness.

His was a remarkable story. He had come to Seattle eight years ago after spending several years working for nationally based programs like Habitat for Humanity and Child Risk. He worked for the Union Gospel Mission and Treehouse, then, after three years, founded Fresh Start. He began with an all-volunteer staff and an old warehouse on Jackson Street. Within a year, he had secured sufficient funding to lease the building where Fresh Start was presently housed, to hire a full-time staff of three, including Ray Hapgood, and to begin generating seed money for his next project, Pass/Go. He wrote a book on homeless women and children, entitled *Street Lives*. A documentary filmmaker became interested in his work and shot a feature that won an Academy Award. Shortly afterward, Simon was nominated for the prestigious Jefferson Award, which honors ordinary citizens who do extraordinary things in the field of community service. He was one of five statewide winners, was selected as an entry for national competition, and was subsequently a winner of the Jacqueline Kennedy Onassis Award.

From there, things really took off. The media began to cover him regularly. He was photogenic, charming, and passionate about his work, and he gave terrific interviews. His programs became nationally known. Hollywood adopted him as a cause, and he was smart enough to know how to make the most of that. Money poured in. He purchased the buildings that housed Fresh Start and Pass/Go, increased his full-time staff, began a volunteer training program, and developed a comprehensive informational program on the roots of homelessness, which he made available to organizations working with the homeless in other cities. He held several high-profile fund-raisers that brought in national celebrities to mingle with the locals, and with the ensuing contributions established a foundation to provide seed money for programs similar to his own.

He also wrote a second book, this one more controversial than the first, but more critically acclaimed. The title was *The Spiritual Child.* It was something of a surprise to everyone, because it did not deal with the homeless, but with the spiritual growth of children. It argued rather forcibly that children were possessed of an innate intelligence that allowed them to comprehend the lessons of spirituality, and that adults would do better if they were to spend less time trying to impose their personal religious and secular views and more time encouraging children to explore their own. It was a controversial position, but Simon Lawrence was adept at advancing an argument without seeming argumentative, and he pretty much carried the day.

By now he was being referred to regularly as the Wizard of Oz, a name that had been coined early on by *People* magazine when it ran a fluff piece on the miracles he had performed in getting Fresh Start up and running. Wren knew Simon Lawrence wasn't overly fond of the tag, but he also knew the Wiz understood the value of advertising, and a catchy name didn't hurt when it came to raising dollars. He lived in the Emerald City, after all, so he couldn't very well complain if the media decided to label him the Wizard of Oz. Or the Wiz, more usually, for these days everyone seemed to think they were on a first-name basis with him. Simon Lawrence was hot stuff, which made him news, which made Andrew Wren's purpose in coming to see him all the more intriguing.

"An accomplishment," Simon said softly, repeating Wren's words. He shook his head. "Andrew, I'm like the Dutch boy with his finger in the hole in the dike and the sea rising on the other side. Let me give you some statistics to think about. Use them or not when you write your next story, I don't care. But remember them.

"There are two hundred beds in this facility. With the new building, we should be able to double that. That will give us four hundred. Four hundred to service homeless women and children. There are twelve hundred school-age homeless children, Andrew. That's children, not women. Twenty-four percent of all our homeless are under the age of eighteen. And that number is growing every day.

"Ours is a specific focus. We provide help to homeless women and children. Eighty percent of those women and children are homeless because of domestic violence. The problem of domestic violence is growing worldwide, but especially here, in the United States. The statistics regarding children who die violently are all out of proportion with the rest of the world. An American child is five times more likely to be killed before the age of eighteen than a child living in another industrialized nation. The rate of gun deaths and suicides among our children is more than twice that of other countries. We like to think of ourselves as progressive and enlightened, but you have to wonder. Homelessness is an alternative to dying, but not an especially attractive one. So it is difficult for me to dwell on accomplishments when the problem remains so acute."

Wren nodded. "I've seen the statistics."

"Good. Then let me give you an overview of our response as a nation to the problem of being homeless." Simon Lawrence leaned back again in his chair. "In a time in which the homeless problem is growing by leaps and bounds worldwide—due, to varying extents, to increases in the population, job elimination, technological advances, disintegration of the family structure, violence, and the rising cost of housing—our response state by state and city by city has been an all-out effort to look the other way. Or, as an alternative, to try to relocate the problem to some other part of the country. We are engaged in a nationwide effort to crack down on the homeless by passing new ordinances designed to move these people to where we can't see them. Stop them from panhandling, don't let them sleep in our parks and public places, conduct police sweeps to round them up, and get them the hell out of town—that's our solution. Is there a concerted effort to get at the root problems of homelessness, to find ways to rehabilitate and reform, to address the differences between types of homelessness so that those who need one kind of treatment versus another can get it? How many tax dollars are being spent to build shelters and provide showers and hot meals? What efforts are being made to explore the ways in which domestic violence contributes to the problem, especially where women and children are concerned?"

He folded his arms across his chest. "We have thousands and thousands of people living homeless on the streets of our cities at the same time that we have men and women earning millions of dollars a year running companies that make products whose continued usage will ruin our health, our environment, and our values. The irony is incredible. It's obscene."

Wren nodded. "But you can't change that, Simon. The problem is too indigenous to who we are, too much a part of how we live our lives."

"Tell me about it. I feel like Don Quixote, tilting at windmills." Simon shrugged. "It's obviously hopeless, isn't it? But you know something, Andrew? I refuse to give up. I really do. It doesn't matter to me if I fail. It matters to me if I don't try." He thought about it a moment. "Too bad I'm not really the Wizard of Oz. If I were, I could just step behind the old curtain and pull a lever and change everything—just like that."

Wren chuckled. "No, you couldn't. The Wizard of Oz was a humbug, remember?"

Simon Lawrence laughed with him. "Unfortunately, I do. I think about it every time someone refers to me as the Wiz. Do me a favor, Andrew. Please refrain from using that hideous appellation in whatever article you end up writing. Call me Toto or something; maybe it will catch on."

There was a soft knock, the door opened, and Stefanie Winslow walked in carrying the lattes Simon had sent her to purchase from the coffee shop at Elliott Bay Book Company. Both men started to rise, but she motioned them back into their seats. "Stay where you are, gentlemen, you probably need all your energy for the interview. I'll just set these on the desk and be on my way."

She gave Wren a dazzling smile, and he wished instantly that he was younger and cooler and even then he would probably need to be a cross between Harrison Ford and Bill Gates to have a chance with this woman. Stefanie Winslow was beautiful, but she was exotic as well, a combination that made her unforgettable. She was tall and slim with jet-black hair that curled down to her shoulders, cut back from her face and ears in a sweep so that it shimmered like satin in sunlight. Her skin was a strange smoky color, suggesting that she was of mixed ancestry, the product of more than one culture, more than one people. Startling emerald eyes dominated an oval face with tiny, perfect features. She moved in a graceful, willowy way that accentuated her long limbs and neck and stunning shape. She seemed oblivious to how she looked and comfortable within herself, radiating a relaxed confidence that had both an infectious and unsettling effect on the people around her. Andrew Wren would have made the journey to Seattle just to see her in the flesh for ten seconds.

She set the lattes before them and started for the door. "Simon, I'm going to finish with the SAM arrangements, then I'm out of here. John has your speech all done except for a once-over, so we're going out for a long, quiet, intimate dinner. See you tomorrow."

"Bye, Stef." Simon waved her out.

"Nice seeing you, Mr. Wren," she called back.

The door closed behind her with a soft click. Wren shook his head. "Shouldn't she be a model or an actress or something? What sort of hold do you have over her, Simon?"

Simon Lawrence shrugged. "Will you be staying for the dedication on Wednesday, Andrew, or do you have to get right back?"

Wren reached for his latte and took a long sip. "No, I'm staying until Thursday. The dedication is part of what I came for. It's central to the article I'm writing."

Simon nodded. "Excellent. Now what's the other part, if you don't mind my asking? Everything we've talked about has been covered in the newspapers already—ad nauseam, I might add. *The New York Times* didn't send its top investigative reporter to interview me for a rerun, did it? What's up, Andrew?"

Wren shrugged, trying to appear casual in making the gesture. "Well, part of it is the dedication. I'm doing a piece on corporate and governmental involvement—or the lack thereof—in the social problems of urban America. God knows, there's little enough to write about that's positive, and your programs are bright lights in a mostly shadowy panorama of neglect and disinterest. You've actually done something where others have just talked about it—and what you've done works."

"But?"

"But in the last month or so the paper has received a series of anonymous phone calls and letters suggesting that there are financial improprieties in your programs that need to be investigated. So my editor ordered me to follow it up, and here I am."

Simon Lawrence nodded, his face expressionless. "Financial improprieties. I see." He studied Wren. "You must have done some work on this already. Have you found anything?"

Wren shook his head. "Not a thing."

"You won't, either. The charge is ridiculous." Simon sipped at his latte and sighed. "But what else would I say, right? So to set your mind at ease, Andrew, and to demonstrate that I have nothing to hide, I'll let you have a look at our books. I don't often do this, you understand, but in this case I'll make an exception. You already know, I expect, that we have accountants and lawyers and a board of directors to make certain that everything we do is above reproach. We're a high-profile operation with important donors. We don't take chances with our image."

"I know that," Wren demurred, looking vaguely embarrassed to deflect the implied criticism. "But I appreciate your letting me see for myself."

"The books will show you what comes in and what goes out, everything but the names of the donors. You aren't asking for those, are you, Andrew?"

"No, no." Wren shook his head quickly. "It's what happens to the money after it comes in that concerns me. I just want to be certain that when I write my article extolling the virtues of Fresh Start and Pass/Go and Toto the Wonder Wizard, I won't be shown up as an idiot later on." He tacked on a sheepish smile.

Simon Lawrence gave him a cool look. "An idiot? Not you, Andrew. Not likely. Besides, if there's something crooked going on, I want to know about it, too."

He stood up. "Finish your latte. I'll have Jenny Parent, our bookkeeper, bring up the records. You can sit here and look them over to your heart's content." He glanced down at his watch. "I've got a meeting with some people downtown at five, but you can stay as long as you like. I'll catch up with you in the morning, and you can give me your report then. Fair enough?"

Wren nodded. "More than fair. Thank you, Simon."

Simon Lawrence paused midway around his desk. "Let me be honest with you about my feelings on this matter, Andrew. You are in a position to do a great deal of harm here, to undo an awful lot of hard work, and I don't want that to happen. I resent the hell out of the implication that I would do anything to subvert the efforts of Fresh Start and Pass/Go and the people who have given so much time and effort and money in support of those programs, but I understand that you can't ignore the possibility that the rumors and innuendos have some basis in fact. You wouldn't be doing your job if you did. So I am trusting you to be up front with me on anything you find—or, more to the point, don't find. Whatever you need, I'll try to give it to you. But I'm giving it to you in the belief that you won't write an article where rumors and accusations are repeated without any basis in fact."

Wren studied Lawrence for a moment. "I don't ever limit the scope of an investigation by offering conditions," he said quietly. "But I can also say that I have never based a report on anything that wasn't backed up by solid facts. It won't be any different here."

The other man held his gaze a moment longer. "See you tomorrow, Andrew."

He walked out the door and disappeared down the hallway, leaving Wren alone in his office. Wren sat where he was and finished his latte, then stood up and walked over to the window again. He admired the Wiz, admired the work he had done with the homeless. He hoped he wouldn't find anything bad to write about. He hoped the phone calls and letters were baseless—sour grapes from a former employee or an errant shot at troublemaking from an extremist group of "real Americans." He'd read the letters and listened to the tapes of the phone calls. It was possible there was nothing to them.

But his instincts told him otherwise. And he had learned from twenty-five years of experience that his instincts were seldom wrong.

The demon gave Andrew Wren the better part of an hour with the foundation's financial records, waiting patiently, allowing the reporter enough time to familiarize himself with the overall record of donations to Fresh Start and Pass/Go, then checked to make certain the hallway was empty and slipped into the room behind him. Wren never heard the demon approach, his back to the door, his head lowered to the open books as he ran his finger across the notations. The demon stood looking at him for a moment, thinking how easy it would be to kill him, feeling the familiar hunger begin to build.

But now was not the time and Wren had not been lured to Seattle to satisfy the demon's hunger. There were plenty of others for that.

The demon moved up behind Andrew Wren and placed its fingers on the back of the man's exposed neck. Wren did not move, did not turn, did not feel anything as the dark magic entered him. His eyes locked on the pages before him, and his mind froze. The demon probed his thoughts, drew his attention, and then whispered the words that were needed to manipulate him.

I won't find what I'm looking for here. Simon Lawrence is much too clever for that. He wouldn't be stupid enough to let me look at these books if he thought they were incriminating. I have to be patient. I have to wait for my source to contact me.

The demon spoke in Andrew Wren's voice, in Andrew Wren's mind, in Andrew Wren's thoughts, and it would seem to the reporter as if the words were his own. He would do as the demon wanted without ever realizing it; he would be the demon's tool. He would think that the ideas the demon gave him were his own and that the conclusions the demon reached for him were his. It was easy enough to arrange. Andrew Wren was an investigative reporter, and investigative reporters believed that everyone was covering up something. Why should Simon Lawrence be different?

Andrew Wren hesitated a moment as the demon's words took root, and then he closed the book before him and began to stack it with the others.

The demon smiled in satisfaction. It wouldn't be long now until everything was in place. Another two days was all it would take. John Ross would be turned. A Knight of the Word would become a servant of the Void. It would happen so swiftly that it would be over before Ross even realized what was taking place. Even afterward, he would not know what had been done to him. But the demon would know, and that would be enough. A single step was all that was required to change John Ross's life, a step away from the light and into the dark. Andrew Wren would help make that happen.

The demon lifted its fingers from Andrew Wren's neck, slipped back out the door, and was gone.

CHAPTER 8

In the aftermath of San Sobel, John Ross decided to return to the Fairy Glen and the Lady.

It took him a long time to reach his decision to do so. He was paralyzed for weeks following the massacre, consumed with despair and guilt, replaying the events over and over in his mind in an effort to make sense of them. Even after he had reached his conclusion that the demon had subverted a member of the police rescue squad, he could not lay the matter to rest. To begin with, he could never know for certain if his conclusion was correct. There would always be some small doubt that he still didn't have it right and might have done something else to prevent what had happened. Besides, wasn't he just looking for a way to shift the blame from himself? Wasn't that what it all came down to? Whatever the answer, the fact remained that he had been responsible for preventing the slaughter of those children, and he had failed.

So, after a lengthy deliberation on the matter, he decided he could no longer serve as a Knight of the Word.

But how was he to go about handing in his resignation? He might have decided he was quitting, but how did he go about giving notice? He had already stopped trying to function as a Knight, had ceased thinking of himself as the Word's champion. He had retreated so far from who and what he had been that even the nature of his dreams had begun to change. Although he still dreamed, the dreams had turned vague and purposeless. He still wandered a grim and desolate future in which his world had been destroyed and its people reduced to animals, but his part in that world was no longer clear. When he dreamed, he drifted from landscape to landscape, encountering no one, seeing nothing of value, discovering nothing of his past that he might use as a Knight of the Word. It was what he wanted, not to be burdened with knowledge of events he might influence, but it was vaguely troubling as well. He still carried the staff bequeathed to him by the Word, the talisman that gave him his power, but he no longer used it for its magic, only as a walking stick. He still felt the magic within, a small tingling, a brief surge of heat, but he felt removed and disconnected from it.

He no longer saw himself as a Knight of the Word, had quit thinking of himself as one, but he needed a way to sever his ties for good. He decided finally that to do this he must go back to where it had all begun.

To Wales, to the Fairy Glen, and to the Lady.

He had not been back in more than ten years, not since he had traveled to England in his late twenties, a graduate student permanently mired in his search for his life's purpose, not since he had drifted from postgraduate course to postgraduate course, a prisoner of his own indecision. He had gone to England to change the direction of his life, to travel and study and find a path that had meaning for him. In the course of that pursuit, he had journeyed into Wales to stay at the cottage of a friend's parents in the village of Betwys-y-Coed in Gwynedd in the heart of the Snowdonia wilderness. He had been studying the history of the English kings, particularly of Edward Longshanks, who had built the iron ring of fortresses to subdue the Welsh in the Snowdonia region, and so was drawn to the opportunity to travel there. Once arrived, he began to fall under the spell of the country and its people, to become enmeshed in their history and folklore, and to sense that there was a purpose to his being there beyond what was immediately apparent.

Then he found the Fairy Glen and the ghost of Owain Glyndwr, the Welsh patriot, who appeared to him as a fisherman and persuaded him to come back at midnight so that he could see the fairies at play. Skeptical of the idea of fairies and a little frightened by the encounter, but captivated as well by the setting and the possibility that there was some truth to the fisherman's words, he eventually did as he was asked. It was there, in the blackness of the new moon and the sweep of a thousand stars on a clear summer night, that the Lady appeared to him for the first and only time. She told him of her need for his services as a Knight of the Word. She revealed to him his blood link to Owain Glyndwr, who had served her as a Knight in his lifetime. She showed to him a vision of the future that would be if her Knights failed to prevent it. She persuaded him to accept her, to accept the position she offered him, to accept a new direction in his life.

To accept the way of the Word.

Now, to abandon that way, to sever the ties that bound him to the Word's path, he decided he must return to her.

He bought a ticket, packed a single bag, and flew east. He arrived at Heathrow, boarded a train, and traveled west to Bristol and then across the border into Wales. He found the journey nostalgic and unsettling; his warm memories of the past competed with the harsh reality of his purpose in the present, and his emotions were left jumbled, his nerves on edge. It was late fall, and the countryside was beginning to take on a wintry cast as the colors of summer and autumn slowly drained away. The postage-stamp fields and meadows lay fallow, and the livestock huddled closer to the buildings and feeding troughs. Flowers had disappeared, and skies were clouded and gray with the changing weather.

He reached Betwys-y-Coed after expending several days and utilizing various forms of transportation, and he booked himself at a small inn. It began to rain the day he arrived, and it kept raining afterward. He waited for the rain to stop, spending time in the public rooms of the inn and exploring various shops he remembered from his visit before. A few of the residents remembered him. The village, he found, was substantially unchanged.

He spent time thinking about what he would say to the Lady when he came face-to-face with her. It would not be easy to tell her he could no longer be in her service. She was a powerful presence, and she would try to dissuade him from his purpose. Perhaps she would even hurt him. He still remembered how she had crippled him. After his return to his parents' home in Ohio, her emissary, O'olish Amaneh, had come to him with the staff, and he had sensed immediately that his life would change irrevocably if he accepted it. His determination and conviction had been eroding steadily since his return from England, but now there was no time left to equivocate. The staff was thrust upon him, and the moment his hands touched the polished wood, his foot and leg cramped and withered, the pain excruciating, and he was bound to the talisman forever.

Would that change now? he wondered. If he was no longer a Knight of the Word, would his leg be healed, be made whole and strong again? Or would his decision to abandon his charge cost him even more?

He tried not to dwell on the matter, but the longer he waited, the harder it became to convince himself to carry through on his resolve. His imagination was working overtime after a week of deliberation, stimulated by the rain and the gray and his own fears, turned gloomy and despairing of hope. This was a mistake, he began to believe. This was stupid. He should not have come here. He should have stayed where he was. It was sufficient that he refused to act as a Knight of the Word. His decision did not require the Lady's validation. He barely dreamed at all anymore, his dreams so indistinct by now that they lacked any recognizable purpose. They were closer to real dreams, to the ones normal people had that involved bits and pieces of events and places and people, all of it disjointed and meaningless. He was no longer being shown a usable future. He was no longer being given clues to a past he might act upon. Wasn't that sufficient proof that he was severed from his charge as a Knight of the Word?

But in the end he decided that he was being cowardly. He had come a long way just to turn around and go home again, and he should at least give it a try. He put on a slicker and boots and hitched a ride out to the Fairy Glen. He went at midday, thinking that perhaps the daylight would lessen his trepidation. But it was a slow, steady rain that fell, turning everything gray and misty, and the world had taken on a hazy, ephemeral look in which nothing seemed substantive, but was all made of shadows and the damp.

His ride dropped him right next to the white board sign with black letters that read FAIRY GLEN. Ahead, a rutted lane led away from the highway and disappeared over a low rise, following a wooden fence. A small parking lot was situated on the left with a box for donations, and a wooden arrow pointed down the lane, saying TO THE GLEN.

It was all as he remembered.

The car drove away, and he was left alone. The forest about him on both sides of the road was deep and silent and empty of movement. He could see no houses. Fences ran along the road at various points, bent with its curves, and disappeared into the gray. He took a long moment to stare at the signs, the donation box, the parking lot, and the rutted lane, and then at the countryside about him, recalling what it had been like when he had come here for the first time. It had been magical. Right from the beginning, he had felt it. He had been filled with wonder and expectation. Now he was weary and uncertain and burdened with a deep-seated sense of failure. As if all he had accomplished had gone for nothing. As if all he had given of himself had been for naught.

He walked up the rutted lane to find the break in the fence line that would lead him down into the glen. He walked slowly, placing his feet carefully, listening to the patter of the rain and the silence behind it. The branches of the trees hung over him like giants' arms, poised to sweep him up and carry him off. Shadows moved and drifted with the clouds, and his eyes swept the haze uneasily.

At the opening in the fence, he paused again, listening. There was nothing to hear, but he kept thinking there should be, that something of what he remembered of his previous visit would reveal itself. But everything seemed new and different, and while the terrain looked as he remembered, it didn't feel the same. Something was missing, he knew. Something was changed.

He went through the gate in the fence and started down the pathway that wound into the ravine. Leaning heavily on his staff, he worked his way slowly ahead. The Fairy Glen was a jumble of massive boulders and broken rock and isolated patches of wildflowers and long grasses. A waterfall tumbled out of the high rocks to become a meandering stream of eddies and rapids, with pools so clear and still he could see the colored pebbles they collected. Rain dripped from the trees and puddled on the trail and ran down the steep sides of the ravine in rivulets that eroded the earth in intricate designs. No birdsong disturbed the white noise of the water's rush or the fall of the rain. No movement disrupted the deep carpet of shadows.

As he reached the floor of the ravine, he glanced back to where the waterfall spilled off the rocks, but there was no sign of the fairies. He slowed and looked around carefully. The Lady was nowhere to be seen. The Fairy Glen was cloaked in shadow and curtained by rain, and it was empty of life. It was as he remembered, but different, too. Like before, he decided, when he had stood at the gate opening, it seemed changed. He took a long moment to figure out what the nature of that change might be.

Then he had it. It was the absence of any magic. He couldn't feel any magic here. He couldn't feel anything.

His hand tightened on the staff, searching. The magic failed to respond. He stood staring at the Fairy Glen in disbelief, unable to accept that this could be so. Were the Lady and the fairies gone from the glen? Was that why he could not sense the magic? Because the magic was no longer here?

He walked along the rugged bank of the rain-choked stream, picking his way carefully over the litter of broken rock and thick grasses. On a flat stone shelf, he knelt and peered down into a still pool. He could see his reflection clearly. He looked for something more, for something different, for a sign. Nothing revealed itself. He watched the rain pock his reflection with droplets that sent glistening, concentric rings arcing away, one after the other. His image grew shimmery and distorted, and he looked quickly away.

When he lifted his head, a fisherman was standing on the opposite shore a dozen yards away, staring at him. For a moment, Ross couldn't believe what he was seeing. He had convinced himself that the Fairy Glen was abandoned; he had given up hope of finding anyone here. But he recognized the fisherman instantly. His clothes and size and posture were unmistakable. And his look. Because he was a ghost and was not entirely solid, his body shifted and changed as the light played over it. When he tilted his head, as he did now, a slight movement of his broad-brimmed hat, his familiar features were revealed. It was Owain Glyndwr, his ancestor, the Welsh patriot who had fought against the English Bolingbroke, Henry IV—Owain Glyndwr, dead now for hundreds of years, but given new life in his service to the Lady. He looked just as he had years earlier, when Ross had first come upon him in the Fairy Glen.

Seeing him like this, materialized unexpectedly, would have startled John Ross before, but not now. Instead, he felt his heart leap with gratitude and hope.

"Hello, Owain," he greeted with an anxious wave of his hand.

The fisherman nodded, a spare, brief movement. "Hello, John. How are you?"

Ross hesitated, suddenly unsure of what he should say. "Not well. Something's happened. Something terrible."

The other man nodded and turned away, working his line carefully through the rapids that swirled in front of where he stood. "Terrible things always happen when you are a Knight of the Word, John. A Knight of the Word is drawn to terrible things. A Knight of the Word stands at the center of them."

Ross adjusted the hood of his slicker to ward off the rain that blew into his eyes. "Not any longer. I'm not a Knight of the Word anymore. I've given it up."

The fisherman didn't look at him. "You cannot give it up. The choice isn't yours to make."

"Then whose choice is it?"

The fisherman was silent.

"Is she here, Owain?" Ross asked finally, coming forward to the very edge of the rock shelf on which he stood. "Is the Lady here?"

The fisherman gave a barely perceptible nod. "She is."

"Good. Because I couldn't feel her, couldn't feel anything of the magic when I walked down." Ross groped for the words he needed. "I suppose it's because I've been away for so long. But . . . it doesn't feel right." He hesitated. "Maybe it's because I'm here in the daylight, instead of at night. You told me, the first day we met, that if it was magic I was looking for, if I wanted to see the fairies, it was best to come at night. I'd almost forgotten about that. I don't know what I was thinking. I'll come back tonight—"

"John." Owain's soft voice stopped him midsentence. "Don't come back. She won't appear for you."

John Ross stared. "The Lady? She won't? Why not?"

The fisherman took a long time before answering. "Because the choice isn't yours to make."

Ross shook his head, confused. "I don't understand what you're saying. Which choice? The one for her to appear or the one for me to stop being a Knight of the Word?"

The other man worked his pole and line without looking up. "Do you know why you can't feel the magic, John? You can't feel it because you don't admit that it's inside yourself anymore. Magic doesn't just happen. It doesn't just appear. You have to believe in it."

He looked over at Ross. "You've stopped believing."

Ross flushed. "I've stopped believing in its usefulness. I've stopped wanting it to rule my life. That's not the same thing."

"When you become a Knight of the Word, you give yourself over to a life of service to the Word." Owain Glyndwr ran his big, gnarled hands smoothly along the pole and line. Shadows from passing clouds darkened his features. "If it was an easy thing to do, anyone would be suitable to the task. Most aren't."

"Perhaps I'm one of them," Ross argued, anxious to find a way to get his foot in the door the Lady had apparently closed on him. "Perhaps the Word made a mistake with me."

He paused, waiting for a response. There was none. This was stupid, he thought, arguing with a ghost. Pointless. He closed his eyes, remembering San Sobel. "Listen to me, Owain. I can't go through it anymore. I can't live with it another day.

The dreams and the killing and the monsters and the hate and fear and all of it endless and purposeless and stupid! I can't do it. I don't know how you did it."

The big man turned to face him again, taking up the pole and line, looking away from the stream. "I did it because I had to, John. Because I was there. Because maybe there was no one else. Because I was needed to do it. Like you."

Ross clenched his hands on the walnut staff. "I just want to return the staff," he said quietly. "Why don't I give it to you?"

"It doesn't belong to me."

"You could give it to the Lady for me."

The fisherman shook his head. "If I take it from you, how will you leave the Fairy Glen? You cannot walk without the staff. Will you crawl out on your hands and knees like an animal? If you do, what will you find waiting for you at the rim? When you became a Knight of the Word, you were transformed. Do you think you can be as you were? Do you think you can forget what you know, what you've seen, or what you've done? Ever?"

John Ross closed his eyes against the tears that suddenly welled up. "I just want my life back. I just want this to be over."

He felt the rain on his hands, heard the sound of the drops striking the rocks and trees and stream, small splashes and mutterings that whispered of other things. "Please, help me," he said quietly.

But when he looked up again, the ghost of Owain Glyndwr was gone, and he was alone.

He climbed out of the Fairy Glen and returned—walking more than half the distance before he found a ride—to his inn. He ate dinner in the public rooms and drank several pints of the local ale, thinking on what he would do, on what he believed must happen. The rain continued to fall, but as midnight neared it eased off to a slow, soft drizzle that was more mist than rain.

The innkeeper let him borrow his car, and Ross drove out to the Fairy Glen and parked in the little parking lot and walked once more to the gap in the fence. The night was clouded and dark, the world filled with shadows and wet sounds, and the interlaced branches of the trees formed a thick net that looked as if it were poised to drop over him. He eased his way through the gap and proceeded carefully down the narrow, twisting trail. The Fairy Glen was filled with the sound of water rushing over the rocks of the rain-swollen stream, and the rutted trail was slick with moisture. Ross took a long time to reach the floor of the ravine, and once there he stood peering about cautiously for a long time. When nothing showed itself, he walked to the edge of the stream and stood looking back at the falls.

But the fairies, those pinpricks of scattered, whirling bright light he remembered so well, did not appear. Nor did the Lady. Nor did Owain Glyndwr. He stood in the darkness and rain for hours, waiting patiently and expectantly, willing them to appear, reaching out to them with his thoughts, as if by the force of his need alone he could make them materialize. But no one came.

He returned to his rooms in disappointment, slept for most of the day, rose to eat, waited anew, and went out again the following night. And again, no one appeared. He refused to give up. He went out each night for a week and twice more during the days, certain that someone would appear, that they could not ignore him entirely, that his determination and persistence would yield him something.

But it was as if that other world had ceased to exist. The Lady and the fairies had vanished completely. Not even Owain returned to speak with him. Not a hint of the magic revealed itself. Time after time he waited at the edge of the stream, a patient supplicant. Surely they would not abandon him when he needed help so badly. At some point they would speak to him, if only to reject his plea. His pain was palpable. They must feel it. Wasn't he entitled to at least the reassurance that they understood? The rain continued to fall in steady sheets, the forests of Snowdonia stayed dark and shadowy, and the air continued damp and cold in the wake of fall's passing and the approach of winter.

Finally he went home to America. He despaired of giving up, but there seemed to be no other choice. It was clear he was to be given no audience, to be offered no further contact. He was wasting his time. He packed his bags, bussed and trained his way back to Heathrow, boarded a plane, and flew home. He thought more than once to turn around and go back to the Fairy Glen, to try again, but he knew in his heart it was futile. By choosing to give up his office, he had made himself an outcast. Perhaps Owain Glyndwr was right, that once you gave up on the magic, it gave up on you, as well. He no longer felt a part of it, that much was certain. Even when he touched the rune-scrolled length of his staff, he could find no sign of life. He had wanted to distance himself from the magic, and apparently he had done so.

He accepted that this was the way it must be if he was to stop being a Knight of the Word. Whatever ties had bound him to the Word's service were apparently severed. The magic was gone. The dreams had nearly ceased. He was a normal man again. He could go about finding a normal life.

But he remembered Owain Glyndwr's words about how, by becoming a Knight of the Word, he had been transformed and things could never be the same again. He found himself thinking of a time several years earlier in Hopewell, Illinois, when Josie Jackson had made him feel for just a few hours of his nightmarish existence what it was like to be loved, and of how he had walked away from her because he knew he had nothing to give her in return. He recalled how Nest Freemark had asked him in despair and desperation if he was her father, and he remembered wishing so badly he could tell her that he was.

He thought of these things, and he wondered if anything even remotely resembling a normal life would ever be possible again.

CHAPTER 9

It was already dark when John Ross and Stefanie Winslow exited the offices of Fresh Start, turned down Main Street, and headed for Umberto's. Daylight saving time was over for another year, and all the clocks had been reset Sunday morning in an effort to conserve daylight—spring forward, fall back—but the approach of winter in the northwest shortened Seattle days to not much more than eight hours anyway. Streetlights threw their hazy glare on the rough pavement of the roadways and sidewalks, and the air was sharp and crisp with cold. It had rained earlier in the day, so shallow puddles dotted the concrete and dampness permeated the fall air. Traffic moved sluggishly through a heavy concentration of mist, and the city was wrapped in a ghostly pall.

Ross and Stefanie crossed Second Avenue and continued west past Waterfall Park, a strange, secretive hideaway tucked into an enclosure of brick walls and iron fences that abutted the apartment building where they lived. One entire wall and corner of the park's enclosure was devoted to a massive waterfall that tumbled over huge rocks with such a thunderous rush that conversation attempted in its immediate vicinity was drowned out. A walkway dropped down along a catchment and circled back around to a narrow pavilion with two additional features involving a spill of water over stone, and a cluster of tables and chairs settled amid a collection of small trees and flowering vines. In better weather, people employed in the vicinity would come into the park on their lunch breaks to watch the waterfall and to eat. John and Stefanie did so frequently. From their bedroom window, they could look down on the park and across at the offices of Fresh Start.

Adjoining Waterfall Park was Occidental Park, a broad open space paved with cobblestones that overlapped Main from Jackson to Yesler and fronted a series of shops and restaurants and a parking lot that serviced the entire Pioneer Square area. The new Seattle was built on the old Seattle, the earlier version of the city having burned to the ground in a turn-of-the-century fire. An underground tour of portions of the old city began just a few blocks to the north. By passing through a nondescript door and descending a steep, narrow flight of stairs, you could step back in time.

But the present was above ground, and that was what most people came to see. Pioneer Square was an eclectic collection of art galleries, craft outlets, bookstores, bars, restaurants, souvenir shops, and oddities, funky and unassuming and all-embracing, and John Ross had felt at home from the day he arrived.

He had come to Seattle with Stef more than a year ago. They had been together for several months by then, were drifting more or less, and had read about Fresh Start and thought it would be a good place for them to work. They had come on a whim, not even knowing if there might be jobs available, and there hadn't been, not at first, but they had fallen in love with the city and particularly with Pioneer Square. They had rented a small apartment to see how things would go, and while he had been pessimistic about their chances of catching on at Fresh Start—they had been told, after all, that there were no paid openings and none expected anytime soon—Stef had just laughed and told him to be patient. And sure enough, within a week Simon Lawrence had called her back and said he had something, and within a month after that, after spending his time doing volunteer work at the shelter, Ross had been offered full-time employment, too.

He glanced over at Stef surreptitiously as they crossed Occidental Park. He was wearing his greatcoat with the huge collar turned up and his heavy wool scarf with the fringed ends trailing behind, and as he limped along with the aid of his heavy walking staff, he looked a little like a modern-day Gandalf. Stefanie matched her pace to his, all sleek and smooth and flawless with her shimmering black hair and long limbs. She seemed entirely out of place amid the jumble of old buildings, antique street lamps, and funky people. She looked odd walking past the trolley that was stopped at the little island across from The Paper Cat, as if she had gotten off at the wrong stop on her way to the glass and steel towers of the high-rent district uptown. You might have thought she was slumming amid the homeless men who were clustered together next to the carved wooden totems and on the benches and under the mushroom-shaped pavilion across the way.

But you would have been wrong. If there was one thing Ross had learned about Stefanie Winslow, it was that notwithstanding how she looked and dressed, she was right at home anywhere. You might think you could tell something about her by just looking at her, but you couldn't. She was comfortable with herself in a way that astonished him. Stef was one of those rare people who could walk into any situation, anyplace, anytime, and find a way to deal with it. It was a combination of presence and attitude and intelligence. It was the reason Simon Lawrence had hired her. And subsequently hired him, for that matter. Stefanie made you feel she was indispensable. She made you believe she was up to anything. It was, in large part, he knew, why he was in love with her.

They rounded the corner at Elliott Bay Book Company and walked down First Avenue to King Street, then turned into the door of Umberto's Ristorante. The hostess checked off their names, smiled warmly at Stef, and said that their table was ready. She led them down several steps to the dining area, past the salad island toward the neon sign that said IL PICCOLO, which was the tiny corner bar, then turned right down a hallway covered with posters of upcoming Seattle arts events. Ross looked at Stef in surprise. The dining room was behind them now; where were they going? Stef gave him a wink.

At the end of the hallway was the wine cellar, a small room closed away behind an iron gate in which a single table had been set for dinner. The hostess opened the wrought-iron door and seated them inside. A white tablecloth, green napkins, and silver and china seemed to glow in soft candlelight amid the racks of wines surrounding them.

"How did you manage this?" Ross asked in genuine amazement as the hostess left them alone.

Stef tossed back her long hair, reached for his hand, and said, "I told them it was for you."

* * *

He had been back from Wales for almost a month when he met her. He had returned defeated in spirit and bereft of hope. He had failed in his effort to speak with the Lady or return the staff of power. His parents were dead, and his childhood home sold. He had lost contact with his few relatives years earlier. He had nowhere to go and no one to go to. For lack of a better idea, he went up from New York to Boston College, where he had studied years earlier, and began auditing classes while he worked out his future. He was offered a position in the graduate-studies program in English literature, but he asked for time to think about it, uncertain if he wanted to go back into academia. What he really wanted was to do something that would allow him to make a difference in people's lives, to take a job working with people he could help. He needed human contact again. He needed validation of his existence. He worked hard at thinking of himself as something other than a Knight of the Word. He struggled bravely to develop a new identity.

Each day he would take his lunch in the student cafeteria, sitting at a long table, poring through his study books and staring out the windows of the dining hall. It was winter, and snow lay thick and white on the ground, ice hung from the eaves, and breath clouded in the air like smoke. Christmas was approaching, and he had nowhere to spend it and no one to spend it with. He felt incredibly lonely and adrift.

That was when he first saw Stefanie Winslow. It was early December, only days before the Christmas break. He wasn't sure if she had been coming there all along and he just hadn't noticed her or if she had suddenly appeared. Once he saw her though, he couldn't look away. She was easily the most beautiful woman he had ever seen—exotic, stunning, and unforgettable. He couldn't find words to give voice to what he was feeling. He watched her all through the lunch hour and stayed afterward when he should have been auditing his class, continuing to stare at her until she got up and walked away.

The next day she was back, sitting at the same table, off to one side, all alone. He watched her come in and sit down to have her lunch for five days, thinking each time that he had to go over to her and say something, had to introduce himself, had to make some sort of contact, but he always ended up just sitting there. He was intimidated by her. But he was compelled, as well. No one else tried to sit with her; no one else even tried to approach. That gave him pause. But his connection with her was so strong, so visceral, that he could not ignore it.

Finally, at the beginning of the following week, he just got up and walked over, limped over really, feeling stupid and inadequate with his heavy staff and rough look, and said hello. She smiled up at him as if he were the most important thing in her life, and said hello back. He told her his name, she told him hers.

"I've been watching you for several days," he said, giving her a deprecatory shrug.

"I know," she said, arching one eyebrow speculatively.

He flushed. "I guess I overdid it if I was that obvious. I was wondering if you were a student at the college."

She shook her head, her black hair catching the winter light. "No, I work in administration."

"Oh. Well, I'm auditing some classes." He let the words trail away. He didn't know where else to go with it. He felt suddenly awkward about what he was doing, sitting here with her. He glanced about. "I didn't mean to intrude, I just . . ."

"John," she interrupted gently, drawing his eyes back to hers, holding them. "Do you know why I've been sitting here alone every day?"

He shook his head slowly.

"Because," she said, drawing out the word, "I've been waiting for you to join me."

She always knew the right thing to say. He had been in love with her from the beginning, and his feelings had just grown stronger over time. He sat watching her now as she gave their order to the waiter, a young man with long sideburns and a Vandyke beard, holding his attention with her eyes, with her voice, with her very presence. The waiter wouldn't look away if a bomb went off, Ross thought. When he left with the order, the wine steward, who had been by earlier, reappeared with the bottle of Pinot Grigio Stef had ordered. He poured it for Ross to taste, but Ross indicated Stef was in charge. She tasted it, nodded, and the wine steward filled their glasses and disappeared.

They sat close within the dim circle of candlelight and stared at each other without speaking. Silently Ross hoisted his glass. She responded in kind, they clinked crystal softly, and drank.

"Is this some sort of special occasion?" he asked finally. "Did I forget an important date?"

"You did," she advised solemnly.

"And you won't tell me what it is, will you?"

"As a matter of fact, I will. But only because I don't want to see how long it takes you to remember." She cocked her head slightly in his direction. "It was one year ago today, exactly, that Simon Lawrence hired you to work at Fresh Start."

"You're kidding."

"I don't kid. Josh, yes. Tease, now and then. Never kid." She took a sip of her wine and licked her lips. "Cause for celebration, don't you think? Who would have thought you would end up writing speeches for the Wizard of Oz?"

Ross shook his head. "Who would have thought I would have ended up living with Glinda the Good?"

Stef arched her eyebrows in mock horror. "Glinda the Good? Wasn't she a witch?"

"A good witch. That's why she was called Glinda the Good."

Stef gave him a considering look. "John, I love you deeply, madly, truly. But don't call me Glinda the Good. Don't call me anything that smacks of the Wizard of Oz or the Emerald City or Munchkins or Dorothy or the yellow brick road. I get quite enough of that at work. Our life is separate and distinct from all this Wiz business."

He leaned back, looking hurt. "But it's the date of my hiring. Isn't the analogy appropriate under those circumstances?"

The waiter returned with their salads, and they began to eat. The sounds of the main dining room seemed distant and disconnected from their little haven. Ross thought about all the years he had dreaded night's coming and sleep, plagued by the knowledge that when he slept he was condemned to dream of the future he must prevent and of the horror he must live if he failed. Once, he had thought he would never escape that life, and that even if he did, its memories would haunt him forever. Stefanie had saved him from that, helped him find his way free of the labyrinth of his past, and brought him back into the light of possibility and hope.

"Have you finished your polish of the Wiz's speech?" she asked. "Hmm, good salad. I like the bits of walnuts and blue cheese."

"It's all done," he replied with a sigh. "Another masterpiece. Simon will be quoted for weeks afterward." He grinned. "I shall live vicariously through him, his words my own."

"Yes, well, I don't know how much of this vicarious-living business you want to indulge in," she mused, lifting her wineglass and studying it speculatively. "He seemed pretty on edge after Andrew Wren's visit."

Ross looked up from his salad. "Really? What was that all about anyway, did you ever find out?"

She shook her head. "But it's never good news for a public figure when an investigative reporter comes calling."

"No, I suppose not."

"Jenny told me Simon asked for the books cataloguing donations and expenditures to be brought up for Wren to look at. What does that suggest to you?"

"Financial impropriety." Ross shrugged. "Wren will hunt a long time before he'll find evidence of that. Simon's a fanatic about keeping clean books. He can account for every penny received or spent."

He went back to eating his salad. Stef continued to study her wineglass, finally taking a sip from it. "I just don't like the way Simon is behaving," she said finally. "He isn't himself lately. Something is bothering him."

Ross finished chewing, kept his eyes lowered, then forced himself to look up at her and smile. "Something is bothering almost everyone, Stef. The thing to remember is, mostly we have to work these things out by ourselves."

John Ross dreams. It is the same dream, the only dream he has anymore that he can remember upon waking. It is a dream of the future he was sworn to prevent as a Knight of the Word, and each time it reoccurs it is a little darker than it was before.

This time is no exception.

He stands on a hillside south of Seattle, watching as the city burns. Hordes of once-men and demons pour through gaps in the shattered defenses and drive the defenders steadily back toward the water that hems them in on all sides but his. Feeders cavort through the carnage and drink in the terror and frenzy and rage of the dying and wounded. It is a nightmarish scene, the whole of the scorched and burning landscape awash in rain and mist, darkened by clouds and gloom, wrapped in a madness that finds voice in the screams and cries of the humans it consumes.

But the feelings that fill Ross are unfamiliar ones. They are not of frustration or anger, not of despair or sadness, as they have been each time before. His feelings now are dull and empty, devoid of anything but irritation and a faint boredom. He stands with a group of the city's survivors, but he has no regard for them either. Rather, he is a shell, armored and invulnerable, but emotionless. He has no idea how he became this way, but it is a transcending experience to realize it has happened. He is no longer a Knight of the Word; he is something else entirely. The humans he stands with are not a part of him. They do not meet his gaze as he looks over at them speculatively. They cower in his presence and huddle submissively before him. They are frightened of him. They are terrified.

Then the old man approaches and whispers that he knows him, that he remembers him from years earlier. His hollow-eyed gaze is vacant, and his voice is flat and toneless. He looks and speaks as if he is disconnected from his body. He repeats the familiar words. You were there, in the Emerald City! You killed the Wizard of Oz! It was Halloween night, and you were wearing a mask of death! They were celebrating his life, and you killed him!

He shoves the old man away roughly. The old man collapses in a heap and begins to sob. He lies helpless in the dirt and rainwater, his ragged clothes and beard matted with mud, his frail body shaking.

Ross looks away. He knows the words the old man speaks are true, but he does not care. He has walled away all guilt long since, and killing no longer means anything to him.

He realizes in that moment that he is no longer part of the humans clustered at his feet. He has shed his humanity; he has left it behind him in a past he can barely remember.

Suddenly, he understands why the humans look at him as they do.

He is the enemy who has come to destroy them.

Ross and Stef walked slowly back along First Avenue after leaving Umberto's, arms linked, shoulders hunched against the cold. The air was still hazy and damp and the sky still gray, but there was no rain yet. The street lamps of Pioneer Square blazed above them, casting their shadows on the sidewalk as they passed, dark human patterns lengthening and then fading with each bright new circle.

The dream had come again last night, for the first time in several weeks, and Ross was still wrestling with its implications. In this latest version of the future, Simon Lawrence was still dead, and Ross was still his killer. But now Ross was one of the bad guys, no longer a Knight of the Word, no longer even a passive observer as he had been every time the dream came to him before. He was some sort of demon clone, a creature of the Void and only barely recognizable as having ever been human.

He frowned into the upturned collar of his coat. It was ridiculous, ludicrous to think that any of this could ever come to pass.

So why was he having this dream?

Why was he being plagued with visions of a future he would never let happen?

"The state legislature is going to pass a bill before the end of the week that will cut back on state funding for welfare recipients to match what the federal government has already done in cutting back its funding to the state." Stef's voice was soft and detached in the gloom. "Maybe that's what has got Simon so upset."

"Well, by all means, let's put more people back on the streets." Ross shook his head, thinking of other things.

"Welfare encourages people not to work, John. You know that. You hear it all the time. Cutting off their aid will force them to get out there and get a job."

"Good thing it's all so simple. We can just ignore the culture of poverty. We can just pretend that poor people are just rich people without money. We can tell ourselves that educational, social, and cultural opportunities are the same for everyone. We can ignore the statistics on domestic violence and teen pregnancy and rate of exposure to crime and disease and family stability. Cut off welfare and put 'em to work. I don't know why anyone didn't think of it before. We can have everyone off the street and working by the end of the month, I bet."

"Yep. Then we can tackle a cure for cancer and get that out of the way, too." She snuggled her face into his shoulder, her dark hair spilling over him like silk.

"I liked our dinner," he ventured, trying to take the edge off his frustration.

She nodded into his coat. "Good. I liked it, too."

They rounded the corner of Main at Elliott Bay Book Company and started for home. Occidental Park sprawled ahead of them, empty of life, watched over by the wooden totems, spectral sentinels in the gloom. The homeless had moved on to warmer spots for the night, abandoning their daytime haunt. Some would find a bed in one of the shelters. Some would make their bed on the streets. Some would wake up in the morning. Some would not.

"There are just not enough of us," Ross said quietly.

She lifted her head to look at him. "Not enough of who?"

"Not of who. Of what. I misspoke. Not enough shelters for the homeless. Not enough schools for displaced children. Not enough food banks. Not enough care facilities. Not enough churches working with the needy. Not enough charities. Not enough programs or funding or answers. Not enough of anything."

She nodded. "There's a lot of competition for people's money and time, John. The choices aren't always easy."

"Maybe it would be easier if people remembered there's a lot of competition for their souls, as well."

She stared hard at him for a moment. "Then everyone should be able to figure out what to do, shouldn't they?"

They crossed Main to Waterfall Park, peering into the blackness where the sound of rushing water welled up and reverberated off the brick walls. Amid the cluster of rocks and trees and garden tables, shadows shifted with barely perceptible movements. Ross thought he caught a glimpse of lantern eyes peering out at him. He didn't see the feeders much anymore—only brief glimpses. It bothered him sometimes that he couldn't see them better. He had wanted to remove himself from their world, and it didn't help knowing they were there and not being able to see them.

It reminded him of something Owain Glyndwr had asked of him.

Do you think you can ever be as you were?

He found himself thinking of the dream again, of the way he had appeared in it, of the way it made him feel. He might not ever be as he was, but at least he could keep himself from being like that. He could manage that much, couldn't he?

He stared into the shadows in silence, Stefanie clinging to his arm, and dared the things that lurked within to come into the light. It seemed to him as he did so that he could feel them daring him, in turn, to come into the dark.

Chapter 10

Even though its hunger had become all-consuming, the demon waited until after midnight to hunt.

It crept from its lair as silent as the death that awaited its victims and slipped out onto the empty streets of Pioneer Square. The weeknight city had closed its eyes early, and even the bars and restaurants had shuttered their doors and clicked off their lights. The air was damp and heavy with mist and the beginnings of a fresh rain, and the moisture glistened on the concrete in a satiny sheen. Cars eased past in ones and twos, carrying their occupants to home and bed, strays following in the wake of the early evening rush. The demon watched from the shadows close by Occidental Park, wary of being seen. But the park and sidewalks and streets were empty and still. The demon was alone.

It crept from its hiding place in human form, standing upright, maintaining its guise as it made its way to the place where the hunt would begin. It wore running shoes and sweats to mask the sound of its passing, keeping to the shadows as much as possible, sliding along the walls of the darkened buildings, across the shadowed stretches of the park, and through the blackened tunnels of the alleys and walkways. The homeless who spent their days in the park had all gone elsewhere, and the Indian totems loomed above the empty stone spaces like hunters in search of prey, eyes fearsome and staring, beaks and talons at the ready.

But the demon's hunt was not for food. Its hunger was of a different sort. Its hunger was more primal and less easily understood. The demon hunted because it needed to kill. It hunted to feel the struggles of its victims as it rent their flesh, cracked their bones, and spilled their blood. It hunted to experience that exquisite moment of fulfillment when its efforts claimed another human life—that last shudder of consciousness, that final exhalation of breath, that concluding gasp as death arrived. The demon's need for killing humans was indigenous to its makeup. It had been human itself once, long ago, and to continue to be what it was, it was necessary for it to keep killing its human self over and over again. It accomplished this through the killing of others. Its own humanity was drowned completely in the madness that drove it, but it was necessary that it pretend at being human so that it could move freely among its victims, and there was danger in this. Killing kept the pretense from ever threatening to become even a momentary reality.

At the corner of First Avenue and Yesler, the demon paused a final time in the shadows to look about. Seeing neither cars nor people approaching, it slipped quickly across First to the line of old doorways and basement windows that fronted the street, and hunkered down beside a set of concrete steps that led into a kite and banner shop. Again, it paused to look about and listen. Again, it saw and heard nothing.

Scooting forward like a crab, it paused in front of an old, wood-frame basement window with its glass painted out, levered the window open with practiced ease, slithered through the opening into the darkness beyond, and was gone.

Inside, it dropped softly to the basement floor and waited for its eyes to adjust. It took only a moment, for the demon's sight was as keen in darkness as in light. It saw with all its senses, unlike the human it had once been, unlike the humans it hunted. It despised the weaknesses of flesh and blood and bone it had long ago discarded. It despised the humanity that it had shed like a snake's skin. It was not burdened by moral codes or emotional balance or innate sensibility or anything even approaching responsibility. The demon functioned in its service to the Void without any restrictions save one—to survive. It did not question that it served the Void; it did so because it could not conceive of any other way to be and because the Void's interests were a perfect fit with its own. The demon's purpose in life was to destroy the humans of whom it had once been part. Its purpose was to wipe them from the face of the earth. That it served the Void in doing so seemed mostly chance.

It stood motionless in the darkness for a long moment, then began to strip off its clothes. It would hunt better once it had transformed. Its human guise was uncomfortable and restrictive, and it served only to remind the demon of the shell it had been trapped inside for so many years. All demons were mutable and, given time, could become whatever they chose. But this demon was particularly adept. It could change forms effortlessly, which was not usually the case. Most demons were required to keep to the form they adopted because it took so long to build another. But this demon was different. It could change forms with the speed of a chameleon changing colors, rebuilding itself in moments. Its ability had served it well as a creature of the Void. It specialized in ferreting out and subverting the more powerful servants of the Word. It had destroyed many of them. It was working now at destroying John Ross.

Of course, it was only the part of Ross that was human that the demon sought to destroy. It would keep the rest. It would keep his magic. It would keep his knowledge. It would set free the dark underside that he worked so hard to contain and give it mastery over what remained of his spirit.

When its clothes lay on the floor, the demon began to change. Its human form disappeared as its body swelled and knotted with muscle and its skin sprouted thick, coarse hair. Its head lengthened, its jaws widened, and its teeth grew long and sharp. It took on the appearance of something that was a cross between a huge cat and a massive dog, but it resembled most closely a monstrous hyena—all powerful neck and sinewy shoulders and fanged muzzle.

Altered, it dropped down on all fours and began to make its way through the darkness. It passed from the basement down a set of open stairs to another level. Now it was inside the burned-out shell of old Seattle, of the ruin that served as the foundation for the city above. This was not a part of the old city that was covered by the underground tour. It was a part that was closed off, inaccessible to most. The streets and alleyways ran on for hundreds of yards, mysterious and empty. Parts of it collapsed from time to time, and sometimes its darkened corridors flooded with runoff from the streets and sewers during heavy rains. Few knew it even existed. No one ever came down at night.

Except for the homeless.

And the demon who liked to hunt them.

The demon was thinking of John Ross, imagining what it would be like to close its massive jaws about his throat, to crush the life from him, to feel the blood spurt from his torn body. The demon hated Ross. But the demon was attracted to him, too. All that magic, all that power, the legacy of a Knight of the Word. The demon would like to taste that. It would like to share it. It hungered for killing, but it hungered for the taste of magic even more.

Its feral eyes cast about in the black as it loped through the darkness on silent paws, ears pricked forward, listening. All about, feeders kept pace. There would be killing, they sensed. There would be terror and rage and desperation, and they were anxious to taste them all. Just as the demon hungered after magic and killing, the feeders hungered for the residual emotions in humans that both evoked.

John Ross belongs to me, the demon was thinking. *He belongs to me because I have found him, claimed him, and understand his uses. I will subvert him, and I will set him free. I will make him over as I have made myself over. It will happen soon, so soon. The wheels of the machine that will make it possible are in motion. No one can stop them. No one can change what I intend.*

John Ross is mine.

Ahead, distant still through the seemingly unending darkness, the faint sound of voices rose. The demon's jaws hung open and its tongue lolled out. The eyes of the feeders gleamed more brightly and their movements grew more intense.

Head lowered, nose sniffing expectantly at the cobblestones of the underground city's abandoned streets, the demon began to creep forward.

Above ground and unaware of the demon's presence, Nest Freemark was less than two blocks away.

It had taken her all day to get to Seattle, and she had arrived too late to make a serious effort at contacting John Ross until tomorrow—which, by now, was today, because it was after midnight. Fending off endless questions regarding her travel plans and misguided offers of help, she had booked a United flight leaving O'Hare at three-fifteen in the afternoon and, as planned, ridden into Chicago that morning with Robert. Robert meant well, but he still didn't know when to back off. She avoided telling him exactly what it was she was doing or why she was going. It was an unexpected trip, a visit to some relatives, and that was all she would say. Robert was beside himself with curiosity, but she thought it would do him good to have to deal with his frustration. Besides, she wasn't entirely unhappy with the idea of letting him suffer a little more as penance for his behavior at her grandfather's funeral.

He dropped her at the ticketing entrance to United, still offering to come along, to accompany her, to meet her, to do whatever she asked. She smiled, shook her head, said good-bye, picked up her bag, and walked inside. Robert drove away. She waited to make sure.

She hadn't seen Ariel since the night before and had no idea how the tatterdemalion planned to reach Seattle, but that wasn't her problem. She checked her bag, received her boarding pass, and was advised that the departure time had been moved back to five o'clock due to a problem with the plane.

She walked down to the assigned gate, took a seat, and resumed reading the book she had begun the night before. It was titled *The Spiritual Child*, and it was written by Simon Lawrence. She was drawn to the book for several reasons—first, because it made frequent reference to the writing of Robert Coles, and to his book *The Spiritual Life of Children* in particular, which she had read for a class in psychology last semester and enjoyed immensely, and second, because she was on her way to find John Ross, who was working for Lawrence at Fresh Start, and she wanted to know something about the thinking of the man with whom a failed Knight of the Word would ally himself. Of course, it might be that this was only a job for Ross and nothing more, but Nest didn't think so. That didn't sound like John Ross. He wasn't the sort to take a job indiscriminately. After abandoning his service to the Word, he would want to find something he felt strongly about to commit to.

In any case, she had whiled away the time reading Simon Lawrence, the airplane still hadn't shown, the weather had begun to deteriorate with the approach of a heavy thunderstorm, and the departure time had been pushed back yet again. Growing concerned that she might not get out at all, Nest had gone up to the gate agent and asked what the chances were that the flight might not leave. The agent said she didn't know. Nest retraced her steps to customer service and asked the agent on duty if she could transfer to another flight. The agent looked doubtful until Nest explained that a close friend was dying, and she needed to get to Seattle right away if she was to be of any comfort to him. It was close enough to the truth that she didn't feel too bad about saying it, and it got her a seat on a flight to Denver connecting on to Seattle.

The flight had left a little after five, she was in Denver by six forty-five, mountain time, and back on a second plane to Seattle by seven-fifty. The flight up took another two hours and something, and it was approaching ten o'clock Pacific time before the plane touched down at Sea-Tac. Nest disembarked carrying her bag, walked outside to the taxi stand, and caught a ride downtown. Her driver was Pakistani or East Indian, a Sikh perhaps, wearing one of those turbans, and he didn't have much to say. She still hadn't seen a sign of Ariel, and she was beginning to worry. She could find her way around the city, locate John Ross, and make her pitch alone if she had to, but she would feel better having someone she could turn to for advice if she came up against a problem. She was already composing what she would say to Ross. She was wondering as well why he would pay any attention to her, the Lady's assurances notwithstanding.

She missed Pick terribly. She hadn't thought their separation would be so bad, but it was. He had been with her almost constantly from the time she was six years old; he was her best friend. She had been able to leave him to go off to school, but Northwestern University was only a three-hour drive from Hopewell and it didn't feel so far away. She supposed her grandfather's death contributed to her discomfort as well; Pick was the last link to her childhood, and she didn't like leaving him behind. It was also the first time she had done anything involving the magic without him. Whatever the reason, not having him there made her decidedly uneasy.

The taxi driver had taken her to the Alexis Hotel, where she had booked a room the night before by phone. The Alexis was situated right at the north end of Pioneer Square, not far from the offices of Fresh Start. It was the best hotel in the area, and Nest had decided from the start that if she was going to travel to a strange city, she wanted to stay in a good place. She had been able to get a favorable rate on a standard room for the two-night stopover she had planned. She checked in at the front desk, took the elevator to her room, dropped her bag on the bed, and looked around restlessly.

Despite the fact that she had been traveling all day, she was not tired. She unpacked her bag, glanced through a guide to Seattle, and walked to the window and looked out. The street below glistened with dampness, and the air was hazy with mist. All of the shops and offices she could see were closed. There were only a few cars passing and fewer people. It was just a little after eleven-thirty.

She had decided to go for a walk.

Nest was no fool. She knew about cities at night and the dangers they presented for the unwary. On the other hand, she had grown up with the feeders in Sinnissippi Park, spending night after night prowling the darkness they favored, avoiding their traps, and surviving confrontations far more dangerous than anything she was likely to encounter here. Moreover, she had the magic to protect her, and while she hadn't used it in a while and didn't know what stage of growth it was in at the moment, she had confidence that it would keep her safe.

So she had slipped on her heavy windbreaker, ridden the elevator back down to the lobby, and gone out the door.

She was no sooner outside and walking south along First Avenue toward the banks of old-fashioned street lamps that marked the beginning of Pioneer Square than Ariel had appeared. The tatterdemalion materialized out of the mist and gloom, filling a space in the darkness beside Nest with her vague, transparent whiteness. Her sudden appearance startled Nest, but she didn't seem to notice, her dark eyes cast forward, her silken hair flowing out from her body as if caught in a breeze.

"Where are you going?" she asked in her thin childlike voice.

"Walking. I can't sleep yet. I'm too wound up." Nest watched the shadows whirl and spin inside the tatterdemalion's gauzy body. "How did you get here?"

Ariel didn't seem to hear the question, her dark eyes shifting anxiously. "It isn't safe," she said.

"What isn't safe?"

"The city at night."

They had crossed from the hotel and walked into the next block. Nest looked around cautiously at the darkened doorways and alcoves of the buildings. There was no one to be seen.

"I remember about cities," Ariel continued, her voice small and distant. She seemed to float across the pavement, a ghostly hologram. "I remember how they feel and what they hide. I remember what they can do to you. They are filled with people who will hurt you. They are places in which children can disappear in the blink of an eye. Sometimes they lock you away in dark places and no one comes for you. Sometimes they wall you up forever."

She was speaking from the memories of the children she had been once, of the only memories she had. Nest decided she didn't want to know about those memories, the memories of dead children.

"It will be all right," she said. "We won't go far."

They walked quite a distance though, all the way down First Avenue under Pioneer Square's turn-of-the-century street lamps past shuttered shops and galleries to where they could see the Kingdome rising up against the night sky in a massive hump. The mist thickened and swirled about them, clinging to Nest's face and hands in a thin, cold layer of moisture. Nest drew her windbreaker tighter about her shoulders. When the character of the neighborhood began to change, the shops and galleries giving way to warehouses and industrial plants, Nest turned around again, with Ariel hovering close, and started back.

They were approaching a small, concrete, triangular park with benches and shade trees fronting a series of buildings that included one advertising Seattle's Underground Tour when the screams began.

They were so faint that at first Nest couldn't believe she was hearing them. She slowed and looked around doubtfully. She was all alone on the streets. There was no one else in sight. But the screams continued, harsh and terrible in the blackness and mist.

"Something hunts," Ariel hissed as she shimmered brightly, darting left and right.

Nest wheeled around, looking everywhere at once. "Where are they coming from?" she demanded, frantic now.

"Beneath us," Ariel said.

Nest looked down at the concrete sidewalk in disbelief. "From the sewers?"

Ariel moved close, her childlike face smooth and expressionless, but her eyes filled with terror. "There is an old city beneath the new. The screams are coming from there!"

The demon worked its way ahead slowly through the blackness of the underground city, following the scent of the humans and the sound of their voices. It wound through narrow streets and alleyways and in and out of doors and gaps in crumbling walls. It was filled with hunger and flushed with a need to kill. It was driven.

Scores of feeders trailed after it, lantern eyes glowing in the musky gloom.

After a time, the demon saw the first flicker of light. The voices of the humans were clear now; it could hear their words distinctly. There were three of them, not yet grown to adulthood, a girl and two boys. The demon crept forward, eyes narrowing, pulse racing.

"What's that?" one of them said suddenly as stone and earth scraped softly under the demon's paw.

The demon could see them now, huddled about a pair of candles set into broken pieces of old china placed on a wooden crate. They were in a room in which the doors and windows had long since fallen away and the walls had begun to collapse. The ceiling was ribbed with pipes and conduits from the streets and buildings above, and the air was damp and smelled of rotting wood and earth. The boys and the girl had made a home of sorts in the open space, furnishing it with several wooden crates, a couple of old mattresses and sleeping bags, several plastic sacks filled with stuff they had scavenged, and a few books. Where they had come from was anybody's guess. They must have found their way down from the streets where they spent their days, taking shelter each night as so many did in the abandoned labyrinth of the older city.

The demon rounded the corner of a building across from them and paused. Feeders crowded forward and hovered close. The older of the two boys came to his feet and stood looking out into the dark. The other two crouched guardedly to either side. There was only one way in or out of their shelter. The demon had them trapped.

It advanced slowly into the light, showing itself gradually, letting them see what it was. Fear showed on their faces and in their eyes. Frantic exclamations escaped their lips—low, muttered curses that sounded like prayers. The demon was filled with joy.

The older boy produced a long-bladed knife. "Get away!" he warned, and swore violently at the demon. The demon came forward anyway, the feeders trailing in its wake. The girl and the younger boy shrank from it in terror. The girl was already crying. Neither would challenge it; the demon could tell from what it saw in their eyes. Only the older boy would make a stand. The demon's tongue licked out across its hooked teeth, and its jaws snapped hungrily at the air.

The demon crept through the doorway in a crouch, eyes fixed on the knife. All three of its intended victims retreated toward the back wall of the room. Foolish choice, the demon thought. They had let it inside, let it block their only escape.

Then the younger boy wheeled away in a flurry of arms and legs and threw himself toward one of the broken windows, intent on breaking free that way. But the demon was too quick. It lunged sideways and caught the unfortunate boy in a single bound. It dragged him to the earthen floor, closed its massive jaws on his neck as he screamed and thrashed frantically, and crushed the life from him with a single snap.

The boy fell back lifelessly. Feeders piled onto the body, tearing at it. The demon swung its bloodied muzzle toward the other two, showing all its teeth. The girl was screaming now, and the older boy was cursing and shouting and brandishing the knife more as a talisman than as a weapon. They might have made a run for the open doorway while the demon was engaged in killing their companion, but they had failed to do so. Or even to try. The girl was on her knees with her arms about her head, keening. The older boy was standing his ground, but it seemed to the demon that he was doing so because he could not bring himself to move.

The demon advanced on the older boy, stiff-legged, alert. When it was close enough, it waited until the boy lunged with the knife, then hurled itself under the gleaming blade, jaws closing on the hand that wielded it. Bones crunched and muscles tore, and the boy screamed in pain. The demon knocked the boy backward against the wall and tore out his throat while he was still staring at his ruined hand.

Feeders sprang out of the darkness in knots of black shadow, falling on the dying boy, lapping up the life that drained away from him, feeding on the raw feelings of terror and despair and pain.

The girl had begun to crawl toward the open door, a futile attempt to get free. The demon moved quickly to intercept her. She crouched before it in a shivering heap, her arms clasped over her head, her eyes closed. She was crying and screaming and begging—*Don't, please, don't, please, don't*—over and over again. The demon studied her for a moment, intrigued by the way the madness had enveloped her. It was no longer in a hurry, its hunger appeased with the killing of the boys. It felt languorous and sleepy. It watched the girl through lidded eyes. There were feeders crawling all over her, savoring the emotions she expended, licking them up anxiously. Perhaps she could feel them, perhaps even see them by now, with death so close. Perhaps she sensed what death held in store for her. The demon wondered.

Then it closed its jaws almost tenderly about the back of the girl's exposed white neck and crushed the slender stalk to pulp.

* * *

Abruptly, the screams faded to silence. Nest froze, staring into the mist and gloom, into the faint pools of streetlight, listening. She couldn't hear a thing.

Ariel drifted close. The tatterdemalion hung suspended on the air, spectral, barely a presence at all. "It is over."

Nest blinked. Over. So quickly. Her mind spun. "What was it?" she asked quietly.

"A creature of the Void."

Nest stared into the tatterdemalion's eyes and knew exactly which creature. She felt a chill sweep through her body and settle in her throat. "A demon," she whispered.

"Its stink is in the air," Ariel said.

"What was it hunting?"

"The humans who live under the streets."

Homeless people. Nest closed her eyes in despair. Could she have helped them, if she had been quicker, if she had known where to go, if she had summoned her magic? If, if, if. She took a deep breath. She wondered suddenly if these killings were connected in some way with John Ross. Was this monster hunting for him, as well? Mustn't it be, if it was here, so close to where he was working?

"We have to go," said Ariel. Her childlike voice was a ripple of breeze in the silence. "It isn't safe for us to remain here."

Because it might come for us next, Nest thought. She stood her ground a moment longer, tempted to invite it to try, riddled with anger and disgust. But staying would be foolish. Demons were too strong for her. She had learned that lesson from her father five years earlier.

She began to walk, Ariel skimming the air beside her, moving toward the hotel once more. She had been searching the shadows for feeders the entire time they had walked, a habit she would never break, but she hadn't seen any. Now she understood why. They were all underground with the demon, drinking in the detritus of its kills.

She stared off into the night, down the darkened corridors of side streets and alleyways, into blackened doorways and landings, and along shadowy eaves and overhangs. It isn't safe for us to remain here, Ariel had said, urging her to move quickly away, to flee.

Maybe so, she thought. Not with a demon present. But demons seemed to be everywhere in her life. Demons and dark magic, the workings of the Void.

It isn't safe for us here.

But maybe it was no longer safe anywhere.

Tuesday, October 30

Chapter 11

When Nest Freemark awoke the following morning, the sun was streaming so brightly through her window that she thought she must have overslept. The clock radio she had set the night before was playing softly, which meant that the alarm had gone off, and she leaned over quickly to check the time. But it was only nine o'clock, the hour she had chosen for her wake-up, so she was right on schedule. She glanced over at the window, and she realized that the reason it was so bright was that she had forgotten to draw the blinds.

She laid her head back on her pillow sleepily for a moment, still disoriented from her sudden awakening. She could hear the sounds of traffic on the street below, brash and jarring, but her room was a bright cocoon of silence and warmth. She had read somewhere that it rained a lot in Seattle, but apparently that wasn't going to be the case today.

She closed her eyes and then opened them again, searching her mind. Last night's memories of her walk into Pioneer Square seemed distant and vague, almost as if they were part of a dream. She stared at the ceiling and forced herself to remember. Walking alone with Ariel. Hearing the screams. Feeling frightened and helpless. Hearing Ariel's words.

Something hunts.

A demon, she had replied.

She rose and walked to the window and looked down at the street. Same street as last night, only brighter and more populated in the daylight. She watched the people and cars for a few minutes, organizing her scattered thoughts and gathering up the shards of confusion and uncertainty that littered her mind. Then she went into the bathroom and showered. She stood beneath the hot stream of water for a long time, eyes closed, thinking. She was a long way from home, and she was still uncertain of her purpose in coming to find John Ross. She wished she had a better idea of what she was going to do when she found him. She wished she knew what she was going to say. She wished she were better prepared.

She toweled dry and dressed, thinking once again of the demon. She would tell Ross of last night; she knew that much, at least. She would tell him of the Lady's concern, of her warning to him. She would try to convince him of his danger. But what else could she do? What did she really know about all this, after all? She knew what Ariel had told her, but she couldn't say for certain that it was the truth. If Pick's response was any measure of things, it probably wasn't. The truth wasn't something you got whole cloth from the Word anyway; it came in bits and pieces, riddles and questions, and self-examination and deductive reasoning that, if you were lucky, eventually led to some sort of revelation. She had learned that much from her father. The truth wasn't simple; it was complex. Worse, it wasn't easily decipherable, and it was often difficult to accept.

She sighed, looking about the room, as if the answer to her dilemma might be hidden there. It wasn't, of course. There were no answers here; the answers all lay with John Ross.

She went down to the lobby for her breakfast, pausing to stare out through large plate-glass doors at the busy city streets. Although the day was bright and sunny, people out walking were bundled up in coats and scarves, so she knew it must be cold. She continued on to the dining room and ate alone at a table near the back, sipping at her coffee and nibbling on her toast and scrambled eggs as she formulated her plan for the day.

She would have preferred to talk things over with Ariel, but there was no sign of the tatterdemalion. Nor was there likely to be. She remembered Ariel saying to her last night, just before she went back into the hotel, "Don't worry. I'll be close to you. You won't see me, but I'll be there when you need me."

Reassuring, but not particularly satisfactory. It made her wish Pick was with her. Pick would have appeared whether she needed him or not. Pick would have talked everything over with her. She still missed him. She found herself comparing the sylvan and the tatterdemalion and decided that, given the choice, she still preferred Pick's incessant chatter to Ariel's wraithlike presence.

She tried to remember the rest of what Pick had told her about tatterdemalions. It wasn't much. Like sylvans they were born fully formed, but unlike sylvans they lived only a short time and didn't age. Both were forest creatures, but sylvans never went beyond the territory for which they were given responsibility, while tatterdemalions rode everywhere on the back of the wind and went all over the world. Sylvans worked at managing the magic, at its practical application, at keeping the balance in check. Tatterdemalions did none of that, cared nothing for the magic, were as insubstantial in their work as they were in their forms. They served the Word, but their service was less carefully defined and more subject to change than that of sylvans. Tatterdemalions were like ghosts.

Nest finished the last of her orange juice and stood up. Tatterdemalions were strange, even as fairy creatures went. She tried to imagine what it must be like to be Ariel, to have lived without experiencing a childhood and with no expectation of ever becoming an adult, to know you would be alive only a short time and then be gone again. She supposed the concept of time was a relative one, and some creatures had no concept of time at all. Maybe that was the way it was with tatterdemalions. But what would it be like to live your entire life with the memories of dead children, of lives come and gone before your own, to have only their memories and none of your own?

She gave it up. She would never be able to put herself in Ariel's place, not even in the most abstract sense, because she had no reference point to help her gain any real insight. They were as different as night and day. And yet they both served the Word, and they were both, in some sense, creatures of magic.

Nest stopped thinking about it, went back to her room, brushed her teeth, put on her heavy windbreaker and scarf, and went out to greet the day.

She had looked up the address to Fresh Start and consulted a map of Pioneer Square, so she pretty much knew where she was going. The map was tucked in her pocket for ready reference. She walked down First Avenue, retracing her steps from the night before, until she reached the triangular open space where she had heard the death screams of the demon's victims. She stood in the center of the little concrete park and looked around. No one acted as if anyone had died. No one seemed to think anything was amiss. People came and went along the walk—workers, shoppers, and tourists. A few sad-looking homeless people sat with their backs to the walls of buildings fronting the street, holding out hand-lettered cardboard signs and worn paper cups as they begged for a few coins. The former mostly ignored the latter, looking elsewhere as they passed, engaging in conversations that kept their eyes averted, acting as if they didn't see. In a way, she supposed, they didn't. She thought that was an accurate indicator of how the world worked, that people frequently managed to find ways of ignoring what troubled them. Out of sight, out of mind. Maybe that was how the demon got away with killing homeless people; everyone was ignoring them anyway, so when a few disappeared, no one even noticed.

Maybe that was the cause that John Ross had taken up in joining forces with Simon Lawrence. Maybe that was his passion now that he was no longer a Knight of the Word. The thought appealed to her.

She walked on, doing her best to turn away from the gusts of cold wind that blew at her. Winter was coming; she didn't like to think of her world turning to ice and snow and temperature drops and wind-chill factors. She didn't like thinking of everything turning white and gray and mud-streaked. She glanced back at the people begging. How much worse it would be for them.

At the corner of Main, she turned east and walked through a broad open space that was marked on her map as Occidental Park. It wasn't much of a park, she thought. Cobblestones and concrete steps, with a few shade trees planted in squares of open earth, a scattering of bushes, a few scary totem poles, some benches, and a strange steel and Plexiglas pavilion. Clusters of what looked to be homeless were gathered here, many of them Native Americans, and a couple of police officers on bicycles. She followed the sidewalk east and found herself at the entrance to an odd little enclosure formed of brick walls and iron fencing with a sign that identified it as Waterfall Park. The space was filled with small trees, vines, and tables and chairs, and was backed by a thunderous man-made waterfall that cascaded into a narrow catchment over massive rocks stacked up against the wall of the building it attached to.

She glanced back at Occidental Park, then into Waterfall Park once again. The parks here weren't much like the parks she was familiar with, and nothing like Sinnissippi Park, but she supposed you made do with what you had.

She crossed Second Avenue and began to read the numbers on the buildings. There was no sign identifying Fresh Start, but she found the building number easily enough and went through the front door.

Once inside, she found herself in a lobby that was mostly empty. A heavyset black woman sat at a desk facing the door, engaged in writing something on a clipboard, and a Hispanic woman sat holding her baby on one of a cluster of folding chairs that lined the windowless walls of the room. Behind the black woman and her desk, a hallway led to what looked like an elevator.

Almost immediately, Nest experienced an odd feeling of uneasiness. She glanced around automatically in an effort to locate its source, but there was nothing to see.

Shrugging it off, she walked up to the desk and stopped. The black woman didn't look up. "Can I help you, young lady?"

"I'm looking for John Ross," Nest told her. "Does he work here?"

The black lady's eyes lifted, and she gave Nest a careful once-over. "He does, but he's not here right now. Would you like to wait for him? He shouldn't be gone long."

Nest nodded. "Thanks." She looked around at the empty seats, deciding where to sit.

"What's your name, young lady?" The black woman regained her attention.

"Nest Freemark."

"Nest. Now, that's an unusual name. Nest. Very different. I like it. Wish I had a different name like that. I'm Della, Nest. Della Jenkins."

She stuck out her hand and Nest shook it. The handshake was firm and businesslike, but warm, too. "Nice to meet you," Nest said.

"Nice to meet you, too," Della said, and smiled now. "I work intake here at the center. Been at it from the start. How do you know John? Isn't anyone ever came in before that knows John. I was beginning to think he didn't have a life before he came here. I was beginning to think he was one of those pod people." She laughed.

Nest grinned. "Well, I don't know him very well. He was a friend of my mother's." She shaded the truth deliberately, unwilling to give anything away she didn't have to. "I was in town, and I thought I ought to stop in and say hello."

Della nodded. "Well, how about that? John was a friend of your mother's. John doesn't talk much about his past life with us. Hardly at all. A friend of your mother's. How about that." She seemed amazed. Nest blushed. "Oh, now, don't you be embarrassed, Nest. I'm just making conversation to hide my surprise at anybody knowing John from before him coming here. You know, really, he spends all his time with Stef—that's Stefanie Winslow, his . . . oh, what do you call it, I always forget? Oh, that's right, his 'significant other.' Sounds so awkward, saying it like that, doesn't it? His significant other. Anyway, that's what Stefanie is. Real pretty girl, his sweetheart. Do anything for him. They came here together about a year ago, and neither one of them talks hardly at all about what went on before."

Nest nodded, distracted. The uneasiness was stealing over her again, a persistent tugging that refused to be ignored. She couldn't understand where it was coming from. She had never experienced anything like it.

Della stood up abruptly. "You want a cup of coffee while you wait, Nest? Tell you what. Why don't you come with me, and I'll introduce you to a few of the people who work here, some of John's friends, let them catch you up on what he's been doing? He's downtown at the Seattle Art Museum checking things out for tomorrow night. Big dedication party. Simon's giving a speech John wrote, thanking the city and so forth for the building, their support and all. You probably don't know about that, but John can fill you in later. C'mon, young lady, right this way."

She led Nest around the intake desk and down the hallway toward the elevator. Nest followed reluctantly, still trying to sort out the reason for her discomfort. Was Ariel responsible? Was the tatterdemalion trying to communicate with her in some way?

As they reached the elevator doors, a tall, lean, mostly balding black man walked through a doorway from further down the hall and came toward them.

"Ray!" Della Jenkins called out to him at once. "Come over here and meet Nest Freemark. Nest is an old friend of John's, come by to say hello."

The black man strolled up, grinning broadly. "We talking about John Ross, the man with no past? I didn't think he had any old friends. Does he know about this, Nest, about you being his old friend? Or are you here to surprise him with the news?"

He held out his hand and Nest took it. "Ray Hapgood," he introduced himself. "Very pleased to meet you, and welcome to Seattle."

"Ray, you take Nest on down and get her some coffee, will you? Introduce her to Stef and Carole and whoever, and keep her company until John gets back." Della was already looking over her shoulder at the lobby entrance as the elevator doors opened. "I got to get back out front and keep an eye on things. Go on now."

She gave Nest a smile and a wave and walked away. The doors closed, leaving Nest alone with Ray Hapgood.

"What brings you to Seattle, Nest?" he asked, smiling.

She hesitated. "I was thinking of transferring schools," she said, inventing a lie to suit the situation.

He nodded. "Lot of good schools in Washington. You'd like it out here. So tell me. You know John a long time? I meant what I said; he never talks about his past, never mentions anything about it."

"I don't know him all that well, actually." She glanced up at the floor numbers on the reader board. "Mostly, my mother knows him. Knew him. She's dead. I didn't know him until a few years ago, when he came to visit. For a few days, that's all."

She was talking too much, giving up too much, but her uneasiness was increasing with every passing moment. She was beginning to hear voices—vague whispers that might be coming from her, but might also be coming from someone else.

"Oh, I'm sorry about that. About your mother." Ray Hapgood seemed genuinely embarrassed. "Has she been gone a long time?"

Nest suddenly felt trapped in the elevator. She thought that if she didn't get out right away, right this instant, she might start to scream. She was racked with shivers and her skin was crawling and her breathing was coming much too quickly. "She's been dead since I was little," she managed.

The elevator doors opened, and she burst through in a near panic, feeling stupid and frightened and confused all at the same time. Ray Hapgood followed, looking at her funnily. "I don't like close places," she lied.

Oh, he mouthed silently, nodded, and gave her a reassuring smile.

They were in a basement room filled with long, multipurpose tables and folding chairs, a coffee machine, shelves with dishes, and storage cabinets. There were mingled smells of cooking and musty dampness, and she could hear a furnace cranking away from behind a closed door at the back of the room. Fluorescent lighting from low-hung fixtures cast a brilliant white glare over the whole of the windowless enclosure, giving it a harsh, unnatural brightness. A young man sat alone at a table to one side, poring through a sheaf of papers. Two women sat together at another table close to the coffee machine, talking in low voices. The women looked up as Nest appeared with Ray Hapgood. One was middle-aged and unremarkable, with short blond hair and a kind face. The other was probably not yet thirty and strikingly beautiful. Nest knew at once that she was Stefanie Winslow.

"Ladies," Ray greeted, steering Nest toward their table. "Say hello to Nest Freemark, an old friend of John's. Nest, this is Carole Price, our director of operations here at Fresh Start, and Stefanie Winslow, the boss's press secretary and all-around troubleshooter."

Nest shook hands with each in turn, noting the looks of surprise that appeared on both faces when Ray mentioned her connection to Ross. It was becoming clear that when John Ross had ceased to be a Knight of the Word, he had turned his back on his past entirely. The women smiled at Nest, and she smiled back, but this whole business of her relationship with Ross was growing awkward, and she wished he would just hurry up and get back so that she could get this visit over with.

"Sit down, Nest," Carole Price suggested, pulling out a chair. "I can't believe we have someone here who actually knows John from . . . well, from when?"

"A long time ago," Nest answered, trying not to sound evasive. She sat down. "It was my mother who knew him, really."

"Your mother?" Carole Price prompted.

"They went to school together."

"Good heavens!" Carole Price seemed amazed. "Even Stef doesn't know much about our boy from those days."

Stefanie Winslow shook her head in quick agreement. "He never talks about himself, about what he was doing or who he was before we met." Her smile was dazzling. "Tell us something about him, Nest. Before he gets back. Tell us something he won't tell us himself."

"Yeah, go on," Ray Hapgood urged, drawing up a chair across from her.

What Nest Freemark wanted to do most right then was to get out of there. The room felt impossibly close and airless, the fluorescent light hot and revealing, and the presence of these people she didn't know a weight she could barely shoulder. What was happening inside her was indescribable. The uneasiness had taken on a life of its own, and it was careening about in her chest and throat like a pinball, shrieking unintelligibly and battering her senses. It was taking all her energy to keep it from getting completely out of control, to prevent it from breaking free in a form she could only begin to imagine. She had never experienced anything like it before. She was frightened and confused. She was wishing she had never come looking for John Ross.

"Come on, Nest, tell us something," Stefanie Winslow urged cheerfully.

"He was in love with my mother," she blurted out, saying the first thing that came to mind, not caring if it was true or not, just wanting to shift their focus to something else. What in heaven's name was wrong with her?

There was a flicker of uncertainty in Stefanie Winslow's eyes. Then Ray Hapgood said, "Her mother died some years ago, Stef. This was a college romance, I'd guess."

"It was," Nest agreed quickly, realizing what Stefanie Winslow must be thinking. "It happened a long time ago."

"Let's get you some coffee, Nest," Hapgood announced. "I don't want Della on my case for not keeping my promises."

He stood up and walked over to the coffee machine and drew down a cup and filled it. "Cream or sugar?"

Nest shook her head. She no longer wanted the coffee. She thought if she drank it, she would throw it right back up. She was physically sick to her stomach, her head was throbbing, and there was a buzzing in her ears. But it was the uneasiness that roiled through her like a riptide that commanded her focus.

"Nest, you don't look well," Carole Price said suddenly, concern shadowing her blunt features.

"I am a little queasy," she admitted. "I think maybe it was something I ate at breakfast."

"Do you want to lie down for a little while? We've got some beds that aren't in use, up on two."

Nest shook her head. "No, I just need to . . . you know, maybe what I need is to go back up and get some fresh air for a moment."

Carole Price was on her feet instantly. "Here, I'll take you right up. Ray, forget about that coffee. I don't think it's what she needs just now. C'mon, Nest, come with me."

She took Nest's arm and led her toward the elevator. "Nice meeting you, Nest," Stefanie Winslow called after her. "Maybe I'll see you later."

"Bye, Nest," Ray Hapgood said. "You take care."

Carole Price had her almost to the elevator when the doors opened and Simon Lawrence stepped out. She knew him right away from his pictures in the magazine articles and books. He was dressed in jeans with the sleeves of his plain blue workshirt rolled up, but there was something polished and elegant about the way he held himself as he stepped out of the lift and smiled at her.

He held out his hands. "Here, here, what's this? Carole, where are you taking her? She just got here. I haven't even met her yet. Is everything all right?"

"She's feeling a little queasy, that's all," Carole replied, slowing. "I was taking her up for some air."

Simon Lawrence took Nest's hands in his own and held them. "Well, we can't have you getting sick," he said. "You go on upstairs, Nest, and we'll talk later. I want you to know that I'm very pleased you've come to see us. I didn't realize you were a friend of John's, but I certainly know who you are."

Everyone stared at them, confused. Simon Lawrence laughed. "You don't recognize her, do you?" He shook his head. "I have got to get you out of the office more, all of you. Or at least reading the papers about something besides the homeless once in a while. Ray, I'm especially disappointed in you." He squeezed Nest's hands. "This young lady is the best college distance runner in the nation—maybe in the world. She's been written up in any number of articles as the next Mary Decker Slaney—except that Nest isn't going to fall when she runs in the next Olympics, are you, Nest? You're going to win."

Nest knew she was expected to say something, but she couldn't think of what it should be. Finally she said, "It's a long way off yet."

Simon Lawrence laughed and released her hand. "Good point, young lady. We shouldn't get ahead of ourselves. But you'll do fine, I know. It's very nice to meet you. Now you go on up with Carole, and I'll see you later."

He walked past Nest with a smile, already back to kidding Ray Hapgood about his failure to recognize Nest Freemark when he was such an avid sports fan. Stefanie Winslow was on her feet, grinning and joking, as well. Nest stepped into the elevator with Carole Price and let the doors close behind them.

She rode back up to the ground floor with something approaching panic, but she made it down the hall past a wondering Della Jenkins and out the front door, where she stood with Carole holding on to her while she took huge gulps of fresh air in an effort to steady herself. The deep breathing seemed to work. The nausea and headache went away. Her uneasiness lingered, but gradually it began to lessen. Her insides quit churning, and the whispers and buzzing receded into the sounds of the city about her.

"Are you feeling better?" Carole asked her after a few minutes.

Nest nodded. "I am, thanks. Much better." She straightened, gently freeing herself from Carole's proprietorial grip. She tried out a fresh smile. "I didn't come here to get underfoot. I know you must have work to do, and I'm fine now. I'll just wait out here for John. Maybe I'll come back inside in a few minutes."

Carole seemed uncertain, but Nest reassured her, and the other woman left her alone. Nest leaned against the wall of the building and stared out at the people and traffic, trying to make sense of what had happened. She could not account for it. This odd uneasiness was an entirely new experience. It was like having a sudden bout of flu coupled with a good scare. It didn't make any sense. The feeling had started when she entered the building and talked with the people who worked there. Was it something connected with that? Was it her magic, reacting to something? If so, her magic was taking a new direction; it hadn't ever done anything like this before.

She whispered Ariel's name as she stood with her back against the building wall, thinking that the tatterdemalion might appear and reveal to her the source of her discomfort. But Ariel stayed hidden.

Nest stood to one side of the doorway and considered the matter from every angle she could imagine, but the answer she was seeking eluded her.

She was still deliberating when a taxi pulled up in front of her and the man she had come to Seattle to find stepped out.

CHAPTER 12

John Ross.

She recognized him immediately. Even though it had been five years since she had seen him last and she had been only a girl at the time, she recognized him. He didn't look as if he had changed at all. His boyish face was still weathered and rugged, still all planes and angles, still the face of the boy next door grown up. He still wore jeans and a blue denim shirt with worn walking shoes and a silver-buckled belt, looking as if he might be one meal or one paycheck from being homeless himself. He still wore his long brown hair tied back from his face with a bandanna, and he still carried the heavy black staff.

It was as if he had been frozen in time, and while she had changed, grown into a young woman, he had remained exactly the same.

She watched him climb gingerly from the taxi, leaning heavily on the staff, reach back to pay the driver, then start toward the front door of Fresh Start. She straightened and moved away from the wall. He looked at her without recognition and smiled pleasantly.

Then surprise shadowed his face and turned quickly to astonishment mingled with something else. He stared at her, slowing, then came forward again, an uncertain smile chasing the feelings back into hiding.

"Nest?" he asked carefully. "Is that you?"

"Hello, John," she greeted.

"I don't believe it," he said.

He stopped in front of her and stood there awkwardly, shaking his head, the smile broadening. His clear green eyes looked her up and down, assessing her, comparing her with what he remembered. She could read everything in his expression—how much she had changed, and at the same time, how familiar he found her.

She started to extend her hand, then stopped, feeling it wasn't enough. He glanced down, then up again, meeting her gaze, and their arms extended toward each other at the same moment and they embraced warmly.

"Nest, Nest, Nest," he whispered, and he said it with such tenderness that it made her want to cry.

She drew back after a moment and grinned. "Guess I've changed a bit from what you remember."

He returned her grin. "Guess you have. You look good, Nest. You look . . . terrific."

She blushed in spite of herself. "Well, gee." She shook her head in embarrassment. "You look pretty terrific yourself."

They stood in the middle of the sidewalk staring at each other. People walked by, a few glancing over curiously, but neither one paid the least attention. For Nest, it was as if time had stopped completely. She wasn't prepared for how good it was to see him. She wasn't prepared for how good it made her feel. She had come looking for John Ross because she believed she must if she did not want his death on her conscience, and not because she felt she needed to see him. She had lived five years with such ambivalent feelings about him that she could not come to terms with whether she ever wanted to see him again. Now, in an instant's time, five years of uncertainty were swept away, and she knew that coming to find him, that seeing him, was exactly the right thing.

"I just can't believe that you're standing here." He opened his arms to emphasize the extent of his amazement. "I suppose I should have written you or called, but I wasn't sure . . . well, that you would want to speak to me."

She smiled sadly. "Neither was I. Not until right now."

"How did you ever find me?"

She shrugged. "I had some help."

"I didn't think anyone knew where I was. I haven't talked to anyone, told anyone here about . . ."

"I know. They told me you've kept your life a mystery."

"You've been inside already?" He glanced toward the doorway. "You met Simon?" She nodded. "And Stef?" She nodded again. "Ray, Carole, all the others?"

"Some of them, anyway. The lady at the reception desk, Della, sent me downstairs to wait for you. I met everyone there. They were amazed you had any friends from the past." She gave him a meaningful look. "They were amazed you even had a past."

He nodded slowly. "I expect so. I don't ever talk about it." He hesitated. "I don't know what to say. Or where to begin. Things have changed for me, Nest. A lot of things."

"I know that, too," she said.

He looked closely at her now, and suddenly there was suspicion as well as curiosity mirrored in his eyes. "I've read some articles about you," he said, his words tentative, cautious. "I know you're a student at Northwestern University, that you're still running competitively, that you're good enough that you're expected to represent the United States in the next Olympics." He hesitated. "Is that why you're here?"

She waited a heartbeat, meeting his intense gaze. "No. I came here looking for you. I was sent. By the Lady."

He stared at her, astonishment filling his eyes. When he spoke, his voice was unsteady. "The Lady sent you?"

"Is there somewhere we could talk about it?" she asked, no longer comfortable standing out in the open where they could be heard. "Just for a little while."

He seemed distracted, uncertain. "Sure, of course." He glanced toward the building.

"No, not in there," she said quickly. "Somewhere else, please."

He nodded slowly. "All right. It's almost noon. Why don't we go down to the waterfront, and I'll buy you a northwest kind of lunch. Some clam chowder, some fish and chips. How would that be?"

"That would be good," she said.

He didn't bother with going in to tell anyone he was leaving. He didn't even pause to consider doing so. He simply motioned her toward the direction from which she had come, and they began to walk. They crossed Second Avenue, passed by Waterfall Park, and moved over to the island platform in the center of Main where the trolley stopped on its way down to the waterfront. They sat together on the wrought-iron bench and stared out over the cobblestones of Occidental Park, waiting.

"Do you know what I do now?" he asked after a minute. His tone of voice was distant and weary, as if he were at the start of a long journey.

"I know you work for Simon Lawrence at Fresh Start," she replied. "I know about the work Fresh Start does."

He nodded. "It's important work, Nest. The most important work I've done in a long time. Maybe ever." He paused. "Did the Lady tell you about me?"

Nest nodded, saying nothing.

"Then you know I'm no longer a Knight of the Word?"

She nodded a second time. *It's what you believe anyway,* she thought, but she didn't speak the words.

They didn't say anything further for a time, wrapped in their separate thoughts amid the jumbled noise of traffic and people's voices. *This is going to be hard,* Nest thought. He was not going to want to hear what she had to say. Maybe he would simply refuse to listen. Maybe he would just walk away. She could see him doing that. He had walked away already from the most important part of his life.

"Do you still live on the park?" he asked finally.

"Yes." She glanced at him. "But Grandpa died last May, so I live there alone."

She could see the pain reflect in his face. He was remembering the time he had spent in their house, pretending to be someone he was not. He was remembering how he had left things with her grandfather. "I'm sorry he's gone," he said finally. "I liked him very much."

Nest nodded. "Everybody did. Pick is still there, looking after the park. He wants me to come back and help him like I used to."

"That would be very hard for you now, I expect," he said.

"It is," she agreed.

"Things change. Life changes. Nothing stays the same."

She wasn't sure she agreed with this, but she nodded anyway, not wanting to get into a debate about it.

A few moments later, the trolley arrived and they boarded. Ross gave the conductor two tokens, and they took a seat near the front. They rode the trolley down a hill between rows of buildings, under a two-tiered viaduct that supported an expressway, over some railroad tracks, and then turned right on Alaskan Way to follow the waterfront north. It was too noisy inside the open-air trolley for conversation, so they rode in silence.

At the Madison Street stop, they got off and walked across Alaskan Way to the piers. Orange cranes stretched steel limbs skyward at the edges of the loading docks along Elliott Bay, dominating the skyline. Huge container ships piled with freight sat at rest beneath their cabled lifts, some being unloaded of the shipments they had brought from abroad and others loaded with whatever was being exported. Trawlers were tied up at the ends of several piers, winches cinched, nets drawn up and folded. To their immediate left, a terminal buttressed by huge clumps of wooden pilings provided docking slips for the ferries that serviced the islands and the Olympic Peninsula. Tour boats filled with passengers nosed their way along the waterfront, poking into the channels that ran back to the ends of the docking slips of Harbor Island and into the Duwamish River. Small sailboats with brightly colored, wind-filled spinnakers rode the crest of the silver-tipped blue waves, and tiny fishing boats dotted the bay, straddling the shipping lanes on the open water.

The piers closest to where they departed the trolley were dominated by long, wooden buildings housing shops and restaurants. The one to which John Ross took Nest was painted yellow with red letters that identified it as Pier 56. They navigated the noonday crowd strolling the walkways out front and pushed through the doors of a glassed-in entryway beneath a sign that announced they were guests of Elliott's Oyster House. The entryway was stuffy and hot. A hostess greeted them and led them to a booth near the back of the dining area, further out on the pier toward the water. Nest seated herself across from Ross and looked out at the view. The sun shone brightly through scattered clouds, and the sky was azure and depthless. In the distance, beyond the bay and the sound, the peaks of the Olympics gleamed whitely against the horizon.

The waitress brought them water and menus and asked if they were ready to order. Nest glanced at the menu, then at Ross, arching one eyebrow. "Two bowls of chowder, two orders of the fish and chips, and two iced teas," he told the waitress, and she picked up the menus and left.

Nest looked out the window again. "This is a wonderful city," she told him.

"People who visit when it's not raining always say that," he advised, shrugging.

"I guess I'm lucky to be here now."

"Stay a few more days, and you can see what it's like the rest of the time."

She looked out at the tour boats, which were anchored right next to where they were sitting. A small crowd of tourists was boarding one of two tied up in the docking slips, filing through the interior and out onto the upper and lower decks. They were bundled up against the chill, and they all carried cameras at the ready. Nest thought she would like to be going out with them. She would like to look back at the city from the water, see if the view was as spectacular from that direction. Maybe she would do so later.

"So you like your new life," she said to him, looking for a place to start.

He nodded slowly. "I like what I do at Fresh Start. I like Simon Lawrence and the others who work for him. I've met someone I'm very much in love with, and who is very much in love with me—something I thought would never happen. Yes, I like my life. I'm happy."

"Stefanie is beautiful," she said.

"She is. But she's more than that. A lot more. She saved me when I thought there wasn't anything left worth saving. After San Sobel."

Nest wondered suddenly if he ever thought about Josie Jackson. Early on, not long after he left, Josie had asked Nest if she had heard from him; from the way she asked, Nest had known that there had been something between them. But that was a long time ago. He probably didn't think of Josie at all these days. Maybe she had stopped thinking about him, too. "What happened at San Sobel must have been awful," she said.

"It was, but it's over." He looked up as the waitress reappeared with their iced teas. When she left again, he took a careful sip of his, and then said, "Why did the Lady send you to find me, Nest?"

Nest shook her head doubtfully. "To talk with you. To tell you something you probably already know. I'm not sure." She looked away from him, out over the water. "The truth is, I came because I don't want to hear later that something bad has happened to you and find myself wishing I'd tried to prevent it."

He grinned cautiously. "What is it you think might happen?"

She sighed. "Let me start at the beginning, all right? Let me tell it my way, maybe work up to the part about what might happen. I'm not really sure about any of this myself. Maybe you can fill in the gaps for me. Maybe you can even persuade me I came here for no better reason than to see you again. That would be all right."

She told him then about Ariel's appearance in the park two days earlier, the tatterdemalion's purpose in coming as a messenger, and the Lady's request that Nest come to Seattle to find him in the hope he might heed her warning that his life was in peril.

Nest paused. "So I gather you've already been told that you're in some kind of danger."

He seemed to consider the statement, to weigh it in a way she didn't understand. Then he nodded. "I've been told. I don't know that any warning is necessary."

She shrugged. "I don't know that it is, either. But here I am, delivering the message anyway. I guess you don't have any concerns about it, huh?"

He smiled unexpectedly. "Nest, let me tell you what happened at San Sobel."

And he did so, retelling the story from his perspective, recounting it carefully and thoroughly, obviously trying to make her understand how terrible it was for him, to help her see why he had been unable to continue as a Knight of the Word. She listened attentively, for he kept his voice low and his words shielded from the people eating around them, pausing once when he came to the aftermath of the killings to gather his thoughts so that he could relate clearly what the experience had done to his psyche, pausing a second time when the bowls of clam chowder arrived and the waitress was standing over them.

At the conclusion of his tale, he told her something he had never been able to tell anyone. He told her how close to suicide he had been when he realized the fault might be his. He had managed to get past that, but only by determining he could never revisit that place in his mind, could never again put himself in a position where he might have to hold himself responsible for people dying.

Nest let him finish, then shook her head doubtfully. "If you do nothing, people die anyway, John. What would have happened to me if you hadn't come to Hopewell? I don't know that you can say any of it is your fault."

"It feels like it is. That's enough." He looked down at the soup cooling before him. He hadn't eaten a bite. "I don't mean to argue with you on this, but you can't know what it's like if you're not me. You don't have to live with the dreams. You don't have to live with the responsibility for what happens if they come true." He shook his head. "It's a special kind of hell."

"I know," she said. "I wouldn't even try to put myself in your shoes. I wouldn't presume."

She finished her soup. All the bad feelings she had experienced at Fresh Start had evaporated, and she found herself hungrier than expected.

"I drifted afterward, looking for something to do, some place to be, a reason for being alive." Ross began to eat a little. "Then I found Stef, and everything changed. She gave me back what I had lost at San Sobel. Or maybe lost even before that. She made me feel good about something again. So here we are, working at Fresh Start with the Wizard of Oz, and doing something important. I don't want to go back to what I was. Let's face it; I can't go back. How could I? It would change everything."

He shrugged. "I don't know what to tell you about being in danger, Nest. I don't feel as if I'm in any danger. I'm not part of that life anymore. I don't have any connection to what I was or did. I don't even dream anymore—or hardly ever, anyway. It's all in the past."

The fish and chips arrived, and they paused while the waitress set down their plates, asked if there was anything else she could get them, and walked away. Nest picked up a piece of deep-fried halibut and bit into it. "Mmmm, this is wonderful," she said.

"Told you." He picked up a piece of his own fish and began eating.

"Ariel said the Lady thinks the Void will try to subvert you, whether or not you think you're still involved in its battle with the Word." Nest studied his face. "She says you can't stop being a Knight of the Word. She says you can't quit unless the Word allows it."

He nodded soberly. "I've heard it all before. I don't think I believe it. What have I been doing for the past year if she's right? Haven't I quit, if I haven't served? What else do I have to do? Write a letter of resignation? I don't dream, I don't use the magic, I don't go out looking for demons. I'm done with all of it."

"She says you can't ever be done with it." Nest paused, moving a french fry around in a paper cup filled with ketchup. "Here's the part that bothers me—the reason I came looking for you, I guess. She says you've had a dream, and the events of the dream will take place on Halloween. She says your involvement with the dream will place you in danger of becoming ensnared by the Void."

She watched his reaction closely. He said nothing, but she could tell at once that he knew what she was talking about, that in fact there had been a dream, and that in some way he was a part of it.

"The Lady told Ariel something else, John. She told her she will never let that happen, she will never allow a Knight of the Word to be subverted. She has sent someone to prevent it."

A flicker of recognition crossed his lean face.

"The way you were sent to me maybe, five years ago," she finished quietly.

For an instant she thought he would tell her everything. She could see in his eyes that he wanted to, that a part of him was looking for a way. But he stayed silent. She watched him a moment longer, then went back to eating. The voices around them filled the sudden silence.

"She told you all this?" His anger was laced with irony. "When I went back to Wales and the Fairy Glen to ask her to release me from my duty, she wouldn't even speak to me."

Nest said nothing, didn't even look up at him, continuing to eat.

"All the times I waited for her to come to me, to tell me what I had to do, to help me . . ." He trailed off, staring fixedly at her. "Nothing is going to happen," he said finally.

She nodded. "But you know about the dream, don't you?"

"It's only a dream. It won't happen. It can't happen, because I won't let it."

She straightened and locked her eyes on his. "You taught me about being strong, John. I learned that from you in Hopewell. But I learned about caution, as well. You don't seem cautious enough to me. You think you can't be hurt, no matter what, unless you do something to invite it. But I don't think that's how life works."

"I think I can control what I do," he snapped. "That's all I'm saying."

She shook her head. "What if Stefanie's life is threatened, and you have to choose between doing what the Void wants or letting her die? What will you do? If you love her as much as you say, what will you do? I don't think you can just shrug this off."

Pushing back his lunch, he shook his head emphatically. "I'm not shrugging anything off. I'm not taking this lightly. But there's no reason for the Void to try to subvert me. I'm worthless. I have nothing left to give. I gave up everything already."

She looked at him. "Did you?" She looked over very deliberately at the black staff, resting against the window ledge beside him.

"It doesn't work," he insisted quietly, but she could tell from the way he said it that he was hedging.

"What if the Lady has sent someone to kill you, just to be sure you don't switch sides?" She flushed. "Are we going to pretend that what happened five years ago couldn't happen again today? That war between the Word and the Void is still going on, and the creatures that fight in it still exist. There are still feeders out there, multiplying in the wake of the bad things that happen. Humans are still working hard at destroying themselves. Nothing has changed, John. You act as if it has. The fact that your life is different doesn't mean the world is. And it doesn't mean your connection to it has stopped having significance. Some things you can't walk away from. Wasn't that the lesson you taught me?"

He stared at her for a moment without replying, then shook his head. "It isn't the same."

He was lying to himself, and he didn't even realize it. She saw it clearly, a truth so obvious that she was appalled. Why was he refusing to listen to her? She remembered him as being so clearheaded, so focused on the reality of the world's harsh demands and unexpected treacheries. What had happened to him?

"Did you know there's a demon in Pioneer Square?" she asked quietly.

That got his attention. She watched his reaction with satisfaction, a quick shifting of the pale green eyes, a hint of shock and disbelief on the angular face. "It was hunting homeless people last night in the catacombs of the old city. I was out walking with Ariel, after midnight, because I couldn't sleep. We could hear its victims screaming."

"You didn't see it?"

She shook her head. "Ariel could smell it. She wouldn't let me go after it. She was terrified."

He glanced down at his food. "Maybe she was mistaken."

Nest gave him a moment to consider what he had said, then replied, "Maybe she wasn't."

She could tell what he was thinking. He was wondering what a demon would be doing so close to home. He was wondering why he hadn't known, then deciding it was because he had given up his position as a Knight of the Word, then realizing how vulnerable that made him. She let him work it through, saying nothing.

"If there is a demon, it has nothing to do with me," he said after a moment, sounding like a man trying hard to convince himself.

She finished her iced tea and looked over at him. "You don't believe that for a moment." She paused. "You wouldn't care to tell me about your dream, would you?"

He shook his head.

She smiled. "Okay, John. I did my good deed. I came here to warn you, and I've warned you. The rest is up to you. I'm here until tomorrow. We can talk about this some more, if you'd like. Just give me a call. I'm staying at the Alexis."

She rose. It was better to leave things where they were, not to say anything more, to let him think about it. He stared at her, perplexed by her abruptness. She reached for her purse. "Can I help pay for the lunch?"

He shook his head quickly. "Wait, I'll walk back with you."

"I'm not going back," she said. "I'm staying down on the waterfront for a while, have a look around."

They stared at each other, neither saying anything. She could see the indecision mirrored in his green eyes. "You believe what she's saying about me, don't you?" he asked finally. "What the Lady's saying?"

"I don't know that I do," she answered him. "I don't know what I believe. It's difficult to decide. But I think you have to look carefully at the possibility that she might be telling you the truth. I think you have to protect yourself."

He reached for his staff and levered himself to his feet. The waitress saw them rise, and she came over to give them the check. Ross took it, thanking her. When she was gone, he held out his hand to Nest.

"I'm glad you came, Nest. Whether or not it turns out there was a good reason for it, I'm glad you came. I've wondered about you often."

She nodded, brushing back her curly hair. "I've wondered about you, too."

"I didn't like leaving things with you in Hopewell the way I did. I've always felt bad about that."

She smiled. "It's over with, John."

"Sometimes it doesn't feel as if any of it will ever be over, as if the past will ever really be the past." He stepped around the table and bent to kiss her cheek. "I'll think about what you've told me, I promise. I'll think about it carefully. And I'll talk with you before you leave."

"All right," she said, content to leave it at that.

They left together, walking out into the brilliant afternoon sunshine and coolish fall air, and he left her standing on the sidewalk in front of the harbor tours ticket booth, then limped across the street for the trolley. He looked older to her then, as if he had aged all at once, his movements more studied, his stoop more pronounced. She wished she could do more to help him with this, but she had done everything she could think to do.

Even so, she could not shake the feeling that it wasn't enough.

CHAPTER 13

Nest was debating what to do with the rest of her day when Ariel unexpectedly reappeared. The tatterdemalion was gossamer thin and spectral in the sunlight, and she floated close against Nest, as if human contact had become suddenly necessary. Nest glanced around quickly to see if passersby were looking, but no one was. It was clear they couldn't see Ariel. Only Nest could.

"Where have you—" she began, but the tatterdemalion cut her short with a sudden rush of movement.

"Did you say everything to John Ross that you came to say?" the forest creature hissed in her soft, childlike voice.

Nest stared in surprise. "Yes, I guess so, pretty much."

Ariel was hunched close against her, and Nest could feel her small, transparent body vibrating as if it were a cord pulled taut in a high wind.

"Then stay away from him." The tatterdemalion's dark eyes were wide and staring as she watched John Ross depart. "Stay far away."

Nest followed Ariel's gaze across the roadway to where Ross was boarding the trolley. "What do you mean, *stay away*?"

The tatterdemalion darted behind her as the trolley moved down the tracks, and Nest realized that she was trying to conceal herself. Nest didn't think Ariel was even conscious of the movement, that she was reacting to something instinctual. The vibrating had increased, turned to a violent trembling, and Ariel was pressed so closely against her that parts of them were beginning to blend together. Nest shuddered at the feeling of invasion, inundated by a wave of dark emotions and terrifying memories. She realized that she was reliving with Ariel snippets of the lives of the children the magic had assimilated to create the tatterdemalion, caught in their overpowering flow. She tried to close her mind against them, to seal herself away, but Ariel's closeness made it impossible. Nest recoiled with the impact of their assault and stepped back in revulsion. She tried to move away from Ariel, to free herself of the other's presence, and she nearly collided with an elderly couple passing behind her.

"Sorry, I'm sorry," she said hastily, then turned away and walked to the railing overlooking thc slips where the tour boats docked. She took several deep gulps of air, staring down at the choppy waters, waiting for her mind to clear, for the dizziness to pass.

Ariel reappeared at her side, but did not try to touch her. "I didn't mean to do that," she said.

Nest nodded. "I know. But it was so, so . . ."

"Sometimes, I forget myself. Sometimes, all the children inside me come together in a knot and claim me. They want to be alive again. They want to be who they were. Their memories are so strong that they overwhelm me. I can feel everything they feel. I can remember everything they knew. They fight to get out of me, to become free. They need to touch another human being. They want to be inside a human body, to feel it warm and alive around them, to be real children again."

Her small voice faded away in a whisper, and her dark eyes seemed to lose their focus. "It scares me when that happens. I think that if they succeed, there will be nothing left of me."

Nest swallowed the dryness in her throat. "It's all right, I wasn't hurt. And you're still here." She forced herself to look into the tatterdemalion's opaque eyes. "Tell me, Ariel. What is it that bothers you about John Ross? Why did you tell me to stay away from him?"

"He is lost," the tatterdemalion replied softly.

"Lost?" Nest shook her head. "Lost how? I don't understand."

"You can't save him. Nothing you can do can save him. It is too late."

Nest stared in confusion. "Why would you say that? Why is it too late?"

The strange childlike face looked at her wonderingly. "Because he has demon stink all over him. He is already claimed."

They stood facing each other in the shadow of the overhang that protected the pier walkway, eyes locked. Nest started to speak again and then stopped. There were people moving all around them, passing on their way to someplace else, talking, laughing, unaware. She did not want to draw attention to herself; she did not want them to hear.

The sun broke through the high clouds and blinded her. She turned away. Demon stink? On John Ross? She shook her head slowly. This wasn't making sense.

"We have to go," Ariel said suddenly, and she started to move away.

"Wait!" Nest called out to her, saying the word so loudly that heads turned. She tried to look nonchalant as she detached herself from the pier railing and walked over to where Ariel hovered, glancing out at the boats as she did so. "Go where?" she whispered fiercely.

Ariel pointed north, down the trolley line, away from the direction they had come. "Someone is waiting to see you."

"Who?"

"Someone you know. Hurry, we have to go."

Ariel moved out to the sidewalk and Nest followed reluctantly. They turned north along the waterfront, passing Elliott's on Pier 56 and the shops on Pier 57. The wind whipped off the bay, cold and sharp, and in spite of the sunshine, Nest hunched down into her windbreaker, wishing she had brought something warmer.

Her mind raced as her eyes followed the movement of her feet. She spoke without looking up. "Ariel, were you in the building with me at Fresh Start, when I talked to John's friends?"

The tatterdemalion nodded. "I was."

"Was the demon stink there, too?"

"Yes, everywhere."

"Was it as strong?"

"Yes, as strong."

Nest tried to decide what this meant. Something had made her violently ill inside the rooms of Fresh Start. Could it be demon stink? If there was demon stink all over John Ross, wouldn't she have felt sick around him, too? Besides, she hadn't been able to detect demon stink five years ago, when her demon father had come back into her life, so why should she be able to detect it now?

Had something changed since then?

Maybe something about her?

She walked up Alaskan Way, keeping pace with Ariel, her head lowered against the bite of the October wind. The tatterdemalion seemed unaffected by the cold and wind, her ephemeral form a steady presence, her light silken coverings hanging limp and unruffled. Ariel did not look at her, but kept her gaze directed ahead, toward wherever it was they were going.

They crossed Alaskan Way at Pier 59, which housed the Seattle Aquarium, passed under the viaduct, and moved toward the broad, concrete steps of a hillclimb that led up to the city. There was another possibility, she realized, still thinking about what Ariel had said. Maybe what had happened at Fresh Start had nothing to do with demon stink. Maybe it had to do with the demon itself. If there was demon stink all over Fresh Start and John Ross, then it stood to reason the demon made its home close to both. So maybe the reason she became sick at Fresh Start was that the demon had been right there beside her.

One of Ross's friends and coworkers.

One of the people he trusted.

It made sense. The Lady said that the Void would send someone to subvert Ross, that maybe it had already happened. Ariel seemed to think it had. Ross did not. But maybe Ross couldn't see what was happening and that was the whole problem. Maybe her job in coming to find him was to make him take a closer look at himself.

Had she done that by speaking to him as she had? Had she given him enough cause to reexamine his situation? She couldn't be sure. But she knew now that she had to find out.

She climbed the steps past a small Mexican restaurant and a series of shops to Western Avenue, then turned up toward Pike Place Market. She knew where she was from the time she had spent studying the map of Seattle. Pike Place Market was a Seattle landmark, a long, low building that consisted of stalls and kiosks and display tables that were leased by vendors of fresh fish, fruits and vegetables, flowers, and crafts. Western ran below the market through warehouses and buildings that had been converted into microbreweries, restaurants, retail shops, and parking garages. The street sloped steadily upward from where she left the hillclimb, passing beneath several overpasses that connected the waterfront to the market and the surrounding shops. The crowds had dissipated to a scattering of people working their way between the parking lots and shopping areas. She wondered anew where it was that Ariel was taking her.

They passed a ramp leading down into an open-sided parking garage that abutted the expressway, and the sound of passing cars was a dull whine of tires on concrete. Then a park came into view. It was a small park, barely more than an open space with a grassy knoll at its center, clusters of small trees, and a sidewalk winding out from the street to a railing that overlooked Elliott Bay. Wooden benches lined the sidewalk and quarter-slot telescopes pointed out toward the Olympics. A juncture of streets leading down to the Market from the city fronted the little park, and traffic crawled past sluggishly in the afternoon sun.

A blue and red sign at the edge of the lawn proclaimed that this was Victor Steinbrueck Park.

"Here," said Ariel.

Nest walked up into the park for a closer look, drawn by the vista of the bay and the distant mountains, by the bright, sunny mix of blue water, green trees, and white-capped mountain peaks. She glanced around at the people in the park. They were an eclectic group. There were schoolchildren clustered at the railing with their supervising teachers and parents. There were shoppers on their way to and from the market. Businessmen and women were reading newspapers and magazines in the warmth of the sun as they munched sandwiches and sipped coffee.

But mostly there were Native Americans. They occupied the majority of the benches, particularly those fronting Western. They sat together in small groups on the grassy knoll. One or two lay sleeping in the sunshine, wrapped in old blankets or coats. They were a ragged, sullen group, their copper faces weathered, their black hair lank, and their clothes shabby. The ones sitting on the benches fronting the sidewalk on Western had placed paper cups and boxes in front of them to solicit handouts from passersby. They kept their faces lowered and their eyes on each other, seldom bothering even to look up at the people they begged from. Some drank from bottles wrapped in brown paper sacks. Most were men, but there were a few women, as well.

Nest turned to find Ariel, to ask who it was that they had come to meet, but the tatterdemalion was gone.

"Hello, little bird's Nest," someone growled from behind.

She knew the voice instantly, and even so she couldn't quite believe it. She turned around, and there stood Two Bears. The Sinnissippi was as ageless and unchanging as John Ross, his copper-colored features blunt and smooth, his long hair ink black and woven into a single braid, and his eyes so dark they seemed depthless. He wore the familiar army fatigue pants and boots, but here, where it was cooler, he also wore a heavy jacket over a checked flannel shirt. The silver buckle of his belt was tarnished and the leather scarred. He was as big and imposing as she remembered, with huge shoulders and thick, gnarled fingers. He was a solid and immutable presence.

"O'olish Amaneh." She spoke his Indian name carefully, as if it were made of glass.

"You remember," he said approvingly. "Good."

"Are you the one I'm supposed to meet?"

He cocked his head. "I don't know. Have you come here to meet someone, little bird's Nest?"

She nodded. "My friend Ariel brought me. She said . . ."

"Your friend? Have you come with a friend? Where is she?"

Nest looked around. "Gone, I guess. Hiding."

"Ah, just like your friend in the park five years ago. Mr. Pick." Two Bears seemed amused. His broad face creased with his smile. "All your friends want to hide from me, it seems."

She colored slightly. "Maybe you frighten them."

"Do you think so?" He shrugged, as if disclaiming responsibility. "You've changed, little bird's Nest. Maybe I can't call you that anymore. Maybe you're too old, too grown up."

"You haven't changed," she replied. "You look just the same. What are you doing here?"

He looked around speculatively. "Maybe I've come to be with my brothers and sisters. The Sinnissippi are gone, but there are still plenty of other tribes. Some of them have prospered. They run casinos and sell fireworks. They have councils to govern their people and rules to enforce their proclamations. The government in Washington recognizes their authority. They call them Native Americans and pass laws that give them special privileges. They don't call them Indians or Redskins anymore. At least, not to their faces."

He cocked an eyebrow at her. "There is even a segment of the population who believes that my people were wronged once, long ago, when white Europeans took away their land and their way of life. Can you imagine that?"

Nest shook her head noncommittally. "Are you sure Ariel didn't bring me here to see you?"

His face remained expressionless. "Why don't we sit down and talk, little bird's Nest?"

He led her to a bench facing out toward the water. A group of weathered men was sitting there, passing around a bottle and speaking in low voices. Two Bears said something to them in another language, and they rose at once and moved away. Two Bears took their place on the bench, and Nest sat down next to him.

"What did you say to them?" she asked.

He shrugged. "I told them they have no pride in themselves and should be ashamed." The copper skin of his blunt features tightened around his bones. "We are such a sad and hopeless people. Such a lost people. There are some of us, it is true, who have money and property. There are some who have found a way of life that provides. But most of us have nothing but empty hearts and alcohol and bad memories. Our pride in ourselves was stripped away a long time ago, and we were left hollow. It is a sad thing to see. Sadder to live."

He looked at her. "Do you know what is wrong with us, little bird's Nest? We are homeless. It is a bad way to be in the world. But that is how we are. We are adrift, tiny boats in a large ocean. Even those of us who have land and houses and friends and neighbors and some sort of life. It is a condition indigenous to our people. We bear a legacy of loss passed down to us by our ancestors. We bear the memory of what we had and what was taken. It haunts us."

He shook his head slowly. "You can be homeless in different ways. You can be homeless like those of my people you see here, living on the streets, surviving on handouts, marking time between the seasons. But you can be homeless in your heart, too. You can be empty inside yourself because you have no spiritual center. You can wander through life without any real sense of who you are or where you belong. You can exist without purpose or cause. Have you ever felt like that, little bird's Nest?"

"No," she said at once, wondering where he was going with this.

"Indians know," he said softly. "We have known for a long time. We are homeless in the streets and we are homeless in our hearts as well. We have no purpose in the world. We have no center. Our way of life was changed for us long ago, and it will never return. Our new life is someone else's life imposed on us; it is a false life. We struggle to find our home, our center, but it is as faded as the Sinnissippi. A building is a home if the people who inhabit it have memories and love and a place in the world. Otherwise, it is just a building, a shelter against the elements, and it can never be anything more. Indians know."

He bent close to her, pausing. "There are others who know this, too. A few, who have been uprooted and displaced, who have been banished to the road and a life of wandering, who have lost any sense of who they are. Some of these are like us—men and women whose way of life has been taken from them. Some of them are looking for a way back home again. Maybe you even know one."

Nest stared at him in silence.

"Do you still have your magic?" he asked suddenly.

Caught off guard by the question, she fumbled for an answer. "I think so."

"Not sure, are you? Perhaps it has changed as you have grown?" He nodded his understanding. "It may be so. Everything changes with time's passage. Only change itself is constant. So you must adapt and adjust and remember to keep close what is important and not to forget its purpose. Remember when we sat in the park and watched the spirits of the Sinnissippi dance?"

She did. On the Fourth of July weekend five years earlier, at midnight, she had gone into the park she had grown up in, the park that Pick warded, to see if the spirits would speak to her. The spirits had come on Two Bears' summons, and they had danced in the starlit darkness and shown to Nest in a vision a secret her family had hidden from her. It had been the catalyst for her terrifying confrontation with her father, and it had probably saved her life. She had not understood it that way at the time; she had not understood much of what had happened to her that weekend until much later.

"We were searching for truths, you and I—me, about my people, and you, about your father." He shook his head. "Hard questions were needed to uncover those truths. But the truths define who we are. They measure our place in the world. That is why they have worth. We search and we learn. It is how we grow."

He looked out over the bay. "Do you think this country has changed much since we spoke last, little bird's Nest? Since you were a girl, living in the park of the Sinnissippi? This is a hard question to answer, but the truth it masks needs uncovering. As a country, as a people, have we changed? On the surface we might appear to have done so, but underneath I think we are still the same. Our change is measurable, but not significant. We remain bent on destroying ourselves. We still kill each other with alarming frequency and for foolish reasons, and we begin the killing at a younger age. We have much to celebrate, but we live in fear and doubt. We are pessimistic about our own lives and the lives of our children. We trust almost no one.

"It is the same everywhere. We are a people under siege, walled away from each other and the world, trying to find a safe path through the debris of hate and rage that collects around us. We drive our cars as if they were weapons. We use our children and our friends as if their love and trust were expendable and meaningless. We think of ourselves first and others second. We lie and cheat and steal in little ways, thinking it unimportant, justifying it by telling ourselves that others do it, so it doesn't matter if we do it, too. We have no patience with the mistakes of others. We have no empathy for their despair. We have no compassion for their misery. Those who roam the streets are not our concern; they are examples of failure and an embarrassment to us. It is best to ignore them. If they are homeless, it is their own fault. They give us nothing but trouble. If they die, at least they will provide us with more space to breathe."

His smile was bitter. "Our war continues, the war we fight with one another, the war we wage against ourselves. It has its champions, good and bad, and sometimes one or the other has the stronger hand. Our place in this war is often defined for us. It is defined for many because they are powerless to choose. They are homeless or destitute. They are a minority of sex or race or religion. They are poor or disenfranchised. They are abused or disabled, physically or mentally, and they have forgotten or never learned how to stand up for themselves.

"But you and me, little bird's Nest, we are different. We have advantages others do not. We have magic and knowledge and insight. We know of the ways men destroy themselves and of the reasons they do so. We know the enemy who threatens us all. Because we know these truths, we are empowered and we can choose the ground we would defend. We have an obligation and a responsibility to decide where we will stand."

He paused. "I chose my ground a long time ago, when I returned from the Nam. I did so because after I died and came back to life, I was no longer afraid. I did so because even though I was the last of my people, I was made strong by the fire that tested me, and I was given purpose. You have been tested and given purpose, as well. You have been made strong. Now it is your turn to choose where you will stand."

Nest waited, impatient for the rest, guarded and edgy. On the sidewalk in front of her, close by the railing, the schoolchildren shrieked as a seagull dove over their heads in a wide sweep and soared away.

Two Bears locked her eyes with his. "Let me tell you a story. It is just a story, but maybe it will speak to you. A long time ago, a servant of a very powerful lady carried a talisman to a man who had agreed to become her champion. This man was conscripted to fight in a good and necessary cause. He was to wield the talisman as a weapon in an effort to help turn aside an evil that threatened to destroy all. He was fearful of his responsibilities, but he was determined as well. He took the talisman from the servant and bore it into battle, and for many years he fought bravely. His task was not easy, because the people he fought to protect often acted badly and foolishly, and by doing so they did harm to themselves. But he remained their champion nevertheless.

"Then something happened to him, and he lost faith in his cause. He abandoned hope; he gave up his fight. He became one of those who are homeless in their hearts. He despaired of who he was, and he thought to change everything about himself. He ran away to find a place to start over."

Two Bears looked around speculatively. "He might even have come to a city like this. This is the kind of city a man might flee to, if he were looking to begin again, don't you think, little bird's Nest?"

Her heart was hammering in her chest.

"Now the lady who had sent her servant to give this man her talisman was very disappointed in his failure to keep his promise to her. Shhhh, listen now, don't interrupt. Ask yourself what you would do if you were the lady in question. Your talisman is in the hands of a man who will not use it, but cannot give it back. A talisman once given cannot be returned. The magic does not allow for it."

He smiled. "Or so the story goes. At any rate, the lady sent someone to talk to this man, a young woman. As a matter of fact, she was someone very much like you. She was the man's friend, and the lady thought she might be able to persuade him of the danger he faced if he continued to ignore who he was and what he had promised. The lady thought the young woman was his best hope."

His eyes glistened. "Picture how this must be for the young woman. She is faced with a difficult task. She must find a way to help her friend, even though he does not wish her help. She must help him, because he has no one else and no other hope. The young woman is like you, little bird's Nest. She has magic at her command, and she has been tested by fire. She has a strength and purpose lacking in others."

He paused. "And so she must decide where she will stand. Because of who she is. Because, as with you and me, she has an obligation and a responsibility to do so."

Nest shook her head in dismay. "But I don't know what . . ."

A big hand came up swiftly to cut her short. "Because, if the young woman does not help him," he said carefully, his rough voice leaning heavily on each word, "he will be lost forever."

She nodded, her breath tight in her throat.

"Because, if the young woman fails, the lady has made other arrangements." Two Bears leaned so close that his broad face was only inches from her own. His voice became a whisper. "She cannot allow her champion to serve another cause, one that would be harmful to her own. She cannot allow her talisman to fall into the hands of her enemies."

There was no mistaking his meaning. It was the same message the Lady had given Ariel. If John Ross succumbed to the Void, he would be killed. But how did you kill a Knight of the Word? Who was strong enough? Who had a weapon more powerful than his?

Two Bears rose abruptly, and she with him. They stood close, looking out over the bay. The wind blew in chilly gusts off the water, causing Nest to shiver.

"As I said, it is only a story. Who knows if it is true? There are so many stories like it. Fairy tales. But the young woman reminded me of you." Two Bears folded his massive arms. "Tell me. If you were the young woman in this story, what would you do?"

She looked up at him, tall, broad-shouldered, and implacable. She was suddenly frightened. "I don't know."

He smiled at her, and the smile was warm. "Don't be so sure of that. Maybe you know better than you think."

She took hold of his arm. "If this is only a story, then it must have an ending. Tell it to me."

He said nothing, and his smile turned chilly. Her hands fell away. "There are many endings to this story. They change over time and with the teller. The stories of the Sinnissippi were all changed when my people perished. The endings would be different if they had survived, but they did not. I know this much. If you make the story your own, then the ending becomes yours to tell as you wish."

He was leaving, and when he did so she would lose any chance of gaining his help. She fought down the desperation that flooded through her. "Don't go," she begged.

"Our paths have crossed twice now, little bird's Nest," the Sinnissippi said. "I would not be surprised if they were to cross again."

"You could help me," she hissed, pleading with him.

He shook his head and placed his big hands on her slender shoulders. "Perhaps it is for you to help me. If I were the lady in the story, in the event all else failed, I would send someone to take back the talisman from my fallen champion, someone strong enough to do so, someone who knew much about death and did not fear it, because he had embraced it many times before." He paused. "Someone like me."

Nest's throat knotted in horror. Images of the past flooded through her mind. In Sinnissippi Park, on the Fourth of July, five years earlier, when he had appeared so mysteriously and done so much to help her find the courage she needed to face her father, she had seen nothing of this. She stared at him in disbelief, unable to give voice to what she was thinking.

"Speak my name," the big man said softly.

"O'olish Amaneh," she whispered.

He nodded. "It sounds good when you say it. I will remember that always."

One hand pointed. "Look. Over there, where the mountains and the forests and the lakes shine in the sunlight. Look closely, little bird's Nest. It will remind you of home."

She did as he asked, compelled by his voice. She stared out expectantly at a vista of white and green and blue, at a panorama that extended for miles, at a sweep of country that was so beautiful it took her breath away. Ferry boats churned through the bay below. Sailboats tacked into the wind. The late afternoon sun beat down on the foaming waters, reflecting in bright silver bursts off the wave caps. The forests of the islands and peninsula were lush and inviting. The mountains shone.

Two Bears was right, she thought suddenly. It did make her think of home.

But when she turned to tell him so, he was gone.

Chapter 14

John Ross had told Nest he had already been warned of the consequences of his refusal to continue as a Knight of the Word. What he hadn't told her was that the warning had been delivered by O'olish Amaneh.

As he rode the trolley back up to Pioneer Square and the offices of Fresh Start, thinking through everything Nest had said, he recalled anew the circumstances of that visit.

It was not long after he met Stef and before they started living together. He was still residing in Boston and auditing classes at the college. It was just after Christmas, sometime in early January, and a heavy snow had left everything blanketed in white. The sky was thickly clouded, and a rise in the temperature following a deep cold spell had created a heavy mist that clung to the landscape like cotton to Velcro and slowed traffic to a crawl. It was the perfect day to stay indoors, and that was what he was doing. He was in his apartment, finished with his classes, working his way through a book on behavioral science, when the door (which he was certain he had locked) opened and there stood the Indian.

Ross remembered his panic. If he had been able to do so, he would have bolted instantly, run for his life, consequences and appearances be damned. But he was settled back in his easy chair, encumbered by his book and various notepads, so there was no possibility of leaping up to escape. His staff lay on the floor beside him, but he didn't bother to reach for it. He knew, without having ever been given any real proof of it, that trying to use the staff's magic against O'olish Amaneh, even in self-defense, would be a big mistake.

"What do you want?" he asked instead, fighting to keep his voice steady.

O'olish Amaneh stepped inside and closed the door softly behind him. He was wearing a heavy winter parka, which he unzipped and removed. Underneath, he wore fatigue pants and combat boots, a checked flannel shirt with the sleeves rolled up, and a fisherman's vest with mesh pockets. A wide leather belt with a silver buckle bound his waist, metal bracelets encircled his wrists, and a beaded cord held back his long, black hair. His blunt features were wind-burnt and raw with the cold, and his dark eyes were flat and empty as they fixed on Ross.

He crossed his arms over his massive chest with the parka folded between them, but made no move to come closer. "You are making a mistake," he rumbled.

Ross put aside the book and notepads and straightened slightly. "Did the Lady send you?"

"What did I tell you, John Ross, about trying to cast off the staff?"

"You told me not to. Ever."

"Did you not believe me?"

"I believed you."

"Did you fail to realize that when I told you not to cast off the staff, I meant spiritually as well as physically?"

Ross's mouth and throat went dry. This was the Lady's response to his attempt to return the staff at the Fairy Glen. This was her answer to his abdication of his responsibilities as a Knight of the Word. She had sent O'olish Amaneh to discipline him. He still remembered the Indian delivering the staff to him fifteen years earlier, forcing him to take it against his will. He remembered the pain when he had touched the staff for the first time and the magic had bound them as one, joining them irrevocably and forever. He was terrified then. And now.

"What are you going to do?" he asked.

O'olish Amaneh studied him expressionlessly. "What should I do?"

Ross took a deep breath. "Take back the staff. Return it to the Lady."

The Indian shook his head. "I cannot do that. It is not permitted. Not while you remain a Knight of the Word."

Ross leaned forward in the chair and pushed himself to his feet. Whatever was going to happen, he wanted to be standing for it. He reached for the staff and used it to lean upon as he faced the big man. "I am no longer a Knight of the Word. I quit. I tried to tell the Lady, but she wouldn't speak to me. Maybe you can tell her. I just can't do it anymore. The truth is, I don't want to do it."

O'olish Amaneh sighed impatiently. "Listen closely to me. When you become a Knight of the Word, you become one forever. You cannot stop. The choice is not yours to make. You accepted a charge, and the charge is yours until it is lifted. That has not been done. The staff cannot be returned. You cannot send it back. That is the way things are."

Ross came forward a step, stumbling against a pile of books and magazines and nearly falling. "Do you know what happened to me?" he asked angrily. "At San Sobel?"

The Indian nodded. "I know."

"Then why is it so hard for you to understand that I want to quit? I don't want to have what happened at San Sobel ever happen again! I can't stand for it to happen again! So I quit, now, forever, and that's the end of it, and I don't care what the rules are!"

He knew he had crossed some line, but he didn't care. Even his fear could not control him. He hated who and what he had been. He had met Stefanie, and there was something special happening there. For the first time in years, he was feeling alive again.

The Indian walked right up to him, and Ross flinched in spite of himself, certain he was about to be struck. But the big man stopped before reaching him, and the flinty eyes bore deep into his own.

"Did you think, when you accepted your charge, you would make no mistakes in carrying it out? Did you think no innocents would die as a result of your actions? Did you think the world would change because you had agreed to serve, and the strength of your convictions alone would be enough to save the lives you sought to protect? Is that what you thought, John Ross? Were you so full of pride and arrogance? Were you such a fool?"

Ross flushed, but held his tongue.

"Let me tell you something about yourself." The Indian's words were as sharp as knives. "You are one man serving a cause in which many have given their lives.

You are one man in a long line of men and women, one only, and not so special that you could ever afford to hope you might make a significant difference. But you have done the best you could, and no more was ever asked. The war between the Word and the Void is a long and difficult one, and it has been waged since the beginning of time. It is in the nature of all life that it must be waged. That you were chosen to take up the Word's cause is an honor. It should be enough that you have been given a chance to serve.

"But you disgrace yourself and our cause by denigrating its purpose and abdicating your office. You shame yourself by choosing to renounce your calling. Who do you think you are? The burden of those children's deaths is not yours to bear. Yours is not the hand that took their lives; yours was not the will that decreed those lives must be sacrificed. Such choices and acts belong to a power higher than your own."

Ross felt the tendons in his neck go taut with his rage. "Well, it feels as if they are my responsibility, and I'm the one who has to live with the consequences of their dying because of my efforts or lack thereof, and blaming it on the Word or fate or whatever is a whole lot of bullshit! Don't try to tell me it isn't something I should think about! Don't try to tell me that! I do think about it! I think about it every day of my life. I see the faces of those children, dying in front of me. I see their eyes . . ."

He wheeled away, tears blurring his vision. He felt defeated. "I can't do it anymore, and that's all there is to it. You can't make me do it, O'olish Amaneh. No one can."

He went silent, waiting for whatever was going to happen next, half believing this was the end for him and not caring if it was.

But the Indian did not move. He was so still he might have been carved from stone.

"The consequences of accepting responsibility for the lives of others are not always pleasant. But neither are the consequences of abdicating that same responsibility. What is certain is that you cannot pretend to be someone other than who you are. You made a choice, John Ross. Failure and pain are a part of the price of your choice, but you cannot change that by telling yourself the choice was not binding. It was. It is."

The big man's voice dropped to a whisper. "By behaving as you do, you present a danger to yourself. Your self-deception places you at great risk. Whatever you believe, you are a Knight of the Word. You cannot be otherwise. The creatures of the Void know this. They will come for you. They will steal your soul away. They will make you their own."

Ross shook his head slowly. "No, they won't. I won't let them."

"You won't be able to stop it."

Ross met his gaze. "If they make the attempt, I will resist. I will resist to the point of dying, if that's what it takes. I may no longer be in service to the Word, but I will never serve the Void. I will never do that."

O'olish Amaneh looked out the window into the snow-covered landscape, into the somnolent white. "The Void wants your magic at its service, and it will do what it takes to obtain it. Subverting you will take time and effort and will require great deception, but it will happen. You may not even realize it until it is too late. Think, John Ross. Do not lie to yourself."

Ross held out the black staff. "If you take this from me now, the Void can do nothing. The solution is simple."

The Indian made no move. He kept his gaze directed away, his body still. "Others have suffered a loss of faith. Others have tried to abandon their charges. Others like you. They have been warned. Some thought they were strong. They have all been lost. One way or the other, they have been lost."

He looked at Ross, solemn-faced and sad-eyed. "You will go down the same path if you do not heed me."

They faced each other in silence, eyes locked. Then O'olish Amaneh turned without a word and went out the door and was gone, and John Ross did not see him again.

But he thought about him now, riding the trolley to Pioneer Square, stepping off onto the platform at Main, and walking back to the offices of Fresh Start. He thought about everything Two Bears had told him. The Indian and Nest had given him essentially the same warning, a veiled suggestion that the danger he posed by refusing to continue as a Knight of the Word would not be ignored and that measures would be taken to bring him back in line.

But did those measures include eliminating him? Would the Lady really send someone to kill him? He thought maybe she would. After all, five years ago he had been sent to kill Nest Freemark in the event she failed to withstand the assault of her demon father. Why should it be any different now, with him? They could not chance losing him to the Void. They could not let him become a weapon for their enemy.

Lost in thought, he slowed as he approached the entry to the shelter. Why did everyone think such a thing could happen? What could the Void possibly do to subvert him that he wouldn't recognize and resist? There was his dream, of course, and the danger that it might somehow come to pass and he would kill Simon Lawrence. But the events of that dream would never happen. There was no reason for them to happen. And in any case, he didn't really believe his dream and the Lady's warning were connected.

He shook his head stubbornly. Only one thing bothered him about all this. Why had the Lady sent Nest to warn him? She could just as easily have sent Ariel. He would have given the tatterdemalion's warning the same consideration he was giving Nest's. Why send the girl? The Lady couldn't possibly believe that Nest would have a greater influence on him than O'olish Amaneh. No, something else was going on, something he didn't understand. His instincts told him so.

He walked into the reception area at Fresh Start, said hello to Della, gave Ray Hapgood a perfunctory wave on his way back to the office, and closed the door behind him. He sat in his chair with his elbows on his desk and his chin in his hands, and tried to think it through.

What was he missing? What was it about Nest's coming to find him that was so troubling?

He was getting exactly nowhere when Stefanie Winslow walked in.

"You're back," she said. "How did it go?"

He blinked. "How did what go?"

She gave him an incredulous look. "Your lunch with your old flame's daughter. I assume that's where you've been." She took the chair across from him. "So tell me about it."

He shrugged, uncomfortable with the subject. "There's nothing to tell. She was in town and decided to look me up. I don't know how she even knew I was here. I haven't seen or spoken with her in five years. And that stuff about her mother is—"

"I know, I know. It was a long time ago, and her mother is dead. She told us before you came back." Stef brushed back her dark hair and crossed her long legs. "It must have been quite a shock to see her again."

"Well, it was a surprise, anyway. But we had a nice talk."

He had never told Stef anything about his past or the people in it, save for stories about his boyhood when he was growing up in Ohio. He had never told her about his service as a Knight of the Word, about the Lady or Owain Glyndwr or O'olish Amaneh. She did not know about his dreams. She did not know of the war between the Word and the Void or the part he had played in it. She did not know of his magic. As far as he knew, she had no concept of the feeders. Having Nest Freemark appear unexpectedly, come out of a past he had so carefully concealed from her, was unnerving. He did not want to tell her about any of that. He traced his present life to the moment he had met her, and everything that went before to another life entirely.

Stef studied his face. "Simon says she's some kind of world-class runner, that she might even win a gold medal in the next Olympics. That's pretty impressive."

He nodded noncommittally. "I gather she's pretty good."

"Is she in town for very long? Did you think to ask her to have dinner with us?"

He took a deep breath, wishing she would stop talking about it. "I mentioned dinner, but she said she might have other plans. She said she would call later. I don't think she's here for very long. Maybe only a day or so."

Stef looked at him. "You seem uneasy about this, John. Is everything all right? This girl hasn't announced that she's your love child or something, has she?"

The words shocked Ross so that he started visibly. Five years earlier Nest had indeed thought he was her father, had wished it were so. He had wished it were so, too.

He laughed quickly to mask his discomfort. "No, she didn't come here to tell me that. Or anything like that." He pushed back in his chair, feeling trapped. "I guess I'm just a little nervous about the speech. I haven't heard back from Simon on it. Maybe it wasn't so good."

Stef smirked. "The speech was fine. He told me so himself." Her smile brightened the whole room. "Matter of fact, he loved it. He'll tell you himself when he sees you again, if the two of you are ever in the office at the same time. He's gone again just now. There's a lot of preparation left for tomorrow night."

He nodded. "I suppose so." He fidgeted with his pens and paper, gathering his thoughts. "You know, I don't feel so well. I think I'm going to go back to the apartment and lie down for a while. You think they can get along without me for an hour or so?"

She reached across and took his hand in her own. "I think they can get along just fine. It's me I'm not sure about."

"Then come back with me."

"I thought you were sick."

"I'll get better."

She smirked. "I'll bet. Well, you're out of luck. I have work to do. I'll see you later." She frowned. "Or maybe not. I just remembered, I'm supposed to go with

Simon to the KIRO interview, then maybe to some press things after that. He hasn't given me the final word yet. Sorry, sweetie, but duty calls. Ring me if you hear from Nest, okay? I'll try to break free to join you."

She smiled and went out the door, blowing him a kiss. He stared after her without moving, then pushed the pens and paper away and got to his feet. Might as well follow through on his plan and get out of there, he decided. He was already back to thinking about something else Nest had said—that a demon in Pioneer Square was killing homeless people in the underground city. No one would miss them; no one would know. Except the feeders, of course. And he didn't see the feeders much anymore, so he couldn't tell if their current behavior reflected the demon's presence or not.

He stared down at his desk, unseeing. Sometimes he was tempted to try out his magic, just for a minute, just to see if he still had the use of it. If he did that, he might see the feeders clearly and maybe be able to determine if there was a demon in their midst.

But he refused to do that. He had sworn an oath that he wouldn't, because using magic was integral to acting as a Knight of the Word, and he had given all that up.

He walked out of his office, down the hall, past Della and a cluster of new arrivals huddled about her desk, and through the front door. The midday sunshine was fading, masked by heavy clouds blown in from the west on a sharp wind. The air had turned cold and brittle, and the light was autumn gray and pale. He glanced skyward. A storm was moving in. There would be rain by tonight.

His thoughts drifted.

A demon in Pioneer Square.

Someone sent to kill him.

Someone sent to subvert him.

The Word and the Void at play.

He crossed the street and moved past Waterfall Park toward the doorway to his apartment building. The waterfall tumbled down over the massive rocks and filled the walled enclosure with white noise. The park was empty, the afternoon shadows falling long and dark over the tables and chairs, benches and planters, and fountains. He didn't like how the emptiness made him feel. He didn't care for the thoughts it provoked. It seemed to reflect something inside.

In the shadows pooled among the boulders of the waterfall, something moved. The movement was quick and furtive, but unmistakable. Feeders. He paused to look more closely, to spy them out, but he could not do so. Those days were gone. He was someone different now. Something rough-edged brushed up against his memory—a reluctance, a wistfulness, a regret. The past had a way of creeping into the present, and his attempts at separating the two were still difficult. Even now. Even here.

Why had Nest Freemark been sent to him?

For just a moment he experienced an almost overpowering urge to flee. Just pack his bags, pick up Stefanie, and catch the first bus out of town. He stood facing into the park, and the movement in the shadows seemed to be reaching for him. He felt trapped in his life and by his decisions, and he could feel his control over things slipping away.

Then the moment passed. He took a deep breath and exhaled slowly, and he was all right again. He studied the shadows and saw nothing. The park was still and empty. He felt foolish and slightly embarrassed. He supposed he was not yet entirely free of the emotional fallout of San Sobel. He guessed that's what it was.

That was what he told himself as he turned away from the park and went down the sidewalk. That was how he dismissed the matter.

But deep inside, where hunches and instinct kept separate counsel, he wasn't really sure.

Chapter 15

After Two Bears disappeared, Nest Freemark sat back down on the bench they had shared and stared out at the bay. Her thoughts kept returning to five years ago when she had first met him. She kept trying to reconcile what she remembered from then with what she knew from now. She kept trying to make the parts fit.

I fought in Vietnam. I walked and slept with death; I knew her as I would a lover. I was young before, but afterward I was very old. I died in the Nam so many times, I lost count. But I killed a lot of men, too.

He had told her that right after he had told her his name. He had told her he was a killer. But nothing else he had told her had made him seem so. There had been no hint of violence about him. He had gone out of his way to dispel her concerns.

I am a stranger, a big man, a combat veteran who speaks of terrifying things. You should be afraid. But we are friends, Nest. Our friendship was sealed with our handshake. I will not hurt you.

But he might hurt John Ross. He might have to, because that was what he had been sent to do. She pondered the idea, thinking that in some strange way they had all changed places from five years ago. John Ross was on trial instead of her, and Two Bears might become his executioner. Ross now stood in her shoes, and Two Bears stood in his.

But where did she stand?

She was aware after a while that there were eyes watching her, and she glanced around cautiously. The shabby, sad-eyed Native Americans whom Two Bears had dismissed from their bench were staring at her from a short distance away. They huddled together on the grass, sitting cross-legged, their coats pulled over their shoulders, their heads hunched close, their dark eyes haunted. She wondered what they were thinking. Maybe they were wondering about her. Maybe about Two Bears. Maybe they just wanted their bench back.

I'm afraid, she had said five years ago to Two Bears. And he had replied, *Fear is a fire to temper courage and resolve. Use it so.*

She was afraid again, and she wondered if she could use her fear now as he had taught her to use it then.

Speak my name once more, he had asked her, and she had done so. *O'olish Amaneh. Yes,* he had said. *Say it often when I am gone, so that I will not be forgotten.*

Speak my name, he asked her again, just moments ago. As if by saying it, she could keep him alive.

The last of his kind, the last of the Sinnissippi, appearing and disappearing like a ghost. But his connection to her, while she didn't pretend to understand it completely, was as settled as concrete. They were linked in a way that transcended time and distance, and she felt her kinship to him so strongly it seemed as if they had been joined always. She wondered at its meaning. She knew now he was a servant of the Word, just like John Ross. So he shared with her a knowledge of the war with the Void, and they were possessed of magic, and they knew of demons and feeders, and they walked a line between two worlds that others didn't even know existed.

But there was more. In some strange way, she knew, they needed each other. It was hard to explain, but it was there. She took strength from him, but he took something from her, as well. Something. Her brow furrowed. Something.

She rose and walked to the railing, abandoning the bench. She stared out over the bay to the mountains, their jagged peaks cutting across the horizon. What was it he took from her? A hope? A comfort? A companionship? Something. It was there, a shape, a form at the back of her mind, but she could not quite put a name to it.

The afternoon was lengthening. Already the sun was sliding rapidly toward the horizon, its light tinting the clouds that masked it in myriad colors of purple and rose. It would be dark soon. She glanced at her watch. Four-fifteen. She wondered what she should do. She had already decided to meet John Ross for dinner, to tell him of her conversation with O'olish Amaneh, to try again to persuade him of the danger he was in. But it was too early yet to go back to the hotel and call him.

She walked out of the park and through the market, ambling along through the stalls of fruits and vegetables, fish and meats, and flowers and crafts, pausing now and again to look, to listen to the itinerant musicians, and to talk with the vendors. Everyone was friendly, willing to spend a few minutes with a visitor to the city. She bought a jar of honey and a fish pin, and she tasted a cup of apple cider and a slice of fresh melon. She reached the brass pig that marked the far end of the market, turned around, and walked back again.

When she had made the circuit, she went back into the park and looked around. The park was almost empty, dappled with shadows and splashed with light from the street lamps. Even the Indians had moved on, all but one who was asleep on the grass, wrapped head to foot in an old green blanket, long black hair spilling out of the top like silk from an ear of corn.

Nest looked around. She kept thinking that Ariel would reappear, but so far there was no sign of her. She checked her watch again. It was five o'clock. Maybe she should call Ross. She had the phone number of Fresh Start written on a slip of paper in her pocket. She could probably reach him there. She looked around for a phone and didn't see one. But there were several restaurants close at hand, and there would be phones inside.

Then she heard her name called in an excited whisper. "Nest! Come quickly!"

Ariel was right next to her, hovering in the fading light, a pale shimmer of movement.

"Where have you been?" she demanded.

The tatterdemalion's face brushed against her own, and she could feel the other's urgency. "Out looking. There are sylvans everywhere, and sometimes they can tell you things. I went to find the ones who live here. There are three in the city, and all of them make their homes in its parks. One is east in the Arboretum, one is north in Discovery, and one is west in Lincoln."

She paused, and then the words exploded out of her in a rush. "The one in Lincoln," she hissed, "has seen the demon!"

"Some kids set fire to a homeless man under the viaduct last night," Simon Lawrence announced, looking into his tonic and lime as if it were a crystal ball. "They doused him with gasoline and lit him up. Then they sat around and watched him burn. That's how the police caught them; they were so busy watching, they forgot to run." He shook his head. "Just when you think some measure of sanity has been restored to the world, people find a way to prove you wrong."

Andrew Wren sipped at his scotch and water and nodded. "I thought that sort of thing only happened in New York. I thought Seattle was still relatively civilized. Goes to show."

They were sitting across from each other in easy chairs on the upper level of the lobby bar in the Westin. It was five o'clock, and the hotel was bustling with activity. Participants from a handful of conferences the hotel was hosting were streaming in, identified by plastic badges that announced their company name in abbreviated block letters, one tag indistinguishable from another. With the day's meetings and seminars concluded, drinks and dinner and evening entertainment were next on the agenda, and the attendees were ready to rock and roll. But the corner of the bar in which Simon Lawrence and Andrew Wren sat was an island of calm.

Wren watched the Wiz check his watch. He seemed distracted. He had seemed so since his arrival, as if other things commanded his attention and he was just putting in his time here until he could get to them. They had agreed to meet for drinks after Simon had been detained earlier in the day at a meeting with the mayor and been unable to keep their noon appointment. When he was done here, the Wiz had a TV interview scheduled. Maybe that was what he was thinking about. No rest for the wicked, Wren thought sourly, then immediately regretted it. He was being perverse because he hadn't found anything bad to write about Simon Lawrence. No skeletons had emerged from the closet. No secrets had revealed themselves. The anonymous tips had not panned out. His instincts had failed him. He sipped at his drink some more.

"I appreciate your meeting me, Andrew," Simon said, smiling now. He was dressed in a dark shirt, slacks, and sport coat, and he looked casually elegant and very much at ease amid the convention suits. Wren, in his familiar rumpled journalist's garb, looked like something the cat had dragged in. "I know I haven't been able to give you as much time as you would like, but I want to make sure you feel you've been given full access to our records."

Wren nodded. "I've got no complaints. Everyone has been very cooperative. And you were right. I didn't find so much as a decimal point out of place."

The smile widened. "You sound a tad disappointed. Does this mean you will be forced to write something good about us?"

Wren pushed his glasses up on his nose. "Looks that way. Damned disappointing to have it end like this. When you're an investigative reporter, you like to find something to investigate. But you can't win them all."

Simon Lawrence chuckled. "I've found that to be true."

"Not lately, I'll wager." Wren cocked an eyebrow expectantly. "Lately, you've been winning them all. And you're about to win another."

The Wiz looked unexpectedly skeptical. "The shelter? Oh, that's a victory all right. It counts for something. But I wonder sometimes what it is that I'm winning. Like that general, I keep thinking I'm winning battles, but losing the war."

Wren shrugged. "Wars are won one battle at a time."

Simon Lawrence hunched forward, his dark eyes intense. The distracted look was gone. "Sometimes. But some wars can't be won. Ever. What if mine against homelessness is one?"

"You don't believe that."

The Wiz nodded. "You're right, I don't. But some do, and they have cogent arguments to support their position. A political scientist named Banfield posited back in the early seventies that the poor are split into two groups. One is disadvantaged simply because it lacks money. Give them a jump start and their middle-class values and work ethic will pull them through. But the second group will fail no matter how much money you give them because they possess a radically present-oriented outlook on life that attaches no value to work, sacrifice, self-improvement, or service. If that's so, if Banfield was right, then the war effort is doomed. The problem of homelessness will never be solved."

Wren frowned. "But your work is with women and children who have been disenfranchised through circumstances not of their own making. It's not the same thing, is it?"

"You can't compartmentalize the problem so easily, Andrew. There aren't any conditions of homelessness specifically attributable to particular groups that would allow us to apply different solutions. It doesn't work like that. Everything is connected. Domestic violence, failed marriages, teen pregnancy, poverty, and lack of education are all a part of the mix. They all contribute, and ultimately you can't solve one problem without solving them all. We fight small battles on different fronts, but the war is huge. It sprawls all over the place."

He leaned back again. "We treat homelessness on a case-by-case basis, trying to help the disadvantaged get back on their feet, to reclaim their lives, to begin anew. But you have to wonder sometimes how much good we are really doing. We shore up people in need, and that's good. But how much of what we do is actually solving the problem?"

Wren shrugged. "Maybe that's best left to somebody else."

Simon Lawrence chuckled. "Who? The government? The church? The general population? Do you see anyone out there addressing the specific causes of homelessness or domestic violence or failed marriages or teen pregnancy in any meaningful way? There are efforts being made to educate people, but the problem goes way beyond that. It has to do with the way we live, with our values and our ethics. And that's exactly what Banfield wrote decades ago when he warned us that poverty is a condition that, to a large extent at least, we cannot alleviate."

They stared at each other across the little table, the din of the room around them closing in on the momentary silence, filling up the space like water poured in a glass. Wren was struck suddenly by the similarity of their passion for their work. What they did was so different, yet the strength of their commitment and belief was much the same.

"I'm sounding pessimistic again," the Wiz said, making a dismissive gesture. "You have to ignore me when I'm like this. You have to pretend that it's someone else talking."

Wren drained the last of his drink and sat back. "Tell me something about yourself, Simon," he asked the other man suddenly.

Simon Lawrence seemed caught off guard. "What?"

"Tell me something about yourself. I came out here for a story, and the story is supposed to be about you. So tell me something about yourself that you haven't told anyone else. Give me something interesting to write about." He paused. "Tell me about your childhood."

The Wiz shook his head immediately. "You know better than to ask me about that, Andrew. I never talk about myself except in the context of my work. My personal life isn't relevant to anything."

Wren laughed. "Of course it is. You can't sit there and tell me how you grew up doesn't have anything to do with how you came to be who you are. Everything connects in life, Simon. You just said so yourself. Homelessness is tied to domestic violence, teen pregnancy, and so forth. Same with the events of your life. They're all tied together. You can't pretend your childhood is separate from the rest of your life. So tell me something. Come on. You've disappointed me so far, but here's a chance to redeem yourself."

Simon Lawrence seemed to think about it a moment, staring across the table at the journalist. There was a dark, troubled look in his eyes as he shook his head. "I've got a friend," he said slowly, reflecting on his choice of words. "He's the CEO of a big company, an important company, that does some good work with the disadvantaged. He travels the same fund-raising circuits I do, talks to some of the same people. They ask him constantly to tell them about his background. They want to know all about him, want to take something personal away with them, some piece of who he is. He won't give it to them. All they can have, he tells me, is the part that deals directly with his work—with the present, the here and now, the cause to which he is committed.

"I asked him about it once. I didn't expect him to tell me anything more than he told anyone else, but he surprised me. He told me everything."

The Wiz reached for his empty glass, studied it a moment, and set it down. A server drifted over, but he waved her away. "He grew up in a very poor neighborhood in St. Louis. He had a brother and a sister, both younger. His parents were poor and not well educated, but they had a home. His father had a day job at a factory, and his mother was a housewife. They had food on the table and clothes on their backs and a sense of belonging somewhere.

"Then, when he was maybe seven or eight, the economy went south. His father lost his job and couldn't get rehired. They scraped by as long as they could, then sold their home and moved to Chicago to find work there. Within months, everything fell apart. There was no work to be found. They used up their savings. The father began to drink and would sometimes disappear for days. They drifted from place to place, often living in shelters. They started taking welfare, scraping by on that and the little bit of income the father earned from doing odd jobs. They got some help now and then from the churches.

"One day, the father disappeared and didn't come back. The mother and children never knew what happened to him. The police searched for him, but he never turned up. The younger brother died in a fall shortly afterward. My friend and his little sister stayed with their mother in a state-subsidized housing project. There wasn't enough food. They ate leftovers scavenged from garbage cans. They slept on old mattresses on the floor. There were gangs and drugs and guns in the projects. People died every day in the rooms and hallways and sidewalks around them."

He paused. "The mother began to go out into the streets at night. My friend and his sister knew what she did, even though she never told them. Finally, one night, she didn't come home. Like the father. After a time, the state came looking for the children to put them in foster homes. My friend and his sister didn't want that. They preferred to stay on the streets, thinking they could stay together that way.

"So that was how they lived, homeless and alone. My friend won't talk about the specifics except to say it was so terrible that he still cries when he remembers it. He lost his sister out there. She drifted away with some other homeless kids, and he never saw her again. When he was old enough to get work, he did so. Eventually, he got himself off the streets and into the schools. He got himself a life. But it took him a lot of hard years."

Simon Lawrence shrugged. "He had never told this to anyone. He told it to me to make a point. What difference did any of this make, he asked me, to what he did now? If he told this story to the people from whom he sought money—or if he told the press—what difference would it make? Would they give him more money because he'd had a hard life? Would they give him more money because they felt sorry for him? Maybe so. But he didn't want that. That was the wrong reason for them to want to help. It was the cause he represented that mattered. He wanted them to help because of that, not because of who he was and where he came from. He did not want to come between the donors and the cause. Because if that happened, then he risked the possibility he would become more important than the cause he represented. And that, Andrew, would be a sin."

He stood up abruptly, distracted anew. "I'm sorry, but I've got to run. You're staying over for the dedication tomorrow night, aren't you?"

Wren nodded, rising with him. "Yes, but I'd like to . . ."

"Good." Simon took his hand and gave it a firm shake. "If the newspaper's paying, try Roy's, here at the hotel, for a good dinner. It's first-rate. I'll see you tomorrow."

He was gone at once, striding across the lobby toward the front door, tall form scything through the crowd with catlike grace and determination. Andrew Wren stared after him, and it wasn't until he was out of sight that it occurred to the journalist that maybe, just maybe, Simon Lawrence had been talking about himself.

Nest Freemark found a phone booth across from the park and dialed the number for Fresh Start. It was after five now, the sun slipped below the horizon, the last color fading fast in a darkening sky. Ariel was hovering invisibly against the building walls behind her, and the streets were filling with traffic from people on their way home from work. The park had emptied long ago, and the grassy rise was a shadowed hump against the skyline.

It was beginning to rain, a slow, chilly misting that clung to Nest's skin. On the sound, a bank of fog was beginning to build over the water.

The lady who answered the phone was not Della, and she did not know Nest. She said John Ross wasn't there and wasn't expected back that day and she couldn't give out his home number. Nest told her it was important she speak to him. The lady hesitated, then asked her to hold on a minute.

Nest stared off into the gathering darkness, itching with impatience.

"Nest? Hi, it's Stefanie Winslow." The familiar voice sounded rushed and out of breath. "John's gone home, and I think he's shut off the phone, because I just tried to call him a little while ago and I couldn't reach him. Are you calling about dinner?"

Nest hesitated. "Yes. I don't think I can make it."

"Well, neither can I, but I think maybe John was planning on it. Will you be by tomorrow?"

"I think so." Nest thought furiously. "Can you give John a message for me?"

"Of course. I have to go by the apartment for a few minutes. I could even have him call you, if you want."

"No, I'm at a pay phone."

"All right. What should I tell him?"

For just an instant Nest thought about dropping the whole matter, just hanging up and leaving things the way they were. She could explain it all to Ross later. But she was uncomfortable with not letting him know there was new reason for him to be concerned about his safety, that something was about to happen that might change everything.

"Could you just tell him I'm meeting a friend of Pick's over in West Seattle who might know something about that trouble we were talking about at lunch? Tell him Pick's friend might have seen the one we were looking for."

She paused, waiting. Stefanie Winslow was silent. "Have you got that, Stefanie?" she pressed. "I know it's a little vague, but he'll know what I'm talking about. If I get back in time, I'll call him tonight. Otherwise, I'll see him tomorrow."

"Okay. Listen, are you all right? This sounds a little . . . mysterious, I guess. Do you need some help?"

Nest shook her head at the phone. "No, everything's fine. I have to go now. I'll see you tomorrow. Thanks for helping."

She hung up the phone and went looking for a taxi.

The demon walked into the lobby of the Westin through a side door, paused to look around, then moved quickly to the elevators across from the lobby bar. It didn't have much time; it had to hurry. An empty elevator was waiting, doors open, and the demon rode alone to the sixth floor. It stepped off into a deserted hallway, checked the wall numbers for directions, and turned left.

Seconds later, it stood before Andrew Wren's room. It listened carefully for a moment to make certain the room was empty, then slipped a thin manila envelope under the door. When Wren returned, he would find all the evidence he needed to confront the Wiz with the threat of exposure and a demand for an explanation that the latter would be unable to provide. The consequences of that would be inescapable. By tomorrow night, the Wiz would be history and John Ross would have taken his first step toward entering into the service of the Void.

There was only one additional matter to be settled. Nest Freemark was a threat to everything. The demon had sensed her magic when they had talked earlier that day at Fresh Start. It was raw and unrealized, but it was potent. She could prove dangerous. Moreover, she had a tatterdemalion with her, and the tatterdemalion, if given the right opportunity, could expose the demon. If that happened, everything would be ruined.

The demon was not about to allow that. It didn't know what the girl and the forest creature were doing here, if they had been sent by the Word or come on their own, but it was time to be rid of them.

The demon turned and walked to the exit sign above the stairs and descended the six flights to the lobby. No one saw it leave.

In the parking garage, it claimed its car and headed for West Seattle.

CHAPTER 16

The night was cool and dark. As Nest Freemark rode through the city, rain misted on the windshield of the taxi, smearing the glass, blurring the garish neon landscape beyond. The taxi passed back down First Avenue in front of the Alexis Hotel, then climbed a ramp to the viaduct. Suspended above the waterfront, with the piers and ferries and colored lights spread out below and the orange cranes lifting skyward overhead, the taxi wheeled onto the lower tier of the expressway and sped south.

It had taken longer to find transportation than Nest had expected. She couldn't find anything in the market area, so she had walked down to a small hotel called the Inn at the Market, situated just above the Pike Place Market sign, and had the doorman call for her. Ariel had disappeared again. How the tatterdemalion would reach their destination was anybody's guess, but since she had gotten there once already, Nest guessed she would manage this time, too.

The canopy of the northbound viaduct lowered and leveled to join with the southbound, and Nest was back out in the rain again. The taxi eased around slower cars, its tires making a soft, steady hiss on the damp pavement. Nest watched the cranes and loading docks appear and fade on her right, prehistoric creatures in the gloom. The driver was a motionless shape in front of her. Neither of them spoke. Brightly lit billboards whizzed by, advertisements for beer, restaurants, sports events, and clothing. She read them swiftly and forgot them even quicker, her thoughts tightly focused on what lay ahead.

The taxi took the off-ramp onto the West Seattle Bridge, and headed west. Nest settled back in the seat, thinking. Ariel had found a sylvan in one of the parks who had seen the demon a few months ago and gotten a good look at it. More important, at least from Ariel's point of view, was the story behind that sighting. She wouldn't elaborate when Nest asked for details. She wanted the sylvan to tell the story. She wanted Nest to hear for herself.

The freeway took a long, sweeping turn up a hill past a sign announcing their arrival in West Seattle. Residential lights shone through the rain. Fog cloaked the wooded landscape, clinging in thick patches to the heavy boughs of the conifers. Nest peered into the deepening gloom as the city dropped away behind her. They crested the hill and passed through a small section of shops and fast-food outlets. Then there were only residences and streetlights, and the city disappeared entirely.

The taxi wound its way steadily down the far side of the hill, took a couple of wide turns, then straightened out along a broad, straight, well-lit roadway. Ahead, she could see the dark wall of her destination. Lincoln Park was south of West Seattle proper, bordering Puget Sound just above the Vashon Island Ferry terminal. She found it on the map while she was riding in the taxi, checking its location, situating herself so that she wouldn't become turned around. When she was satisfied that she knew where she was, she stuck the map back in her pocket.

The taxi passed a park sign, then pulled into an empty parking area fronting a thick mass of trees. Nest could just make out the flat, earthen threshold of a trailhead next to it. There was no one in sight. Within the trees, nothing moved.

She paid the driver and asked him where she could call a taxi to get back into the city. The driver told her there was a pay phone at the gas station they had passed just up the road. He gave her a business card with the phone number of his company.

She stepped out into the mist and gloom, pulling up the hood of her windbreaker as the taxi drove away. Standing alone at the edge of the park, she glanced around uncertainly. For the first time that night, she began to have doubts.

Then Ariel was next to her, appearing out of nowhere. "This way, Nest! Follow me!"

The silken white image floated onto the trailhead, and Nest Freemark dutifully followed. They entered the wall of trees, and within seconds the parking lot and its lights disappeared behind them. Nest's eyes adjusted slowly to this new level of darkness. There were no lights here, but the low ceiling of clouds reflected the lights of the city and its homes to provide a pale, ambient glow. Nest could pick out the shapes of the massive conifers—cedar, spruce, and fir—interspersed with broad-leaved madrona. Thick patches of thimbleberry and salal flanked the pathway, and fern fronds drooped in feathery clusters. Rain carpeted the grass and leaves in crystal shards, and mist worked its way through the branches and trunks of the trees in snakelike tendrils. The park was silent and empty-feeling. It could have been Sinnissippi Park on a cold, wet fall night, except that the limbs of the northwest conifers, unlike their deciduous midwest cousins, were still thick with needles and did not lift bare, skeletal limbs against the sky.

The trail branched ahead, but Ariel chose the way without hesitation, her slender childish body wraithlike in the gloom. Nest glanced right and left at every turn, her senses pricked for movement and sound, wary of this dark, misty place. The uneasiness she had felt earlier was still with her. At times like these, she wished she had Wraith to protect her. The big ghost wolf had been a reassuring presence. She did not think often of him these days, not since he had disappeared. She was surprised to discover now that she missed him.

The trail climbed and she went with it, working her way through heavy old growth, fallen limbs, and patches of thick scrub. Clearings opened every so often to either side, filled with dull, gray light reflected off the heavy clouds. The rain continued to mist softly, a wetness that settled on her face and hands and left the air tasting of damp earth and wood. Now and again, her shoes slipped on patches of mud and leaves, causing her to lose her balance. Each time, she righted herself and continued, keeping Ariel in sight ahead of her.

They topped a rise, and Nest could just make out the black, choppy surface of Puget Sound through the trees. They were atop a bluff that dropped away precipitously beyond a low rail fence. The trail they followed branched yet again, following the edge of the cliff both ways along the fence into the darkness.

Ariel turned left and led Nest to a small clearing with a rain-soaked wooden bench that looked out over the sound.

"Here," she said, stopping.

Nest drew even with her and looked around doubtfully. "What happens now?"

Ariel was insistent. "We wait."

The minutes ticked by as they stood in the chilly darkness, listened to the rain falling softly through the trees, and watched the mist float in and out of the damp, shiny trunks in shifting forms. Wind rustled the topmost branches in sudden gusts that showered them with water. Out on the sound, ferry boats and container ships steamed by, their lights steady and bright against the black waters.

Nest hugged herself with her arms and dug the toe of her shoe into the wet earth, growing impatient.

Then a familiar shadow flitted across the darkness, appearing abruptly from out of the woods. It swept down to the bench in a long glide and settled on the back rest, folding into itself. It was an owl, and on its back rode a sylvan, twiggy legs and arms entwined within the feathers of the great bird's neck.

The sylvan jumped off the owl with a quick, nimble movement, slid down the back rest, and stood facing her on the bench seat. She peered through the gloom in an effort to make out his features. He was younger than Pick, his wooden face not so lined, his beard not so mossy, and his limbs not so gnarled. He wore a bit of vine strapped about his waist, and from the vine dangled a small tube.

"You Nest?" he asked perfunctorily.

She nodded, coming forward several steps, closing the distance between them to six feet.

"I'm Boot, and this is Audrey." The sylvan indicated the owl. It was a breed with which she was not familiar, something a little larger and lighter colored than the barn owls she was used to. "We're the guardians of this park."

"Pleased to meet you," she said.

"You grew up in a park like this, I understand. You're friends with another sylvan."

"His name is Pick."

"You can do magic, too. That's unusual for a human. What sort of magic can you do?"

Nest hesitated. "I'm not sure I can do any magic. I haven't used it for a while. I have some problems with it. It hurts me to use it sometimes."

Ariel came forward, a delicate white presence in the night, dark eyes shifting from one to the other. "Tell her about the demon, Boot," she whispered anxiously.

The sylvan nodded. "Don't rush me. There's plenty of time to do that. All night, if we need it, and we don't. Where demons are concerned, you don't want to rush things. You want to step carefully. You want to watch where you go."

"Tell her!"

The sylvan harrumphed irritably. Nest thought of Pick. Apparently sylvans became curmudgeons at a young age.

Audrey ruffled her feathers against a rush of wind and damp, and resettled herself on the bench back, luminous round eyes fixing on Nest. Boot folded his skinny arms and muttered inaudibly into his beard and gave every appearance of refusing to say another word.

"I have a friend who is in danger from this demon," Nest announced impulsively, not wanting to lose him to a mood swing. "Whatever you can tell me might help save his life."

Boot stared at her. "All right. No reason not to, I guess. You've come a long way, haven't you? Well, then."

The arms unlocked and dropped to his sides. "The demon came to this park about three months ago. I'd never seen it before. I'd seen others from time to time, but they were always passing through on their way to somewhere else, and they were cloaked in their human guise and had been for a long time. But this one came deliberately. This one came with a purpose. It was night, midsummer, and it walked into the park just after sunset and came up to the cliffs and waited in the trees where the paths don't go. It was hiding, waiting for something. I was patrolling the park on Audrey and saw it from the air. I knew what it was right away. So Audrey and I circled back behind it, keeping to the high limbs, and found a place to watch."

"What did it look like?" Nest asked quickly.

"I'm getting to that, if you please," the sylvan informed in a no-nonsense tone of voice. "Don't rush me." He cleared his throat. "It was a man. He was tall and thin, rather different looking—dark hair and small features. He wore a long coat, no hat. I got a good look at him through the scope." He held up the tube tied to his waist. "Spyglass. Lets me see everything. Anyway, he stood there in the shadows for a long time. Maybe an hour or more. The park emptied out. It was a bright, moonlit night, so I could see what happened next very clearly."

He paused meaningfully. "Another demon appeared. It crawled up the cliff face from somewhere below, from the shoreline. I don't know where it came from before that. This one was huge, barely recognizable as human, its disguise sort of thrown together. It was thick-limbed and hunched over and all hairy and twisted. It looked more like an animal than a human, but a human is what it was trying to play at being, sure enough.

"So the first demon steps out from its hiding place to talk to the second. I have good ears, so I could hear them. 'What are you doing here?' the first one asks. 'I've come to kill him,' says the second. 'You can't kill him, he's mine, he belongs to me, and I want him alive,' says the first. 'It doesn't matter what you want. He's too dangerous to be allowed to live, and besides, I want to taste his magic. I want to make it my own,' says the second.

"Then they begin shrieking at each other, making threatening gestures, calling each other names." Boot shook his leafy head. "Well, you can imagine. I'm watching all this and wondering what in the world is going on. Two demons fighting over a human! I'd never heard of such a thing! Why would they do that when there's a whole world full of them, and more than a few ready, willing, and eager to be made victims?"

The sylvan came forward to the very edge of the bench, head inclined conspiratorially. "So then the first demon says, 'You have no right to interfere in this. The Knight belongs to me. His magic and his life are mine.' Well, now I know what they're talking about. They're quarreling over a Knight of the Word. For some reason, they seem to think there's one out there waiting to be claimed! I've heard of this happening. Rarely, but now and then. But I don't know about this Knight. I don't know much of anything that happens outside the park, so I'm a little surprised to hear about this. I pay close attention."

Boot glanced around at the darkness as if someone else might be listening. "So this is what happens next. The second demon pushes the first and says, 'I was sent to make certain of him. I tracked him before you, in other cities and other towns.

You stole him from me. I want him back.' The first demon backs away. 'Don't be stupid! You don't have a chance with him! I'm the one who can turn him! I can make him one of us! I have already started to do so!'

"But the second demon isn't listening. Its hair is bristling and its eyes are narrowed and hard. I can feel Audrey trembling next to me, her talons digging into the limb from which we watch. 'He has made you weak and foolish. You think like the humans you pretend to be,' says the second demon, advancing again on the first. 'You are not strong enough to do what is needed. I must do it for you. I must kill him myself.'

"Then the second demon pushes the first demon hard and sends it sprawling into the brush."

Nest felt the skin on the back of her neck crawl with the idea of two demons fighting over possession of John Ross. She should have taken the time to find him and bring him with her. He should be listening to this. If he were, he would be hard-pressed to argue that he wasn't in any real danger.

Boot nodded, as if reading her mind. "It was a bad moment. The first demon gets back to his feet and says, 'All right, he's yours. Take him. I don't care anymore.' The second demon grunts and sneers at the first, then turns and moves off down the path. The first demon waits until the second is out of sight, then starts to undress. It takes off its coat and the clothes underneath. Then it begins to transform into something else. It happens quickly. I have heard of creatures like this, but I have never seen one—a changeling, a special kind of demon, able to shift from one form to another in moments where it takes the others days or even weeks to assume a new disguise."

The sylvan took a deep breath. "It becomes a four-legged creature, a monster, a predator like nothing I've ever seen. It has these huge jaws and this massive neck and shoulders. A hellhound. A raver. It lopes off into the brush after the second demon. Audrey and I take to the air and follow, watching. The changeling catches up to the second demon in seconds. It doesn't hesitate. It attacks instantly, charging out of the brush. It knocks the second demon to the ground despite its size and holds it there with its body weight. It tears the bigger demon's head from its shoulders, then rips its body down the middle and fastens on the dark thing inside that is its soul. There is a horrible shriek, and the second demon thrashes and goes limp. It begins to dissolve. It turns to ash and blows away in the summer's night breeze.

"The first demon says—growls, actually, and I can hear it even from atop the trees where Audrey and I watch it begin to change again—'He belongs to me, he is mine.' "

Rain gusted suddenly through the trees, blown on a fresh wind, and Nest started as the cold droplets blew into her face. The weather was worsening, the mist turning to a steady downpour. Nest tried to make sense of what the sylvan was telling her, why it was that the first demon would be so desperate to protect its interest in John Ross, to keep him alive so that he could be subverted. Something in the back of her mind nudged at her, a memory of something that had happened before, but she could not quite manage to identify it.

Ariel floated past her in the dark, her childlike form looking frail and exposed against the rush of wind and rain. "Is that all?" she asked Boot. "Is that the end of the story?"

"Not quite," replied the sylvan, dark eyes bright. "Like I said, the demon begins to change again, but—it's the strangest thing—this time it changes into . . ."

Something huge tore through the woods. Thick masses of brush shivered suddenly, shedding water and scattering shadows. Boot wheeled toward the movement in frightened recognition, his voice faltering and his dark eyes blinking in shock. Ariel gasped sharply and screamed at Nest.

Then the brush exploded in a shower of branches and leaves, and a massive black shape hurtled out of the night.

On the advice of Simon Lawrence, Andrew Wren enjoyed a leisurely dinner at Roy's, topping it off with the chocolate soufflé because everyone around him seemed to be doing the same. He was not disappointed. Then he went back out into the lobby for a nightcap. He drank a glass of port and engaged in conversation with a computer-software salesman from California who was in town to do a little business with Microsoft, picking up a few new tidbits of information on Bill Gates in the process (he never knew what was going to prove useful in his business). So it was nearing nine o'clock when he went up to his room to turn in.

He saw the manila envelope as soon as he opened the door, a pale square packet lying on the dark carpet. Wary of strange deliveries and having known more than one investigative journalist who had been the recipient of a letter bomb, he switched on the light and knelt to examine it. After a careful check, and noting how thin it was, he decided it was safe and picked it up. No writing on it anywhere. He carried it over to the small table by the window and set it down. Then he walked to the closet and hung his coat, turned on a few more lights, called the message service to retrieve a call that had come in over the dinner hour from his editor, and finally went back to the table, sat down in the straight-backed chair tucked under it, and picked up the envelope once more.

He knew what it was before he opened it. His intuition told him in a loud, clear voice. It was the material he had been looking for on Simon Lawrence. It was the evidence he had come to find. Maybe it was from his mysterious source. Maybe it was from someone else. Whoever it was from, it was either going to propel the stalled investigation of the Wiz to a new level or it was going to end it once and for all.

Wren separated the flap from the envelope and slipped out the sheaf of papers nestled inside. He set the envelope aside and began to read. It took him a long time because the material consisted mostly of photocopies of bank accounts, transfer slips, records of deposits and withdrawals, and ledger pages, and it was difficult to follow. Besides, he didn't want to jump to conclusions. After a while, he loosened his tie and rolled up his sleeves. His glasses slid down his nose, and his face assumed an intense, professorial look that accompanied deep thought. His burly body slouched heavily in the hard-backed chair, but he paid no attention to his discomfort. Outside, on the rain-slicked streets below, a stream of traffic crawled by, and every so often someone would forget what city they were in and honk their horn in irritation.

When he was done reading, he picked up the phone and called down for a bottle of scotch, a bottle of Evian, and some ice. He was treating himself, but he was fortifying himself as well. He knew what he had here, but it was going to take him half the night to sort it out. He wanted everything in order when he went to see Simon Lawrence in the morning. He wanted it all clear in his own head as well as on paper, so that he could analyze quickly any explanations that the Wiz chose to give. Not that he was likely to give any, if Wren was reading this right. Not that he was likely to want ever to see Andrew Wren again.

Because what someone had uncovered was evidence of a systematic siphoning of funds from the accounts of Fresh Start and Pass/Go, an elaborate and intricate series of transfers from accounts set up to receive charitable donations that dispersed them to other accounts within the corporations, applied them to payments of charges that didn't actually exist, and eventually deposited them in noncorporate accounts. The corporate books he had reviewed yesterday, and which presumably the corporate auditors reviewed as well, disguised the transfers in various ways, none of which could be uncovered readily in the absence of a comprehensive audit, the kind you didn't usually get unless the IRS came calling.

That hadn't happened as yet, and there was no reason to think it would happen anytime soon. The embezzling had been going on for less than a year, and from what Andrew Wren could tell, it involved only two people.

Or maybe only one.

Wren paused, rethinking the matter. Two, if they were both participating. One, if the second was being used as a front. Wren couldn't tell which from the photocopies alone. It would require an analysis of the signatures on the deposits and withdrawals. It would require an extensive investigation.

He shook his head. The photocopies showed the stolen funds being deposited into the private accounts of two people. One was Simon Lawrence. But why would the Wiz steal from his own foundation? Stranger things had happened, sure. But Simon Lawrence was so committed to his work, and his work had brought him nationwide recognition. If all he wanted out of this was more money, he could quit tomorrow and go to work as a CEO for any number of corporations. The thefts were recent. Why would the Wiz decide now, after achieving so much, to start stealing from his company? The thefts were clever, but they weren't perfect. Sooner or later, someone would find out what was happening in any event, and the Wiz would be exposed. He had to know that.

Wren poured two fingers of scotch into a glass of ice and sipped at it thoughtfully. The alcohol burned pleasantly as it slipped down his throat. Something wasn't right about this. The Wiz wouldn't steal from himself without a very strong reason, and then he would steal more than this because he had to know he wouldn't be able to get away with it for very long, so he had to make his killing early.

Wren stared out the window into the night. It was more likely the second man was the one doing all the stealing, and he had siphoned some of the funds into Simon's account so that if he were discovered, he could always claim he was just a flunky acting on orders. The public outcry would pass right over him and settle directly on the Wiz, a high-profile figure just ripe for lynching.

Andrew Wren nodded slowly. Yes, that made better sense. The second man was doing all the real stealing, and the Wiz was guilty merely of bad judgment in hiring him. That was what he believed. That was what his instincts told him was the truth. Of course, he would write the article based on the facts and let the chips fall where they may, because that was his job. So it might be the end of Simon Lawrence in any event. In the wake of a scandal like this, the Wiz would be hard-pressed to escape the fallout.

He sighed. Sometimes he hated being right so often, having those infallible instincts that prodded him on and on until he uncovered the harsh truth of things. Of course, it hadn't been so difficult this time. He wondered who his source was. It had to be someone inside the organization, someone who resented Simon and wanted to see him brought down.

Or possibly, he acknowledged with a lifting of his glass and a small sip of the scotch, someone who wanted to see John Ross brought down as well.

CHAPTER 17

Nest Freemark sprang aside at the sound of Ariel's warning, skidding headfirst across a slick of mud and dead needles as the dark shape hurtled past. In a rain-streaked blur she watched it catapult into Boot and Audrey. The sylvan was back astride the owl, and the owl was lifting away into the night. Both disappeared in a shower of blood and feathers and bits of wood, there one second and gone the next. The dark shape went right through them, bearing them away like a strong wind, the force of its momentum carrying it back into the night.

"Demon!" Ariel was screaming as she fled. "Demon! Demon!"

Nest scrambled to her feet and began to run after the tatterdemalion. She had no idea where she was going, only that she had to get away. She tore down the dirt path that paralleled the cliffs, tennis shoes slipping and sliding on the muddied track. She was nearly blind in the darkness and rain, and she was riddled with fear. Boot and Audrey were gone, dead in one terrible second, and the image of them exploding apart burned in the air before her as she ran, raw and terrible.

"Faster, Nest!" Ariel cried frantically.

Nest could hear the demon behind her, pursuing them. She could hear the wet sound of its paws on the muddy path over the steady thrum of the rain. What sort of creature had it made itself into? She had only caught a glimpse, and she had never seen anything like it before. Her heart pounded in her chest, and her breath was fiery in her throat. She was deep in the woods and there was nowhere to hide, but if she didn't reach a place of safety in the next few seconds, the demon would have her.

Her eyes flicked left and right, and a new well of fear opened within. Running with her were dozens of feeders, come out of nowhere in the rainy gloom, faceless squat shapes keeping pace as they darted through the trees, eyes filled with excitement and anticipation.

She glanced over her shoulder and saw the demon closing fast, its black shape stretched out low to the ground and hurtling forward. A surge of adrenaline propelled her ahead, and for a few seconds she managed to increase her speed enough to put a little more distance between them. But then the beast was closing on her again, and she could see the gleam of its teeth and eyes in the misty gloom.

Ahead and to her left, there were only more trees and darkness. To her right, beyond the low rail fence, the cliff fell away into a void. There were lights from houses and streets, but they were distant pinpricks through the woods, still far, far away.

She knew she was not going to escape. She was fit and strong; she was a world-class distance runner. But the thing pursuing her was too much for any human. She faltered slightly, preparing to turn and fight. The demon burst out of the night, a silent black predator, gathering itself to strike. She saw it clearly, revealed for just an instant in a patch of gray light, some sort of monstrous hyena, all neck and blunt muzzle, with huge jaws and rows of teeth. She swerved through the trees and out again, scattering feeders everywhere, trying to throw the demon off, but it was quick and agile, and it followed her easily.

"Nest, no!" she heard Ariel scream a final time, turning.

The demon caught up to her at a wide spot where the trail took a slow bend to the left, away from the cliff. She looked back and saw that it was right on top of her. She watched it gather itself, preparing to bear her struggling and helpless to the ground. Her fear enveloped her like a death shroud, choking off her breath, suffocating her. Something wild and fierce blossomed inside her in response, and for just an instant she thought it was her magic, trying to break free. But her mind was frozen by the demon's closeness, by the gleam of its yellow eyes and the certainty of what was going to happen next, and she could not find a way to help it.

Feeders streamed through the trees, leaping wildly, shadows with eyes, gathered for the kill.

But as the demon lunged for Nest, rising up against the night, Ariel threw herself into its path, a white blur against the dark, and collapsed around its head like a child's bedsheet. Demon and tatterdemalion went down in a tangled heap, rolling over and over on the muddied earth. Nest backed away, staring in horror at the thrashing dark knot. In seconds all that remained of Ariel was a silken white shroud that clung tenaciously to the momentarily blinded demon.

Then even that was gone, and the demon was clawing its way back to its feet, snarling in fury.

Nest, momentarily transfixed by the struggle taking place before her, wheeled to flee once more. But she had lost her sense of direction entirely, forgetting the bend in the trail and the low rail fence at her back. She took one quick stride and toppled right over the fence. She was up again instantly, thrashing at the heavy brush, trying to escape its clinging embrace. Then the ground disappeared beneath her feet, and she was falling head over heels down a rain-slicked slope. She groped futilely for something to hang on to, skidding and sliding along slick bare earth and through long grass, careening off bushes and exposed tree roots, the darkness whirling about her in a kaleidoscope of distant lights and falling rain. Her stomach lurched with each sudden change of direction, and she tucked in her arms and legs and covered her head with her hands, waiting for something to slow her.

When she hit the base of the precipice, the breath was knocked from her lungs and her head was left spinning. She lay where she was for an instant, listening to the sound of the rain. Then she was back on her feet and running, dazed and battered, but otherwise unhurt. A wide, grassy embankment stretched along the base of the cliffs, fronting the dark, choppy waters of Puget Sound, and a concrete path paralleled the water's edge. She wheeled left down the path, heading for the lights of the residences that lay closest.

Already she could hear the sounds of the demon's pursuit. It was coming down the cliff face after her, scrambling through the brush and grasses, branches and roots snapping as it tore through them. She gritted her teeth against her fear and rage. Feeders ran at her side, an unshakable presence. Her windbreaker was muddied and torn, pieces of it flapping wildly against her body. If she could reach the houses outside the park, she would have a chance. Her lungs burned as she forced herself to run faster. Again she thought to turn and face the thing that chased her, to summon up the magic that had protected her so often before. But she had no way of knowing if she still had the use of it, and no time to find out.

Her feet splashed loudly through the rain that puddled on the concrete, spraying surface water everywhere. Her clothing was soaked through, and her curly hair was plastered to her head. She could no longer see or hear the demon, but she knew it was back there. She thought of Ariel, and tears filled her eyes. Dead because of her. All of them—Boot, Audrey, and Ariel—dead because of her. She ran faster, sweeping past grassy picnic areas with tables and iron cookers, swing sets and benches, and a small pavilion with a wooden roof and a concrete floor. To her right, the sound lapped against the shoreline, driven by the wind. The world about her was a vast, empty, rain-swept void.

She wished desperately that Wraith was there. Wraith would protect her. Wraith would be a match for the demon. A part of her, deep inside, shrieked defiantly that he *was* still there and would come if she summoned him. She almost thought to do so, to wheel back and call for him, to bring him to her side once more. But Wraith was gone, disappeared over a year ago, and there was no reason to think he would come to her now, after so long.

She cast aside the last of her futile wishes for what couldn't be, and concentrated on gaining the safety of the city streets. She could see the residences clearly now, bulky shapes hunkered down against the misty gloom, lights a blurry yellow through rain-streaked windows. She could see cars moving on the street further south, distant still, but recognizable.

She risked a quick glance over her shoulder. In the darkness, beyond the feeders trailing after her, the demon's larger shape was visible.

The concrete path rose ahead of her, leading out of the park's lower regions. She swept up the rise without slowing, ignoring the hot, raw feeling in her lungs and the cramping in her stomach. She was not going to give up. She was not going to die. She gained the summit of the rise, broke through the empty parking lot, and was on the street.

She crossed in a gust of wind and rain that blew sideways at her, making for the houses on the other side. The park was a black mass behind her, an impenetrable wall of darkness, the jagged tips of the ancient trees piercing the skyline. The street was momentarily empty of cars; she would find no help there. The feeders stayed with her, keeping pace easily, yellow eyes gleaming in the night. She ignored them, concentrating on the houses ahead. Several were dark or poorly lit, and there was no sign of life. She passed them by. *Please,* she prayed silently, *let someone be home!* Out of the corner of her eye, she saw movement behind her at the head of the pathway leading out of the park. The demon was coming.

There was a brightly lit picture window in a brick cottage that lay ahead, and she could see a man reading a newspaper in an easy chair. She crossed the lawn in a rush, leaped onto the cement steps, and tried to wrench open the screen door. It was locked. She pounded on it wildly, looking over her shoulder as she did. The demon was in the middle of the street, its massive body stretched out as it ran, coming straight for her. All around her the feeders leaped and scrambled anxiously. She hissed at them and pounded on the door again.

The heavy inner door opened and the man stood there, staring at her through the screen with a mix of irritation and surprise that quickly changed to shock when he got a better look.

"Please, let me in," she begged, trying to keep her voice even, to keep the fear out of it. She could see herself reflected in his glasses, disheveled, muddied, scraped, and bruised.

"Good Lord, young lady!" he exclaimed, wide-eyed. He was an older man, white-haired and slightly stooped. He peered at her doubtfully. "What happened to you?"

He was still talking to her through the screen. She felt her desperation threaten to overwhelm her, felt the demon's breath on her neck, its claws and teeth on her body. "An accident!" she gasped. "I need to call for help! Please!"

He unfastened the latch now, finally, and the moment he began to crack the door, she wrenched it open and rushed inside, ignoring his startled surprise as she pushed him aside, slamming the screen door, then the inner door, and locking them both.

The man stared at her. "Young lady, what in the world . . ."

"There's something chasing me . . ." she began.

The demon slammed into the screen door from the other side with such force that it tore it off entirely. Then it hammered into the inner door, once, twice, and the hinges began to loosen.

"What in God's name?" gasped the older man as he stumbled backward in fright.

"Get out of here!" she shouted, racing past him for the back of the house. "Call the police!"

The demon was hammering into the door, pounding at it in fury. It meant to have her, and it didn't care what stood in its way. She raced down a hall into a kitchen, where an older woman stood washing dishes at a sink. The woman looked up in surprise, blinked, and stared at her with the same look of shock as the man.

"Get out of the house now!" Nest screamed at her.

Sorry, sorry, sorry! she apologized silently as she raced out the back door into the night.

Rain and wind beat at her. The storm was growing worse. She glanced left and right into the darkness, then broke across the backyard, heading north once more. If she could reach the service station the taxi driver had told her about, she could call for help there. Porch lights came on in a few of the houses around her. She could no longer hear the sound of the demon trying to break down the door of the house she had abandoned. That meant it knew she was gone and was coming for her again.

She crossed through several backyards before coming to a fence. She would have to climb it or go back out front. Rain and sweat streaked her forehead and spilled into her eyes. Her strength was ebbing. She wheeled left along the fence and raced for the street once more.

When she broke into the open, she was alone but for one or two feeders; the rest had fallen away. There was no sign of the demon. She felt a moment of elation, then saw a flicker of movement behind her. In a panic, she raced toward the street. A car swept out of the darkness, its tires throwing up spray, and she ran for it, waving her arms and yelling. But the car never slowed, and a moment later she was alone again. In the fading sweep of the car's headlights, she caught a momentary glimpse of the demon charging toward her. She turned back to the houses, searching. There was a two-story with a glassed-in porch and lights in almost every window. She made for that one. Cars lined the curbing in front. A party was in progress. She felt a hot rush of satisfaction. This time she would find the help she needed.

She raced up the steps and yanked on the handle of the porch door. The door opened easily, and she was inside in the blink of an eye. She slammed the door behind her, threw the lock, rushed to the front door, and began to pound. Inside, she could hear the sound of laughter and music. She pounded harder.

The door opened. A young woman dressed in a sweater and jeans stood there, holding a drink in her hand and staring in disbelief.

"Please let me in!" Nest began once more. "There's someone after me, and I need to call—"

A storm window flew apart in an explosion of jagged shards as the demon crashed onto the porch and slammed into the front wall of the house, snarling and snapping at the air with its massive jaws and hooked teeth. The young woman screamed in terror, and Nest shoved her back inside the house, followed her in, slammed the door shut, and threw the bolt lock. The young woman went down in a heap and lay there, sobbing. They were in a hallway leading to a series of rooms, the nearest of which was filled with other young people who stared out at them in surprise. Laughter and light conversation gave way to exclamations. Nest went past them down the hall in a rush. Behind her, the demon was tearing at the door, stripping away the wooden facade as if it were cardboard.

Party-goers spilled out into the entry to help the young woman back to her feet, some calling after Nest, some staring wide-eyed toward the sounds coming from outside the door. "Don't open it!" Nest shouted back at them. Not that anyone was that stupid, she thought in a sudden moment of giddiness.

At the end of the hallway lay the kitchen. Inside, she found a phone and dialed 911. Maybe the old couple down the block had already done so, but maybe not. She told the operator there was a forcible entry in progress at a house just north of Lincoln Park. She said there was screaming. She gave the phone number of the house and then hung up. That ought to bring someone.

There was a new sound of glass breaking, this time from somewhere at the side of the house. The demon was trying to get in another way. She leaned against the kitchen counter, listening to the sounds, staring into space. If she remained where she was, she was risking the safety of the people in the house. If she went out again, she was risking her own safety. She closed her eyes and tried to think. She was so tired. But she was alive, too, and that was more than she could say about Boot and Audrey and Ariel. She pushed away from the counter and went through a laundry room to a back door. The demon was still trying to break in from the other side of the house. She could hear the party-goers shouting and screaming, crowding down the hallway, trying to get away from the intruder. She could hear the phone begin to ring.

She yanked open the door and fled once more into the night.

She was running through a tall hedge into a neighbor's backyard when she heard the boom of a gun. Maybe the shooter would get lucky. You couldn't kill a demon with a gun, but you could destroy its current guise and force it to take time to reform. If that happened, it would be done chasing after her.

But she knew she couldn't count on that. She couldn't count on anything except that the demon would keep coming. She crossed through several more backyards, then caught sight of something that might save her. A transit bus was just pulling to a stop down the street. She broke from between the houses and raced for it, yelling at the top of her lungs, waving her arms wildly. She saw the bus driver turn and look at her. The look was a familiar one by now. She didn't care. She raced around the front of the bus and through the open door.

"Hey, what's going on?" the driver demanded as she dug frantically into her pockets for some change.

"Just close the door and start driving," she ordered, glancing quickly over her shoulder.

Whatever he saw on her face convinced him not to argue. He closed the doors and put the bus in gear. The bus swung away from the curb and into the street, rain beating against its wide front windows.

She had just begun to make her way down the aisle when something heavy crashed into the doors, causing the metal to buckle and the glass to splinter. There were only three other passengers on the bus, and all three froze, eyes bright with shock and fear. The driver cursed and stepped on the gas. Nest wheeled back toward the damaged doors, hanging on the metal bar of a seat back for support, searching the darkness beyond.

A huge, wolfish shadow was running next to the bus, eyes gleaming brightly in the night.

Then a police car crested the hill in front of them, coming fast, lights flashing. It swept past without slowing, searchlight cutting through the rainy dark.

The shadow disappeared.

Nest exhaled slowly and slipped into the seat beside her, heart pounding in her chest. When she looked down at her hands, she saw that they were shaking.

The ride back into the city was a blur. Once she determined that the bus was going in the right direction, she quit paying attention. People got on and off, but she didn't look at their faces. She stared out the window into the darkness, thinking.

It took a long time for the fear to subside, and when it did she was filled with cold rage. Three lives had been snuffed out quicker than a candle's flame, and no one but she even knew about it and no one but she cared. Boot, Audrey, and Ariel—a sylvan, an owl, and a tatterdemalion. Creatures of the forest, of magic and imagination. Humans didn't even know they existed. What difference did their loss make to anything? The unfairness of it burned inside her. She struggled for a time with the possibility that she was to blame for what had happened, that she had brought the demon down on them. But there was no reason to believe this was so, and her guilt stemmed mostly from the fact they were dead and she was alive. But barely alive, she kept reminding herself. Alive, because she had been fortunate enough to step off a cliff and survive the fall. Alive, because she had evaded a handful of serious attempts by a monster to rip her to shreds.

She blinked in the sudden glare of a passing truck's headlights. How had the demon found out about her meeting? There was a question that screamed for an answer. She stared harder at the darkness and tried to reason it through. The demon might have followed her. But to do so, it must have been following her all day. Was that possible? Could it have done so without Ariel or Two Bears knowing? Without her feeling something, a twinge of warning initiated by her dormant magic? Maybe. The magic wasn't so dependable anymore. But if the demon hadn't been following her, then it must have intercepted her message to John Ross. It must have been listening in when she called. Or learned something from Stefanie Winslow or from John himself.

She gritted her teeth at the idea that she had been caught so unaware, so vulnerable, and that she had run—*run!*—rather than stand and fight. She hated what had happened, and she was not pleased with how she had behaved. It didn't matter that she could explain it away by telling herself what she had done had kept her alive and that she had reacted on instinct. She had fled and not stood her ground, while three other lives had been taken, and no amount of rationalization could change how that made her feel.

As she rode through the darkness and the rain, struggling with the rush of emotions churning inside, she was reminded of how she had felt at Cass Minter's funeral. She had stood there during the graveside services on a beautiful, sun-filled day trying to make herself believe that her best and oldest friend was gone. It hadn't seemed possible. Not Cass, who was only eighteen and had lived so little of her life. Nest had stood there and tried to will her friend alive again, furious at having had her taken away so unexpectedly and abruptly and pointlessly. She had stood in a rage as the minister read from his Bible in a soft, comforting voice, trying in vain to make sense of the arbitrary nature of one young woman's life and death.

She felt like that now, thinking back on the events in Lincoln Park. She had been in Seattle for less than twenty-four hours. She had come with simple expectations and a single purpose to fulfill. But it had all gotten much more complicated than anything she might have imagined. It had become rife with madness.

She watched the lights and the buildings of the downtown rise out of the darkness, sitting sodden, muddied, and exhausted in her seat. West Seattle fell away behind her, disappearing into the dark, and her rage faded with her fear, and both were replaced by an immense sadness. She began to cry. She cried softly, soundlessly, and no one around her appeared to notice. She wanted to go home again. She wanted none of this ever to have happened. A huge, empty well opened inside, echoing with the sounds of voices she would never hear again. Some came from Lincoln Park and the present. Some came from Hopewell and the past. She felt abandoned and alone. She could not find a center for the downward spiral in which she was caught.

She left the bus at a downtown stop and walked through the mostly empty streets of the city to her hotel. She wondered vaguely if the demon might be tracking her still, but she no longer cared. She almost hoped it was, that it would come for her again and she would have another chance to face it. It was a perverse wish, unreasonable and foolish. Yet it made her feel better. It gave her renewed strength. It told her she was still whole.

But no one approached her or even tried to speak to her. She reached the hotel and went into the lobby and up to her room, locking the door behind her, throwing the deadbolt and fastening the chain. She stripped off her ruined clothes, showered, and climbed into bed.

There, in the warm enfolding dark, just before she fell asleep, with images of Ariel and Boot and Audrey spinning in a wash of streetlight shining brightly through her bedroom window, she made herself a promise that she would see this matter through to the end.

Wednesday, October 31

Chapter 18

When Stefanie Winslow woke him at midnight, John Ross was so deeply asleep that for a few seconds he didn't know where he was. The bedside clock flashed the time at him, so he knew that much, but his brain was fuzzy and muddled and he could not seem to focus.

"John, wake up!"

He blinked and tried to answer, but his mouth was filled with cotton, his tongue was glued to the roof of his mouth, and there was a buzzing in his ears. He blinked in response to her words, recognizing her voice, hearing the urgency in it. She was shaking him, and the room swam as he tried to push himself up on one elbow.

He felt as if he were drugged.

"John, there's something wrong!"

His memory returned through a haze of confusion and sluggishness. He was in his bedroom—their bedroom. He had come back there after his lunch with Nest, to think things over, to be alone. He had thought about her warning, about the possibility of a demon's presence, about the danger that might pose to him. The afternoon had passed away into evening, the weather outside slowly deteriorating, sunshine fading to clouds as the rain moved in. Stef had come in from work, stopping off to deliver a message from Nest and to see how he was. She had made him pasta and tea and gone out again. That was the last he remembered.

He blinked anew, struggling with his blurred vision in the darkness, with the refusal of his body to respond to the commands from his brain. Stefanie bent over him, trying to pull him upright.

The message from Nest . . .

That she was going to West Seattle for a meeting with a sylvan. That the sylvan had seen the demon she was looking for. That this was her chance to prove to him her warning was valid. Her words were coded, but unmistakable. Stef had asked him if he knew what they meant, and he had, but couldn't tell her, so he had been forced to concoct an explanation.

The message had been very upsetting. He didn't like the idea of Nest wandering around the city looking for a demon. If there actually was one and it found out what she was doing, it would try to stop her. She was resourceful and her magic gave her a measure of protection against creatures of the Void, but she was no match for a demon.

But when he had started to go after her, Stef had quickly intervened. She had felt his forehead and advised him he had a fever. When he insisted he was going anyway, she had insisted with equal fervor that at least he would have something to eat first, and she had made him the pasta. Then she had left for her press conference with Simon, promising to be home soon, and he had moved to the sofa to finish his tea, closed his eyes for just a moment, and . . .

And woken now.

Except that he had a vague memory of Simon Lawrence being there, too, coming in through the door right after Stef had gone, saying something . . . he couldn't remember . . .

He rubbed his eyes angrily and forced his body into a sitting position on the side of the bed, Stef helping to guide him into position.

"John, damn it, you have to wake up!" she hissed almost angrily, shaking him.

His head drooped, heavy and unresponsive. What in the world was wrong with him?

He slept like this often these days, ever since the dreams had stopped and he had ceased to be a Knight of the Word. He had given up his charge and his responsibilities and his search, and the dreams had faded and sleep had returned. But his sleep had turned hard and quick; it frequently felt as if he were awake again almost immediately. There was no sense of having rested, of slumbering as he once had. He was gone and then he was back again, but there had been no journey. Stef marveled at the soundness of his sleep, commenting more than once on how peaceful he seemed, how deeply at rest. But he felt no peace or rest on waking, and save for the few times he had dreamed of the old man and the burning of the city, he had no memory of having slept at all.

"What's wrong?" he managed to ask finally, his head lifting.

She bent close, a black shape in the room's darkness. Streetlight silhouetted her against the curtained window. "I think there's a fire at Fresh Start."

His mind was still clouded, and her words rolled through its jumbled landscape like thick syrup. "A fire?"

"Will you just get up!" she shouted in frustration. "I don't want to call it in unless I'm sure! I called over to the night manager and no one answered! John, I need you!"

He lurched to his feet, an effort that left him dizzy and weak. It was as if all the strength had been drained from his body. He was like a child. She helped him over to the window, and he peered out into the rainy darkness.

"There," she said, pointing, "at the back of the building, in the basement windows."

Slowly his vision focused on the dark, squarish bulk of the shelter. At first he didn't see anything. Then he caught a flicker of something bright and angry against a pane of glass, low, at ground level. He waited a moment, saw it again. Flames.

He braced himself on the windowsill and tried to shake the cobwebs from his mind. "Call 911. Tell them to get here right away." He squinted against the gloom, peering down the empty streets of Pioneer Square. "Why hasn't the fire alarm gone off?"

She was on the phone behind him, lost in the dark. "That's what I wondered. That's why I didn't call it in right away. You'd think if there was a fire, the alarm . . . Hello? This is Stefanie Winslow at 2701 Second Avenue. I want to report a fire at Fresh Start. Yes, I can see it from where I'm standing . . ."

She went on, giving her report to the dispatcher. John Ross moved away from the window to find his clothes. He tried a light switch and couldn't get it to work, gave up, and dressed in the dark. He was still weak, still not functioning as he should, but the rush of adrenaline he had experienced on realizing what was happening had given him a start on his recovery. He pulled on jeans, shirt, and walking shoes, not bothering with socks or underwear, anxious to get moving. There should be someone on duty at the center. Whoever it was should have detected the smoke—should have answered the phone, too, when Stef called over to see what was wrong.

She was hanging up the phone behind him and heading for the door. "I've got to get over there, John!" she called back to him as she swept out into the living room.

"Stef, wait!"

"Catch up to me as quick as you can! I'll wake as many people as I can find and try to get them out!"

The door slammed behind her. Cursing softly, he finished tying the laces of his shoes, stumbled through the darkness to the front closet, pulled on his all-weather coat, grabbed the black walking stick, and followed her out.

He didn't waste time on the elevator, which was notoriously slow, heading instead for the stairs, taking them as quickly as he could manage with his bad leg, hearing her footsteps fading ahead of him followed by the closing of the stairway door below. His mind was clearer now, and his body was beginning to come around as well. He limped down the stairs in a swift shamble, using the walking stick and the railing for support, and he was into the entryway and out the front door in moments.

Rain beat down in torrents, and the streetlights were murky and diffuse in the storm-swept gloom. Second Avenue was deserted and eerily quiet. Where were the fire engines? He left the sidewalk and crossed through the downpour, head lowered against gusts of wind that blew the rain into his face with such force that he could barely make out where he was going.

Ahead, he watched Stefanie's dark figure pause at the front door of the shelter, pounding at it, then fumbling with her keys to release the lock. The building was dark, save for a glimmer of night-lights in the upper dormitories and front lobby. Inside, everything was silent and still.

Then the front door was open and Stef was inside, disappearing into the gloom. As he drew nearer, he saw rolling gray smoke leaking from the basement windows and the front entry, escaping the building to mix with the mist and rain outside. His chest tightened with fear. In an old building like this, a fire would spread quickly. He shouted after Stefanie, trying to warn her, but his words were blown away on the wind.

He reached the front door, still open from Stef's entry, and rushed inside. The interior was murky with smoke, and he could barely see well enough to make his way across the lobby to the hallway and the offices beyond. The stairway door to the upper floors was open, and he could hear shouts and cries from above. He coughed violently, covered his mouth with his wet sleeve, and tried to find some sign of the night manager. He couldn't remember who had the duty this week, but whoever it was, was nowhere to be found. He searched the length of the hallway and all the offices without success.

The basement door was closed. Smoke leaked from its seams, and it was hot to the touch. He ignored his instincts and wrenched it open. Clouds of smoke billowed forth, borne on a wave of searing heat. He shouted down the stairs, but there was no response. He started down, but the heat and smoke drove him back. He could see the flames spreading along the walls, climbing to the higher floors. Wooden tables, filing bins and cabinets, records and charts, and even the stairway were burning.

He slammed the door shut again, backing away.

There were footsteps on the stairway behind him, the women and children coming down from the upper floors. He limped over to meet them so that he could direct them to the front door. They appeared out of the gloom, dim shapes against the haze of smoke. They stumbled down in ones and twos, coughing and crying and cursing in equal measure, the children clinging to their mothers, the mothers clinging back, the women without children helping both, the whole bunch wrapped in robes and coats and even sheets. The smoke was growing thicker and the heat increasing. He shouted at them to hurry, urging them on. He tried to count heads, to determine how many had come out so he could know how many were still inside. But he couldn't remember the number in residence, and he didn't know how many might have been admitted that afternoon after he left. Twenty-one, twenty-two, twenty-three—they were filing past him in larger groups now, bumping up against one another in their haste to get out. Thirty-five, thirty-six. There had to be at least ninety, probably more like a hundred.

He peered through the haze, feeling the heat grow about him, seeing red flickers from down the hallway at the back of the building. The fire was climbing through the air vents.

There was still no sign of Stef.

Sirens screamed up to the front doorway, and firefighters clad in flame-retardant gear rushed inside in a knot. Ross was down on one knee now, coughing violently, eyes burning with the smoke, head spinning. They reached out for him and pulled him to his feet. He was too weak to resist, barely able to keep hold of his staff.

Hoses were being dragged through the doorway, and he could hear the sound of glass being broken.

"Who else is in here?" he heard someone ask.

He shook his head. "More women and children . . . upstairs. Stef is up there . . . helping them." He retched violently and doubled over. "A night manager . . . somewhere."

They hauled him outside into the cool, rainy night, propped him against the side of an ambulance, and gave him oxygen. He gulped it down greedily, his eyes gradually beginning to clear, his sight to return. Knots of women and children huddled all around him, shivering in the cold night air.

His gaze settled on Fresh Start. Flames were climbing the exterior of the walls, shooting out of the second- and third-story windows.

Stef!

He lurched to his feet and tried to push his way back inside, but hands closed tightly on his arms and shoulders and pulled him back again. "You can't do that, sir," a voice informed him quickly. "Get back now, please."

Windows exploded, showering the street with shards of glass. "But she's still in there!" he gasped frantically, trying to make them understand, fighting to break free.

More women and children were being hustled out, escorted by firefighters. A hook and ladder truck had rolled into position, and the extension was being run up toward the roof. Police cars had arrived to protect the firefighters and control traffic, and there were flashing lights everywhere. At the fringe of the action, a crowd was gathering to watch from behind cordoned lines. The mix of rain and hydrant water had turned the streets to rivers.

Still struggling, Ross was moved back to the makeshift shelter, overpowered by the combined weight of his protectors. Fear and anger swept through him in a red haze, and he felt himself losing control.

Stef! He had to go back in for Stef!

And then she appeared, stumbling out the smoke-filled doorway of the shelter, a small child clutched in her arms. Firefighters clustered around her, taking charge of the child, moving both of them away from the blaze, the building behind them bright with flames.

Ross broke free of the restraining hands and went to her. She collapsed into his arms, and they sank to the rain-soaked pavement.

"Stef," he murmured in relief, hugging her tightly.

"It's all right, John," she whispered, nodding into his shoulder, firefighters rushing past them in dark knots, hoses trailing after like snakes. "It's all right."

Fresh Start burned for another hour before the fire was extinguished. The blaze did not spread to the nearby buildings, but was contained. The shelter was a total loss. All of the women and children housed in the building were safely evacuated, in large part because of Stef's quick action in getting to them before the blaze spread to the sleeping rooms.

Only the night manager did not escape. His ruined body was found in the basement, lying near the charred filing cabinets and records bins. It took only a short time to make a tentative identification. It was a man, not a woman, and Ray Hapgood had been on duty and was unaccounted for.

It was three in the morning when Ross and Stef reentered their apartment and closed the door softly behind them. They stood holding each other in the darkness for a long time, breathing into each other's shoulders in the silence, saying nothing. Ross could not stop thinking about Ray.

"How could this have happened?" he whispered finally, his voice still tight with shock.

Stef shook her head and said nothing.

"What was Ray doing there?" he pressed, lifting his head away from her shoulder to look at her. "It wasn't his duty. He was supposed to go out to his sister's in Kent. He told me so."

Her fingers tightened on his arms. "Let it go, John."

A stubborn determination infused him. "I don't want to let it go. Who had the duty tonight? Who?"

She lifted her head slightly and he could see the angry welts and bruises on her face. "Simon makes up the list, John. Ask him."

"I'm asking you. Who had the duty?"

She blinked back the tears that suddenly filled her eyes. "You did. But when you went home sick, Ray offered to fill in."

He stared at her in disbelief. He had the duty? He couldn't remember it. Why hadn't he known? Even before he was sick, why hadn't he known? It should have been posted. It must have been. He was certain he had looked at the list. So why didn't he remember seeing his name?

He felt worn and defeated. He stood in the dark holding Stef and looking into her eyes, and for the first time in a long time he was uncertain about everything. "Did you see my name?"

"John . . ."

"Did you, Stef?"

She nodded. "Yes." She touched his face. "This isn't your fault, John. Just because you weren't there and Ray was doesn't mean it's your fault."

He nodded because that was what she expected him to do, but he was thinking that it felt like it was his fault, just as it had felt like it was his fault at San Sobel. Any failure of responsibility or neglect of duty belonged to him, and nothing could change that. He closed his eyes against what he was feeling. Ray Hapgood had been his friend, his good friend, and he had let him die.

"John, listen to me." Stef was speaking again, her face close to his, her body pressing against him in the darkness. "I don't know why this happened. I don't know how it happened. No one does. Not yet. So don't go jumping to conclusions. Don't be shouldering the blame until you know the facts. I'm sorry Ray is dead. But you didn't kill him. And if it had to be someone, I would rather it was him than you."

He opened his eyes, surprised by her vehemence. "Stef."

She shook her head emphatically. "I'm sorry, but that's how I feel."

She kissed him hard, and he kissed her back and held her tightly against him. "I just can't believe he's gone," he whispered, his hand stroking her slender back.

"I know."

They held each other for a long moment, and then she led him to the bedroom. They undressed in the dark and crawled into the bed and held each other again in the cool of the sheets. The streets beyond their window were silent and empty. All the fire trucks, police cars, ambulances, and bystanders were gone. The rain had faded away, and the air was damp and cold in the wake of its passing. Ross hugged Stef's smooth body against his own and listened to the soft, velvet sound of her breathing.

"I could have lost you tonight," he whispered.

She nodded. "But you didn't."

"I was scared I had." He took a long, slow breath and let it out. "When you were inside, bringing out the last of those children, and I saw the flames climbing the walls, I thought for sure I had."

"No, John," she whispered, kissing him gently, over and over, "you won't lose me ever. I promise. No matter what, you won't lose me."

The dream comes swiftly, a familiar acquaintance he wishes now he had never made. He stands once more on the hillside south of Seattle, watching as the city burns, as the hordes of the Void swarm through the collapsed defenses and begin their ritual of killing and destruction. He sees the battle taking place on the high bridge where a last, futile defense has been mounted. He sees the steel and glass towers swallowed in flames. He sees the bright waters of the bay and sound turn red in the reflected glare.

He finds he is cold and indifferent to what he witnesses. He is detached in a way he cannot explain, but seems perfectly normal in his dream, as if he has been this way a long time. He is himself and at the same time he is someone else entirely. He pauses to examine this phenomenon and decides he has changed dramatically from when he was a Knight of the Word. He is a Knight no longer, but he remembers when he was. Oddly, his memories are tinged with a wistfulness he can't quite escape.

Before him, Seattle burns. By nightfall, it will have ceased to exist. Like his old life. Like the person he once was.

There are people huddled about him, and they glance at him fearfully when they think he is not looking. They are right to fear him. He holds over them the power of life and death. They are his captives. They are his to do with as he chooses, and they are anxious to discover what he has planned for them. The exercise of such power is a curious feeling because it both attracts and repels him. He wonders in a vague sort of way how he got to this point in his life.

From the long, dark span of the high bridge, bodies tumble into an abyss of smoke and fire like rag dolls. Their screams cannot be heard.

The old man approaches, as he has approached each time in the dream, and points his bony finger at Ross and whispers in his hoarse, ruined voice, I know you.

Get away from me, Ross orders in disgust and dismay, not wanting to hear the words he will speak.

I know you, the old man repeats, undeterred, the bright light of his madness shining in his strange, milky eyes. You are the one who killed him. I was there.

Ross stands his ground because he cannot afford to turn away. His captives are watching, listening, waiting for his response. They will measure his strength accordingly. The old man sways as if he were a reed caught in a stiff wind, stick-thin and ragged, his mind unbalanced, his laughter filled with echoes of his shattered life.

Get away from me, Ross says once more.

The Wizard of Oz! You killed him! I remember your face! I saw you! There, in the glass palace, in the shadow of the Tin Woodman, in the Emerald City, on All Hallows' Eve! You killed the Wizard of Oz! You killed him! You!

The words fade and die, and the old man begins to cry softly. Oh, God, it was the end of everything!

Ross shakes his head. It is a familiar litany by now. He has heard it before, and he turns away in curt dismissal. It is all in the past, and the past no longer matters to him.

But the old man presses closer, insistent. I saw you. I watched you do it. I could not understand. He was your friend. There was no reason!

There was a reason, he thinks to himself, though he cannot remember it now.

But, the young woman! The old man is on his knees, his head hanging doglike between his slumped shoulders. What reason did you have for killing her?

Ross starts, shaken now. What young woman?

Couldn't you have spared her? She was just trying to help. She seemed to know you . . .

Ross screams in fury and shoves the old man away. The old man tumbles backward into the mud, gasping in shock. Shut up! Ross screams at him, furious, dismayed, because now he remembers this, as well, another part of the past he had thought buried, a truth he had left behind in the debris of his conversion . . .

Shut up, shut up, shut up!

The old man tries to crawl away, but he has crossed a line he should not have, and Ross cannot forgive him his trespass. He strides to where the old man cringes, already anticipating the punishment he will deliver, and he lifts the heavy black staff and brings it down like a hammer . . .

Ross jerked upright in the darkness of his bedroom, eyes snapping open, body rigid, awash in terror. His breath came in quick, ragged gulps, and he could hear the pounding of his heart in his ears. Stef lay sleeping next to him, unaware of his torment. The bedside clock read five-thirty. He could hear a soft patter against the window glass. Outside, it was raining again.

He held himself motionless beneath the sheet, staring at nothing, remembering. The dream had been real. The memories were his. He squeezed his eyes shut in dismay. He knew who the young woman was. He knew who it must be.

And for the first time since the dream had come to him, he was afraid it might really happen.

Chapter 19

When the phone rang, Nest was buried beneath her blankets where it was pitch-black, and she was certain it was still the middle of the night. She let the phone ring a few times, her mind and body warm and lazy with sleep. Then memories of last night's horror at Lincoln Park flooded through her, and she crawled from under the covers into shockingly bright daylight.

Squinting uncertainly against the glare, she picked up the phone. "Hello?"

"Nest, it's me. Are you all right?"

John Ross. She recognized his voice. But what an odd question. Unless he knew what had happened to her in the park, of course, but she didn't know how he could. She hadn't spoken to anyone afterward. She'd come back and fallen asleep almost immediately.

"I'm fine," she answered, her mouth and throat dry and cottony. What time was it? She glanced at the bedside clock. It was almost noon. She had forgotten to set the alarm and slept more than ten hours.

"Did I wake you?" he asked quickly. "I'm sorry if I did, but we have to talk."

She nodded into the phone. "It's okay. I didn't mean to sleep this late." She could feel the pain begin even as she spoke the words. Her entire body was throbbing, an ache building steadily from a low whine to a sharp scream. "Where are you?"

"Downstairs, in the lobby." He paused. "I called earlier and there was no answer. I was afraid something had happened to you, so I decided to come over. Can you come down?"

She took a deep breath, still working at waking up. "In about a half hour. Can you wait?"

"Yes." He hesitated a long time. "I've been thinking. Maybe you were right about some of the things we talked about. Maybe I was wrong."

She blinked in surprise. "I'll be down as quick as I can."

She returned the receiver to its cradle and rolled onto her back. Whatever had happened to him must have been every bit as significant as what had happened to her. She didn't know for sure that he was ready to concede the point, but it sounded as if he might be. She stared at the sunlight pooling on the floor in a golden rectangle in front of the tall window. Not only had she forgotten to set the alarm, she hadn't even bothered to close the drapes. She looked out at the sliver of blue sky visible through the walls of the surrounding buildings. Last night's storm had given way to better weather, it seemed.

She rolled slowly out of the big bed, her joints and muscles groaning in protest. Every part of her body ached from last night's encounter, and when she looked down at herself, she found bruises the size of Frisbees on her ribs and thighs, and scratches on her hands and arms that were caked with dried blood. She could hardly wait to see what her face looked like. She glanced at the blood-streaked sheets and pillow cases and grimaced. She was grateful she wouldn't have to explain all this to the day maids when they came around to clean up.

She went into the bathroom and showered. She was reminded by the heap of damp towels and washcloths that she had showered just last night, but she needed to perform the ritual again to prepare for her encounter with John Ross. Last night seemed far away, and the deaths of Ariel, Boot, and Audrey more distant in time than they actually were. At first, as she stood beneath the stream of hot water, they didn't even seem real to her, as if she had dreamed them, as if they were imagined. But as the details recalled themselves, the images sharpened and solidified, and by the time she was pulling on her jeans and an NU sweatshirt, she was surprised to find she was crying.

She picked up the dirty clothes, stuffed them into a laundry bag, and shoved the bag into her suitcase. Her windbreaker was in tatters, so she dropped it into the wastebasket. She would have to buy a new one before she went outside. She paused, wondering exactly where she was going out to. She had taken the room for two nights, and her plane ticket home was for four-thirty that afternoon. Was she really leaving? Was her part in all of this over? She remembered her promise to herself the night before that she would see things through to the end. She had made that promise for Ariel and Audrey and Boot, but for herself, as well.

She looked around the room. Well, what she would do next depended on what John Ross had to say.

The long, dark, feral shape of the demon chasing her through the park flashed unexpectedly in the back of her mind. She hugged herself and set her jaw determinedly. She was done with running out of fear and a lack of preparation. She would be ready if the demon came at her again. She would find a way to deal with it.

But it was John Ross who needed strengthening. It was Ross the demon was really after, not her. She was just a distraction, an annoyance, a threat to its plans for him. Once Ross was subverted, it wouldn't matter what she did.

She went out the door and rode the elevator down to the lobby. Ross was sitting in a chair across from her when she stepped out, and he came to his feet immediately, leaning heavily on the walking stick.

"Good morning," he said as she came up to him. She saw the shock in his expression as he got a closer look at her face.

"Good morning," she replied. She gave him a wry smile. "The rest of me looks just as bad, in case you're wondering."

He looked distraught. "I was. Did this happen at Lincoln Park? I got your message from Stef."

"I'll tell you everything over breakfast. Or lunch, if you prefer. I'm starving. I haven't eaten since yesterday about this same time. Come on."

She led him into the dining room and asked for a table near the back wall, some distance apart from those that were occupied. They sat down facing each other and accepted menus from the waitress. Nest studied hers momentarily and put it aside.

"You said something's happened," she prodded, studying his face.

He nodded. "Fresh Start burned down last night. Ray Hapgood was killed. They made a positive identification this morning." His voice sounded stiff and uncomfortable. "Ray was working the night shift for me, it turns out. I didn't know this. I didn't even know I was scheduled to work it this week. I don't know why I didn't know, but that's the least of what's bothering me." He shook his head. "Ray was a good friend. I'm having a lot of trouble with that."

"When did this happen?" she asked right away. "What time, I mean?"

"Sometime after midnight. I was asleep. Stef woke me, got me up to take a look out the window, to make sure of what she was seeing. We called 911, then rushed over to wake the people in the building. Stef went all the way to the top floor. She got everyone out but Ray."

Nest barely listened to him as he filled in the details, her mind occupied with working out the logistics of the demon's movements between Lincoln Park and Pioneer Square. It couldn't have been both places at once if the events happened concurrently, but there was an obvious gap in time between when it was chasing her and when it would have set the fire. It would have had to rush right back after she had escaped, but it could have done so.

But why would it bother setting fire to Fresh Start? What reason could it possibly have for doing that?

"I know what you're thinking," he said suddenly. "I've been thinking it, too. But the fire marshall's office says the fire started because of frayed or faulty wiring in the furnace system. It wasn't arson."

"You mean, they don't have any evidence it was arson," she said.

He studied her carefully. "All right. I don't believe it was an accident either. But why would a demon set fire to Fresh Start?"

Same question she was asking herself. She shook her head. The waitress returned to take their order and left again. Nest tried to think the matter through, to discover what it was she had missed, because her instincts told her she had missed something.

"You said on the phone you'd been thinking about what I told you," she said finally. "You said that maybe you were wrong. What made you change your mind? It wasn't just the fire, was it? It must have been something else." She paused. "You said you came over because you thought maybe something had happened to me. Why did you think that?"

He looked decidedly uncomfortable, but there was a hard determination reflected in his eyes. "Do you remember the dream I told you about?"

"I remember you didn't exactly tell me about it at all."

He nodded. "I didn't think it was necessary then. I do now."

She studied him silently, considering what this meant. It couldn't be good. "All right," she said. "Tell me."

Her face was so battered and scraped that it was all he could do to keep his voice steady. He could not help feeling responsible, as if by having had last night's dream he had set in motion the events prophesied for today. He wanted to know what had happened to her, but he knew she would not tell him until she was satisfied he was reconsidering his position on the Lady's warning. He felt a sense of desperation grip him as he began his narrative, a growing fear that he could not accomplish what he had come here to do.

"I've been having this dream for several months," he began. "It's always the same dream, and it's the only dream I ever have. That's never happened to me before. For a long time after I stopped being a Knight of the Word, there were no dreams—not of the sort I used to have, just snippets of the sort everyone has. So when I began having this dream, I was surprised. It was the same dream, but it changed a little every time, showing me a little bit more of what was to happen.

"The dream goes like this. I'm standing on a hill south of Seattle watching the city burn. Like all the old dreams I had as a Knight of the Word, it takes place in the future. The Void has besieged the city and taken it. There is a battle going on. I am not a Knight of the Word in this dream, and I am not involved in the fighting. But I am standing there with captives all around me, and in the dreams of late, I am their captor. I don't understand why this is, but I am.

"Then an old man approaches, and he accuses me of killing someone long ago. He says he was there, that he saw me do it. He says I killed Simon Lawrence, the Wizard of Oz, in Seattle, on Halloween. He says I killed him at the art museum. He doesn't say it exactly that way. He says it happened in the Emerald City, in the glass palace, in the shadow of the Tin Woodman. But I know what he means. The art museum is mostly glass and outside there is a piece of sculpture called *Hammering Man*, a metal giant pounding his hammer on a plate. There's no mistaking what he means. Besides, in the dream I can remember it happening, too. I can't remember the details—maybe because I don't know them. But I know he is telling the truth."

He stopped talking as the waitress arrived with their food. When she departed, he bent forward to continue.

"I didn't learn this all at once. It was revealed in pieces. But I put the pieces together. I knew what the dream was telling me. But I didn't believe it. There is no reason for me to kill Simon Lawrence. I respect and admire him. I want to work for him as long as he'll let me. Why would I ever even consider killing him? When you asked me yesterday about the dream, I didn't see any point in going into it. Whether or not I was a Knight of the Word, I wouldn't let the events of the dream ever happen. To tell you the truth, I was afraid that the dream was a tactic by the Word to bring me back into line, to scare me into changing my mind about serving. I even considered the possibility that it was the work of the Void. It didn't matter. I wasn't going to allow it to affect me."

She was wolfing down her club sandwich as he talked, but her eyes were fixed on him. He glanced down at his own food, which he had not touched. He took a sip of his iced tea.

"Last night, after the fire, I had the dream again." He shook his head. "I don't know why. I never do. The dreams just come. It was the same dream, with the same troubling aspects. But this time there was a new wrinkle. The old man reminded me of something else. He said that I had killed another person at the same time as I killed Simon Lawrence. He said it was a young woman, someone I knew."

She stopped eating and stared at him. "I know," he said quietly. "I felt the same way. The shock woke me. I was awake after that until it was light, thinking. I don't believe it could ever happen. I don't think I would let it." His voice thickened. "But in the dream, it had, so I can't discount the possibility that I might be wrong. I also remember what I was sent to do in Hopewell five years ago. If I was prepared for it to happen once . . ."

He trailed off, his hands knotting before him, his eyes shifting away. "I've gambled as much as I dare to with this business. I don't know if there's a demon out there or not. I don't know if the Void is setting a trap for me. I don't know what's going on. But whatever it is, I don't want you involved. At least not any further than you already are. I want you to get on a plane right now and get out of here. Get far away, so far away you can't possibly be a part of whatever happens next."

She nodded slowly. "And what happens to you?"

He shook his head. "I don't know yet. I have to figure that out. But I can tell you one thing. I'm not so sure anymore I'm not in danger."

She finished the last of her sandwich and wiped her mouth carefully, wincing as she brushed one of the deeper cuts on her chin. "Good for you," she said. There was neither approval nor condemnation in her voice. Her gaze was steady. "But you don't know the half of it. Let me tell you the rest."

She was shaken by the revelations of his dream and more than a little frightened and angered by the idea that she might be his target once again, but she kept it all hidden. She could not afford to let her feelings interfere with her purpose in coming to him in the first place. She could stew about the ramifications of his having had such a dream later, but for now she must concentrate on convincing him he needed to do something to protect himself.

"I watched three forest creatures die last night," she began. "One of them was Ariel, one was a sylvan named Boot, and the third was an owl named Audrey. A demon killed them, a demon that is attempting to claim your soul, John. Ariel, Audrey, and Boot died trying to stop that from happening. So please pay close attention to what I have to say."

She told him everything that had happened. She started with Ariel's appearance in the market, summoning her to West Seattle and Lincoln Park, where Boot and Audrey lived. Boot had seen the demon and had a story to tell. She called to let him know what she was doing, perhaps to persuade him to come, as well. But she couldn't reach him, so she left a message with Stef that she believed only he would understand. She took a taxi to the park and went in. At the rim of the cliffs overlooking Puget Sound and the park embankment, the sylvan and the owl appeared.

She related Boot's tale, repeating the conversation that had taken place between the two demons as accurately as she could remember it, then telling of how the first demon had killed the second to protect its claim on Ross. Boot was about to tell her more, she finished, when the attack occurred that snuffed out Boot's and Audrey's lives and led to the chase along the heights that ended up costing Ariel her life, as well.

"I went over the cliff by mistake or I would be dead, too," she finished. "I fell all the way to the base of the embankment, but I didn't break anything. I got up and ran out of the park with the demon still chasing me. There were houses where I thought I could get help. Twice I managed to get inside and twice the demon broke down doors and windows to get at me. I was lucky, John. It almost had me several times. In the end, I managed to get on a bus just ahead of it. Even then, it slammed into the bus doors with such force that the glass broke and the metal bent. It was in such a frenzy it didn't seem to care what it had to do. If the police hadn't arrived, I think it would have kept coming. It has to be really worried about me to go to such efforts. Maybe it thinks I know something. Maybe I do, but the truth is I haven't figured out what it is yet."

She watched the skin grow taut across his face and his eyes lose their focus, as if he was looking at something beyond her. "I wanted to come after you, and then something happened and I couldn't," he said softly.

She waited. His eyes came back to her. "The demon has to be someone I know, doesn't it?"

She nodded. "I guess so. Someone you know well, for that matter. Someone at Fresh Start, if you want my further opinion. When Ariel appeared to me after our lunch, she said I should stay away from you, that you were lost, that there was demon stink all over you. She said it was all over Fresh Start, as well. I was there earlier, and I was physically sick while I was inside the building. It might have been demon stink or it might have been the demon itself. This is all new to me. But it isn't idle speculation anymore. It's real. Something is after you."

He didn't say anything for a moment, thinking it through. "Who was at Fresh Start yesterday morning when you were there?"

She shook her head. "I can't be sure. Stef, Simon Lawrence, Ray Hapgood, Carole someone, Della Jenkins, some others. There were a lot of people. I don't think we can pin it down that way."

"You're right, it's too hard. How about the park? How did the demon manage to track you there? It must have followed you . . ."

"Or intercepted my message," she finished. "I already thought of that. Who besides Stef and yourself would have known where I was going?"

He hesitated. "I don't know. Stef took the message at Fresh Start and gave it to me. I don't think she would have told anyone else, but she might have."

Nest took a deep breath, not liking what she was about to say. "So the demon might be Stef."

The look John Ross gave her was unreadable. "That isn't possible," he said quietly.

She didn't say anything.

Ross looked around, took in the nearby diners. "Let's continue this somewhere else."

She charged the bill to her room, and they went out into the lobby. There was a small library bar on the other side and no one inside. They went in and took a table at the back on the upper level. The bartender, who was working the bar alone, came up and took their order for two iced cappuccinos and left. Surrounded by shelves of books and a cloud of suspicion and doubt, they faced each other anew.

"She saved all those people last night," Ross insisted. "She risked her life, Nest. A demon wouldn't do that."

"A demon would do anything that suited its purpose."

"It isn't possible," he said again.

"This demon is a changeling. A very adept changeling."

Ross shook his head. "I would know. I could be fooled, but not that completely."

She wasn't going to change his mind. Besides, she wanted to believe him. "So the demon found out where I was going and what I was doing some other way. What way would that be?"

Ross rubbed his lean jaw with one hand and shook his head slowly. "I don't know. None of this makes much sense. There's something not right about all of it. If the Void wanted to turn me, why wouldn't it take a more direct approach? Just suppose for a moment the dream comes to pass, and I do kill Simon Lawrence. That would be a terrible thing, but it wouldn't persuade me to begin serving the Void. It would probably do just the opposite."

Nest looked at him doubtfully. "But the Lady said it begins with a single misstep. You don't change all at once. You change gradually."

They stared at each other some more, neither speaking. Nest thought suddenly of Two Bears, and the reason he was in Seattle. Perhaps she should tell Ross. But what would that accomplish? How would it help him at this point?

His green eyes were intense. "Remember when I said earlier I wanted to come after you, but something happened and I couldn't? There was something wrong with me yesterday after I left you. I went back to the apartment and practically passed out. Stef stopped off just long enough to give me your message. Then I seem to recall Simon being there, too. That's the last thing I remember before waking up at midnight. It's been bothering me. I don't even remember going to bed. I just remember sitting in the living room, thinking it was odd that Simon was there, then waking up in bed when Stef shook me."

He hesitated. "I was pretty well out of it. Maybe there was someone else there, too. Maybe I said something about your message, and I can't remember."

He was looking for help from her, but she had none to give. He waited a moment, then leaned forward. "When are you scheduled to fly back to Chicago?"

"Today, at four-thirty."

He nodded. "Good. Get on that plane and get out of here. We have to do something to disrupt the flow of things, something to sidetrack this dream. Getting you out of here is the first step. I'll nose around a little and see what I can learn. Maybe I can uncover something. If I can't, I'll leave, too. I've got a few days coming. I'll just take them. If neither of us is here, the events in the dream won't happen."

She studied him. "You'll leave before dark, before tonight's celebration?"

His lips compressed tightly. "I won't go anywhere near the Seattle Art Museum. I'll stay far away."

She was thinking about the promise she had made to herself to see things through to the end. But if she insisted on staying, he would stay, too. She couldn't allow that. And if they both left, then the matter was ended—for the moment, at least. If Ross accepted he was in danger, that there was a demon out there working to subvert him, he would be on his guard. That ought to be enough. She had delivered the Lady's message, and that was all she was expected to do.

"All right," she said. "I'll go."

"Now?"

"As soon as I can pack my bag and check out. I'll catch a taxi to the airport. You won't have to worry about me anymore."

He exhaled slowly. "Fair enough."

"Just promise me you won't forget to keep worrying about yourself. This isn't going to end until you find out who the demon is."

"I know," he said.

And it wouldn't end then either, and they both knew it. It wouldn't end, because even if he unmasked this demon, there would be another, and another, until one of them succeeded in destroying him. It wouldn't end until he either found a way to give back the staff or agreed to resume his life as a Knight of the Word. It was not a choice that would be easily resolved, and neither one of them wanted to examine it too closely.

"Will you call me in Hopewell and at least leave a message?" she asked him in the ensuing silence.

"Yes."

She sighed. "I hate leaving this business unfinished." She saw the sudden look of concern in his eyes. "But I'll keep my bargain, John. Don't worry."

"That's just the trouble. I do."

She stood up. "I'd better go. Good-bye, John. Be careful."

He rose, as well, and she walked around to embrace him, kissing his cheek. The gesture was stiff and awkward and uncertain.

"Good-bye, Nest," he said.

She stepped back. "I'll tell you something," she said. "I don't know that saying good-bye feels any better this time than it did the last. I'm still not sure about you."

His smile was bitter and sad, and he suddenly looked older than his years. "I know, Nest. I'm sorry about that. Thanks for coming. It means a lot that you did."

She turned and walked out of the bar, crossed the lobby to the elevators, and did not look back.

Chapter 20

Andrew Wren woke early that same morning despite the fact he had been up very late tracing the transfers of funds from the corporate accounts of Fresh Start and Pass/Go to the private accounts of Simon Lawrence and John Ross. It was well after midnight by the time he completed his work and satisfied himself he knew exactly how all the withdrawals and deposits had been made and the routes through which various funds had traveled. He was exhausted by then, but a little bit of sleep did wonders for him when he was hot on the trail, and he felt energized and ready to go once more shortly after first light.

Nevertheless, he took his time. He had calls to make and faxes to send. He wanted to check on balances and signatures. He wanted to make very sure of what he had before he started writing anything. So he showered and shaved at a leisurely pace, thinking things through yet again, formulating his plans for the day.

It wasn't until he went downstairs for breakfast and was engaged in perusing Wednesday's *New York Times* that he overheard a conversation at an adjoining table and learned Fresh Start had burned down during the night.

At first he couldn't quite believe what he was hearing, and he paused in his reading to listen more closely as the conversation revealed the details. The building was a total loss. There was only one fatality, an employee. Arson wasn't thought to be the cause. Simon Lawrence would be holding a press conference on the future of the program at two o'clock that afternoon.

Andrew Wren finished his breakfast and bought a copy of the *Post-Intelligencer*, Seattle's morning paper. There were pictures and a short piece on the fire on the front page, but it had happened too late for an in-depth story.

Wren walked back to his room with the papers and sat down at his work desk with his yellow pad and notes and the packet of documentation on the illegal funds transfers spread out before him. He tried to decide if the fire had anything to do with what he was investigating, but it was too early to make that call. If it wasn't arson, then it wasn't relevant. If it was arson, then it might be. He stared out the window, deciding what to do next. It was only nine-fifteen.

He made up his mind quickly, the way he always did when he was closing in on something. He sent his faxes to the home office and to various specialists he worked with from time to time, requesting the information he needed, then began calling all the banks at which personal accounts had been opened in the names of Simon Lawrence and John Ross for the deposit of Fresh Start and Pass/Go funds. He used a time-tested technique, claiming to be in accounting at one or the other of the nonprofit corporations, giving the account number and the balance he had before him, and asking to verify the amounts. From there he went on to gather other information, building on the initial rapport he had established with whoever was on the other end of the line to complete his investigation. It was practically second nature to him by now. He knew all the buttons to push and all the tricks and ploys.

He was done by a little after ten-thirty. He called the number at Pass/Go and asked for Stefanie Winslow. When she came on the line, he told her he was coming over to see the Wiz. She advised him that Simon wouldn't be available until late in the day, if then. He assured her he understood, he had heard about the fire and knew what Simon must have been going through, but he needed only a few minutes and it was imperative they meet immediately. He added it involved the matter they had discussed yesterday, and he was sure Simon would want to see him.

She put him on hold. When she came back on, she said he could come right over.

Andrew Wren put down the phone, pulled on his rumpled jacket with the patches on the elbows, picked up his briefcase, and went out the door, humming softly.

Ten minutes later, he was climbing out of a taxi in front of Pass/Go. The educational center was situated right next door to Fresh Start, but separated by a narrow alleyway. Before last night, the two buildings had looked substantially the same—1940s brick buildings of six stories facing on Second Avenue with long glass windows, recessed entries with double wooden doors, and no signs. But Pass/Go had survived the fire where Fresh Start had not. Fresh Start was a burned-out, blackened shell surrounded by barricades and yellow tape, its roof and floors sagging or collapsed, its windows blown out by the heat, and its fixtures and furnishings in ruins.

As he stood staring at the still-smoking wreck, Stefanie Winslow came out the front door of Pass/Go.

"Good morning, Mr. Wren," she said cheerfully, her smile dazzling, her hand extended.

As he offered his own hand in response, he was shocked to see the marks on her arms and face. "Good heavens, Ms. Winslow! What happened to you?"

She gave a small shrug. "I was involved in getting people out last night, and I picked up a few bumps and bruises along the way. It's nothing that won't heal. How are you?"

"Fine." He was somewhat nonplussed by her attitude. "You seem very cheerful given the circumstances, if you don't mind my saying so."

She laughed. "Well, that's my job, Mr. Wren. I'm supposed to put a good face on things, my own notwithstanding. We lost the building, but all the clients got out. That doesn't help much when I think about Ray, but it's the best I can do."

She filled him in on the details of Ray Hapgood's death and the efforts of the fire department to save the building. Ross had been present when it took place, but he had been sleeping earlier and she'd had to wake him to help her, so it didn't look like he was involved in any way. Wren listened without seeming overly interested, taking careful mental notes for later.

"The building was fully insured," she finished, "so we'll be able to rebuild. In the meantime, we've been given the use of a warehouse several blocks away that can be brought up to code pretty easily for our purposes and will serve as a temporary shelter during the rebuilding. We've been given a number of donations already to help tide us over and there should be more coming in. Things could be much worse."

Wren smiled. "Well, I'm very glad to hear that, Ms. Winslow."

"Stefanie, please." She touched his arm. "Ms. Winslow sounds vaguely authoritarian."

Wren nodded agreeably. "Do you suppose I could see Mr. Lawrence now for those few minutes you promised me? Before he becomes too tied up with other things? I know he has a news conference scheduled for two o'clock."

"Now would be fine, Mr. Wren." She took his arm as she might an old friend's. "Come with me. We've got him hidden in the back."

They went inside through a lobby decorated with brightly colored posters and children's drawings, past a reception desk, and down a hall with doors opening into classrooms and offices. Through tall glass windows, Wren could see a grassy play area filled with toys and playground equipment shoehorned between the surrounding buildings.

"The nursery, kitchen facilities, dining rooms, Special Ed, and more classrooms are upstairs," Stefanie informed him, waving to one of the teachers as she passed by an open door. "Life goes on."

Simon Lawrence had set up shop in a tiny office at the very back of the building. He sat at an old wooden desk surrounded by cartons of supplies and forms, his angular frame hunched forward over a mound of papers, files, notepads, and pens and pencils. He was on the phone talking, but he motioned Wren through the open door and into a folding chair identical to the one he was occupying. Stefanie Winslow waved good-bye and went out the door, closing it softly behind her.

The Wiz finished his conversation and hung up. "I hope this isn't bad news, Andrew," he said, smiling wearily. "I've had just about all the bad news I can handle for the moment."

"So I gather." Wren glanced around at the boxes and bare walls. "Quite a comedown from your last digs."

Simon snorted derisively. "Doesn't mean a thing compared to the cost to Fresh Start. It will take a minimum of three to four weeks to get the warehouse converted and the program up and running again. How many women and children will we lose in that time, I wonder?"

"You'll do the best you can. Sometimes that has to be enough."

Simon leaned back. His handsome face looked worn and haggard, but his eyes were bright and sharp as they fixed on the reporter. "Okay, Andrew, what's this all about? Lay it out on the table and get it over with."

Andrew Wren nodded, reached into his briefcase, took out the copies he had made of the documents with which he had been provided, and placed them on the desk in front of the Wiz. Simon picked them up and began scanning them, quickly at first, then more slowly. His face lost some color, and his jaw tightened. Halfway through his perusal, he looked up.

"Are these for real?" he asked carefully. "Have you verified they exist?"

Wren nodded. "Every last onc."

The Wiz went back to his examination, finishing quickly. He shook his head. "I know what I'm seeing, but I can't believe it." His eyes fixed on Wren. "I don't know anything about this. Not about the accounts or any of the transfers. I'd give you an explanation if I could, but I can't. I'm stunned."

Andrew Wren sat waiting, saying nothing.

The Wiz leaned back again in his folding chair and set the papers on the desk. "I haven't taken a cent from either program that wasn't approved in advance. Not one. The accounts with my name on them aren't really mine. I don't know who opened them or who made the transfers, but they aren't mine. I can't believe John Ross would do something like this, either. He's never given me any reason to think he would."

Wren nodded, keeping silent.

"If I were going to steal money from the corporations, I would either steal a lot more or do a better job of it. This kind of petty theft is ridiculous, Andrew. Have you checked the signatures to see if they match mine or John's?"

Wren scratched his chin thoughtfully. "I'm having it done professionally. I should know something later today."

"Who brought all this to you?" The Wiz indicated the incriminating papers with a dismissive wave of his hand.

Wren gave a small shrug. "You know I can't tell you that."

Simon Lawrence shook his head in dismay. "Well, they say these things come in threes. Last night I lost a good friend and half of five years' hard work. Today I find I'm about to lose my reputation. I wonder what comes next?"

He rose from the desk and paced to the door and back again, then turned to face Wren. "I'm betting that when you check the signatures, you won't find a match."

"Quite possibly not. But that doesn't mean you aren't involved, Simon. You could have had someone else act for you."

"John Ross?"

"Ross, or even a third person."

"Why would I do this?"

"I don't know. Maybe you were desperate. Desperate people do desperate things. I've given up trying to figure out the reasons behind why people do the things they do. I've got all I can handle just uncovering the truth of what's been done."

The Wiz sat down again, his eyes smoldering. "I've spent five years building this program, Andrew. I've given everything I have to make it work. If you report this, it will all go down the tubes."

"I know that," Wren acknowledged softly.

"Even if there's nothing to connect me directly, even if an inquiry clears me of any wrongdoing, the program will never be the same. I'll quit in order to remove any lingering doubts about the possibility of impropriety, or I'll stay and fight and live with the suspicion that something is still going on, but either way Fresh Start and Pass/Go will always be remembered for this scandal and not for the good they've accomplished."

Andrew Wren sighed. "I think maybe you're overstating your case a bit, Simon."

The Wiz shook his head. "No, I'm not. You know why? Because the whole effort is held together by the slenderest of threads. Helping the homeless isn't a program that attracts support naturally. It isn't a program people flock to just because they believe in aiding the homeless. What happens to the homeless is a low priority in most people's lives. It isn't a glamorous cause. It isn't a compelling cause. It's balanced right on the edge of people's consciousness, and it could topple from view with just a nudge. It took me years to bring it to people's attention and make it a cause they would choose to support over all the others. But it can lose that same support in the blink of an eye."

He sighed. "I know you're just doing your job, Andrew," he said after a moment. "I wouldn't ask you to do anything less. But be thorough, please. Be sure about this before you act. An awful lot rides on what you decide to do."

Andrew Wren folded his hands in his lap and looked down at them. "I appreciate what's at stake better than you think, Simon. That's why I came to talk with you first. I wanted to hear what you had to say. As far as making any decisions, I have a lot more work to do first. I won't be rushing into anything."

He rose and held out his hand. "I'm sorry about this. As I told you earlier, I admire the work you've done here. I'd hate to think it would suffer for any reason."

Simon Lawrence took his hand and shook it firmly. "Thank you for coming to me about this. I'll do what I can to look into it from this end. Whatever I find, I'll pass along."

Andrew Wren opened the door and walked back down the hall to the reception area. There was no sign of Stefanie Winslow, who was probably out working on preparations for the press conference. He paused as he neared the front door, then turned back.

The young woman working the intake desk looked up as he approached, smiling. "Can I help you?"

"I was wondering," he said, returning the smile, "if you know where I could find John Ross."

Chapter 21

It was nearing two o'clock by the time Nest packed her bag, checked out of the Alexis, and caught a taxi to the airport. She rode south down I-5 past Boeing Field on one side and lines of stalled traffic heading north on the other. She stared out the window, watching the city recede into the distance, wrestling with the feeling that her connection with John Ross was fading with it.

She was riddled with doubt and plagued by a sense of uneasiness she could not explain.

She had done everything she had come to do and a little more. She had found John Ross, she had given him the Lady's warning, she had persuaded him he was in danger, and she had extracted his solemn promise he would take whatever steps were necessary to protect himself. She kept telling herself there was really nothing else she could do—nothing else, in fact, that she could justify—but none of the monolog seemed to help.

Maybe it had something to do with the fact that Ariel and Audrey and Boot were still dead and some part of the guilt for that was still hers. Maybe it had something to do with her discomfort at having done so little to help them. She knew she was dissatisfied with the idea of leaving the demon who had killed them loose in the city of Seattle. But what was she supposed to do? Track it down and exact revenge? How would she do that and what difference would it make now? It wouldn't bring back the forest creatures. It wouldn't make things whole or right in any meaningful way. Maybe it would give her a measure of satisfaction, but she wasn't even sure of that.

Mostly, she decided, she was bothered by the prospect of leaving behind so many loose ends. She was a runner, a competitor, and she was used to seeing things through to the finish, not giving up halfway. And that's what her leaving felt like.

For a time she managed to put it aside and think about what waited at the other end of her flight. Northwestern University, with classes first thing in the morning, three days of homework waiting to be made up, and her lapsed training regimen. Her grandparents' home, now hers, and the papers sitting on the kitchen counter, which would permit its sale. Pick, with his incessant questions about her commitment to Sinnissippi Park. Robert, waiting patiently for a phone call or letter telling him everything was all right.

As she would wait for a phone call or a letter from John Ross telling her the same thing.

Or would she never hear another word?

The taxi took the airport exit, wound its way along a series of approaches, and pulled onto the ticketing ramp. She looked over at the big airplanes parked at the boarding gates and contemplated the idea of flying home. It didn't seem real to her. It didn't seem like something that was going to happen.

She got out at the United terminal, paid the driver, and walked inside. She checked in at the ticketing counter and received her boarding pass and gate assignment. She decided to keep her bag with her because it was not very big and she did not want the hassle of trying to retrieve it through baggage claim at O'Hare. She walked toward the shops and gate ramps, remembering suddenly, incongruously, she still hadn't replaced her windbreaker. She had thrown on her sweatshirt, but that wasn't going to provide her with enough warmth when she had to go outside in Chicago.

She glanced around, then walked into a Northwest Passage Outdoor Shop, a clothing store that sold mostly logo products. After rooting around in the parkas for a while, she found a lightweight down jacket she could live with, carried it up to the register, and paid for it with her charge card.

As she carried it out of the store, under her arm, she found herself wondering if the dead children's memories that had helped make up Ariel would be used to make another tatterdemalion or if they would be blown about by the wind forever. What happened to tatterdemalions when their lives ended? Little more than scraps of magic and memories to begin with, did they ever come together again in a new life? Pick had never said.

She moved to a seating area facing a security check and sat down. She was back to thinking about John Ross. Something was very wrong. She didn't know what it was, but she knew it was there. She was trying to pretend everything was fine, but it wasn't. On the surface maybe, but not down deep, beneath the comfortable illusion she was trying to embrace. She held up her anxiety for examination, and it glared back at her defiantly.

What was it she was missing?

What was it she needed to do in order to make the discomfort go away?

She began to examine the John Ross situation once again. She went through all of its aspects, stopping abruptly when she came to his dream. The Lady had warned Nest about the dream, that it would come to pass in a few short days, and that to the extent Ross was a part of the events it prophesied, he risked becoming ensnared by the Void. The dream foretold that Ross would kill Simon Lawrence, the Wizard of Oz.

It also foretold that he would kill her. But it hadn't done that until last night.

Because until these past few days, she hadn't been a part of his present life at all, had she?

She stared at the lighted window of a newsstand across the way, thinking. John Ross had told her about his dreams five years earlier. His dreams of the future were fluid, because the future was fluid and could be changed by what happened in the present. It was what he was expected to accomplish as a Knight of the Word. It was his mission. Change those events that will hasten a decline in civilization and the fall of mankind. Change a few events, only a few, and the balance of magic can be maintained and the Void kept at bay.

What if, in this instance, the Lady was playing at the same game? What if the Lady had sent Nest to John Ross strictly for the purpose of introducing a new element into the events of his dream? Ross would listen to Nest, the Lady had told her through Ariel. Her words would carry a weight that the words of others could not.

But it hadn't worked out that way, had it? It wasn't what she'd said to Ross that had made a difference. It was what had happened to her in the park. It was the way in which her presence had affected the demon that, in turn, had affected him. Like dominos toppling into one another. Could that have been the Lady's purpose in sending her to Ross all along?

Nest took a slow, deep breath and let it out again. It wasn't so strange to imagine there were games being played with human lives. It had happened before, and it had happened to her. Pick had warned her the Word never revealed everything, and what appeared to be true frequently was not. He had warned her to be careful.

That triggered an unpleasant thought. Perhaps the Lady knew Nest's presence would affect John Ross's dream, would change it to include her, jolting Ross out of his complacent certainty he was not at risk.

If so, it meant the Word was using her as bait.

When John Ross left Nest, he didn't go back to Pass/Go or to his apartment. He walked down First Avenue to a Starbucks instead, stepped inside, bought a double-tall latte, took it outside to a bench in Occidental Park, and sat down. The day was still sunny and bright, the cool snap of autumn just a whisper on the back of the breezes blowing off the sound. Ross sipped at his latte thoughtfully, warmed his hands on the container, and watched people walk by.

He kept thinking he would have a revelation regarding the demon's identity. He was certain that if he thought about the puzzle hard enough, if he looked at it in just the right way, he would figure it out. There were only a handful of possibilities, after all. A lot of people worked at Fresh Start and Pass/Go, but only a few were close to him. And once you eliminated Ray Hapgood and Stef and certainly Simon, there weren't many candidates left.

But each time he considered a likely suspect, some incongruity or contradictory piece of evidence would intervene to demonstrate he was on the wrong track. The fact remained that no one seemed to be the right choice. His confusion was compounded by his complete failure to understand what his dream about killing Simon Lawrence had to do with anything. The demon's subterfuge was so labyrinthine he could not unravel it.

He finished the latte and crumpled the empty container. He was running out of ideas and choices. He would have to keep his promise to Nest and subtract himself from the equation.

Dumping the latte container in a trash can, he began walking back to his apartment. He wouldn't even bother going in to work. He would just pack an overnight bag, call Stef, have her meet him, and walk down to the ferry terminal. Maybe they would go up to Victoria for a few days. Stay at the Empress. Have high tea. Visit the Buchart Gardens. Pretend they were real people.

He was almost to the front door of his apartment building when he heard his name called. He turned to watch a heavyset, rumpled man come up the sidewalk to greet him.

"Mr. Ross?" the man inquired, as if to make sure.

Ross nodded, leaning on his walking stick, trying to place the other's face.

"We haven't met," the newcomer said, and extended his hand. "I'm Andrew Wren, from *The New York Times*."

The investigative reporter, Ross thought warily. He took the proffered hand and shook it. "How do you do, Mr. Wren?"

The professional face beamed behind rimless glasses. "The people at Pass/Go thought I might find you here. I came by earlier, but you were out. I wonder if I could speak with you a moment?"

Ross hesitated. This was probably about Simon. He didn't want to talk to Wren, particularly just then, but he was afraid that if he refused it would look bad for the Wiz.

"This won't take long," Wren assured him. "We could sit at one of those tables in the little park right around the corner, if you wish."

They walked back to the entrance to Waterfall Park and took seats at a table on the upper level where the sound of the falls wasn't quite so deafening. Ross glanced across the street at the offices of Pass/Go, wondering if anyone had seen him. No, he amended wordlessly, not if anyone had seen him. If the demon had seen him.

He grimaced at his own paranoia. "What can I do for you, Mr. Wren?"

Andrew Wren fumbled with his briefcase. "I'm doing a piece on Simon Lawrence, Mr. Ross. Last night, someone dropped off some documents at my hotel room." He extracted a sheaf of papers from the case and handed them across the table. "I'd like you to take a look."

Ross took the packet, set it before him, and began to thumb through the pages. Bank accounts, he saw. Transfers of funds, withdrawals and deposits. He frowned. The withdrawals were from Fresh Start and Pass/Go. The deposits were into accounts under Simon Lawrence's name. And under his.

He glanced up at Andrew Wren in surprise. Wren's soft face was expressionless. Ross went back to the documents. He worked his way through, then looked up again. "Is this some sort of joke?"

Wren shook his head solemnly. "I'm afraid not, Mr. Ross. At least not the sort anyone is laughing at. Particularly Simon Lawrence."

"You've shown these to Simon?"

"I have."

"What did he say?"

"He says he's never seen them."

Ross pushed the packet back across the table at Wren. "Well, neither have I. I don't know anything about these accounts other than the fact they're not mine. What's going on here?"

Andrew Wren shrugged. "It would appear you and Simon Lawrence have been siphoning funds from the charitable corporations you work for. Have you?"

John Ross was so angry he could barely contain himself. "No, Mr. Wren, I have not. Nor has Simon Lawrence, I'm willing to bet. Those signatures are forgeries, every last one of them. Mine looks pretty good, but I know I didn't sign for any of those transfers. Someone is playing a game, Mr. Wren . . ."

The minute he said it, he knew. The answer was there in ten-foot-high neon lights behind his eyes, flashing.

"Do you have any idea who that someone might be, Mr. Ross?" Andrew Wren asked quietly, folding his hands over the documents, his eyes bright and inquisitive.

Ross stared at him, his mind racing. Of course, he did. It was the demon. The demon was responsible. But, why?

He shook his head. "Offhand, I'd say whoever provided you with the information, Mr. Wren."

The other man nodded thoughtfully. "I've considered that."

"Someone who doesn't like Simon Lawrence."

"Or you."

Ross nodded. "Perhaps. But I'd say Simon is the more likely target." He paused. "But you've thought this through already, haven't you? That's what an investigative reporter does. You've already considered all the possibilities. Maybe you've even made up your mind."

Wren grimaced. "No, Mr. Ross, I haven't done that. It's too early for making up one's mind about this mess. I have tried to consider the possibilities. One of those possibilities relies on your analysis that the Wiz is the primary target. But for that to be true, it must also be true that someone is setting him up. That requires a motive. You seem to have a rather good one. If you were looking for a way to protect yourself in the event your own theft was discovered, salting an account or two in Simon Lawrence's name might just do the trick."

Ross thought it through. "Oh, I get it. I steal a little for me, a little for him, then claim it was all his idea if I get caught. That gets me a reduced sentence, maybe even immunity."

"It's happened before."

"You know something, Mr. Wren?" Ross looked off at the waterfall for a minute, then back again. His eyes were hard and filled with a rage he could no longer disguise. "I'm just about as mad as I've ever been in my life. I love my work with Fresh Start. I would never do anything to jeopardize that. Nor would I do anything to jeopardize a program I strongly believe in and support. I've never stolen a penny in my life. Frankly, I don't care much about money. I've never had it, and I've never missed it. Nothing's happened to change that."

He rose, stiff-legged and seething. "So you go right ahead and do what you have to do. But let me tell you something. If you don't find out who's behind this, I will. That's a promise, Mr. Wren. I will."

"Mr. Ross?" Andrew Wren stood up with him. "Could you just give me another minute? Mr. Ross?"

But John Ross was already walking away.

Bait.

Nest Freemark considered the implications of the word as calmly as she could, which wasn't easy to do. The thought that she had been dispatched to Seattle to find John Ross, not with any expectation she could influence him by virtue of well-reasoned argument, but solely for the purpose of influencing his dreams and forcing him to rethink his position at the same time she was being put at risk was almost more than she could bear.

She fumed for a moment, then wondered how the Lady could know how her presence would affect things. Could she know the dream would be changed in a way that would make Ross reconsider? If the Lady knew what the dream was, it wasn't such a long shot she knew how to change it.

Nest put her face in her hands and closed her eyes. She was jousting with shadows. She was just guessing.

She left behind the dream and its implications and went back to what she knew.

There was a demon. The demon was in Seattle. The demon was after Ross. The demon was someone he knew, probably well. The demon was determined to claim him—so determined it had been willing to attack and kill another demon who challenged it for possession of his soul.

So far, so good. Nest nodded into her hands. What else?

The demon had recognized Nest and decided she was a threat. But not enough of a threat to do anything about her until after she had gone to Lincoln Park to speak with Boot. Boot was going to tell her something when the demon attacked, something about the demon changing again, only not in the same way.

She backed off, knowing all she could do with that approach was to speculate, that the answers she needed had to be reached from another direction.

She glanced at her watch. Three-thirty. Her plane would begin boarding around four. She looked down at her bag, glanced over at the security check and the people lined up to go through the metal detector, and went back to thinking.

The demon had been present when she had gone to Fresh Start to find John Ross. Her magic, into whatever form it had evolved, had reacted to the demon and made Nest physically sick. The demon had tracked her or followed her or intercepted her message and found her later at Lincoln Park. Which? It had killed Boot, Audrey, and Ariel, and had tried to kill her. And then it had gone back to the city and set fire to Fresh Start. Why?

Her head hurt. Nothing fit. She walked down the concourse with her bag to an SBC stand and ordered a decaf cappuccino. Then she found a different seat and thought about the demon some more.

What was she missing?

Stay away from him, Ariel had warned her of John Ross. He has demon stink all over him. He is already lost.

Seemed right to her, given his refusal to accept the possibility he was in danger, that he might be fooling himself about his vulnerability. But John Ross genuinely seemed to believe that he was a different person, no longer a Knight of the Word, no longer a keeper of the magic. He was shattered by San Sobel, and now he was in love with Stefanie Winslow and committed to the work of Simon Lawrence, and his life was all new.

Like her own was new, she thought suddenly. She had left the past behind as well, back in the park of the Sinnissippi, back with the passing of Gran and Old Bob, back with the end of her childhood.

She thought suddenly of her mother. There was no reason for it, but all of a sudden she was thinking about how much she missed not having her there while she was growing up. Gran and Old Bob had done the best they could, which was pretty good, but the gap in her life that her mother's death had left wasn't something anyone could fill. She wondered if that was how John Ross had felt before Stef had come into his life. He had wandered alone for more than ten years in service to the Word, living with his terrible dreams of the future and the responsibility they forced on him in the present. It was so hard to be without someone who loved you. Everyone was affected by the absence of love. Even her father, who was a demon . . .

The words froze in midsentence, crystallized in her mind, and hung there like shards of ice. She had been trying to think of something earlier, something that spoke to the issue of the demon's behavior with Ross, something from her past. Now she knew what it was. It was her father's behavior toward Gran, years ago.

It was the same. It was exactly the same.

In a moment's time, everything came together, all the loose ends, all the answers she had been unable to locate, all the missing clues. She felt her breath catch in her throat as she thought it through, trying it out, seeing if it fit.

She knew who the demon was.

She knew why John Ross could not escape it.

A wave of heat rushed through her. Maybe she had been wrong about the Lady after all. Maybe the Lady knew Nest would see what Ross could not.

But was there still time enough to save him?

She was on her feet, her bag flung over one shoulder, running for the exit and the taxi stand.

CHAPTER 22

John Ross went up to his apartment and stood at the window looking down at the ruins of Fresh Start, fuming. A crew from the fire marshall's office was picking its way carefully through the debris, searching for clues. He scanned the busy streets for Andrew Wren, but the reporter was nowhere to be seen.

Why was the demon working so hard to discredit him? What did it hope to gain?

Where the Wiz was concerned, the answer was obvious. The demon hoped that by discrediting Simon, it would derail the progress of his programs. If enough doubt was cast and suspicion raised as to the integrity of the work being done at Fresh Start and Pass/Go, donors would pull back, political and celebrity sponsors would disappear, and support from the public would shift to another cause. Worse, it would reflect on programs assisting the homeless all across the country. It was typical demon mischief, a sowing of discontent that, given enough time and space, would reap anarchy.

The more difficult question was why the demon had chosen to paint him with the same brush. What was the point? Was this phony theft charge supposed to send him into a tailspin that would lead to an alliance with the Void? Given that the demon intended to subvert him and claim his magic, this business of manipulating bank accounts and transfers seemed an odd way to go about it.

He chewed his lip thoughtfully. It might explain the fire, though. Burning down Fresh Start at the same time Simon Lawrence was being discredited would only add to the confusion. If the plan was to bring down Simon and put an end to his programs, an attack from more than one front made sense.

He shoved his hands in his jeans pockets angrily. He wanted to walk right over to Pass/Go and deal with his suspicions. But he knew there wasn't really anything he could do. Andrew Wren was still in the middle of his investigation. He was checking signatures and interviewing bank personnel. Maybe the signatures wouldn't match. Certainly the bank people wouldn't remember seeing either him or Simon.

Except, he remembered suddenly, the demon was a changeling and could have disguised itself as either of them.

He turned away from the window and stared at the interior of the apartment in frustration. The best thing he could do was to follow through on his promise to Nest and get out of town. Do that, put a little distance between himself and whatever machinations the demon was engaged in, and take a fresh look at things in a few days.

Don't take any chances with the events of the dream.

He glanced at his watch. It was already approaching four o'clock, and the festivities at the Seattle Art Museum were scheduled to begin at six sharp.

Dropping into his favorite wing chair, he dialed Pass/Go and asked for Stefanie. Told that she was in a meeting, he left a message for her to call him.

He went into the bedroom, pulled his duffel bag out of the closet, and began to pack. It didn't take long. There wasn't much packing to do for this sort of trip, and he didn't have much to choose from in any case. It gave him pause when he realized how little he owned. The truth was, he had never stopped living as if he were just passing through and might be catching the morning bus to some other place.

He was reading a magazine when the door burst open and Stefanie stalked into the room and threw a clump of papers into his lap.

"Explain this, John!" she demanded coldly, standing rigid with fury before him.

He looked down at the papers, already knowing what they were. Photocopies of the bank transfers Andrew Wren had shown him earlier. He looked up again. "I don't know anything about these accounts. They aren't mine."

"Your signature is all over them!"

He met her gaze squarely. "Stef, I didn't steal a penny. That's not my signature. Those aren't my accounts. I told the same thing to Andrew Wren when he asked me about it an hour ago. I wouldn't do anything like this."

She stared at him silently, searching his face.

"Stef, I wouldn't."

All the anger drained away, and she bent down to kiss him. "I know. I told Simon the same thing. I just wanted to hear you say it."

She put her hands on his shoulders and ran them down his arms, her tousled black hair falling over her battered face. Then she knelt before him, her eyes lifting to find his. "I'm sorry. This hasn't been a good day."

You don't know the half of it, he thought to himself. "I was thinking we might go away for a few days, let things sort themselves out."

She smiled up at him sadly. "A few days, a few weeks, a few months, we can take as much time as we want. We're out of a job."

He felt his throat tighten. "What?"

"Simon fired you. When I objected and he wouldn't change his mind, I quit." She shrugged.

He shook his head in disbelief. "Why would Simon fire me without giving me a chance to explain?"

"He's cutting his losses, John. It's the smart thing to do." Her dark eyes studied him. "He's frightened. He's angry. A lot of bad things are happening all at once, and he has to do something to contain the damage. If word of this leaks to the mayor's office or the local press, it's all over for Simon."

"So his solution is to fire me?"

"That's what I asked him." She brushed her hair aside, her mouth tight and angry. Then she stood up and walked across the room and threw herself on the couch, staring up at the ceiling. "There's nothing back yet on the transfer signatures, and no one he's talked to at the banks involved remembers anything about who opened the accounts. But when Wren suggested the possibility that you were trying to set Simon up, Simon bought into it. He thinks you're responsible, and he wants to distance himself from you right now before you become a liability he can't explain."

She looked over at him. "There's more. He claims he came by last night after I left. He claims he found you drunk and irrational, and you threatened him. I told him that wasn't possible, that you weren't drinking. I told him you were sick and half asleep when I left you, so maybe he misinterpreted what he heard. He refused to listen." She exhaled sharply, her bitterness evident. "He fired you, just like that. So I quit, too."

Ross was staring at the space between them, stunned. First the business of the demon hunting him, then Andrew Wren's accusations, and now this. He felt as if he was caught in some sort of diabolical whirlpool that was sucking him under where he couldn't breathe.

"This isn't like Simon, John," Stef was saying. "This isn't like him at all. He hasn't been the same lately. I don't know what the problem is, but it's almost as if he's someone else completely."

Ross was thinking the same thing. A glimmer of suspicion had surfaced inside, hot and fierce. It couldn't be, he was thinking. Not Simon. Not the Wiz.

Stef crossed her long legs and stared down the length of her body at her feet. "I don't understand what he's thinking anymore."

Ross looked at her. "How did his TV interview go last night?" he asked casually.

She pursed her lips. "It didn't. He canceled it. I didn't even find out until I showed up and no one was there. That's when I came back here and found you collapsed on the couch. I hauled you off to bed and read my book in the living room until around midnight, when I woke you about the fire."

His suspicion burned inside like an inferno. "You know that message you got over the phone from Nest Freemark? The one about meeting her in West Seattle? Did you mention it to anyone else? Or could anyone else have overheard?"

Stefanie sat up slowly, puzzled. "I don't know. Why?"

"Just think about it. It might be important."

She was silent a moment. "Well, Simon knew, I guess. He was there talking with me when I took Nest's call. He asked me afterward what it was about, and I said it was from Nest and she wanted you to meet her in Lincoln Park. He laughed, said it was an odd place to meet someone. I said it had something to do with a friend of somebody named Pick."

Ross felt the blood drain from his face.

Stef sat up slowly, her brow furrowing with concern. "John, what's going on?"

He shook his head. Simon Lawrence knew about the meeting with Nest. If he was the demon, he had time and opportunity to get over there, intercept her at her meeting with the forest creatures, and still get back to set the fire at Fresh Start.

He almost laughed out loud. No, this was ridiculous!

But the idea had taken root. Who was in a better position than Simon Lawrence to sabotage the work of Fresh Start and Pass/Go? Simon was the whole program. If he came under suspicion, if he was forced to quit, if—just suppose now—he disappeared at a crucial juncture in the investigation, everything would go down the drain. There would be national coverage. Every homeless program in the country would be adversely affected.

"John?" Stef was on her feet. She looked frightened.

He smiled. "It's all right, I'm just thinking. Would you mind getting me a root beer from the fridge?"

She nodded, smiling back at him uncertainly. He waited until she was out of the room, then resumed his deliberation. Simon Lawrence as the demon—it made a certain amount of sense. Simon could ruin his own programs. He could sabotage homeless programs nationwide by wrecking his own. And he was in a great position to wreck Ross's life, as well. He could implicate him in the theft of corporate funds, terminate his job, maybe even have him sent to prison. If the demon intended to turn him to the Void's service, it would be a perfect place to begin.

It might even cost him his relationship with Stef.

His head throbbed fiercely. One misstep was all it took, the Lady had cautioned. One misstep that led to another. He considered the possibility that the demon might take that step for him. It wasn't too difficult to imagine.

But Simon Lawrence? He still couldn't bring himself to accept that the Wiz was a demon.

Stefanie reentered the room. He came to his feet, facing her. "Stef, I can't go away just yet. I have to do something first. I have to see Simon."

She sighed. "John, no."

He took hold of her arms and held her gently, but firmly, in place. "I can call him up right now or I can just go over. It won't take but a moment."

She shook her head, her eyes angry. "It won't do you any good, John. He's made up his mind. I already argued your case for you, and it didn't change anything."

He studied her face, thinking she was right, that it was pointless. "I have to try," he insisted anyway. "I have to make the attempt myself. I'll be right back."

She grabbed his arm as he started to turn away. "John, he's not even there. He's already gone down to the art museum to help put things in place for tonight's benefit. He's doing interviews and . . . Look, forget this. Let it go. Give me five minutes to pack a bag and we're out of here. We'll deal with it when we get back, okay?"

But he was already committed. He could not just walk away, not even for three or four days. He had to know the truth about Simon. He had no idea how he was going to find it out, but he could at least speak with him face-to-face and see how he responded.

Then a very strange thought occurred to him. What if the dream about killing the Wizard of Oz wasn't a warning at all? What if it were an admonition? Perhaps he had been mistaken about the purpose of the dream, and he was having it not because he was supposed to avoid the Wiz, but because he was supposed to go after him. His dreams of the future had been windows into mistakes that had been made in the present and might yet be corrected. He had assumed this was the case here. But he was no longer a Knight of the Word, and it was possible this dream, the only dream he was having anymore, the one he had experienced so often, was meant to work in a different way.

Maybe he was supposed to kill Simon Lawrence because Simon was a demon.

It was a stretch, by any measure, and he had no way of knowing if it were so. But if Simon was a demon, it would give new meaning to his dream. It would lend it a purpose and a reason for being that had been missing before.

Stefanie was still holding the root beer. He looked down at it and shook his head. "I've changed my mind. I don't want it after all."

She put her free hand on his arm. "John . . ."

"Stef, I'm going down to the art museum to find Simon. I won't be long. I just want to ask him why he didn't wait a little longer. I just want to hear him tell me why he won't give me the benefit of the doubt."

She set the can of root beer down on the table. "John, don't do this."

"What can it hurt?"

"Your pride, for one thing." She was seething. Her exquisite features were calm and settled, but her eyes were angry. "You don't have anything to prove to Simon Lawrence, certainly not anything more than he should have to prove to you. Those are his signatures on those bank accounts, too. Why isn't it just as likely he's to blame?"

Ross put his finger to her lips. "Because he's the Wiz, and I'm not."

She shook her head vehemently, her anger edging closer to a breakout. "I don't care who he is. You don't have to prove anything."

"I just want to talk with him."

She didn't say anything for a moment, studying him with a mix of resignation and dismay, as if realizing all the arguments in the world had been suddenly rendered useless. "I'm not going to change your mind on this, am I?"

He smiled, trying to take the edge off the moment. "No, but I love you for trying. Go pack your bag. Wait for me. I'll be back inside of an hour, and then we'll go."

He kissed her mouth, then walked over to the front closet and pulled on his greatcoat. She was still standing there, staring after him, as he went out the door.

Nest Freemark rode back into the city from the airport in impatient silence, staring out at the sun as it dropped westward toward the Olympics. It was already growing dark, the days shortened down to a little more than eight hours, the nights lengthening in response to the coming of the winter solstice. Shadows crept and pooled all across the wooded slopes of the city's hills, swallowing up the last of the light.

She had thought to call ahead, to reach Ross by telephone, but what she had to say would be better coming from her in person. He might believe her then. She might stand a chance of convincing him.

She exhaled wearily, peering out at the descending dark. This was going to be a much harder task than the one the Lady had given her.

The taxi rolled onto the off-ramp at Seneca and down to Pioneer Square. The district's turn-of-the-century lamps were already lit, the shadows of the city's tall buildings stretching dark fingers to gather in dwindling slivers of daylight. The taxi pulled up at the curb beside the burned-out hulk of Fresh Start, and she paid the driver and jumped out, bag in hand. The taxi drove away, and she stood there, gathering her thoughts. She realized how cold it had gotten, a brisk wind whipping out of the northwest down Second Avenue's broad corridor, and she slipped hurriedly into her new jacket.

She turned and looked across the intersection at Waterfall Park and the apartment building where John Ross lived with Stefanie Winslow. The wind buffeted her gangly form as she stood there and tried to decide what she should do.

Finally, she picked up her bag and turned the corner to walk up Main Street to Pass/Go. She entered the reception area and glanced around. Except for the lady working the intake desk, the room was empty.

She moved over to the desk, taking several deep breaths to slow the pounding of her heart, masking her trepidation and urgency with a smile. "Is John Ross here?" she asked.

The woman at the desk shook her head without looking up. She seemed anxious to stick with her paperwork. "He didn't come in today. Can I help you?"

"My name is Nest Freemark. I'm a friend. I need to speak with him right away. It's rather urgent. Can you give him a call for me at his apartment? Or would you let me have his number?"

The woman smiled in a way that let Nest know right off the bat she wasn't about to do either. "I'm sorry, but our policy is—"

"Well, look who's back!" Della Jenkins strolled into the room, smiling like this was the best thing that had happened all day. "I thought you was flying home, Nest Freemark. What're you doing, back in my kitchen?"

She saw Nest's face, and the smile faded away. "Good gracious, look at you! If I didn't know better, I'd say you'd been in a cat fight with Stef Winslow! She looks just the same!"

Nest flinched as if she had been struck. "I'm sorry to barge in like this, but something's come up and I really need to find John."

"Lord, if this isn't a day for finding John! Everyone wants to find John! You'd think he'd won the lottery or something. He hasn't, has he? 'Cause if he has, I want to be sure and get my share. Marilyn, let me use the phone there, sweetie."

Della moved the woman at the intake desk out of the picture with an easy exercise of authority that didn't leave much room for doubt as to who was boss. She picked up the receiver, punched in a number, and waited, listening. After a long time, she set the receiver down.

"John's been home all day, far as I know. He's stayed clear of here, and I don't expect him in. Stefanie's gone, too. Left here a short time ago. There's no answer at the apartment, so maybe they're out together somewhere."

Nest nodded, her mind racing over the possibilities. Had they left town? Had John Ross done as he promised? She didn't think so. She didn't think there was a prayer of that happening. He would still be in the city . . .

"Is Mr. Lawrence here?" she asked quickly.

"Oh, no, he's gone, too," Della answered, surrendering her seat to Marilyn once more. She came around the desk and put her finger to the side of her cheek. "You know, Nest—oh, I do love that name! Nest! Anyway, Nest, John might be down at the art museum, helping set up for tonight. That's where Simon's gone, so maybe John's gone there, too."

Nest was already starting for the door, shouldering her bag. "Thanks, Della. Maybe you're right."

"You want me to call and ask?"

"No, that's okay, I'll just go down. If John shows up here or calls in, tell him I'm looking for him and it's really important."

"Okay." Della made a face. "Here, where are you going with that bag? You don't want to be carrying that all over the place. You leave it with me, I'll keep it safe."

Nest came back and handed her bag to the big woman. "Thanks again. I'll see you."

She raced across the lobby, thinking, *I'm going to be too late, I'm not going to be in time!*

"Slow down, for goodness' sake, this ain't the fifty-yard dash!" Della called after her, but she was already out the door.

Andrew Wren spent the remainder of the afternoon following investigative roadways that all turned into dead ends. He was not discouraged, though. Investigative reporting required patience and bulldog determination, and he had an abundance of both. If the research took until Christmas, that was all right with him.

What wasn't all right was the way his instincts were acting. He trusted his instincts, and up until this morning they had been doing just fine. They had told him the anonymous reports of wrongdoing at Fresh Start were worth following up. They had told him the transfer records that had been slipped under his door were the real thing.

But what they were telling him now, barely eighteen hours later, was that something about all this was screwy.

For one thing, even though he had proof of the funds transfers from the corporate accounts of Fresh Start and Pass/Go to the private accounts of Simon Lawrence and John Ross, he couldn't find a pattern that made any sense. The withdrawals and deposits were regular, but the amounts transferred were too low given the amounts that might have been transferred from the money on hand. Sure, you wouldn't take too much, because you didn't want to draw attention. But you wouldn't take too little either, and in several cases it appeared this was exactly what the Wiz and Mr. Ross had done.

Then there was the matter of identifying the thieves. No one at any of the various banks could remember ever seeing either Mr. Lawrence or Mr. Ross make a deposit. But some of the deposits had been made in person, not by mail. Andrew Wren had been circumspect in making his inquiries, cloaking them in a series of charades designed to deflect the real reason for his interest. But not one teller or officer who had conducted the personal transactions could remember ever seeing either man come in.

But it was in the area of his personal contact with the two men he was investigating that his instincts were really acting up, telling him that the two men didn't do it. When someone was guilty of something, he could almost always tell. His instincts lit up like a scoreboard after a home run, and he just knew. But even after bracing both Simon and John Ross on the matter, his instincts refused to celebrate. Maybe they just weren't registering the truth of things this time out, but he didn't like it that they weren't flashing even a little.

Well, tomorrow was another day, and tonight was the gala event at the Seattle Art Museum, and he was anxious to see if he might learn something there. It wasn't an unrealistic expectation, given the circumstances. He would have another shot at both the Wiz and Ross, since both were expected to attend. He would have a good chance to talk with their friends and maybe even one or two of their enemies. One could always hope.

He reached the Westin just after five and rode up to his room in an otherwise empty elevator. He unlocked his door, slipped out of his rumpled jacket, and went into the bathroom to wash his face and hands and brush his teeth. When he came out again, he located his invitation, dropped it on top of his jacket, and poured himself a short glass of scotch from what remained of last night's bottle.

Then he sat down next to the phone and called Marty at the lab in New York. He let it ring. It was three hours later there, but Marty often worked late when there was no one around to interrupt. Besides, he knew Wren was anxious for a quick report.

On the seventh ring, Marty picked up. "Lab Works."

"Hello, Marty? It's Andrew. How are you coming?"

"I'm done."

Wren straightened. He'd sent Marty the transfer records by fax for signature comparison late that morning, marked "Urgent" in bold letters, but he hadn't really expected anything for another day.

"Andrew? You there?" Marty sounded impatient.

"I'm here. What did you find?"

"They don't match. Good forgeries, very close to the real thing, but phony. In some cases the signatures were just tracings. Good enough to pass at first glance, but nothing that would stand up in court. These boys are being had."

Andrew Wren stared into space. "Damn," he muttered.

Marty chuckled. "I thought you'd like that. But hang on a second, there's more. I checked the forgeries against all the other signatures you sent—friends, acquaintances, fellow workers, so on and so forth."

He paused meaningfully. "Yeah, so?" Wren prodded.

"So while there isn't a match there either, there is a singular characteristic in one other person's writing style that suggests you might have a new suspect. Again, not enough to stand up in court, but enough to make me sit up and take notice. It only appears on the signatures copied freehand, not on the ones traced, which is good because it's their freehand writing we're interested in."

Wren took a long drink of his scotch. "Enough with the buildup, Marty. Whose signature is it?"

Chapter 23

John Ross stepped out of the bus tunnel onto Third Avenue, walked right to University Street, and started down the steep hill. The evening air was brittle and sharp, tinged with a hint of early frost, and he pulled the collar of his coat closer about his neck. He moved slowly along the sidewalk, his gaze lowered to its surface, conscious of a slippery glaze encrusting the cement, relying on his staff for support.

Still bound to my past, he thought darkly. *Crippled by it. Unable to escape what I was.*

He tried to organize his thoughts as he passed close by the imposing glass lobby of the symphony hall, brilliant light spilling out across the promenade and planting areas to where he walked. But his mind would not settle. The possibilities of what he might discover when he confronted Simon Lawrence did not lend themselves readily to resolution. He wanted to be wrong about Simon. But a dark whisper at the back of his mind told him he was not and warned him he must be careful.

At the next intersection, he paused, waiting for the light to change, and allowed himself his first close look at his destination. The high, curved walls of the Seattle Art Museum loomed ahead, filling the entire south end of the block between Second and First. The Robert Venturi–designed building had a fortresslike look to it from this angle, all the windows that faced on First hidden, the massive sections of exposed limestone confronting him jagged, rough, and forbidding. In the shadowy street light, the softening contours and sculpting were invisible, and there was only a sense of weight and mass.

He crossed with the light and began his descent of a connecting set of terraces and steps that followed the slope of the hill down to the museum's primary entrance. He limped uneasily, warily, seeing movement and shadows everywhere, seeing ghosts. He peered into the brightly lit interior, where service people were bustling about in preparation for the night's festivities. He could see a scattering of tables on the broad platform of the mezzanine outside the little café, and more on the main floor of the entry. Stacks of trays and plates were being set out along with bottles of wine and champagne, chests of ice, napkins, silver, and crystal. The waiters and waitresses were dressed in skeleton suits, their painted bones shimmering with silver incandescence. One or two had already donned their skull masks. It gave the proceedings an eerie look: no guests had arrived yet, but the dead were making ready.

Ahead, the *Hammering Man* rose fifty feet into the night, stark and angular against the skyline of Elliott Bay and the mountains. A massive, flat steel cutout painted black, it was the creation of Jonathan Borofsky, who had intended it to reflect the working nature of the city. A hammer held in the left hand rose and fell in rhythmic motion, giving the illusion of pounding and shaping a bar that was held firmly in the right. The head was lowered in concentration to monitor the work being done, the body muscular and powerful as it bent to its endless task.

Ross stopped at the sculpture's base and looked up at it. An image of the dream that had haunted him these past six months clouded his vision, the old man accusing him anew of slaying the Wizard of Oz, in the glass palace of the Emerald City, where the Tin Woodman kept watch. He had recognized the references instantly, known them to be the museum and the *Hammering Man*. He had sworn to stay away, to do anything required to keep the dream from becoming reality. Yet here he was, as if in perverse disregard of all he had promised himself, because now there was reason to believe the dream was meant to happen.

He stood rooted in place then, thinking desperately. If he entered the museum, he was accepting he might not be meant to foil the dream, but to facilitate it. Such logic flew in the teeth of everything he had learned while he was a Knight of the Word, and yet he knew the past was not always an accurate measurement for the present and what had once been reliable might no longer be so. If he turned around now and walked away, he would not have to find out. But he would be left with unanswered questions about the demon who sought to destroy him and about Simon Lawrence, and he would have no peace.

He held the staff before him and stared into its rune-scrolled length. He gripped it in frustration, as if to break it asunder, giving way to an inner core of rage and heat that sought to drag the recalcitrant magic from its hiding place. But no magic appeared, and he was forced to consider anew that perhaps it was forever gone. As he had often wished, he reminded himself bitterly. As he had often prayed.

Cars moved past him on the streets in a steady line of headlights, rush-hour traffic heading home. Horns honked, more in celebration than in irritation. It was Halloween, and everyone was feeling good. Some passersby wore masks and costumes, waving their hands and yelling, holding up plastic weapons and icons against the night. Ross gave them a momentary glance, then faced the museum anew. The magic of the staff was a crutch he did not require. He would not have to do more than ask Simon why. There need not be a confrontation, a struggle, or a death. The dream need not come about. It was the truth he was seeking, and he thought it would make itself known quickly when he had Simon Lawrence before him.

But still he hesitated, torn in two directions, caught between choices that could change his life inalterably.

Then he took a deep breath, hefted the staff, set the butt end firmly on the ground, and walked into the museum.

It was loud and cavernous in the lobby, where the servers were scurrying about in final preparation. He stood in the doorway, glancing about for an indication of where to go. Ahead and to his left was a reception desk, the museum shop, and doors opening into an auditorium where the announcement of the dedication of city land for a new building for Fresh Start would be made. To his right, the Grand Stairway climbed through a Ming dynasty marble statuary of rams, camels, and guardians past the mezzanine to the upper floors. The prominent, distinctive arches draped from the ceiling were spaced at regular intervals so that Ross could imagine how the inside of the whale must have looked to Jonah. Where the rough-edged exterior was formed of limestone, sandstone, and terra-cotta, the softer interior was comprised of polished floors of terrazzo set in cement and of walls of red oak. Ross had visited the museum only once during the time he had lived in Seattle. He admired the architectural accomplishments, but still preferred the green, open spaces of the parks.

One of the security guards walked up to him and asked to see his invitation. Staying calm when he felt anything but, he said he had forgotten it, but he was employed at Fresh Start and was on the guest list. The guard asked for identification, which Ross produced. The guard seemed satisfied. Ross asked him if he had seen Simon Lawrence, but the guard said he had been working the door and hadn't seen anyone who might have entered another way.

Ross thanked him and walked past, eyes scanning the lobby, then the upper levels. There was no sign of Simon. He was feeling edgy again, thinking Stef had been right, he shouldn't have come, he should have let it go.

One of the servers came up to him with a mask. "Everyone gets a mask at this party," she enthused, handing him his. "Do you want me to take your coat?"

Ross declined her offer, not expecting to stay beyond talking with Simon, and then, because she seemed to expect it, he slipped on the mask. It was a black nylon sheath that covered the upper half of his face. It made him feel vaguely sinister amid the skeleton suits and Halloween trimmings.

He looked around some more without success for Simon and was about to move on to the reception desk when a security guard from the upper mezzanine area came down the steps toward him, waving to catch his attention.

"Mr. Ross?" he asked. When Ross nodded, the guard said, "Mr. Lawrence is waiting for you on the second floor in the Special Exhibition Hall. He said to go on up."

Ross caught himself staring at the guard in surprise, but then thanked him quickly and moved away. Simon was waiting for him? He began to climb the Grand Stairway without even considering the elevator, the broad steps leading up from the brightness of the lobby and mezzanine to the more shadowy rooms of the display halls above. He ascended at a steady pace through the rams and camels, through the civilian and military guardians, their eyes blank and staring, their expressions fixed, sculptures warding artifacts and treasures of the dead. Servers bustled by, skeleton costumes rippling, masks in place. He glanced at his watch. The evening's events were scheduled to begin in less than thirty minutes.

At the top of the stairs, he stopped and looked around. Below, the Grand Stairway stretched downward in a smooth flow of steps, arches, and glass windows to the array of finger foods, drinks, and serving people. Ahead, the hallway wound back on itself up a short flight of stairs to the exhibition rooms. Simon Lawrence was nowhere to be seen.

A ripple of apprehension ran down his spine. What was Simon doing up here?

He climbed the short flight of stairs and walked down the hallway into the exhibition rooms. The lights were dim, the red oak walls draped with shadows. There was a display of Chihuly glass that shimmered in bright splashes of color beneath directional lighting. Fire reds, sun-bright yellows, ocean blues, and deep purples lent a festive air to the semidark. Ross walked on, passing other exhibits in other areas, searching. The sound of his footfalls echoed eerily.

Then abruptly, shockingly, Simon Lawrence stepped out from behind a display directly to one side and said, "Why are you here, John?"

Ross started in spite of himself, then took a quick breath to steady the rapid beating of his heart and faced the other man squarely. "I came to ask you if what Stef told me was true."

Simon smiled. He was dressed in a simple black tuxedo that made him look taller and broader than Ross knew him to be and lent him an air of smooth confidence. "Which part, John? That I fired you for stealing money from the project? That I chose to do it without talking to you first? That I did it to distance myself from you?" He paused. "The answer is yes to all."

John stared at him in disbelief. Somehow, he hadn't expected Simon to find it so easy to say it to his face. "Why?" he managed, shaking his head slowly. "I haven't done anything, Simon. I didn't steal that money."

Simon Lawrence moved out of the shadows and came right up to Ross, stopping so close to him that Ross could see the silvery glitter of his eyes. "I know that," Simon said softly. "I did."

Ross blinked. "Simon, why—"

The other man interrupted smoothly, dismissing the question with a wave of his hand. "You know why, John."

John Ross felt the ground shift under his feet, as if the stone had turned to quicksand and was about to swallow him up. In that instant of confusion and dismay, Simon Lawrence snatched away his staff, wrenching it from his grasp with a sudden, vicious twist, then stepped back swiftly out of reach, leaving Ross tottering on his bad leg.

"I set fire to Fresh Start as well, John," Simon went on smoothly, cradling the staff beneath one arm. "I killed Ray Hapgood. Everything you think I might have done, I probably did. I did it to destroy the programs, to undermine the Simon Lawrence legend, the mystique of the Wiz, which, after all, I created in the first place. I did it to further the aims I really serve and not those I have championed as a part of my disguise. But you guessed as much already, or you wouldn't be here."

Ross was fighting to keep from attempting to rush Simon—or the thing that pretended at being Simon. An attack would only result in Ross falling on his face. He had to hope the other might come close enough to be grappled with, might make a mistake born of overconfidence.

"You fooled us all," he said softly. "But especially me. I never guessed what you really were."

The demon laughed. "I hired you in the first place, John, because I knew what *you* were and I was certain I could make good use of you. A Knight of the Word fallen from grace, an exile by choice, but still in possession of a valuable magic. The opportunity was too good to pass up. Besides, it was time to abandon this charade, to put an end to Simon Lawrence and his good works. It was time to move on to something else. All I had to do was to destroy the persona I had created by discrediting him. You were the perfect scapegoat. So willing, John, to be seduced. So I used you, and now you will take the blame, I will resign in disgrace, and the programs will fail. If it works as I intend, it will have a ripple effect on homeless programs all over the country. Loss of trust is a powerful incentive for closing up pocketbooks and shutting off funds."

The demon smiled. "Was that what you wanted to hear, John? I haven't disappointed you, have I?"

It took the staff from beneath its arms and flung it into the space behind, where it skidded across the stone floor and clattered into the wall. Then it reached out and took Ross by his shirt front and dragged him forward. Ross fought to escape, but the demon was too strong for him and backhanded him across the face. The blow snapped Ross's head back, and a bright flash of pain left him blinded and stunned. The demon lifted Ross and held him suspended above the floor. Ross blinked to clear his vision, then watched as the demon lifted its free hand. The hand began to transform, changing from something human to something decidedly not. Claws and bristling hair appeared. The demon glanced at its handiwork speculatively, then raked the claws across Ross's midsection. They tore through coat and shirt, shredding the flesh beneath, bringing bright welts of blood.

The demon threw John Ross down, sending him sprawling back onto the floor. "You really are pathetic, John," it advised conversationally, walking to where he lay gasping for breath and bleeding. "Look at you. You can't even defend yourself. I was prepared to offer you a place in service to the Void, but what would be the point? Without your staff, you're nothing. Even with the staff, I doubt you could do much. You've lost your magic, haven't you? It's all dried up and blown away. There's nothing left."

The demon reached down, picked Ross up, and slashed him a second time, this time down one shoulder. It struck Ross across the face again, dropping him as it might a thing so foul it could not bear to hold him longer. Ross collapsed in a heap, fighting to stay conscious.

"You're not worth any more of my time, John," the demon sneered softly, standing over him once more. "I could kill you, but you're worth more to me alive. I've still use for you in destroying Simon Lawrence and his fine works. I've still plans for you."

It bent down, leaning close, and whispered, "But if I see you again this night, I will kill you where I find you. Don't test me on this, John. Get out of here and don't come back."

Then it rose, pushed Ross down with its foot, held him pinned helplessly against the floor as it studied him, then turned and walked away.

For a long time Ross lay where the demon had left him, a black wave of nausea and pain threatening to overwhelm him with every breath he took. He lay on his back, staring up at a ceiling enveloped in layers of deep shadows. He might have given in to the despair and shame that swept through him if he were any other man, if he had not once been a Knight of the Word. But the seeds of his identity ran deeper than he would have thought possible, and amid the darker feelings wound an iron cord of determination that would have required him to die first.

After a while, he was strong enough to roll onto his side and sit up. Dizziness threatened to flatten him anew, but he lowered his head between his legs, braced himself with his hands, and waited for the feeling to pass. When it did, he lurched to his knees, dropped back to his hands, and began to crawl. Streaks of blood from his wounds marked his slow passage, and shards of fire traced the deep furrows the demon's claws had left on his body. The hallway and exhibit areas were silent and empty of life, and he worked his solitary way across the polished stone with only the sound of his breathing for company.

He had been a fool, he told himself over and over again. He had misjudged badly, been overconfident of what he could accomplish when he would have been better served by being more cautious. He should have listened to Stef. He should have trusted his instincts. He should have remembered the lessons of his time in service to the Word.

Twice he slipped in pools of his own excretions and went down. His arms and hands were wet from blood and sweat, and every movement he made trying to cross the museum floor racked his body with pain.

Damn you, Simon, he swore silently, resolutely, a litany meant to empower. *Damn you to hell.*

When he reached the staff, he rose again to his knees and wiped his bloodstained palms on his pants. Then he took the staff firmly in his hands and levered himself back to his feet.

He stood there for a moment, swaying unsteadily. When the dizziness passed, he moved to an empty bench in the center of the hall, seated himself, slipped off the greatcoat, then the tattered shirt, and used the shirt to bind his ribs and chest in a mostly successful effort to slow the flow of his blood. He sat staring into space after that, trying to gather his strength. He didn't think anything was broken, but he had lost a lot of blood. He could not continue without help, and the only help he could count on now would have to come from within.

Hard-eyed and ashen-faced, he leaned forward on the bench, wrapped in the tatters of his shirt, his upper torso mostly bare and red-streaked with his blood. He straightened with an effort and tightened his grip on the staff, his abandoned choices swirling around him like wraiths, his decision of what he must do fully embraced. He no longer cared about consequences or dreams. He could barely bring himself to think on the future beyond this night. What he knew was that he had been driven to his knees by something so foul and repulsive he could not bear another day of life if he did not bring an end to it.

So he called forth the magic of the staff, called it with a certainty that surprised him, called it with full acceptance of what it meant to do so. He renounced himself and what he had become. He renounced his stand of the past year and took up anew the mantle he had shed. He declared himself a Knight of the Word, begged for the right to become so once more, if only for this single night, if only for this solitary purpose. He armored himself in his vow to become the thing he had tried so hard to disclaim, accepting as truth the admonitions of Owain Glyndwr and O'olish Amaneh. He bowed in acknowledgment to the cautions of the Lady as delivered by Nest Freemark and her friends, giving himself over once more to the promises he had made fifteen years earlier when he had taken up the cause of the Word and entered into His service.

Even then, the magic did not come at once, for it lay deep within the staff, waiting for the call to be right, for the prayer to be sincere. He could sense it, poised and heedful, but recalcitrant. He strained to reach it, to make it feel his need, to draw it to him as he would a reluctant child. His eyes were closed and his brow furrowed in concentration, and the pain that racked his body became a white-hot fury at the core of his heart.

Suddenly, abruptly, the Lady was before him, there in the darkness of his mind, white-gowned and ephemeral, her hands reaching for him. Oh, my brave Knight Errant, would you truly come back to me? Would you serve me as you once did, without reservation or guilt, without doubt or fear? Would you be mine as you were? Her words filtered like the slow meandering of a forest stream through rocks and mud banks, soft and rippling. He cried at the sound of her voice, the tears filling his lids and leaking down his bloodied face. I would. I will. Always. Forever.

Then she was gone, and the magic of the staff stirred and gathered and came forth in a swift, steady river, climbing out of the polished black walnut into his arms and body, filling him with its healing power.

Silver light enfolded the Knight of the Word with bright radiance, and he was alive anew.

And dead to what once he had hoped so strongly he might be.

John Ross lifted his head in recognition, feeling the power of the magic flow through him, rising out of the staff, eager to serve. He let it strengthen him as nothing else could, not caring what it might cost him. For the cost was not his to measure. It would be measured in his dreams, when they returned. It would be measured in the time he would spend unprotected in the future he had sworn to prevent and, as a Knight of the Word once more, must now return to.

But before that happened, he vowed, climbing to his feet as the damage to his body was swept aside by the sustaining magic, he would find Simon Lawrence, demon of the Void.

And he would destroy him.

Nest Freemark arrived at the museum with the first crush of invited guests, and it took her a while just to get through the door. When she was asked for her invitation and failed to produce it, she was told in no uncertain terms that if her name wasn't on the guest list, she couldn't come in. She tried to explain how important this was, that she needed to find John Ross or Simon Lawrence, but the security guards weren't interested. People behind her were getting impatient with the delay, and she might have been thwarted altogether if she hadn't caught sight of Carole Price and called her over. Carole greeted Nest effusively and told the security guards to let her through.

"Nest, what are you doing here?" the other woman asked, steering her to an open spot amid the knots of masked guests and skeleton-costumed servers. "I thought you'd gone back to Illinois."

"I postponed my flight," she replied, keeping her explanation purposefully vague. "Is John here?"

"John Ross?" A waiter came up to them with a tray filled with champagne glasses, and Carole motioned him away. "No, I haven't seen him yet."

"How about Mr. Lawrence?"

"Oh, yes, Simon's here somewhere. I saw him just a little while ago." Her brow furrowed slightly. "You heard about the fire, didn't you, Nest?"

Nest nodded. "I'm sorry about Mr. Hapgood." There was an awkward silence as she tried to think of something else to say. "I know John was very upset about it."

Carole Price nodded. "We all were. Look, why don't you go on and see if you can find him. I haven't seen him down here, but maybe he's up on the mezzanine. And I'll tell Simon you're here. He'll want to say hello."

"Thanks." Nest glanced around doubtfully. The lobby was filling up quickly with guests, and everyone was wearing a mask. It made recognizing people difficult. "If you see John," she said carefully, "tell him I'm here. Tell him it's important that I speak with him right away."

Carole nodded, a hint of confusion in her blue eyes, and Nest moved away before she could ask any questions.

A passing server handed her one of the black nylon masks, and she slipped it on. All around her, people were drinking champagne. Their talk and laughter was deafening in the cavernous space. Eyes scanning the crowd, she moved toward the wide staircase with the massive stone figures warding its various levels and began to climb. As she did so, a troubling realization came to her. She had forgotten about the dream, the one that had haunted Ross for months, the one in which the old man accused him of killing the Wizard of Oz—and perhaps of killing her as well. She had been thinking so hard about Ross and the demon and what she suspected about both that it had slipped her mind. It was supposed to happen here, in the Seattle Art Museum, on this night. He had wanted her far away from this place, so it could never happen. He had wanted himself far away as well. But she suspected events and demon schemes were at work conspiring to thwart his wishes. Simon Lawrence was already here. She was here. If he wasn't already, soon John Ross would be here too.

She reached the mezzanine and glanced around anew. She did not see Ross. She felt a growing desperation at her inability to locate him. The longer he remained ignorant of what she suspected, the greater the risk his dream would come to pass. But all she could do was to keep looking. She walked over to a security guard and asked if he had seen John Ross. He told her he didn't even know who Ross was. Frustrated with his response, she asked if he'd seen Simon Lawrence. The guard said no, but asked her to wait and walked over to speak with a second guard. After a moment he came back and told her the second guard had sent a man upstairs not long ago to talk with Mr. Lawrence—a man who walked with a limp and carried a walking stick.

Stunned by her blind good luck, she thanked him and moved quickly to the stairway. She had never even thought to ask if a man with a walking staff and a limp had come in. Stupid, stupid! She tore off the nylon mask and went up the stairs in a rush, wondering what Simon and Ross were doing up there, wondering if somehow she was already too late. There was still too much she didn't know, too much about the circumstances surrounding the events portended in Ross's dream that was hidden from her. There was a tangle of threads in this matter that needed careful unraveling before it ensnared them all.

She reached the second-floor landing and wheeled left to where a dozen steps rose to a dimly lit corridor and the exhibition rooms beyond. She was halfway up this second set of stairs when she drew up short.

John Ross walked out of the shadows, a luminous, terrifying apparition. His clothes were torn and bloodied, and his tattered coat billowed out from his half-naked body like a cape. The black, rune-scrolled staff that was the source of his magic shimmered with silver light, and the radiance it emitted ran all about him like electricity. His strong, sharply angled face was hard-set and drawn, and his green eyes were fierce with determination and rage.

When he saw her, he faltered slightly, and with recognition came a hint of fear and shock. "Nest!" he hissed.

Her breath caught in her throat. "John, what happened?" When he shook his head, unwilling to answer, she wasted no further time on the matter. "John, I had to come back," she said quickly. "I took a chance I might find you here. I have to talk with you."

He shook his head in horror, seeing something that was hidden from her, some truth too terrible to accept. "Get out of here, Nest! I told you to get away! I warned you about the dream!"

"But that's why I'm here." She tried to get closer, but he held up one hand as if to ward himself against her. "John, you have to forget about the dream. The dream was a lie."

"It was the truth!" he shouted back at her. "The dream was the truth! The dream is meant to happen! But some of it can still be changed, enough so that you won't be hurt! But you have to get out of here! You have to leave now!"

She brushed back her curly hair, trying to understand what he was saying. "No, the dream doesn't have to happen. Don't you remember? You're supposed to prevent the dream!"

He came forward a step, wild-eyed and shining with silver light, the magic a living thing as it raced up and down his body and across his limbs. "You don't understand!" he hissed at her in fury. "I'm supposed to *make* it happen!"

There were footsteps and voices on the Grand Stairway, and Nest turned in surprise. She heard Simon Lawrence speaking, and she rushed to where she could see him climbing out of the brightly lit mezzanine toward the second-floor shadows.

She wheeled back to find John Ross striding toward her. "Get out of the way, Nest."

She stared at him, appalled at what she saw in his eyes and heard in his voice. "No, John, wait."

The footsteps stopped momentarily, the voices still audible. Nest could hear Simon Lawrence distinctly, calling to someone below. A woman. Carole Price? Nest went back toward Ross, holding out her hands pleadingly. "John, it isn't him!"

His laugh was brittle. "I saw him, Nest! He did this to me, moments ago, up there!" He gestured back in the direction from which he had come. "He told me everything, admitted it! Then he attacked me! He's the demon, Nest! He's the one who stalked you in the park, the one who destroyed Ariel and Audrey and Boot! He's the one who set fire to Fresh Start! He's the one who killed Ray Hapgood!"

He slammed the butt end of his black staff against the stone floor, and white fire ran up its length like a rocket, searing the dark. "This dream isn't like the others, Nest! It's a prophecy!" His voice was ragged and uneven, choked with anger. "It's a revelation meant to put things right! It's a window into a truth I was trying wrongly, foolishly to ignore! I have to act on it! I have to make it happen!"

She held up her hands to slow his advance. "No, John, listen to me!"

The footsteps were approaching again, the voices growing stronger. She could hear Simon joking with someone, could hear muffled responses, sudden laughter, the clink of glasses. Ross was staring past her, the staff's magic gathering about his knotted hands, growing brighter as he waited for Simon to come into view so that he could unleash it.

"Step aside, Nest," he said softly.

In desperation she backed away from him, but slowly and with measured steps, so he did not advance immediately, but stood watching to see what she intended. She backed until the sweep of the stairway came into view, then wheeled on the knot of people approaching. Simon Lawrence was foremost, smiling, at ease, exchanging remarks with Carole Price and three weathered, worn-looking men who looked to have seen hard times and few respites. They had not seen her yet, and she did not wait for them to do so. She acted on instinct and out of need. She called on her own magic, on the magic she had been born with but had forsworn since the death of Gran. She called on it without knowing whether it would come, but with certainty that it must. She drew Simon Lawrence's gaze to her own, just a glimpse and no more, just enough to bind them for an instant, then used the magic to buckle his legs and drop him nerveless and limp upon the stairs.

She stepped quickly from view as his companions gathered around him, kneeling to see what had happened. It surprised her how quickly she was able to regain her use of a skill she had not tested for so long. But calling on it had an unexpected side effect. It had awakened something else inside of her, something much larger and more dangerous. She felt it stir and then rise, growing large and ferocious, and for a terrifying moment she felt as if it might get away from her completely.

Then she recovered herself, all in an instant, and turned back to face Ross. He hadn't moved. He was standing where she had left him, a puzzled look on his face. He had seen something that had escaped her, and whatever it was, it had left him confused and momentarily distracted.

She did not wait for him to recover. She went to him immediately, crossed the open space between them, and came right up to where he stood, aswirl in his magic, enfolded by the staff's power, the rage and fierce determination returning to his eyes as he recovered his purpose.

"No, John," she said again, quickly, firmly, taking hold of his arms, ignoring the feel of the magic as it played across her skin. She was not afraid. There was no place for her fear in what he required of her. Her eyes met his and she held him bound. "You've been tricked, John. We've all been tricked."

"Nest," he whispered, but there was no force behind the speaking of her name, only a vague sort of plea.

"I know," she replied softly, meaning it without understanding how exactly, knowing mostly that he needed to feel it was true. "But it isn't him, John. It isn't Simon. He isn't the demon."

And then she told him who was.

Chapter 24

So now, with his memory of the dream that had started it all fading like autumn color, John Ross began to cross the shadowed cobblestone expanse of Occidental Park in Pioneer Square, his topcoat pulled close about his battered, bloodied torso, a wraith come down out of Purgatory to find the demon who had sentenced him to Hell. The night air was cold and sharp with the smell of winter's coming, and he breathed in the icy scents. Wooden totems loomed overhead as he passed beneath their watchful, fierce gaze, and the homeless who scurried to get out of his way cast apprehensive glances over their shoulders, wary of the silver glow that emanated in a faint sheen from the long black staff that supported him. On the hard surface of the cobblestones, the butt end of the staff clicked softly to mark his progress, and a sudden rush of wind blew debris in a ragged scuttle from his path. The feeders who had gathered at his return trailed silently in his wake, eyes watchful, movements quick and furtive. He could sense their anticipation and their hunger for what lay ahead.

He was a Knight of the Word once more, now and forever, bound by the pledge he had given in persuading the magic to return to him. He was become anew what he had sought so hard to escape, and in his recognition and acceptance of the futility of his efforts he found a kind of solace. It was the home he had looked for and not found in his other life. It was the reality of his existence he had sought to deny. In his renunciation of the Word, he had lost his way, been deceived, and very nearly given himself over to a fate that even on brief reflection made his skin crawl.

But all that was past. All of who he had been and sought to be in these last twelve months was past. His life, the only life he would ever have now, he supposed, was given back to him, and he must find a way to atone for casting it aside so recklessly.

Even if it meant giving it up again as payment for the cost of setting things right.

Street lamps burned with fierce bright centers through the Halloween gloom. All masks were off, all secrets revealed, the trickery finished. By dawn, there would be an accounting and a retribution and perhaps his own death. It would depend on how much of himself he had rescued, how much of the warrior he had been he could summon anew.

He looked ahead to the lights of his apartment, and beyond to the smoking ruins of Fresh Start and the mostly darkened bulk of Pass/Go. The buildings lined the corridor of Main Street, safeholds hiding the secrets of the people within. Ross experienced a sense of futility in thinking of the disguises that obscured the truths in human existence. It was so easy to become lost in the smug certainty that what happened to others really mattered very little to you. It was so easy to ignore the ties that bound humanity on its collective journey in search of grace.

A solitary car passed down the broad corridor of Second Avenue and disappeared. In the distance rose voices and music, laughter and shouts, the sounds of celebration on All Hallows' Eve. For those people, at least, the dark side of witchery and demons was only a myth.

He passed Waterfall Park, the rush of the waterfall a muffled whoosh in the dark confines of the park's walls, the courtyard a vaguely defined spiderweb of wrought-iron tables, chairs, and trellises amid the blockier forms of the stone fountains and sculptures. He turned on hearing his name called, looking back the way he had come. Nest Freemark was running toward him, her unzipped parka flying out behind her, her curly hair jouncing about her round, flushed face. Feeders melted away into the darkness at her approach, into the rocks of the park, into the tangle of tables and chairs, but she seemed heedless of them. She came up to Ross in a rush and stood panting before him, eyes quickly searching his own.

"I came to help," she said.

He smiled at her earnest expression, at the determination he found in her young voice. "No, Nest," he told her quietly.

"But I want to. I need to."

He had left her behind at the museum when he had departed. She had gone down the stairs to intercept Simon Lawrence and his companions, to delay them long enough for Ross to slip out a side door so he wouldn't be seen. Even so, in leaving another way besides the main entrance he set off an alarm that brought security guards from the lower level. As he crossed the street toward a dark alleyway, he watched them stumble unaccountably in their efforts to navigate the Grand Stairway, Nest studying them intently from her position beside a recovering Simon.

"For Ariel," she said firmly. "For Boot and Audrey."

He felt a rush of hot shame and anger, the revelations she had provided burning through him in a fresh wave of shock and disbelief. But truth has a way of making itself known even to the most skeptical, and he had stripped away the blinders that had kept him deceived and was empowered by his new knowledge and the determination it generated.

"For myself, John," she finished.

But she had not seen herself as he had, back at the museum, in the shadowy confines of the Exhibition Hall, where the two of them had come face-to-face in a confrontation that might have led to the horrific fulfillment of his dream. She did not realize yet what she had revealed to him that even she did not know, of the way her magic had evolved, of the secret she now held inside. Powerful forces were at work in Nest Freemark that would change her life yet again. He should tell her, of course. But he could not bring himself to do so now, when the secrets of his own life weighed so heavily on his mind and demanded their own resolution.

He stepped closer to her and put his hands on her shoulders. "I am a Knight of the Word, Nest. I am what I was always meant to be, and I owe much of that to you. But I cannot claim the right to serve if I do not resolve first the reason I lost my way. I have to do that. And I have to do it alone. This is personal to me, so close to the bone that to settle it in any other way would leave me hollowed out. Do you see?"

She studied his face a long time. "But you're hurt. You've lost a lot of blood."

He took his hands away from her shoulders and settled them on the polished length of his staff. "The magic will give me the strength I need for this."

She shook her head. "I don't like it. It's too dangerous."

He looked at her, thinking it odd that someone so young should speak to him of what was too dangerous. But then the dangers in her own life had been, on balance, no less than his.

"Wait for me here, Nest," he told her. "Keep watch. If I don't come out, at least one other person will know the truth."

He didn't wait for her response but wheeled away quickly and went down the sidewalk to the corner, turned left along Second, and walked to the apartment entrance. Feeders reappeared in droves, creeping over the walls of Waterfall Park, coming up from the gutters and out of the alleyways between the buildings. They materialized in such numbers that he experienced an unexpected chill. Their yellow eyes were fixed on him, empty of everything but their hunger. So many, he mused. He could feel the weight of their expectations in the way they pressed forward to be close to him, and he knew they understood with primal instinct what was at stake.

He entered the foyer, using his key, walked to the elevator, and took it up to the sixth floor. The feeders did not follow. He imagined them scaling the outside wall, climbing steadily, relentlessly closer to the windows of his apartment. He envisioned an enormous tidal wave washing toward a sleeping town.

He exited the elevator and moved to his apartment door, used his key again, and entered.

The apartment was shadowy and silent, with only a single lamp burning at one end of the old couch. Stefanie sat reading in the halo of its light, her exquisite face lifting to greet him, her strange, smoky eyes filling with shock as he closed the door and came into the light.

"John, what happened?" she whispered, rising quickly.

He put out his hand, a defensive gesture, and shook his head. "Don't get up, Stef. Just stay where you are, please." He leaned heavily on his staff, studying her perplexed face, the way she brushed back her dark hair, cool and reserved, watchful. "Simon Lawrence isn't dead," he said quietly.

He saw a flicker of something dark in her eyes, but her face never changed. "What do you mean? Why *would* he be dead? What are you talking about, John?"

He shrugged. "It's simple. I went to the museum to speak with him. He was waiting for me. He admitted everything—firing me without giving me a hearing, stealing the money himself, working to destroy Fresh Start, all of it. Then he attacked me. He overpowered me, threw me down, and walked away. When he left, I went after him. I wanted to kill him. I would have, too, except for Nest Freemark. She came back from the airport to warn me. It wasn't Simon Lawrence I was looking for at all, she said." He paused, watching her carefully. "It was you."

She shook her head slowly, a strange little smile playing over her lips. "I have no idea what you are talking about."

He nodded indulgently. She was so beautiful, but everything about her was a lie. "The fact of the matter is, I was ready to believe everything you wanted me to believe. That Simon Lawrence was the demon. That he was responsible for all the bad things happening. That he was intent on ruining my life, on using me, on breaking me down. I had convinced myself. Then, when you tricked me into coming upstairs at the museum, when you disguised yourself as Simon and attacked me, humiliated me, taunted me, and cast me aside as if I were worthless, I was primed and ready to kill him the moment I found him again. And I would have killed him, too, if not for Nest."

"John—"

"She told me it was you, Stef, and after I got past the initial shock that such a thing could possibly *be*, that I could have been fooled so *completely*, that I could have been so *stupid*, I began to realize what had happened. You were so clever, Stef. You used me right from the beginning. You let me approach you in Boston, played me like a fish on a line, and then reeled me in. I was hooked. I loved you. You made yourself so desirable and so accessible I couldn't help myself. I wanted to believe you were the beginning, the cornerstone, of a new life. I was through being a Knight of the Word; I wanted something else. You understood what that something was better than I did, and you gave it to me. You gave me the promise of a life with you.

"But you know, what really made it all work was that I couldn't imagine it wasn't real. Why would it be anything else? Why wouldn't you be exactly who you said you were? When Nest first suggested you might be the demon, I dismissed the idea out of hand. It made no sense. If you were the demon, why wouldn't you just kill me and be done with it? Of what possible use was I alive? A former Knight of the Word, an exile, a wanderer—I was just further proof you had made the right choice a long time ago when you embraced the Void."

She wasn't saying anything. She was just sitting there, listening attentively, waiting to see if he had really worked it out. He could tell it just by looking at her, by the way she was studying him. It infuriated him; it made him feel ashamed for the way he had allowed himself to be used.

"Nest figured it out, though," he continued. "She explained it to me. She said you saw me in the same way her father had seen her grandmother, when her grandmother was a young girl. Her father was drawn to her grandmother's magic, and you were drawn to mine. But demons need to possess humans, to take control of them in order to make the magic their own, and sometimes they mistake this need to possess for love. Their desire for the magic confuses them. I think maybe that's what happened to you."

"John—"

"No. Don't say a word to me. Just listen." His fingers knotted about his staff more tightly. "The fact remains, I was no good to you dead. Because if I were dead you couldn't make use of the magic trapped inside the staff. And you wanted that magic badly, didn't you? But to get it, you had to do two things. You had to find a way to persuade me to recover it from the dark place to which I had consigned it and then to use it in a way that would make me dependent on you. If I could be tricked into killing Simon Lawrence, if I could be made to use the magic in such a terribly wrong way, then I would share something in common with you, wouldn't I? I would have taken the first step down the path you had chosen for me. I was halfway there, wasn't I? I was already very nearly what you wanted me to be. You'd worked long and hard to break me down, to give me the identity you wanted. Only this one last thing remained."

He shook his head in amazement. "You killed that demon in Lincoln Park to protect your investment. Because it wanted me dead, so it could claim victory over a Knight of the Word. But you wanted me alive for something much grander. You wanted me for the magic I might place at your command."

She stared at him, her perfect features composed, still not moving. "I love you, John. Nothing you've said changes that."

"You love me, Stef? Enough that you might teach me to feed on homeless children, like you've been feeding on them?" He spit out the words as if they were tinged with poison. "Enough that you might let me help you hunt them down in the tunnels beneath the city and kill them?"

Her temper flared. "The homeless are of no use. No one cares what happens to them. They serve no real purpose. You know that."

"Do I?" He fought down his disgust. "Is that why you killed Ariel and Boot and Audrey? Because they didn't serve any real purpose either? Is that why you tried to kill Nest? That didn't work out so well, did it? But you were quick to cover up, I'll give you that. Burning down Fresh Start, that was a nice touch. I assumed at first that you burned it down just to undermine its programs. But you did it to hide the truth about what happened in Lincoln Park. You marked yourself up pretty good going after Nest, smashing down doors and hurtling through windows. You couldn't hide that kind of damage. So you killed two birds with one stone. You'd drugged me earlier so I wouldn't be able to meet Nest. When you woke me, after you'd set fire to Fresh Start, you did so in the dark so I couldn't see your face, and while I was still barely coherent, you ran on ahead on the pretext of waking the women and children sleeping on the upper floors on the building, thereby providing yourself with a perfect excuse for the cuts and bruises on your face and hands."

His laugh was brittle. "It's funny, but Nest figured that out, too. When she came looking for me, she stopped by Pass/Go, and Della told her she looked just like you. Nest got the connection immediately. She knew what it meant."

She leaned forward. "John, will you listen . . . ?"

But he was all done listening, and he pushed relentlessly on. "So you set me up with this story about Simon firing me, and you quitting, and how strangely he's been acting, and how every time something bad happens, he's among the missing, and I'm just like a loaded gun ready to go off. I take the bus down to the museum, which you know I'll do, and it takes me a while because I don't walk very well with my bad leg, and you catch a cab, and there you are, waiting, disguised as Simon, ready to point me in the right direction."

He was so angry now he could barely contain himself, but his voice stayed cool and detached. "I really hate you, Stef. I hate you so much I can't find the words to express it!"

She studied him a moment, her perfect features composed in thoughtful consideration, and then she shook her head at him. "You don't hate me, John. You love me. You always will."

His shock at hearing her say it left him momentarily speechless. He had not expected her to be so perceptive. She was right, of course. He loved her desperately, even now, even knowing what she was.

"You aren't as honest with yourself as you think," she continued calmly, her dark eyes locking on his own. "You don't want any of this to be so, but even knowing it is, you can't get around how you feel. Is that so bad? If you want me, I'm still yours. I still want you, John. I still love you. Think about what you're doing. If you give me up, you become the thing you fought so hard to escape being. You become a Knight of the Word again. You give up everything you've found this past year with me. You go back to being solitary and lonely and rootless. You become like the homeless you've spent so much time trying to help."

She rose, a smooth, lazy motion, and he tensed in response, remembering how strong she was, what she was capable of doing. But she didn't try to approach him. "With me, you have everything that's made you happy these past twelve months. I can be all the things I've been to you from the beginning. Are you worried you might see me another way? Don't be. You never will. I'll be for you just what you want. I've made you happy. You can't pretend I haven't."

He smiled at her, suddenly sad beyond anything he had ever known. "You're right," he acknowledged softly, and all the rage seemed to dissipate. "You have made me happy. But none of it was real, was it, Stef? It was all a sham. I don't think I want to go back to that."

"Do you think other people live any differently than we do?" she pressed. She took a step away from the couch, then another, moving out of the circle of lamplight, edging into the shadows beyond. Ross watched, saying nothing. "Everyone keeps secrets. No one reveals everything. Even to a lover." He winced at the words, but she didn't seem to notice. She brushed back her hair, seemingly distracted by something behind him. He kept his eyes on her. "We can do the same," she said. "You won't ever find anyone else who feels about you the way I do."

The irony of that last statement must have escaped her entirely, he thought. "How you feel about me is rooted mostly in the ways you hope to use me, Stef."

He was moving with her now, a step and then two, a slow circling dance, a positioning for advantage.

"You can make your own choices about everything, John," she said. "I won't interfere. Just let me do the same. That's all I require."

His laugh was brittle. "Is that all it would take to make you happy, Stef? For me to ignore what you are? For me to let you go on feeding on humans? For me to pretend I don't care that you won't ever stop trying to turn the Word's magic to uses it was never intended for?" She was shaking her head violently in denial. "Just forget about the past? Forget about Boot and Audrey and Ariel and Ray Hapgood and several dozen homeless people? Forget about everything that's gone before? Would that do the trick?"

He saw a glimmer of something dark and wicked come into her eyes. He took a step toward her. "You crossed the line a long time ago, and it's way too late for you to come back. More to the point, I don't intend to let you try."

She was silhouetted against the bay window that looked down on Waterfall Park, her slender body gone suddenly still. Outside, feeders were pressed against the glass, yellow eyes gleaming.

There was a subtle shift in her features. "Maybe you can't stop me, John."

He straightened, clasping the staff in both hands, the magic racing up and down its length in slender silver threads.

Her smile was faint and tinged with regret. "Maybe you never could."

In a single, fluid motion she dropped into a crouch, wheeled away, and catapulted herself through the plate glass of the window behind her. Before he could even think to try to stop her, she had dropped from sight and was gone.

Nest Freemark was standing on the sidewalk outside Waterfall Park when the apartment window exploded as if struck by a sledgehammer, raining shards of glass into the night and sending feeders scattering into the shadows like rats. She turned toward the sound, her first thoughts of John Ross, but the dark thing that plummeted through the gloom was screaming in another voice entirely. Nest stood frozen in place, watching as it began to twist and re-form in midair, as if its flesh and bones were malleable. It had been human at first, but now it was something else entirely. It struck the jumble of rocks midpoint on the waterfall, bounced away, and tumbled into the catchment.

Nest raced for the narrow park entrance, her heartbeat quick and hurried and anxious. She burst through the ungated opening as the dark thing climbed free of the trough, a two-legged horror that was already losing what remained of its human identity, dropping down on all fours and shape-shifting into something more primal. Its legs thinned and lengthened and turned crooked, its torso thickened from haunches to chest, and its head grew elongated and broad-muzzled.

Stefanie Winslow, she thought in horror. The demon.

Re-formed into something that most closely resembled a monstrous hyena, the demon shook itself as if to be rid of the last of the disguise that had confined it and lifted its blunt snout toward the heights from which it had fallen. Feeders leaped and scrambled about it in a frenzy, like shadows flowing over one another, eyes bright against the dark. The demon snarled at them, snapped at the air through which they passed, and started to turn away.

Then it caught sight of Nest and wheeled quickly back again.

Even in the scattered light of the street lamps, Nest could see the hard glitter of its eyes fix on her. She could see the hate in them. The big head lowered, the muzzle parted, and rows of hooked teeth came into view. A low-pitched, ugly snarl rose from its throat. Maybe it intended to finish what it had started in Lincoln Park. Maybe it was just reacting on instinct. Nest held her ground. She felt her magic gather and knot in her chest. She had fled from this monster once; this time she would stand and face it. The demon, it seemed, had made up its mind as well. It could have turned away from her, could have scaled the park fence and escaped without forcing a confrontation. But it never wavered in its approach.

In a scrabbling of claws on stone and with a bone-chilling howl, it attacked. Feeders converged in its wake, leaping and darting through the shadows in a wave of yellow eyes. Nest had only a moment to react, and she did so. She locked eyes with the demon and threw out the magic she had been born with, her legacy from the Freemark women, thinking to stun it, to throw it off stride, to cause it to falter. She need only delay it long enough for John Ross to reach her. He would be coming; the demon was clearly in flight from him. A few moments was all she needed, and her magic would give her that. She had used it on Simon Lawrence and the security guards at the museum not two hours earlier. It was an old and familiar companion, and she could feel its presence stir deep inside even before she called it forth.

Even so, she wasn't prepared for what happened next.

The magic she had called upon did not respond.

Another magic did.

It came from the same place as the magic she had been born to, from inside, where her soul resided in a conjoining of heart and mind and body. It exploded out of her in a rush of dark energy, taking its own distinctive form, unleashed by instincts that demanded she survive at any cost. Its power was raw and terrifying, and she could not control it. It did not release from her as she had expected, but swept her along, borne within its storm-racked center, and it was as if she were caught inside a whirlwind.

She was seeing the demon now through darker, more primitive eyes, and she realized suddenly, shockingly, that those eyes belonged to Wraith. She was trapped inside the ghost wolf. She had become a part of him.

Then she was hurtling into the demon, with no time left to think. Claws and teeth ripped and tore, and snarls filled the air, and she was fighting the demon as if become Wraith, herself grown massive through the shoulders and torso, rough-coated with fur, gimlet-eyed and lupine.

Back against the rocks she drove the demon, steeped in the ghost wolf's strength and swift reactions. The demon twisted and fought, intertwined so closely with her she could feel the bunching of its muscles and hear the hissing of its breath. The demon tried to gain a grip on her throat, failed, and leaped away. She gave pursuit, a red veil of hot rage and killing need blinding her to everything else. They rolled and tumbled through the wrought-iron furniture, against the maze of rocks and fountains, and she no longer thought to wonder what was happening or why, but only to gain an advantage over a foe she knew she must destroy.

Perhaps she would have succeeded. Perhaps she would have prevailed. But then she heard her name called. A sharp cry, it was filled with despair and anguish.

John Ross had reached her at last.

White fire lashed the air in front of her, turning her aside. But the fire was not meant for her. It struck the demon full on, a rope of searing flame, and threw it backward to land in a bristling heap. She caught sight of Ross now, standing just inside the park entrance, his legs braced, the black staff bright with magic. Again the fire lanced from the Knight of the Word into the demon, catching it as it tried to twist away, knocking it down once more. Ross advanced, his face all planes and sharp edges, etched deep with shadows and grim determination.

The demon fought back. It counterattacked with a stunning burst of speed and fury, snapping at the scorched night air. But the Word's magic hammered into it over and over, knocking it back, flinging it away. Ross closed the distance between himself and his adversary, ignoring Nest, his concentration centered on the demon. The demon wailed suddenly, as if become human again, a cry so desperate and affecting that Nest cringed. Ross screamed in response, perhaps to fight against the feelings the cry generated somewhere back in the dark closets of his heart, perhaps simply in fury. He went to where the demon lay broken and writhing, a thing barely recognizable by now. It was trying to change again, to become something else—perhaps the thing Ross had loved so much. But Ross would not allow it. The black staff came down, and the magic surged forth, splitting the demon asunder, ripping it from neck to knee.

Feeders swarmed over it, rending and digging hungrily. The winged black thing that formed its twisted soul tried to break free from the carnage, but Ross was waiting. With a single sweep of his staff, he sent it spinning into the darkness, a tiny, flaming comet trailing fire and fading life.

What remained of the demon collapsed on itself and scattered in the wind. Even when the last of its ashes had blown away, John Ross stayed where he was, silhouetted against the shimmer of the waterfall, staring down at the dark smear that marked its passing.

THURSDAY, NOVEMBER 1

CHAPTER 25

It was a little after ten-thirty the following morning when Andrew Wren walked into the offices of Pass/Go, announced himself to the receptionist, and was told Simon Lawrence would see him. He thanked her, advised her that he knew the way, and started back. He proceeded down the hall past the classrooms and offices, contemplating a collage of children's finger paintings that decorated one section of a sun-splashed wall. He was dressed in his corduroy jacket with the patches at the elbows and had worn a scarf and gloves against the November chill. He carried his old leather briefcase in one hand and a newsboy cap in the other. His cherubic face was unshaved, and his hair was uncombed. He had overslept and been forced to forgo the niceties of personal grooming and had simply pulled on his clothes and headed out. As a result, he looked not altogether different from some of the men standing in the soup line at Union Gospel Mission up the street.

Rumpled and baggy, he shuffled through the doorway of the Wiz's cramped office and gave a brief wave of his hand. "Got any coffee, Simon?"

Simon Lawrence was immersed in paperwork, but he gestured wordlessly toward a chair stacked with books, then picked up the phone to call out to the front desk to fill Wren's order and one of his own.

Wren cleared the chair he had been offered and sat down heavily. "I watched you perform for the assembled last night with something approaching awe. Meeting all those people, shaking hands, answering questions, offering prognostications, being pleasant. To tell you the truth, I don't know how you do it. I couldn't possibly keep up the kind of pace you do and stay sane."

"Well, I don't do it every night, Andrew." Simon stretched and leaned back in his chair. He gave Wren a suspicious look. "I'm almost afraid to ask, but what brings you by this time?"

Wren managed to look put upon. "I wanted to see how you were, for one thing. No more episodes, I hope?"

The other man spread his hands. "I still don't know what happened. One moment I was standing there on the stairs, talking with Carole and those workers from Union Gospel, and the next I was down on the floor. I just seemed to lose all my strength. I'm scheduled to see a doctor about it this afternoon, but I don't think it's anything more than stress and a lack of sleep."

Wren nodded. "I wouldn't be surprised. Anyway, I also wanted to congratulate you on last night. It was a huge success, as you know. The gift of the land from the city, the offer of additional funding, the pledges of support from virtually every quarter. You should be very pleased about that."

Simon Lawrence sighed, arching one eyebrow. "About that, yes, I'm very pleased. It helps take the edge off a few of the less pleasant aspects of the day's events."

"Hmmm," Wren murmured solemnly. "Speaking of which, have you seen her today?"

Simon didn't have to ask who he was referring to. "No, and I don't think I'm going to. Not today or any other. I went by her apartment early this morning, thinking I might surprise her with the news, but she was gone. Her clothes, luggage, personal effects, everything. The door to the apartment was wide open, so I had no trouble getting in. At first I thought something might have happened to her. A chair had been thrown through the living room window. It was lying down in the park with pieces of glass all over the place. But nothing else in the apartment seemed disturbed. There was no sign of any kind of violence having occurred. I called the police anyway."

Wren studied him thoughtfully. "Do you think she suspected we were onto her?"

Simon shook his head. "I don't see how. You and I were the only ones who knew the lab results—and I didn't know until after the dedication, when you told me." He paused, reflecting. "I tell you, Andrew, I'd never have guessed it was her. Not in a million years. Stefanie Winslow. I still can't believe it."

"Well, the handwriting analysis of the signatures on the deposit slips were pretty conclusive." Wren paused. "Why do you think she did it, Simon?"

Simon Lawrence shrugged. "I can't begin to answer that question. You'll have to ask her, if she ever resurfaces from wherever she's gone to ground."

"Maybe John Ross can tell us something."

Simon pursed his lips sourly. "He's gone, too. He left this. It was on my desk when I came into work this morning, tucked into an envelope."

He reached into his desk and produced a single sheet of white paper with a handwritten note. He handed it to Wren, who pushed up his glasses on the bridge of his nose and began to read.

Dear Simon,

I regret that I am unable to deliver this in person, but by the time you read it I will already be far away. Please do not think badly of me for not staying. I am not responsible for the thefts that occurred at Fresh Start. Stefanie Winslow is. I wish I could tell you why. As it is, I feel that even though all the money will be returned, my continued involvement with your programs will simply complicate matters. I will not forget the cause you have championed so successfully and will endeavor in some small way to carry on your work wherever I go.

I am enclosing a letter authorizing transfer back to Fresh Start of all funds improperly deposited to my accounts.

John

Wren looked up speculatively. "Well, well."

The coffee arrived, delivered by a young volunteer, and the two men accepted the cups and sat sipping at the hot brew in the silence that followed the intern's departure.

"I think he was as fooled as the rest of us," the Wiz said finally.

Wren nodded. "Could be. Anyway, there's no one left who can tell us now, is there?"

Simon put down his coffee cup and sighed. "If you want to have dinner tonight, I can try to fill you in on the details of this mess so you can keep your article for the *Times* as accurate as possible."

Wren smiled, relinquished his own cup, and rose to his feet. "I can't do that, Simon. I'm flying out this afternoon, back to the Big Apple. Besides, the article's already written. I finished it at two this morning or something like that."

The Wiz looked confused. "But what about . . ."

Wren held up one chubby hand, assuming his most professional look. "Did you get all the money transferred back to Fresh Start out of Ross's accounts?"

Simon nodded.

"And your own?"

Simon nodded again. "First thing this morning."

"Then it's a story with a happy ending, and I think we ought to leave it at that. No one wants to read about a theft of charitable funds where the money is recovered and the thief is a nobody. It doesn't sell papers. The real story here is about a man whose vision and hard work have produced a small miracle—the opening of a city's stone heart and padlocked purse in support of a cause that might not gain a single politician a single vote in the next election. Besides, what point is there in writing about something that would serve no other purpose than to muddy up such beautiful, pristine waters?"

Andrew Wren picked up his briefcase and donned his cloth cap. "Someday, I'll be back for the story of your life. The real story, the one you won't talk about just yet. Meantime, go back to work on what matters. Just remember, for the record, you owe me one, Simon."

Then he walked out the door, leaving the Wizard of Oz staring after him in bemused wonder.

Nest Freemark spent the first day of November traveling. After spending another night at the Alexis, she caught a midmorning flight to Chicago, which arrived shortly before four in the afternoon. She had debated returning to Northwestern for the one remaining day of the school week and quickly abandoned the idea. She was tired, jittery, and haunted by the events of the past few days, and not fit company for herself, let alone anyone else. Her studies and her training would have to wait.

Instead, she chartered a car to pick her up at the airport and drive her to Hopewell. What she needed most, she decided, was to just go home.

She slept most of the way there, on the airplane and in the car, curled up in the warmth of her parka, drifting in and out of a light, uneasy sleep that mixed dreams with memories, so that by the time her journey was over, with daylight gone and darkness returned, with Seattle behind her and Hopewell at hand, they seemed very much the same.

Nest, as a part of Wraith, as a part of a magic different from anything she knew, returned slowly to herself on the empty walkway in Waterfall Park. She felt the magic withdraw and her vision change. She felt Wraith slip silently away on the night breeze. She stood swaying in the wake of his departure, feeling as if she had returned from a long journey. She drew in deep gulps of air, the cold burning down into her lungs, sending a rush of adrenaline through her body and sharp-edged clarity to her dizzied head.

Oh, my God, my God! she whispered soundlessly, and she hugged herself against the first onslaught of willful despair.

John Ross turned from the demon's remains and limped to her side. He reached for her, drew her into the cradle of his arms, and held her close. Nest, it's all right, he whispered into her hair, stroking it softly, comfortingly. It's all over. It's finished.

Did you see? Did you see what happened? She gasped, broke down, and could not finish.

He nodded quickly. I know. I saw it begin at the museum. It didn't happen there, but I saw that it could. Wraith is inside you, Nest. You said he just walked into you and was gone, that last time you saw him. It's like Pick said. Magic doesn't just cease to exist. It takes another form. It becomes something else. Don't you see? Wraith has become a part of you.

She was shaking now, enraged and despairing. But I don't want him inside me! He's got nothing to do with me! He belongs to my father! Her head jerked up violently. John, what if my father's come back to claim me? What if Wraith is some part of him trying to reach out to me still!

No, no, he said at once, holding her away from him, bracing her shoulders with his strong hands. He released the black staff, and it clattered to the concrete. His eyes held her own. Listen to me, Nest. Wraith wasn't your father's. He was never that. He saved you from your father, remember? Gran made him over with her own magic to protect you. He was yours. He belonged to you.

The lean, weathered face bent close. Perhaps he's only done what he was supposed to do. When you became of age and strong enough to look after yourself, perhaps his job as your protector was finished. Where does magic go when it has served its purpose and not been fully expended? It goes back to its owner. To serve as needed.

So maybe, he whispered, Wraith has just come home.

She spent every waking moment of her journey back to Hopewell wrestling with that concept. Wraith had come home. To her. To become part of her. The idea was terrifying. It left her grappling with the prospect that at any moment she might jump out of her skin. Literally. It made her feel as if she were a character out of *Alien*, waiting for that repulsive little head to thrust out of her stomach, all teeth and blood.

But the image was wrongly conceived, and after a while it diminished and faded, giving way to a more practical concern. How could she control this newfound magic? It didn't seem as if she had done much of a job so far. What was to prevent it from reappearing again without warning, from jeopardizing her in ways she couldn't even begin to imagine?

Then she realized this image was wrongheaded, as well, that Wraith's magic had lived inside her for a long time before it had surfaced. What had triggered its appearance last night was the presence of other magic, first the magic of John Ross and then the magic of the demon. She remembered how strangely she had felt that first day at Fresh Start, then later that night in Lincoln Park, both times when she was in close proximity to the demon. She hadn't understood that it was Wraith's magic, threatening to break free. But in each instance, his magic was simply responding to the perceived threat another magic offered.

Realizing that gave her some comfort, but she still struggled with the idea that the big ghost wolf was locked inside her—not just as magic, but as the creature in which the magic had been lodged. Why did it still exist in that form?

It wasn't until she was almost home, the lights of the first cluster of outlying residences breaking through the evening darkness, that she decided she might still be misreading things. In the absence of direction, magic took the form with which it was most familiar. It didn't act independently of its user. Pick had taught her that a long time ago, when he was instructing her on the care of the park. If Wraith had still been whole, still her shadow protector, he would have come to her defense instinctively. It was not strange to think that bereft of form and independent existence, his magic would still do so. After all, the magic had been given to her in the first place, hadn't it? And in making its unexpected appearance, absent any direction from her, was it surprising it would assume the same form it had occupied for so many years?

What was harder for her to reconcile, she discovered, was that in seeking its release it had required her to become one with it.

She rode through the streets of Hopewell, slumped in the darkness of the car's rear seat, curled into the cushions like a rag doll, looking out at the night. She would be a long time coming to terms with this, she knew.

She found herself wondering, somewhat perversely, if the Lady had known about Wraith in sending her to John Ross. She wondered if she had been sent with the expectation that in aiding Ross she would discover this new truth about herself. It was not inconceivable. Any contact with a strong magic would have released Wraith from his safehold inside her. Knowledge of his continued existence was something Nest would have had to come to grips with sooner or later. The Lady might have believed it was better she do so now.

As they passed the Menards and the Farm and Fleet, she gave the driver directions to her house. She sat contemplating the tangled threads of her life, of what was known and what was not, until the car turned into her driveway and parked. She climbed out, retrieved her bag, signed the driver's receipt, said good-bye, and walked into the house.

It was dark and silent inside, but the smells and shadows of the hallways and rooms were familiar and welcome. She turned on some lights, dropped her bags in the living room, and walked back to the kitchen to fix herself a sandwich from a jar of peanut butter and last week's bread.

She sat eating at the kitchen table, where Gran had spent most of her time in her last years, and she thought of John Ross. She wondered where he was. She wondered how much success he was having at coming to terms with the truths in his life. He had not said much when they parted. He thanked her, standing there in the shadowy confines of Waterfall Park, his breath billowing out in smoky clouds as the cold deepened. He would never forget what she had done for him. He hoped she could forgive him for what he had done to her, five years earlier. She said there was nothing to forgive. She told him she was sorry about Stefanie. She told him she knew a little of how he must feel. He smiled at that. If anyone did, it was she, he agreed.

Did he feel trapped by being what he was? What was it like to be a Knight of the Word and realize your life could never change?

She had not told him of Two Bears. Of the reason O'olish Amaneh had come to

Seattle for Halloween. Of the terrible responsibility the last of the Sinnissippi bore for having given him the Word's magic.

She finished the sandwich and a glass of milk and carried her dishes to the sink. The contracts for the sale of the house still sat on the kitchen counter. She glanced down at them, picked them up, and carried them to the table. She sat down again and read them through carefully. In the hallway, the grandfather clock ticked steadily. When she was finished reading, she set the contracts down in front of her and stared off into space.

What we have in life that we can count our own is who we are and where we come from, she thought absently. For better or worse, that's what we have to sustain us in our endeavors, to buttress us in our darker moments, and to remind us of our identity. Without those things, we are adrift.

Her gaze shifted to the darkness outside the kitchen window. John Ross must feel that way now. He must feel that way every day of his life. It was what he gave up when he became a Knight of the Word. It was what he lost when he discovered the truth about Stefanie Winslow.

She listened to the silence that backdropped the ticking of the clock. After a long time, she picked up the real estate contracts, walked to the garbage can, and dropped them in.

Moving to the phone, she dialed Robert at Stanford. She listened to four rings, and then his voice mail picked up.

At the beep, she said, "Hey, Robert, it's me." She was still looking out the window into the dark. "I just wanted to let you know that I'm home again. Call me. Bye."

She hung up, stood looking around her at the house for a moment, then walked back down the hallway, pulled on her parka, and went out into the cold, crisp autumn night to find Pick.

It was just after four in the morning when John Ross woke from his dream. He lay staring into the empty blackness of his room for a long time, his breathing and his heartbeat slowing as he came back to himself. On the street outside his open window, he could hear a truck rumble by.

It was the first dream he had experienced since he had resumed being a Knight of the Word. As always, it was a dream of the future that would come to pass if he failed to change things in the present. But it felt new because it was his first such dream in a long time.

Except for the dream of the old man and the Wizard of Oz, of course, but he did not think he would be having that dream anymore.

He closed his eyes momentarily to gather his thoughts, to let the tension and the fury of this night's dream ease. In the dream, he had been stripped of his magic, as he knew he would be, because he had chosen to expend his magic in the present, and when he made that choice, the price was always the same: For the span of one night's sleep, there was no magic to protect him in the future. He often wondered how long the loss of magic lasted in real time. He could not tell, for he was given only a glimpse of what was to be before he came awake. If he used the magic often enough in the present, he sometimes wondered, would he at some point lose the use of it completely in the future?

His eyes opened, and he exhaled slowly.

In his dream, he had run through woods at the edge of a nameless town. He had a vague sense of being hunted by his enemies, of being tracked like an animal. He had a sense of being at extreme risk, bereft of any real protection, exposed to attack from all quarters without being able to offer a defense, at a loss as to where he might go to gain safety. He moved swiftly through the darkened trees, using stealth and silence to aid him in his flight. He tried to make himself one with the landscape in which he sought to hide. He burrowed into the earth along ditches and ravines, crawled through brush and long grasses, and edged from trunk to trunk, pressing himself so closely to the terrain he traversed that he could feel and smell its detritus on his skin. There was a river, and he swam it. There were cornfields, and he crept down their rows as if navigating a maze that, if misread, would trap him for all time.

He did not see or hear his pursuers, but he knew they were back there. They would always be back there.

When he awoke in the present, he was still running to stay alive in the future.

He rose now and picked up the black staff from where it lay beside the bed. He limped over to the window, leaning heavily on the staff, and stood for a time looking down at the street. He was in Portland. He had come down on the train early this morning and spent the day walking the riverfront and the streets of the city. When he was so tired he could no longer stay awake, he had taken this room.

Thoughts of Stefanie Winslow crowded suddenly into the forefront of his mind. He let them push forward, unhindered. Less painful now than yesterday, they would be less painful still tomorrow. It was odd, but he still thought of her as human, maybe because it made thinking of her at all more bearable. Memories of a year's time spent with someone you loved couldn't be expunged all at once. The memories, he found, were bittersweet and haunting. They marked a rite of passage he could not ignore. If not for Stefanie, he would have no sense of what his life might have been were he not a Knight of the Word. And in an odd sort of way, he was better off for knowing. It gave him perspective on the worth of what he was doing by revealing what he had given up.

He studied the empty street as if it held answers he could not otherwise find. He might have been a decent sort of man in an ordinary life. He might have done well over the years working with Simon Lawrence on the programs at Fresh Start and Pass/Go. He might have made a difference in the lives of other people.

But never the kind of difference he would make as a Knight of the Word.

His eyes drifted from empty doorway to empty doorway, through shadows and lights. He had been wrong in thinking that successes alone were the measure of his worth in the Word's service. He had been wrong in fleeing his mistakes as if they marked him a failure. It was not as simple as that. All men and women experienced successes and failures, and their tally at death was not necessarily determinative of one's worth in life. This was true, as well, for a Knight of the Word. It was trying that mattered more. It was the giving of effort and heart that lent value. It was the making of sacrifices. Ray Hapgood had said it best. Someone has to take responsibility. Someone has to be there.

That was the real reason he was a Knight of the Word.

Such a hard lesson, in retrospect, but Stefanie Winslow had taught him well the price for not understanding it.

He thought back to last night. When he left Nest, he had gone back up to the apartment to write Simon a short note of explanation and a letter of authorization for transfer of the misplaced funds. He had packed his duffel bag, then packed Stefanie's suitcases, removing everything of a personal nature from the apartment. Tossing the wooden desk chair out the window to provide an explanation for the glass breakage had been an afterthought. He had taken the note and authorization, put them in an envelope, and carried them over to Pass/Go.

Then he had gone down to the train station with his duffel and Stefanie's bags in hand to wait for the six-ten commuter. When he reached Portland, he disembarked and dumped Stefanie's bags in a Dumpster not a block away from the station.

He turned away from the window and looked around the little room. He wondered how Nest Freemark was doing. She had come to Seattle to help him, to give him a chance he might not otherwise have gotten, and it had cost her a great deal. He was sorry for that, but he did not think it his fault. The Lady had sent her, knowing to some extent the likely result. The Lady had placed her in a dangerous situation, knowing she would be forced to use her magic and would discover the truth about Wraith. It would have happened at another time in another place if not here. And it had saved his life. It did not make him feel better knowing this. But recognizing truths seldom achieved that result anyway.

He thought about how much alike they were, both of them gifted with magic that dominated their lives, both of them pressed into service by an entity they would never fully understand or perhaps ever satisfy. They were outsiders in a world that lacked any real comprehension of their service, and they would struggle on mostly alone and largely unappreciated until their lives were ended.

There was one glaring difference, of course. In his case, the choice to be what he was had been his. In hers, it had not.

He went into the bathroom, showered and shaved, and came out again and dressed in the light of the bedside lamp. When he was finished, he packed his duffel bag. He went downstairs to the lobby, dropped his key on the desk, and walked out.

Sunrise was brightening the eastern sky, a faint, soft glow against the departing night. The day was just beginning. By nightfall, John Ross would be in another town, looking to make a change in the way the world was going. His dreams would begin to tell him again what he could do that would make a difference.

It wasn't the worst sort of way to live one's life. In his case, he concluded hopefully, perhaps it was the best.

ANGEL FIRE EAST

TO MY FATHER, DEAN BROOKS
Who made sacrifices as an aspiring writer then so that I could be a published writer now.

PROLOGUE

He stands at the edge of a barren and ravaged orchard looking up from the base of a gentle rise to where the man hangs from a wooden cross. Iron spikes have been hammered through the man's hands and feet, and his wrists and ankles have been lashed tightly in place so he will not tear free. Slash wounds crisscross his broken body, and he bleeds from a deep puncture in his side. His head droops in the shadow of his long, lank hair, and the rise and fall of his chest as he breathes is shallow and weak.

Behind him, serving as a poignant backdrop to the travesty of his dying, stands the fire-blackened shell of a tiny, burned-out country church. The cross from which the man hangs has been stripped from the sanctuary, torn free from the metal brackets that secured it to the wall behind the altar, and set into the earth. Patches of polished oak glisten faintly in the gray daylight, attesting to the importance it was once accorded in the worshipping of God.

Somewhere in the distance, back where the little town that once supported this church lies, screams rise up against the unmistakable sounds of butchery.

John Ross stands motionless for the longest time, pondering the implications of the horrific scene before him. There is nothing he can do for the man on the cross. He is not a doctor; he does not possess medical skills. His magic can heal and sustain only himself and no other. He is a Knight of the Word, but he is a failure, too. He lives out his days alone in a future he could not prevent. What he looks upon is not unusual in the postapocalyptic horror of civilization's demise, but is sadly familiar and disturbingly mundane.

He can take the man down, he decides finally, even if he cannot save him. By his presence, Ross can give the man a small measure of peace and comfort.

Beneath a wintry sky that belies the summer season, he strides up the rise to the man on the cross. The man does not lift his head or stir in any way that would indicate he knows Ross is present. Beneath a sheen of sweat and blood, his lean, muscular body is marked with old wounds and scars. He has endured hardships and abuse somewhere in his past, and it seems unfair that he should end his days in still more pain and desolation.

Ross slows as he nears, his eyes drifting across the blackened facade of the church and the trees surrounding it. Eyes glimmer in the shadows, revealing the presence of feeders. They hover at the fringes of his vision and in the concealment of sunless corners, waiting to assuage their hunger. They do not wait for Ross. They wait for the man on the cross. They wait for him to die, so they can taste his passing from life into death—the most exquisite, fulfilling, and rare of the human emotions they crave.

Ross stares at them until the light dims in their lantern eyes and they slip back into darkness to bide their time.

A shattered length of wood catches the Knight's attention, and his eyes shift to the foot of the cross. The remains of a polished black staff lie before him—a staff like the one he carries in his hands. A shock goes through him. He stares closely, unable to believe what he has discovered. There must be a mistake, he thinks. There must be another explanation.

But there is neither. Like himself, the man on the cross is a Knight of the Word.

He moves quickly now, striding forward to help, to lower the cross, to remove the spikes, to free the man who hangs helplessly before him.

But the man senses him now and in a ragged, whispery voice says, Don't touch me.

Ross stops instantly, the force of the other's words and the surprise of his consciousness bringing him to a halt.

They have poisoned me, the other says.

Ross draws a long, slow breath and exhales in weary recognition: Those who have crucified this Knight of the Word have coated him in a poison conjured of demon magic. He is without hope.

Ross steps back, looking up at the Knight on the cross, at the slow, shallow rise and fall of his breast, at the rivulets of blood leaking from his wounds, at the shadow of his face, still concealed within the curtain of his long hair.

They caught me when I did not have my magic to protect me, the stricken Knight says softly. I had expended it all on an effort to escape them earlier. I could not replenish it quickly enough. Sensing I was weak, they gave chase. They hunted me down. Demons and once-men, a small army hunting pockets of resistance beyond the protection of the city fortresses. They found me hiding in the town below. They dragged me here and hung me on this cross to die. Now they kill all those who tried to help me.

Ross finds his attention drawn once more to the shrieks that come from the town. They are beginning to fade, to drain away into a deep, ominous silence.

I have not done well in my efforts to save mankind, the Knight whispers. He gasps and chokes on the dryness in his throat. Blood bubbles to his lips and runs down his chin to his chest.

Nor have any of us, Ross says.

There were chances. There were times when we might have made a difference.

Ross sighs. We did with them what we could.

A bird's soft warble wafts through the trees. Black smoke curls skyward from the direction of the town, rife with the scent of human carnage.

Perhaps you were sent to me.

Ross turns from the smoke to look again at the man on the cross, not understanding.

Perhaps the Word sent you to me. A final chance at redemption.

No one sent me, Ross thinks, but does not speak the words.

You will wake in the present and go on. I will die here. You will have a chance to make a difference still. I will not.

No one sent me, Ross says quickly now, suddenly uneasy.

But the other is not listening. In late fall, three days after Thanksgiving, once long ago, when I was on the Oregon coast, I captured a gypsy morph.

His words wheeze from his mouth, coated in the sounds of his dying. But as he speaks, his voice seems to gain intensity.

It is my greatest regret, that I found it, so rare, so precious, made it my own, and could not solve the mystery of its magic. The chance of a lifetime, and I let it slip away.

The man on the cross goes silent then, gasping slowly for breath, fighting to stay alive just a few moments longer, broken and shattered within and without, left in his final moments to contemplate the failures he perceives are his. Eyes reappear in the shadows of the burned-out church and blighted orchard, the feeders beginning to gather in anticipation. Ross can scorch the earth with their gnarled bodies, can strew their cunning eyes like leaves in the wind, but it will all be pointless. The feeders are a part of life, of the natural order of things, and you might as well decide there is no place for humans either, for it is the humans who draw the feeders and sustain them.

The Knight of the Word who hangs from the cross is speaking again, telling him of the gypsy morph, of how and when and where it will be found, of the chance Ross might have of finding it again. He is giving Ross the details, preparing him for the hunt, thinking to give another the precious opportunity that he has lost. But he is giving Ross the chance to fail as well, and it is on that alone his listener settles in black contemplation.

Do this for me if you can, the man whispers, his voice beginning to fail him completely, drying up with the draining away of his life, turning parched and sandy in his throat. Do it for yourself.

Ross feels the implications of the stricken Knight's charge razor through him. If he undertakes so grave and important a mission, if he embraces so difficult a cause, it may be his own undoing.

Yet, how can he do otherwise?

Promise me.

The words are thin and weak and empty of life. Ross stares in silence at the man.

Promise me . . .

John Ross awoke with sunshine streaming down on his face and the sound of children's voices ringing in his ears. The air was hot and sticky, and the smell of fresh turned earth and new leaves rose on a sudden breeze. He blinked and sat up. He was hitchhiking west through Pennsylvania, and he had stopped at a park outside Allentown to rest, then fallen asleep beneath the canopy of an old hardwood. He had thought only to doze for a few minutes, but he hadn't slept well in days, and the lack of sleep had finally caught up to him.

He gazed around slowly to regain his bearings. The park was large and thickly wooded, and he had chosen a spot well back from the roads and playgrounds to rest. He was alone. He looked down at his backpack and duffel bag, then at the polished black staff in his hands. His throat was dry and his head ached. A spot deep in his chest burned with the fury of hot coals.

His dream shimmered in a haze of sunlight just before his eyes, images from a private hell.

He was a Knight of the Word, living one life in the present and another in the future, one while awake and another while asleep, one in which he was given a chance to change the world and another in which he must live forever with the consequences of his failure to do so. He had accepted the charge almost twenty-five years ago and had lived with it ever since. He had spent almost the whole of his adult life engaged in a war that had begun with the inception of life and would not end until its demise. There were no boundaries to the battlefield on which he fought—neither of space nor of time. There could be no final resolution.

But the magic of a gypsy morph could provide leverage of a sort that could change everything.

He reached in his backpack and brought forth a battered water bottle. Removing the cap, he drank deeply from its lukewarm contents, finding momentary relief for the dryness in his throat and mouth. He had trouble fitting the cap in place again. The dream had shaken him. His dreams did so often, for they were of a world in which madness ruled and horror was commonplace. There was hope in the present of his waking, but none in the future of his sleep.

Still, this dream was different.

He climbed to his feet, strapped the backpack in place, picked up the duffel bag, and walked back through the park toward the two-lane blacktop that wound west toward Pittsburgh. As always, the events of his dream would occur soon in his present, giving him a chance to affect them in a positive way. It was June. The gypsy morph would be born three days after Thanksgiving. If he was present and if he was quick enough, he would be able to capture it.

Then he would have roughly thirty days to change the course of history.

That challenge would have shaken any man, but it was not the challenge of the gypsy morph that haunted Ross as he walked from the park to begin his journey west. It was his memory of the man on the cross in his dream, the fallen Knight of the Word. It was the man's face as it had lifted from the shadow of his long hair in the final moments of his life.

For the face of the man hanging on the cross had been his own.

Sunday, December 21

CHAPTER 1

Nest Freemark had just finished dressing for church when she heard the knock at the front door. She paused in the middle of applying her mascara at the bathroom mirror and glanced over her shoulder, thinking she might have been mistaken, that she wasn't expecting anyone and it was early on a Sunday morning for visitors to come around without calling first.

She went back to applying her makeup. A few minutes later the knock came again.

She grimaced, then glanced quickly at her watch for confirmation. Sure enough. Eight forty-five. She put down her mascara, straightened her dress, and checked her appearance in the mirror. She was tall, a shade under five-ten, lean, and fit, with a distance runner's long legs, narrow hips, and small waist. She had seemed gangly and bony all through her early teens, except when she ran, but she had finally grown into her body. At twenty-nine, she moved with an easy, fluid model's grace that belied the strength and endurance she had acquired and maintained through years of rigorous training.

She studied herself in the mirror with the same frank, open stare she gave everyone. Her green eyes were wide-set beneath arched brows in her round, smooth Charlie Brown face. Her cinnamon hair was cut short and curled tightly about her head, framing her small, even features. People told her all the time she was pretty, but she never quite believed them. Her friends had known her all her life and were inclined to be generous in their assessments. Strangers were just being polite.

Still, she told herself with more than a trace of irony, fluffing her hair into place, you never know when Prince Charming will come calling. Best to be ready so you don't lose out.

She left the mirror and the bathroom and walked through her bedroom to the hall beyond. She had been up since five-thirty, running on the mostly empty roads that stretched from Sinnissippi Park east to Moonlight Bay. Winter had set in several weeks before with the first serious snowfall, but the snow had melted during a warm spot a week ago, and there had been no further accumulation. Patches of sooty white still lay in the darker, shadowy parts of the woods and in the culverts and ditches where the snowplows had pushed them, but the blacktop of the country roads was dry and clear. She did five miles, then showered, fixed herself breakfast, ate, and dressed. She was due in church to help in the nursery at nine-thirty, and whoever it was who had come calling would have to be quick.

She passed the aged black-and-white tintypes and photographs of the women of her family, their faces severe and spare in the plain wooden picture frames, backdropped by the dark webbing of trunks and limbs of the park trees. Gwendolyn Wills, Carolyn Glynn, and Opal Anders. Her grandmother's picture was there, too.

Nest had added it after Gran's death. She had chosen an early picture, one in which Evelyn Freemark appeared youthful and raw and wild, hair all tousled, eyes filled with excitement and promise. That was the way Nest liked to remember Gran. It spoke to the strengths and weaknesses that had defined Gran's life.

Nest scanned the group as she went down the hallway, admiring the resolve in their eyes. The Freemark women, she liked to call them. All had entered into the service of the Word, partnering themselves with Pick to help the sylvan keep in balance the strong, core magic that existed in the park. All had been born with magic of their own, though not all had managed it well. She thought briefly of the dark secrets her grandmother had kept, of the deceptions she herself had employed in the workings of her own magic, and of the price she had paid for doing so.

Her mother's picture was missing from the group. Caitlin Anne Freemark had been too fragile for the magic's demands. She had died young, just after Nest was born, a victim of her demon lover's treachery. Nest kept her pictures on a table in the living room where it was always sunlit and cheerful.

The knock came a third time just as she reached the door and opened it. The tiny silver bells that encircled the bough wreath that hung beneath the peephole tinkled softly with the movement. She had not done much with Christmas decorations—no tree, no lights, no tinsel, only fresh greens, a scattering of brightly colored bows, and a few wall hangings that had belonged to Gran. This year Christmas would be celebrated mostly in her heart.

The chill, dry winter air was sharp and bracing as she unlatched the storm door, pushed it away, and stepped out onto the porch.

The old man who stood waiting was dressed all in black. He was wearing what in other times would have been called a frock coat, which was double-breasted with wide lapels and hung to his knees. A flat-brimmed black hat sat firmly in place over wisps of white hair that stuck out from underneath as if trying to escape. His face was seamed and browned by the wind and sun, and his eyes were a watery gray as they blinked at her. When he smiled, as he was doing, his whole face seemed to join in, creasing cheerfully from forehead to chin. He was taller than Nest by several inches, and he stooped as if to make up for the disparity.

She was reminded suddenly of an old-time preacher, the kind that appeared in southern gothics and ghost stories, railing against godlessness and mankind's paucity of moral resolve.

"Good morning," he said, his voice gravelly and deep. He dipped his head slightly, reaching up to touch the brim of his odd hat.

"Good morning," she replied.

"Miss Freemark, my name is Findo Gask," he announced. "I am a minister of the faith and a bearer of the holy word."

As if to emphasize the point, he held up a black, leather-bound tome from which dangled a silken bookmark.

She nodded, waiting. Somehow he knew her name, although she had no memory of meeting him before.

"It is a fine, grand morning to be out and about, so I won't keep you," he said, smiling reassuringly. "I see you are on your way to church. I wouldn't want to stand in the way of a young lady and her time of worship. Take what comfort you can in the moment, I say. Ours is a restless, dissatisfied world, full of uncertainties and calamities and impending disasters, and we would do well to be mindful of the fact that small steps and little cautions are always prudent."

It wasn't so much the words themselves, but the way in which he spoke them that aroused a vague uneasiness in Nest. He made it sound more like an admonition than the reassurance it was intended to be.

"What can I do for you, Mr. Gask?" she asked, anxious for him to get to the point.

His head cocked slightly to one side. "I'm looking for a man," he said. "His name is John Ross."

Nest started visibly, unable to hide her reaction. John Ross. She hadn't seen or communicated with him for more than ten years. She hadn't even heard his name spoken by anyone but Pick.

"John Ross," she repeated flatly. Her uneasiness heightened.

The old man smiled. "Has he contacted you recently, Miss Freemark? Has he phoned or written you of late?"

She shook her head no. "Why would he do that, Mr. Gask?"

The smile broadened, as if to underline the silliness of such a question. The watery gray eyes peered over her shoulder speculatively. "Is he here already, Miss Freemark?"

A hint of irritation crept into her voice. "Who are you, Mr. Gask? Why are you interested in John Ross?"

"I already told you who I am, Miss Freemark. I am a minister of the faith. As for my interest in Mr. Ross, he has something that belongs to me."

She stared at him. Something wasn't right about this. The air about her warmed noticeably, changed color and taste and texture. She felt a roiling inside, where Wraith lay dormant and dangerously ready, the protector chained to her soul.

"Perhaps we could talk inside?" Findo Gask suggested.

He moved as if to enter her home, a subtle shift of weight from one foot to the other, and she found herself tempted simply to step aside and let him pass. But she held her ground, the uneasiness becoming a tingling in the pit of her stomach. She forced herself to look carefully at him, to meet his eyes directly.

The tingling changed abruptly to a wave of nausea.

She took a deep, steadying breath and exhaled. She was in the presence of a demon.

"I know what you are," she said quietly.

The smile stayed in place, but any trace of warmth disappeared. "And I know what you are, Miss Freemark," Findo Gask replied smoothly. "Now, is Mr. Ross inside or isn't he?"

Nest felt the chill of the winter air for the first time and shivered in spite of herself. A demon coming to her home with such bold intent was unnerving. "If he was, I wouldn't tell you. Why don't you get off my porch, Mr. Gask?"

Findo Gask shifted once more, a kind of settling in that indicated he had no intention of moving until he was ready. She felt Wraith stir awake inside, sensing her danger.

"Let me just say a few things to you, Miss Freemark, and then I'll go," Findo Gask said, a bored sigh escaping his lips. "We are not so different, you and I. When I said I know what you are, I meant it. You are your father's daughter, and we know what he was, don't we? Perhaps you don't care much for the reality of your parentage, but truth will out, Miss Freemark. You are what you are, so there isn't much point in pretending otherwise, though you work very hard at doing so, don't you?"

Nest flushed with anger, but Findo Gask waved her off. "I also said I was a minister of the faith. You assumed I meant your faith naturally, but you were mistaken. I am a servant of the Void, and it is the Void's faith I embrace. You would pretend it is an evil, wicked faith. But that is a highly subjective conclusion. Your faith and mine, like you and I, are not so different. Both are codifications of the higher power we seek to comprehend and, to the extent we are able, manipulate. Both can be curative or destructive. Both have their supporters and their detractors, and each seeks dominance over the other. The struggle between them has been going on for eons; it won't end today or tomorrow or the day after or anytime soon."

He stepped forward, kindly face set in a condescending smile that did nothing to hide the threat behind it. "But one day it will end, and the Word will be destroyed. It will happen, Miss Freemark, because the magic of the Void has always been the stronger of the two. Always. The frailties and weaknesses of mankind are insurmountable. The misguided belief that the human condition is worth salvaging is patently ridiculous. Look at the way the world functions, Miss Freemark. Human frailties and weaknesses abound. Moral corruption here, venal desires there. Greed, envy, sloth, and all the rest at every turn. The followers of the Word rail against them endlessly and futilely. The Void embraces them, and turns a weakness into a strength. Pacifism and meek acceptance? Charity and goodwill? Kindness and virtue? Rubbish!"

"Mr. Gask—"

"No, no, hear me out, young lady. A little of that famous courtesy, please." He cut short her protestation with a sharp hiss. "I don't tell you this to frighten you. I don't tell it to you to persuade you of my cause. I could care less what you feel or think about me. I tell it to you to demonstrate the depth of my conviction and my commitment. I am not easily deterred. I want you to understand that my interest in Mr. Ross is of paramount importance. Think of me as a tidal wave and yourself as a sand castle on a beach. Nothing can save you from me if you stand in my way. It would be best for you to let me move you aside. There is no reason for you not to let me do so. None at all. You have nothing vested in this matter. You have nothing to gain by intervening and everything to lose."

He paused then, lifting the leather-bound book and pressing it almost reverently against his chest. "These are the names of those who have opposed me, Miss Freemark. The names of the dead. I like to keep track of them, to think back on who they were. I have been alive a very long time, and I shall still be alive long after you are gone."

He lowered the book and put a finger to his lips. "This is what I want you to do. You will have no trouble understanding my request, because I will put it to you in familiar terms. In the terms of your own faith. I want you to deny John Ross. I want you to cast him out of your heart and mind and soul as you would a cancer. I want you to shun him as a leper. Do this for yourself, Miss Freemark, not for me. I will have him anyway, in the end. I do not need to claim you as well."

Nest was buffeted by so many emotions she could no longer distinguish them. She had kept quiet during the whole of his noxious, execrable presentation, fighting to keep herself and an increasingly agitated Wraith under control. She didn't think Findo Gask knew of Wraith, and she did not want him to discover Wraith was there unless that became unavoidable. She needed to know more of what was going on first, because she wasn't for a moment thinking of acceding to a single demand he had made.

"John Ross isn't here," she managed, gripping the storm-door frame so tightly with one hand her knuckles turned white.

"I accept that, Miss Freemark," Findo Gask said with a slight dip of his flat-brimmed hat. "But he will be."

"What makes you so sure?"

She could see in his eyes that he believed he had won her over, that she was trying to find a way to cooperate with him. "Call it a hunch. I have been following his progress for a time, and I think I know him pretty well. He will come. When he does, or even if he tries to make contact another way, don't do anything to help him."

"What does he have that you want?" she pressed, curious now.

The demon shrugged. "A magic, Miss Freemark. A magic he would attempt to use against me, I'm afraid."

She nodded slowly. "But that you will attempt to use against him, instead?"

Findo Gask stepped back, reaching up to touch the brim of his hat. "I have taken up enough of your time. Your Sunday worship awaits. I'll look forward to your call."

"Mr. Gask," she called to him as he started down the porch steps toward the walk. He turned back to her, squinting against the bright December sunlight. "My grandfather kept a shotgun in his bedroom closet for duck hunting. When my father tried to come back into this house fifteen years ago, my grandmother used that shotgun to prevent him from doing so. I still have that shotgun. If you ever step foot on my property again, I will use it on you. I will blow away your miserable disguise and leave you naked in your demon form for however long it takes you to put yourself back together and all the while be hoping to God you won't be able to do so!"

Findo Gask stared at her speechless, and then his face underwent such a terrible transformation that she thought he might come at her. Instead he turned away, strode up the walk to the roadway without looking back, and disappeared.

Nest Freemark waited until he was out of sight, then walked back inside and slammed the door so hard the jolt knocked the pictures of the Freemark women askew.

CHAPTER 2

On the drive to church, Nest considered the prospect of another encounter with John Ross.

As usual, her feelings about him were mixed. For as little time as she had spent with him, maybe seven days all told over a span of fifteen years, he had made an extraordinary impact on her life. Much of who and what she was could be traced directly to their strange, sad relationship.

He had come to her for the first time when she was still a girl, just turned fourteen and beginning to discover that she wasn't at all who she thought she was. The secrets of her family were unraveling around her, and Ross had pulled on the ends of the tangle until Nest had almost strangled in the resulting knots. But her assessment wasn't really fair. Ross had done what was necessary in giving her the truth. Had he not, she would probably be dead. Or worse. Her father had killed her mother and grandmother, and tried to kill her grandfather. He had done so to get to her, to claim her, to subvert her, to turn her to the life he had embraced himself long ago. Findo Gask had been right about him. Her father was a demon, a monster capable of great evil. Ross had helped Nest put an end to him. Ross had given her back her life, and with it a chance to discover who she was meant to be.

Of course, he would just as quickly have taken her life had she been turned to the demon's cause, which was a good part of the reason for her mixed feelings about him. That, and the fact that at one time she believed Ross to be her father. It seemed strange, thinking back on it. She had rejoiced in the prospect of John Ross as her father. She found him tender and caring; she thought she probably loved him. She was still a girl, and she had never known her father. She had made up a life for her father; she had invented a place for him in her own. It seemed to her John Ross had come to fill that place.

Gran warned her, of course. In her own way, without saying as much, she indicated over and over that her father was not somebody Nest would want to know. But it seemed as if Gran's cautions were selfish and misplaced. Nest believed John Ross was a good man. When she learned that he was not her father and the demon was, she was crushed. When she learned that he had come to save her if he could but to put an end to her otherwise, the knowledge almost broke her heart.

Most of her anger and dismay had abated by the time she encountered him again five years later in Seattle, where he was the victim and she the rescuer. Ross was the one in danger of being claimed, and if Nest had not been able to save him, he would have been.

Ten years had passed since then, and she hadn't seen or heard from him.

She shook her head, watching the houses of Hopewell, Illinois, drift past as she drove her new Taurus slowly along Lincoln Highway toward downtown. The day was bright and sunny, the skies clear and blue and depthless. Another storm was predicted for Tuesday, but at the moment it was hard to imagine.

She cracked a window to let in some fresh air, listening to the sound of the tires crunch over a residue of road dirt and cinders. As she drove past the post office, the Petersons pulled up to the mail drop. Her neighbors for the whole of her life, the Petersons had been there when Gran was still young. But they were growing old, and she worried about them. She reminded herself to stop by later and take them some cookies.

She turned off Fourth Street down Second Avenue and drove past the First Congregational Church to find a parking space in the adjoining bank lot. She climbed out of the car, triggered the door locks, and walked back toward the church.

Josie Jackson was coming up the sidewalk from her bake shop and restaurant across Third, so Nest waited for her. Bright and chipper and full of life, Josie was one of those women who never seemed to age. Even at forty-eight, she was still youthful and vivacious, waving and smiling like a young girl as she came up, tousled blond hair flouncing about her pretty face. She still had that smile, too. No one ever forgot Josie Jackson's smile.

Nest wondered if John Ross still remembered.

"Good morning, Nest," Josie said, falling into step with the younger woman, matching her long stride easily. "I hear we've got baby duty together this morning."

Nest smiled. "Yes. Experience counts, and you've got a whole lot more than me. How many are we expecting?"

"Oh, gosh, somewhere in the low teens, if you count the three- and four-year-olds." Josie shrugged. "Alice Wilton will be there to help out, and her niece, what's-her-name-Anna."

"Royce-Anna."

"Royce-Anna Colson." Josie grimaced. "What the heck kind of name is that?"

Nest laughed. "One we wouldn't give our own children."

They mounted the steps of the church and pushed through the heavy oak doors into the cool dark of the narthex. Nest wondered if Josie ever thought about John Ross. There had been something between them once, back when he had first come to Hopewell and Nest was still a girl. For months after he disappeared, she asked Nest about him. But it had been years now since she had even mentioned his name.

It would be strange, Nest thought, if he was to return to Hopewell after all this time. Findo Gask had seemed sure he would, and despite her doubts about anything a demon would tell her, she was inclined to think from the effort he had expended to convince her that maybe it would happen.

That was an unsettling prospect. An appearance by John Ross, especially with a demon already looking for him, meant trouble. It almost certainly foreshadowed a fresh upheaval in her life, something she didn't need, since she was just getting used to her life the way it was.

What would bring him back to her after so long?

Unable to find an answer, she walked with Josie down the empty, shadowed hallway, stained glass and burnished wood wrapping her in a cocoon of silence.

She spent the next two hours working in the nursery, having a good time with the babies and Josie, doing something that kept her from thinking too much about things she would just as soon forget. She concentrated instead on diaper changing, bottle feeding, telling stories, and playing games, and left the world outside her bright, cheery room of crayon pictures and colored posters to get on by itself as best it could.

Once or twice, she thought about Paul. It was impossible for her to be around babies and not think about Paul, but she had found a way to block the pain by taking refuge in the possibility that she was not meant to have children of her own but to be a mother to the children of others. It was heartbreaking to think that way, but it was the best she could do. Her legacy of magic from the Freemark women would not allow her to think otherwise.

Josie helped pass the time with wry jokes and colorful stories of people they both knew, and mostly Nest found herself thinking she was pretty lucky.

When the service was over, a fellowship was held in the reception room just off the sanctuary. After returning her small charges to their proper parents, Nest joined the congregation in sipping coffee and punch, eating cookies and cake, and exchanging pleasantries and gossip. She wandered from group to group, saying hello, asking after old people and children come home for the holidays, wishing Christmas cheer to all.

"What's the world coming to, young lady?" an indignant Blanche Stern asked when she paused to greet a gaggle of elderly church widows standing by the narthex entry. She peered at Nest through her bifocals. "This is your generation's responsibility, these children who do such awful things! It makes me weep!"

Nest had no idea what she was talking about.

"It's that boy shooting those teachers yesterday at an outing in Pennsylvania," Addie Hull explained, pursing her thin lips and nodding solemnly for emphasis. "It was all over the papers this morning. Only thirteen years old."

"Takes down his father's shotgun, rides off to school on his bike, and lets them have it in front of two dozen other students!" Winnie Ricedorf snapped in her no-nonsense teacher's voice.

"I haven't read the papers yet," Nest explained. "Sounds awful. Why did he do it?"

"He didn't like the grades they were giving him for his work in some advanced study program," Blanche continued, her face tightening. She sighed. "Goodness sakes alive, he was a scholar of some promise, they say, and he threw it all away on a bad grade."

"Off to his Saturday Challenge Class," Winnie said, "armed with a shotgun and a heart full of hate. What's that tell you about today's children, Nest?"

"Remember that boy down in Tennessee last year?" Addie Hull asked suddenly. Her thin hands crooked around her coffee cup more tightly. "Took some sort of automatic rifle to school and ambushed some young people during a lunch break? Killed three of them and wounded half a dozen more. Said he was tired of being picked on. Well, I'm tired of being picked on, too, but I don't go hunting down the garbage collectors and the postal delivery man and the IRS examiner who keeps asking for those Goodwill receipts!"

"That IRS man they caught dressing in women's clothes earlier this month, good heavens!" Winnie Ricedorf huffed, and took a sip of her coffee.

"His wife didn't mind, as I recall," Blanche Stern advised primly, giving Nest a wink. "She liked to dress up as a man."

Nest excused herself and moved on. Similar topics of conversation could be found almost everywhere, save where clusters of out-of-season golfers looking forward to a few weeks in Florida replayed their favorite holes and wrestled with the rest of the sports problems of the world while the teenagers next to them spoke movie and rap and computer talk. She drifted from group to group, able to fit in anywhere because she really belonged nowhere at all. She could talk the talk and pretend she was a part of things, but she would never be anything but an outsider. She was accepted because she had been born in Hopewell and was a part of its history. But her legacy of magic and her knowledge of Pick's world and the larger life she led set her apart as surely as if she had just stepped off the bus from New York City.

She sipped at her coffee and looked off at the blue winter sky through the high windows that lined the west wall. What was she doing with herself anyway?

"Wish you were out there running?" a friendly voice asked.

She turned to find Larry Spence standing next to her. She gave him a perfunctory smile. "Something like that."

"You could still do it, girl. You could still get back into training, be ready in time for St. Petersburg."

The Olympics in four years, he was saying. "My competitive days are over, Larry. Been there, done that."

He was just trying to make conversation, but it felt like he was trying to make time as well, and that annoyed her. He was a big, good-looking man in his mid-thirties, athletic and charming, the divorced father of two. He worked as a deputy sheriff with the county and moonlighted nights as a bouncer at a dance club. His family were all from Hopewell and the little farm towns surrounding. She had known him only a short while and not well, but somewhere along the line he had decided he wanted to change the nature of their relationship. He had asked her out repeatedly, and she had politely, but firmly, declined. That should have been the end of it, but somehow it wasn't.

"You were the best, girl," he said, putting on his serious-guy mask. He always called her "girl." Like it was some sort of compliment, an endearment intended to make her feel special. It made her want to smack him.

"How are the kids?" she asked.

"Good. Growing like weeds." He edged closer. "Miss having their mother with them, though. Like there was ever anything about her for them to miss."

Marcy Spence had not been what anyone could call dependable even before she had children, and having children hadn't improved her. She was a party girl with a party girl's tastes. After numerous flings with just about anyone inclined to show her a good time, and a number of screaming knock-down-drag-outs with her husband, the marriage was over. Marcy was on the road and out of Hopewell even before the papers were filed, husband and kids be damned. She was twenty-four when she left. "Babies raising babies," Nest had heard the old ladies tut-tut.

"Got any plans for Christmas?" Larry asked her suddenly. His brow furrowed. "You know, it would be good for the kids to have a woman around for the present opening and all."

Nest nodded, straight-faced. "Sort of a stand-in mother."

Larry paused. "Well, yeah, sort of, I guess. But I'd like it if you were there, too."

She gave him a pointed look. "Larry, we barely know each other."

"Not my fault," he said.

"Also, I've met your children exactly once. They probably don't even know who I am."

"Sure, they do. They know."

She shook her head. "The timing's not right," she said diplomatically. "In any case, I have my own plans."

"Hey, just thought I'd ask." He shrugged, trying to downplay the importance of the request. "No big deal."

It was, of course, as any teenage girl, let alone a woman of Nest's age, could see in a heartbeat. But Larry Spence had already demonstrated with Marcy that he was far from wise in the ways of women. In any case, he was in way over his head with Nest. He had no idea what he was letting himself in for by pursuing her, and she was not about to encourage him by spending Christmas at his home with his children. In this instance ignorance was bliss. Let him tie up with someone normal; he would be far better off.

She caught sight of Robert Heppler across the room. "Larry, I see someone I need to talk to. Thank you for the invitation."

She hurried past him before he could respond, anxious to forestall any other misguided offers he might be inclined to make. Larry was a nice guy, but she had no interest in him at all. Why he couldn't see that was a mystery to her, but it was the sort of mystery commonplace in relationships between men and women.

She came up to Robert with a grin. "Hey," she said.

"Hey, there you are," he replied, grinning back.

She reached out and gave him a hug and a kiss on the cheek. Still rail thin and towheaded, still looking very much like a mischievous little boy, Robert might have been mistaken by those who hadn't seen him in a while for the same smart-ass kid he had been all through school. But Robert had grown up when no one was looking. Right out of graduate school, he had married a small, strong-minded young woman named Amy Pruitt, and Amy had set him straight. Forthright, no-nonsense, and practical to a fault, she loved Robert so much she was willing to take him on as a project. Robert spent most of his life with his head somewhere else, developing codes, languages, programs, and systems for computers. Always convinced of his own brilliance and impossibly impatient with the perceived shortcomings of others, he had gotten as far as he had mostly on grades and the high expectations of his professors that one day they could point to him with pride in cataloging their academic accomplishments. But the real world has an entirely different grading system, and Amy was quick to recognize that Robert was ill equipped to succeed in the absence of a serious attitude adjustment.

She performed the surgery with flawless precision. Nest could hardly believe the difference in Robert between the time he met Amy and the time he married her, scarcely ten months later. Robert seemed totally unaware of the transformation she had wrought, believing he was just the same as he had always been. But after getting to know her a little better, Nest was quick to realize that Amy was the best thing that could have happened to her old friend.

Now they had one child, a boy of two who was clinging to Robert's leg playfully, and another on the way. Robert had a family and a life. He was a real person at last.

"Hey there, Kyle," she said, bending down to ruffle the boy's blond hair. "We missed you downstairs today."

"Was 'n churtch," the little boy mumbled, then blew her a kiss.

"I kept him with me," Robert admitted, shrugging. "I wanted some companionship. Amy stayed home. Not feeling so good this morning when she woke. This pregnancy has been a little rough."

"Is everything okay?"

"Yeah, sure. You know Amy. Tough as nails. But she's being careful. She's a little over six months. Kind of a touchy time."

"You'll let me know if I can do anything?"

Robert laughed. "I'll let you know if *I* can do anything. With my parents and my sister and her husband hovering over her twenty-four hours a day, I can't get close enough to find out!"

He glanced over at Larry Spence, who was watching surreptitiously from behind his coffee cup. "I see you can still draw bees like honey. Or maybe *horseflies* would be a better choice of word."

She arched one eyebrow. "I see you still haven't lost your rapierlike wit, Robert."

He shrugged. "I'm just being protective. He reminds me a little of that guy who kept coming on to you the summer before we entered high school, the one I would have decked if you hadn't hypnotized him into falling over his own feet. What was his name, anyway? Bobby something?"

"Danny Abbott," she said quietly.

"Yeah. That was a summer, wasn't it? I was in trouble all the time. Of course, you were the one playing around with magic."

He meant it as a joke, but it was closer to the truth than he realized. Nest forced a smile.

"You remember that business on the Fourth with John Ross and those fireworks exploding all over the place?" he pressed. "I was chasing after you through the park, and I fell down or something, hit my head. I can still remember the way you looked at me. You said afterward you used magic." He paused, suddenly thoughtful. "You know, I never did understand what really happened."

Nest reached down abruptly, snatched up a squealing Kyle, and thrust him at his father. "Here, Kyle, you explain it to him," she urged.

"Splane," Kyle repeated, giggling.

Robert took his son into his arms, jiggling him gently. "Don't forget the Christmas party Tuesday night," he said to Nest, kissing Kyle's fat cheeks. "You got the invitation, didn't you?"

She nodded. "Sure. I'll be there."

"Good. My parents are sure to find a way to blame me, if you aren't."

"Serve you right," she said, moving away. "See you later, Robert. Bye, Kyle." She wiggled her fingers at the boy, who hid his face in his father's shoulder.

"Hey, don't scare him like that!" Robert threw after her.

She put her coffee cup on a tray near the kitchen door, ready to leave. Larry Spence was still watching her, but she tried not to notice. *Life in a small town is filled with moments of trying not to notice,* she thought wearily.

She was just departing the reception room to retrieve her coat from the narthex when a tall, angular young woman with wild red hair and acrylic green eyes came up to her.

"Are you Nest Freemark?" the young woman asked, eyes wide and staring like a cat's. Actually, on closer inspection, she seemed more a girl barely out of her teens than a woman. Nest nodded. "I'm Penny," the other announced.

She stuck out her hand, and Nest took it in her own. Penny's grip was strong and sure. "I just wanted you to know how much I admire you. I've followed your career, like, ever since the Melbourne Olympics. I was just a little girl, but you were such a great inspiration to me! I wanted to be a runner, but I didn't grow up with strong enough lungs or something. So I became an actress. Can you tell?" She giggled. "Anyway, I thought you should know there's someone who still remembers you. You know, when you were famous." She giggled some more. "Hey, it was nice meeting you. You'll be seeing me around, I expect. Bye-bye."

She was gone before Nest could reply, disappearing into the crowd gathered by the coffee urn. *Someone who remembers you from back when you were famous?* Nest grimaced. What a strange remark! She had never seen the young woman before and had no idea who she was. She didn't even look like anyone Nest knew, so it was impossible to match her up to a Hopewell family.

Must be someone new in town, she thought, still staring after the young woman. *Things around here change so quickly,* she thought, mimicking Alice in Wonderland.

Speaking of which, there was Larry Spence, moving in her direction with a decidedly hopeful look in his eye. She turned as if remembering something and hurried out the door.

CHAPTER 3

Findo Gask stood across the street from the First Congregational Church, just in front of the Hopewell Gazette, waiting patiently for Penny's return. He was an incongruous figure standing there in his frock coat and flat-brimmed hat, his tall, stooped figure silhouetted against the white stone of the newspaper building by the bright winter sunlight. With his black book held in front of him like a shield, he might have been a modern-day prophet come to pronounce judgment on an unsuspecting populace.

The truth, however, was a good deal scarier.

Even as demons went, Findo Gask was very old. He was centuries old, and this was unusual. For the most part, demons had a tendency to self-destruct or fall prey to their own peculiar excesses rather early in their careers. In completing their transformations, demons shed their human trappings, reducing themselves to hard, winged husks, so that when stripped of their disguises they looked not unlike bats.

But as hard as they worked to shed their human skins, they remained surprisingly dependent on their origins. To disguise themselves, they were forced to resume looking like the creatures they had been. To satisfy their desperate need to escape their past, they were forced to prey upon the creatures they pretended to be. And to survive in their new forms, they were forced to struggle constantly against a small but intransigent truth—they hungered endlessly and helplessly for contact with the creatures they despised.

As a direct result, they were torn by the dichotomy of their existence. In their efforts to give vent to their schizophrenic personalities, they descended swiftly into madness and bestiality. Their control over themselves collapsed, their sanity fragmented, and they disintegrated like wheels spinning so fast and so hard they succumbed to the heat of their own friction.

Findo Gask had avoided this end because he was not driven by emotion. He was not hungry for power or personal gratification. Revenge did not interest him. Validation of his existence was never a cause he was tempted to pursue. No, he was simply curious. Curiosity provided a limitless supply of inspiration for Findo Gask. He was smart and inventive and able. As a man, he might have uncovered secrets and solved riddles. He might have accomplished great things through research. But a man lived a finite number of years and was hampered by rules Findo Gask did not necessarily accept. A demon, he was quick to see, could do so much more. If he was willing to let go of the part of him that was human, a part he considered of no particular consequence or purpose in any case, he could explore and discover and dissect forever.

Moreover, he realized early on, humans made great subjects for his studies. They fit with his needs and his wants perfectly. All that was required was that he separate himself.

He had done so with surprising ease. It was difficult to recall the details now. He had been alive for so long, a demon for so many centuries, that he no longer remembered anything of his human history. Even the century of his transformation had been forgotten. He was the oldest of his kind perhaps, though it didn't matter to him if he was because he took no satisfaction from it. The Void was his master, but his master was a vague, substanceless presence who pretty much left him alone to do what he wished, appearing only now and then as a brief presence—a whisper, a shadow, a dream of something remembered.

Other demons envied him. Some hated him openly. He had what they wanted and did not know how to get. He was older and wiser and stronger and more immune to the trappings of humanness that still tore at them like razors. His insights into humans were deeper. His assimilation of both demon and human worlds was more complete. He undertook the challenges that interested him and gave himself over to the studies that intrigued him.

Except that every once in a while the Void reminded him there was a price for everything and choice was not always an option, no matter who he was . . .

He watched Penny emerge from the church, red hair uncoiling from her head like a mass of severed electrical wires, gawky form working its way along the sidewalk and across the street, a poorly made marionette, jerked and tugged by invisible strings. He smiled indulgently, watching her progress. Outwardly, she was a mess, but one couldn't always judge a book by its cover. Inside, she was twisted and corrosive and lethal. Penny Dreadful. She'd heard that the name applied to the dime-store crime novels of an earlier century. That's me, she'd said with a wicked grin, and took the name as her own.

She came up to Findo Gask with a skipping motion, putting on her little-girl facade, coquettish and sly. "Greetings, Gramps," she gushed, circling him once, then throwing her arms around him with such abandon that two elderly ladies passing on the other side of the street paused to have a look.

Gently, patiently, he disengaged himself from her grasp. He understood her excesses, which were greater than those of most demons. Unlike himself, she had no interest in staying alive. Penny Dreadful was intent on self-destructing, was enamored of the idea in fact, ensnared by her own special blend of madness and looking to write her finish in a particularly spectacular manner. Gask considered her a live hand grenade, but he was hopeful she would last long enough to be of some use to him in this matter.

"Did you do as I asked?" he inquired, arching one eyebrow in what might have been misinterpreted as a conciliatory gesture.

Penny, missing nothing, played dumb anyway. "Sure. Hey, you know something, Gramps?" She called him that all the time, emphasizing their age difference in a continuing, if futile, effort to annoy him. "That girl isn't anything special, you know? Nest Freemark. She isn't anything at all. I could snuff her out just like that."

She snapped her fingers lightly, grinning at him.

He took her by the arm without a word and guided her down the sidewalk to the car. "Get in," he ordered, not bothering even to look at her.

She did, snickering and casting small glances in his direction, a clever little girl playing to an indulgent grandfather. Findo Gask felt like rolling his eyes. Or perhaps hers.

When they were seated inside, relatively secluded from passersby, he took a long moment to study her before speaking. "Who did you find?"

She sighed at his unwillingness to play along with her latest game. She shrugged. "Some dork named Larry Spence. He's a deputy sheriff, got some clout in the department 'cause he's been there ten years or so. He was happy to tell me all about himself, little me, all wide-eyed and impressed. He's got it real bad for Tracy Track Shoes. Like, totally. Do anything if he thought it would help her. He's perfect, for what you seem to want."

She arched her eyebrows and met his gaze for the first time. "Which is what exactly, Gramps? Why are we wasting our time on this creepo?"

"Watch the church door," he said, ignoring her questions. "When you see him come out, tell me."

She held his gaze only a moment, then huffed disdainfully, slouched behind the steering wheel, and did as he asked. She was pretty good at that, for all the back talk she liked to give him. He let her get away with it precisely because back talk never went any further than talk with Penny. With Twitch, it was another matter, of course.

They sat silently in the warmth of the Sunday morning sunshine as midday came and went. The congregation was filing out in steadily increasing numbers, bundled in their coats, heading home for the noontime meal.

"Wish he'd hurry it up," Penny groused.

"Let me give you some advice," Findo Gask said quietly. "Grandfatherly advice, if you prefer. Don't underestimate Nest Freemark. She's tougher than you think."

She glanced at him with a sneer, about to say something in rebuttal, but he shook his head at her and pointed back toward the church.

A few moments later, Larry Spence emerged, a small girl hanging off one hand, a boy only slightly older hanging off the other. Penny identified him, and Findo Gask told her to start the car. When Spence pulled out of the parking lot with his children, Findo Gask told Penny to follow. It was annoying having to issue all these instructions, but he couldn't rely on any of them to do what was necessary on their own. Three demons, each one more difficult to manage than the others, each a paradox even in demon terms. He had recruited them after Salt Lake City, realizing that in Ross he was up against someone who might prove his undoing. After all, by then he knew the Void's wishes, and he understood there was not going to be any margin for error.

He sighed wearily and looked out the window at the passing houses as Penny followed Larry Spence and his children down First Avenue toward the north end of town. He had been in Hopewell for almost a week, waiting patiently for Ross to show, knowing Ross would come, sensing it instinctively, the way he always did. It was an advantage he enjoyed over other demons, although he did not understand exactly why he had this power. Perhaps his instincts were sharper simply because he had lived so long and survived so much. Perhaps it was because he was a seeker of answers and more attuned to the possibilities of human behavior than others of his kind. Whatever the case, he would succeed where they would not. Demons would be hunting Ross all over the United States, peeking in every closet and looking under every bed. But he was the one who had found Ross the last time, and he would be the one to find him this time, too.

His hands moved lovingly over the worn leather cover of his Book of Names. He called it that, a simple designation for his record of the humans he had dispatched in one way or another over the centuries. He didn't bother with times or dates or places when he recorded their passing. The details didn't interest him. What he cared about was collecting lives and making them his own. What interested him was the nature of their dying, what they gave up, how they struggled, what they made him feel as they took their last breath. Something in their dying could be possessed, he discovered early on. Something of them could be claimed. It was a tribute to his continuing interest in collecting the names that he could always remember who they belonged to. Common memories were pale and insubstantial. But a memory of death was strong and lasting, and he kept each one, many hundreds in all, carefully catalogued and stored away.

He sighed. When he quit being interested in seeing them die, he supposed, he would quit collecting their names.

"He's home, Gramps," Penny advised, cutting into his reverie.

He shifted his eyes to the front, watching as Larry Spence turned his car into a driveway leading to a small bungalow on Second Avenue, just off LeFevre Road.

"Drive past a couple of blocks and then turn around and come back," he instructed.

Penny took the car up Second for a short distance, then turned into someone's drive, backed out, and came down the street from the other direction. Just before they reached Spence's house, she pulled the car over to the curb and parked. Switching off the ignition, she looked over. "Now what, Grampa Gask?"

"Come with me," he said.

Larry Spence was already inside the house with his kids, and Gask and Penny heard the ticking of his still-warm engine as they walked up the drive. The house seemed small and spare from the outside, shorn by winter's coming of the softening foliage of the bushes and trees surrounding it, its faded, peeling paint and splintered trim left bare and revealed. Findo Gask reflected on the pathetic lives of humans as he knocked on the front door, but only for a moment.

Larry Spence appeared almost immediately. He was still wearing his church clothes, but his tie was loosened and he had a dish towel in his hand. He pushed open the storm door and looked at them questioningly.

"Mr. Spence?" Findo Gask asked politely, his voice friendly but businesslike. Spence nodded. "Mr. Larry Spence?"

"What do you want?" Spence replied warily.

Findo Gask produced a leather identification holder and flipped it open. "Special Agent George Robinson, Mr. Spence. I'm with the FBI. Can you spare a moment?"

The other's confidence turned to uncertainty as he studied the identity card in its plastic slipcase. "Something wrong?"

Now Gask gave him a reassuring smile. "Nothing that involves you directly, Mr. Spence. But we need to talk with you about someone you know. This is my assistant, Penny. May we come inside?"

Larry Spence's big, athletic frame shifted in the doorway, and he brushed back his dark hair with spread fingers. "Well, the kids are here, Mr. Robinson," he replied uncertainly.

Findo Gask nodded. "I wouldn't come to you on a Sunday, Mr. Spence, if it wasn't important. I wouldn't come to your home if I could handle the matter in your office." He paused meaningfully. "This won't take long. Penny can play with the children."

Spence hesitated a moment longer, his brow furrowed, then nodded. "All right. Come on in."

They entered a small hallway that led to a tiny, cramped living room strewn with toys and magazines and pieces of the Sunday *Chicago Tribune*. Evidently Larry Spence hadn't done his housework before going off to church. The little boy appeared at the end of a hallway leading farther back into the house and looked at them questioningly.

"It's okay, Billy," Spence said quickly, sounding less than certain that it was.

"Mr. Spence, perhaps Billy would like to show Penny his room," Findo Gask suggested, smiling anew. "Penny has a brother just about his age."

"Sure, that would be fine." Spence jumped on the suggestion. "What do you say, Billy?"

"Hey, little man," Penny said, coming forward to greet the boy. "You got any cool stuff to show me?"

She guided him back down the hallway, talking at him a mile a minute, Billy staring up at her like a deer caught in the headlights. Findo Gask hoped she would behave herself.

"Why don't we sit down, Mr. Spence," he suggested.

He didn't bother removing his coat. He didn't bother putting down the book. Larry Spence wasn't seeing either one. He wasn't even seeing Findo Gask the way he appeared. Gask had clouded his vision the moment he opened the door, leaving him only vaguely aware of what the man he was talking to looked like. The trick wouldn't work with someone like Nest Freemark, but Larry Spence was a different matter. Already beset by doubts and confusion, he would probably stay that way until Findo Gask was done with him.

They moved over to a pair of worn easy chairs and seated themselves. Sunlight filtered, sharp-edged, through cracks in the drawn blinds, and Matchbox cars lay overturned on the carpet like miniature accidents.

"Mr. Spence, as a law enforcement officer yourself, you are undoubtedly familiar with the work we do," Findo Gask opened the conversation. "I'm here in Hopewell because of my work, and I need your help. But I don't want anyone else to know about this, not even your superiors. Usually, we try to work openly with the local law enforcement agencies, but in this case that isn't possible. At least, not yet. That's why I've come to your house rather than approach you at your office. No one but you even knows we are here."

He paused. "I understand you are acquainted with a young woman named Nest Freemark."

Larry Spence looked startled. "Nest? Sure, but I don't think she would ever—"

"Please, Mr. Spence, don't jump to conclusions," Gask interrupted smoothly, cutting him short. "Just let me finish. The bureau's interest in Miss Freemark is only peripheral in this matter. Our real interest is in a man named John Ross."

Spence was still holding the dish towel, twisting the fabric between his big hands nervously. He saw what he was doing and set the towel aside. He cleared his throat. "I never heard of anyone named John Ross."

Findo Gask nodded. "I didn't think you had. But Nest Freemark knows him quite well. Their friendship was formed some years ago when she was still a little girl and highly impressionable. He was an older man, good looking in a rugged sort of way, and very attentive toward her. He was a friend of her dead mother, and Nest was eager to make the connection with him for that reason if for no other. I suspect that she had quite a crush on him. She formed a strong attachment to him in any case, and she still thinks of him as her close friend."

Gask chose his words carefully, working on the assumption that Larry Spence already felt possessive about Nest and would not welcome the idea of a rival, particularly one to whom she was attracted.

"John Ross is not the man Miss Freemark thinks he is, Mr. Spence," he continued earnestly. "He is a very dangerous criminal. She believes him to be her knight in shining armor, the man she knew fifteen years ago, the handsome, older man who paid so much attention to a young, insecure girl. She has deceived herself, and she will not be quick to change her thinking."

He was laying it on a bit thick, but when dealing with a man as enamored of a woman as Larry Spence was of Nest Freemark, he could get away with it.

"What's he done?" Spence demanded, stiffening in his seat, ready to charge out and do battle with his duplicitous, unsavory rival. Gask smiled inwardly.

"I'd prefer not to discuss that aspect of the case with you, Mr. Spence." *Let him use his imagination,* Gask thought. "What should be of concern to you, as it is to us, is not so much what he's done elsewhere, but what he may do once he comes here."

"He's coming to Hopewell?" Spence swallowed. "So you think he'll look up Nest?"

Gask nodded, pleased that the deputy was doing all the work for him. "There is every reason to believe he will try to contact her. When he does, he will ask her to keep his presence a secret. He will lay low for the duration of his visit. He will not show himself readily. That's where you come in."

Larry Spence leaned forward, his hands knotted. "What do you want me to do?"

Findo Gask wished everything in life were this easy. "Miss Freemark is your friend. She knows of your interest in her, and she will not be suspicious if you find an excuse to visit her. Do so. Do so at least once every day. Get inside her house any way you can and look around. You may not see Ross, but you may see some sign of his presence. If you do, don't do anything foolish. Just call this number immediately."

Gask drew out a white business card and handed it to Larry Spence. It bore his fake identity and rank and a local number to which an answer phone would respond.

"I don't have to tell you how grateful the bureau is for your cooperation, Mr. Spence," Gask announced, rising to his feet. "I won't take up any more of your time today, but I'll stay in touch."

He shook the deputy's hand, leaving a final imprint of his presence so that the other would not be quick to forget what he had been told. "Penny!" he called down the hallway.

Penny Dreadful emerged on cue, smiling demurely, trying to hide the hungry look in her eyes. She was like this every time she got around children. Gask took her by the arm and steered her out the front door, nodding in the direction of Larry Spence as they departed.

"I was just starting to have fun," she pouted. "I had some of my toys out, and I was showing him how to cut things. I took off one of my fingers with a razor." She giggled and held up the severed digit, then stuck it back in place, ligaments and flesh knitting seamlessly.

"Penny, Penny, Penny," he sighed wearily.

"Don't get your underwear in a bundle, Gramps. I made sure he won't remember any of it until tonight, after he's asleep, when he'll wake up screaming. Deputy daddy will think it's just a bad dream."

They climbed back into the car, clicking their seat belts into place. Findo Gask wondered how much longer he was going to be able to keep her in line. It was bad enough with Twitch, but to have Penny pushing the envelope as well was a bit much. He rolled down the window and breathed in the winter air. The temperature had risen to almost forty, and the day felt warm and crisp against his skin. Odd, he thought, that he could still feel things like that, even in a body that wasn't his.

He thought for a moment about the enormity of the struggle between the Word and the Void. It had been going on since the dawn of time, a hard-fought, bitter struggle for control of the human race. Sometimes one gained the upper hand, sometimes the other. But the Void always gained a little more ground in these exchanges because the Word relied on the strengths of humans to keep in balance the magic that held the world together and the Void relied on their weaknesses to knock it askew. It was a foregone conclusion as to which would ultimately prevail. The weaknesses of humans would always erode their strengths. There might be more humans than demons, but numbers alone were insufficient to win this battle.

And while it was true that demons were prone to self-destruct, humans were likely to get there much quicker.

"Home, Penny," he instructed, realizing she was waiting for him to tell her what to do.

She pulled out into the street, swerving suddenly toward a cat that just barely managed to get out of the way. "I was listening to you in there," she declared suddenly.

He nodded. "Good for you."

"So what's the point of having this dork hang around Miss Olympic Big Bore to find out if this Ross guy is staying with her?"

"What's the matter, Penny? Don't you believe in cooperating with your local law enforcement officers?"

She was staring at the road intently. "Like that matters to you, Gramps. We could find out easy enough if Ross is out there without help from Deputy Dawg. I don't get it."

He stretched his lanky frame and shrugged. "You don't have to get it, Penny. You just have to do what you're told."

She pouted in silence a moment, then said, "He'll just get in the way, Gramps. You'll see."

Findo Gask smiled. *Right you are, Penny,* he thought. *That's just exactly what he'll do. I'm counting on it.*

CHAPTER 4

Driving home from church, Nest Freemark brooded some more about John Ross. It was a futile exercise, one that darkened her mood considerably more than she intended. Ross was a flashpoint for all the things about her life that troubled her. Even though he wasn't directly responsible for any of them, he was the common link. By the time she parked the car in her driveway and climbed out, she was ready to get back in again and start driving to some other time zone.

She went inside resignedly, knowing there was nothing she could do to stop him from coming to see her if that's what he intended to do, nothing she could do to prevent yet another upheaval in her life. She changed into jeans and a sweatshirt and pulled on heavy walking shoes, then went into the kitchen to fix herself some lunch. She sat alone at the worn, wooden table she had shared with Gran for so many years, wondering what advice the old lady would give her about John Ross. She could just imagine. Gran had been a no-nonsense sort, the kind who took life's challenges as they came and dealt with them as best she could. She hadn't been the sort to fantasize about possibilities and what-ifs. It was a lesson that hadn't been lost on her granddaughter.

Polishing off a glass of milk and a sandwich of leftover chicken, she pulled on her winter parka and walked out the back door. Tomorrow was the winter solstice, and the days had shortened to barely more than eight hours. Already the sun was dropping westward, marking the passing of the early afternoon. By four-thirty, it would be dark. Even so, the air felt warm this winter day, and she left her parka open, striding across her backyard toward the hedgerow and the park. Her old sandbox and tire swing were gone, crumbled with age and lack of use years ago. The trees and bushes were a tangle of bare, skeletal limbs, webbing across the blue sky, casting odd shadows on the wintry gray-green grass. It was a time of sleep, of the old year and its seasons passing into the new, of waiting patiently for rebirth. Nest Freemark wondered if her own life was keeping pace or just standing still.

She pushed through a gap in the bare branches of the hedge and crossed the service road that ran behind her house. Sinnissippi Park stretched away before her, barren and empty in the winter light. The crossbar at the entrance was down. Residents living in the houses that crowded up against its edges walked their dogs and themselves and played with their kids in the snow when there was snow to be played in, but there was no one about at the moment. In the evenings, weather permitting, the park opened from six to ten at night for tobogganing on the park slide and ice skating on the bayou.

If the temperature dropped and the forecast for snow proved out, both would be open by tomorrow night.

She hiked deliberately toward the cliffs, passing through a familiar stand of spruce clustered just beyond the backstop of the nearest baseball diamond, and Pick dropped from its branches onto her shoulder.

"You took your sweet time getting out here!" he snapped irritably, settling himself in place against the down folds of her collar.

"Church ran a little long," she replied, refusing to be baited. Pick was always either irritable or coming up on it, so she was used to his abrupt pronouncements and sometimes scathing rebukes. "You probably got a lot done without me anyway."

"That's not the point!" he snapped. "When you make a commitment—"

"—you stick to it," she finished, having heard this chestnut at least a thousand times. "But I can't ignore the rest of my life, either."

Pick muttered something unintelligible and squirmed restlessly. A hundred and sixty-five years old, he was a sylvan, a forest creature composed of sticks and moss, conceived by magic, and born in a pod. In every woods and forest in the world, sylvans worked to balance the magic that was centered there so that all living things could coexist in the way the Word had intended. It was not an easy job and not without its disappointments; many species had been lost through natural evolution or the depredations of humans. Even woods and forests were destroyed, taking with them all the creatures who lived there, including the sylvans who tended them. Erosion of the forest magic over the passing of the centuries had been slow, but steady, and Pick declared often and ominously that time was running out.

"The park looks pretty good," she offered, banishing such thoughts from her mind, trying to put a positive spin on things for the duration of her afternoon.

Pick was having none of it. "Appearances are deceiving. There's trouble brewing."

"Trouble of what sort?"

"Ha! You haven't even noticed, have you?"

"Why don't you just tell me?"

They crossed the entry road and walked up toward the turnaround at the west end that overlooked the Rock River from the edge of the bluffs. Beyond the chain-link fence marking the park's farthest point lay Riverside Cemetery. She had not been out to the graves of her mother or grandparents in more than a week, and she felt a pang of guilt at her oversight.

"The feeders have been out," Pick advised with a grunt, "skulking about the park in more numbers than I've seen in a long time."

"How many?"

"Lots. Too many to count. Something's got them stirred up, and I don't know what it is."

Shadowy creatures that lurked on the edges of people's lives, feeders lapped up the energy given off by expenditure of emotions. The darker and stronger the emotions, the greater the number of feeders who gathered to feast. Parasitic beings who responded to their instincts, they did not judge and they did not make choices. Most humans never saw them, except when death came violently and unexpectedly, and they were the last image to register before the lights went out for good. Only those like Nest, who were born with magic themselves, knew there were feeders out there.

Pick gave her a sharp look, his pinched wooden face all wizened and rough, his gnarled limbs drawn up about his crooked body so that he took on the look of a bird's nest. His strange, flat eyes locked on her. "You know something about this, don't you?"

She nodded. "Maybe."

She told him about Findo Gask and the possibility that John Ross was returning to Hopewell. "A demon's presence would account for all the feeders, I expect," she finished.

They walked up through the playground equipment and picnic tables that occupied the wooded area situated across the road from the Indian mounds and the bluffs. When they reached the turnaround, she slowed, suddenly aware that Pick hadn't spoken a word since she had told him about Findo Gask and John Ross. He hadn't even told her what work he wanted her to do that day in the park.

"What do you think?" she asked, trying to draw him out.

He sat motionless on her shoulder, silent and remote. She crossed the road to the edge of the bluffs and moved out to where she could see the frozen expanse of the Rock River. Even with the warmer temperatures of the past few days, the bayou that lay between the near shore and the raised levee on which the railroad tracks had been laid remained frozen. Beyond, where the wider channel opened south on its way to the Mississippi, the Rock was patchy with ice, the swifter movement of the water keeping the river from freezing over completely. That would change when January arrived.

"Another demon," Pick said softly. "You'd think one in a lifetime would be enough."

She nodded wordlessly, eyes scanning the tangle of tree trunks and limbs immediately below, searching for movement in the lengthening shadows. The feeders, if they were out yet, would be there, watching.

"Some sylvans go through their entire lives and never encounter a demon." Pick's voice was soft and contemplative. "Hundreds of years, and not a one."

"It's my fault," she said.

"Not hardly!"

"It is," she insisted. "It began with my father."

"Which was your grandmother's mistake!" he snapped.

She glanced down at him, all fiery-eyed and defensive of her, and she gave him a smile. "Where would I be without you, Pick?"

"Somewhere else, I expect."

She sighed. Over the past fifteen years she had attempted to move away from the park. To leave the park was unthinkable for Pick; the park was his home and his charge. For the sylvan, nothing else existed. It was different for her, of course, but Pick didn't see it that way. Pick saw things in black-and-white terms. Even an inherited obligation—in this case, an obligation passed down through six generations of Freemark women to help care for the park—wasn't to be ignored, no matter what. She belonged here, working with him, keeping the magic in balance and looking after the park. But this was all Pick knew. It was all he had done for more than one hundred fifty years. Nest didn't have one hundred fifty years, and she wasn't so sure that tending the magic and looking after the park was what she wanted to spend the rest of her life doing.

She looked off across the Rock River, at the hazy midafternoon twilight beginning to steal out of the east as the shortened winter day slipped westward. "What do you want to do today, Pick?" she asked quietly.

He shrugged. "Too late to do much, I expect." He did not say it in a gruff way; he simply sounded resigned. "Let's just have a look around, see if anything needs doing, and we can see to it tomorrow." He sniffed and straightened. "If you think you can spare the time, of course."

"Of course," she echoed.

They left the bluffs and walked down the road from the turnaround to where it split, one branch doubling back under a bridge to descend to the base of the bluffs and what she thought of as the feeder caves, the other continuing on along the high ground to the east end of the park, where the bulk of the woods and picnic areas were located. They followed the latter route, working their way along the fringes of the trees, taking note of how everything was doing, not finding much that didn't appear as it should. The park was in good shape, even if Pick wasn't willing to acknowledge as much. Winter had put her to sleep in good order, and the magic, dormant and restful in the long, slow passing of the season, was in perfect balance.

The world of Sinnissippi Park is at peace, Nest thought to herself, glancing off across the open flats of the ball diamonds and playgrounds and through the skeletal trees and rolling stretches of woodland. Why couldn't her world be the same?

But she knew the answer to that question. She had known it for a long time. The answer was Wraith.

Three years earlier, she had been acclaimed as the greatest American long-distance runner of all time. She had already competed in one Olympics and had won a pair of gold medals and set two world records. She had won thirty-two consecutive races since. She owned a combined eight world titles in the three and five thousand. She was competing in her second Olympics, and she had won the three by such a wide margin that a double in the five seemed almost a given.

She remembered that last race vividly. She had watched the video a thousand times. She could replay it in her own mind from memory, every moment, frame by frame.

Looking off into the trees, she did so now.

She breaks smoothly from the start line, content to stay with the pack for several laps, for this longer distance places a higher premium on patience and endurance than on speed. There are eight lead changes in the first two thousand meters, and then her competitors begin boxing her in. Working in shifts, the Ukrainians, the Ethiopians, a Moroccan, and a Spaniard pin her against the inside of the track. She has gone undefeated in the three- and five-thousand-meter events for four years. You don't do that, no matter how well liked or respected you are, and not make enemies. In any case, she has never been all that close to the other athletes. She trains with her college coach or alone. She stays by herself when she travels to events. She keeps apart because of the nature of her life. She is careful not to get too close to anyone. Her legacy of magic has made her wary.

With fifteen hundred meters to go, she is locked in the middle of a pack of runners and unable to break free.

At the thousand-meter mark, a scuffle for position ensues, and she is pushed hard, loses her balance, and tumbles from the track.

She comes back to her feet almost as quickly as she has gone down and regains the track. Furious at being trapped, jostled, and knocked sprawling, she gives chase, unaware that she is bleeding profusely from a spike wound on her ankle.

Zoning into that place where she sometimes goes when she runs, where there is only the sound of her breathing and beat of her heart, she catches and passes the pack. She doesn't just draw up on them gradually; she runs them down. There is something raw and primal working inside her as she cranks up her speed a notch at a time. The edges of her vision turn red and fuzzy, her breathing burns in her throat like fire, and the pumping of her arms and legs threatens to tear her body apart.

She is running with such determination and with so little regard for herself that she fails to realize that something is wrong.

Then she hears the gasps of the Ethiopians as she passes them in the three and four positions and sees the look of horror on the face of the Spaniard when she catches her two hundred meters from the finish.

A tiger-striped face surges in the air before her, faintly visible in the shimmer of heat and dust. Wraith is emerging from her body. He is breaking free, coming out of her, unbidden and out of control. Wraith, formed of her father's demon magic and bequeathed to her as a child. Wraith, created as her protector, but become a presence that threatens in ways she can barely tolerate. Wraith, who lives inside her now, a magic she cannot rid herself of and therefore must work constantly to conceal.

It happens all at once. Emerging initially as a faint image that clings to her in a shimmer of light, he begins to take recognizable shape. Only those who are close can see what is happening, and even they are unsure. But their uncertainty is only momentary. If he comes out of her all the way, there will be no more doubt. If he breaks free entirely, he may attack the other runners.

She fights to regain control of him, desperate to do so, unable to understand why he would appear when she has not summoned him and is not threatened with harm.

Powering down the straightaway, her body wracked by pain and fatigue and by her struggle to rein in the ghost wolf, she catches the Moroccan at fifty meters. The Moroccan's intense, frightened eyes momentarily lock on her as she powers past. Nest's teeth are bared and Wraith surges in and out of her skin in a flurry of small, quick movements, his terrifying visage flickering in the bright sunlight like an iridescent mirage. The Moroccan swerves from both in terror, and Nest is alone in the lead.

She crosses the finish line first, the winner of the gold medal by ten meters. She knows it is the end of her career, even before the questions on how she could have recovered from her fall and gone on to win turn to rumors on the use of performance-enhancing drugs. Her control over Wraith, always tenuous at best, has eroded further, and she does not understand why. His presence is bearable when she can rely on keeping him in check. But if he can appear anytime she loses control of her emotions, it marks the end of her competitive running days as surely as sunset does the coming of night.

"I'm getting old," Pick said suddenly, kicking at her shoulder in what she supposed was frustration.

"You've always been old," she reminded him. "You were old when I was born. You've already lived twice as long as most humans."

He glared at her, but said nothing.

She watched clouds fill the edges of the western sky beyond the scraggly tops of the bare hardwoods, rolling out of the plains. The expected storm was on its way. She could feel a drop in the temperature, a bite in the wind that gusted out of the shadows. She pulled the parka tight against her body and zipped it up.

"Hard freeze coming in," Pick said from his perch on her shoulder. "Let's give it up for today."

She turned and began the long walk home. Dead leaves rustled in dry clusters against the bare ground and the trunks of trees. She kicked at pieces of deadwood, her thoughts moody and unsettled, fragments of the race and its aftermath still playing out in her mind.

It had taken months to put an end to the newspaper reports, even after she had taken a voluntary drug test in an effort to end the speculation. Everyone wanted to know why she would quit competitive running when she was at the peak of her career, when she was so young, after she had won so often. She had given interviews freely on the subject for months, and finally she had just given up. She couldn't explain it to them, of course. She couldn't begin to make them understand. She couldn't tell them about the magic or Wraith. She could only say she was tired of running and wanted to do something else. She could only repeat herself, over and over and over again.

Only a month ago, she had received a phone call from an editor at the sports magazine Paul worked for. The editor told her the magazine wanted to do a story on her. She reminded him she didn't give interviews anymore.

"Change your policy, Nest," he pressed. "Next summer is the Olympics. People want to know if you'll come out of retirement and run again. You're the greatest long-distance runner in your country's history—you can't pretend that doesn't mean something. How about it?"

"No, thanks."

"Why? Does it have anything to do with your quitting competitive running after your race in the five thousand in the last Olympics? Does it have anything to do with the rumors of drug use? There was a lot of speculation about what happened—"

She'd hung up on him abruptly. He hadn't called back.

In truth, quitting was the hardest thing she had ever done. She loved the competition. She loved how being the best made her feel. She couldn't deny giving it up took something away from her, that it hollowed her out. She still trained, because she couldn't imagine life without the sort of discipline and order that training demanded. She stayed fit and strong, and every so often she would sneak back into the city and have herself timed by her old coach. She did it out of pride and a need to know she was still worth something.

Her life had been a mixed bag since. She lived comfortably enough on money she had saved from endorsements and appearance fees, earning a little extra now and then by writing articles for the running magazines. The writing didn't pay her much, but it gave her something to do. Something besides helping Pick with the park. Something besides charity and church work. Something besides sitting around remembering her marriage to Paul and how it had fallen apart.

She crossed out of the ravine that divided the bulk of the park from the deep woods and climbed the slope toward the toboggan slide and the pavilion. From out of the distance came the piercing wail of a freight-train whistle followed by the slow, thunderous buildup of engines and wheels. She paused to look south, seeing the long freight drive out of the west toward Chicago, stark and lonely against the empty expanse of the winter landscape.

She waited until it passed, then continued on. Oddly enough, Pick hadn't said a word in complaint. Perhaps he sensed her sadness. Perhaps he was wrestling with concerns of his own. She let him be, striding across the open ball diamonds toward the service road and the hedgerow that marked the boundary between the park and her backyard. Pick left her somewhere along the way. Lost in thought, she didn't see him go. She just looked down and he wasn't there.

As she crossed the yard Hawkeye skittered along the rear of the house, stalking something Nest couldn't see. A big, orange stray who had adopted her, he was the sort of cat who put up with you if you fed him and expected you to stay out of his way the rest of the time. She liked having a mouser about, but Hawkeye made her nervous. His name came from the way he looked at her, which she caught him doing all the time. It was a sort of sideways stare, full of trickery and cool appraisal. Pick said he was just trying to figure out how to turn her into dinner.

As she came up beside the garage, she saw a young woman and a little girl sitting on her back steps. The little girl was bundled in an old, shabby red parka with the hood drawn up. Her face was bent toward a rag doll she held protectively in her lap. The woman was barely out of her teens, if that, short and slender with long, tangled dark hair spilling down over her shoulders. She wore a leather biker's jacket over a miniskirt and high boots. No gloves, no hat, no scarf.

Her head came up at Nest's approach, and she climbed to her feet watchfully. The pale afternoon light glinted dully off the silver rings that pierced her ears, nose, and one eyebrow. The deep blue markings of a tattoo darkened the back of one hand where it folded into the other to ward off the cold.

Nest came up to her slowly, thinking, *I know this girl.*

Then, for just a moment, something of the child she remembered from fifteen years ago surfaced in the young woman's face.

"Ben Ben?" Nest asked in disbelief.

A smile appeared. "Guess what, Nest? I've come home."

Sure enough, it was Bennett Scott.

Chapter 5

The demon who called himself Findo Gask climbed out of the passenger seat of the car and let Penny Dreadful pull ahead into the narrow garage. He stretched, smoothed down the wrinkles in his frock coat, and glanced around at his new neighborhood. The homes were large, faded mansions that had seen better days. The neighborhood had been one of Hopewell's finest, once upon a time, when only the well-to-do and wellborn lived there. Most of the homes sat on a minimum of two acres of rolling lawn and enjoyed the benefits of swimming pools, tennis courts, ornamental gardens, and gazebos. Lavish parties were held under the stars as fine brandies and ports were sipped and imported cigars smoked and live music played until dawn.

All that was before Midwest Continental Steel began expanding its plant west out of the city just below the back property lines, forming a wall of corrugated iron, scrap metal shriek, and molten fire between itself and the river. When that happened, the well-to-do and wellborn migrated to less offensive, more secluded sections of the city, and property values began to plummet. For a time, upper-middle-class families raised their children in these old homes, happy to find a neighborhood that exuded a sense of prestige and provided real space. But such families lasted only a short decade or so, when it became clear to all that the cost of upkeep and the proximity of the mill far outweighed any benefits.

After that, most of the homes were converted to apartments and town houses, save for a few where the original owners, now in their late seventies or eighties, had made the decision to hang on till the end. But even the conversions to multifamily dwellings had mixed results. Because the homes were old, they lacked reasonable heating, cooling, plumbing, and wiring, and even with modifications and improvements they were still dated, cavernous, and vaguely spooky. Besides, nothing could be done about the obvious presence of MidCon Steel, sitting right outside the back door at the end of the yard, and most people who might have considered renting at the rates sought wanted someplace with at least a modicum of tranquillity and ambiance.

Soon, rents dropped to a level that attracted transients and what was commonly referred to in the community as trailer trash. Renters came and went with the regularity of midseason TV shows. The banks and mortgage companies sold what they could of their inventory and put off any repairs or improvements that weren't absolutely necessary. The neighborhood continued its steady decline toward rock bottom, and eventually those renting were pretty much the kind of people who got through life by preying on each other.

Findo Gask had learned all this from the real estate lady at ERA with whom he had inspected his present home two days earlier. It was an old Victorian, four bedrooms, three baths, living room, dining room, study, powder room, basement recreation room, two screened porches, a swimming pool that had been converted to a pathetic Japanese rock garden, and a spacious lawn that ran down to a tall line of spruce trees that effectively screened away the sights, if not the smells and sounds, of MidCon and was the best feature of the property. The house was painted lavender and blueberry, and there were flower boxes set at all the windows on the lower floor.

The real estate lady had insisted it was a real bargain.

He smiled now, thinking of her. She had been quite anxious to sell him the place, poor woman. What she didn't realize was that he wasn't even considering renting, let alone buying. It took him a few, ugly moments to convince her of this. When he was done, she was so frightened she could barely manage to draw up the necessary papers, but at least she had given up on the sales pitch. By the time she recovered her wits enough to realize what she had done, he would be long gone.

Findo Gask left Penny to her own devices and walked up the drive to the front of the house. Leather-bound book held in both hands, he stood surveying the old building, wondering at its endurance. It was sagging and splintering and cracking at every corner and seam. He thought that if he took a deep breath and exhaled sharply enough, it would simply collapse.

He shook his head. It was just another crumbling, pathetic edifice in a crumbling, pathetic world.

He walked up the steps and through the front door. The hallway was dark and cool, and the house silent. It was always like that when Penny was out. The other two never made any noise. He wouldn't have known Twitch was even there if he hadn't listened closely for the television, which Twitch watched incessantly when he wasn't hanging around bars, looking for someone to traumatize.

Findo Gask frowned. At least with Twitch, there was the television to home in on when you wanted to know if he was around. With the other . . .

Where could it be, anyway?

He glanced into the living and dining rooms out of habit, then started upstairs. He climbed slowly and deliberately, letting each step take his full weight, making certain the creaking of the old boards preceded him. Best not to appear too unexpectedly. Some demons didn't like that, and this one was among them. You could never be certain of its reaction if you caught it by surprise.

Findo Gask searched through all the bedrooms, bathrooms, closets, nooks, and crannies. It would be up here rather than in the basement with Twitch, because it didn't like Twitch and it didn't like lights or television. Mostly, it liked being alone in silent, dark places where it could disappear entirely.

Gask looked around, perplexed. *Come out, come out, wherever you are.*

Findo Gask didn't like Twitch either. Or lights or television or Penny or anything about this house and the time he spent in it. He endured all of it solely because he was intrigued by the prospect of adding John Ross to his book.

And perhaps, he thought suddenly, *of adding Nest Freemark as well.* He nodded to himself. *Yes, perhaps.*

A small noise caught his attention—a scrape, no more. Gask peered up at the ceiling. The attic, of course. He walked down the hall to the concealed stairway, opened the door, and began to climb. The ceiling light was out, so the only illumination came from sunlight that seeped through a pair of dirt-encrusted dormer windows set at either end of the chamber. Gask reached the top of the stairs and stopped. Everything was wrapped in shadows, inky and forbidding, layer upon layer. The air smelled of dust and old wood, and he could hear the sound of his own breathing in the silence.

"Are you up here?" he asked quietly.

The ur'droch brushed against him before he even realized it was close enough to do so, and then it was gone again, melting back into the shadows. Its touch made him shudder in spite of himself. He wished it would talk once in a while, but it never said a word or uttered a sound. It rarely even showed itself, and that was all to the good as far as Gask was concerned. There weren't many demons like the ur'droch, and the few he knew about were universally shunned. They didn't take the forms of humans like most demons; they didn't take any form at all. Something in their makeup made them feel more comfortable in a substanceless form, a part of the shadows they hid within.

Not that this made them any less capable of killing.

"We're going out tonight," he advised, his eyes flicking left and right in a futile effort to find the other. "I want you along."

No response. Nothing moved. Findo Gask was tempted to have the whole house lighted from top to bottom just to expose this weasel to a clinical examination, but the effort would be pointless. The ur'droch was useful precisely because of what it was, and putting up with its shadowy presence was part of the price paid for its services.

Gask turned and walked back down the stairs and shut the door behind him. His mouth tightened as he stood in the upstairs hallway and ran his fingers over the cover of his book. Penny, Twitch, and the ur'droch. They were a strange and unpredictable bunch, but they were also what was needed.

He had learned that lesson in Salt Lake City.

The biggest of the five men he had hired bent close to the hotel room door, listening. The dimly lighted hallway was empty and silent at one o'clock in the morning. Findo Gask could hear the sound of his own breathing.

The man with his ear to the door straightened, shaking his head at the other two and Gask. No snores, no heavy breathing, no television, nothing.

Gask motioned impatiently. *Go in. Get it over with.*

The big man glanced at the two who flanked him, then down the hallway to where the other two were positioned, one each in front of the elevator and the stairway doors. Then he took out the Glock with the screwed-on silencer, stepped back a pace, and carefully inserted the key in the door.

Findo Gask's search for John Ross had begun three weeks earlier with a summoning. He was in Chicago at the time, working the projects on the south side, stirring up dissension and playing on frustrations, an invisible presence in an intellectual and cultural wasteland where hope was a mirage and reality a hammer. The riots of summer had been his work, as had the tenement fires of fall. Winter brought freezing cold and no heat, good building blocks for the instigation of further carnage.

The summoning came to him in the middle of the night as a child's wailing. It was inaudible to human ears, but perfectly clear to his. He knew at once what it was. He had been summoned before, and he recognized the feelings the call invoked. Hunger, blood-lust, fury, and a deep and pervasive emptiness. It was as if the Void were hollowing him out, dredging his insides, his heart and mind and soul, with a tiny metal scoop. The pain was excruciating, and he went quickly from his room in search of relief.

He found it in the basement of the abandoned project in which he had constructed his spider's web of hate, a place where gangs carried out acts so unspeakable there were no names for them. The wail had its source in a dark corner where rats prowled and the detritus of expended human lives was discarded as casually as yesterday's newspapers. There were no windows in the concrete-block walls, but gaps in the ceiling served the purpose. Streetlamps lent just enough illumination to the chamber for Findo Gask to pick his way to where the summoning originated.

The wail died to a rustle as he appeared, a voice speaking to him not from the shadows but from inside his head. The Void's presence was unmistakable, cold, empty, and lifeless, a whisper of the passing of all things and the beginning of none.

Listen carefully, the rustle cautioned. *A gypsy morph has been captured by a Knight of the Word at a place called Cannon Beach, Oregon. The Knight's name is John Ross. He is a seasoned, dangerous veteran of our wars. He seeks to unlock the morph's magic. He must be found and destroyed. Findo Gask. Findo Gask.*

The words echoed and died into silence. The dark of the basement shifted and tightened about him as he waited for the rest.

Bring me the morph. Findo Gask. Findo Gask.

Something like an electric shock jolted him, lifting him clear of the floor, filling his vision with red fire, then retreating in a light as clear as glass. Within the light was a vision of John Ross and the gypsy morph on a day as hard and gray as slate. They emerged onto a beach from a cavern cut into the side of an embankment of stone and brush, the morph caught in a strange netting, all bright lights and speed, the Knight of the Word already beginning to check for the enemies he knew would be coming for him.

The vision faded, and Findo Gask found himself slumped on his knees on the cold concrete basement floor, rats skittering away in the dark, shadows again gone still, silence everywhere.

Not many demons were summoned, Findo Gask knew. Only the oldest and most experienced, the ones the Void depended on most. A gypsy morph was rare and dangerous. Formed of loose, wild magics come together in the ether, a morph had the potential of becoming a weapon of incredible power. How a Knight of the Word had managed to capture one was unimaginable. It must have taken an incredible stroke of luck. Whatever the case, the Knight's luck was about to change.

Findo Gask left the basement and the projects and Chicago that night. One or two other demons would be dispatched by the Void as well. But Findo Gask knew he was the one who would have the best chance of succeeding.

In the beginning, tracking John Ross was not difficult. Every time the gypsy morph underwent a new transformation, which was sometimes hourly, it emitted a pulse of expended magic. Like a beacon, the pulses could be homed in on, leading a hunter to his target. But human behavior was complex, and John Ross would know he was being hunted and that the gypsy morph was giving them away. He would be evasive. He would not stand around waiting to be caught.

Findo Gask tracked John Ross for eighteen days before he found him. He read the pulse of the gypsy morph at each change and relied on his instincts to tell him what Ross would do. He found the Knight of the Word in Salt Lake City ten days before Christmas in a seedy hotel at the north edge of the downtown area. With five very tough, well-paid thugs in tow, he entered the empty lobby of the hotel on the night shift, walked up to the clerk, produced his fake U.S. marshal's identification, and asked for the key to Ross's room. The clerk, young and stupid and scared, handed it over without a word.

"There's not gonna be no trouble, is there?" he asked.

Gask smiled reassuringly. "Tell me what Mr. Ross brought with him to his room," he ordered.

The clerk stared at him dumbly, trying to figure out what was being asked of him. "I dunno. A duffel bag and a knapsack's all. Came in off a bus." He paused, thinking. "Oh, yeah, he's got a ferret, too. Must be some sort of pet."

Gask took the men up to the third floor where Ross was staying. One man would position himself at the elevator, one by the stairs, and the other three would go in after Ross. They had been told Ross was a dangerous man, a traitor and a spy. They were not to try to subdue him; they were to kill him. He would be armed, and he would kill them if they did not kill him first. They had been issued Glocks with silencers and sworn in as deputy U.S. marshals. They would face no adverse consequences for their actions. All were under the protection of the United States government. Everything they did was fully sanctioned.

A demon could persuade violent men of anything, and Findo Gask had no trouble with these. Kill John Ross, he emphasized, but under no circumstances harm the ferret. Leave the ferret to him.

Standing at the far end of the hall in the shadows, Findo Gask watched it all. The room key went into the lock smoothly, the door cracked open, the big man kicked out the chain, and the three primary assailants burst through the opening, their weapons firing—*phfft, phfft, phfft.* One heartbeat later, there was a brilliant flash of light, as if a thousand cameras had all gone off at once. The wall separating the room from the hallway shattered as the broken bodies of two of the assailants hurtled through it. The third assailant, he discovered later, was thrown through the window to the street.

Then John Ross came through the door in a crouch, his staff ablaze with magic, his knapsack slung over his shoulder, his duffel abandoned. For just an instant he looked in Findo Gask's direction, but the demon remained in the shadows, holding himself perfectly still.

The man by the elevator began firing his weapon. Ross knocked him twenty feet through the air with a single surge of power from the staff, and when his head struck the metal-bound edge of the wall where it angled around the main heating vent, Gask heard the vertebrae crack. By now, the last man was firing as well, but Ross knocked him down with a sweep of his staff and was past him so quickly he might as well have been armed with a flyswatter.

In less than two minutes, the Knight of the Word had disposed of all five assailants and disappeared through the fire door. Four of the five were dead, and Findo Gask finished off the last on his way out, pausing as he passed through the lobby to silence the night clerk as well.

It was a messy business, and it netted him nothing. What he learned, however, was that if he was to have any chance at all with John Ross, he would need help of a special sort.

Help of a kind only other demons could supply.

But three days earlier, while he was continuing his search for Ross, something unexpected happened.

That the morph continued to change shape on a regular basis not only provided a way to trace it, but showed that it hadn't settled on a form or been revealed. John Ross had not found the key to unlock its magic. His time was running out. A morph, on average, survived for only thirty days before it began to break up. If Ross was to solve its riddle, he must do so quickly. The odds against his succeeding were enormous. Only on a handful of occasions in the course of history had the servants of either the Word or the Void found a way to unlock the magic.

But then, sometime in the middle of the night three days ago, the gypsy morph had found the shape it wanted. It had not changed since, not once, not even for the briefest moment. Findo Gask had searched the power lines that embraced the earth carefully for any disturbance, and there had been none.

Even more unexpected than the morph's settling into a permanent shape was that it had spoken. A morph lacked a voice. It was energy, pure and simple. But somehow it had communicated, one word only, spoken three times. Undoubtedly, the word had been meant for the ears of John Ross alone, yet it was delivered with such intensity of purpose and need that it snagged on the lines of power that conveyed all the magics of the world and filtered through the ether in a whisper that Findo Gask overheard.

The word was *Nest*.

Findo Gask walked down the hallway of the old Victorian toward the stairs, musing over his good fortune. No other demon had heard, he was certain; no other had his talent and instincts. The find was his alone, and he would be the one to make use of it. John Ross would come to Hopewell because he would draw the same conclusion as Findo Gask. He would come in the hope that Nest Freemark could provide the clue that would unlock the secret of the gypsy morph's magic. He would come to seek help from someone he trusted and respected. He would come because he had nowhere else to go.

When he did, Findo Gask would be waiting.

CHAPTER 6

I've come home.

The words didn't register for a moment, Nest struggling with the idea that it was really Bennett Scott standing in front of her, no longer a little girl, but someone so far removed from the child she remembered she could barely bring herself to accept that such a transition was possible.

"Home?" she echoed in confusion.

Bennett looked embarrassed. "Yeah, well, I know it's been a long time since I lived here. I should have written or called or something. But you know me. I was never much good at keeping in touch."

Nest stared at her, still trying to make sense of the fact that she was here at all. "It's been almost ten years," she said finally.

Bennett's smile faltered slightly. "I know. I'm sorry." She brushed at her lank hair. "I was hoping it would be all right if I just showed up."

Her words had taken on a defensive tone, and there was an unmistakable hint of desperation in her voice. She looked used and worn, and she did not look well. Nest suddenly felt the cold and grayness of the day more acutely. The sun had slipped all the way west, and darkness hung in the bare-limbed trees like a shroud.

"Of course, it's all right," she told Bennett softly.

The smile returned. "I knew it would be. You were always my big sister, Nest. Even when I was back with Big Momma and the other kids, moved to that southern Indiana redneck farming town . . ."

Her voice tightened, and she shivered with more than the cold.

"Mommy?" the little girl at her side said, tugging on her sleeve.

Bennett reached down and touched her round cheek. "Hey, pumpkin, it's okay. This is your Aunt Nest. Nest, this is my baby girl, Harper."

Nest came forward and dropped to one knee in front of the little girl. "Hello, Harper."

"Say hello to Aunt Nest, baby," Bennett encouraged.

The little girl lifted her eyes doubtfully. "Lo, Neth."

Bennett picked her up and hugged her close. "She's kind of shy at first, but once she gets to know you, she's real friendly. Talks all the time. She can say a lot of words, can't you, baby?"

Harper dug her face into her mother's shoulder, entwining her tiny fists in Bennett's dark hair. "Appo juss."

Nest straightened. "I might have some apple juice in the fridge. Come on inside."

Bennett picked up a small satchel sitting to one side and, still carrying Harper, followed Nest through the back porch door and into the house. Nest took them into the kitchen and sat them down at the table. She accepted a baby cup from Bennett and filled it with apple juice. The baby began to suck the liquid down with steady, hungry gulps.

Nest busied herself with emptying the dishwasher while Bennett bounced Harper gently on one knee. Every so often Nest would glance over, still trying to convince herself that it was really Bennett Scott. Piercings and tattoos aside, the young woman sitting at her kitchen table didn't look anything like the girl she remembered. All of the softness and roundness was gone; everything was sharp and angular. Bennett had been full of life and bright-eyed; she had been a repository of fresh possibilities. Now she looked hollowed out, as if her life had been reduced to harsh truths that boxed her in.

"Would you like something to eat?" she asked impulsively, still worried about the way Bennett looked.

"What have you got?" Bennett Scott asked.

"How about some chicken noodle soup for you and Harper? It's only Campbell's, but it might take the edge off the chill." She looked over. "Are you hungry?"

"Sure." Bennett was looking down at Harper. "We haven't had anything to eat . . ."

Nest put on a can of chicken noodle soup, made some peanut butter and jelly sandwiches, and peeled an orange. She didn't take any for herself, which was just as well. Harper and Bennett ate everything.

As she watched them eating, Nest found herself recalling how long it had been since she had seen Bennett. Bennett had lived with her for almost two years while her alcoholic mother drifted in and out of rehab facilities and struggled to get her life together. Fifteen years ago, when Nest was fourteen, Enid Scott's boyfriend had beaten her oldest boy, Nest's close friend Jared, so badly he had almost died. The result was a court action that stripped Enid of her children and put them in foster homes. Old Bob was still alive then, and Nest had begged him to bring little Bennett, who was only five, home to live with them. Old Bob, perhaps remembering Gran's promise to Enid to do what she could for her, applied for temporary custody of the little girl, and the court agreed to give it to him.

It was a hard time in everyone's life. Nest and Bennett had gone through a traumatic and life-altering experience over a Fourth of July weekend that saw John Ross come and go from Hopewell like a one-man wrecking crew. Gran was dead. Enid was in recovery. All of the Scott children were in separate homes. Something of what they had survived brought them closer together. They became like sisters in the weeks and months that followed, and Nest remembered even now how happy Bennett had been living with her.

But eventually Enid returned, sufficiently dried out and stable to reclaim her children from their foster homes. It was a wrenching ordeal for both Bennett and Nest, and Old Bob even asked Enid to reconsider moving Bennett back until she was older. But Enid was determined to reunite her family, and it was hard to blame a mother for wanting that. Bennett went home with the others, and after a year's probation, Enid was allowed to move the children out of state to a small town in Indiana where a handful of Enid's relatives lived.

There were letters from Bennett at first, but she was only nine, and nine-year-olds don't make it a point to write without encouragement. After a time, the letters stopped coming. Nest continued to write on her own, then tried calling. She found out that Enid was back in detox and the children were living with relatives. She began getting cards from Bennett again. Then the cards stopped for good.

When Old Bob died, Nest lost all track of Bennett Scott. Her own life was consumed with training for the Olympics and the demands of college. The relationship, like so many in her life, just drifted away.

Nest cleared the dishes from in front of Bennett and Harper. The little girl had fallen asleep in her mother's lap, moppet's head buried in a deep crease in the leather jacket. Nest motioned for Bennett to pick Harper up and led the way to one of the spare bedrooms in back. Together, they deposited Harper on the king-size bed, slipped off her shoes and parka, covered her with a blanket, and tiptoed out the door.

"I'll make us some tea," she advised, placing Bennett back at the kitchen table.

As she boiled water and fished about in the cupboard for some herbal tea bags, she wondered what had happened to Bennett Scott in those ten years gone. Nothing good, she suspected; very little remained of the child Bennett had been when she lived in Hopewell. She looked used and worn and hard. The tattoos and piercings suggested things Nest would rather not think about.

But maybe she was being small-minded and jumping to conclusions; she brushed the thoughts away angrily.

"Is Harper's father traveling with you?" she asked, handing Bennett a cup of the tea and sitting down across from her.

Bennett shook her head. "It's just Harper and me."

"Are you meeting him for Christmas?"

"Not unless they decide to let him out of the pen."

Nest stared.

"Sorry, Nest, that's a lie." Bennett looked away, shaking her head. "I tell it all the time. I tell it so often, I get to believing it. Bobby thinks he's the father 'cause I told him so once when I needed money. But he isn't. I don't know who Harper's father is."

The old clock in the hallway ticked in the ensuing silence. Nest sighed wearily. "Why didn't you write me to come for you, Bennett?" she said finally. "I would have."

Bennett nodded. "I know that. You were my big sister, Nest. You were the only one who cared about me, except for Jared. He ran off as soon as he turned sixteen. I haven't seen him since. I should have called you when I had the chance. But I wasn't sure. I just wasn't. Big Momma kept telling me that everything was going to be all right, even after she started drinking again and bringing home trash from the bars. And I kept right on believing, because I wanted it to be true."

She put her teacup down and stared out the window. "She's dead, you know. Drank herself to death, finally. Five years ago. Pneumonia, they said, but I heard the doctor tell Uncle Timmy that every organ in her body was ruined from her drinking.

"So I did what Jared did. I ran away from home. I lived on the streets, in the parks, on beaches, anywhere I could. I grew up real fast. You can't imagine, Nest. Or if you can, you don't want to. I was alone and scared all the time. The people I was with did things to me you wouldn't do to a dog. I was so hungry I ate out of garbage cans. I was sick a lot. Several times I was in hospitals, then farmed out to foster homes. I always ran away."

"But not here," Nest said quietly.

Bennett Scott blew out a short breath and laughed. "You got a cigarette, Nest?" Nest shook her head. Bennett nodded. "Didn't think so. World champion runner like you wouldn't smoke, would you? Bet you don't drink, either?"

"Nope."

"Do any drugs?"

"Why didn't you come here, Bennett?"

Bennett stretched, then slipped out of her leather jacket. She was wearing a sleeveless cotton sweater that hugged her body and retained almost no warmth. Nest got up, took the throw from behind the couch, walked over, and placed it over her shoulders. Bennett pulled it around her without a word, staring down at her teacup on the table.

"I've done a lot of drugs," she said after a minute, still not looking up. She sipped at the tea. "I've done just about every drug you could name and a few besides. For a while I was doing them all at once sometimes, just to get away from myself and my crappy life. But the high never lasts; you always come down again, and there you are, the old you, and nothing's changed."

She looked up now. "I was sixteen when I was doing all of it at once, but I started a lot earlier." She shook her head slowly. "That's why I didn't call you or write you or try to come see you. I didn't want you to see me like that. I didn't want you to know what I'd become. My life was . . ." She shrugged.

"It wouldn't have mattered to me, you know," Nest said.

Bennett shook her head reprovingly. "Pay attention, Nest. I know it wouldn't have mattered to you. But it would have mattered to me. That's the whole point." She shivered inside the throw, her slim body hunching down and tightening into stillness. "When I got pregnant with Harper, I tried to stop using. I couldn't do it. I wanted to stop, I wanted it bad. I knew what my using might do to her, but I couldn't help myself. I tried a couple of programs, but they didn't work out. Nothing worked."

She brushed back her dark hair. "When Harper was born, I checked into Hazelden. You've probably heard of it, big drug-rehab program out of Minneapolis. I got into a treatment center for new mothers, something long term. It was better there. We were all women on drugs with children just born or about to be born. I went there because Harper was born clean, and that was a real miracle. My higher power gave me another chance, and I knew I'd be a fool not to take it. I was turning into Big Momma." She snorted. "Who am I kidding? I was already there, worse than she ever was. You got any more of that tea, Nest?"

Nest got up and brought over the hot water and fresh tea bags. She poured them both another cup, then sat down again. "Are you better now?" she asked.

Bennett laughed bitterly. "Better? No, I'm not better! I'll never ever be better! I'm an addict, and addicts don't get better!"

She glared at Nest angrily, defiantly. Nest waited a moment, then said, "You know what I mean."

Bennett's sigh was sad and empty. "Sorry. I'm not mad at you. Really, I'm not. I'm mad at me. Twenty-four hours a day, seven days a week, all year long, I'm mad at me. Loser me." She shrugged. "Anyway, I'm not better. I'm 'between treatments' again. I stay good for a while, then I fall off the wagon. Look under *relapse* in the dictionary and you'll find a picture of me. It's pitiful. I don't want it to happen, but I'm just not strong enough to stop it. Each time I go in for help, I think maybe this is the time I'll get off drugs for good. But I can never quite manage it."

"I guess it's not easy," Nest said.

Bennett Scott smiled. "Nope." She exhaled sharply and set down the tea. "It wasn't so much of a problem when it was just me. But now there's Harper, and she's almost three, and she hasn't ever seen me clean for more than a few months in a row. First year or so, I got into rehabs where they'd let me keep her with me. Now they won't do that. I don't have many friends so I have to leave her with anyone who will take her."

She looked down at her hands where they rested on the tabletop. They were cracked and dry, and the nails were dirty. She folded them together self-consciously. "I just got out again a couple of weeks ago. I don't plan on going back."

"If you needed to," Nest said quietly, "you could leave Harper with me."

Bennett's eyes lifted. For a moment, she didn't say anything. "Thanks, Nest. That's nice of you to offer."

"She would be safe here."

"I know that."

Nest looked out the window into the crisp black night. It was almost five in the afternoon. "Would you like to stay for dinner?" she asked.

Bennett Scott looked down again at her hands. "We wouldn't want to be any trouble."

In those few words, Nest heard a plea so desperate that she knew things were much worse than she believed. Then she remembered the dilapidated satchel Bennett was carrying. It was sitting inside the back door where Bennett had left it. Nest had thought it was just a baby bag, but now she wondered if it might not contain everything they had.

"Maybe you'd like to stay over for the night, too," she said carefully, feeling her way across this treacherous ground. "Is someone else expecting you? Are you visiting anyone here?"

Bennett shook her head. "No. No one." She was quiet for a long moment, as if she were making up her mind about something, and then she looked up. "The truth is, Harper and me came here because we don't have anywhere else to go."

Tears glistened at the corners of her eyes, and she looked down again quickly. Nest reached across the table and put her hand over Bennett's. "I'm glad you came. You're welcome to stay as long as you need to."

She rose and walked around the table. "Come on," she urged, gently drawing the other to her feet. "I want you to go in and take a long, hot bath, soak everything out, just let it all go. I'll look after Harper. When you're done, we'll talk some more."

She walked Bennett into the guest bathroom, helped her out of her clothes, and deposited her in the big claw-foot tub that used to be Gran's. Leaving Bennett to soak, she looked in on Harper, then went back out into the kitchen to clean up. Feeling as she did about herself, it must have taken a strong mix of courage and desperation for Bennett to come back to her after all this time. It made Nest wonder how much of what had happened to her she couldn't bring herself to talk about and was keeping hidden somewhere deep inside.

When she finished the dishes, she began preparing dinner. She put together a tuna and noodle casserole and stuck it in the refrigerator so Bennett could heat it up later on. Nest had agreed to accompany the church youth group as a chaperone while they went caroling to the elderly sick and shut-in, and she would have to leave soon. She would get herself something to eat when she returned.

Finished with her preparations, she stood at the sink and stared out the window at the darkness. The park lay directly in front of her, just across the backyard, but the moon and stars were masked by clouds, so there was little to see. The temperature had dropped to well below freezing, and she doubted that it would snow tonight. When she lifted her hand and placed her fingers against the window glass, the cold pierced her skin like needles.

How did Pick stay warm on a night like this? Did he burrow down in a tree somewhere or was his bark skin impervious to cold? She had never asked him. She must remember to do so.

She thought about the ways in which magic ruled both their lives, its influence pervasive and inexorable. Sometimes she wished she could talk about it with someone, but for the whole of her life there had been only Pick and Gran. Gran had been willing, but Pick regarded talk of magic the same way he regarded talk about the weather—a pointless exercise. He would instruct, but he didn't know how to empathize. Having magic didn't mean the same thing to him that it did to her. To him, it was a natural condition of who and what he was. To her, in spite of her heritage, it was an aberration.

The back porch light clicked on at the Peterson house, and she was reminded of her promise to herself to look in on them. She walked to the kitchen doorway and listened down the hall for signs of stirring from Bennett or Harper. All was quiet, so she went back into the kitchen and set about baking sugar cookies. Gran had taught her how to cook when Nest was still a girl, and she had made it a point to stay in practice even after she was living alone. She baked all the time for the church and the neighbors. There was something comforting and satisfying in baking; it always left her feeling good about herself.

The cookie sheets went into the oven, and the sweet, doughy smell wafted through the kitchen. She took down the red and green sprinkles and set them on the counter. Hawkeye came in through the cat door and padded to his food bowl, pointedly ignoring her. He ate noisily, tossing bits of food around as he nosed about his bowl, chewing each bit loudly. When he was done, he left the way he had come without so much as a glance in her direction.

Moments later, Harper Scott appeared in the kitchen doorway, all sleepy-eyed and lost-looking. "Mommy?" she asked.

Nest walked over and gathered her up. "Mommy's taking a bath, pumpkin. She'll be right out. How would you like a fresh-baked sugar cookie while you're waiting?"

Great dark eyes regarded her solemnly. A small nod followed. Nest sat her down at the table, poured milk into her baby cup, and went to work on the first batch of cookies, taking them from the oven and off the cookie sheet, stacking them on a plate. She gave one to Harper when it had cooled enough to hold and watched the little girl nibble around the edges as she held the cookie carefully in both hands.

Oh, child, child.

Fifteen years ago, she had saved Bennett Scott's life when the feeders had lured the frightened sleepy child to the top of the bluffs at the turnaround. When Pick and

Nest found her, she had been close to walking off the edge of the cliffs. Terrified and confused, the little girl had barely known where she was.

That was a long time ago, Nest thought, watching Harper eat her cookie. Bennett hadn't been much older than her daughter then—just a little girl herself. It was hard to reconcile the grownup with the child. She remembered how Bennett had looked back then and how she had looked an hour earlier when Nest had helped her step into the old bathtub. How had Bennett gotten so far away from herself? Oh, it was easy to rationalize when you factored in drug usage and child abuse. But it was emotionally jarring nevertheless; the memory of who she had been was not easy to dismiss.

By the time Harper was working on the last few bites of her sugar cookie, Bennett reappeared, wrapped in the old terry cloth robe Nest had left for her by the tub. She gave Harper a hug and sat down to share a cookie with her. Her pale skin looked translucent in the kitchen light, and her dark eyes were sunken and depthless. Beneath the robe, needle tracks walked up and down her arms and legs; Nest had seen them, and the image flashed sharply in her mind.

She smiled at Nest. "You were right about the bath. I feel a lot better."

Nest smiled back. "Good. Stick Harper in the tub next. Borrow anything you need in the way of clothes. There's a casserole in the fridge for dinner; just heat it up. I have to go out with the church youth group, but I'll be back around eight or nine."

She finished up with the cookies, shutting down the oven and washing up the metal sheets. She glanced at the clock. Five-fifty. Allen Kruppert and his wife, Kathy, were picking her up in their big Suburban at six-thirty. She had just enough time to take a plate of cookies over to the Petersons.

She picked up the phone and called to see if they had started dinner, which they hadn't.

"I've got to be going," she called over her shoulder to Bennett as she finished putting together her cookie offering. "Don't worry about the phone; the answer machine will pick up. And don't wait up. You need to get some sleep."

She went out into the hall to pull on her parka, scarf, and gloves, then came back for the cookies and whisked them out the back door.

The cold was hard and brittle against her skin as she tromped down the porch steps, and she shivered in spite of herself. The clouds were breaking up, and moonlight illuminated the stark, skeletal limbs of the trees, giving them a slightly silver sheen. All about her, the darkness was hushed and still. She blew out a breath of white vapor, tucked her chin into her chest, and hurried across the backyard toward her neighbors' home.

She had gone only a few steps when she saw the feeders. They were gathered at the lower end of her yard, tucked up against the hedgerow in formless clumps, their yellow eyes blinking in the night like fireflies. She slowed and looked at them. She hadn't seen any feeders this close to her home in months. She glanced in either direction from the hedgerow and found others at the edges of the house and garage, shadowy forms creeping stealthily, silently through the cold night.

"Get out of here!" she hissed in a low voice.

A few disappeared. Most simply moved off a bit or shifted position. She glanced around uneasily. There were too many for coincidence. She wondered suddenly if they knew about John Ross, if the prospect of his coming was drawing them.

More likely it was just the stink of the demon who had visited her earlier that was attracting them.

She brushed the matter aside and hurried on across the frosted carpet of the lawn.

She saw nothing of the figure who stood at the top of her walk in the deep shadow of the cedars.

Chapter 7

Findo Gask waited for Nest to cross the lawn to the Petersons', then for her to come out again when the big Suburban pulled into her driveway. He stood without moving in the darkness, virtually invisible in his black frock coat and black flat-brimmed hat, his leather-bound book held close against his chest. The night was bitter cold, the damp warmth of the sunny day crystallized to a fine crust that covered the landscape in a silvery sheen and crunched like tiny shells when walked on. Even the blacktop in front of the Freemark house glimmered in the streetlight.

When Nest Freemark climbed inside the Suburban and it backed out of her driveway and disappeared down the street, Findo Gask waited some more. He was patient and careful. He watched his breath cloud the air as it escaped his mouth. A human would have been freezing by now, standing out there for better than an hour. But demons felt little of temperature changes, their bodies shells and not real homes. Most of Findo Gask's human responses had been shed so long ago that he no longer could recall how they made him feel. Heat or cold, pain or pleasure, it was all the same to him.

So he waited, unperturbed by the delay, cocooned within the dark husk to which he had reduced himself years ago, biding his time. It had taken a bit of effort to find out Nest would be gone this evening. He didn't want that effort to be wasted.

He passed the time keeping watch on the house, intrigued by the shadowy movements inside. There were lights on in a few of the rooms, and they revealed an unexpected presence. Nest had left someone at home. The wrinkled old face creased suddenly with smile lines. Who might that someone be?

When everything was silent with the cold and the dark and there was no longer any reasonable possibility that Nest Freemark might be returning for something she had forgotten, Findo Gask left his hiding place and walked up onto the front porch and knocked softly.

The door opened to reveal a young woman wrapped in a terry cloth bathrobe. She was rather small and slender, with lank hair and dark eyes. It was the eyes that caught his attention, filled with pain and disappointment and betrayal, rife with barely concealed anger and unmistakable need. He knew her instantly for what she was, for the life she had led, and for the ways in which he might use her.

She stood looking out through the storm door, making no move to admit him. "Good evening," he said, smiling his best human smile. "I'm Reverend Findo Gask?" He made it a question, so that she would assume she was supposed to be expecting him. "Is Nest ready to go with me?"

A hint of confusion reflected on her wan face. "Nest isn't here. She left already."

Now it was his turn to look confused. He did his best. "Oh, she did? Someone else picked her up?"

The young woman nodded. "Fifteen minutes ago. She went caroling with a church group."

Findo Gask shook his head. "There must have been a mix-up. Could I use your phone to make a call?"

His hand moved to the storm-door handle, encouraging her to act on his request. But the young woman stayed where she was, arms folded into the robe, eyes fixed on him.

"I can't do that," she announced flatly. "This isn't my house. I can't let anybody in."

"It would take only a moment."

She shook her head. "Sorry."

He felt like reaching through the glass and ripping out her heart, an act of which he was perfectly capable. It wasn't anger or frustration that motivated his thinking; it was the simple fact of her defiance. But the time and place were wrong for acts of violence, so he simply nodded his understanding.

"I'll call from down the road," he offered smoothly, taking a step back. "Oh, by the way, did Mr. Ross go with her?"

She pursed her lips. "Who is Mr. Ross?"

"The gentleman staying with her. Your fellow boarder."

A child's voice called to her from somewhere out of view, and she glanced over her shoulder. "I have to go. I don't know Mr. Ross. There isn't anyone else staying here. Good night."

She closed the door in his face. He stood staring at it for a moment. Apparently Ross still hadn't arrived. He found himself wondering suddenly if he had been wrong in coming to Hopewell, if somehow he had intuited incorrectly. His instincts were seldom mistaken about these things, but perhaps this was one of those times.

He couldn't afford to have that happen.

He turned around and walked back out to the street. The ur'droch joined him after a dozen paces, all shadowy presence and rippling movement at the edges of the light.

"Anything?" he asked.

When the shadow-demon gave no response, he had his answer. It was not unexpected. It wasn't likely Ross was there if the young woman hadn't seen him. Who was she, anyway? Where had she come from? *Another pawn on the board, waiting to be moved into position,* he thought. It would be interesting to see how he might make use of her.

He walked back down the road to where he had left the car parked on the shoulder and climbed inside. The ur'droch slithered in behind him and disappeared onto the floor of the backseat. He would give Ross another three days, until Christmas, before he gave up his vigil. It wasn't time to panic yet. Panic was for lesser demons, for those who relied on attributes other than experience and reasoning to sustain them.

He started the car and wheeled it back onto the roadway. It was time to be getting home so that he could enjoy the little surprise he had prepared for Nest Freemark.

Nest climbed in beside Kathy Kruppert, squeezing her over toward her husband on the Suburban's bench seat. In the back, somewhere between six and nine teens and preteens, two of them Krupperts, jostled and squirmed while trading barbs and gossip. She exchanged hellos with everyone, then leaned back against the padded leather while Allen backed the big Chevy onto Woodlawn and headed for the next pickup.

Her thoughts drifted from John Ross and Findo Gask to Bennett and Harper Scott and back again.

"Everything okay, Nest?" Kathy asked after a few minutes of front-seat silence amidst the backseat chaos. She was a big-boned blond carrying more weight than she wanted, as she was fond of saying, but on her the weight looked good.

Nest nodded. "Sure, fine."

"You seem awfully quiet tonight."

"For a basically noisy person," Allen added, straight-faced.

Nest gave him a wry grin. "I'm just saving myself for later, when the singing starts."

"Oh, is that it?" Allen said, nodding solemnly. He glanced at her over the top of his glasses, beetle-browed and balding. "You know, Kath, it's always the quiet ones you have to look out for."

They hit a bump where weather and repeated plowing had hollowed out a section of the roadway. *Ouch! Hey, watch it!* the kids all began yelling at once in back, offering myriad, unnecessary pieces of driving advice.

"Quiet down, you animals!" Allen shouted over his shoulder, giving them a mock glare. When they did, for what must have been a nanosecond, he declared with a smirk, "Guess I showed them."

Kathy patted his leg affectionately. "Father always knows best, honey."

Allen and Kathy had been married right out of high school, both graduating seniors, six or seven years older than Nest. Allen began working as a salesman with a realty firm and found he had a gift for it. Ten years later, he was running his own business. Ten years earlier, he had approached Nest with an offer for her house at a time when she was seriously considering selling. Even though she had decided against doing so, she had been friends with the Krupperts ever since.

"How are the Petersons?" Kathy asked her suddenly.

"Pretty frail." Nest dug her hands into her parka pockets with a sigh. The truth was, time was running out on the Petersons. Their health was deteriorating, there was no one to look after them, and nothing anyone said or did could convince them to consider moving into a care facility.

"You do the best you can for them, Nest," Kathy said.

Allen shifted his weight in the driver's seat and brushed back his thinning black hair. "They're determined people. You can only do so much to help them. There's no point in fussing about it. They'll go on, just like they have been, until something happens to force them to change their way of life. You have to respect that."

"I do, but I worry anyway. It's like sitting around waiting for the other shoe to fall."

"Sure enough," Kathy agreed with a sigh. "My uncle Frank was like that."

"Gran, too," Nest said.

Allen chuckled. "Good thing you two understand the problem so well. That way, you won't become part of it later on. That'll sure be a relief to a lot of folks."

They picked up two more teens from the Moonlight Bay area, then headed back into town for a rendezvous with a van-load of kids driven by Marilyn Winthorn, one of the older ladies who still worked assiduously with the youth groups. From there, they started on their rounds, following a list of names and addresses supplied by Reverend Andrew Carpenter, who had taken over the ministry after Ralph Emery retired three years ago. At each stop, they sang a few carols at the front door, deposited a basket of Christmas goodies supplied by the ladies' guild, exchanged Merry Christmases and Happy New Years, and moved on.

By the twelfth visit, Nest had stopped thinking about anything but how good this was making her feel.

It was sometime around eight-thirty when they pulled into the driveway of an old Victorian home on West Third, an area of fallen grandeur and old money gone elsewhere. The name on the list for this home was smudged, and no one could quite make it out. Hattie or Harriet something. It wasn't a name or address anyone recognized, but it might be a church member's relative. They climbed out of the vehicles, walked to the front entry, and arranged themselves in a semicircle facing the door.

There were lights on, but no one appeared to greet them. Allen stepped up to the door, knocked loudly, and waited for a response.

"Creepy old place, isn't it?" Kathy Kruppert whispered in Nest's ear.

Nest nodded, thinking that mostly it seemed rather sad, a tombstone to the habitation it had once been. She glanced around as the kids whispered and shuffled their feet, waiting impatiently to begin. It was a neighborhood of tombstones. Everything was dark and silent along the rows of old homes and corridors of ancient trees. Even the street they bracketed was empty.

Someone came to the door now and inched back the curtain covering the glass. A face peeked out, its features vague and shadowy in the gloom.

The door cracked open, and a frail voice said, "Goodness."

Taking that as a cue to begin, Allen stepped off the porch, and the youth group began singing "Joy to the World." Their voices rang out through the darkness and cold, and their breath clouded the air. The door remained cracked, but no one appeared.

They had begun the refrain, "Let heaven and nature sing," when the door burst open with such force that it shattered the glass pane, and a huge, hulking figure stormed through the opening and down the steps. Albino white and hairless, he stood seven feet tall and weighed three hundred pounds, but he moved with such quickness that he was on top of the group almost as quickly as their singing turned to shrieks of fear and shock.

"Joy to the world! Joy to the world! Joy to the world!" the big man shouted tunelessly.

The kids were scattering in every direction as he reached Allen Kruppert, knotted one massive fist into the startled realtor's parka, and snatched him right off his feet. Holding him aloft with one arm extended, he shook Allen like a rag doll, yelling at him in fury.

"Joy to the world! Joy to the world! Joy to the world!"

Fists pressed against her mouth, Kathy Kruppert was screaming Allen's name. Marilyn Winthorn was herding the kids back toward the vehicles, intent on loading them in as quickly as she could manage, her face tight and bloodless.

Allen was kicking and shouting, but the big man held him firm, continuing to shake him as if he meant to loosen all his bones and empty out his skin.

"Joy to the world! Joy to the world!"

It all happened in seconds, and for the brief length of time it took, Nest Freemark was frozen with indecision. Her first impulse was to use her magic on the big man, the magic that caused people to lose control of their muscles and collapse in useless heaps, that she had used on Danny Abbott and Robert Heppler all those years ago, that she had used on her father.

But if she invoked it now, she risked setting Wraith loose. It was the reality she had lived with since she was nineteen. She could never know what might trigger his release. She had discovered that three years ago at the Olympics, and she had not used her magic since.

Now, it seemed, she had no choice.

She shouted at the big man, striding toward him, small and inconsequential in his shadow. He barely looked at her, but his shaking movement slowed, and he let Allen sag slightly. He was all misshapen, she saw, as if he had not been put together in quite the right way and his parts did not fit as they should, some too large and some too small. He had the look of something formed of castoffs and leftovers, the detritus of the human gene pool.

Nest shouted harder, and now the strange pink eyes fixed on her. Screwing up her courage and tightening her hold on Wraith, who was already awake and pressing for release inside her, she hammered at the big man with her magic, trying to make him take a sudden misstep in her direction, to lose his balance and release Allen. But it was as if she had run into a wall. He shrugged aside her magic as if it weren't even there, and in his eyes she found only an empty, blank space in which nothing human lived.

Nothing human . . .

He tossed Allen aside, and the realtor collapsed in a crumpled heap, head lowered between his shoulders like a broken fighter as he struggled to his hands and knees, Kathy racing over to kneel next to him, tears streaming down her cheeks.

The big man wheeled on Nest. "Joy to the world! Joy to the world!"

He came at her, and she hit him with another jolt of magic, eyes locked on his. This time he slowed, staggered slightly by the force of her attack. The kids were still screaming in the background, some of them calling to her to run, to get away, thinking she was paralyzed with fear and indecision. She stood her ground, watching as Kathy tried in vain to pull a battered Allen to his feet.

The big man snarled at her, an animal sound, a deep, throaty growl that brought Wraith right up into her throat, so close to breaking free she could see the tiger striping of his wolfish face and feel the thick, coarse fur of his powerful body. She backed away, trying to keep him in check. If she failed to do so, everyone would discover the truth about her. Whatever else happened, she could not permit that.

"Joy to the world!" the big man howled as he lumbered toward her. "Joy to the world!"

"Twitch!" a voice shrilled.

The big man stopped as if he had been reined in by invisible wires, jerking upright, his strange, misshapen head lifting like a startled bird's.

"You come right into this house!" the voice ordered. "You are so bad! I mean it! Right now!"

On the porch stood a solitary figure bundled in a heavy coat and scarf, frizzy red hair sticking out all over. It was the young woman who had introduced herself at church that morning, the one called Penny. At the sound of her voice, the giant slowly turned away and trudged back toward the old house. Nest took a deep, calming breath as the screaming behind her died away into hushed whispers and sobs.

The young woman stood aside as the giant lumbered past her sheepishly and disappeared inside. Then she came down the porch, shaking her head in exasperation.

"Nest, I'm really, really sorry about this." She came up and took Nest's gloved hand in her own and held it. "That's my brother. He isn't right in the head. He doesn't mean any harm, but he doesn't know how strong he is."

She looked over at Allen, who was finally climbing back to his feet. "Are you all right, mister? Did he hurt you at all?"

Allen Kruppert looked as if he had just climbed out of a working cement mixer. He tried to speak, coughed hard, and shook his head.

"I think he's okay," Kathy offered quietly, bracing him against her with both arms wrapped tightly about his bulky form. "That was a very scary thing your brother did, miss."

Penny nodded quickly in agreement. "I know. I should have been watching him more closely, but I was upstairs working. My grandmother answered the door, but she is so old and feeble she can't do anything with him. He just pushed her aside and came out." She looked quickly from Nest to the Krupperts. "He just wanted to play. That's what he thought all this was about. Playing."

Nest gave her a brief, uncertain smile. She had the oddest queasy feeling. Penny seemed sincere in her apology, but there was just a hint of something in her voice that suggested maybe she wasn't.

Nest glanced up at the house. "Do you live here, Penny?" she asked conversationally.

"Sometimes." Penny's red hair gave her the look of something that had shorted out. Her green eyes glittered. "Right now I'm just visiting."

"With your brother?"

"Yeah. With Twitch. We call him Twitch."

"Is it your grandmother who belongs to the church?"

Penny shrugged. "I suppose."

"What is your grandmother's name?"

Penny smiled. "I better get back inside, Nest. I don't like leaving Twitch alone after an episode. You know how it is. Thanks for coming by with the church group, though. It was really nice of you."

She walked back up the steps and through the broken door, closing the windowless frame carefully behind her. Nest watched until she was gone, then gave the windows a casual sweep as she swung back toward the others.

The interior of the house had gone completely dark.

She helped Kathy get Allen back in the Suburban, settling him into the passenger seat and buckling him in. He insisted he was all right, and it seemed he was. The youth group was noticeably subdued, and there was talk of calling it a night. But Allen wouldn't hear of it. There were four more names on the list, including the Northway Nursing Home. All those people were counting on them. Allen wasn't the sort to let anyone be disappointed on account of him. He insisted they finish what they started.

It was nearing ten o'clock when Nest finally got home. Everyone else, Allen included, seemed to have put the incident on West Third behind them, but she was still uneasy about it. Two encounters in one day with Penny Whoever-she-was seemed a bit of a stretch for coincidence and two encounters too many in any case. The whole business troubled her, particularly since it had forced her to confront anew what it meant to employ her magic as a weapon. It was something she had hoped never to have to do again. Tonight's incident suggested her thinking was incredibly naive.

She walked up the drive and slipped in through the back door. There were lights on, but the house was quiet. Hawkeye was curled up on his chair in the kitchen, the one he had adopted for this week anyway, and he did not even open his eyes as she passed through. She left her coat, scarf, and gloves in the hall closet and eased down the hall to the den, where the television was playing. Bennett was dozing in her grandfather's big leather easy chair.

She opened her eyes as Nest entered. "Hi," she murmured.

"Hi," Nest replied, sitting at the desk chair. "Harper asleep?"

Bennett stretched and yawned. "About an hour ago. She was pretty worn out." She stood up. "Me, too. I'm going to bed. Did Reverend Gask ever catch up with you? He was here earlier."

Nest went cold, her whole body stiffening. She had forgotten to warn Bennett about Gask. But then, what could she have said? "No, he must have missed me."

"He said he was here to pick you up. He wanted to come in, but I told him I couldn't let anyone in someone else's house. I hope that was all right."

Nest responded to the wave of relief that washed through her by giving the other a big hug. "You did good."

"Thanks." Bennett trundled toward the door. "Oh, I almost forgot. He was looking for someone named John Ross, too. Said he thought he was staying here, but I told him I didn't think so."

"You told him right," Nest assured her, growing angry again with Gask. "Go on to bed. I'll see you in the morning."

Alone, she sat thinking anew of John Ross and Findo Gask and what their conflict meant. Gask was not going to give up. He would keep coming around until he found Ross and whatever it was that he thought Ross was hiding from him. Demons are persistent. Time means nothing to them; they operate on a schedule as foreign to humans as life on Mars. She had dealt with demons half her life, and she had a pretty good idea what she was in for.

She got up and turned off the television, then sat down again, staring out the window into the darkness. At times like this, she wished Gran was still alive. Gran, with her no-nonsense approach to life's problems and her experience with the ways of demons and forest creatures, would know better than she how to deal with this mess. Gran might have some thoughts about what to do with Bennett and Harper, too. Nest would have to try her best to think like Gran and hope that would be enough to see her through.

After a time, she went out into the kitchen and made herself some dinner. She ate a small portion of the leftover tuna and noodle casserole and drank a glass of milk, sitting at the kitchen table, listening to the ticking of the clock and to the whisper of her scattered thoughts. It wasn't as if John Ross wouldn't show, she realized. Too much of what Gask had told her suggested he would. The problem was what to do about him when he did. Or, more specifically, what to do about the fact that he was coming to find her, which was really the only reason he would come back.

She shook her head at the idea. So much time had passed with no contact between them. What would bring him to her now? What did he need?

Surrounded by memories of her past, of a childhood and girlhood linked inextricably to him, she searched in vain for an answer.

She was still awake at midnight when the knock on the front door came. She had turned off most of the lights and moved to the living room. She was sitting there in the dark, staring out the window once more, her thoughts drifting through the frosty landscape of the park. She was not sleepy, her mind spinning out possibilities that might explain the day's events, her magic alive and singing in her blood with strange energy. Sitting there, working her way through the past to conjecture on the future, she found herself wanting to do what Gran had done as a girl, to go out into the park and run with the feeders who lived there, wild and uninhibited and free. It was a strange feeling, and she was mildly shocked by the idea that after all she had gone through to escape her grandmother's past, she was still somehow drawn to it.

The knock brought her to her feet and scattered her thoughts. There was never any doubt in her mind as to who it was. She walked quickly through the darkness of the living room to the hallway, where a solitary light glimmered weakly from farther down the corridor. The porch light was on as well, but she never even bothered to look out the peephole. She knew who it was. She knew who it had to be. She simply opened the door to confirm it, and there he was.

"Hello, Nest," he said.

He stood in the halo of the porch light, clear-eyed and expectant, looking younger and fitter than when she had seen him last in Seattle, ten years ago. She was astonished at the transformation, and immediately suspicious of what it meant.

A small, slender boy of maybe four or five years stood at his side, honey-colored hair tousled and shaggy, blue eyes bright and inquisitive. He stared at her with such intensity that she was momentarily taken aback.

She looked from the boy to Ross, and for just a moment Findo Gask's dark warning whispered from the closet in the back of her mind to which she had consigned it. She stood at the edge of a precipice, and she could feel a tremendous mix of attraction and repulsion roiling within her. Whichever way she turned, whatever choice she made, her life would never be the same again.

She cracked the storm door wide open. "Come on inside, John." She gave him a warm smile. "I've been expecting you."

Monday, December 22

Chapter 8

After he awoke from the dream of the Knight on the cross, John Ross began his search for the gypsy morph.

It wasn't so much the Knight's words of advice that guided him in his efforts. He had forgotten those almost immediately, shards of sound buried in the wave of emotion he experienced on seeing that the Knight bore his own face. But in the Knight's eyes, in eyes that were undeniably his own, he found a road map he would never forget. In a moment's time, that map became indelibly imprinted on his consciousness. All the Knight's memories of where and how the gypsy morph could be found were made his. To recall them, to remember what they showed, he need only look inside himself.

It was early summer when he set out, the weather still mild almost everywhere. In Pennsylvania, where he began his journey, the air smelled of new grass and leaves, the green beginnings of June fresh and pungent. By the time he reached the west coast, the July heat had settled in, all scorched air and damp heat, thick and barely breathable, an ocean of suspended condensation bearing down with suffocating determination. On the colored weather charts that appeared in *USA Today*, seven-eighths of the country was shaded in deep reds and oranges.

The sole exception was the Pacific Northwest, where Ross had gone to await the morph's coming. In Oregon, where he would make his preparations, the heat was driven inland by the breezes off the ocean, and the coastal bluffs and forests west of the Cascades stayed green and cool. Like a haven, the windward side of the mountains gave shelter against the burning temperatures that saturated everything leeward to the Atlantic, and the coast was like a world apart.

John Ross knew what he had to do. The crucified Knight's memories of what was needed were clear and certain. He could not tell if the dream had shown him his own fate, if he was the Knight on the cross and he had witnessed his own death. He could not know if by being told of the morph he was being given a second chance at changing his own life. To accept that his dream had allowed him to step outside himself completely in bearing witness to the future he was working so hard to prevent, he must conclude that there was an extraordinary reason for such a thing to happen because it had never happened before.

It was easier to believe that seeing his own face on the crucified Knight of the Word was a trick of his imagination, a deception wrought by his fear that he would fail as this other Knight had failed and come to a similar end. It was not difficult to believe. The odds against his successfully capturing and exploiting a gypsy morph were enormous. It had been done only a handful of times in all of history. The methods employed and the differing results had never been documented. There was no standard procedure for this. But if necessity was the mother of invention, John Ross would find a way.

The stories of gypsy morphs were the stuff of legends. Ross had heard tales of the morphs during the twenty-five-odd years he had served the Word. Mostly they were whispered in awe by forest creatures, stories passed down from generation to generation. When the consequences of an intervening magic were particularly striking, either for good or evil, it was always suggested that it might have been due to the presence of a morph. No one living, as far as Ross could tell, had ever seen one. No one knew what they looked like at the moment of their inception. No one knew what they would turn out to be because no two had ever turned out the same. There were rumors of what they might become, but no hard evidence. One, it was said, had become an antibiotic. Another had become a plague. Gypsy morphs were enigmas; he had to be able to accept that going in.

What John Ross knew for sure when he went to Oregon was that whoever gained control over a gypsy morph acquired the potential to change the future in a way no one else could. It was a goal worth pursuing, even knowing it was also virtually impossible to achieve. He had little working for him, but more than enough to know where to begin. The crucified Knight's memories had told him the morph would appear in a low-tide coastal cave on the upper coast of Oregon near the town of Cannon Beach three days after Thanksgiving. In those memories he found a picture of the cave and the landscape surrounding it, so he knew what to look for.

What his dream of the crucified Knight had revealed to him was not so different from what his dreams usually told him—a time and a place and an event he might alter by his intervention. But usually he knew the details of the event, the course it had taken, and the reason things had gone amiss. None of that was known to him here. He did not know the form the gypsy morph would take when it came into being. He did not know how to capture it. He did not know what would happen afterward, either to the morph or to himself.

It was reassuring in one sense to have it so. Not knowing suggested he was someone other than the Knight on the cross, their resemblance notwithstanding. But it was odd, too, that the Knight's memories ceased with the moment of the morph's appearance, as if the slate afterward had been wiped clean or never come into being. Clearly the Knight felt he had failed in his attempt to secure the morph's magic and unlock its secret. Was this because he had failed even to capture the morph? Or was it because he was hiding the truth of what had happened afterward, not wanting Ross to see? There was no way for Ross to know, and speculation on the matter yielded nothing.

Cannon Beach was a small, charming oceanfront town a little more than an hour directly west of Portland. Bustling with activity generated by the annual appearance of summer vacationers, the town's shops and residences were clustered along a bypass that looped down off Highway 101 to run parallel to the edge of the ocean for about three miles. A second, smaller town, called Tolovana Park, which was really less town and more wide spot in the road, occupied the southernmost end of the loop. Together the two communities linked dozens of inns, hotels, bed-and-breakfasts, and vacation cottages through a tangle of shingle-shake and wood-beam restaurants and fast-food emporiums, souvenir and craft shops, art galleries, and clothing stores. There was a theater, a bakery, two wine shops, a gas station, a general store, a post office, and a whole clutch of real estate agencies. To its credit,

Cannon Beach seemed to have resisted the pervasive onslaught of name-brand chains that had invaded virtually every other vacation spot in the country, so that the familiar garish signs touting burgers and tacos and chicken and the like were all blessedly missing.

Ross arrived on a Sunday, having caught a ride west out of Portland with a trucker hauling parts for one of the lumber mills. He was dropped five miles inland and walked the rest of the way to the coast on a sunny, pleasant afternoon. It was still light when he arrived. Cannon Beach was so busy that Ross judged it impossible to differentiate Sunday from any other day of the week. Vacationers thronged the streets, pressing in and out of the shops, eating ice cream and chewing fudge, with shopping bags, small children, and dogs in hand.

Carrying his duffel and his backpack, he limped down the sidewalk with the aid of his black walking stick, the sun glinting off its bright surface and etching out in shadowed nuance the rune carvings that marked its otherwise smooth surface. He looked a transient, and the impression was not far from wrong. He was not indigent or bereft of hope or purpose, but he was homeless and rootless, a citizen of the world. He had lived this way for twenty-five years, and he had become used to it. His service to the Word required that he travel constantly, that he be able to respond to his dreams by moving to wherever they directed him, that when he had finished acting on them he be prepared to move again. It was a strange, wearing existence, and if he did not believe so strongly in the work he was doing, it would have quickly done him in.

Once, ten years earlier, he had lost his faith and given up on himself. He had settled in one place and tried to make a life as other men do. He had failed at that. His past had caught up with him, as he now understood it always would, and he had gone back to being what he now understood he must always be.

Thoughts of that past and this present drifted through his mind as he walked the business district of Cannon Beach. Hemlock, its main north-south street, was the center of almost everything of note, and he did not deviate from its path in the forty minutes his walk required. He was looking for a beginning, as he always did. Sometimes when he was in a larger city, he would simply take a room at a YMCA and go from there. That approach would not do in a vacation town or in the circumstances of his present endeavor. He would be in Cannon Beach until close to the end of November. He needed more than just a six- or seven-day room at the Y.

He found what he was looking for more quickly than he had expected. A small, hand-lettered sign in the window of the Cannon Beach Bookstore, which was located at the south end of Hemlock where the shops and galleries began to peter out, read HELP WANTED. Ross went into the store and asked what sort of help they were looking for. The manager, a sallow-faced, pleasant man of fifty named Harold Parks, told him they were looking for summer sales help. Ross said he would like to apply.

"That's summer sales, Mr. Ross," Harold Parks said pointedly. "It doesn't extend beyond, oh, maybe mid-September. And it's only thirty, thirty-five hours a week." He frowned at Ross through his beard. "And it only pays seven-fifty an hour."

"That suits my purposes," Ross replied.

But Parks was still skeptical. Why would John Ross want a job for only two months? What was his background concerning books and sales? How had he found out about the position?

Ross was ready with his answers, having been through this many times before. He was a professor of English literature, currently on leave so that he could try his hand at writing his own work of fiction, a thriller. He had decided to set it on the Oregon coast, and he had come to Cannon Beach to do the necessary research and to begin writing. He needed a job to pay expenses, but not one that would take up too much of his time. He admitted to having almost no sales experience, but he knew books. He gave Parks a small demonstration, and asked again about the job.

Parks hired him on the spot.

When asked about lodging, Parks made a few calls and found Ross a room with an elderly lady who used to work at the store and now supplemented her own small retirement income with rent from an occasional boarder. At present, both rented rooms were open, and Ross could have his pick.

So, by Sunday evening he had both living quarters and a job, and he was ready to begin his search for the gypsy morph—or, more particularly, for the place the morph would appear just after Thanksgiving. He knew it was somewhere close by and that it was a cave the elements and time's passage had hollowed into the side of the bluffs that ran along the ocean beaches. He knew the cave was flooded at high tide. He knew what the cave looked like inside and a little of what it looked like from without.

But the beaches of the Oregon coast ran all the way from Astoria to the border of California in an unbroken ribbon of sand, and there were thousands of caves to explore. For the most part, the caves lacked identifiable names, and in any case, he didn't know the name of the one he was searching for. He believed he would have to walk the coast for a dozen miles or so in either direction to find the right one.

He began his search during his off hours by walking north to Seaside and south to Arch Cape. He did so during low tide and daylight, so his window of opportunity was narrowed considerably. It took him all of July and much of August to complete his trek. When he was done, he had nothing to show for it. He had not found the cave.

His progress as a bookseller was meeting with better results. He had a gift for selling, and since he was familiar with and a believer in the value of his product, he was able to impress Harold Parks with his effort. His landlady, Mrs. Staples, liked him well enough to give him the run of the house, including the use of her own refrigerator, and she came to visit him frequently at work, always insisting that Mr. Ross be the one to help with her buying selections.

It was Mrs. Staples who suggested he talk with Anson Robbington.

By now it was nearing September, and he was beginning to be concerned about his lack of success. He had not found the cave in which the gypsy morph would appear, and he still had no idea what the morph would look like or how he would capture it. He had not asked for help from anyone, thinking that he could manage the search on his own and not involve others. When it became clear his plan was not working, he then had to decide how to ask for the help he needed without revealing what he was really up to.

So he mentioned to a few carefully chosen people, rather casually, that he was looking for someone to talk to who knew the Oregon coast around Cannon Beach.

"The man you want," Mrs. Staples advised at once, "is Anson Robbington. He's explored every inch of the coastline from Astoria to Lincoln City at one time or another in his life. If there's something you want to know, he's the one who can tell you."

Ross found Robbington two mornings later holding down the fort at Duane Johnson Realty, where he worked part-time as a salesman. He was big and weathered and bearded, and he dressed like the prototypical Northwest iconoclast. He was slow talking and slow moving, and he seemed lost in his own thoughts during much of their conversation, rather as if he were busy with something else entirely and could give Ross only a small portion of his time and attention.

Ross approached his inquiry in a circumspect manner, asking a few general questions about the geological underpinnings of the bluffs, offering a short synopsis of his imaginary book's premise, then detailing, as if it were his personal vision for his writing, a description of the cave he was thinking of including.

"Oh, sure," Robbington said after a long pause, gray eyes wandering back from whatever country they'd been viewing. "I know one just like it. Just like you described." He nodded for emphasis, then went away again for a bit, leaving Ross to cool his heels. "Tell you what," he began anew when he returned, "I'll take you out there myself Monday morning. Can you get some time off?"

The bright, sunny Monday morning that followed found them driving south along the coast in Robbington's rackety old Ford pickup, motoring out of Cannon Beach, past Tolovana Park, the turnoff to Arcadia Beach, and onward toward Arch Cape. The cave he was thinking of, Anson Robbington advised, lay just below Arch Cape on the other side of the tunnel, cut into the very rock that the tunnel burrowed through. It was six o'clock in the morning, and the tide was out. At other times, when the tide was either coming in, all the way in, or going out, you wouldn't know the cave was even there.

When they reached their destination, they parked the truck, climbed out, and worked their way along the bluff edge to a narrow trail, so hidden in underbrush it was invisible until they were right on top of it. The trail led downward toward the beach, winding back and forth amid outcroppings and ledges, switchbacking in and out of precipitous drops and deep ravines. It took them almost fifteen minutes to get down, mostly because of the circuitous route. Robbington admitted they could have gone farther down the beach to an easier descent and then walked back, but he thought Ross ought to experience something of the feel of bluffs if he was going to be writing about their features. Ross, making his way carefully behind the old man, his bad leg aching from the effort, held his tongue.

When they reached the cave, Ross knew immediately it was the one he was looking for. It was cut sideways into the rock where the bluff formed a horseshoe whose opening was littered with old tree trunks, boulders, and broken shells. It was farther south by less than a half mile from where Ross had given up his own search, but he might not have found it even if he had kept on, so deep in shadow and scrub did it lie. You had to get back inside the horseshoe to see that it was there, warded by weather-grayed cedar and spruce in various stages of collapse, the slope supporting them slowly giving way to the erosion of the tides. It bore all the little exterior landmarks he was looking for, and it felt as it had in the eyes of the crucified Knight of the Word.

They went inside with flashlights, easing through a split in the rock that opened into a cavern of considerable size and several chambers. The air and rock were chill and damp and smelled of dead fish and the sea. Tree roots hung from the ceiling like old lace, and water dripped in slow, steady rhythms. The floor of the cave rose as they worked their way deeper in, forming a low shelf where the rock had split apart in some cataclysmic upheaval thousands of years ago. On the right wall of the chamber into which the shelf disappeared, a strange marking that resembled a bull's head had been drawn over time by nature's deft hand.

Ross felt a wave of relief wash through him at the discovery. The rest, he felt, would come more easily now.

He explored the cave with Robbington for twenty or thirty minutes, not needing to, but wishing to convince his guide that he was working on descriptive material for the book. When they departed, they walked the beach south to a more gentle climb, and then returned along the shoulder of the highway to where they had left the pickup.

As they climbed into the cab, Ross thanked Anson Robbington and promised he would make mention of him in the book when it was published. Robbington seemed content with the fact that he had been of help.

John Ross worked in the bookstore that afternoon, and that night he treated himself and Mrs. Staples to dinner out. He was feeling so good about himself that he was able to put aside his misgivings and doubts long enough to enjoy a moment of self-congratulation. It was little enough compensation for the agonizing burden of his life. All the while he had been engaged in this endeavor, his dark dreams of the future had continued to assail him on a regular basis. Once or twice, they had shown him things he might otherwise have acted upon, but he had not, for fear of jeopardizing his search for the morph. It was difficult to ignore the horror of the future he lived each night in his dreams, and his first impulse each morning on waking was to try to do something about what he had witnessed. But there was only so much he could do with his life, only so much one man could accomplish, even as a Knight of the Word, even with the magic he could summon. He must make his choices, stand his ground, and live with the consequences.

In the days that followed, he returned to the cave many times, seeking something more that would help him when the gypsy morph finally appeared. He studied the configuration and makeup of the walls, of the separate chambers, of the entry. He tried to figure out what he might do to trap something found in that cave. He did his best to imagine in what way he might win over the creature he would snare so that it might trust him enough to reveal itself.

It was a hopeless task, and by the close of September, he was no closer to finding answers to his questions than he had been on waking from his dream. He had thought he might have the dream again, that he might see once more the Knight on the cross and be given further insight into what he must do. But the dream never returned.

He was beginning to despair when, on a dark still night as he thrashed awake from a particularly bad dream of the future, a tatterdemalion appeared to him, sent by the Lady, and summoned him to Wales.

Chapter 9

John Ross paused in his narrative and took a long, slow drink of his coffee. His gaze drifted to the curtained windows, where the sunrise burned with a golden shimmer through the bright, hard, cold December dawn.

Nest Freemark sat across from him at the kitchen table, her clear, penetrating gaze fixed on him, assessing his tale, measuring it for the consequences it would produce. She looked pretty much as he remembered her, but more self-assured, as if she had become better able to cope with the life she had been given. He admired the calm acceptance she had displayed the night before on finding him on her doorstep after ten long years, taking him in, asking no questions, offering no conditions, simply giving him a room and telling him to get some sleep. She was strong in ways that most people weren't, that most couldn't even begin to approach.

"So you went to Wales," she prodded, ruffling her thick, curly hair.

He nodded. "I went."

Her eyes never left his face. "What did you learn there?"

"That I was up against more than I had bargained for." He smiled ruefully and arched one eyebrow. "It works out that way more often than not. You'd think I'd learn."

The big house was quiet, the ticking of the old grandfather clock clearly audible in the silences between exchanges of conversation. The sun was just appearing, and darkness cloaked the corners and nooks with layered shadows. Outside, the birds were just waking up. No car tires crunched on the frosted road. No voices greeted the morning.

The boy who had come with him to Nest Freemark—the boy the gypsy morph had become only a handful of days ago—knelt backward on the living room couch, chin resting on folded arms as he leaned against the couch back and stared out the window into the park.

"Is he all right?" Nest asked softly.

Ross shook his head. "I wish I knew. I wish I could tell. Something. Anything. At least he's quit changing shapes. But I don't have a clue about what he's doing or why."

Nest shifted in her high-backed wooden chair, adjusting her robe. "Didn't the Lady give you any insight into this?"

"She told me a little of what to expect." He paused, remembering. "She gave me a kind of netting, so light and soft it was like holding a spiderweb. It was to be used to capture the morph when it appeared in the cave after Thanksgiving."

He cleared his throat softly. "She told me how the morph was formed, that it was all wild magic come together in shards to form a whole. It doesn't happen often, as I've said. Very rare. But when it does, the joining is so powerful it can become almost anything. I asked her what. A cure or a plague, she said. You could never tell; it was different each time and would seek its own shape and form. She wouldn't elaborate beyond that. She said wild magic of this sort was so rare and unstable that it only held together for a short time before breaking up again. If it could find a form that suited it, it would survive longer and become a force in the war between the Word and the Void. If not, it would dissipate and go back into the ether."

He twisted his coffee cup on its saucer, eyes dropping momentarily. "The gypsy morph is not a creation of the Word, as most other things are, but a consequence of other creations. It comes into being because the world is the way it is, with its various magics and the consequences of using them. The Word didn't foresee the possibility of the morph, so it hasn't got a handle on its schematic yet. Even the Word is still learning, it seems."

Nest nodded. "Makes sense. There are always unforeseen consequences in life. Why not for the Word as well as for us?"

Hawkeye wandered in from outside, trudged through the hallway and into the kitchen for a quick look around, then moved on to the living room. Without pausing, he jumped onto the couch next to the boy and began to rub against him. The boy, without looking, reached down absently and stroked the cat.

"I've never seen Hawkeye do that with anyone," Nest said quietly. Ross smiled faintly, and her gaze shifted back to him. "So, she gave you a net?"

He nodded. "When the gypsy morph appeared for the first time, she told me, it would materialize in a shimmer of lights, a kind of collection of glowing motes. As soon as that happened, I was to throw the net. The light would attract it, and the net would close about it all on its own, sealing it in. Immediately, she warned, the morph would begin to change form. When it did, I was to get out of there as quickly as possible because the expenditure of magic that resulted from the morph's changes would attract demons from everywhere."

"And did it?"

He lifted the coffee cup from its saucer and held it suspended before him.

He remembered how it had begun, his words as he spoke them recalling the moment. He had gone to the cave at sunrise on the day of the event, having rehearsed his role many times, having explored the grotto and its surroundings so thoroughly he could detail everything with his eyes closed. It was bitter cold and damp that day, the rains of the past two having ceased sometime during the night, leaving the chill and the wet to linger in the earth and air. Mist clung to the edges of the beach and the surface of the water in a thick, impenetrable curtain. Clumps of it had broken away from the main body and wandered inland to hunker down among the trees and rocks like fugitives in hiding. The ocean surf, calm this windless morning, rolled in a steady, monotonous *whoosh* onto the beach, advancing and receding, over and over in hypnotic motion. Gulls screamed their strange, challenging cries as they flew in search of food, smooth and bright against the gray.

He had once again borrowed Mrs. Staples's Chevy. It had carried him back and forth to the cavern often enough over the past three months that it probably could find the way on its own. Leaving it on the shoulder of the road where the beach access was easiest, he descended through the mist and gray and damp, a solitary hunter in the dim dawn light, and made his way back along the broad, sandy expanse to his destination.

Inside, it was dark enough that he was required to use his flashlight to find his way to the rock shelf, where he began his vigil. He did not know exactly how long he would have to wait, only that the morph would appear this day before sunset. Besides his flashlight and the spiderweb netting given to him by the Lady, he carried a blanket and a small basket of food and drink. The dead Knight's memories carried with them a clear image of where the morph would appear, and so Ross knew how to position himself.

After a time, he began to see the feeders. There were only a couple at first, then a couple more, then half a dozen, all of them hanging back in the darkened corners and nooks, eyes glinting as they kept watch. Ross was not surprised to see them; feeders were always watching him, drawn by his magic, waiting in anticipation of its expenditure. He could not think of a time when there hadn't been feeders close by, so he thought nothing of seeing them now.

But as midmorning crawled toward noon, their numbers increased, and soon there were so many he could not begin to count them. They sensed that something unusual was going to happen. Perhaps they even sensed what it was. But so many gathered in one place was not a good thing. Other creatures of magic would sense their presence and be drawn as well.

Ross rose and stalked from one end of the cave to the other, chasing the feeders back into the darkness. Their eyes winked out, then reappeared in the wake of his passing. Light from the midday sun, hazy and weak, brightened the entrance to the cave through the leafy curtain of tree branches and scrub. He peered out cautiously at the beach, open and flat and empty. There was no sign of life beyond the gulls. The ocean rolled in a low smooth surf of white noise.

At midday, he ate his lunch and drank a bottle of water, growing increasingly uneasy with the long wait. The number of feeders was now immense, and people were beginning to appear on the beach, strolling, walking dogs, playing with children, all of them passing by without stopping or even pausing, but all of them worrisome nevertheless. He knew now from the crush of feeders and his own heightened sense of a foreign magic's presence that the morph was going to appear. Wild magic was present, careening through the ether in waves that shocked his conscience and sharpened his instincts.

He was on his feet, the netting in hand, his parka cast aside, when the magic finally came together. It did so in a rush of wind and sound that brought him to his knees as it tore through the rock chamber with ferocious purpose. Damp spray flew into his face, and the eyes of the feeders gleamed and closed. Hunching his shoulders, he squinted at the movement he saw materializing above the shelf of rock, a darkness at first, then a slow brightening. It was happening! He crept forward amid the sound and fury, the gossamer netting clutched tightly to his chest. The wind alone would rip it to shreds, he feared. But it was all he had and what the Lady had given him to use.

The brightening grew more intense, a kind of wash in the air that slowly began to coalesce. Motes appeared, whirling through the shimmering haze, taking incandescent form against the backdrop of shadows and gloom. Ross was on his feet, ignoring the deep whistle of the wind, the spray of dampness, and the thrust of movement from the magic's gathering. He must be ready when the moment came, he knew. He must not falter.

When the dancing motes tightened suddenly, beginning to take form in the air before him, he cast the net. It billowed in the wind as if it had become a sail, taking shape as it flew through the darkness to close about the gathering light.

Instantly, the wind died away and the light went out. An abrupt, blanketing silence descended over everything. John Ross stood frozen in place, his ears still ringing and his shoulders hunched, his eyes trying to readjust to the sudden change in light. He breathed slowly and deeply, listening, watching, and waiting.

Then the eyes of the feeders began to reappear, lantern bright against the gloom in which they crouched. Outside, the screams of gulls and the roll of the surf could be heard. He edged forward on the rock shelf, feeling his way over the smooth, cold, wet rock. He did not want to turn on the flashlight, afraid of the reaction the light might bring.

He found the netting with its prize nestled in a hollow at the center of the shelf. The netting was opaque and still until he touched it, and then its captive moved and light emanated from within. He picked it up and carried it to the cave's entrance, where the dim sunlight fell upon and revealed it.

The netting was changing shape with such rapidity that he could barely follow what was happening. It squirmed and shook and twitched, and with each movement, a small amount of light escaped.

A quick check of the beach outside the cave revealed it was momentarily deserted. Clutching the netting and its writhing contents to his chest, he started back down the beach at a rapid walk.

He had almost reached his car when the first demon appeared.

A young woman and a little girl appeared suddenly in the kitchen doorway, and John Ross went silent. The young woman was thin and worn looking, and she had the look of someone with problems sleep alone could not solve. Her dark eyes fixed boldly on Ross and stayed there, assessing him, reading him, seeing him in some secret way.

Nest, her back to the entry, turned in her chair. "Good morning," she said, smiling at them. "Did you sleep well?"

The young woman nodded, her dark, intense eyes still on Ross. "Did we miss breakfast?"

"No, we were waiting for you." Nest glanced at Ross. "This is John Ross. John, this is Bennett Scott and her daughter, Harper."

Ross nodded. "Nice to meet you."

"Nice to meet you," Bennett Scott replied, but looked doubtful about it. "Guess you got in late."

"After midnight sometime."

"Is that your son?" She gestured toward the living room, where the boy who was the gypsy morph kneeled on the sofa and stared into the park.

Ross hesitated, not sure what to say. "Yes."

"What's his name?"

Ross glanced at Nest. "John Junior. We call him Little John."

"Little John," Bennett repeated thoughtfully.

"Kind of corny, I guess." Ross gave her a rueful smile.

"Appo juss," Harper said softly, tugging on her mother's hand.

Nest rose to retrieve the container from the refrigerator and pour some into one of the sealed cups the little girl drank from, leaving Ross to deal with Bennett, who continued to stare boldly at him.

"How old is Little John?" she asked casually, but there was an edge to her voice.

"Four years and two months." Ross held the smile. "We're just visiting for a few days, and then we'll be on our way."

Bennett Scott pursed her lips. "There was a minister here last night looking for you. Findo Gask. Odd name. I told him I didn't know you. But now I kind of think maybe I do."

He shook his head, holding her gaze. "I don't think so."

She brushed at her lank hair, then folded her arms under her breasts. "Nest doesn't seem to think much of this minister. I guess I don't either. He was kind of pushy."

Ross stood up slowly, levering himself to his feet by leaning on the tabletop. "I'm sorry if he caused you any trouble, Miss Scott. I don't know who this man is or what he wants." *But I can guess,* he thought to himself.

The young woman pointed at him suddenly. "I do know who you are. I remember now. You were here, oh, fifteen years ago or so. I was just a little girl. You came to see Nest's grandparents. You knew her mother, didn't you?"

His throat tightened. "Yes. That was a long time ago."

"Sit down," she urged, concern mirrored in her dark eyes. Her hands gestured, and he did as she asked. "I shouldn't expect you to remember me after all that time. I guess I wasn't sure where . . ."

She trailed off, looking around quickly for Harper, who was sucking on her juice cup. "Are you hungry, sweetie?"

Harper's eyes were on the boy in the living room. "Boy," she said, not seeming to hear her mother. She trundled past Bennett into the living room and climbed up on the couch next to the gypsy morph. She knelt as he did, drinking her juice and staring out at the park. The morph did not look at her.

"Why don't you get dressed," Nest suggested to Bennett, coming back to the table. "Harper can play with Little John. I'll keep an eye on her. She'll be fine. When you come out, we'll have breakfast."

Bennett considered the matter, then nodded and went down the hallway to her bedroom, closing the door softly behind her. Ross watched her go without comment, wondering why she had been so worried about who he was. It was more than uneasiness she had demonstrated; it was fear. He recognized it now, considering her response to him, to the possibility that their paths had crossed somewhere before. Yet once the mystery of their previous encounter was cleared up, she seemed fine. Perhaps *relieved* was a better word.

Nest reseated herself at the table. "Little John?" she inquired, arching one eyebrow.

He shrugged. "It was all I could come up with on the spur of the moment. He's only been a boy for four days. I haven't had any reason to think of a name for him before."

"Little John will do. Tell me about the demons before Bennett gets back."

Pushing the empty coffee cup away from him as if to distance himself from his narrative, he did as she asked.

* * *

He hadn't even reached the car before the first demon appeared. Carrying the netting that contained the morph in one hand and gripping his walnut staff with the other, he clambered awkwardly up the sandy trail from the beach to the shoulder of Highway 101 and immediately caught sight of the longhaired young man standing several dozen feet away, occupying the space between himself and the car. He was paying Ross no attention whatsoever, his eyes directed out at the ocean. But Ross felt his instincts prickle, the magic that warded him surfacing in a rush, and he knew what was coming.

He walked up the road as if indifferent to the young man's presence, keeping close to the paving so as to pass behind the other. He saw the young man's posture shift, then watched him step back and shade his eyes as if to get a better look at something on the beach. When Ross came abreast of him, the young man wheeled to attack, but Ross was already moving, bringing his staff around to catch the other squarely across the forehead. Fire lanced from the rune-scrolled wood, and the young man's head exploded in a shower of blood. Revealed for what it was and stripped of its disguise, the demon's ruined shell went backward over the bluff and tumbled from view.

Wiping away the blood with an old rag, Ross climbed hurriedly into the car, backed onto the road, and drove toward Cannon Beach. They would be waiting for him at Mrs. Staples's by now, converging from all directions to intercept him. But he had anticipated this and had no intention of returning to Cannon Beach. He hadn't stayed alive this long by being predictable.

He drove past the turnoff without slowing and caught Highway 26 east toward Portland. In the seat beside him, the morph continued to change shape and emanate light, the magic pulsing like a beacon with each re-forming, leading his enemies right to it. Ross knew that if he was to have any chance at all, he needed to lose himself in a large population. If he remained in Cannon Beach or tried to find sanctuary in any other small town, the demons would find him in a heartbeat. But in a city he could disappear. The number and frequency of the morph's changes would diminish after a time, and while he could not hope to avoid entirely the demons seeking him, he could make it harder for them to determine where he was. When the morph was not changing, it was less identifiable; the Lady had advised him of this. Gradually, Ross would become the focus of their hunt. As one among thousands, he would not be so easy to find.

But he had to get to Portland to have any chance at all, and the demons were already in place. A logging truck ran him off the road just above the turnoff to Banks. He escaped into the woods, found a dirt road farther in, and caught a ride with an old woman and her daughter to a town so small he didn't even see a sign with a name. He felt bad about Mrs. Staples's car, but there was nothing he could do. He felt bad about the car he stole in the nameless town, too, but there was nothing he could do about that either. He abandoned it outside Portland and caught a metro bus into the city.

In a cavernous train station on the west side, while waiting to board a train south to San Francisco, he was attacked again. Two men came at him in the men's room, armed with iron pipes and buttressed by lives of willful destruction. He took them both out in seconds, but the demon who had dispatched them and was waiting outside surprised him as he tried to sneak out the back. The demon was savage and primal, but intelligent as well. It picked a good spot for an ambush, and if it had been a little luckier, it might have succeeded in its effort. But his instincts saved John Ross once more, and the demon died in a fiery conflagration of magic.

Ross called Mrs. Staples from the bus station after the cab dropped him off to tell her of the car and apologize for what he had done. He told her he would send her money. She took it very well, considering. Then he picked up his ticket, boarded the bus, waited until it was ready to leave, and got off again. He walked out of the station and down the street to a used-car agency, took a clunker out for a test drive after leaving the salesman the purchase price in cash as security, and kept going. He drove north to Vancouver, abandoned the car, caught another bus south, and was in California the next day.

He continued on like this for more than a week, twisting and turning, dodging and weaving, a boxer under attack. Over and over again he picked up and moved, sometimes not even bothering to unpack. He slept infrequently and for brief periods, and he was tired and edgy all the time, his energy slowly draining away. It did not help that he was forced to defend himself so often that he was spending all of his time in his dreams of the future without protection, a fugitive there as well, constantly on the run, hunted and at risk. That he stayed alive in both worlds was impressive. That he managed to hold on to the gypsy morph was a genuine miracle.

The morph continued to change rapidly for the first seven days before finally slowing down. It stayed in the netting all this time, never even trying to venture forth, going through its multitude of transformations. It was animal, vegetable, insect, bird, reptile, and a whole slew of other things that Ross was unable or unwilling to identify. At one point it seemed to disappear entirely, but when he peeked inside, he found it was a slug. Another time, it was a bee. A third time it was some sort of mold. Ross quit looking after that and, until it took the shape of something possessing bulk, just assumed it was in the net. It never made a sound and never seemed in need of food or drink. Somehow it had the capacity to sustain itself during this early period, so he didn't need to be concerned for its well-being beyond keeping it safe and alive.

By the time of the incident in Salt Lake City in mid-December, it was changing on the average of only once a day. For two days during that period, it was a cat. For a day and a half, it was a chimp. Once, for a matter of only a few hours, it was a wolf with a tiger-striped face, an uncanny reminder of Wraith.

Shortly after that, it changed into the little boy it was now and spoke a single word—*Nest.* When it said her name twice more in the space of a single day, Ross decided to take a chance and come back to Hopewell.

"Because he said 'Nest' and you thought he was talking about me," she said quietly.

"Because I thought he *might* be talking about you, yes." She watched his face grow intense and troubled. "Because I had just watched him turn into a miniature Wraith, and it made me wonder. But mostly because I was at my wits' end—am at my wits' end still, for that matter—and I had to try something."

He leaned back in his chair. "I am exhausted and almost out of time, and I haven't gotten anywhere. I've been with him for twenty-two days, and I don't have a clue how to reach him. I thought I would learn something in that time, thought I would tip to some secret about his magic. But all I've managed to do is to keep the two of us alive and running. There's been no communication, no exchange of information, no discovery of any sort at all. Your name was the first breakthrough. That, and the fact that he's stayed a little boy for four days now. Maybe it means something."

She nodded, then rose to pour them both a fresh cup of coffee and reseated herself. Outside, the day was bright and clear and cold, the early morning frost still visible in the shadowed spaces and on the tree trunks in crystalline patches. Ross could hear the oil furnace thrum as it pumped out heat to ward against the freeze.

"He doesn't seem especially interested in me now that he's here," she observed carefully.

He sipped at the coffee. "I know. He hasn't spoken your name either. Hasn't said a single word. So maybe I was wrong."

"How much time is left?"

"Before he disappears altogether?" Ross shook his head. "Several days, I guess. They give a morph on the average of thirty days of life, and that leaves this one down to eight."

"Interesting," she said, "that he's become a little boy."

"Interesting," he agreed.

They talked a bit longer about the propensities of gypsy morphs, but since morphs came without blueprints and tended to be wholly inconsistent in their development, there was really little to conclude about the intentions of this one. Nest would have liked to understand more about the strange creatures, but the fact remained that she understood little enough even about Pick, whom she had known for most of her life. Creatures of the forest and magic tended to be as foreign to humans as plankton, even to those as attuned to them as she was.

Bennett reappeared wearing jeans and an old sweatshirt she'd pulled from Nest's closet and a pair of her walking shoes, so they set about making breakfast. It was served and consumed at the larger dining room table, with everyone eating except the morph, who picked at his food and said nothing.

"Lo, boy," Harper said to him midway through the meal.

The gypsy morph studied her solemnly.

"Is he always this quiet?" Bennett asked Ross, frowning.

He nodded. "He understands everything, but he doesn't speak." He hesitated. "The fact is, we're on our way to Chicago after the holidays to see a specialist on the matter."

"Better have his appetite checked at the same time," she advised pointedly. "He hasn't eaten a thing."

"He ate some cereal earlier," Nest said.

"Mommy?" Harper asked, looking up, big eyes curious. "Boy talk?"

"Maybe later, sweetie," Bennett said, and went back to her breakfast.

Afterward, she bundled up Harper and told Nest they were going for a walk in the park. She asked Ross if Little John wanted to come with them, but Ross said he hadn't seemed well and should probably stay in. Her intentions were good, but he couldn't take a chance on letting the gypsy morph out of his sight.

Bennett and Harper went out the back door, across the lawn, and into the frozen expanse of the park. It was still not even noon. From his position on the couch, the gypsy morph watched them go, staring out the window anew. Ross stood beside him for a time, speaking in low tones, eliciting no response at all.

Finally he walked back into the kitchen and picked up a towel to help dry the dishes Nest was washing.

"You have a dishwasher," he pointed out, indicating the machine in front of her.

"I like doing it by hand. I like how it makes me feel."

They worked in silence for a while, falling into a comfortable rhythm. Then Ross said, "They'll come looking for me, you know."

She nodded. "They already have. One of them, at least. Findo Gask, minister of the faith."

"There will be more. It will be dangerous if I stay."

She looked at him. "No duh, as Robert would say."

He didn't know who Robert was, but he got the message. "So maybe I should go after tonight."

"Maybe you should. But maybe coming here was the right thing to do. Let's give it some time and see." She handed him a juice glass. "Let's get one thing straight, John. I'm not asking you to leave. We crossed that bridge last night."

He finished drying all the glasses, stacking them on a towel spread out atop the counter. "It means a lot. I don't know when I've been this tired."

She smiled. "It's funny, but I thought I was going to end up spending Christmas all alone this year. Now I have a house full of people. It changes everything."

"Life has a way of doing that." He smiled ruefully. "It keeps us from becoming too complacent."

They had just finished putting away the dishes when a knock sounded at the front door. Nest exchanged a quick glance with Ross, then walked down the hall to answer it. He stayed in the kitchen for a few minutes listening to the slow drift of conversation that ensued, then walked to the kitchen window and looked out.

A county sheriff's car was parked in the drive.

CHAPTER 10

Bennett Scott walked out of Nest Freemark's backyard and into Sinnissippi Park, head lowered, wincing against the brightness of the sun. A crystalline coating of frost lingered in shadowed patches of brittle grass and crunched beneath her boots when she walked on it. She watched Harper skip ahead of her, singing softly to herself, lost in that private child's world where adults aren't allowed. She recalled it from her own childhood, a not-so-distant past tucked carefully away in her memory. It was a world she had gone into all the time when growing up, often when she was seeking escape from Big Momma and the unpleasantness of her real life. She supposed Harper did the same, and it made her want to weep.

"Mommy, birdies!" the little girl called out, pointing at a pair of dark shadows winging through the trees.

"Robins," Bennett guessed, smiling at her daughter.

"Obbins," Harper parroted, and skipped ahead once more, watching the fluid movement of her shadow as it stretched out beside her.

Bennett tossed back her dark hair and lifted her face bravely against the sunlight. It would be better here, she thought. Better than it had been on the streets, when she was using all the time. Better than in the shelters, where she always kept her switchblade in one hand and Harper's wrist in the other. Better, even, than in the rehab units where she always felt used up and hopeless, where she went through the litany of recovery and still craved a fix all the time. She had tried to shield Harper, but the truth was, everything originated with her. There was no protection without separation, and she couldn't bear that.

But it had happened a few times, just because it was necessary if she was to survive. That was behind her now, so she could bear to think of it again, if only just. But she had left Harper in places rats called home and with people she wouldn't trust a dog with if she were thinking straight, and it was something of a miracle that nothing bad had happened to her baby. Coming back to Hopewell and to Nest was an attempt to set all that straight, to prevent any more incidents, to stop exposing Harper to the risks her mother had chosen to embrace. The men, the sex, the sickness, the drugs, the life—all rolled up into one big ball of evil that would drag her down and bury her if she gave it enough space in her life.

No more, she thought. *Not ever.*

They crossed the ball diamonds to the roadway fronting the bluffs and walked to the crest of the slope to look down over the bayou and the river beyond. Harper had found a stick and was dragging it through patches of frost, making designs. Bennett took out a cigarette, lit it, inhaled deeply, and sighed. She was a mess. She wasn't using, but her health was shot and her head was all fuzzy inside where reason warred with need and emotions fragmented every few days in a fireworks display that was truly awesome. She thought of her mother and hoped she was burning in hell, then immediately regretted the thought. Tears filled her eyes. She had loved her mother, loved her desperately, the way she hoped Harper loved her. But her mother had abandoned her, disappointed her, and rejected her time and again. What was left for her when it happened so often but to flee, to try to save herself? Her flight had saved her life, perhaps, but had cost her in measurable increments her childhood innocence and sense of self-worth and any chance of escaping her mother's addict life.

But it would be different for Harper. She had made that vow on the morning she had learned at the free clinic she was pregnant and had decided whatever higher power had given her this one last chance at something good, she wasn't going to mess it up.

So here she was, come back to where she had started, back to where a few things still seemed possible. She was dressed in another woman's clothing, and the clothes her child wore had been stolen from or discarded by others, but even so she felt new and hopeful. Nest Freemark had been so good to her in the past. If anyone could help her find a way back from the dark road she had traveled, it was Nest.

A train whistle sounded, distant and forlorn in the midday silence, echoing across the gray, flat surface of the Rock.

"Choo choo," Harper said, and she made some train noises. She shuffled around in a circle, dragging her stick, chuffing out clouds of breath into the sunshine.

I can make this work, Bennett thought, staring off into the distance, out where the whistle was still echoing through the winter silence.

"Hi, there, cutie," a voice behind her said. "You are about the sweetest little muffin I've ever seen."

Bennett turned quickly, shifting in a smooth, practiced motion to place herself between the newcomer and Harper. The young woman facing her smiled and shrugged, as if apologizing for her abrupt appearance while at the same time saying, so what? She was close to Bennett's age, tall and lanky, with wild red hair that stuck out. Her bright, green eyes fastened on Harper with an eagerness that was disconcerting. "Hey, you."

Then she glanced at Bennett, and the look cooled and hardened. "You are one lucky mom, to have someone like her. How are you doing? My name is Penny."

She stuck out her hand. Bennett hesitated before accepting it. "I'm Bennett. This is Harper."

Penny shifted her stance without moving her feet, loose and anticipatory. "So, are you from around here or just passing through, like me?" Penny grinned. "I'm visiting my granny for the holidays, but you can believe me when I tell you this place is in a time warp. Nothing to do, nowhere to go, no one to see. I can't wait to get out. You?"

"I'm from here, back for a visit with a . . . friend, an old friend." Bennett held her ground, watchful, the hand in her pocket fastened on the switchblade. "We're staying on awhile."

Penny sniffed. "Whatever. I'm outta here December twenty-sixth and good riddance."

She looked off into the distance as the freight train swung into view out on the levee, wheeling down the tracks with a slow-building rumble of iron wheels and pistons. They stood motionless, the three of them, staring out at the train as it bisected the horizon in a seemingly endless line of cars, a zipper motion against the still backdrop of water and winter woods. When it disappeared, the sound faded gradually, still audible when the train was several miles up the track.

"So, you having fun here in the park, Harper?" Penny asked suddenly, shifting her gaze once more.

Harper nodded wordlessly and edged closer to Bennett. She sensed the same thing about this woman her mother did, that something wasn't quite right. Bennett felt suddenly exposed and vulnerable, standing at the edge of the wooded slope, away from everyone and everything in the hard edge of the winter chill. Clouds had crept out of the northwest, obscuring the sun, and the gray sky was melting down into the backdrop of the skeletal trees.

"We've got to be going," Bennett advised, reaching down for Harper's hand, keeping her eyes on Penny.

"Oh, sure," Penny replied, smiling cheerfully, the light in her green eyes dancing, shrugging her shoulders and shifting away. "You go, girl, you need to. But, hey, you look a little uptight. Know what I mean?"

"No." Bennett shook her head quickly, not wanting to hear any more, already sensing what was coming. "I'm fine."

She started away, but Penny moved with her. "Well, you can say you're fine if you want, but you are most definitely not, you know? I can tell. And I don't blame you. I wouldn't be fine if I didn't have a little something to help me get by, let me tell you."

Bennett wheeled on her. "Look, I don't know who you are—"

"Hey, I'm just another victim of life, just another sister fighting to make it through another day." Penny held up her hands placatingly. "You don't need to worry about me. You think I'm the law? I'm not, girlfriend. Not hardly." She winked. "Hope you're not the law either, because I got something for you, you want it, something to make you feel a little better."

Bennett heard the blood pounding inside her head. She felt the familiar pumping of adrenaline, her body's automatic response to the possibility of a fix. Everything seemed to kick in at once, all the familiar expectancies, all the insatiable needs. She was surprised at how strong they were, even in the face of her resolve to put them aside.

Penny eased closer to her, eyes bright. "What I got, is a little white dust that doesn't take but a single whiff to sweep you away to la-la land, smooth and easy and cream-puff sweet. You can live on this stuff for days, girl. Keeps you sharp and strong and focused, but takes the edge off, too. I got it before I came to Dullsville, knowing what it would be like. I used it day before last, and I'm still flying high."

"No, thanks," Bennett told her abruptly, shaking her head, starting off again. It took everything she had to say it, to make her feet move, to keep her mind focused, but she managed. "We've got to go."

"Hey, wait up, Bennett!" Penny came after her quickly, keeping pace as she walked. "Don't be mad. I wasn't trying to jerk you around or anything. I was just trying to be nice, trying to make conversation. Hey, I'm lonely here, I admit it. You seem like me, that's all. I was just looking for some company." She paused. "I wasn't going to ask you for money, you know. I was going to share, to give it to you for free."

Bennett kept walking, trying to shut the words out, trying to make Penny go away. *Even here,* she was thinking. *Even here, someone's got the stuff and wants me to use.* She was walking faster, practically dragging Harper, needing to escape and not wanting to, both at once.

"We could meet later and do some together," Penny was suggesting, keeping pace effortlessly. "My place, maybe. You know, just the two of us. Granny doesn't know what's going on anyway, so she won't be a bother."

"Owee, Mommy," Harper was complaining, trying to pull free from her mother's grip.

Bennett shifted her hand on the little girl's arm and looked over at Penny angrily. "I can't—"

"What do you say?" Penny cut her short. "You want a little now? Just a taste to see if it's worth doing some more later?"

Bennett stopped and stood with her head lowered and her eyes closed. She wanted nothing more. She wanted it so bad she could hardly wait for it to happen. She felt empty and sick inside, and she found herself thinking, *What the hell difference does it make after all the other drugs I've done?*

Penny's hand was on her shoulder, and her frizzy red head was bent close. "You won't be sorry, babe, I promise. Just a taste to get you by until, oh, maybe tonight, okay? Come on. I know the signs. You're all strung out and uptight and you want a little space for yourself. Why shouldn't you have it?"

Bennett felt her defenses shutting down and her addictive needs sweeping through her with relentless purpose. The itch was working its way up her spine and down her throat, and she thought—knew—that if she didn't take what was being offered, she would self-destruct in spectacular fashion. Besides, a taste was not so much, and Nest could help her later, give her the strength she lacked now so she could start over again.

"Come on, I'll do a little with you," Penny persisted, whispering now, so close that Bennett could hear her breathing.

Her eyes were still closed, but now, on the verge of capitulating, on the edge of a hunger so intense she could not find words to define it, she opened them.

It was then she saw the Indian.

Nest Freemark opened her front door and found Deputy Sheriff Larry Spence waiting, his big hands clasped around his leather gloves. He was dressed in his uniform, brown over tan, and he wore a leather jacket with the collar and cuffs trimmed in dark fur. Bits and pieces of metal stays and accents glinted dully in the graying light, giving him that armored look that lawmen and the military favor.

"How you doing, girl," he greeted pleasantly.

She glanced past him to the empty sheriff's car. He had come alone. "Can I help you, Larry?"

He shoved his gloves into his coat pocket, eyes shifting away. "I'd like to speak with you for just a minute, if it's okay."

She studied him pointedly, waiting. He flushed. "It's business, you know, not personal."

She smiled, but held her ground. "Sure. Go right ahead."

He cleared his throat, looking past her for just a moment. "I wonder if we might speak inside?"

The last thing she wanted was Larry Spence in her house. On the other hand, it was rude to make him stand out in the cold and she couldn't come up with a good reason for not inviting him in long enough to tell her what he wanted.

She stood aside. "Sure."

He moved into the entry, and she shut the door behind them. He glanced around, nodding appreciatively. "You have a very nice home. Very warm. Sort of reminds me of my folks' old two-story."

"Would you like some hot tea?" she asked. "We can sit in the kitchen."

She led him down the hall and through the kitchen doorway. John Ross stood with his back to the sink, leaning on his staff, a mix of curiosity and wariness mirrored in his green eyes. But it was the look on Larry Spence's face that surprised her, changing from friendly to antagonistic and back again so fast she almost missed it. Something was very wrong, but she had no idea what it was.

"John, this is Larry Spence," she said. "Larry, my friend John Ross. He's visiting for the holidays with his son."

The men shook hands, a firm, measured sort of greeting that lacked warmth and advised caution. Nest put Larry Spence at the old wooden table and gave both men fresh cups of tea. Leaving Ross at the sink, she sat down across from Spence. "So, tell me what you need, Larry."

He cleared his throat and straightened. "There's been some rumors of drug dealing in the park, Nest. I'm making a few inquiries, just in case anyone's seen anything unusual this past week or so. You haven't noticed any strangers around, have you?"

This was the first Nest had heard about the matter. If there was any drug dealing going on in Sinnissippi Park, Pick would have noticed and said something. She frowned. "Pretty hard for anyone to hide out there in the park at this time of the year, Larry."

"Maybe. What you need to know is that these people are pretty dangerous."

She shrugged. "I haven't seen anyone."

He looked at Ross. "How about you, Mr. Ross? Do you know anything about this business?"

His tone of voice and the emphasis he gave to his words turned his question into an accusation. Nest was stunned.

John Ross merely shook his head."I just got here last night."

"Didn't see anyone out in the park when you drove up?"

"I came in on the bus."

"Are you from around here, Mr. Ross?"

"No, I—"

"Just a minute, John." Nest had had enough. She fixed Larry Spence with a withering look. "As a sheriff's deputy, you make a great Nazi, Larry. What are you doing? John is an old friend and a guest in my house. I invited you in out of kindness, not to give you a chance to practice your interrogation skills."

The big man nodded, a gesture intended to placate, as if anything else might invite further attack. He brushed at his mop of blond hair. "His name came up during my investigation, Nest."

"What?" She stared. "How?"

He shrugged. "Anonymous source."

"Anonymous source? How convenient!"

He took a slow, steadying breath. "I'm just doing my job, girl, asking these questions. And I'm concerned about your safety. Mr. Ross is a stranger, and I just want to be sure—"

She came to her feet abruptly, incensed. "You don't have to be sure in my house, Larry. You just have to be courteous. I think you better go."

He rose reluctantly, then nodded at Ross. "I apologize for any rudeness, Mr. Ross. I didn't come here to make trouble."

John Ross nodded back. "You don't need to apologize to me, Deputy."

Larry Spence looked down at the floor. "Nest, I'm sorry. But I worry about you. Rumors have a way of sneaking up on you, if you don't keep an eye on them. If there's drug dealing going on in the park, I don't want you to be associated with it."

Nest stared at him. For just an instant she sensed that he was talking about something else entirely, that he was trying to tell her something. She shook her head slowly and stepped up to him. "Larry, I appreciate your concern. But drugs have never been a part of my life and certainly not of John's. I promise you, if we see anything suspicious, we'll give you a call."

The big man nodded, turned, and started back down the hall. He caught sight of Little John perched on the sofa, staring out at the park, and turned back to Ross. "Your son?"

Ross nodded.

Spence looked at the boy, puzzlement etched in his rough features, as if he found the boy's presence difficult to accept. Then he continued down the hall to the front door, where he paused.

"The offer for Christmas is still open. Kids would love it."

"I don't think so, Larry," she replied, wondering what in the world he was thinking.

He nodded, opened the door, and went back outside. Nest stood in the doorway and watched as he climbed into his sheriff's car and drove slowly off. Her hands were clenched and her throat was tight with anger.

Larry Spence, she decided, was an idiot.

The Indian seemed to come out of nowhere, appearing amidst the bare trees in a wooded stretch behind the toboggan slide, all size and dark shadows in the graying light. He was big all over, dressed in camouflage pants, ribbed army sweater, mesh vest, and combat boots. His black hair glistened with a gunmetal sheen, braided and drawn tight against his scalp, and his coppery skin shone like orange fire. He carried a rucksack and a rolled blanket over one shoulder, and his eyes, even from so far away, were bright pinpricks beneath his heavy brow.

Bennett Scott forgot about Penny and the drugs and everything else, and simply stared at him as he approached, his slow, heavy steps carrying him steadily closer, until he seemed to take up all the space in her screen of vision.

At the last minute, Penny, still whispering sweet enticements and urgent pleas, realized something was wrong. She backed away quickly and turned as the Indian loomed over her. Bennett heard her gasp of surprise and shock turn an instant later to a hiss of warning.

"Afternoon," the Indian said, his copper face expressionless, his deep voice smooth. He was addressing Bennett and Harper, looking right through Penny. "Beautiful day for a walk in the park."

No one replied. The women and the little girl stood frozen in place, as if turned to ice. The Indian glanced from Bennett to Harper, unperturbed. "Ah, little one," he said softly to the child. "Do you wait for tonight's snow so that tomorrow you might go out and build a snowman with Mama?"

Harper gave a slow nod. "Yeth."

The Indian smiled faintly. "Mama," he said to Bennett, speaking past a seething Penny as if she weren't even there. "Do you know a woman named Nest Freemark?"

Bennett swallowed against the dryness in her throat, so frightened she could barely bring herself to do that much. The Indians she had encountered had mostly been street people, drunks and indigents and welfare dependents, barely able to get from street corner to soup line. This one was a different sort entirely, big and powerful and self-assured. He had not threatened Harper or her, but he seemed capable of anything.

"Do you know Nest Freemark?" he pressed gently.

Bennett nodded. "She lives right over there," she managed, suddenly in control of herself again, her mind clear.

"She is your friend?"

"Yes. I'm staying with her."

"Would you go to her and tell her Two Bears is waiting in the park to speak with her?"

It was an odd request. Why didn't he just walk over there and tell her himself? But she didn't feel inclined to argue the matter, and it gave her the excuse she needed to get away from Penny. "Okay," she said. "Come on, Harper."

She reached for the little girl's hand, but Penny moved instantly to block their way, wheeling back on the Indian. "Why don't you just push off, Tonto? Run your own errand. We were talking."

For the first time, he looked at her. And Penny, well, Penny with her drugs and smart-ass talk, looked as if she might turn into a pillar of salt. She shrank from him as if struck, retreating into a protective crouch. Then something ugly and dark surfaced in her eyes, and she took on the appearance of a feral creature. She lunged at the Indian, snake-quick. There was a glint of metal, but the metal went spinning out into the gray, and Penny shrieked and dropped to one knee, holding her wrist and baring her teeth at Two Bears. A knife lay on the ground a dozen feet away, knocked free from her hand. Bennett had never even seen the Indian move.

"You should be more careful," the big man told Penny, then dismissed her as if she were already gone. He bent to Harper. "Come, little one," he said, taking her tiny hand in his. "I will walk part of the way with you."

Harper went obediently, saying nothing. Bennett followed, leaving Penny kneeling on the ground where the Indian had put her. She did not look back.

CHAPTER 11

Nest Freemark pulled on her parka, not bothering with snaps or zippers, and banged her way out through the storm door onto the back porch, down the steps, and into the yard. She exhaled her frustration in a frothy cloud, her mind racing. First Larry Spence comes by with his bizarre story about drug dealing in the park and now O'olish Amaneh reappears. Today was turning into a replay of yesterday, and she wasn't sure she was up to it.

She was already scanning the park, searching for the Indian's familiar silhouette when Pick dropped onto her shoulder.

"Getting to be old home week around here, isn't it?" he offered brightly, fastening on her collar with both twiggy hands. "Hey, watch what you're doing!"

She was hunching down into the coat, jostling Pick as she did so, working the Gore-Tex into a more protective position. It was colder out than she had believed. The temperature was dropping again, the afternoon chill deepened by the sun's disappearance behind a thick bank of clouds, the morning's brightness faded to memory.

"Try thinking about someone besides yourself!" Pick snapped, regaining his balance.

"Quit griping." She was in no mood for sylvan nonsense. Pick meant well, but sometimes he was an out-and-out annoyance. She had enough to deal with. "You saw him, I gather?"

"Which one do you mean? That deputy sheriff, John Ross, or the Indian? I saw them all. What's going on?"

She shook her head. "I'm not sure."

She pushed through the bushes and onto the service road separating the Freemark property from the park. Ahead, the dead grass of the ball diamonds and central play area stretched away in a gray and windburned carpet. Beyond, along the ridge of the bluffs ahead, right toward Riverside Cemetery, and left past the toboggan slide, the bare trunks and limbs of the broad-leaves were framed like dark webbing against the steely sky.

Two Bears was nowhere in sight.

"I don't see him," she said, casting about as she proceeded.

"He's there," Pick insisted. "He was there early this morning, sitting all by himself at one of the picnic tables."

"Well, I don't see him now."

"And you want *me* to stop griping? Criminy!" He rode her shoulder in silence for a moment. "What does he want this time? Did the Scott girl say?"

"Nope. I don't think she knows."

Nest's boots crunched and skidded against the frosty dampness that had melted earlier and was now refreezing. She'd left both children with Bennett, who seemed confused and out of sorts from her encounter with Two Bears. There's an Indian waiting outside in the park, she'd reported. Bear Claw, she'd called him. Ross was in the shower. Maybe he didn't need to know about this. Maybe he didn't even have to find out O'olish Amaneh was there. Maybe cows could fly.

She wasn't kidding herself about what the Indian's appearance meant. When Two Bears showed up, it meant trouble of the worst kind. She could have predicted his coming, she realized, if she had let herself. With Findo Gask sniffing around in search of the gypsy morph, John Ross bringing the morph to her in an effort to save it, and a deadly confrontation between the paladins of the Word and the Void virtually assured, it was inevitable that O'olish Amaneh would be somewhere close at hand.

A dog came bounding across the park, a black Lab, but its owner's whistle brought it around and back toward where it had come from. She glanced behind her at the house, shadowed in the graying light and heavy trees, remote and empty-seeming. She found herself wondering anew about the unexpected appearance of Larry Spence. One thing was certain. He had come to her for something more than a warning about drug sales in the park, and it clearly had to do with John Ross. Larry didn't like Ross, but she couldn't figure out why. She didn't think they had even met when Ross had come to Hopewell fifteen years ago. Even if they had, Larry wouldn't be carrying a grudge that long, not without more reason than she could envision. It was something else, something more recent.

"There he is," Pick said.

Two Bears stood next to the toboggan slide, a dark shadow within the heavy timbers. He was O'olish Amaneh in the language of his people, the Sinnissippi. He had told Nest once that he was the last of them, that his people were all gone. She shivered at the memory. But Two Bears was much more than a Native American. Two Bears was another of the Word's messengers, a kind of prophet, a chronicler of things lost in the past and a seer of things yet to come.

He moved out to meet her as she approached, as imperturbable as ever, big and weather-burnt, black hair braided and shining, looking for all the world as if he hadn't aged a day. Indeed, even after fifteen years, he didn't seem to have aged at all.

"Little bird's Nest," he said with that slow, warm rumble, hands lifting to clasp her own.

"O'olish Amaneh," she said, and placed her hands in his, watching them disappear in the great palms.

He did not move to embrace her, but simply stood looking at her, dark eyes taking her measure. She was nearly as tall as he was now, but she felt small and vulnerable in his presence.

"You have done much with your life since we spoke last," he said finally, releasing her hands. "Olympics, world championships, honors of all sorts. You have grown wings and flown far. You should be proud."

She smiled and shook her head. "I have a failed marriage, no family, no future, a ghost wolf living inside me, and a house full of trouble." She held his steady gaze with her own. "I don't have time for pride."

He nodded. "Maybe you never did." His eyes shifted to Pick. "Still have your shy little friend, I see. Mr. Pick, the park looks tended and sound, the magic in balance. You are a skilled caretaker."

Pick frowned and gave a small *humph*, then nodded grudgingly. "I could use a little help."

Two Bears smiled faintly. "Some things never change." His eyes shifted back to Nest. "Walk with me. We can talk better down by the river."

He started away without waiting for her response, and she found herself following. They moved beyond the slide and down into the trees, edging slowly toward the icy skin of the bayou. The temperature was dropping quickly as the afternoon lengthened and the skies darkened further, and their breath formed white clouds in the air before them. Nest was tempted to speak first, to ask the obvious, but Two Bears had asked to speak with her, so she thought it best to wait on him.

"It feels good to hear you speak my name, to know that you have not forgotten it," he said, looking off into the distance.

As if she could, she thought without saying so. As if it were possible. She had encountered Two Bears only twice, but both times her life had been changed forever. O'olish Amaneh and John Ross, harbingers of change: she wondered if they ever thought of themselves that way. Both served the Word, but in different ways, and their relationship was something of a mystery. Two Bears had given Ross the rune-carved staff that was both the talisman of his power and the chain that bound him to his fate. Ross had tried at least once to give the staff back and failed. Each had come to Nest both as savior and executioner, but the roles had shifted back and forth between them, and in some ways they remained unclear. They were fond of her, but not of each other. Perhaps their roles placed restrictions on their feelings. Perhaps fondness for her was allowed, while fondness for each other was not.

She was not certain how she felt about them. She guessed she liked Ross better for having witnessed his vulnerability ten years ago in Seattle, when a demon had almost claimed him through misguided love. He had lost almost everything then, stripped of illusion and hope. In a few seconds of blinding recognition, he discovered how deeply pervasive evil was and how impossible it would be to walk away from his battle against it. He had taken up the black staff of his office once more, reclaimed his life as a Knight of the Word, and gone on because there was nothing else for him to do. She found him brave and wonderful because of that.

By the same token, she guessed, she had distanced herself from Two Bears. It wasn't for what he had done, but for what she had discovered he might do. In Seattle, he had come to observe, to see if she could change the direction in which John Ross had drifted and by doing so enable him to escape the trap that was closing about him. Two Bears had come to watch, but if she had failed in her efforts, he had come to act as well, to make certain that whatever else happened, John Ross would not become a servant of the Void. He had made that clear to her in urging her to go to Ross, even after John had rejected her help, and it had given her an understanding of Two Bears that she would just as soon not have.

But that was long ago, she thought, walking through the park with him, *and these are different times.*

"I'm surprised you showed yourself to Bennett," she said finally, abandoning her resolve to wait longer on him.

"She needed someone to protect her from evil spirits." He kept his gaze directed straight ahead, and she could not determine if he was serious.

"I had a visit from a demon named Findo Gask," she said.

"An evil spirit of the sort I was talking about. One of the worst. But you already know that."

She scuffed at the frozen ground impatiently. "John Ross is here as well. He brought a gypsy morph to me."

"A houseful of trouble, as you claim, when you add in the young woman and her child." He might have been talking about the weather. "What will you do?"

She made a face. "I was hoping you might tell me." On her shoulder, Pick was muttering in irritation, but she couldn't tell who or what he was upset with.

Two Bears stopped a dozen yards from the riverbank in a stand of winter grasses and gray hickory. He looked at her quizzically. "It is not my place to tell you what to do, little bird's Nest. You are a grown woman, one possessing uncommon strength of mind and heart and body. You have weathered difficult times and harsh truths. The answers you seek are yours to provide, not mine."

She frowned, impatient with his evasiveness. "But you asked to speak to me, O'olish Amaneh."

He shrugged. "Not about this. About something else." He began walking again, and Nest followed. "A houseful of trouble," he repeated, skirting a stand of hackberry and stalks of dried itch weed, moving toward the ravine below the deep woods, following a tiny stream of snowmelt upstream from the bayou. "A houseful of trouble can make a prisoner of you. To get free, you must empty your house of what is bad and fill it with what is good."

"You mean I should throw everybody out and start over?" She arched one eyebrow at him. "Bring in some new guests?"

Still walking steadily ahead, as if he had a destination in mind and a firm intention of reaching it, he did not look at her. "Sometimes change is necessary. Sometimes we recognize the need for it, but we don't know how to achieve it. We misread its nature. We think it is beyond us, failing to recognize that our inability to act is a problem of our own making. Change is the solution we require, but it is not a goal that is easily reached. Identifying and disposing of what is troubling to us requires caution and understanding."

He was telling her something in that obscure, oblique way he employed when talking of problems and solutions, believing that everyone must resolve things on their own, and the best he could do was to offer a flashlight for use on a dark path. She struggled with the light he had provided, but it was too weak to be of help.

"Everyone in my house needs me," she advised quietly. "I can't ask them to leave, even if allowing them to stay places me in danger."

He nodded. "I would expect nothing less of you."

"So the trouble that fills my house, as you put it, will have to be dealt with right where it is, I guess."

"You have dealt with trouble in your house before, little bird's Nest."

She thought about it a moment. He was speaking of Gran and Old Bob, fifteen years earlier, when John Ross had come to her for the first time, and she had learned the truth about her star-crossed family. But this was different. The secrets this time were not hers, but belonged to the gypsy morph. Or perhaps to John Ross.

Didn't they?

She looked at him sharply, sensing suddenly that he was talking about her after all, that he was giving her an insight into her own life.

"Not all the troubles that plague us are ours to solve," Two Bears advised, walking steadily on. "Life provides its own solutions to some, and we must accept those solutions as we would the changing of the seasons." He glanced at her expectantly.

"Well, I'm not much good at sitting back and waiting for life to solve my problems for me."

"No. And this is not what you should do. You should solve those problems you understand well, but leave the others alone. You should provide solutions where you are able and accept that this is enough." He paused, then sighed. "In a houseful of trouble, not everything can be salvaged."

Well, okay, she was thinking, you save what you can and let go of the rest. Fair enough. But how was she supposed to save anything if she didn't know where to start?

"Can you tell me something about the gypsy morph?" she tried hopefully.

He nodded. "Very powerful magic. Very unpredictable. A gypsy morph becomes what it will, if it becomes anything at all, which is rare. Mostly it fails to find its form and goes back with the air, wild and unreachable. Spirits understand it, for they occupy space with it. They brush against it, pass through it, float upon it, before it becomes a solid thing, while it is still waiting to take form." He shrugged. "It is an enigma waiting for an answer."

She blew out a cloud of breath. "Well, how do I go about finding out what that answer is? This morph has become a little boy. What does that mean? Is that the form it intends to take? What does it want with me? It spoke my name to John Ross, but now that it's here it doesn't even look at me."

They stopped on the rickety wooden bridge that crossed the nearly frozen trickle of the winter stream. Two Bears leaned on the railing, hands clasped.

"Talk to him, little bird's Nest."

"What?"

"Have you said anything to him? This little boy, have you spoken to him on your own?"

She thought about it a moment. "No."

"The solution is often buried somewhere in the problem. If the gypsy morph requires you, it may choose to tell you so. But perhaps it needs to know you care first."

She thought about it a moment. The gypsy morph was a child, a newborn less than thirty days formed, and as a four-year-old boy, it might be necessary that he be reassured and won over. She hadn't done that. She hadn't even tried, feeling pressed and rushed by Ross. The morph might need her badly, but needing and trusting were two different things entirely.

"All right," she said.

"Good." He lifted away from the bridge, straightening. "Now I will explain my reason for asking to speak with you. It is simple. I am your friend, and I came to say good-bye. I am the last of the Sinnissippi, and I have come home to be with my people. I wanted you to know, because it is possible I will not see you again."

Nest stared, absorbing the impact of his words. "Your people are all dead, O'olish Amaneh. Does this mean you will die, too?"

He laughed, and his laugh was hearty and full. "You should see your face, little bird's Nest! I would be afraid to die with such a fierce countenance confronting me!

Mr. Pick! Look at her! Such fierce resolution and rebuke in her eyes! How do you withstand this power when it is turned on you?"

He sobered then, and shook his head. "This is difficult to explain, but I will try. By joining with my ancestors, with my people, who are gone from this earth, I do not have to give up my own life in the way you imagine. But I must bond with them in a different form. By doing so, I must give up something of myself. It is difficult to know beforehand what this will require. I say good-bye as a precaution, in the event I am not able to return to you."

"Transmutation?" she asked. "You will become something else."

"In a sense. But then, I always was." He brushed the matter off with a wave of his big hand. "If I leave, I will not be gone forever. Like the seasons, I will still be in the seeds of the earth, waiting." He shrugged. "My leaving is a small thing. I will not be missed."

She exhaled sharply. "Don't say that. It isn't true."

There was a long silence as they faced each other in the graying winter light, motionless in the cold, breath clouding the air before their intense faces. "It isn't true for you," he said finally. "I am grateful for that."

She was still fighting to accept the idea that he would not be there anymore, that he would be as lost to her as Gran and Old Bob, as her mother and her father, as so many of her friends. It was a strange reaction to have to someone she had encountered only twice before and had such mixed feelings about. It was an odd response no matter how she looked at it. The closest parallel she could draw was to Wraith, when he had disappeared on her eighteenth birthday, gone forever it seemed, until she discovered him anew inside her.

Would it be like that with O'olish Amaneh?

"When will this happen?" she asked, her voice tight and small.

"When it is time. Perhaps it will not happen at all. Perhaps the spirits of my people will not have me."

"Perhaps they'll throw you back when they find out you talk in riddles all the time!" Pick snapped.

Two Bears' laughter boomed through the empty woods. "Perhaps if they do, I will have to come live with you, Mr. Pick!" He glanced at Nest. "Come, walk with me some more."

They retraced their steps down the ravine toward the bayou, then along the riverbank where the woods hugged the shoreline, the dark, skeletal limbs crisscrossing the graying skies. The air was crisp and cold, but there was a fresh dampness as well, the smell of incoming snow, thick and heavy. The Rock was frozen solid below the toboggan run, and there would be sleds on the ice by nightfall.

When they reached the edge of the woods and were in sight of the wooden chute where it opened onto the ice, Two Bears stopped.

"Even when I am with my people, you may see me again, little bird's Nest," he said.

She wrinkled her nose. "Like a ghost?"

"Perhaps. Are you afraid of what that might mean?"

She gave him a look. "We're friends, aren't we?"

"Always."

"Then I have no reason to be afraid."

He shook his head in contradiction. "If I come to you, I will do so as my ancestors did for me in the park fifteen years ago—in dreams. They came to you as well that night. Do you remember?"

She did. Fifteen years ago, her dreams of the Sinnissippi had shown Gran as a young girl, running with a demon in the park, feeders chasing after her, a wild, reckless look in her dark eyes. They had revealed truths that had changed everything.

"There is always cause to be afraid of what our dreams will show us," he whispered. One hand lifted to touch her face gently. "Speak my name once more."

"O'olish Amaneh," she said.

"No one will ever say it and give me greater pleasure. The winds bear your words to the heavens and scatter them as stars."

He gestured skyward, and her eyes responded to the gesture, searching obediently.

When she looked back again, he was gone.

"Just tell me this," Pick said after a long moment of silence. "Do you have any idea what he was talking about?"

John Ross came down the hallway to the living room and found Bennett Scott sitting in a chair reading a *Sports Illustrated* while Harper colored paper on the floor. The gypsy morph knelt on the couch and stared out the window as if turned to stone.

Bennett looked up, and he asked, "Where's Nest?"

She shrugged. "Out in the park, talking with some Indian."

A cold space settled in the pit of his stomach. Two Bears. He leaned heavily on his staff, thinking that it was all going to happen again, a new confrontation between the Word and the Void, another battle in an endless war. What was expected of him this time? To unlock the secret of the morph, he knew. But if he failed . . .

He brushed his thoughts aside, finding they spiraled down into a darkness he didn't care to approach. He thought back suddenly to the Fairy Glen and the Lady, to his last visit there, and to the secret he had discovered and could never share with anyone. Thinking on it made him suddenly weary of his life.

"Are you all right?" Bennett Scott asked him.

He almost laughed, thinking that he would never be all right, thinking the question strange coming from her. "Yes," he said, and walked into the kitchen.

He had poured himself a fresh cup of coffee and was halfway through it when the doorbell rang. When it rang a second time, he walked to the kitchen entry and looked into the living room. Harper was in her mother's lap, a storybook in her hands. Bennett glanced up and shrugged indifferently, so Ross limped down the hallway instead.

When he opened the front door, Josie Jackson was waiting.

CHAPTER 12

It had been fifteen years since they had seen each other, but it might just as easily have been yesterday. Physically, they had changed, weathered and lined by the passing years and life's experiences, settled into midlife and aware of the steady approach of old age. But emotionally, they were frozen in time, locked in the same space they had occupied at the moment they had spoken last. Their feelings for each other ran so deep and their memories of the few days they had shared were so vivid and immediate that they were reclaimed instantly by what they had both thought lost forever.

"John?" Josie said his name softly, but the shock mirrored in her dark eyes was bright and painful.

She was older, but not enough so that it made more than a passing impression on him. Mostly, she was the way he remembered her. She still had that tanned, fresh look and that scattering of freckles across the bridge of her nose. Her blond, tousled hair was cut shorter, but it accentuated her face, lending it a soft, cameo beauty.

Only the smile was missing, that dazzling, wondrous smile, but he had no reason to expect she would be inclined to share it now with him. When he met her, the attraction was instantaneous and electric. Even though he knew that a relationship with her would be disastrous, particularly one in which he fell in love, he let it happen anyway. For two days, he allowed himself to imagine what it would be like to have a normal life, to share himself with a woman he cared about, to pretend it might lead to something permanent. Together, they spent an evening in Sinnissippi Park at a picnic and dance. When he was attacked and beaten by men who believed him someone other than who he was, she took him home, washed him, bandaged him, soothed him, and gave herself to him. When he left her in the morning for a final confrontation with the demon who was Nest Freemark's father, walking away from her as she sat in her car looking after him, he had thought he would never see her again.

"Hello," she said, and he realized he hadn't said anything, but was simply standing there in the doorway, staring.

"Hello, Josie," he managed, his own voice sounding strange to him, forced and dry. "How are you?"

"Good." The shock in her eyes had eased, but she didn't seem to be having any better luck than he was with conversation. "I didn't know you were here."

"My coming was kind of unexpected."

He felt slow and awkward in her presence, aware of his ragged appearance in old jeans, plaid work shirt, and scuffed boots. His long hair, tied back from his face and still damp from his shower, was shot through with gray and had receded above his temples. He bore the scars from his battles with the minions of the Void across his sun-browned face and forearms, and the damage to his leg ached more often these days. He found Josie as fresh and youthful as ever, but believed that to her he must look old and used up.

He glanced down at the plate of cookies she was holding in her hands, seeing them for the first time.

Her eyes lowered. "I brought them for Nest. She always bakes cookies for everyone else, so I thought someone ought to bake some for her. Can I come in?"

"Of course," he said hurriedly, stepping back. "Guess my mind is somewhere else. Come in." He waited until she was inside and then closed the door. "Nest is out in the park, but she should be back in a few minutes."

They stared at each other in the shadowed entry, hearing the ticking of the grandfather clock and the low murmur of Bennett reading to Harper.

"You look tired, John," she said finally.

"You look wonderful."

The words were out of his mouth before he could stop them. Josie flushed, then released that blinding smile, and he felt as if nothing on earth would ever be more welcome.

"That smile—now there's something I've thought about often," he admitted, shaking his head at what he was feeling inside, knowing already he shouldn't allow it, unable to help himself.

She held his gaze, the smile in place. "I've missed you, too. Isn't that remarkable?"

"It's been a long time," he said.

"Not so long that you felt the need to call or write?"

He gave her a rueful look. "I've never been much good at either. I tell myself to do it, but I just don't follow through. I don't really know what to say. It feels strange trying to put down what I'm thinking on paper or to say it into a phone. I don't know. Ask Nest. I haven't called or written her either."

The smile faded, and she shook her head slowly. "It's all right. I guess I never really thought you would." She handed him the plate of cookies. "Here, hold these for a moment, will you?"

She shrugged out of her coat and hung it on the coatrack, draping her scarf on top and shoving her gloves into the pockets. She brushed back her hair self-consciously, smoothed her blouse where it tucked into her pants, and took the cookies back.

"Pour me a glass of milk and I'll share," she offered, the smile back in place again.

They walked down the hall past the living room, and Bennett and Harper looked up. Little John, kneeling on the couch, never moved. Josie leaned around Ross to say hello and asked if anyone would like a snack. The women didn't seem to know each other, but neither made an effort to introduce herself, so Ross let the matter alone. He went into the kitchen with Josie, helped her with glasses of milk, then remained leaning against the counter looking off into the tree-shrouded distance while Josie carried a tray for Bennett and the children into the living room.

When she returned, he sat with her at the old wooden table, the cookies and milk between them. For a moment, no one spoke.

"Do you still have the coffee shop?" he asked finally.

"Yep. Mostly the same customers, too. Nothing changes." She arched one eyebrow. "You?"

"Traveling," he said. "Working odd jobs here and there, trying to make sense of my life. You know. How's your daughter?"

"Grown up, married, two kids. I'm a grandmother. Who would have thought?"

"Not me. I don't see you that way."

"Thanks. How long are you here for?"

He shook his head. "I don't know yet. Through Christmas, I guess. It depends."

She nodded slowly. "On them?" She indicated the living room with a nod of her head.

"Well, on the boy, at least."

She waited, watching him carefully. When he didn't say anything, she asked, "Who is he?"

He cleared his throat softly. "He's my son. I'm taking him to Chicago to see a specialist. He doesn't speak."

She went very still. "Is that your wife and daughter with him?"

"What?"

"The woman and the little girl?"

He blinked. "No. Why would you—No, she's barely twenty, and I don't . . ."

"You seemed a little awkward about introducing them," she said.

"Oh, well, maybe so." He shook his head. "I don't know them, is the problem. I just got here last night, and they were already here, and I don't know much more about them than you do."

She took a bite of cookie and a sip of milk, eyes shifting away. "Tell me about your son. Where is his mother?"

He shook his head again. "I don't know." He caught himself too late, the lie already spoken, and quickly added, "He's adopted. Single-parent adoption." His mind raced. "That's another reason I'm here. I'm not much good at this. I'm hoping Nest can help."

He was getting in deeper, but he couldn't seem to stop himself. He had never thought he would have to explain the gypsy morph to anyone except Nest, that he would slip in at night, tell her why he was there, then wait for something to develop, and slip out again. Instead, he found himself in a situation where he was forced to make things up almost faster than he could manage.

"What is it you think Nest can do?"

He stared at her wearily. "I don't know," he admitted, realizing he was saying the same thing over and over, but this time speaking the truth. "I'm in over my head, and I don't know who else to turn to."

Her face softened instantly. "John, you can ask Nest for anything. You know that. If she can help you, she will." She paused. "I hope you know that you can ask me, as well."

He grinned ruefully. "It helps hearing you say it. I wasn't sure how things stood between us."

She nodded slowly. "They stand the way they have always stood. Can't you tell?"

The way she looked at him when she said it, he guessed maybe he could.

* * *

Deputy Sheriff Larry Spence pulled over at the Quik Stop and went inside to buy some gum. When he came out, hunching down into his heavy leather coat for warmth, taking note of the graying skies and gusting winds, he paused at the pay phone attached to the side of the building and dialed the number FBI Agent Robinson had given him. He still wasn't sure about this whole business, but he didn't want to take any chances with Nest.

He drummed his fingers on the metal phone shell while he waited for someone to pick up. He didn't much like Robinson or that woman agent, especially after their visit to his house. His kids didn't seem to like them much either. Neither had slept very well last night, and Billy had come awake half a dozen times screaming about knives. No, he didn't much like it. It seemed to him they might have found a better place to talk to him about John Ross. He'd thought about calling the bureau, checking up on the agents, but he was afraid it would make him look foolish to do so. Anyway, all they wanted to know was whether or not Ross was out there. Once he told them that, he was done with the matter.

Then, maybe, the buzzing in his ears would lessen and the headaches would go away and he wouldn't be spending all his time arguing within himself about what he should do.

The phone picked up on the other end, and a man said, "Yes?"

The buzzing stopped. "Agent Robinson?"

"Good afternoon, Deputy Sheriff Spence." Robinson's voice was smooth and reassuring. "What do you have for me?"

Spence looked off into the distance, unsure once more. Ross didn't seem like much of a threat to him. Hell, he could barely walk with that bum leg. Nest didn't seem all that taken with him either, not in the way Robinson had suggested she was. He was pretty old for her, more like a father. It just didn't feel right.

"Deputy?"

"Sorry, I was checking on something." He brushed his concerns aside, hearing whispers of derision and urgency that warned him of the dangers of equivocation. He was anxious to get this over with. "I was out at Nest Freemark's house just a little while ago. John Ross was there."

"Good work, Deputy. What did you tell them was the reason for your visit?"

"Oh, I made something up about checking on drug sales in the park, said it was a rumor we were investigating. I just asked if they'd seen anything, either of them." He flashed on the angry response he'd gotten from Nest when he'd pushed the matter with Ross, and decided not to say anything about that part.

There was a pause on the other end. "Did you notice anything unusual? Was Ross carrying anything?"

Spence frowned. "Like what?"

"I don't know, Deputy. I'm asking you."

Spence flushed at the rebuke. "He was carrying a walking stick. He's got a bad leg."

"Yes. Anything else?"

"Not that I could see." His breath clouded the air in front of him. The buzzing returned, working its way around inside of his head, making him crazy. He pushed hard at his temples. "I don't get it. What am I supposed to be looking for?"

Robinson's voice was iron sheathed in velvet. "You know better than to ask me that, Deputy. This is an ongoing investigation. I'm not at liberty to reveal everything just now."

The whispers burned their way past the buzzing, filling Larry Spence's head with sound and pain. Don't ask stupid questions! Don't go into places you don't belong! Do what you're told! Remember what's at stake!

Nest! Nest was at stake!

He pictured her in his mind, upset with him now, and it was all because of John Ross. He pressed at his temples anew and leaned into the shelter of the call box, suddenly angry and belligerent. It wasn't right, the way she protected him. What was he doing here, anyway? He was taking up all the space in her life, so that there was no room for anyone else.

Like me! She should be with me!

Just do as you're told, and everything will be all right, someone seemed to say. Then he heard Robinson add, "I'll be in touch."

He caught his breath. "But I thought that was all you wanted me to do," he said, and the line went dead.

Ross and Josie finished their cookies and milk, waiting on Nest's return. Josie talked about life in Hopewell, about working still at Josie's, about the people who came in and the way they were. Ross mostly listened, not having much he could tell her that wouldn't reveal things he wanted kept secret. He did say he had gone back to university a couple of times, audited some courses, taught a few classes. He talked a little of some of the places he had been. Josie listened and didn't press, taking what he would give her, giving him the space he required when he chose to back away.

"I'd better be going," she said finally. "You can tell Nest I dropped by."

She rose, and he stood with her, levering himself up with his staff. "You sure you don't want to wait?"

"I don't think so." She carried their glasses and the empty plate to the sink and began rinsing them. "Will I see you again before you leave?" she called over her shoulder.

The question startled him. "I don't know," he said automatically. Then he added, "I hope so."

She turned, her eyes meeting his. "Would you like to come to dinner tomorrow night?"

The back door opened and closed, and they both looked toward the hall. A moment later Nest appeared, rubbing her hands briskly. "Cold out there. Hi, Josie." She looked from one to the other. "Have I missed anything?"

"We were just visiting," Josie Jackson offered brightly. "I stopped by with some cookies, Nest. John was keeping me company." She hesitated only a moment. "I was just asking if he might like to come to dinner tomorrow night."

Nest never looked at John Ross. She walked over to the sink, picked up a cookie from the tray, and began munching on it. "Sounds like a good idea to me. Why don't you go, John?"

Ross felt himself transfixed by Josie's eyes. "You're all invited, of course," she added, her smile warm and encouraging.

"No, thanks anyway," Nest interjected quickly. "I have a Christmas party to attend. I was planning on taking Bennett and Harper with me. I'll just take Little John, too. There will be lots of other kids there."

She looked at Ross. "John, you go to Josie's."

Ross was thinking that he shouldn't do this. He wanted to, but it could only lead to the same sort of problem he had encountered with Josie Jackson fifteen years ago. It didn't make any sense to let history repeat itself when he knew he couldn't change it. Besides, it meant leaving the morph alone with Nest, which was dangerous for her. It meant taking a risk of the sort he should never even consider.

On the other hand, Nest Freemark seemed to be the gypsy morph's only hope. He had brought the morph to her in an effort to save it. He would have to give it up to her at some point, and time was running out. Maybe it would help if they could spend some time together without him.

"John?" Nest said quietly.

He was still looking at Josie, taking in her familiar features, her face and body, so much of it remembered so well after all these years. Everything about Josie was just right, a composite so perfectly formed that he couldn't imagine her being any other way. Being with her made him feel as if anything was possible and none of it mattered. Only her, and only now.

Fifteen years, and she still made him feel like this. A sweet ache filled him, then a small whisper of despair. No matter how she made him feel, it would end in the same way.

"I'd better take a rain check."

Josie stared at him without speaking for a moment. "All right, I understand." She started for the kitchen entry, her eyes lowered. "Bye, Nest."

She went down the hall, stopped to pull on her coat, scarf, and gloves, and went out the front door. Her car started up in the drive and pulled out onto Woodlawn.

Nest busied herself at the kitchen counter, putting away the rest of the cookies. When she looked at Ross again, her expression was neutral. "Sit down, and I'll tell you what happened in the park."

He did as she asked and listened patiently as she talked about her meeting with Two Bears. But his mind drifted like smoke on the wind.

Outside, it was beginning to snow.

CHAPTER 13

By nightfall, eight inches had fallen and more was on the way. Local forecasts called for as much as two feet by morning, and a second storm was expected by Christmas. Ross listened to the weather report on the radio and stared out the kitchen window at the thick white fluff that blanketed everything for as far as the eye could see—which wasn't far, because snow continued to fall in big, swirling flakes that reflected the street and porch lights in gauzy yellow rainbows and curtained away the night.

Bennett Scott was sitting on the living-room floor with Harper, working on an old wooden puzzle. Harper would lift each piece and study it, then set it down again and move on. The puzzle had only twelve pieces, but she seemed to regard the preparation process as more important than actually building anything. Little John had turned away from the window and was sitting on the floor beside them, watching intently. He still wasn't saying anything. He still barely paid attention when he was spoken to. He was still a complete enigma.

Nest put together a stew for dinner, chopping up potatoes, onions, carrots, and celery, adding frozen peas, and throwing the whole mess in with chunks of browned chuck roast and some beef broth. She worked on memory and instinct, not from a recipe, and every now and then she would hesitate and consider before choosing or passing on an ingredient. She spoke sparingly to Ross, who sat there with his gaze directed out toward the snowfall and his thoughts drifting to Josie.

It bothered him that he found himself so obsessed with her. It wasn't as if he hadn't thought of her before he'd seen her this afternoon; he'd done so often. But his memories of Josie had seemed part of a distant past that was unconnected to his present. He supposed that seeing her again and remembering how strongly he felt about her simply pointed up the emptiness of his life. Bereft of family and friends, of loved ones, of relationships, of an existence of the sort other people enjoyed, he was one of the homeless he had worked with years ago in Seattle. It was only natural, he supposed, that he should want those things that others had and he did not.

Once or twice he pondered the appearance of Two Bears, but there was nothing he could make of the Sinnissippi that wasn't self-evident. A pivotal moment in the war between the Word and the Void was at hand, and Two Bears was there to monitor what happened. Perhaps he was there to attempt to tip the balance, as he had done twice before in Nest Freemark's life, but Ross knew it was pointless to try to guess what O'olish Amaneh intended. The Indian lived in a sphere of existence outside that of normal men, and he would do what was required of him. For Ross to dwell on the matter was a waste of time.

But so was thinking of Josie. So there he was.

It was after six and dark two hours already when Robert Heppler called. He wanted to know if Nest would go tobogganing in the park. A check of the ice by the park service people revealed it was strong enough to take the weight of an eight-man sled, and with the snow packed down on the chute, the slide was slick and ready. Robert was taking Kyle while Amy stayed home with his parents, but he needed a few more bodies for weight. How about it?

While she was listening to Robert and before Ross even knew the nature of the conversation, he saw her do something odd. She started to say it probably wasn't a good time or something of the sort, and then she looked off into the living room where Harper and Little John were sitting with Bennett, hesitated a moment, her gaze lost and filled with hidden thoughts, and then said she would come if she could bring her houseguests, two adults and two children. Robert must have said yes, because she said they would meet him at the slide at eight, and hung up.

She relayed the conversation to Ross, then shrugged. "It might be good for the children to get out of the house and do something kids like."

He nodded, thinking she was jeopardizing the morph's safety by taking it out where it would be exposed and vulnerable, but thinking as well that the morph was useless if she couldn't get close enough to it to discover what it wanted of her and that maybe doing something together would help. There was no rational reason to believe going down a toboggan slide would make one iota of difference to anything, but nothing else seemed to be working. Nest had gone out to Little John several times before starting dinner, sitting with him, trying to talk to him, and there had been absolutely no response. She was as baffled by the morph's behavior as he was, and trying something different, anything, no matter how remote any chance of it working might seem, was all that was left.

"Maybe Little John will like Kyle," she offered, as if reading his thoughts. "Maybe he'll talk with someone closer to his age."

Ross nodded, moving to help with silverware and napkins as she carried plates to the table and began arranging the place settings. The morph had taken the form of a child for a reason, so treating it like a child might reveal something. He thought it a long shot at best, but he couldn't think of anything better. He felt drained by the events of the past twenty-odd days, and the gypsy morph was a burden he wasn't sure he could carry much longer.

They sat at the table and ate stew with hot rolls and butter and cold glasses of milk, the morph eating almost nothing, Harper eating enough for three. Then they cleared the dishes and bundled into sweaters, parkas, boots, scarves, and gloves, and headed out into the night. Nest had enough extra clothing that she was able to outfit everyone, even Ross, who wore spares she had kept from her days with Paul. The night was crisp and still, and the wind had died away. Snow continued to fall in a hazy drifting of thick, wet flakes, and the ground squeaked beneath their boots. No other tracks marred the pristine surface across her backyard and into the ball diamonds, so they blazed their own trail, heads bent to the snowy carpet, breath pluming the air before them.

Ross limped gingerly at the rear of the group, his staff making deep round holes where he set it for support. All the while, he glanced around watchfully, still not trusting Little John's safety. As they crossed the service road, he caught a flicker of movement out of the corner of his eye. An owl winged its way through the trees bordering the residences, lifting away across the park, a tiny shadow attached to its neck—Pick, on patrol.

"Mommy, look!" Harper called out, dancing this way and that with her mouth open and her tongue out, trying to catch snowflakes. "Mmmm, stawbury! Mmmm, 'nilla!"

They crossed the open spaces of the ball diamonds toward the east end of the park and the toboggan slide. Lights blazed from the parking area, which was filled with cars, and shouts and screams rose from the slopes where the sleds were making their runs. Ross peered through the snowfall, which was slowing now, turning to a lazy drifting of scattered flakes against a stark backdrop of black sky and white, snow-covered earth. The toboggan slide came into view, timbers blocky, dark struts against the haze of lights, looking like the bones of a creature half-eaten.

"Mommy, Mommy!" Harper was calling excitedly, pulling on Bennett's arm, trying to get her to move faster.

They found Robert waiting with the toboggan and Kyle throwing snowballs at another boy. Nest made quick introductions. Robert seemed pleased to see Bennett Scott and Harper and wary of Ross. Ross didn't blame him. Robert Heppler had no reason to remember him with any fondness. But Robert shook his hand firmly, as if to prove his determination to weather the unexpected encounter, and beckoned them onto the slide.

The toboggan slide had been in Sinnissippi Park since Nest was a small child. Various attempts had been made to dismantle it as unsafe, a climbing hazard that would eventually claim some unfortunate child's life or health and result in a serious lawsuit against the park district. But every time the subject came up for discussion, the hue and cry of the Hopewell populace was so strident that the park board let the matter drop.

The slide was built on a trestle framework of wood timbers fastened together by heavy iron bolts and sunk in concrete footings. A fifteen-foot-high platform encircled by a heavy railing was mounted by ladder. Two teams could occupy the platform at any given time, one already loaded and settled in the chute, the other waiting to take its place. The slide ran down from the top of the bluff to the edge of the bayou, where it opened onto the ice. A space had been cleared of snow all the way to the levee and the railroad tracks. A good run with enough weight could carry a sled that far.

At the top of the slide, a park district employee stood just to the right of the chute with a heavy wooden lever that locked the sled in place while it was being loaded and released to free the sled when it was ready to make its run.

When he got a close look at how it all worked, Ross took Nest aside. "I can't do this," he told her quietly. "Getting up there is just too hard."

"Oh." She glanced at his staff. "I forgot."

His eyes shifted to the others. "I'd better wait here."

She nodded. "Okay, John. I'll watch him."

He didn't have to ask whom she was talking about. He stood aside as Robert got the rest of them in line, carrying the toboggan tipped on end with its steering rope hanging down the bed. When they reached the ladder and began to climb, Nest took the lower end of the toboggan to help boost it up. Ross glanced downhill to where the toboggan chute rested comfortably in its cradle of support timbers, lowering toward the earth as it neared the ice in a long, gradual incline. Lights brightened the pathway, leaving the chute revealed until it reached the ice. On the ice, everything was dark.

Robert's group climbed the platform and stood waiting for the sled ahead of them to load and release. Ross shifted his weight in the snow, leaning on his staff, his eyes wandering off into the trees. A pair of feeders slid like oil through the shadows. He tensed, then shook his head admonishingly. *Stop worrying,* he told himself. There were lights and people everywhere. A few feeders creeping around in the darkness didn't necessarily mean anything.

He glanced skyward for Pick, but didn't see him.

Moments later, Robert's group was climbing onto the sled, Robert steering, Kyle behind him, then Bennett, Harper, Little John, and Nest. They tucked themselves in place. Except for Robert, each had legs wrapped around the waist of the person ahead, hands and arms locked on shoulders. Kyle and Harper were laughing and shouting. Little John was staring off into the dark.

When the lock bar was released, the sled slid away from the loading platform into the night, picking up speed as it went, the sound of its flat runners on the frozen snow and ice a rough, loud *chitter*. Down the sled went, tearing through a wave of cold and snow, of freezing air, of shouts and screams. Ross watched until it reached the ice and disappeared from view.

All around him, families were lining up for another run.

One run, however, was more than enough for Bennett Scott. Harper, crazy little kid, was eating it up, screaming and howling like a banshee all the way down the run, laughing hysterically when it was over, then begging all the way back up the slope to do it again.

"Mommy, Mommy, go fast, go fast!" she trilled.

If the ride wasn't enough to give Bennett heart failure, the climb would finish the job, and by the time she'd reached the top again, she was gasping for breath and desperate for a cigarette.

"Mind if I sit this one out?" she asked Nest as they lined up for another run. That creepy guy Ross was standing off to the side, looking like he was about to be jumped or something, and if he didn't have to go with his kid, then Bennett didn't see why she should feel obligated to go with hers.

"Sure," Nest agreed, peering at her. "Are you okay?"

Bennett shrugged. "Define *okay*. I just need a cigarette, that's all." She looked at Harper. "Honey, can you go with Nest, let Mommy take a break?"

The little girl gave her a questioning look, then nodded and turned away to say something to Kyle. He appeared to have hit it off with her, even if Little John hadn't. Creepy kid for a creepy father. She felt sorry for him, but that's the way things worked out. She should know.

Deliberately avoiding John Ross, who was looking somewhere else anyway, she moved away as the others took their place in line. She took a deep breath, her lungs aching with cold and fatigue, fished in her pocket for her cigarettes, knocked one loose from the pack, and reached for her lighter.

Someone else's lighter flared right in front of her face, and she dipped her cigarette tip to catch the fire. Drawing in a deep lungful of heat and smoke, she looked into Penny's wild green eyes.

"Hey, girlfriend," Penny said, snapping shut the lighter.

Bennett exhaled and blew smoke in her face. "Get away from me."

Penny smiled. "You don't mean that."

"Try me." Bennett began to move away.

"Wait!" Penny caught up to her and kept pace as she walked. "I got something for you."

"I don't want it."

"Sure you do. It's good stuff. White lightning and mellow smoke. It'll make you fly and glide all night. I took some earlier. Let me tell you, this town becomes a better place in a hurry."

Bennett sucked on her cigarette and kept her gaze turned away. "Just leave me alone, all right?"

"Look, you hate it here as much as me. Don't pretend you don't." Penny brushed at her wild hair, eyes darting everywhere at once, feral and hungry. "This town is for losers. It's nowhere! I keep trying to find something to do besides sit around listening to Grandma snore. There's not even a dance club! Bunch of bars with redneck mill workers and farmers. 'How's the crop this year, Jeb?' 'Oh, pretty fair, Harv.' Like that. Only way to get past losing your mind is doing a little something to keep sane."

"I'm off drugs." Bennett stopped at the edge of the trees where the darkness grew so heavy she couldn't make out even the trunks. She was already too far away from the light. "I'm clean and I'm staying clean."

"State of mind, girl," Penny sniffed. "There's clean and there's clean. You do what you want, what you need. You still stay clean."

"Yeah, right."

Penny shrugged. "So now what? You gonna go back up there for more toboggan fun?" Her eyes were on the platform, clearly outlined in the light. "Gonna join your friends?"

Bennett glanced up. Nest, Robert, and the children were standing on the platform, waiting to go next. "Maybe."

Penny laughed, her angular frame twisting for emphasis. "You lie like a rug. You wouldn't go back up there on a bet! But you make believe all you want, if it gets you through your pain. Me, I got a better way. Have a look at this."

She took out a plastic pouch filled with brilliant white powder, took a little of the powder on her finger, and snorted it in. She gasped once, then grinned. "Mother's milk, girl. Try a little?"

Bennett wet her lips, eyes fixed on the pouch. The need inside her was so strong she didn't trust herself to speak or move. She wanted a hit so bad she could hardly stand the thought. Just a little, she was thinking. Just this one time. Penny was right. She was all twisted up inside, fighting to stay straight and not really believing there was any hope for it.

It wouldn't hurt anything. I've used before and kept going. Besides, Harper will be all right, no matter what. Nest is here. Nest is looking after her, probably better than me. Harper likes Nest. She doesn't need me. Anyway, doing a little coke would probably give me some focus. Just a little. I can take as much as I want and stop. I've always been able to do that. I can quit anytime. Anytime I want.

Oh, God, she thought, and squeezed her eyes shut until it hurt. *No. No.* She folded her thin arms against her body and looked back at the toboggan slide. "You keep it."

Penny kept looking at her for a minute, then tucked the pouch back into her coat pocket. She glanced up at the platform, where Nest and the others were climbing onto the sled.

Her smile was a red slash on her pale face. "Better get back with your friends, take another ride down the chute," she said. She smiled in a dark sort of way, giving Bennett a look that whispered of bad feelings and hard thoughts.

Then she walked over to the edge of the rise and looked down at the bayou. "Be a good mom, why don't you? Keep your kid company." She reached into her pocket, brought out a flashlight, pointed it downhill, and clicked it on and off twice.

She turned back to Bennett, stone-faced. "Maybe later, girlfriend," she said. "There's always later."

She waved casually over her shoulder as she walked off.

Standing in the shelter of the big oaks and scrub birch bordering the bayou's edge, back where the lights from the toboggan run didn't penetrate, Findo Gask watched Penny Dreadful's flashlight blink twice from the top of the rise and smiled. Time to start demonstrating to Nest Freemark the consequences of engaging in uncooperative behavior. He'd wasted enough time on her, and he wasn't inclined to waste any more.

He stepped from the shadows to walk down to the water's edge. The water was all ice just now, of course. But everything was subject to change. It was just a matter of knowing how to apply the right sort of pressure. It was a lesson that Nest Freemark would have done well to learn before it was too late.

Garbed in his black frock coat and flat-brimmed hat, he might have been a preacher come to the river to baptize the newly converted. But the demon had something more permanent in mind than a cleansing of the soul. Baptism wasn't really up his alley in any case. Burial was more his style.

Aware of the clutch of feeders creeping hungrily out of the shadows to be close to him, he knelt beside the ice. Feeders were fond of Findo Gask; they could always depend on him for a good meal. He saw no reason to disappoint them now.

He reached down and touched the ice with his fingers, eyes closing in concentration. Slowly, a crack in the surface appeared, broadened and spread, then angled off into the darkness toward the clearing on the ice where the sleds usually ended their runs, close to where the levee that supported the railroad tracks rose like a black wall. He lifted his hand away from the ice and listened carefully. Out in the darkness where the crack had gone, dispatched by his magic, he could hear snapping and splintering, then the soft slosh of water.

A nice surprise would be waiting for Nest Freemark and her friends when they came down this time.

He stood up in time to catch a glimpse of a large bird streaking out of the trees behind him, bolting from cover toward the slide.

Atop the loading platform, the locking lever released.

The toboggan slid out of the starting gate with a crunching of ice crystals under wood runners, easing down the chute, quickly picking up speed. There were only five of them riding the sled now, Robert in front, gloved hands fastened on the steering ropes, Kyle behind him, Harper and Little John next, and Nest in the rear. Hunched close against each other, legs looped over hips and around waists, arms clasped about shoulders, and heads bent against the rush of wind and cold and snow, they watched the landscape of dark trees and hazy trail lights gradually begin to blur and lose shape.

"Hang on!" Robert shouted gleefully, grinning back over his shoulder.

"Hang on!" Harper repeated happily.

The chittering sound of runners pounding over packed snow, ice, and wooden boards grew louder as their speed increased, mixing with a rush of air until they could only barely hear themselves shouting and yelling in response to their excitement. Nest clutched at Little John, trying for a response, but the boy continued his stoic silence, blue eyes fastened on something out in the night, his pale child's face expressionless and distant.

"Eeeeek!" Harper screamed in mock horror, burying her face in Kyle's parka. "Too fast! Too fast!"

They were halfway down the slide, the darkness of the ice drawing steadily closer, the toboggan flying over the packed surface of the chute. Nest grinned, the burn of the wind on her cheeks sharp and exhilarating. It was a good run. Even with only five of them to give the sled weight, they were getting a smooth, fast ride, one that should carry them all the way to the levee. Ahead, Robert was bent all the way forward toward the sled's curled nose, trying to cut down wind resistance, anxious for more speed.

"Go, Robert!" she yelled impulsively.

They were almost to the end of the chute when a dark, winged shadow streaked out of the night, angling close, pulling even with Nest as she rode the sled. Huge wings and a barrel body hove into view, barely within her line of sight, and Pick's voice cried out in her ear, "Get off the sled, Nest! Gask's cracked the ice right ahead of you! Get off!"

At first she thought she was imagining things—catching a blurred glimpse of the owl, listening as Pick yelled at her out of nowhere, hearing words that sounded crazy and dangerous. She turned her head in response, half expecting the shadow and the words to disappear, to prove a figment of her imagination. Instead the shadow swung closer, barely clearing the heads of riders pulling their sleds uphill for another run, shouts of surprise breaking out as the sled on the chute and the trailing shadow swept past.

"Nest, get off now!" Pick screamed.

She felt a jolt of recognition, a moment of deep shock. She wasn't mistaking what she saw or heard. It was real.

The toboggan launched itself clear of the chute and onto the ice, tearing away through sudden darkness as the trail lights disappeared behind.

"Robert, turn the sled!" she screamed at him.

Robert glanced over his shoulder, confused. She reached forward with a lunge, jamming all three children together as she did so, grabbed Robert's right arm, and hauled back, causing him to jerk sharply on the steering rope and yank the sled out of its smooth run. But the ropes gave only minimal control, and the sled continued to rush ahead, skidding slightly sideways, but still on track.

"Nest, stop it!" Robert shouted back, yanking his arm free. "What are you doing?"

The darkness ahead was a black void beneath the clouded, snowy sky, and only a pair of very distant track lights provided any illumination. Nest felt her stomach clutch as she imagined what waited, and she yanked on Robert's arm anew.

"Robert! There's a hole in the ice!"

Finally, in desperation, she grabbed him by both shoulders, the children locked between them, shouting and screaming in protest, and launched herself sideways off the sled, pulling all of them with her. The toboggan tipped wildly, careened on its edge for a moment, then went over, spilling them onto the ice. Riders and sled separated, the former skidding across the ice into a snowbank, the latter continuing on into the dark.

Lying in a pile of bodies, gasping for breath and fighting for purchase on the bayou's slick surface, with Harper crying and Robert cursing, Nest heard a sudden sloshing of water. A dark premonition burned through her.

"Hush!" she hissed at the others, grabbing at them for emphasis, needing their silence in order to hear what was happening, but fearful of what might be listening for them as well. "Hush!"

They responded to the urgency of her words and went still. In the silence that followed, there was a rush of freezing wind across the open expanse of the bayou, and the temperature dropped thirty degrees and what little warmth the night had provided was suddenly sucked away. Ice cracked and snapped, shifting and reforming as the cold invaded its skin. Swiftly, the gap closed. There was a crunching of wood as the ice seized the toboggan, trapped it like a toothpick in a giant's dark maw, and sealed it away.

Nest took Harper in her arms and soothed her with soft words and a hug, quieting her sobs. Kyle was staring out into the darkness with eyes the size of dinner plates. Little John was staring with him, but with no expression on his face at all.

"Damn!" Robert whispered softly as the last of the terrifying ice sounds died away. "What was that?"

You don't want to know, Robert, Nest thought in the dark silence of her anger and fear.

Chapter 14

They trudged back up the slope from the now empty ice, Nest and Robert herding the children in front of them, no one saying much of anything in the aftermath of the spill. Toboggan runs had been suspended after they went over. Now the slide attendant, a twenty-year park employee named Ray Childress, a man Nest had known since she was a little girl, had dropped the locking bar across the chute, emptied the loading platform of people, and hurried down the hill to find out what had happened. On reaching them, he fell into step beside Robert, warned off of Nest, perhaps, by the look on her face. Robert did his best to explain, but the truth was he didn't understand either, so the best he could do was improvise and suggest that further runs that night probably weren't safe and the park service could investigate the matter better in daylight.

Bennett was next on the scene, bounding down the slope in a flurry of arms and legs, snatching up Harper with such force that the little girl cried out.

"Baby, baby, are you all right?" Still hugging and kissing her, she wheeled angrily on Nest. "What did you think you were doing out there? She's just a little girl! You had no right taking chances with her safety, Nest! I thought I could trust you!"

It was an irrational response, fueled by a mix of fear and self-recrimination. Nest understood. Bennett was an addict, and she viewed everything that happened as being someone else's fault, all the while thinking deep inside that it was really hers.

"I'm sorry, Bennett," she replied. "I did the best I could to keep Harper from any danger. It wasn't something I planned. Anyway, she did very well when we tipped over. She kept her head and held on to me. She was a very brave little girl."

"Sorry, Mommy," Harper said softly.

Bennett Scott glanced down at her, and all the anger drained away in a heartbeat. "It's okay, baby." She didn't look up. "Mommy's sorry, too. She didn't mean to sound so angry. I was just scared."

When they arrived at the top of the slope, Ray Childress told those still standing around to go home, that the slide was closed for the evening and would open again tomorrow if things worked out. The adults, already cold and thinking of warmer places, were just as happy, while the kids grumbled a bit before shuffling away, dragging their sleds behind them. Cars started up and began to pull out of the parking lot, headlights slashing through the trees, tires crunching on frozen snow. Flurries blew sideways in a sudden gust of wind, but the snowfall had slowed to almost nothing.

Nest checked the sky for some sign of Pick, but the sylvan had disappeared. Undoubtedly, Findo Gask was gone as well. She chastised herself for being careless, for thinking that the demon wouldn't dare try anything in a crowd—no, she corrected herself angrily, wouldn't dare try anything *period*, because that had been the level of arrogance in her thinking. She had been so stupid! She had believed herself invulnerable to Gask, too seasoned a veteran in the wars of the Word and the Void for him to challenge her, too well protected by the magic of Wraith. Or perhaps it had simply been too long since anything had threatened her, and she had come to believe herself impervious to harm.

"You look like you could chew nails," Robert said, coming over to stand beside her.

She put a hand on his shoulder and leaned on him. "Maybe I'll just chew the buttons off your coat. How about that?"

"I don't have any buttons, just zippers." He sighed. "So tell me. What happened down there? I mean, what really happened?"

She shrugged and looked away. "There was a hole in the ice. I caught a glimpse of it just in time."

"It was pitch-black, Nest. I couldn't see anything."

She nodded. "I know, but I see pretty well at night."

He brushed at his mop of blond hair and looked over at John Ross, who was kneeling in front of Little John, speaking softly to him, the boy looking somewhere else. "I don't know, Nest. Last time something weird like this happened, he was here, too. Remember?"

"Don't start, Robert."

"Fourth of July, fifteen years ago, when the fireworks blew up on the slope right below us, and you went chasing after him, and I went chasing after you, and you coldcocked me in the trees . . ."

She stepped back from him. "Stop it, Robert. This isn't John's fault. He wasn't even with us on the sled."

Robert shrugged. "Maybe so. But maybe it's too bad that he's here at all. I just don't feel good about him, Nest. Sorry."

She shook her head and faced him. "Robert, you were always a little on the pigheaded side. It was an endearing quality when we were kids, and I guess it still is. Sort of. But you'll understand, I hope, if I don't share your one-sided, unsubstantiated, half-baked judgments of people you don't really know."

She took a deep breath. "Try to remember that John Ross is a friend." He looked so chastened, she almost laughed. Instead, she shoved him playfully. "Take Kyle and go home to Amy and your parents. I'll see you tomorrow night."

He nodded and began to move away. Then he looked back at her. "I may be pigheaded, but you are too trusting." He nodded at Ross, then toward Bennett Scott. "Do me a favor. Watch out for yourself."

She dismissed him with a wave of her hand and walked over to Ross, who rose to greet her. "Are you all right?" he asked.

She glanced around to make sure they were out of earshot. Little John stood next to them, but his gaze was flat and empty and directed out at the night. She put a comforting hand on the boy's shoulder, but he didn't respond.

"Gask opened the ice in front of us on that last run," she said quietly. "Pick warned me in time, and I tipped the sled over and threw us into a snowbank. The sled went into the water, and the ice closed over it and crunched it into kindling. I think. It was dark, and I didn't care to go out for a closer look. My guess is that what happened to the sled was supposed to happen to us." She shook her head.

"I'm sorry. I know this is my fault. I'm the one who talked us into coming. I just didn't think Gask would try anything."

Ross nodded. "Don't blame yourself. I didn't think he would, either." His gaze wandered off toward the trees. "I'm wondering who this attack was directed at." He paused and looked back at her. "Do you see what I mean?"

She kicked at the snow with her boot, her head lowering. "I do. Was Gask after us or Little John?" She thought about it a moment. "Does he know Little John is a gypsy morph, and if he does, would he try to destroy him before finding a way to claim the magic for himself?"

Ross exhaled wearily, his breath clouding the air between them. "Demons can't identify morphs unless a morph is using its magic, and that usually happens only when it's changing shape. Little John hasn't changed since we got here." He frowned doubtfully. "Maybe Gask guessed the truth."

Nest shook her head. "That doesn't feel right. This attack was a kind of broadside intended to take out whoever got in the way. It was indiscriminate." She paused. "Gask warned me what would happen if I tried to help you."

A tired and distraught Bennett came up with Harper, saying the little girl was cold and wanted to go home. Harper stood next to her, looking down at her boots and saying nothing. Nest nodded and suggested they all head back to the house for some much needed hot chocolate.

Tightening collars and scarves against the deepening chill, they walked back across the snowy expanse of the ball diamonds toward Sinnissippi Townhomes, pointing for the lights and the thin trailers of smoke from chimneys illuminated by a mix of street and porch lights reflected off the hazy sky. The last of the car lights trailed out of the park and disappeared. From the direction of the homes bordering the service road, someone called out a name, waited a moment, then slammed a door.

Nest cast about for Pick once more, but there was still no sign of him. She worried momentarily that something had happened, then decided it was unlikely and that if it had, she would have sensed it. Pick would show up by morning.

They reached the house and went in, dumped boots, coats, gloves, and scarves by the back door, and moved into the kitchen to sit around the table while Nest heated milk and added chocolate mix and put out more of Josie's cookies. She was still irritated with herself for being so incautious, but she was angry as well with Findo Gask and wondered what she could do to stop him from trying anything else. If he was willing to attack them out in the open, with other people all around, he might be willing to attack them anywhere.

They ate the cookies and drank the hot chocolate, and Bennett took Harper off to bed. When she came back, Nest had finished cleaning up and was sitting alone at the table.

Bennett walked to the sink and looked out the kitchen window. "I'm going out for cigarettes."

Nest kept her expression neutral. "It's pretty late." She wanted to say more, to dissuade Bennett from going anywhere, but she couldn't think of a way to do it. "Maybe you should wait until morning."

Bennett looked down at her feet. "It won't take long. I'll just walk up to the gas station."

"You want some company?" Nest started to rise.

"No, I need some time alone." Bennett moved away from the counter quickly, heading for the door. "I'll be right back."

Nest stood staring after her. A moment later, the back door opened and closed again, and Bennett was gone.

Bennett Scott walked up the drive and turned onto the shoulder of Woodlawn Road, working on the zipper of her coat as the cold burned against her skin, her boots plowing deep furrows through the new-fallen snow. She breathed in the biting air and folded her arms against her slender body. She had never liked the cold. Snowplows hadn't gotten this far out yet, and Woodlawn was still carpeted in white. A few cars eased past, locked in four-wheel drive, but mostly the road was empty and the night silent.

Bennett lowered her head against the cold and hugged her body. She knew she wasn't being rational. She didn't know what had brought her outside again, just knew she had to get away for a while. When she realized the sled had gone over and Harper was out there somewhere in the dark where she couldn't see her, maybe hurt, maybe worse, she just lost it. That was why she had attacked Nest, almost without thinking about it, reacting instinctively to her own fear. She couldn't bear the thought of losing Harper. The little girl was really all she had, the only thing in her life she hadn't managed to screw up. She would do anything to protect her, and she expected everyone else to do the same, though she didn't really think they would, and that was what ate at her. But she'd had confidence in Nest; she'd trusted her big sister.

She trudged through the snow, head lowered, eyes fixed on a moving point in space several feet in front of her boots. It hurt her to be angry then realize her anger was misplaced and wrong. She would walk awhile, wait for things to cool down. Nest wasn't angry with her and wouldn't hold it against her that she had blown up. Not Nest. Never Nest.

When she reached the gas station, she went inside and bought two packs of cigarettes and a coffee. The cold burned her anew when she came back out and started across the parking area toward Woodlawn Road. She lit a cigarette, shielding it in the cup of her hands, and drew the hot, acrid smoke deep into her lungs. Her head swam momentarily with the sensation, and the misery of her life faded to a manageable level. Maybe this would work for her, coming to Nest with Harper, trying to get a new start. Maybe she would find what she needed here, back in good old Hopewell. It wouldn't take all that much to stay straight, if she just worked at it hard enough. Get a job, a little apartment, put Harper in day care, make a few friends. She could do it.

Yeah, right. She shook her head angrily. Like there was any chance at all for someone like her. Who was she kidding? She cried a little, at how messed up her life was and how little chance she had of ever getting it straightened out again.

"It's cold out here, girlfriend," Penny Dreadful said, materializing next to her out of nowhere. "Hey, my car's right over there. Come on. Let me give you a ride."

Bennett looked at her dully, as if she were an inevitability, a constant in her life that refused to change or disappear. She suddenly felt tired and worn and alone. The cold numbed and deadened her, but that wasn't how she wanted to feel. She wanted to feel good about something. Just for a little while. Just for a bit.

Dropping her cigarette into the snow, she allowed Penny to take her by the arm and lead her away.

Deputy Sheriff Larry Spence sat alone in his living room at one end of the big couch, staring at the television set across the way. He was watching it without paying attention to what he was seeing, his mind trying to focus on the voice speaking to him through the telephone receiver he held against his ear. His kids were in bed, asleep or pretending to be, getting ready for a final day and a half of school before the Christmas break, anticipating what Santa was going to bring them. Billy was sleeping better again, not having those nightmares about severed fingers, but he still had a haunted look in his eyes that was troublesome.

"You have to go back out there in the morning and check on him," Special Agent Robinson was saying through the phone, the words resonating inside Spence's confused and distracted mind. "You have to be sure he doesn't hurt her."

"Why would he do that?" Spence asked, staring at nothing. "He doesn't have any reason to."

Robinson paused thoughtfully. "He's dangerous, and dangerous men will do anything. He uses her to give himself a place to hide. He is a drug dealer, and he is here to do business. If she discovers this, what do you think he will do?"

"But she doesn't want me to come there. She practically threw me out. What am I supposed to do?"

"You visit officially, just like you did today. You have every right to conduct an investigation."

"Into what? What am I supposed to be investigating?"

"What do you think, Deputy? What seems possible to you?"

Larry Spence blinked and shook his head. "He's a dealer. So he's here to make a sale. There must be something going down in the park, right?"

"Seems like a good place to start."

"I can say someone saw something, try that out and see if I get a reaction."

"Maybe someone did see something. Someone usually does."

Spence shifted on the couch, his big frame leaning forward. "I can't let that girl be hurt. She doesn't understand how people are. She believes the best about everyone, but she doesn't know."

"Someone has to open her eyes to the truth," Robinson agreed. "She would be very grateful to anyone who did, don't you think?"

Larry Spence nodded slowly. "I could do that for her. I could help her see how things really are. All I have to do is get him to slip up, say the wrong thing. I just have to keep after him, that's all. Yeah, just stay on it."

He didn't know that Findo Gask was listening to him with the same amount of interest that young children evidence when they watch ants before stepping on them. He didn't know that he was just another wild card in a game being played by others, ready to be used when needed. *If nothing else,* the demon thought, *the good deputy sheriff will help distract the troublesome Miss Freemark.* The young lady was proving to be a much larger obstacle than he had anticipated.

But all that would change in the next twenty-four hours. Tonight's events had dictated the need for that.

"It's the right thing to do," Larry Spence was mumbling to himself, nodding for emphasis.

The demon yawned. Bored, he sent a fresh nightmare into the head of the young boy sleeping in the deputy sheriff's back bedroom, then listened idly through the phone as the boy woke, screaming, to run for his father's reassuring arms.

Scattered snowflakes swirled on cold night winds across the mostly darkened expanse of Sinnissippi Park. Like white moths drawn by the incandescent brightness of the pole lights bracketing the roadways, they spun and twisted in small explosions of white. Elsewhere, moonlight peeked through breaking clouds to sparkle off frosted iron stanchions and crusted patches of road ice. Snowdrifts climbed tree trunks and hedges, a soft white draping against the velvet black.

Ray Childress finished locking down the toboggan slide, placing chains across steps and loading ramps, hooking warning signs in place, and closing up the storage shed with its equipment and parts. It was quiet in the park, the last of the cars dispersed, the last of the people gone home. Trail lights still burned down the length of the slide and out along the bayou's edge where the ice had been cleared for skating, but only shadows shifted in the glare.

Ray paused in the act of padlocking the shed and stared out at the darkness below. Damned odd, he was thinking, ice breaking apart like that, all at once. He'd tested it himself earlier in the afternoon. He'd gotten four inches, solid, on several bores and no indication at all of a weakening on the run.

Damned odd.

He had been a park employee for a lot of years, and he'd run this slide during the winter months for most of them. He had seen a lot of strange things in that time, some of them of the head-scratching variety, but never anything like this.

A hole in the ice for no reason.

Standing there, thinking it over, he heard the unmistakable sound, sharp and penetrating in the stillness of the night, of ice tightening—a slow, almost leisurely crackling, like glass crunching underfoot.

He turned and looked. Twenty years, and this had never happened before.

He was a thorough, methodical man, one who followed through on what he started and made sure the job was done right. When something difficult arose in his work, he made it a point to understand the nature of the problem so that it wouldn't happen again, or so that if it did, he would be ready.

Impulsively, almost stubbornly, he snatched up his four-cell flashlight and started down the slope. He took his time, picking his way carefully over the icy spots, finding solid footing with each step. He just couldn't help himself—he had to have a look. He was being silly, doing it now, when it was so dark, instead of waiting for morning. But he wanted to see what had happened before someone else did so he could have a chance to think about it. It wouldn't take long, after all, just to take a look.

Myriad pairs of lantern eyes followed his descent toward the bayou, peering out from the gloom of the surrounding trees, tracking his movements, but he didn't see them.

His breath clouded the air before him as he eased down along the toboggan slide to the riverbank and made his way past the chute where it opened onto the ice. Carol was off with the church guild and wouldn't be back anytime soon, so there was no hurry about getting home. He shuffled his way across the ice with slow, steady steps, keeping to the edges of the shoveled area so that his boots could find purchase. The beam of his flashlight stabbed the darkness, reflecting off the hard, black surface of the frozen river.

It's so quiet, he was thinking. Not even the wind was—

He stopped abruptly, several hundred feet out, and stared at the tombstone shape of the Heppler toboggan where it jutted from the ice, cocked slightly to one side, its curled nose pointing skyward, its lower half trapped in the frigid waters. Parts of the sled were splintered and cracked, slats sticking out in jagged relief, bindings torn and shredded.

Ray shook his head. He had never seen anything like it. A hole opening and then closing again, crushing a toboggan into kindling. Damn, this was weird!

He started forward, intending to go only another few steps, but the ice gave way beneath him all at once, breaking and snapping apart as if formed of the thinnest crust. Ray threw himself backward toward safety, but he was already sliding down into the freezing waters, the shock of the cold taking his breath away. He went all the way under, then fought his way back to the surface, gasping for breath. His heavy boots and coat dragged at him, and he kicked his way out of them, shucking off his gloves as well, all the while groping desperately for a solid piece of ice on which to find a grip.

"Help!" he screamed, his voice thin and high-pitched. "Help! For God's sake!"

Thrashing wildly in the freezing waters, he tried to reach the edge of the ice. But his flashlight was lost, its light gone out, and he could not find the edge of the hole.

"Help me!" he cried in a long, desperate wail.

Then he saw the eyes, yellow and bright and all around, slipping through the darkness just at the edge of his vision, watching him struggle.

Waiting.

The ice began to shift. He heard it crack and snap, then felt the water about him lift in a slow wave. The crunching that followed was deep and resonant and filled the whole of the night's silence. He screamed anew, but something was dragging at his legs, pulling him under. He went down, then flailed back to the surface, gasping for air. *No!* he was screaming inside his head. *Oh, please, no!*

He went down again, and this time when he came back to the surface, the ice was in his face, closing over him. He groped for the edge of the hole and managed to get one arm out before the ice locked about his wrist, trapping everything but his hand beneath the surface. He kicked and lunged frantically from beneath, but the ice would not give way.

From above, just where he could see them, the strange yellow eyes peered down at him hungrily.

For a few moments longer, his bare hand groped and twitched in the night air. When it finally quit moving, frost began to form on the skin until it looked as if the hand wore a white glove.

The eyes watched a little while longer, then disappeared.

Tuesday, December 23

Chapter 15

It was dark the next morning when Nest rose to go running. Light from streetlamps pooled on the snow outside, and the luminous crystals of her bedside clock told her it wasn't yet five. She dressed in the dark, pulling on tights and running shoes, adding sweats, then tiptoed down the hall to the back entry where she picked out a rolled watch cap, gloves, and a scarf. A glance at the coatrack revealed no sign of Bennett's parka. Apparently, she hadn't come home.

The early morning air was so cold it took her breath away. She jogged up the drive, highstepping through drifts to the road, and began to run. The snowplows had been out early, and Woodlawn was already scraped down to the blacktop in a broad swath that cut like a river through the snow. Somewhere in the distance, the plows were still working, the growl of the big engines and the harsh scrape of the metal blades clearly audible in the windless silence. Nothing moved on the road ahead, and she ran alone down its center, picking her way along the cleanest sections, avoiding patches of ice and frozen snow, breathing deep and slow as she moved out toward the country.

Out where, in the solitude and silence, in the deep midwinter calm, she could be at peace.

Streetlights illuminated her path until she was past Hopewell's residences and into the farmland beyond. By then, the eastern sky was showing the first traces of brightness, and the black of night was lightening to deep gray. Stars glimmered in small, distant patches through breaking clouds, and the snow-covered fields reflected their silvery sheen.

She picked up her pace, the adrenaline surging through her body, a humming in her ears, the warmth of her blood pushing past the night chill until she didn't feel it anymore. Her mind worked in response to her body's energy, and her thoughts whirled this way and that, like kids waving their hands in a classroom, eager to ask questions. She wrestled with them in silence as she listened to the pounding of her shoes on the pavement, working through the mix of emotions the thoughts triggered. She should have been smarter about last night, taking them all to the toboggan run and putting them at risk. She should have been smarter about Bennett and not let her go out alone afterward. She probably should have been smarter about a lot of things—like running alone in the early morning hours when she was vulnerable to an attack by the demons stalking John Ross and the gypsy morph, almost as if daring them to try something.

And perhaps, she thought darkly, she was. Let them try contending with Wraith.

She shook off her bravado quickly, recognizing it for what it was, knowing where it led. Reason and caution would serve her better. But it was anger that drove her thinking. She had not asked to be put in this position, she kept telling herself.

She had not wanted Ross to come back into her life, bringing trouble in the form of a four-year-old boy who wouldn't communicate with anyone. That he had spoken her name, bringing them to her, was bad enough. But that her name alone seemed to be the extent of his ability to respond to her, a boundary beyond which he could not go, was infuriating.

Last night, when Ross and Harper were asleep and she was waiting up for Bennett, just beginning to worry that perhaps everything was not as it should be, he had come out of his room to sit with her. As soundless and fluid as a shadow, he had taken a place on the couch next to her. He had looked at her for just a moment, his blue eyes sweeping her face, and then he had turned his attention to the darkness that lay outside, staring once more through the window into the park. She had watched in silence for a time, then turned around to kneel next to him. The lights were all off, save for a nightlight in the hallway, so there was no reflection in the window, and the snowy sweep of the park, its broad expanse white and shimmering, lay revealed beyond the jagged wall of the hedgerow.

"What are you thinking, Little John?" she had asked, again trying out Two Bears' advice. Then added, "What do you see?"

No answer. The boy's features were delicate and fragile, his body slender. His mop of dusky blond hair hung over his forehead and about his ears in ragged wisps. He needed a haircut, she thought, wondering if she should give him one. He needed food and love and a sense of belonging. He was too frail, in danger of fading away.

"Can't you say something, Little John?" she pressed. "Can't you talk to me just a little? You spoke my name once. John told me so. You said 'Nest.' That's my name. Did you know about me? Tell me if you did, Little John. Tell me what you need, and I will try to give it to you."

No answer. The boy's eyes remained fixed on the park.

"I have magic, too," she said finally, easing so close they were touching. She half expected him to flinch or move away, but he stayed perfectly still. "I was born with magic, just like you. It isn't easy having magic, is it? Magic does things to you that you don't always like. It makes you be something you don't necessarily want to be. Has that happened with you?"

She waited, then continued. "I have a magic living inside me that I don't want there. It's my father's magic, and he gave it to me when I was very little. I didn't know it for a long time. I found out when I was fourteen. This magic is a ghost wolf called Wraith. Wraith is very big and scary. When I was little, he followed me everywhere, watching over me. Now he lives inside me. I don't really know how it happened . . ."

She trailed off, not liking how it made her feel to think about Wraith and magic. Flashes of Seattle and her battle with the demon who was trying to subvert John Ross roiled through her mind. It was her confrontation with the demon that had brought Wraith out of her, had revealed his presence. In her memories she felt him rise anew, taking who and what she was with him, sealing them together, so that she felt a part of his dark rage, his terrible power.

He had appeared again, unbidden and unwelcome, at the last race she had ever run . . .

She closed her eyes for a moment and then opened them to the window-framed night. "If you could tell me about your magic, Little John, maybe we could help each other. Maybe we could make each other understand something about what's happened to us. I don't like living with myself like this. Do you?" She placed her hand gently on his thin wrist, feeling his warmth and the beat of his pulse beneath her fingertips. "Maybe we could make each other feel a little better if we talked about it."

But the gypsy morph did not answer, and although she stayed next to him talking for a long time afterward, there was no response, and at last she went to bed, leading him down the hall to his own room. She was tired and dejected, her perceived failures magnified by the lateness of the hour and her inability to make even the smallest progress in unlocking his voice.

She was running smoothly now, the roadway straight and open ahead, leading her on toward Moonlight Bay and the river. Her worries disappeared into the rhythm of her pace, fading away as she ran, left behind as surely as the place she had started from. When she returned, of course, they would be waiting. But they wouldn't seem so bad then; they would be more manageable. That was how running worked.

At the five-mile mark, she turned around and started back again, feeling loose and easy and clearheaded. Her breath clouded the air before her, and her arms and legs pumped smoothly in the cold. She ran almost every day the weather allowed her to, ran because running was what she had done all her life to make herself feel better. It was what had given her strength when she needed it as a girl. It was what had led her to the Olympics and her eight-year professional career as a runner. It was what had, on more than one occasion, saved her life.

Sometimes, she wondered what she would have done without it. It was hard to imagine; running defined who she was, defined her approach to life. It wasn't that she ran from life, but all through it and around it to gain perspective and to find the answers she needed to deal with it. Mostly, she believed, she ran toward it. She was direct in her approach to things, a lesson she had learned from Gran years ago. Nest didn't mind. She thought, on balance, that Gran's way was probably best.

But, at the moment, she was having trouble making that approach to life work.

As she turned up the drive, she saw a fresh set of footprints in the snow. Bennett had returned. She came in the back door quietly, not knowing if anyone was awake yet, and heard voices from the living room. Shucking off her cap, scarf, gloves, and running shoes, she eased quietly down the hallway and peeked around the corner.

"So Little Bear went home to his mother and never, ever went out into the woods again without asking first. The end." Bennett Scott closed the book she was reading to Harper and put it aside. "That's a good lesson for little girls, too. Never go out of your home without asking your mother first. You remember that, sweetie. Okay?"

" 'Kay, Mommy."

Harper sat on her mother's lap, still in her pajamas, nestled in the folds of an old throw Bennett had wrapped about them both. Bennett still wore last night's clothes, and her face was haggard and pale.

" 'Cause Mommy would feel so bad if anything happened to her baby girl. You know that, Harper?" Bennett hugged her. "Mommy just wants to keep you safe always."

"Owee, Mommy," Harper complained, as her mother squeezed too tightly.

"Sorry, sweetie." Bennett rumpled her hair. "Hey, look, the sun's coming up! Look, Harper! It's all gold and red and lavender and pink! Look at all the pretty colors!"

They shifted on the couch, turning to look east out the window where the sun's early light was just cresting the treeline of the park. Nest watched in silence as Bennett drew Harper's small body close to her own and pointed.

"You know what that is, Harper?" she asked softly. "Remember what I told you? That's angel fire. Isn't it beautiful?"

"Bootiful."

"Remember what Mommy told you about angel fire? At the beginning of every day, the angels go all over the world and gather up a little bit of the love that mommies have for their babies. They take bits and pieces, just scraps of it really, because mommies need most of it for themselves, to keep their babies safe. But the angels gather as much as they can, and they bring it all together, before anyone's awake, and they use it to make the sunrise. Sometimes it's really bright and full of colors, like today, because there is more love to spare than usual. But there is always enough to make a sunrise, enough to begin a new day."

She went silent then, lowering her head into Harper's thick hair. Nest slipped past them down the hall to her bedroom. Once inside, she stripped off her running clothes and went into the bathroom. She took a long shower, washed her hair, dressed, and put on makeup, wondering all the while what she was going to say to Bennett. Maybe nothing, she kept thinking. Maybe it was better to just leave things alone.

She was just about to go out and start breakfast when she noticed the message light blinking on her answer machine.

There was one message.

"Hi. It's Paul. I thought I might catch you in, but I guess you're already up and about. Or maybe sleeping, but I bet not. Not you. Anyway, I just wanted to say 'Hi' or maybe 'Merry Christmas.' I've been thinking about you lately. Haven't talked with you for a while, so I decided to call. Hope you're doing okay. Anyway, I'll try again later. Bye."

The machine offered its programmed choices, delete, save, or replay, and she hung up. She stared at the phone, still sitting on the bed. She hadn't heard from Paul in months. Why was he calling her now? Maybe he just wanted to talk, like he said. Maybe it was something else. She wasn't sure she wanted to know.

She went out of her bedroom and down the hall to the kitchen. She was pulling out pots and pans and cooking utensils, trying to decide on a breakfast menu, when Bennett came in and took a seat at the old kitchen table.

Nest glanced over. "Morning."

"Morning," Bennett replied, holding her gaze only a moment before her eyes slid away. She looked a wreck, much worse than Nest had thought earlier. "Can I do something?"

Nest saw Harper playing alone in the living room, content for the moment. "Make yourself some coffee, why don't you?"

Bennett rose and walked over to the machine. She was pulling down the box of filters and opening the coffee tin when her hands began to shake. She couldn't seem to stop them, but continued to try to set the filter in place in the machine, dropping it to the floor in the process.

Nest walked over and took her hands, holding them firmly in her own. "Nobody said this was going to be easy."

Bennett's face turned sullen and stiff. "I'm all right. Leave me alone."

"Where were you last night, Bennett?"

"Out, Nest. Look, I don't want to talk about it, okay? Just leave me alone!"

She wrenched her hands away and threw herself back down at the table, biting her lip. Nest stayed where she was, watching. Then she turned away and began to make the coffee herself.

"You want me to leave?" Bennett asked after a moment, head lowered in the veil of her dark hair. "Just say the word. Harper and I can be gone in a flash. We don't have to stay here."

"I want you to stay," Nest said quietly.

"No, you don't! You want me out! Admit it, okay? Don't lie to me! You want your life back the way it was before I showed up!"

Nest finished with the coffee and walked back to the stove, deciding on pancakes and sausage. "Well, we don't always get what we want in life, and sometimes what we get is better than what we want anyway. Gran used to say that all the time. I think having you and Harper and John and Little John for Christmas is a good example of what she meant. Don't you?"

She waited a minute and then turned around. Bennett was crying, her head buried in her hands, her shoulders hunched and still. Nest walked over and knelt beside her.

"I don't even have a present for her!" Bennett's voice was a whisper of despair and rage. "Not one shitty present! I don't even have the money to buy one! What kind of mother does that make me?"

Nest put her arm around Bennett's shoulders. "Let's make her one, then. You and me. Something really wonderful. I used to do that with Gran, just because Gran liked making presents rather than buying them. She felt they were more special when you made them. Why don't we do that?"

Bennett's nod was barely perceptible. "I'm such a loser, Nest. I can't do anything right. Anything."

Nest leaned closer. "When the holiday is over, Bennett, you and I are going to see a man who works with addicts. He's very good at it. He runs a program out of a group home he supervises. You can live there if you want, but you don't have to. I like him, and I think you will, too. Maybe he can help you get straight."

Bennett shook her head. "Sure, why not?" She didn't sound like she believed it. She sighed and buried her face in her hands, the sobs ending. "God, I hate my life."

Nest left her and went back to the stove. She worked on breakfast until the coffee was ready, then poured a cup and carried it over to Bennett, who hadn't moved from the table. Bennett drank a little, then rose and began setting the dining-room table. After a while, John Ross and Little John appeared, the boy going straight to the couch to kneel facing out the window once more. Harper stared at him for a while from where she sat on the floor, then went back to playing.

They ate breakfast in the dining room with the lights on. The sky clouded over again and the sun disappeared from view until it was only a pale hazy ball, the air turned gray and wintry in its absence. Outside, cars moved on the street like sluggish beetles, the whine of snow tires and the rattle of chains marking their passage.

Andy Wilts came by from the Texaco station to plow out the drive with his four-by-four. Bennett talked with Harper about snow angels and icicle lollipops, and Nest talked about driving out to get a Christmas tree, now that she had company for the holiday. Ross ate in silence, and the gypsy morph looked off into space.

When they were clearing off the table and putting the dishes in the dishwasher, there was a knock at the front door. Nest glanced out the curtained window and saw a county sheriff's car parked in the drive. *Not again,* she thought immediately. Leaving Bennett to finish loading the dishes, she walked down the hall, irritated at the prospect of having to deal with Larry Spence yet again. What could he possibly want this time? Ross was in his room, so maybe she could avoid another confrontation.

"Good morning, Larry," she said on opening the door, fighting down the urge to tell him what she really wanted to say.

Larry Spence stood stiffly in front of her, hat in hand, bundled up in his deputy sheriff's coat. "Morning, Nest. Sorry to have to bother you again."

"That's all right. What can I do for you?"

He cleared his throat. "Well, it might be better if I could come in and we could talk about it there."

She shook her head. "I don't think so. We tried that yesterday, and it didn't work out very well. You better tell me what you want right here on the porch."

His big frame shifted. "All right. We'll do it your way." His tone of voice changed, taking on a slight edge. "It's about the drug dealing in the park. It's still going on. There was a major buy last night. Witnesses saw it going down and called it in. It's possible that someone staying in your house was involved."

She thought at once of Bennett Scott, missing all night. Had Bennett been involved in a drug transaction? She stared at Larry Spence, trying to read his face. How would Bennett have paid for "a major buy" of drugs? She didn't have any money.

"Who did your witnesses think they saw?" she asked quickly.

"I can't tell you that."

"Who are your witnesses?"

"I can't tell you that, either."

"But there are witnesses and they did see someone involved in this drug buy that they can identify, is that right?"

"Right."

But Nest didn't believe it. He was fishing for something. Otherwise, he wouldn't be here asking questions of her. He would be holding a warrant for Bennett's arrest.

"Look, Larry." She closed the door behind her, moved out onto the porch, and stood with her arms folded across her chest. "My guests were all here last night, tucked in their beds, asleep. If you have someone who says differently, trot them out. Otherwise, go investigate someone else."

His face began to redden. "You don't have to be so defensive about this. I'm just doing my job. Drug dealing is a mean business, and the people involved are dangerous. You might be smart to think about that."

"What are you talking about, Larry? I don't know anyone involved in drug dealing, and I'm not friends with people who do. I have four guests in my house—

friends I've known for a long time and a couple of small children. I hardly think they are the kind of people you're talking about."

He shook his head stubbornly. "Maybe you don't know them as well as you think."

"Well, maybe that's so. But what makes you think you know them any better? This is the second time in two days you've been out here, ladling out large helpings of innuendo and unsubstantiated accusations." Her anger surfaced in a rush. "If you know something I don't, why not just tell me instead of waiting for me to break down and confess?"

"Look, Nest, I don't—"

"No, you tell me what you know, or you get the hell off my porch!"

He took a deep breath, his face bright red. "John Ross is a dangerous man. There are people here investigating him. I'm trying to keep you out of it, girl!"

She stared at him. "John Ross? This is about John?" She realized then that this had never been about Bennett, that Larry Spence had been talking about John all along. About John Ross dealing drugs. She wanted to laugh.

Larry Spence looked confused. "Hey, you better wake up about Ross. The people investigating him . . ."

Something clicked in the back of her mind. "What people?" she asked quickly.

"I can't tell you that."

"You don't seem to be able to tell me much of anything. It makes me wonder how much you actually know." She took a step toward him. "Who do these people say they are, Larry? Have you checked them out? Because *I* have a feeling about this."

His mouth tightened. "It's an official investigation, Nest. I've already said more than I should, and I—"

"Is one of them an older man with gray eyes and a leather book, looks like an old-time preacher?"

Larry Spence stared at her, his sentence left unfinished. She sensed his uncertainty. "Listen to me, Larry," she said slowly, carefully. "You're in way over your head. Way over. You stay away from this man, you understand? He isn't who you think. He's the one who's dangerous, not John Ross."

The big man's mouth tightened. "You do know something about this drug-dealing business, don't you?"

"There isn't any drug-dealing business!" she snapped, furious. "Can't you get it through—"

His portable radio squawked sharply in his coat pocket, and he turned away from her as he pulled it out. He spoke softly for a minute, shielding his voice from her, listened, and turned back. "I've got to go. We'll talk about this later. You be careful, girl. I don't think you're clear about what's going on."

Without waiting for her response, he walked off the porch to his car, climbed in, and drove off. She wheeled away as he did so, went back inside, and stood seething in the entryway. Larry Spence was a fool. Findo Gask was using him, that much was certain. But what was he using him for? She thought of the ways the demons she had encountered before had used humans as pawns to get what they wanted. She remembered her father, come back to claim her for his own. She remembered Stefanie Winslow.

History always repeats itself, she thought angrily. *There is nothing you can do to change that. Even in the small things in our lives, we make the same mistakes.* How could she avoid that happening here?

She rubbed her arms through her heavy sweater, chasing away the last of the winter chill from her skin. But the cold that had settled in the pit of her stomach remained.

Chapter 16

When she had calmed down enough to think about something else, Nest loaded everyone into the Taurus and drove them to a tree farm north of town. Picking up a bow saw from the farmer, she marched them out into the Christmas tree forest in search of an acceptable tree. Other customers prowled the long rows, searching for trees of their own. The air was cold and dry against their skins, and a west wind whipped across the snowy fields, kicking up sudden sprays. Heavy clouds rolled in from across the Mississippi, and Nest could taste and smell the impending snow.

Exhilarated, she breathed in the winter air. If she was going to celebrate Christmas, she was going to do it right. Sitting around the house might be the easier choice, but it was also apt to drive her insane. Better to be out doing something. Ever since she was a little girl, she had handled her problems by getting up and doing something. It seemed to help her think, to come to terms with things. It was why she had begun running.

Harper raced ahead, darting in and out of the shaggy trees, playing hide-and-seek with anyone who would do so, leaping out unexpectedly and laughing as the adults feigned surprise and shock. Little John watched her for a time, his face expressionless, his blue eyes intense. He did not join in or respond, but he was not disinterested either. Something about the game seemed to engage his curiosity, and once or twice he slowed long enough to give Harper a chance to spring out at him and run away. Nest watched him do it several times, puzzled by what it meant. Once she encouraged him to join in, but he just walked away.

They found a fat little five-foot fir that Harper hugged and jumped up and down over, so they cut it down and hauled it out to where the farmer measured it and collected their payment. After loading the tree in the trunk and tying down the lid to hold it in place, they drove back to the house. It was not yet noon, and after consuming such a big breakfast, no one was ready to eat again. Nest wanted to keep everyone occupied, so she suggested they stick the tree in a bucket of water on the back porch to give it a chance to relax, and go for a walk.

With snow beginning to fall in fat, lazy flakes, they struck out into the park, Harper in the lead, racing this way and that, Nest, Ross, and Little John following. Smoking a cigarette and hunching her thin shoulders against the cold, Bennett, trailing everyone, had the look of someone who would just as soon be somewhere else. She had grown increasingly moody as the morning progressed, slowly withdrawing from all of them, Harper included. Nest had tried to make conversation, to bring her out of whatever funk she had fallen into, but nothing worked. Bennett's eyes drifted away each time she was addressed, as if she had gone off in search of something. Whatever had happened last night, Nest thought darkly, it was not good.

But she decided to wait on saying anything more. Bennett was already in such a black place that it didn't seem to Nest that it would do much good to emphasize it. After Christmas, maybe she would say something.

They drifted across the snow-covered ball diamonds toward the toboggan slide, drawn at first by their lingering curiosity over last night's accident and then by a clutch of police, fire, and ambulance vehicles that came into view. The deputy sheriff's car belonged to Larry Spence. Nest glanced at Ross, but he shook his head to indicate he had no idea what was happening. Nest moved to the front of the group, directing them west of the parking lot and its knot of traffic, crossing the road farther down. People were gathered along the crest of the slope leading down to the bayou, all of them whispering or standing silent, eyes fixed on a knot of firemen and ambulance workers clustered on the ice.

Nest's group slowed beside the others. The first thing she saw was the twisted length of Robert's toboggan lying to one side. A dark, watery hole glimmered where the ice had been chopped apart by picks and axes to free it. But then she saw that it wasn't the sled they had worked to free. The firemen and ambulance techs were working over a sodden, crumpled form.

"What's going on?" she asked a man standing a few feet away.

The man shook his head. He had owlish features and a beard, and she didn't know him. "Someone fell through the ice and drowned. Must have happened during the night. They just fished him out."

Nest took a steadying breath and looked back at the tableau on the bayou. A body bag was being unrolled and unzipped, its bright orange color brilliant against the dull surface of the ice. "Do they know who it is?" she asked.

The man shrugged his heavy shoulders. "Don't know. No one's been up yet to say. Just some poor slob." He seemed unconcerned.

Someone who fell through the ice, she repeated carefully, trying out the sound of the words in her mind, knowing instantly Findo Gask was responsible.

"They had to chop right through the ice to get him," the man said, growing chummy now, happy to be sharing his information with a fellow observer. "His hand was sticking out when they found him. Ice must have froze right over him after he drowned. The hand was all he got out. Maybe he was a sledder. They found him next to that toboggan. It was froze up, too."

Who was he? Nest wondered. Someone who had ventured out onto the ice while the demon magic was still active? The magic would probably have responded to anyone who got close enough.

The man next to her looked back at the ice. "You'd think whoever it was would have been smarter. Going out on the ice after the slide was shut down and the lights turned off? Stupid, if you ask me. He was just asking for it."

A woman a little farther down the line turned toward them. Her voice was low and guarded, as if she was afraid someone would hear. "Someone said it's a man who works for the park system. They said he was working the slide last night until an accident shut it down, and he must have gone out on the ice afterward to check something and fallen in." She was small and sharp-featured and wore a blue stocking cap with a bell on the tassel. Her eyes darted from the man's face to Nest's, then away again.

Ray Childress, Nest thought dully. *That's Ray down there.*

She turned away and began walking back toward the road. "Let's go," she said to the others.

"Mommy, what's wrong?" Harper asked, and Bennett hushed her softly and took her hand.

Nest kept her eyes lowered as she walked, sad and angry and frustrated. Ray Childress. Poor Ray. He was just doing his job, but he was in the wrong place at the wrong time. This whole thing was her fault. It had happened because she had insisted on bringing everyone out for sledding, even knowing Findo Gask was a danger to them, even after she had been warned not to help John Ross. It wasn't enough that she had saved them on the ice. She should have anticipated that others would be in danger, too. She should have warned Ray. She should have done something. Her eyes teared momentarily as she remembered how long she had known him. Most of her life, it seemed. He had been there when her grandfather had almost died in the fireworks explosion fifteen years ago. He had been one of the men who had dragged Old Bob clear.

Now he was dead, and a pretty good argument could be made that it was because of her.

"Nest!" Ross called sharply.

At first she ignored him, not wanting to talk to anyone, still wrapped in her grief. But then he called to her again, and this time she heard the urgency in his voice and looked up.

Findo Gask stood a dozen yards away at the edge of a clump of alder and blue spruce. He had materialized all at once, his black-garbed form barely distinguishable from the dark, narrow trunks of the alder trees and the slender cast of their shadows. He wore his familiar flat-brimmed black hat and carried his worn leather book. His eyes glittered from beneath his frosted brows as they fixed on her.

"A tragic turn of events, Miss Freemark," he said softly. "But accidents happen sometimes."

She stared at him without speaking for a moment, frightened by his unexpected appearance, but enraged as well. "Who would know that better than you?" she said.

His smile did not waver. "Life is uncertain. Death comes calling when we least expect it. It is the nature of the human condition, Miss Freemark. I don't envy you."

She glanced over her shoulder at Ross, Bennett, Harper, and Little John, who stood in a loose clutch, watching. Then she looked back at the demon. "What can I do for you, Mr. Gask?"

He laughed softly. "You can give me what I want, Miss Freemark. You can give me what I've come here for. You and Mr. Ross. You can give it to me, and I'll go away. Poof—just like that."

She came forward a few steps and stopped, distancing herself from the others. "The gypsy morph?" she asked.

He nodded, cocking his head slightly.

"Just hand it over, and you'll be gone? No more unexpected accidents? No more visits to my home by deluded law enforcement officials inquiring into drug buys in the park?"

His smile broadened. "You have my word."

She matched his smile with her own. "Your word? Why is it I don't find that particularly reassuring?"

"In this case, you can rely on it. I have no interest in you or your friends beyond finding the morph. Where is it, Miss Freemark?"

His eyes locked on hers, probing, and she was struck with a flash of insight. He doesn't know it's Little John he's looking for, she realized. That was the reason for the threats and the attacks; he was stymied unless he could compel her cooperation. He couldn't identify the morph without her.

She almost laughed aloud.

"You seem perplexed by my request, Miss Freemark," Findo Gask said jovially, but there was an edge to his voice now. "Is there something about it you don't understand?"

She shook her head. "No, I understand perfectly. But you know what? I don't like being threatened. Especially by someone like you. Especially now, when I'm not in a very good mood and I'm feeling angry and hurt, and it's mostly because of you. I've known that man you let die on the ice for most of my life. I liked him. He didn't do anything to you, but that wasn't enough to save him. That doesn't matter to you, does it? You don't care. You don't care one bit."

Findo Gask pursed his lips and shook his head slowly. "I thought we were beyond accusations and vitriol. I thought you understood your position in this matter better than it appears you do."

"Guess you thought wrong, huh?" She came forward another step. "Let me ask you something. How safe do you feel out here?"

He stared at her in surprise. His smile disappeared, and his seamed face suddenly lost all expression.

She came forward another step, then two. She was only a few paces away from him now. "I'm not afraid of demons, Mr. Gask. I've faced them before, several times. I know how to stand up to them. I know how they can be destroyed. I have the magic to make it happen. Did you know that?"

He did not give ground, but there was a hint of uncertainty in his frosty eyes. "Don't be foolish, Miss Freemark. There are children to be considered. And I did not come alone."

She nodded slowly. "That's better. Much better. Now I'm seeing you the way you really are. Demon threats are all well and good, but they work best when they are directed toward children and from behind a shield of numbers."

Her words were laced with venom, and hot anger burned through her. Wraith was awake and moving inside, all impatience and dark need, her bitterness fueling his drive to break free and attack. She was tempted. She was close to letting him go, to willing him out of her body and onto the hateful form of the creature in front of her. She wasn't sure how that would end, but it might be worth finding out.

"I made a mistake with you when you came to my house two days ago, Mr. Gask," she said. "I should never have let you leave. I should have put an end to you then and there."

His mouth twisted. "You overestimate yourself, Miss Freemark. You are not as strong as you think."

She smiled anew. "I might say the same for you, Mr. Gask. So now that we know where we stand on matters, why don't we just say good-bye and go our separate ways?"

He considered her silently for a moment, his eyes shifting to Ross and the others, then back again. "Perhaps you should take a closer look at yourself, Miss Freemark, before you expend all of your energy judging others. You are not an ordinary, commonplace member of the human race with which you are so quick to identify. You are an aberration, a freak. You have demon blood in your body and demon lust in your soul. You come from a family that has dabbled more than once in demon magic. You think you are better than us, and that your service to the Word and the human cause will save you. It will not. It will do exactly the opposite. It will destroy you."

He lifted the leather-bound book in front of him. "Your life is a charade. All that you have accomplished is a direct result of your demon lineage. Most of it you have repudiated over the course of time, until now you have nothing. I know your history, Miss Freemark. I made it a point to find out. Your family is dead, your husband left you, and your career is in tatters. Your life is empty and useless. Perhaps you think that by allying yourself with Mr. Ross, you will find the purpose and direction you lack. You will not. Instead, you will continue to discover unpleasant truths about yourself, and in the end your reward for doing so will be a pointless death."

His words were cutting and painful, and there was enough truth in them that she was not immune to their intended effect. But they were the same words she had spoken to herself more than once in the darker moments of her life, when acceptance of harsh truths was all that would save her, and she could hear them again now without flinching. Findo Gask would break down her resolve with fear and doubt, but only if she let him do so.

He smiled without warmth. "Better think on it, Miss Freemark. Should it come to a test of magics between you and me, you are simply not strong enough to survive."

"Don't bet against me, Mr. Gask," she replied quietly. "It may be that this is a battle you will win, that the magic you wield is more powerful than my own. But you will have to find out the hard way. John Ross and I are agreed. We will not hand over the gypsy morph—not because you say we must or because you threaten us or even if you hurt us. We won't cede you that kind of power over our lives."

Findo Gask did not reply. He simply stood there, as black as ink and carved from stone. The wind gusted suddenly, whipping loose snow across the space that separated them. The demon stood revealed for an instant longer before the blowing snow screened him away.

When the wind died again and the loose snow settled, he was gone.

Some lessons you learn early in life, and some of those lessons are hard ones. Nest learned an important one when she was twelve and in the seventh grade. She had only just the year before experienced the consequences of using magic after Gran had warned her not to do so, and she was still coming to terms with the fact that she would always be different from everyone else. She had taken a book from the school library and forgotten to check it out. When she tried to slip it back in place without telling anyone, she got caught. Miss Welser, who ran the library with iron resolve and an obvious distrust of students in general, found her out, accused her of lying when she tried to explain what had happened, and sentenced her to after-school detention as punishment. Nest had been taught not to challenge the authority exercised by adults, particularly teachers, so she accepted her punishment without complaint. Day after day, week after week, she came in after school to perform whatever service Miss Welser required—shelving, stacking, cataloging, and cleaning, all in long-suffering silence.

But after a month of this, she began to wonder if she hadn't been punished enough for a transgression she didn't really believe she had committed in the first place, and she screwed up her courage sufficiently to ask Miss Welser when she would be released. It was almost March, and spring training for track would begin in another few weeks. Running was Nest's passion then as now; she did not believe she should have to give it up just because Miss Welser didn't believe her about the book. But Miss Welser didn't see it that way. She told Nest she would be on detention for as long as it took, that sneaking and lying were offenses that required severe punishment in order to guarantee they would not happen again.

Nest was miserable, trapped in a situation from which it did not seem she could extricate herself. Everything had begun to revolve around Miss Welser's increasingly insufferable control over her life. If Gran noticed what was happening, she wasn't saying, and Nest wasn't about to tell her. At twelve, she was beginning to learn she had to work most things out for herself.

Finally, with only a week to go before the start of track season, she told her coach, Mr. Thomas, she might not be able to compete. One thing led to another, and she ended up telling him everything. Coach Thomas was a big, barrel-chested man who preached dedication and self-sacrifice to his student athletes. Winning wasn't the only thing, he was fond of saying, but it wasn't chopped liver either.

He seemed perplexed by her attitude. "How long have you been going in after school?" he asked, as if maybe he hadn't heard her correctly. When she told him, he shook his head in disgust and waved her out the door. "Tell Miss Welser that track begins on Monday next and Coach Thomas wants you out here training with everyone else and not in the library shelving books."

Nest did what she was told, thinking she would probably end up being sentenced to the library for life. But Miss Welser never said a word. She just nodded and looked away. Nest finished out the week and never went back. After a while, she realized she should have spoken up sooner, that she should have insisted on a meeting with the principal or her adviser. Miss Welser had kept her coming in because she hadn't stood up for herself. She had given Miss Welser power over her life simply by accepting the premise that she wasn't in a position to do anything about it. It was a mistake she did not make again.

Staring at the space Findo Gask had occupied only moments before, she thought about that incident. If she gave the demon power over her by conceding that she was frightened, she lost any chance of ever being free of him.

Of course, there was a certain amount of risk involved in standing up for yourself, but sometimes it was a risk you had to take.

Ross, Bennett, and the children came up to her, Ross's hands knotted about his rune-scrolled staff as he limped past her a few steps to study carefully the tree-thrown shadows. Far back in the hazy gloom of the conifers, there was a hint of movement. Ross started toward it. He looked so tightly strung that Nest was afraid he would lash out at anything that moved.

"John," she said quietly, drawing his dark gaze back to hers."Let him go."

Ross shook his head slowly. "I don't think I should. I think I should settle this here and now."

"Maybe that's what he's hoping you'll try to do. He said he wasn't alone." She paused to let the implication sink in. "Leave it for another time. Let's just go home."

"I don't like that old man," Bennett muttered, her thin face haunted as she pulled Harper close. "What was he talking about, anyway? It was hard to hear."

"Scary man," her daughter murmured, hugging her back.

"Scary is right," Nest agreed, ruffling the little girl's parka hood in an effort to lighten the mood. Her eyes found Bennett's, and she spoke over the top of Harper's head. "Mr. Gask thinks we have something that belongs to him. He's not very rational about the matter, and I can't seem to persuade him to leave us alone. If he comes to the house again, don't open the door, not for any reason."

Bennett's mouth tightened. "Don't worry, I won't." Then she shrugged. "Anyway, Penny said he—"

She caught herself and tried to turn away, but Nest moved quickly in front of her. "Penny? Penny who? What did Penny say?"

Bennett shook her head quickly. "Nothing. I was just—"

It can't be, Nest was thinking, remembering the strange, wild-haired girl at the church. "Penny who?" she pressed, refusing to back off.

"Leave me alone!"

"Penny who, Bennett?"

Bennett stopped moving, head lifting, eyes defiant. She brushed at her lank hair with one gloved hand. "Get over yourself, Nest! I don't have to tell you anything!"

"I know that," Nest said. "You don't. But this is important. Please. Penny who?"

Bennett took a deep breath and looked off into the distance. "I don't know. She didn't tell me her last name. She's just a girl I met, that's all. Just someone I talked to a couple times."

"Someone who knows Findo Gask?"

Bennett flicked her fingers in a dismissive gesture. "She says he's her uncle. Who knows?" She fumbled in her pockets for her cigarettes. "I don't think she likes him any more than we do. She makes fun of him all the time."

"All the time," Nest repeated, watching as Bennett lit a cigarette and inhaled deeply. *Like all last night, maybe. Because that's who you were with.* "What did she say about Findo Gask?" she asked again.

Bennett blew out a thin stream of smoke. "Just that he was leaving town in a day or so and wouldn't be back. Said it was the only thing they'd ever agreed on, him leaving this pissant little town." She sighed. "I just thought that meant we probably wouldn't be seeing him again because he'd be gone, that's all. What's the big deal?"

Ross was staring at both of them, eyes shifting from one to the other.

"Does Penny have wild red hair?" Nest asked quietly.

Bennett's gaze lifted. "Yeah. How did you know that?"

Nest wondered how she could explain. She decided she couldn't. "I want you to listen to me, Bennett," she said instead. "I can't tell you how to live your life. I won't even try. It's not my job. You're here with Harper because you want to be, and I don't want to chase you off by giving you a lot of orders. But I won't look the other way when I think you're in danger. So here it is. Stay away from Penny and Gask and anyone you think might be friendly toward them. You'll have to trust me on this, just like I have to trust you on some other things. Okay?"

"Yeah, okay." Bennett took a last drag on her cigarette and dropped it into the snow. "I guess."

Nest shook her head quickly. "No guessing. I know a few things you don't, and this is one. These are dangerous people. Penny as much as Gask. I don't care what she says or does, she isn't your friend. Stay away from her."

Ross glanced past her to where they were bringing up Ray Childress from the bayou. "Maybe we ought to get back to the house," he said, catching her eye.

Nest turned without another word and started walking. *Maybe we ought to dig ourselves a hole, crawl into it, and pull the ground up over our heads instead,* she thought. *Because not much of anywhere else is looking very safe.*

But she kept the thought to herself.

Chapter 17

They had crossed the park road onto the flats and were starting for home when Nest changed her mind and told the others to go on without her. It was a spur-of-the-moment decision, but she felt a compelling need to visit the graves of her grandparents and mother. She hadn't been up that way recently, although she had intended to go more than once, and her encounter with Findo Gask lent new urgency to her plans. There was a danger in putting things off for too long. Ross, Bennett, and the children could go back to the house and get started on decorating the tree. Everything they needed was in labeled boxes in the garage. She would catch up with them shortly.

Bennett and the children were accepting enough, but Ross looked worried. Without saying so, he made it clear he was concerned that Findo Gask might still be somewhere in the park. Nest had considered the possibility, but she didn't think there was much danger of a second encounter. The park was full of families and dog walkers, and there would be other visitors to the cemetery as well.

"This won't take long," she assured him. "I'll just walk up, be by myself for a few moments, and walk back." She glanced at the sky. "I want to get there before it snows again."

Ross offered to accompany her, rather pointedly she thought, but she demurred. He would be needed to help with the Christmas tree, she told him just as pointedly, nodding toward Bennett and the children. Ross understood.

She set off at a steady pace across the flats until she reached the road again, then began following its plowed surface west toward the bluffs. The sky was blanketed with clouds, and the first slow-spiraling flakes of new snow were beginning to fall. West, from where the weather was approaching, it was dark and hazy. The storm, when it arrived, would be a big one.

A steady stream of vehicles crawled past her, going to and from the parking lot. Some had brought toboggans lashed to the roofs of cars and shoved through the gates and back windows of SUVs. Apparently the word hadn't gotten around yet that the slide was closed. There were sledders on the slopes leading down to the bayou, and kids ran and cavorted about the frozen playground equipment under the watchful, indulgent eyes of adults. Futile efforts to build snowmen were in progress; it was still too cold for the snow to pack.

Watching the children play, Nest was reminded how much of her life had been lived in Sinnissippi Park. When she was little, the park had been her entire world. She had known there were other places, and her grandparents had taken her to some of them. She understood that there was a world outside her own. But that world didn't matter. That world was as distant and removed as the moon. Her family and friends lived at the edge of the park. Pick lived in the park. Even the feeders appeared to her mostly in the park. The magic, of course, had its origins in the park, and Gran and the Freemark women for five generations back had cared for that magic.

It wasn't until the summer of her fourteenth birthday, when her father came back into her life, that everything changed. The park was still hers, but it was never again the same. Her father's deadly machinations forced her to give up her child's world and embrace a much larger one. Perhaps it was inevitable that it should happen, later if not then. Whatever the case, she made the necessary adjustment.

But even after growing up and moving away for a time, even with all she had experienced, she never lost the sense of belonging that she found in the park. She marveled at it now, as she walked down the snow-packed road in the wintry gray light—the way she felt at peace in its confines, at home in its twenty acres of timber and playground and picnic areas. Even now, when there was reason to be wary of what might be lurking there, she did not feel threatened. It was the legacy of her childhood, of her formative years, spent amid magic and magic's creatures, within a world that few others even knew existed.

She wondered if she would ever lose that. She couldn't be sure, especially now. Findo Gask was a powerful and intrusive presence, and his intent was to undo everything in her life. To take her life, she corrected herself quickly, if he could find a way to do so. She looked off across the river, where smoke from fireplace chimneys lifted in the air like streamers. It was the John Ross factor again. Every time she connected with him, her life changed in a way she hadn't imagined was possible. It would do so again this time. It was foolish to believe otherwise.

She shook her head at the enormity of this admission. It would crush her if she tried to accept its weight all at once. She would have to shoulder it a little at a time, and not let herself be overwhelmed. Maybe then she could manage to carry it.

The wind gusted hard and quick down the road, sending a stinging spray of ice needles against her skin and down her throat. The cold was raw and sharp, but it made her feel alive. Despondent over the death of Ray Childress and angered by her confrontation with Findo Gask, she felt exhilarated nevertheless. It was in her nature to feel positive, to pull herself up by her emotional bootstraps. But it was her symbiotic relationship with the park as well. There was that link between them, that tie that transcended every life change she had experienced in her twenty-nine years.

Maybe, she mused hopefully, she could save her connection with the park this time, too. Even with the changes she knew she must undergo. Even with the return of John Ross.

She crossed the bridge where the road split off and curved down to the bayou and to the caves where the feeders lived, making instead for the summit of the cliffs and the turnaround. The parking area was empty, and the snow stretched away into the trees, undisturbed and pristine. In the shadowed evergreens, a handful of feeders crouched, their flat, empty eyes watchful. They had no particular interest in her now, but that could change in a heartbeat.

She found the gap in the cemetery fence that had opened two years ago and not yet been repaired, and she squeezed herself through. Riverside's tombstones and monuments stretched away before her, their bumpy, rolling acres dissected by roads that meandered in long, looping ribbons through clusters of old hardwoods and shaggy conifers. The roads were plowed, and she trudged to the nearest and followed it on toward the edge of the bluffs. The wind had picked up, and the snowflakes were falling more quickly, beginning to form a curtain against the gray backdrop of failing light. It would be dark by four o'clock, the evening settling in early during the winter solstice, the days gone short and the nights made long. She pulled up her collar and picked up her pace.

When she reached the plots of her grandparents and of her mother, she knelt in the snow before them. Snow layered the rough-cut tops of the marble and the well-tended grounds beneath, but the vertical surface of the stone was clear and legible. She read the names to herself in silence. ROBERT ROOSEVELT FREEMARK. EVELYN OPAL FREEMARK. CAITLIN ANNE FREEMARK. Her grandparents and her mother, laid to rest in a tree-shaded spot that overlooked the river. One day she would be there, too. She wondered if she would see them then. If she did, she wondered how it would feel.

"Kind of a cold day for paying your respects to the dead," a voice from behind her remarked.

From her kneeling position, she glanced over her shoulder at Two Bears. He stood a few paces back, beefy arms folded over his big chest. Snowflakes spotted his braided black hair and his ribbed army sweater. One arm encircled his bedroll and gripped his rucksack, which hung down against his camouflage pants and heavy boots. For as little clothing as he wore, he did not seem cold.

"Don't you ever wear a coat?" she asked, swiveling slightly without rising.

He shrugged. "When it gets cold enough, I do. What brings you to visit the spirits of your ancestors, little bird's Nest? Are you lonesome for the dead?"

"For Gran and Old Bob, I am. I think of them all the time. I remember how good they made me feel when they were around. I miss them most at Christmas, when family is so important." She cocked her head, reflecting. "I miss my mother, too, but in a different way. I never knew her. I guess I miss her for that."

He came forward a few paces. "I miss my people in the same way."

"You haven't found them yet, I guess."

He shook his head. "Haven't looked all that hard. Calling up the spirits of the dead takes a certain amount of preparation. It takes effort. It requires a suspension of the present and a step across the Void into the future. It means that we must meet halfway between life and death." He looked out across the river. "No one lives on that ground. Only visitors come there."

She came to her feet and brushed the snow from her knees. "I took your suggestion. I tried talking with the gypsy morph. It didn't work. He wouldn't talk back. He just stared at me—when he bothered looking at me at all. I sat up with him last night for several hours, and I couldn't get a word out of him."

"Be patient. He is just a child. Less than thirty days old. Think of what he has seen, how he must feel about life. He has been hunted since birth."

"But he asked for me!" she snapped impatiently. "He came here to find me!"

Two Bears shifted his weight. "Perhaps the next step requires more time and effort. Perhaps the next step doesn't come so easily."

"But if he would just tell me—"

"Perhaps he is, and you are not listening."

She stared at him. "What does that mean? He doesn't talk!" Then she blinked in recognition. "Oh. You mean he might be trying to communicate in some other way?"

Two Bears smiled. "I'm only a shaman, little bird's Nest, not a prophet. I'm a

Sinnissippi Indian who is homeless and tribeless and tired of being both. I give advice that feels right to me, but I cannot say what will work. Trust your own judgment in this. You still have your magic, don't you?"

Her mouth tightened reproachfully. "You know I do. But my magic is a toy, all but that part that comprises Wraith and belonged to my father. You're not trying to tell me I should use that?"

He shook his head. "You are too quick to dismiss your abilities and to disparage your strengths. Think a moment. You have survived much. You have accomplished much. You are made more powerful by having done so. You should remember that."

A smile quirked at the corners of her mouth. "Isn't it enough that I remember to speak your name? O'olish Amaneh. I say it every time I feel weak or frightened or too much alone. I use it like a talisman."

The copper face warmed, and the big man nodded approvingly. "I can feel it when you do so. In here." He tapped his chest. "When you speak my name, you give me strength as well. You remember me, so that I will not be forgotten."

"Well, I don't know that it does much good, but if you think so, I'm glad." She sighed and exhaled a cloud of frosty air. "I better be getting back." She glanced skyward. "It's getting dark fast."

They stood together without speaking over the graves of her family, flakes of snow swirling about them in gusts of wind, the dark distant tree trunks and pale flat headstones fading into a deepening white curtain.

"A lot of snow will fall tonight," Two Bears said in his deep, soft voice. His black eyes fixed her. "Might be a good time to think about the journeys you have taken in your life. Might be a good time to think back over the roads you have traveled down."

She did not want to ask him why he was suggesting this. She did not think she wanted to know. She did not believe he would tell her anyway.

"Good-bye, little bird's Nest," he said, backing off a step into the white. "Hurry home."

"Good-bye, O'olish Amaneh," she replied. She started away, then turned back. "I'll see you later."

He did not respond. He simply walked into the thickly falling snow and disappeared.

From the concealing shelter of a thick stand of spruce, Findo Gask watched Nest Freemark converse with the big Indian. He watched them through the steadily deepening curtain of new snow until Nest began walking back toward the park, and then he turned to an impatient Penny Dreadful.

"Let's go get her," Penny suggested eagerly.

Findo Gask thought a moment, then shook his head. "I don't think so. Not just yet."

Penny looked at him as if he were newly arrived from Mars. Her red hair corkscrewed out from her head in a fresh gust of wind. "Gramps, are you going soft on me? Don't you want to hurt her after the way she talked to you?"

He smiled indulgently. "I want to hurt her so badly she will never be well again. But the direct approach isn't necessarily the best way to accomplish this."

She made a face. "I'm sick and tired of playing around with Little Miss

Olympics, you know that? I don't get the point of these mind games you love so much. If you want to play games, let's try a few that involve cutting off body parts. That's the way to hurt someone so they won't forget."

Findo Gask watched Nest Freemark begin to fade into the white haze of falling snow. "If we kill her now, John Ross will take the morph and go to ground, and we might not find him again. He is the more dangerous of the two. But he relies on her. She has something he needs. I want to know what it is."

He signaled into the trees behind him where Twitch and the ur'droch were waiting. Then he began walking, Penny right on his heels.

"We're going after the Indian instead," he told her.

She quickened her pace to get close to him. "The Indian? Really?" She looked excited.

He slid through the spruce, shadowy in his dark clothing, his eyes scanning the snow-flecked land ahead. He had heard stories of an Indian who was connected in some way to the Word, either as a messenger or prophet, a powerful presence in the Word's pantheon of magics. He would be the most powerful of Nest Freemark's allies, so it made sense to eliminate him first. It was his plan to strip away Nest Freemark's friends one by one. He wasn't doing this just to weaken her and thereby gain possession of the morph. He wasn't even doing it because he was afraid that killing her outright would scare off John Ross. He was doing it because there was something about her that disturbed him. He couldn't identify it, but it had revealed itself in the way she stood up to him, so confident, so determined. She knew he was dangerous, but she didn't seem to care. Before he killed her, he wanted to find out why. He wanted to break down her defenses, strip away her confidence and determination, and have a close look at what lay beneath.

He would have the morph, of course. It didn't matter what Nest Freemark or John Ross tried to do to stop him. He would have the morph, and their names in his book, before the week was out.

And in the process, he would have their souls as well.

The big Indian was already out of sight, disappeared into the white curtain of blowing snow. But Findo Gask did not need to see the Indian to find him. There were other senses he could call upon besides his sight. There were other ways to find what was hidden.

He glanced left and right, catching just a glimpse of Twitch and the ur'droch to either side. Penny stalked next to him, eyes darting this way and that, pale face intense. She was whispering, "Here, Tonto. Here, big fella. Come to Penny."

Wind gusted and died away, snow swirled and drifted, and Riverside Cemetery was a surreal jungle of dark trunks and ice-capped markers. They were closing on the bluffs overlooking the bayou, where the cemetery ended at a chain-link fence set just back from the cliffs. There was still no sign of the Indian, but Findo Gask could sense him, not far ahead, still moving, but seemingly in no great hurry. The demon's mind was working swiftly. He might lose one or two of his allies in this effort, but demons were replaceable.

All but him, of course.

There was no one else like him.

They came out of the blowing snow on a tree-sheltered flat, close back against the edge of the bluffs, and the Indian was waiting.

* * *

Nest made her way out of the maze of tombstones to the cemetery road and followed it back toward the park. The wind was gusting heavily and the snow blowing so hard it was impossible to see much more than a dozen yards. Banks of storm clouds rolled across the sky, and the light had dimmed to an iron gray that turned the landscape hazy and colorless.

"O'olish Amaneh," she whispered to herself.

A dark shadow whizzed by her head, and she flinched from it automatically, dropping to a guarded crouch. The shadow was gone a moment and then it was back again, appearing out of the whirling snow in a rush of darkness. It was an owl, winging low across the tombstones and monuments, flattened out like a big kite. Without a sound, it flew right at her. At the last minute it banked away, and Pick dropped onto her shoulder with a grunt.

"Criminy, I can't see a thing!" he grumbled, latching on to her collar and pulling himself into the warmth of its folds. "Cold up there, too. I might be made of twigs and leaves, but I'm frozen all the way through!"

"What are you doing?" she asked, coming back to her feet, looking at the white space where the owl had been a moment before.

"What does it look like I'm doing? I'm patrolling the park!"

"In this weather?" She exhaled sharply. "What is that supposed to accomplish?"

"You mean, besides possibly saving your life?" he snapped irritably. "Oh, right, I forgot. That was yesterday, wasn't it? Guess I'm just wasting my time out here today."

"Okay, okay, I'm sorry." She hadn't seen him since last night's incident and had forgotten that she hadn't thanked him. "What can I say? I'm an ingrate. You did save my life. All of our lives, for that matter."

She could feel him puff up. "You are entirely welcome."

"I mean it. It's belated, I know, but thanks."

"It's okay."

"I'm just a little distracted."

He gestured impatiently. "Start walking. It's freezing out here, and I have to see you safely home before I can take cover myself. Mr. Gask is still out here, and he has a couple of his demon cronies with him. They were watching you talk with the Indian."

"With Two Bears?" She glanced around quickly.

"Don't worry, they didn't follow you. I was watching to make sure. Come on, keep moving, don't be looking around like you didn't know the way. I'll keep watch for the both of us."

She made her way to the fence and squeezed through the gap to the other side. Ahead, the park was a white blur. The residences to her left and the bayou and railroad tracks to her right had disappeared completely. But even in weather conditions as bad as this, she could find her way, the park as familiar to her as her own bedroom in darkest night. Head lowered against the stinging gusts of frozen snow and bitter wind, she moved down the road past the Indian mounds.

"Tell me what you know about last night," she suggested, striding steadily forward.

"Not much to tell." Pick was so light she could barely tell he was there. "I was patrolling the park on Jonathan, just like I always do when there's trouble about. After what you'd told me about Mr. Gask, I knew he'd be back. Sure enough, I found him down by the ice, hiding in the trees. He didn't seem to be doing anything, so I took Jonathan high up and out of sight. You went down the toboggan slide once or twice, and Mr. Gask watched. Then someone flashed a light up top by the loading platform, and our demon friend went down to the ice and touched it with his hand. When I saw the cracks start out toward the center, I could see where things were heading. You were already coming down, so I flew out to warn you."

"Good thing," she told him.

He grunted. "There's the understatement of the month. That was a pretty wicked magic he concocted. Lethal stuff. It missed you, but it got that park guy."

"Ray Childress. I know. It makes me sick."

Pick was silent for a time. "You better watch out, Nest," he said finally. "There are bad demons and there are worse-than-bad demons. I think Findo Gask is in a class by himself. He won't give up. He'll keep coming after you until he has what he wants." He paused. "Maybe you ought to just give it to him."

Nest shook her head. "I won't do that. I already told him so."

Pick sighed. "Well, no surprises there. Is John Ross with you on this?"

"Right to the bitter end."

"Good choice of words. That's likely how it will turn out." Pick squirmed on her shoulder to get more comfortable. "Wish this was happening in the summer, when it was warmer. It would make my job a lot easier."

She glanced down at him. "You be careful yourself, Pick."

He snorted. "Hah! You don't have to worry about me. I've got eyes in the back of my head, and Jonathan's got them in his wing tips. We'll be safe enough. You just keep your own instincts sharp."

She swallowed against the cold, moistening her lips. Some Chap Stick was definitely in order. "How come you call him Jonathan? And before that, it was Benjamin and Daniel. What kind of names are those for owls? Can't you come up with something . . . I don't know, not so common?"

He straightened, twiggy hands tightening in her collar. "Those names are only common to you, not to me. I'm a sylvan, remember? We don't use names like Daniel and Benjamin and Jonathan in the normal course of things. Cripes! Try to remember, we're not like you!"

"Okay, already."

"Sometimes, you appall me."

"All right!"

"Well, criminy!"

She trudged on into the snowy gloom, following the dark ribbon of the road as the snow slowly began to hide it away.

Findo Gask was surprised. The Indian was just standing there, watching them. He must have known they were following him, and yet he hadn't tried to escape or hide. Why was that?

"Looky, looky, Gramps," Penny teased. "Someone wants to play."

Gask ignored her, slowing his approach to study his adversary. The Indian was bigger than he had looked earlier, his copper skin dark, his black hair damp and shiny, his eyes hard-edged and penetrating. He had dropped the bedroll and rucksack in the snow, as if anticipating the need to keep his hands free.

"Are you looking for me?" he rumbled softly.

Findo Gask stopped six yards away, close enough that he could see the other's eyes, not so close that he was within reach of those big hands. The Indian did not look at Penny. He did not look to either side, where Twitch and the ur'droch had melted into the trees.

"Hey, Tonto," Penny called out to him. "Remember me?"

Gask let his eyes shift momentarily. She was standing closer to the Indian than he was. She had knives in both hands, their metal blades glinting as she moved them in small circular motions.

The Indian glanced at her, then dismissed her with a shrug. "What is there worth remembering? You are a demon. I have seen many like you before."

"Not like me," she hissed at him.

The Indian looked back at Findo Gask. "Why do you waste my time? What do you want with me?"

Gask brought the leather book in front of him, gripping it with both hands. "What is your name?" he asked.

The Indian was as still as carved stone. "O'olish Amaneh, in the language of my people, the Sinnissippi. Two Bears, in the language of the English. But should you choose to speak my name, it will sear your tongue and scorch your throat all the way down to where your heart has turned to coal."

Findo Gask gave him a considering look. Out of the corner of his eye, he could see Twitch sliding along the fenceline behind the Indian, his movements smooth and silent in the snowfall, his big form barely visible. He could not see the ur'droch, concealed somewhere back in that spruce grove, but he knew it was there. Penny was giggling with anticipation. She was unpredictable, apt to do almost anything in a given situation, this one especially, and it made her useful.

Two Bears seemed oblivious of them. "You are a demon who prides himself on his understanding of humans," he said, studying Gask. "But what you understand is limited by what you feel. Demons feel so little. They lack empathy. They lack the kinder emotions. In the end, this will be your undoing."

Findo Gask smiled without warmth. "I don't think my undoing is the issue at hand, do you?"

"Isn't it?" The Indian's weathered face stayed expressionless. "You would do well not to misjudge your enemies, demon. I think maybe in this case, you have done so."

Gask held the other's dark gaze. "I make it a point never to misjudge my enemies. I think it is you who have misjudged in this instance. You've made a big mistake taking sides in this dispute with Miss Freemark. It is a mistake I intend to correct."

Twitch was behind the Indian now, less than ten paces away. Gask knew the ur'droch would be on his other side. Two Bears was hemmed in, with no place to go. Snow blew in a steady slant out of the northwest. The storm clouds seemed to have dropped all the way down to the treetops, and the light had gone cloudy and gray.

Two Bears shifted his weight slightly, his big shoulders swinging toward Gask. "How would you make this correction, Mr. Demon?"

Findo Gask cocked his head. "I would remove you from this place. I would make you go away so that you could never come back."

Now it was the Indian who smiled. "What makes you think I was ever really here?"

Twitch rushed across the space that separated them and launched himself at the Indian. A flurry of shadowy movement marked the ur'droch's attack from the other side. Penny screamed in glee, dropping into a crouch, right arm cocked for throwing, her knives catching the light.

But in the same instant, snow funneled all about Two Bears, blown straight up out of the earth on which he stood, a cloud of white particles that filled the air. The wind whipped and tore about him, and for a split second everything disappeared.

When the snow settled and the winter air cleared, Two Bears was gone. His rucksack and bedroll lay on the ground, but the Indian had vanished. Big head swiveling left and right, Twitch crouched in the space the Indian had just occupied. The ur'droch was a dark stain sliding back and forth across the rutted snow, searching futilely for its quarry.

Penny hissed in rage as the knives disappeared back into her clothing. "Is this some sort of trick? Where is he?"

Findo Gask stood without moving for a moment, testing the air, casting all about for some indication. "I don't know," he admitted finally.

"Did we kill him or not?" Penny shrieked.

Gask searched some more, but nothing revealed itself, not a trace, not a whisper. The Indian had simply vaporized. His last words whispered in the demon's mind. *What makes you think I was ever really here?* But, no, he had been here in some sense. He had been more than just an image.

Ignoring Penny's rantings, Findo Gask opened the leather-bound book and read the last entry burned onto its weathered pages.

There was nothing after the name of Ray Childress.

He closed the book slowly. A pang of disappointment tweaked his pride. The Indian would have been a nice addition.

"Gone is gone," he said. "A neat trick, but you don't come back for a while after executing it. He's removed himself from the picture, wherever he is." He shrugged dismissively, and his weathered face creased in a slow smile. "Let's go to work on the others."

Chapter 18

John Ross was standing at the living-room window, keeping watch for her, when Nest emerged from the whirling snowfall. She appeared as a dark smudge out of the curtain of white, pushing through the skeletal branches of the hedgerow and trudging across the backyard toward the house. He could tell by the set of her shoulders and length of her stride she was infused with determination and her encounter with Findo Gask had not dampened her resolve. Whether she'd changed her mind regarding her insistence on protecting the gypsy morph remained to be seen. He was inclined to think not.

He limped toward the back door as she came through. Bennett and Harper were already decorating the tree, which had been placed in its stand in the corner across the room from the fireplace. Ross had helped with that and with carrying in the boxes of ornaments, then stood back. Little John had resumed his place on the couch, staring out into the park.

"Whew, it's bad out there now," Nest declared as he came up to her. She stamped her boots on the entry rug and brushed the snow from her coat. "You can hardly see in front of your nose. How's everyone here?"

"Fine." He shifted to let her walk past and followed her down the hall. "They're decorating the tree."

She glanced over her shoulder in surprise. "Little John, too?"

"Well, no." He gave a little shrug. "Me either, actually."

"What's your excuse?"

"I guess I don't have one."

She gave him a look. "That's what I thought. Try to remember, John, it's Christmas. Come on."

She led him back into the living room and put him to work with the others. She brought Little John off the couch and spent time trying to show him how to hang ornaments. He stared at her blankly, watched Harper for a few minutes, hung one ornament, and went back to the couch. Nest seemed unperturbed. She strung tinsel and lights for a time, then went over to sit with him. Kneeling at his side, she began speaking softly to him. Ross couldn't quite catch what she was saying, but it was something about the park and the things that lived in it. He heard her mention Pick and the feeders. He heard her speak of tatterdemalions, sylvans, and the magic they managed. She took her time, not rushing things, just carrying on a conversation as if it was the most natural thing in the world.

When the tree was decorated, she brought out cookies and hot chocolate, and they sat around the tree talking about Santa Claus and reindeer. Harper asked questions, and Nest supplied answers. Bennett listened and looked off into space, as if marking time. Outside, it was growing dark, the twilight fading away, the snowstorm disappearing into a blackness punctured only by the diffuse glow of streetlamps and porch lights, flurries chasing each other like moths about a flame. Cars edged down the roadway, slow and cautious metal beasts in search of their lairs. In the fireplace, the crackling of the burning logs was a steady reassurance.

It was nearing five when the phone rang. Nest walked to the kitchen to answer it, spoke for a few minutes, then summoned John. "It's Josie," she said. She arched one eyebrow questioningly and handed him the receiver.

He looked at her for a moment, then placed the receiver against his ear, staring out the kitchen window into the streetlit blackness.

"Hello."

"I don't mean to bother you, John," Josie said quickly, "but I didn't like the way we left things yesterday. It felt awkward. It's been a long time, and seeing you like that really threw me. I can't even remember what I said. Except that I asked you to dinner tonight, and I guess, thinking it over, I was a little pushy."

"I didn't think so," he said.

He heard her soft sigh in the receiver. "I don't know. It didn't feel that way. You seemed a little put off by it."

"No." He shifted his weight to lean against the counter. "I appreciated the invitation. I just didn't know what to say. I have some concerns about Little John, that's all."

"You could bring him. He would be welcome." She paused. "I guess that's another invitation, isn't it? I'm standing in my kitchen, making this dinner, and I end up thinking about you. So I call to tell you I'm sorry for being pushy yesterday, then I get pushy all over again. Pathetic, huh?"

He still remembered her kitchen from fifteen years earlier, when she had dressed the wounds he had suffered during his fight with the steel-mill workers in Sinnissippi Park. He could picture her there now, the way she would look, how she would be standing, what she would be looking at as she spoke to him.

"I would like to come," he said quietly.

"But?"

"But I don't think I can. It's complicated. It isn't about you."

The phone was silent for a moment. "All right. But if you want to talk later, I'll be here. Give your son a kiss for me."

The line went dead. Ross placed the receiver in its cradle and walked back into the living room. Harper and Bennett were sitting by the tree playing with old Christmas tins. Nest got up from the sofa where she was sitting with Little John.

"I've got to take some soup over to the Petersons," she said, heading for the kitchen. "I'll be back in twenty minutes."

She made no mention of the call and was out the door in moments. Ross stood looking after her, thinking of Josie. It was always the same when he did. It made him consider what he had given up to become a Knight of the Word. It made him realize all over again how empty his life was without family or friends or a lover. Except for Stefanie Winslow, there had been no one in twenty-five years besides Josie Jackson. And only Josie mattered.

Twice, he walked to the phone to call her back and didn't do so. Each time, the problem was the same—he didn't know what to say to her. Words seemed inadequate to provide what was required. The emotions she unlocked in him were sweeping and overpowering and filled with a need to act, not talk. He felt trapped by his circumstances, by his life. He had lived by a code that allowed no contact with others beyond the carrying out of his duties as a Knight of the Word. Nothing else could be permitted to intrude. Everything else was a distraction he could not afford.

When Nest returned, rather more quiet than before, she took Bennett down the hall to the project room to work on a Christmas present for Harper and left Ross to watch the children. With Harper sitting on the sofa next to Little John and pretending to read him a book, Ross moved over to the fireplace and stood looking into the flames. His involvement with the gypsy morph and his journey to find Nest Freemark had been unavoidable, dictated by needs and requiring sacrifices that transcended personal considerations. But his choices here, in Hopewell, were more suspect. The presence of Findo Gask and his allies was not unexpected, but it was disturbing. It foreclosed a number of options. It required pause. Nest was threatened only because Ross was here. If he slipped away, they would lose interest in her. If he took the gypsy morph someplace else, they would follow.

That was one choice, but not the logical one. Another darker and more dangerous one, the one that made better sense, was to seek them out and destroy them before they could do any further damage.

That would allow the morph to stay with Nest. That would give her a better chance of discovering its secret.

For a long moment, he considered the possibility of a preemptive strike. He did not know how many demons there were, but he had faced more than one before, and he was equal to the task. Track them down, turn them to ash, and the threat was ended.

He watched the logs burning in the hearth, and their fire mirrored his own. It would be worth it, he thought. Even if it ended up costing him his life . . .

He recalled his last visit to the Fairy Glen and the truths the Lady had imparted to him. The memory flared in the fire's embers, her words reaching out, touching, stroking. *Brave Knight, your service is almost ended. One more thing you must do for me, and then I will set you free. One last quest for a talisman of incomparable worth. One final sacrifice for all that you have striven to achieve and all you know to have value in the world. This only, and then you will be free . . .*

His gaze shifted to where the children sat upon the couch. Little John had turned around and was looking at the picture book. He seemed intent on a particular picture, and Harper was holding it up to him so that he could better see.

Ross took a deep breath. He had to do something. He could not afford to wait for the demons to come after them again. It was certain they would. They would try a different tactic, and this time it might cost the life not of a park employee but of someone in this house. If it did not come tomorrow, it would come the next day, and it would not end there, but would continue until the demons had possessed or destroyed the gypsy morph.

Ross studied the little boy on the couch. A gypsy morph. What would it become, if it survived? What, that would make it so important? He wished he knew. He wished the Lady had told him. Perhaps it would make choosing his path easier.

Nest and Bennett came out of the work area a few minutes later with a bundle of packages they placed under the tree. Nest was cheerful and smiling, as if the simple act of wrapping presents had infused her with fresh holiday spirit. She went over to the couch to look at the picture book Harper was reading, giving both

Harper and Little John hugs, telling them Santa wouldn't forget them this Christmas. Bennett, in contrast, remained sullen and withdrawn, locked in a world where no one else was welcome. She would force a smile when it was called for, but she could barely manage to communicate otherwise, and her eyes kept shifting off into space, haunted and lost. Ross studied her surreptitiously. Something had happened since yesterday to change her. Given her history as an addict, he could make an educated guess.

"We have to get over to Robert's party," Nest announced a few minutes later, drawing him aside. "There will be lots of other adults and kids. It should be safe."

He looked at her skeptically. "I know what you're thinking," she said. "But I keep hoping that if I expose Little John to enough different situations, something will click. Other children might help him to open up. We can keep a close watch on him."

He accepted her judgment. It probably didn't make any difference what house they were occupying if the demons chose to come after them, and he was inclined to agree that they were less likely to attempt anything in a crowd. Even last night, they had worked hard to isolate Nest and the children before striking.

Nest mobilized the others and began helping the children with their coats and boots. As she did, Ross walked back to the kitchen and looked out the window. It was still snowing hard, with visibility reduced and a thick layer of white collecting on everything. It would be difficult for the demons to do much in this weather. Even though the cold wouldn't affect them, the snow would limit their mobility. In all likelihood, they would hole up somewhere until morning. It was the perfect time to catch them off guard. He should track them down and destroy them now.

But where should he look for them?

He stared out into the blowing white, wondering.

When they were all dressed, they piled into the car and drove down Woodlawn Road to Spring Drive and back into the woods to Robert's house. A cluster of cars was already parked along the drive and more were arriving. Nest pulled up by the front door, and Bennett and the children climbed out and rushed inside.

Ross sat where he was. *If I were Findo Gask, where would I be?*

Nest was staring at him. "I have to do something," he said finally. "It may take me a while. Can I borrow the car?"

She nodded. "What are you going to do?"

"A little scouting. Will you be all right alone with the children and Bennett? You may have to catch a ride home afterward."

There was a long pause. "I don't like the sound of this."

He gave her a smile. "Don't worry. I won't take any chances."

The lie came easily. He'd had enough practice that he could say almost anything without giving himself away.

Her fingers rested on his arm. "Do yourself a favor, John. Whatever it is you're thinking of doing, forget it. Go have dinner with Josie."

He stared at her, startled. "I wasn't—"

"Listen to me," she interrupted quickly. "You've been running for weeks, looking over your shoulder, sleeping with one eye open. When you sleep at all, that is. You're so tightly strung you're about to snap. Maybe you don't see it, but I do. You have to let go of everything for at least a few hours. You can't keep this up."

"I'm all right," he insisted.

"No, you're not." She leaned close. "There isn't anything you can do out there tonight. Whatever it is you think you can do, you can't. I know you. I know how you are. But you have to step back. You have to rest. If you don't, you'll do something foolish."

He studied her without speaking. Slowly, he nodded. "I must be made of glass. You can see right through me, can't you?"

She smiled. "Come on inside, John. You might have a good time, if you'd just let yourself."

He thought about his plan to try tracking the demons, and he saw how futile it was. He had no place to start. He had no plan for finding them. And she was right, he was tired. He was exhausted mentally, emotionally, and physically. If he found the demons, what chance would he have of overcoming them?

But when he glanced over at the Hepplers' brightly lit home, he didn't feel he belonged there, either. Too many people he didn't know. Too much noise and conversation.

"Could I still borrow the car?" he asked quietly.

She climbed out without a word. Leaning back in before closing the door, she said, "She still lives at the same address, John. Watch yourself on the roads going back into town."

Then she closed the door and disappeared inside the house.

It took him a long time to get to where he was going. It was like driving through an exploded feather pillow, white particles flying everywhere, the car's headlights reflecting back into his eyes, the night a black wall around him. The car skidded on patches of ice and through deep ruts in the snow, threatening to spin off the pavement altogether. He could barely make out the roadway ahead, following the tracks of other cars, steering down the corridor of streetlamps that blazed to either side. Now and again, there would be banks of lights from gas stations and grocery stores, from a Walgreens or a Pizza Hut, but even so, it was difficult to navigate.

He thought again of going after the demons, of making a run at them while they were all gathered together somewhere, waiting out the storm. It remained a tempting image. But Nest was right. It was a one-in-a-million shot, and it required energy he did not have to spare.

More debilitating than his exhaustion was his loneliness and despair. He had denied it for a long time, shrugging off the emptiness inside, pretending that for him such things didn't matter. But they did. He was a Knight of the Word, but he was human, too.

It was seeing Josie again that triggered the feelings, of course. But it was returning to Hopewell and Nest Freemark as well, to a town that seemed so much like the one he had grown up in and to the last member of a family that seemed so much like his own. Just being here, he found himself trying to recapture a small part of his past. He might tell himself that he wasn't here for that, but the truth was simple and direct. He wanted to reaffirm his humanity. He wanted to step outside his armor and let himself feel what it was to be human again.

He drove down Lincoln Highway until it became Fourth Avenue, then turned left toward the river. He found his way without effort, the directions still imprinted on his memory, fresh after all these years. He steered the Taurus down the dead-end street to the old wooden two-story and parked by the curb. He switched off the headlights and engine and sat staring at the house, thinking over what he was about to do.

It isn't as if you have to decide now, he told himself. *How can you know what will happen after so long?*

But he did. His instincts screamed it at him. The certainty of it burned through his hesitation and doubt.

He got out of the car, locked it, limped through the blowing snow and drifts, climbed the porch steps, and knocked. He had to knock twice more before she opened the door.

She stared at him. "John?"

She spoke his name as if it were unfamiliar to her, as if she had just learned it. Her blue eyes were bright and wondering, and gave full and open consideration to the fact that he was standing there when by all rights he shouldn't be. She was wearing jeans and a print shirt with the sleeves rolled up. She had been cooking, he guessed. He did not move to enter or even to speak, but simply waited.

She reached out finally with one hand and pulled him inside, closing the door behind him. She was grinning now, shaking her head. He found himself studying the spray of freckles that lay across the bridge of her nose and over both cheeks. He found himself wanting to touch her tousled blond hair.

Then he was looking into her eyes and thinking he was right, there had never been anyone like her.

She brushed snow from his shoulders and began unzipping his coat. "I shouldn't be surprised," she said, watching her fingers as they worked the zipper downward. "You've never been predictable, have you? What are you doing here? You said you weren't coming!"

His face felt flushed and heated. "I guess I should have called."

She laughed. "You didn't call for fifteen years, John. Why should you call now? Come on, get that coat off."

She helped him pull off the parka, gloves, and scarf, and bent to unlace his boots as well. In stocking feet, leaning on his still-damp staff for support, he followed her from the entry into the kitchen. She motioned him to a chair at the two-person breakfast table, poured him a cup of hot cider, and spent a few moments adjusting various knobs and dials on the stove and range. Savory smells rose from casseroles and cooking pans.

"Have you eaten?" she asked, glancing over her shoulder at him. He shook his head. "Good. Me, either. We'll eat in a little while."

She went back to work, leaving him alone at the table to sip cider. He watched her silently, enjoying the fluidity of her movements, the suppleness of her body. She seemed so young, as if age had decided to brush against her only momentarily. When she looked at him and smiled—that dazzling, wondrous smile—he could barely believe that fifteen years had passed.

He knew he loved her and wondered at his failure to recognize it before. He did not know why he loved her, not in a rational sense, because looking at the fact of it too closely would shatter it like glass. He could not parcel it out like pieces of a puzzle, one for each part of the larger picture. It was not so simply explained. But it was real and true, and he felt it so deeply he thought he would cry.

She sat with him after a while and asked about Nest and Bennett and the children, skipping quickly from one topic to the next, filling the space with words and laughter, avoiding close looks and long pauses. She did not ask where he had been or why he had a child. She did not ask why she had not heard from him in fifteen years. She let him be, perhaps sensing that he was here in part because he could expect that from her, that what had drawn them together in the first place was that it was enough for them to share each other's company.

She set the breakfast table for dinner, keeping it casual, serving from the counter and setting the plates on the table. The meal was pot roast with bread and salad, and he ate it hungrily. He could feel his tension and emptiness drain away, and he found himself smiling for the first time in weeks.

"I'm glad you came," she told him at one point. "This will sound silly, but even after you said you couldn't, I thought maybe you would anyway."

"I feel a little strange about that," he admitted, looking at her. He wanted to look at her forever. He wanted to study her until he knew everything there was to know. Then he realized he was staring and dropped his gaze. "I didn't want to be with a lot of people I didn't know. I didn't want to be with a lot of people, period. In a strange house, at Christmas. I thought I would go looking for . . ." He trailed off, glancing up at her. "I don't know what I thought. I don't know why I said I wouldn't come earlier. Well, I do, but it's hard to explain. It's . . . it's complicated."

She seemed unconcerned. "You don't have to explain anything to me," she said.

He nodded and went back to eating. Outside, the wind gusted about the corners and across the eaves of the old house, making strange, whining sounds. Snow blew past the frost-edged windows as if the storm were a reel of film spinning out of control. Ross looked at it and felt time and possibility slipping away.

When he finished his meal, Josie carried their plates to the sink and brought hot tea. They sipped at the tea in silence, listening to the wind, exchanging quick looks that brushed momentarily and slid away.

"I never stopped thinking about you," he said finally, setting down the tea and looking at her.

She nodded, sipping slowly.

"It's true. I didn't write or call, and I was sometimes a long way away from here and lost in some very dark places, but I never stopped."

He kept his eyes fixed on hers, willing her to believe. She set her cup down, fitting it carefully to the saucer.

"John," she said. "You're just here for tonight, aren't you? You haven't come back to Hopewell to stay. You don't plan to ask me to marry you or go away with you or wait for you to come back again. You aren't going to promise me anything beyond the next few hours."

He stared at her, taken aback by her directness. He felt the emptiness and solitude begin to return. "No," he admitted.

She smiled gently. "Because I'd like to think that the one thing we can count on from each other after all this time is honesty. I'm not asking for anything more. I wouldn't know what to do with it."

She leaned forward slightly. "I'll take those few hours, John. I'll take them gladly. I would have taken them anytime during the last fifteen years of my life. I thought about you, too. Every day, I thought about you. I prayed for you to come back. At first, I wanted you to come back forever. Then, just for a few years, or a few months, or days, minutes, anything. I couldn't help myself. I can't help myself now. I want you so badly, it hurts."

She brushed nervously at her tousled hair. "So let's not spend time offering each other explanations or excuses. Let's not make any promises. Let's not even talk anymore."

She rose and came around to stand over him, then bent to kiss him on the mouth. She kept her lips on his, tasting him, exploring gently, her arms coming around his shoulders, her fingers working themselves deep into his hair. She kissed him for a long time, and then she pulled him to his feet.

"I guess you remember I was a bold kind of girl," she whispered, her face only inches from his own, her arms around his neck, and her body pressed against him. "I haven't changed. Let's go upstairs. I bet you remember the way."

As it turned out, he did.

Chapter 19

Bennett Scott stayed at the Heppler party almost two full hours before making her break, even though she had known before coming what she intended to do. She played with Harper and Little John, to the extent that playing with Little John was possible—such a weird little kid—and helped a couple of butter-wouldn't-melt-in-their-mouths teenage girls supervise the other children in their basement retreat. She visited with the adults—a boring, mind-numbing bunch except for Robert Heppler, who was still a kick—and admired the Christmas decorations. She endured the looks they gave her, the ones that took in her piercings and tattoos and sometimes the needle tracks on her arms, the ones that pitied her or dismissed her as trash. She ate a plate of food from the buffet and managed to sneak a few of the chicken wings and rolls into her purse in the process, knowing she might not get much else to eat for a while. She made a point of being seen and looking happy, so that no one, Nest in particular, would suspect what she was about. She hung in there for as long as she could, and much longer than she had believed possible, and then got out of there when no one was looking.

She said good-bye to Harper first.

"Mommy really, really loves you, baby," she said, kneeling in front of the little girl in the darkened hallway leading from the rec room to the furnace room while the other children played noisily in the background. "Mommy loves you more than anything in the whole, wide world. Do you believe me?"

Harper nodded uncertainly, dark eyes intense. "Yeth."

"I know you do, but Mommy likes to hear you say it." Bennett fought to keep her voice steady. "Mommy has to leave you for a little while, baby. Just a little while, okay? Mommy has to do something."

"What, Mommy?" Harper asked immediately.

"Just something, baby. But I want you to be good while I'm gone. Nest will take care of you. I want you to do what she tells you and be a real good little girl. Will you promise me?"

"Harper come, too," she replied. "Come with Mommy."

The tears sprang to her eyes, and Bennett wiped at them quickly, forcing herself to smile. "I would really like that, baby. But Mommy has to go alone. This is big-people stuff. Not for little girls. Okay?"

Why did she keep asking that? *Okay? Okay?* Like some sort of talking Mommy doll. She couldn't take any more. She pulled Harper against her fiercely and hugged her tight. "Bye, baby. Gotta go. Love you."

Then she sent Harper back into the rec room and slipped up the stairs. Retrieving her coat from the stack laid out on the sofa in the back bedroom, she made her way down the hallway through the crowds to the front door, telling anyone who looked interested that she was just going to step out for a cigarette. She was lucky; Nest was nowhere in evidence, and she did not have to attempt the lie with her. The note that would explain things was tucked in Nest's coat pocket. She would find it there later and do the right thing. Bennett could count on Nest for that.

She was not anxious to go out into the cold, and she did not linger once the front door closed behind her. Trudging down the snowy drive with her scarf pulled tight and her collar up, she walked briskly up Spring to Woodlawn and started for home. She would travel light, she had decided much earlier. Not that she had a lot to choose from in any case, but she would leave everything Nest had given her except for the parka and boots. She would take a few pictures of Harper to look at when she wanted to remind herself what it was she was trying to recover, what it was she had lost.

What it was that her addiction had cost her.

All day her need for a fix had been eating at her, driving her to find fresh satisfaction. What Penny had given her last night hadn't been enough. It was always surprising how quickly the need came back once she had used again, pervasive and demanding. It was like a beast in hiding, always there and always watching, forever hungry and never satisfied, waiting you out. You could be aware of it, you could face it down, and you could pass it by. But you could never be free of it. It followed after you everywhere, staying just out of sight. All it took was one moment of weakness, or despair, or panic, or carelessness, and it would show itself and devour you all over again.

That was what had happened last night. Penny had given her the opportunity and the means, a little encouragement, a friendly face, and she was gone. Penny, with her unkempt red hair, her piss-on-everyone attitude, and her disdain for everything ordinary and common. Bennett knew Penny; she understood her. They were kindred spirits. At least for the time it took to shoot up and get high, and then they were off on their own separate trips, and Bennett was floating in the brightness and peace of that safe harbor drugs provided.

By this morning, when she was alone again and coming down just enough to appreciate what she had done, she understood the truth about herself. She would never change. She would never stop using. Maybe she didn't even want to, not down deep where it mattered. She was an addict to the core, and she would never be anything else. Using was the most important thing in the world to her, and it didn't make any difference how many chances she was offered to give it up. It didn't matter that Nest would try to help her. It didn't matter that she was in a safe place. It didn't even matter that she was going to lose Harper.

Or at least it didn't matter enough to make her believe she could do what was needed.

What she could manage, she decided, was to leave Harper with Nest. What she could manage was to give her daughter a better chance at life than she'd been given. Maybe something good would come of it. Maybe it would persuade her to find a way at last to kick her habit. Maybe. Maybe not. Either way, Harper would be better off.

She had been thinking about it all day. She could stand the bad things that happened to her, but not when they spilled over onto Harper. Especially if she was at fault because she was using. She could not bear it; she could not live with it. She was haunted by the possibility. To prevent it from happening, to remove any chance of it, she had to give Harper to Nest.

She shivered inside the parka, the wind harsh and biting as it swept over her in sudden gusts, particles of frozen snow stinging her exposed skin and making her eyes water. Cars lumbered by in the haze, and she wished one would stop and offer her a ride, but none did. When she got to the house, she would be able to get warm for a few minutes before Penny came. Penny would bring drugs and a ride downtown. She would catch the ten o'clock bus out and by morning she would be in another state.

She regretted that she'd had to steal money from Nest to make the break possible, but that was the least of the sins she had committed in her addict's life and the one most likely to be forgiven first. Nest was her big sister, and a good person, and more family to her than Big Momma and the kids, all of whom were lost to her as surely as her childhood, and good riddance. Sometimes, she missed Jared, though. She remembered how sweet Nest had been on him. *Sweet.* She laughed aloud. Where had she picked up that word? She hoped Jared was all right somewhere. It would be nice to know he was.

Big Momma was a different matter. She hoped Big Momma was burning in hell.

It took a long time to reach the house. Her face stung and her fingers and toes were numb with cold. She extracted the house key, unlocked the door, and got herself inside. She stood in the entry and breathed in the warmth, waiting for the cold that had settled in her bones to melt. She was coughing, and her chest rattled. She was sick, but she wondered how sick she really was. It had been a long time since she had been to a doctor. Or Harper. Nest would do a better job with things like that.

Harper's stuffed teddy was sitting by the Christmas tree, and Bennett started to cry. *Harper,* she whispered soundlessly. *Baby.*

She called the number Penny had given her. Penny answered and said she'd be right there, and Bennett hung up. Her bag was already packed, so once the call was made there was little to do but wait. She walked out into the living room from the kitchen and stood looking into space. After a moment, she plugged in the tree. The colored lights reflected in the window glass and hall mirror and made her smile. Harper would have a nice Christmas. She glanced down at the present she had made for Harper—a rag doll with her name stitched on the apron, a project Nest had found in a magazine and helped her finish. She wished she could be there to see Harper's face when she opened it. Maybe she would call from the road, just to say Merry Christmas.

She closed her eyes and hugged herself, thinking of how much better she would feel once Penny came with the drugs. She would do just enough to get her through the night and save the rest for later. She would buy all she could. It was great stuff, whatever it was, some sort of crystal, really smooth. She didn't know how Penny had found anything so good, but it just took you up and up and up. Penny had said she would give it to her for free, but Bennett didn't believe her. You gave it for free the first time, which was last night. Today it would cost. Because it was costing Penny. It had to be.

The phone rang once, but she left it alone. No one would be calling her. She began to worry that Nest would miss her and come after her before Penny arrived. She brought her small bag to the front door and stood looking out at the streetlit darkness. Cars came and went, a few, not many, indistinct and hazy lumps in the blowing snow. She wondered if it would snow all night. She wondered if the bus would be on time. She wished she had a fix.

By the time a car finally pulled into the driveway her anticipation and need were so high she could feel her skin crawl. She peeked out from behind the window curtain, uncertain who it was, torn between hiding and charging out. When the driver's door opened and Penny's Little Orphan Annie head appeared, she let out an audible gasp of relief and rushed to the front door to let her in.

"Ohhh, little girl, you are in some kind of state!" the redhead giggled as she came inside, slamming the door on the wind and the cold and throwing off her coat. "Let's get you back together again right now!"

They shot up right there in the front entry, sitting cross-legged on the wooden floor, passing the fixings back and forth, heads bent close, whispering encouragement and laughing. It didn't matter what was said, what words were used, what thoughts were exchanged. Nothing mattered but the process of injecting the drug and waiting for that first, glorious rush.

Bennett had no idea how much of the stuff she used, but it hit her like a sledgehammer, and she gasped with shock as it began to take hold. She threw back her head and let her mouth hang open, and everything in the world but what she was feeling disappeared.

"There you go," Penny whispered from somewhere far, far away, her voice distant and soft, barely there at all, hardly anything more than a ripple in the haze. "Bring it on, girl. Momma needs her itch scratched good!"

Bennett laughed and soared and watched everything around her change to cotton candy. She was barely awake when Penny climbed to her feet and opened the front door. She was barely aware of the black-clad old man who walked through and stood looking down at her.

"Hey, girlfriend," Penny hissed, and her tone of voice was suddenly sharp-edged and taunting. "How's this for an unexpected surprise? Look who's joining the party!"

Bennett lifted her eyes dreamily as Findo Gask bent close.

It was after nine-thirty before Nest missed Bennett Scott. She was having a good time talking with friends, some of them people she had known since childhood, sharing stories and swapping remembrances. Robert was very much in evidence early on, trying to make up for last night's provocative comments about John Ross by being overly attentive. She tolerated his efforts for a while because she knew he meant well, but sometimes a little of Robert went a long way. Fortunately, Amy was up and about, though not feeling very much better, and when Nest made a point of beginning a discussion with her about pregnancies and babies, Robert quickly disappeared.

Now and then, Nest would drift down to the rec room to see how the children were doing. She had played in this house as a little girl, so she knew the floor plan well. The rec room was safe and secure. A single entry opened down the stairs from the main hallway. There were no exterior doors or windows. The girls who were baby-sitting knew that only parents and friends were allowed to visit and were instructed to ask for help if there was any problem.

Harper fit right in with the other kids, but Little John parked himself in a corner and wouldn't move. She kept checking on him, hoping something would change over the course of the evening, but it never did. Her attempts to persuade him to join in proved futile, and eventually she gave up.

Once or twice she caught sight of Bennett, but since her concerns were primarily for the children and Bennett seemed to be doing all right, she didn't stop to worry about her.

But finally she realized it was getting late and they had to think about making arrangements to get home, and it was then she realized she hadn't seen Bennett for a while. When she had gone through the house twice without finding her, she tracked down Robert and drew him aside.

"I don't want to make too much of this, but I can't find Bennett Scott," she advised quietly. From her look, he knew right away this wasn't good.

He raised and lowered one eyebrow in a familiar Robert gesture. "Maybe she went home."

"Without Harper?"

He shrugged. "Maybe she got sick. Are you sure she's not here somewhere? You want me to ask around?"

She wheeled away abruptly and went back downstairs to the rec room. Kneeling next to Harper as the little girl worked to make something out of Play-Doh, she asked if her Mommy was there.

Harper barely looked up. "Mommy go bye-bye."

Nest felt her throat tighten in panic. "Did she tell you this, Harper? Did she tell you bye-bye?"

Harper nodded. "Yeth."

Nest climbed back to her feet and looked around helplessly. When had Bennett left? How long had she been gone? Where would she go without taking Harper, without telling anyone, without a car? She knew the answer before she finished the question, and she experienced a rush of anger and despair.

She bounded back up the stairs to find Robert. She would have to go looking, of course—even without knowing where to start. She would have to call John home to watch the children while she took the car and conducted a search.

In a snowstorm where everything was shut down and cars were barely moving? On a night when the wind chill was low enough to freeze you to death?

She felt the futility of what she was proposing threaten to overwhelm her, but she shoved aside her doubts to concentrate on the task at hand. She found Robert coming down the stairs from the second floor, shaking his head.

"Beats me, Nest. I looked everywhere I could think—"

Nest brushed the rest of what he was going to say aside with a wave of her hand. "She's gone. I got that much out of Harper. She left sometime back. I don't know why."

Robert sighed wearily. "But you can guess, can't you? She's an addict, Nest. I saw the tracks on her arms." He shook his head. "Look, I know this is none of my business, but—"

"Don't start, Robert. Just don't!" She clenched his wrist so hard he winced. "Don't lecture me about the company I keep, about Bennett and John Ross and all the strange things happening and how you remember it was just like this fifteen years ago on the Fourth of July! Just warm up your car while I get the children into their coats and boots and then drive us home!"

She let go of his wrist. "Do you think you can manage that?"

He looked mortified. "Of course I can manage it! Geez!"

She leaned in and gave him a peck on the cheek. "You're a good guy, Robert. But you require a lot of maintenance. Now get going."

The demons bundled Bennett Scott into her parka and took her out of the house and into the night, letting the drugs in her system do the job of keeping her in line. Snow was flying in all directions, the wind was blowing hard, and it was so cold that nose hairs froze, but Bennett Scott was floating somewhere outside her body, barely aware of anything but the pleasant feeling of not really being connected to reality. Every so often, something around her would come sharply into focus—the bite of the wind, the white fury of the snow, the skeletal shadow of a crooked tree limb, or the faces of Findo Gask and Penny Dreadful, one on either side, propping her up and moving her along. But mostly there was only a low buzzing in her ears and a wondrous sense of peace.

Findo Gask had left everything in the house as he found it, closing the front door behind them without locking it. He wanted Nest Freemark to return home without suspecting he had been there, so he had been careful not to do anything that would scare her off. If she grew too cautious, it would spoil the surprise he had left for her.

With Penny laughing and talking nonstop, they climbed into the car, backed out of the driveway onto Woodlawn, drove to the park entrance, parked in front of the crossbar, and set off on foot. Sinnissippi Park was a black hole of cold and sleet, the darkness unbroken and endless across the flats and through the woods, the snow freezing to ice in the grip of the north wind howling up the river channel. The lights that normally lit the roadway had been lost earlier when a power line went down, and the curtain of blowing snow masked the pale glimmerings of the nearby residences and townhomes. Tonight, the park might as well have been on the moon.

Bennett Scott stumbled and mushed through the deepening snowdrifts, her feet dragging, her body listless, her progress made possible by the fact that the demons who clutched either arm were dragging her. She gulped blasts of frigid air for breath and ducked her head for warmth, automatic responses from her body, but her mind told her almost nothing of what she was doing. She remembered Penny being there, the sharing of drugs that gave her such relief, and the thin, tenuous thread of hope she clung to that somehow, someday, she would find her way back to Harper. Now and again, she would hear her daughter's voice calling to her, small words, little noises, bits and pieces of memories retrieved from the haze of her thoughts.

She saw nothing of the eyes that began to appear in the dark, bright pairs of yellow slits coming out of nowhere in twos and threes until there were dozens.

They crossed the park to the bluffs, then continued west past the Indian mounds to the turnaround and the cliffs. The road had disappeared in the snow, and the entire area was a white carpet beneath the ragged limbs of the leafless hardwoods. Findo Gask was unconcerned about being interrupted; there was no one else in the park. Together with Penny, he nudged Bennett Scott toward the cliff edge, maneuvering her forward until she was only a few yards from the drop.

The feeders pressed closer, eager to become involved.

"Let her go, Penny," Gask ordered.

They stepped back from Bennett, leaving her alone at the cliff's edge, facing out toward the river, her head lolling and her arms hanging loose. The feeders closed on her, touching her softly, cajoling her voicelessly, urging her to give them what they needed.

Bennett stood without moving, her mind in another time zone, gliding through valleys and over peaks, the land all white-edged and golden bright, the singing of her blood in her veins sustaining and comforting. She soared unfettered for a long time, staring at nothing, and then remembered suddenly that she had not come alone.

"Penny?" she managed.

The wind howled at her.

"Penny?"

A child's voice called sharply. "Mommy!"

Bennett lifted her head and peered into the snow and darkness. It was Harper!

"Mommy, can you hear me?"

"Baby, where are you? Baby?"

"Mommy, I need you! Please, Mommy!"

Bennett felt the cold suddenly, a taste of its bite ripping past the armor of her stupor, leaving her shaking and breathing hard. She licked at her dry lips and glanced around. She saw the eyes now, close and watchful and hungry, and she jerked away in shock and fear.

"Harper!" she screamed.

"Mommy, run!" she heard Harper call out.

She saw her daughter then, a faint image just ahead of her in the darkness, lit by a pale white light that brightened and faded with the beating of her own heart, with the pulsing of her blood. She saw Harper and reached for her, but Harper was already moving away.

"Harper!" she wailed.

She couldn't go to her, knew she couldn't, knew there was something very wrong with trying to do so. She had a vague memory of having been in this situation once before, but she could not remember when or why.

"Mommy!" Harper begged, stumbling as she retreated.

Something was pulling at the little girl, dragging her away—something dark and shapeless and forbidding. It was too much for Bennett Scott. She cast off her lethargy and fear and burst through the knot of eyes that pressed against her, lunging after her daughter.

She was close enough to touch Harper, to see the fear in her daughter's eyes, when the ground disappeared beneath her feet and she fell away into the dark.

Chapter 20

Robert Heppler pulled the big Navigator into the empty driveway and put it in park, leaving the engine running. Nest gave a quick sigh of relief. It was blowing snow so hard that the driveway itself and all traces of tire tracks that might have marked its location had long since disappeared, so it was a good thing he knew the way by heart or they could easily have ended up in the front yard. She stared at the lighted windows of the house, but could see no movement. There were more lights on now than when she had left for the party, so someone must have gotten there ahead of her. She felt a surge of hope. Maybe she was wrong about Bennett. Maybe Bennett was waiting inside.

"Do you want me to come in with you?" Robert asked. She shifted her eyes to meet his, and he gestured vaguely. "Just to make sure."

She knew what he meant, even if he wasn't saying it straight out. "No, I can handle this. Thanks for bringing us back, Robert."

He shrugged. "Anytime. Call if you need me."

She opened the door into the shriek of the wind and climbed out, sinking in snow up to her knees. *Criminy,* as Pick would say. "Watch yourself driving home, Robert!" she shouted at him.

She got the children out of the backseat, small bundles of padded clothing and loose scarf ends, and began herding them toward the house. The wind whipped at them, shoving them this way and that as they trundled through its deep carpet, heads bent, shoulders hunched. It was bitter cold, and Nest could feel it reach all the way down to her bones. She heard the rumble of the Navigator as it backed out of the driveway and turned up the road. In seconds, the sound of the engine had disappeared into the wind's howl.

They clambered up the ice-rimmed wooden steps to the relative shelter of the front porch, where the children stamped their boots and brushed snow from their shoulders in mimicry of Nest. She tested the front door and found it unlocked—a sure sign someone was home—and ushered Harper and Little John inside.

It was silent in the house when she closed the door against the weather, so silent that she knew almost at once she had assumed wrongly; no one else was there, and if they had been, they had come and gone. She could hear the ticking of the grandfather clock and the rattle of the shutters at the back of the house where the wind worked them against their fastenings, but that was all.

She glanced down and noticed Bennett's small bag packed and sitting by the front door. Close by, she saw the damp outline of bootprints that were not their own. Then she caught sight of a glint of metal in the carpet. She bent slowly to pick it up. It was a syringe.

She felt a moment of incredible sorrow. Placing the syringe inside a small vase on the entry table, she turned to the children and began helping them off with their coats. Harper's face was red with cold and her eyes were tired. Little John looked the way he always did—pale, distant, and haunted. But he seemed frail, too, as if the passing of time drained him of energy and life and was finally beginning to leave its mark. She stopped in the middle of removing his coat, stared at him a moment, and then pulled him against her, hugging him close, trying to infuse him with some small sense of what she was feeling, trying once again to break through to him.

"Little John," she whispered.

He did not react to being held, but when she released him, he looked at her, and curiosity and wonder were in his eyes.

"Neth," Harper said at her elbow, touching her sleeve. "Appo jus?"

She glanced at the little girl and smiled. "Just a minute, sweetie. Let's finish getting these coats and boots off."

She dropped the coats on top of Bennett's bag to hide it from view, pulled off the children's boots, and laid their gloves and scarves over the old radiator. Outside, a car wearing chains rumbled down the snowy pavement, its passing audible only a moment before disappearing into the wind. Shadows flickered across the window panes as tree limbs swayed and shook amid the swirling snow. Nest stood by the door without moving, drawn by the sounds and movements, wondering if Bennett had been foolish enough to go out. The packed bag by the door suggested otherwise, but the house felt so empty.

"Come on, guys," she invited, taking the children by the hand and leading them down the hallway to the kitchen.

She glanced over her shoulder. It was dark in the back of the house. If Bennett was there, she was sleeping. Her gaze shifted to the shadowy corners of the living room as they passed, and she caught sight of Hawkeye's gleaming orbs way back under the Christmas tree, behind the presents.

Then she looked ahead, down the hall. The basement door was open. She slowed, suddenly wary. That door had been closed when she left. Would Bennett have gone down there for some reason?

She stopped at the kitchen entry and stared at the door. There was nothing in the basement. Only the furnace room, electrical panels, and storage. There were no finished rooms.

Outside, the wind gusted sharply, shaking the back door so hard the glass rattled. Nest started at the sound, releasing the children's hands.

"Go sit at the table," she ordered, gently shooing them into the kitchen.

Standing by the doorway, she picked up the phone to call John Ross, but the line was dead. She put the receiver back in its cradle and looked again at the basement door.

She was being silly, she told herself as she walked over to it swiftly, closed it without looking down the stairs, and punched the button lock on the knob. She stood where she was for a moment, contemplating her act, surprised at how much better it made her feel.

Satisfied, she walked back into the kitchen and began setting out cider and cookies. When the cider and cookies were distributed, she took a moment to check out the bedrooms, just to be sure Bennett was not there. She wasn't. Nest returned to the kitchen, considering her options. Only one made any real sense. She would have to get a hold of the police. She did not like contemplating what that meant.

She was sipping cider and munching cookies with the children when the shriek of ripping or tearing of metal rose out of the bowels of the house. She heard the sound once, and then everything went silent.

She sat for a moment without moving, then rose from her chair, walked out of the kitchen and down the hallway a few steps, and stopped again to listen. "Bennett?" she called softly.

An instant later, the lights went out.

John Ross dreams of the future. The day is gray and clouded, and the light is poor. It is morning, but the sun is only a spot of hazy brightness in the deeply overcast sky. The walls of partially collapsed buildings hem him in on all sides, shutting away the world beyond and giving him the feel of what it must be like to be a rat in a maze. He moves down passageways and streets with quick, furtive movements, sliding from doorway to alcove, from alleyway to darkened corner. He is being hunted, and he feels his hunters drawing close.

He is in a village. He has been hiding there for several days, tired and worn and bereft of his magic. He carries his rune-scrolled black staff, but its magic is dormant. An expenditure of that magic in his past has left him without its use in his present. It has been more than a week since the magic was his to command, the longest time he has spent without its protection. He does not know why the magic has failed him so thoroughly and for so long, but he is running out of time. In the world of the future he has failed to prevent, a week without armor or weapons is a lifetime.

Ahead, he sees the shapes of trees through a haze that never clears. If he can make it to those trees, he may have a chance. Someone in the village has betrayed him, as someone always does. They depend on him, but they do not trust him. The magic he wields is powerful, but it is frightening as well. Sooner or later, someone always decides he is more dangerous than the once-men and the demons he battles. They arrive at the decision out of a misguided belief that by sacrificing him, they can save themselves. It is a condition of humankind brought about by the collapse of civilization. He has long since accepted it as the way of things, but he cannot get used to it. Even as he runs for his life yet another time, he is filled with anger and disgust for those he tries so hard to protect.

The sounds of pursuit are audible now, and he picks up his pace, making for the concealment of the trees. Once clear of the village and deep enough into the woods, he will be difficult to find. He is physically fit, toughened by his years of survival in the brave new world of the Void's ascendancy. He is no longer hampered by the limp that shackled him in the old world, when the Word held sway. He knows how to flee and hide as well as how to attack and fight, and he will not be easily found. He remembers how little he knew of such things in his old life. He was a Knight of the Word then, too, but in the old world there was still hope. Bitterness colors his thoughts; if he had not failed in his efforts there, his survival knowledge would not be necessary here.

Feeders shadow him as he gains the tangle of the trees and melts into their darkened mass. They are always with him, hopeful that one day they will feed on him as they have fed on so many others. Everywhere he goes, they are drawn to him.

He has come to accept this, too. He is a magnet for predators of all sorts, and the feeders are only the most pervasive of the breed. Sometimes they will challenge him, but they cannot stand against his magic. It is only now, when the magic is out of his reach, that they sense they have a chance. He tries to ignore the hunger that reflects in their eyes as they keep pace with him, but he does not completely succeed.

Behind him, screams begin to rise from the village. The demons and once-men are reaping their harvest of death, reducing the village to ashes and rubble. It is unavoidable. All communities of men, whether city fortresses or unwalled villages, are targeted for this end. The destruction of humankind is the goal to which the servants of the Void are pledged. It is a goal that will be attained one day in the not-too-distant future, even though a few like himself struggle still to prevent it. It will be attained because all chance of winning has been lost in the past, and the Word has been reduced to memory and lost in time.

There are movements on his left and right, and he realizes his hunters have flanked him, moving more quickly than he has expected. He slows and listens, trying to judge what he must do. But there is little time for speculation, and after a moment he plunges on, reduced to hoping he can outdistance them. He does not succeed. They come upon him moments later, one or two at first, crying out wildly as they discover him, quickly bringing more, until soon there are so many the trees are thick with them. Still he races on, zigzagging down ravines and up hills, knocking aside the few brave enough to challenge him alone. He tries to call up the magic, hoping that it has returned, that it has not forsaken him when he needs it most, but the magic does not respond.

They catch him in a clearing where there is room enough for them to come at him from all sides. He struggles ferociously, bringing to bear all of his considerable fighting skills, but his attackers overwhelm him by sheer numbers. He is thrown to the ground and pinned fast by many hands, the stench of the once-men thick in his nostrils, their eyes bright with expectation and fever. Feeders swarm over him, finding him helpless at last, already beginning to touch him, to savor the emotions he emits while trapped and helpless.

A demon emerges from the crush of bodies and rips the black staff from his hands. No one has ever been able to do this before, but that is because he has always had the magic to prevent it and now he does not. The demon studies the staff, its twisted face bristling with dark hair and pocked with deep hollows where the leathery skin has collapsed into the bone. It attempts to snap the staff in two, using its inhuman strength, but the staff resists its efforts. Frustrated, the demon throws it down and stamps on it, but the staff will not break. Finally, the demon burns it with magic, scattering the once-men who have gotten too close, leaving the staff charred and smoking within an outline of blackened earth.

They bear him from the clearing then, dozens of hands holding him fast as they move back through the woods toward the village. The demon follows, clutching the remains of the staff. He can hear anew the shrieks and moans of the injured and dying, of the people who first harbored him and then gave him up, guilty and innocent alike. Many will be dead before the day is done, and this time, he knows, he will be one of them. The thought of dying does not frighten him; he has lived with the possibility for too long to fear it now. Nor is he frightened of the pain. There are rents and tears in his skin, and his blood flows down his arms and legs, but he does not feel it. The pain he feels most lies deep inside his heart.

His captors bear him past the village through a ruined orchard and up a small rise to a country church. The church is smoldering from a fire that has mostly burned itself out. The roof has collapsed, the walls are scorched, and the windows have been broken out. A clutch of once-men have brought a large wooden cross from within and laid it on the open ground. The brackets that secured it to the wall behind the altar are still attached, twisted and scarred. Once-men with hammers and iron spikes stand waiting, heads turning quickly at his approach.

Hands lower him roughly to the earth and hold him pinned against the wooden cross, arms outstretched, legs crossed at the ankles. They strip off his boots so that his feet will be unprotected. He does not struggle against them. There is no reason to do so. His time as a Knight of the Word is ended. He watches almost disinterestedly as the demon casts the ruined staff on the ground at his feet and the men with the hammers and spikes kneel beside him. They force one hand open and place the tip of a spike against his palm. He remembers a dream he had—long ago, when there was still hope—of being in this time and place, of hanging broken from a cross. He remembers, and thinks that perhaps the measure of any life is the joining of the past and the future at the moment of death.

Then a hammer rises and falls, and the spike is driven through the bones and flesh of his hand . . .

Ross awoke with a gasp, hands clenching the sheets and blankets, body rigid and sweating. He lay staring into the darkness of the room for several moments, trying to remember where he was. His dreams were always like this—so disturbing that waking from them left him feeling adrift and lost.

Then he felt Josie Jackson stir next to him, folding her body into his, and he remembered that he was in her house, in her bedroom, and had fallen asleep after lovemaking. A sliver of streetlight silvery with frost and cold glimmered through a gap in the window curtains. Josie put her arm around his chest, her fingers settling on his shoulder, smooth and warm. Her body heat infused him with reassurance and a sense of place.

But any contentment he felt was illusory. The dream had told him that his failure to save the gypsy morph, to breach its layers of self-protection, to discover the key to its magic and thereby bring it alive, was locking his future in place.

He lay there for a long time thinking through what that meant, of having to live the rest of his life knowing that even if he stayed alive through everything, his death was already predetermined. He did not know if he could live with that. He did know that his only chance to change things was now.

What then, he asked himself angrily, was he doing here? Nest, at least, was with Little John, monitoring his progress and seeking a way to reach him. What was he doing, away from both, fulfilling needs that had nothing to do with either?

The bitter taste in his mouth compressed his lips into a tight line. He was only human. It wasn't fair to expect more. It wasn't possible for him to give it.

He closed his eyes. Nevertheless, he conceded in the darkness of his mind, it was time to go.

Gently, he extracted himself from Josie's embrace, climbing from the bed, picking up his clothes, and slipping from the room. He dressed in the hallway and walked downstairs to retrieve his coat and boots. The clock in the kitchen told him it was closing on midnight. He glanced around. The old house was dark and silent and felt comfortable. He did not want to leave.

He took a deep breath. He was in love with Josie Jackson. That was why he was here. That was why he wanted to stay. Forever.

He remained where he was for a few moments, then walked to the bottom of the stairway and looked up into the darkness. He should go to her. He should tell her good-bye.

He considered it only briefly. Then he turned and went out the door into the night.

Nest Freemark froze in the sudden darkness, surprised and vaguely uneasy. The lights were all down. The hum of the refrigerator had gone silent. They had lost all power. All she could hear was the ticking of the grandfather clock.

She walked quickly back to the kitchen. The children were sitting at the table, staring around in confusion. "Neth," Harper whispered. "Too dark."

"It's okay, sweetie," she said, walking to the kitchen window to peer outside. Lights blazed up and down the road. Hers were the only ones that had gone out. She glanced around the yard, seeing nothing but blowing snow and the shadows of tree limbs spidering over the drifts. "It's okay," she whispered.

She wished suddenly that John Ross or even Pick was there, to provide some measure of backup. She felt very alone in the old house, in the darkness, with two children to care for. It was silly, she knew. Like the basement door—

The basement steps creaked softly. She heard the sound distinctly. Someone was climbing them. For an instant she dismissed the idea as ridiculous, wanting the sound to be her imagination. Then she heard it again.

She walked to the kitchen table and bent close to the children. "Sit right here for a moment and don't move," she said.

She opened the drawer by the broom closet and brought out Old Bob's four-cell flashlight, the big, dependable one he always carried. She gripped it with determination, the weight of it comforting as she slipped on cat's feet from the kitchen and down the hall to the basement door. She listened a moment, hearing nothing.

Then she took a deep breath, yanked open the door, switched on the flashlight, and flooded the stairwell with its powerful beam.

She almost missed what was there because it had climbed the wall and was hanging from the ceiling. It was shapeless and black, more shadow than substance, a kind of moving stain caught in the edge of the light. When she realized it was there and shifted the light to reveal it more fully, arms and legs unfolded, eyes glimmered out of its spidery mass, a hint of claws and teeth appeared, and it came down off the ceiling in a rush.

Nest reacted instinctively, summoning the magic with which she had been born, the magic that had been the legacy of the Freemark women for six generations. Locking eyes with the dark horror scrabbling up the stairs, she sent the magic spinning into it. It was like burrowing into primal ooze, as if the creature had no bones and there was nothing about it that was solid. But it stumbled and lost its grip anyway, the magic stealing its momentum and twisting its reactions, and it tumbled away into the dark.

Nest slammed the door, punched the button lock, and rushed back into the kitchen. Grabbing one of the high-backed wooden chairs away from the table, she dragged it to the basement door, tilted it so that its back was under the knob, and jammed it in place.

Her breath came in quick gasps. She had to get the children out of there. She hurried back to the kitchen, snatched up Harper, and grabbed Little John by the arm. "Come with me," she urged as calmly as she could manage. "Quick, now."

She got them to the front door and began shoveling them into their coats. Harper was protesting, and Little John was just standing there, looking at her. She fought to keep her composure, listening for the sound of the thing in the basement, thinking, *No lights, no phone, no transportation, trapped.*

The basement door flew open with a crash, the lock giving way, the chair splintering apart.

Keeping the children behind her, she stepped into the hall to face her attacker—only it wasn't there. She speared the darkness with the flashlight, searching for it. She tried the ceiling first, then the walls. Nothing. She backed toward the children, eyes flitting left and right. It must be in the kitchen or living room. It must have ducked through one doorway or the other. She felt her insides churning, her throat and chest going tight with fear. She felt Wraith come awake inside her. In seconds, he would begin to break free. She could not afford to let that happen. Not in front of the children.

Hawkeye shot out from under the Christmas tree, a blur of orange fur as he disappeared down the hall.

She swung the beam of the flashlight back toward the kitchen, frantically searching.

Where is it?

It came from behind her, out of the darkness at the hallway's other end, from the direction of the bedrooms. She sensed it before she heard it and swung about to block its attack just before it launched itself through the beam of her light. It came at her in a rush, a black and formless mass, unexpectedly veering away at the last moment to try to get behind her. She threw the magic at it in a blanket, then swung at it with the flashlight. She saw it twist wildly and stumble, caught in the magic's grip, unable to recover. Some part of it lashed out at her in fury, catching her arms a numbing blow, and the flashlight spun away. Then it was past her and down the hall the other way, lost in shadows.

The flashlight went out and the house was plunged into darkness once more. Nest took the children by the arms and literally dragged them down the hallway to her bedroom. It was too late to get out or to try to summon help now. Her options were all gone. She needed a place where she could stand and fight. She realized something now, after this last attack, that hadn't been apparent before. The thing attacking them wasn't after her. It was after the children.

She got the children into her bedroom and slammed the door behind them, punching the lock. It was the best she could do. Her insides were twisting and roiling, and she knew Wraith would not be kept imprisoned much longer. Besides, there wasn't any choice; if they wanted to stay alive, she would have to let him out. Nothing less than the ghost wolf could protect them. Her own magic was woefully inadequate; it provided a holding action at best. Harper was sobbing, crying for her mother, but there was no time to comfort her. She hurried the children to the closet on the far side of the room, pushed them inside, and told them to get down on the floor and stay there.

She had barely closed the closet door when she heard noises in the hall outside. Her curtains were still open, and the room was brightened by light from a streetlamp. She could see everything clearly. Her eyesight had always been exceptional in any case, a gift of the magic and her heritage, Gran had told her. She could roam the park at night with Pick and see as clearly as he could. She would need that talent now.

The bedroom door flew back, the lock snapped, and the black thing heaved into the room. It didn't come at her right away this time, but floated up the wall to one side. She edged toward the center of the room, away from the bed, but with her back to the closet door, keeping herself between the attacker and the children. The black thing oozed along the wall for a moment, then dropped into a corner. Its movements were fluid and seamless, almost hypnotic.

Slowly it began to spread along the floor in a dark stain, moving toward her.

Wraith broke free then, shattering the restraints she had forged to keep him from doing so. There was no help for it; her need was too great. The big ghost wolf catapulted across the room toward the thing in the corner, tiger-striped face twisted in fury, jaws wide, teeth gleaming. Nest went with him, unable to prevent it, a part of herself trapped inside, her eyes seeing through his, her heart beating within the great sinewy chest. She felt as he did, primal and raw, all hunter and predator, caught up in his dark, compelling instinct to defend her at any cost.

The black thing counterattacked, and for a moment everything became a flurry of teeth and claws, guttural sounds and twisting bodies. Wraith fought ferociously, but the black thing, despite its shapeless, fluid mass, was immensely strong. It hammered into Wraith, and Nest felt the impact as if it were her own body under assault. Slammed violently backward, unable to hold his ground, Wraith went down in a tangle of legs and bristling hair, tiger face contorting in fury.

Up again almost immediately, he swung back to the attack, head lowered, muzzle drawn back.

But the black thing was gone.

It took Nest a moment to realize what had happened. Wraith stalked to the open doorway, gimlet eyes searching the darkness. Down the hall, the front door opened and closed. Wraith froze, a shadow silhouetted in the bedroom doorway, huge and menacing. Nest felt her connection with him unexpectedly loosen.

Then the closet door cracked softly behind her, and Little John slipped into view. He stood frozen in place for a moment, as if mesmerized by the tableau before him. His eyes shifted from Nest to Wraith and back again. Terror and despair were mirrored there; Nest could see both clearly. But there was a dark and haunting need as well. There was an unmistakable plea for contact. Nest was stunned. The gypsy morph was reaching out to her at last, groping in silent, wordless desperation. She was staggered by the depth of his voiceless cry for help. She was terrified.

She reacted instinctively, calling Wraith to her with a thought, drawing him back inside, trying to shield his presence from the boy. The ghost wolf came swiftly, obediently, knowing what was expected of him, but exuding a sense of reluctance, too, that in the heat of the moment she did not even think to question.

But Little John turned frantic. He came at her in a rush, crossing the room in a churning of arms and legs, reaching her just moments after Wraith had disappeared inside. He threw himself at her, this strange, enigmatic boy who would not be understood or revealed, and wrapped his arms around her as if she had become the most precious thing alive.

In the silence that followed, standing there in the center of her bedroom, her arms holding Little John close against her breast as she tried to reassure him that she was there for whatever need he had and would give to him whatever he required, she heard him cry softly.

"Mama," he said in his child's voice. "Mama."

Wednesday, December 24

Chapter 21

Nest was awake by six o'clock the next morning, dressed and ready to go. She walked up the road in the still, cold darkness to the pay phone at the all-night gas station on Lincolnway and spent twenty minutes arranging for repairmen from the electrical and phone companies to make unscheduled early morning stops at her home. Because she had lived in Hopewell all her life, she knew who to call to make this happen. Not that it was all that easy to persuade the people she knew to change things around on the day before Christmas, but in the end she got the job done.

She had taken the time to determine the extent of the damage last night before finally going off to sleep. The phone line was cut where it came into the house, so that wasn't a big deal. But the entire circuit-breaker box had been ripped out of the wall, and she had no idea how difficult it would be to fix that.

She carried back a box of doughnuts and Styrofoam cups of hot chocolate and coffee, thinking that they would at least have that for sustenance. The snow had stopped and the wind had died, so the world around her was still and calm. The children were sleeping, exhausted physically and emotionally from last night's events. It had taken her a long time to get them to sleep, especially Little John, who had done a complete one hundred eighty degree turn toward her. Instead of distancing himself as he had before, going off to a private world to contemplate things hidden from her, he had attached himself so completely that it seemed any sort of separation would break his heart. She could barely get him to release her long enough to greet John Ross, who came through the door less than half an hour after her battle with the thing in the basement and found the gypsy morph clinging to her like a second skin.

She was pleased by Little John's change, but puzzled as well. He had called her *Mama* twice, but said nothing more since. He seemed devastated by her failure to understand what he wanted. She held him and cooed to him and told him it was all right, that she was there and she loved him, but nothing seemed to help. He was disconsolate and bereft in a way she could not understand.

"It has something to do with Wraith," she had told John Ross.

They sat together on the living room couch in the aftermath of the night's events, the children asleep at last and the house secured as best it could be. It was cold in the house and growing colder without any heat, and she had tucked the children into sleeping bags in front of the fireplace and built a fire to keep them warm.

She whispered so as not to wake them. "When he saw me standing there, while Wraith was still across the room, he had such excitement and hope in his eyes, John. But when Wraith came back to me, he was devastated."

"Maybe he was frightened by what he saw." Ross was looking at the sleeping boy, brow furrowed. "Maybe he didn't understand."

Nest shook her head. "He is a creature of magic. He understood what was happening. No, it was something else. It was Wraith that bothered him so. Why would that be? Wraith has been there all along."

"And the gypsy morph hasn't wanted anything to do with you the entire time." Ross looked at her meaningfully.

"No," she agreed.

"Maybe you are being asked to make a choice."

"Between magics? Or between lives? What sort of choice?"

"I don't know. I'm just speculating. Give up one magic for another, perhaps?" Ross shook his head.

She thought about it again, walking home from the gas station. Apparently the gypsy morph couldn't find a way to tell her what it wanted. Little John was a boy, but he wasn't altogether a real boy, rather something like Pinocchio, wooden and jointed and made out of fairy dust. Perhaps he did want her to choose him over Wraith. But how was she supposed to do that? It wasn't as if she hadn't thought of ridding herself of the ghost wolf, of her father's demon magic, time and again. She didn't want that magic inside her. She was constantly battling to keep it under control. Last night she had failed, forced to release it because of a demonic presence. She knew she would never be at peace as long as Wraith stayed locked away inside her. But it wasn't as if the choice was hers.

Snowplows rumbled past her, clearing Woodlawn and the surrounding side streets, metal blades scraping the blacktop in a series of long, rasping whines. Lights glimmered from streetlamps and porches, from solitary windows and passing headlights, but the darkness was still thick and unbroken this Christmas Eve day. The solstice was only just past, and the short days would continue well into January. It would not be light until after eight o'clock, and it would be dark again by four. If the sun appeared at all, they would be lucky. Not much comfort there, if she hoped to find any. Head lowered in thought, she walked on.

Ross was awake and waiting on her return, standing in the kitchen, staring out the window. The children were still asleep. She gave him coffee and a doughnut, took the same for herself, and they sat at the kitchen table.

"I've been awake almost all night," he told her, his gaze steady and alert nevertheless. "I couldn't sleep."

She nodded. "Me, either."

"I should never have gone to Josie's. I should have stayed with you and Little John."

She leaned forward. "It wouldn't have changed anything. You know that. We would have lost Bennett anyway. And if you had been here to protect us from that thing in the basement, Wraith might not have come out and Little John might not have responded to me in the way he did. John, that was the first time he's given me a second look. That was the first positive reaction I've gotten out of him. I'm this close to breaking through. I can feel it."

"If there's time enough left." He shook his head. "I don't know, Nest. This has gotten entirely out of hand. Findo Gask is all over the place, just waiting for a chance to attack us in some new way. I'm sure he was responsible for that thing in the basement. He's probably responsible for Bennett's disappearance as well."

Nest was silent a moment. "Probably," she admitted.

"Did you call the police to report her missing?"

She shook her head. "Not yet. She was gone the night before last, too, and came home on her own. I keep hoping she'll do so now." She exhaled warily. "But if she isn't back by the time the phone is fixed, I'll make the call."

Ross brought the black staff around in front of him and tightened his grip on it. "It's too dangerous for me to be here any longer," he said softly. "I shouldn't have come in the first place. I have to take Little John and get out of here before anything else happens—before some other horror shows up in your basement or your bedroom closet or wherever, and this time you aren't quick enough to save yourself."

Nest sipped at her coffee, thinking the matter through. Outside, the darkness was beginning to lighten. The world glimmered crystalline and white in a faint wash of gray. She replayed last night's battle with the black thing, experiencing again the terror and rage that had overcome her, remembering how it had felt for Wraith to come out of her once again, after so long, after she had worked so hard to keep it from happening. She saw Little John's anguished look of loss and betrayal. She couldn't forget that look. She couldn't stop thinking about what it meant.

"I have an idea, John," she said finally, looking over at him again. "I'll have to talk to Pick about it, but it might give us some breathing space."

Ross did not seem convinced. "If I take Little John and go, it will give you more breathing space."

"If you take Little John and go, we will have given up. Not to mention what effect it would have on him." She held his gaze firmly with her own. "Just let me talk to Pick. Then we'll see. Okay?"

He nodded wordlessly, but didn't look happy. She got up to check on the children before he could say anything else.

The electrician arrived shortly afterward, a big, burly fellow named Mike who looked at the ruined breaker box, shook his head, and wanted to know how in the hell something like that could have happened. His words. Nest told him the house had been broken into and all sorts of damage had been done that didn't seem to have any purpose. Mike shrugged and went to work, apparently accepting her explanation. The phone repairman showed up while she was feeding the rest of the doughnuts and the hot chocolate and some apple juice to Harper and Little John, and fixed the line in about two minutes. The phone guy, unlike Mike, didn't seem all that concerned with being given an explanation. He simply repaired the damage and left.

Nest called the police then to report Bennett missing, making the call out of the children's hearing. This was easier than she had anticipated because Little John had gone back to ignoring her. She had hugged him on waking, and he had barely responded, eyes distant once more, that thousand-yard stare back in place. He sat on the sofa and looked into the park until she led him into the kitchen to eat, then stayed in his seat when he was done, lost in his own private world. She was too busy to be upset yet, but she knew she would be later if he didn't come back to her from wherever he had gone.

The police took down her report and said they would stay in touch. They didn't have any news at their end, which was probably all to the good. Nest still hoped that Bennett would walk through the door on her own, high on drugs or not. She still believed she could help Bennett without involving the police.

But then, while hanging up her coat, which she had tossed aside last night on coming in, she found Bennett's note in the pocket.

Dear Nest,

I am sorry to run off like this, leaving Harper with you, but I have to get away. I used last night, and I know I will use again in a little while. I don't want to, but I can't help myself. I guess I am hopeless. I don't like Harper to be around me when I am using, so I am leaving her with you. I guess maybe I planned to leave her with you all along. I can't take care of her anymore, and I can't leave her with strangers either. Guess that leaves you. Please take care of her, big sister. I trust you. Harper is all I have, and I want to keep her safe and not have her grow up like me. When I am better, I will come back for her. Tell her I love her and will think of her every day. I'm sorry for causing so much trouble. I love you.

Bennett

Nest read the note several times, trying to think what to do. But there was really nothing she could do. Bennett could be anywhere, with anyone. She didn't like to speculate on the possibilities. She did not have any difficulty with the idea of looking after Harper, although she had no way of knowing how the little girl would react when she found out her mother had left her. It had happened before, but that didn't mean it would make things any easier this time.

Mike the electrician wandered up from the basement long enough to announce that he would have everything up and running within the hour, so she left the children in Ross's care, put on her parka, and went out into the park in search of Pick.

He wasn't hard to find. As she trudged across her backyard and into the snowy expanse of the ballpark flats, he soared out of the deep woods east aboard Jonathan. The sky was iron gray and hard as nails. The clouds settled low and threatening above the earth, as if snow might reappear at any moment. Mist filtered through the woods from off the frozen river, long tendrils snaking about the trunks and branches and wandering off into the bordering subdivisions and roadways. The park was empty this day, leaving Nest a solitary watcher as the dark specks that were Pick and Jonathan slowly took on definition with their approach.

The owl swung wide of Nest, then settled in an oak bordering the roadway. Pick climbed off and began to make his way down the trunk. He moved with quick, jerky motions, like a foraging squirrel, dropping from branch to branch, circling the trunk when a better path was needed, stopping every so often to look around. Jonathan folded his broad wings into his body, tucked his head into his shoulders, and became a part of the tree.

Nest walked over and waited until Pick was low enough to jump from the branches onto her shoulder, where he sat huffing from the effort.

"Confound that owl, anyway!" he complained. "You'd think he'd be willing to land on a lower branch, wouldn't you? For an owl, he's a bit on the slow side."

She turned around and sat down in the snow with her back against the tree. "I need your help."

"So what's new?" The sylvan chuckled, pleased with his attempt at humor. "Can you think of a time when you didn't need my help?"

He chuckled some more. It was a rather frightening sound, given that it emanated from a stick figure only six inches high.

Nest sighed, determined not to be baited into an argument. "I need you to concoct some antidemon magic. Something on the order of what you use to protect the trees in the park when there's something attacking them."

"Whoa, wait a minute!" Pick straightened abruptly, suddenly all business. His twiggy finger stabbed the air in her direction. "Are we talking about Findo Gask?"

"We are."

"Well, you can stop right there!" Pick threw up his hands. "What do I look like, anyway? I'm just a sylvan, for goodness sake! I don't have that kind of magic! You've got a real live Knight of the Word living under your roof. Use him! He's got the kind of magic you're talking about, the kind that can strip the skin off a maentwrog in the blink of an eye. What do you need with me when you've got him?"

"Will you calm down and listen to me for a minute?" she demanded.

"Not if the rest of the conversation is going to be like this!" Pick was on his feet, arms windmilling. "I'm a sylvan!" he repeated. "I don't fight demons! I don't charge off into battle with things that eat me for lunch! All I do is take care of this park, and believe me, that's work enough. It takes all of my energy and magic to handle that little chore, Nest Freemark, and I don't need you coming around and asking me to conjure up some sort of . . ."

"Pick, please!"

". . . half-baked magic that won't work on the best day of my life against a thing so black . . ."

"Pick!"

He went silent then, breathing hard from his tirade, glaring at her from under mossy brows, practically daring her to say anything more about the subject of demons and sylvan magic.

"Let me start over," she said quietly. "I don't really expect you to conjure up antidemon magic. That was a poor choice of words."

"Humph," he grunted.

"Nor do I expect you to sacrifice your time and energy in a cause where you can make no difference. I know how hard you work to protect the park, and I wouldn't ask you to do something that would jeopardize that effort."

Her attempt at calming him seemed to be working, she saw. At least he was listening again. She gave him her best serious-business look. It wasn't all that hard considering what she had to say. She told him about what had happened during the snowstorm, with the disappearance of Bennett Scott and the attack by the black thing hiding in her basement. She told him about Wraith coming out to defend them, and of his struggle with their attacker.

"Findo Gask, for sure!" Pick snapped. "You can't mistake demon mischief for anything but what it is."

"Well, you'll understand then when I tell you I am more than a little on edge about all this." She relaxed a hair, but kept her eye on him, waiting for his mercurial personality to undergo another shift. "I can't have this sort of thing hanging over my head every time I walk through the door. I have to find a way to prevent it from happening again. John Ross says he should take the gypsy morph and leave Hopewell. But if he does that, we lose all chance of finding a way to solve its riddle. It will last a few more days, then break apart and be gone. The magic will be lost forever."

Pick shrugged. "The magic might be lost anyway, given the fact that no one knows what it is or how to use it. Maybe Ross is right."

Now it was Nest's turn to glare. "So you think I should just give up?"

"I didn't say that."

"All I should worry about is helping you in the park? The rest of the world can just be damned?"

He grimaced. "Don't swear. I don't like it."

"Well, I don't like the idea of you giving up! Or telling me to give up, either!"

"Will you calm down?"

"Not if you're telling me you won't even try to help!"

"Criminy!" Pick was back on his feet, shuffling this way and that on the narrow ledge of her shoulder. "All right, all right! What is it you want me to do?" He wheeled on her. "What, that is, that doesn't involve antidemon magic?"

She lifted her hands placatingly. "I'm not going to ask you to do anything I know you can't." She paused. "What I want you to create is a kind of early-warning system. I want you to spin out a net of magic and throw it over my house so that the demons can't come in again without my knowing it."

He studied her doubtfully. "You're not asking me to use magic to keep them out?"

"No. I'm asking you to use magic to let me know if they try to get in. I'm asking you to create a warning system."

"Well!" he huffed. "Well!" He threw up his hands again. "Why didn't you say so before? I can do that! Of course, I can!" He glanced at the sky. "Look at the time we've wasted talking about it when we could have been putting it in place. Criminy, Nest! You should have gotten to the point more quickly!"

"Well, I—"

"Come on!" he interrupted, jumping from her shoulder and scrambling back up the tree trunk toward Jonathan.

He flew the owl back across the park to her house while she followed on foot. Midday was approaching, but it was still misty and gray, the clouds low and threatening, the air sharp with cold. The wind had not returned and no new snow had begun to fall, but the return of both seemed altogether likely. Nest stared at the houses bordering the park, indistinct and closed away, their roofs snowcapped, their walls drifted, and their eaves iced. There were cars on the roads, but not many, and they moved with caution on the slick surface. It was Christmas Eve day, but she thought people would try to confine their celebrations to their homes this year.

When she reached the house, Pick was already at work. She had seen him do this before in the park, when warding a tree. The process he used was the same in each case. Here, he flew Jonathan from tree to house, to tree, back to house, and so on, forming a crisscross pattern that draped the threads of magic in an intricate webbing. At each tree he stopped long enough to conjure up a sort of locking device and receptor, invisible to the eye, but there to serve a dual purpose—to anchor the magic in that particular place and to feed its lines of power. No materials were used and nothing of the work was visible, but the result was to render the house as secure as if a fine steel mesh had been thrown over it. All passageways in or out were covered. All entrances were alarmed. Any attempts to pass through, whatever form they took, would be detected instantly.

It took him almost an hour to complete the task, working his way slowly and carefully from point to point, all around the house, spinning out his lines of magic, making certain that nothing was missed. She stayed out of his way as he worked, watching in silence. There would be no more surprises like last night's. If the demons tried to come back again, she would know.

"Now here's the thing to remember," Pick advised when he was done. He sat on her shoulder once more, Jonathan perched in a sycamore some distance off, awaiting his summons. "Any attempt by a demon to get past the net and into your house will trip your alarm. This alarm isn't something that rings or honks or whistles or what have you. It's a feeling, but you won't mistake it."

He lifted a finger in warning. "A human entering the house won't trip the alarm. A human going out won't trip it either. But if you open up a window or door and leave it open, you invite the demon in and the system fails. So close everything up and keep it closed."

She frowned. "I didn't know that part."

"Well, it hardly has any bearing in the park, when we're warding the trees, because there isn't anything living inside the net that would open it up in any case. It's different here. Keep everything shut tight. If you do that, the demons can't get past the system without you knowing. Think you can remember that?"

"I can remember." She gave him a smile. "Thanks, Pick."

"Just remember what I told you. That'll be thanks enough."

He looked exceedingly proud of himself as he jumped from her shoulder and scurried across the yard to climb back aboard Jonathan. Together, they flew off into the haze. She watched them go, thinking that Pick, of all her friends, over all the years, was still the most reliable.

She looked at the house. There was nothing different about it; she felt nothing different inside. She was taking this entire warning system business on faith, but where Pick was concerned, faith was enough. Certainly the demons would detect the system's presence. Maybe that would be enough to keep them at bay for a day or so. Maybe that would be time enough for her to find out what it was that would unlock Little John's secret.

She found herself wondering suddenly how she had ever gotten to this point in her life. She was trapped in her home with a creature she did not understand and under attack from demons. She was struggling with her own magic and with the magics of other beings, the combination of which threatened to overwhelm her at any moment. She was hiding secrets that could destroy her. She was twenty-nine years old, adrift in both the purpose and direction of her life, her future uncertain.

What was her reason for being? Her gift of magic seemed pointless. Her life appeared to have led nowhere. She had been special since birth, but nothing of who she had been gave her insight into who she was meant to be. She was at an impasse, and the events of these past few days only pointed up how thoroughly lost she was.

If Gran were still here, would she be able to tell me what I ought to do? Would she understand the reason for all that has happened in my life? Or would she be as lost as I am?

Likely, she would just tell me to get on with it.

There was no steadying influence in her life. No parents, grandparents, husband, or children. No family. There were friends, but that wasn't the same thing. She felt the lack of an anchor, of a touchstone that would give her a sense of belonging. The house had provided that once. And the park. All the places she had grown up in, the tapestry of her journey out of childhood. But somehow they weren't enough anymore. They served only to trigger memories that locked her in the past.

She stood thinking on the matter for a long time, staring off into space, traveling distances too far to be seen clearly.

Then the door opened, and John Ross stepped out onto the back steps. "Better come inside, Nest," he said quietly. "The sheriff's office is on the phone. They've found Bennett Scott."

CHAPTER 22

As she drove to Community General Hospital, nosing the Taurus between the dirt-and-cinder-encrusted snowbanks plowed up from the streets, Nest found herself reflecting on the cyclical nature of life. Her thinking wasn't so much about the fact of it—that was mundane and obvious—but about the ways in which it happened. Sometimes, in the course of living, you couldn't avoid ending up where you began. You might travel far distances and experience strange events, but when all was said and done, your journey brought you right back around to where everything started.

It was so in an unexpected way for Bennett Scott. She had almost died on the cliffs at Sinnissippi Park fifteen years ago, when she was only five. Nest had been there to save her then, but not this time. It made Nest wonder if the manner of Bennett's death was in some way predetermined, if saving her from the cliffs the first time had only forestalled the inevitable. It was strange and troubling that Bennett should die this way, after escaping once, after it seemed that whatever else might threaten, at least she was safe from this.

Thinking on the cyclical nature of Bennett Scott's life and death reminded Nest of her mother. Caitlin Anne Freemark had also died at the bottom of the cliffs in Sinnissippi Park, shortly after Nest was born. For years, there had been questions about how she had died—whether she had slipped and fallen, wandered off by mistake, or committed suicide. It wasn't until Nest had confronted her demon father that she had discovered the truth. He had instigated the events and emotional trauma that had led to her mother's death. Call it suicide or call it a calculated orchestration, the cause and effect were the same.

Now she wondered if demons were responsible for Bennett's death as well. Had Findo Gask and that girl Penny and whoever else might be aiding them set in motion the events that culminated in Bennett's death? Nest could not escape feeling that they had. As with her mother, as with the children in the park she and Pick had saved so often in that summer fifteen years ago, Bennett Scott had been prey to demon wiles. She could still see Bennett as a five-year-old, standing at the edge of the cliffs atop the bluff at the turnaround, feeders gathered all around her, cajoling her, urging her on, taking advantage of the fear, doubt, and sadness that suffused her life. It wouldn't have been all that different this time. Bennett Scott's life hadn't changed all that much.

It was Larry Spence who called with the news. A young woman had been found at the bottom of the cliffs below the turnaround in Sinnissippi Park, he advised. She fit the description of Bennett Scott, reported missing earlier this morning. Could Nest please come down and identify the body? Nest found herself wondering, irrationally, if anyone else worked at the sheriff's office besides Larry Spence.

She parked the car in the visitor zone of the hospital, went into the lobby, crossed to the elevators, and, following the signs, descended to the morgue.

Larry Spence was waiting when the elevator doors opened and she stepped out. "Sorry about this, girl."

She wasn't sure exactly what he was sorry about, but she nodded anyway. "Let me see her."

Spence walked her through a pair of heavy doors and down a short corridor with more doors on either side. They turned into the second one on the left. Bright light flooded a small chamber with a surgical table supporting a body draped with a sheet. Jack Armbruster, the coroner, stood sipping coffee and watching television. He turned at their entry and greeted Nest with a nod and a hello.

She walked to the table and stood quietly while he lifted the sheet from Bennett Scott's face. She looked almost childlike. Her features were bruised and scraped and her skin was very white. The metal rings and studs from her various piercings gave her the appearance of being cobbled together in some fashion. Her eyes were closed; she might have been sleeping. Nest stared at her silently for a long time, then nodded. Armbruster lowered the sheet again, and Bennett was gone.

"I want her taken over to Showalter's," Nest announced quickly, tears springing to her eyes in spite of her resolve. "I'll call Marty. I want him to handle the burial. I'll pay for everything."

She could barely see. The tears were clouding her vision, giving her the sense that everything around her was floating away. There was an uncomfortable silence when she finished, and she wiped angrily at her eyes.

"You'll have to wait until Jack completes his work here, Nest," Larry Spence advised, his voice taking on an official tone. She glared at him. "There are unexplained circumstances surrounding her death. There has to be an autopsy performed."

She glanced at Armbruster. "To find out how she died?"

The coroner shook his head. "I know how she died. Prolonged exposure. But there's other concerns."

"What he means is that preliminary blood samples revealed the presence of narcotics in her system," Spence interjected quickly. "A lot of narcotics. In addition, she has needle tracks all up and down her arms and legs. You know what that means."

"She was an addict," Nest agreed, casting a withering look in his general direction without making eye contact. "I knew that when she came to see me. She told me she was an addict then. She came back to Hopewell with her daughter to get help."

"That may be so," Spence replied, shifting his weight, hands digging in the pockets of his deputy sheriff's coat. "The fact remains she died under suspicious circumstances, and we need to learn as much about her condition at the time of death as possible. You see that, don't you?"

She did, of course. Rumors of drug sales in the park, an addict living in her house, and mysterious strangers visiting. Larry Spence had already formed his opinion about what had happened, and now he was looking for proof. It was ridiculous, but there wasn't any help for it. He would act on this as he chose, and anything she might say would do nothing to change things.

"Who found her?" she asked suddenly.

Larry Spence shook his head. "Anonymous phone call."

Oh, right, Nest thought.

"There's some damage to her body, but nothing that isn't consistent with her fall," Armbruster observed, already beginning preparations for his work, laying out steel instruments and pans, spreading cloths. "But I don't think that's what killed her. I think it was the cold. Course, I might find the drugs affected her heart, too. I can't tell, until I open her up."

Nest started for the doors. "Just see that she goes over to Showalter's when you're done poking around, okay?"

She was out the door and down the hall in a rush, so angry she could barely manage to keep from breaking down. She was aware of Larry Spence following, hurrying to catch up.

"There's a possibility," he called after her, "that the young lady didn't go over the cliffs by accident. In cases like this, we can't ignore the obvious."

Don't get too close to me, Larry, she was thinking. *Don't even think of trying to touch me.*

She walked back through the heavy doors into the little waiting area and punched the elevator button. The doors opened, and they stepped inside. It was uncomfortably close.

"I told you about the rumors," he persisted. His big hands knotted. "Maybe they weren't just rumors; maybe they were fact. It's possible that this young lady was mixed up in whatever was going on."

You are such a dolt, Larry, she wanted to say, but kept it to herself. He had no idea of what was going on. He couldn't begin to understand what was involved. He had no clue he was being used. He saw things in ordinary terms, in familiar ways, and that sort of thinking didn't apply here. His reality and hers were entirely different. She might try to educate him, but she didn't think he would listen to her. Not about demons and feeders. Not about magic. Not about the war between the Word and the Void, and the way that war used up people's lives.

"I'll have to come out to take a statement from you," he continued. "And from Mr. Ross."

Her anger dissipated, replaced by a cold, damp sadness that filled her with pain and loss. She looked at him dully as they stepped off the elevator and into the hospital lobby.

"Look, Larry, everything I know is in the missing-persons report I made earlier today. If you want me to repeat it, I will. John will give you a statement, too. You come by the house, if that's what you need to do. But I'm telling you right now this isn't about drugs. You can take that for what it's worth."

He stared at her. "What is it about, then?"

She sighed. "It's about children, Larry. It's about keeping them safe from things that want to destroy them." She zipped up her parka. "I have to be going. I have to figure out how to tell a little girl she isn't going to see her mother again."

She stalked out of the hospital, climbed in her car, and drove home through the snowy streets and the iron gray day. That Findo Gask would kill Bennett Scott didn't surprise her. Nothing demons did surprised her anymore. But what purpose did this particular killing serve? Why even bother with Bennett? She wasn't involved in Gask's effort to recover the gypsy morph. She didn't even know what a morph was, or what a demon was, or that anything of their world existed.

Her mood darkened the more she thought about it. This whole business smacked of spitefulness and revenge. It smelled of demon rage. Gask was furious at her—first, for taking in John Ross and the morph, and second, for refusing to give them up. The attacks at the toboggan slide and her house had been designed to frighten her by threatening harm to those she cared about. She was willing to wager that killing Bennett was intended to serve the same purpose.

She was angry and unsettled when she pulled into her driveway and climbed out of the car. The first few snowflakes were beginning to trickle out of the sky, and the light had gone darker even in the time it had taken her to drive to the hospital and back. Another storm was on the way. She hoped it would come soon. She hoped it would trap everyone inside their homes, demons included, for weeks.

Inside, she found John Ross checking the last of the locks on the doors and windows, a job she had left him to complete in her absence after informing him of Pick's efforts at implementing an early-warning system. When she told him about Bennett Scott, he just shook his head wordlessly. Mike the electrician had departed, his work finished, and the heat and lights were back on. She glanced into the living room where Harper and Little John were sitting cross-legged in front of the Christmas tree, playing. Colored tree lights reflected off the Mylar ribbons and paper wrapped about the scattering of presents nestled behind them. The scene had the look of a Hallmark card.

She walked into the kitchen and found the message light blinking on the answer phone. There were two messages. Both had come in this morning. The first was from Paul.

"Hi, it's me again. Just following up yesterday's call. Looks like I missed you. But I'll keep trying. Been thinking about you. Keep a good thought for me, and I'll talk with you later. Happy holidays."

The familiar sound of his voice made her both smile and ache. She found herself wanting to talk with him, too. Just hearing those few words stirred memories and feelings that hadn't surfaced for a long time. Maybe it was because she was so lonely. Maybe it was because she missed what they'd once had more than she was willing to admit.

She closed her eyes a moment, picturing his face, then played the second message. It was a phone number. That was all. But she recognized the voice instantly. The good feelings went away, and she stared at the phone for a long moment before punching in the number.

"Miss Freemark," Findo Gask said when he picked up the receiver on the other end. No hesitation, no greeting. "Why don't you just give me what I want and we can put an end to this business."

Even knowing he would be there, she felt a jolt go through her at the sound of his voice.

"That would be the easiest thing to do, wouldn't it?" she replied. She was surprised at how calm she sounded, given what she was feeling.

"Maybe you could avoid any more unpleasantness," he suggested pointedly. "Maybe no one else would walk off the edge of a cliff. Maybe you wouldn't find any more surprises hiding in your basement. Maybe your life could go back to the way it used to be."

She shook her head at the receiver. "I don't think so. I don't think that's possible anymore."

He chuckled softly, and she hated him so much she could barely keep from screaming it out. "Well, life requires adapting to change, I guess. The trick is to adapt in the way least harmful to yourself and those around you. You haven't done very well with that of late, Miss Freemark. Your choices have cost you the lives of Bennett Scott and Ray Childress. They have resulted in your very nasty encounter with the ur'droch. What did you think of him, Miss Freemark? Would you like him to pay you another visit? He's very fond of children."

She took a deep breath. "I'll be waiting for him next time, Mr. Gask. His visit might have a different ending."

The gravelly voice purred. "Such stubbornness is foolish and pointless. You can't win, Miss Freemark. Don't think you can. Your allies are dropping away. Even that big Indian in the park. You've lost him, too."

Her throat tightened, and she felt her breath catch in shock. Two Bears? No, they couldn't have done anything to him. Not him. She saw him in her mind, a rock, immovable, powerful. O'olish Amaneh. No, not him. She would know.

"I can tell you don't believe me," Findo Gask said quietly. "Suit yourself. What you believe or don't believe changes nothing. He's gone, and he's not coming back. Is Mr. Ross to be next? How about that little sylvan who lives in the park? You're pretty fond of him, aren't you? What do you think about the ur'droch taking him—"

She placed the receiver gently back on its cradle, and the hateful voice died away. She stood staring at the phone, Findo Gask's words echoing in her mind. Her hands were shaking. She waited a long time for the phone to ring again, for Findo Gask to call back, but nothing happened.

Finally, she turned away. She would survive only if she kept her head. Stay busy, take things one at a time, anticipate what might happen without overreaching, and she might have a chance. Findo Gask could talk about making choices and suffering consequences all he wanted. She had made up her mind the moment she had seen Bennett Scott's dead face that she wasn't giving up the gypsy morph and its magic to the demons no matter what happened. A line had been crossed, and there was no going back. She didn't know what her decision might end up costing her, but she did know the cost of capitulating now was too great to live with.

Her resolve surprised her. It wasn't that she was brave or that she believed in the power of right over wrong. She knew Findo Gask was correct about her; she was being unreasonably stubborn. But somewhere along the way—since last night's events, she supposed—she had decided that whatever happened to her or even to those around her, she wouldn't back down. Something important was happening here, and even if she didn't understand exactly what it was, she would fight for it. She had an overpowering conviction that in this instance fighting was necessary, and that she must do so no matter what the consequences.

John Ross would understand, she believed. Certainly he had waged similar battles over the years, championing causes when the issues weren't entirely clear to him, believing that instinct would guide him to make the right decisions when reason wasn't enough.

She glanced out the window into the park. She would have to warn Pick of Gask's threat—although Pick was probably being pretty careful already. But if even O'olish Amaneh couldn't stand against the demons, what chance did the sylvan have—or any of them, for that matter? She couldn't imagine anyone being stronger than Two Bears. She couldn't believe that he might be gone.

She put aside her thoughts on the last of the Sinnissippi and walked into the living room. Harper and Little John were still playing. She smiled at Harper when the little girl looked up. "Come talk to me a minute, sweetie," she said gently.

She took Harper down the hall to her grandfather's den and shut the door behind them. She led Harper over to the big leather recliner that Old Bob had favored for reading and cogitating and naps, sat down, and pulled the child onto her lap.

"When I was little, my grandfather would always bring me into this room and put me on his lap in this chair when he had something important to tell me," she began, cradling Harper in her arms. "Sometimes he wanted to talk about our family. Sometimes he wanted to talk about friends. If I did something wrong, he would bring me in here to explain why I shouldn't do it again."

The little girl was staring at her. "Harper be bad?"

"No, sweetie, you haven't been bad. I didn't bring you in here because you did something bad. But something bad has happened to Mommy, and I have to tell you about it. I don't want to, because it is going to make you very sad. But sometimes things happen that make us sad, and there isn't anything we can do about it."

She exhaled wearily and began to stroke Harper's long hair. "Harper, Mommy isn't coming home, sweetie." Harper went still. "She got very sick, and she isn't coming home. She didn't want to get sick, but she couldn't help it."

"Mommy sick?"

Nest bit her lip. "No, sweetie. Not anymore. Mommy died, honey."

"Mommy died?"

"Do you understand, Harper? Mommy's gone. She's in Heaven with all the angels she used to tell you about, the ones who make the sun bright with all the love that mommies have for their babies. She asked me to take care of you, sweetie. You and I are going to live together right here in this house for as long as you want. You can have your own room and your own toys. You can be my little girl. I would like that very much."

Harper's lip was quivering. "Okay, Neth."

Nest gave her a hug and held her tight. "Your Mommy loved you so much, Harper. She loved you more than anything. She didn't want to die. She wanted to stay with you always. But she couldn't." She looked out the window into the park, where the hazy light was fading toward darkness. "Did you know that my mommy died when I was a little girl, too? I was even younger than you are."

"Wanna see Mommy," Harper sobbed.

"I know, sweetie, I know." Nest stroked her dark hair slowly. "I wanted to see my mommy, too, and I couldn't. But if I close my eyes, I can see her there in the darkness inside my head. Can you do that? Close your eyes and think of Mommy."

She felt Harper go still. "See Mommy," she said softly.

"She'll always be there, Harper, whenever you look for her. Mommies have to go away sometimes, but they leave a picture of themselves inside your head, so you won't forget them."

Harper's head lifted away from her breast. "Does L'il John got a Mommy, Neth?"

Nest hesitated, then smiled reassuringly. "He's got you and me, Harper. We're his mommies. We have to take care of him, okay?"

Harper nodded solemnly, wiping at her eyes with her shirtsleeve. "Harper wanna appo jus, Neth."

Nest stood her on her feet and put her hands on the little girl's shoulders. "Let's go get some, sweetie. Let's go get some for Little John, too." She leaned forward and kissed Harper's forehead. "I love you, Harper."

"Luv 'ou, Neth," Harper answered back, dark eyes brilliant and depthless and filled with wonder.

Nest took her hand and led her from the room. It took everything she had to keep from crying. In that moment, she felt as if her heart was breaking, but she couldn't tell if it was from sadness or joy.

CHAPTER 23

While Nest spoke with Harper Scott in the den, John Ross stood at the living-room entry watching Little John play with the pieces of his puzzle. Sitting in front of the Christmas tree, the boy picked up the pieces one at a time and studied them. He seemed to be constructing the puzzle in his mind rather than on the floor, setting each piece back when he was done looking at it, not bothering with trying to find the way in which it fit with the others. He seemed to be imitating what he had seen Harper doing a couple of days earlier. His blue eyes were intense with concentration, luminous within the oval of his pale face. He had lost color over the last twenty-four hours; there was a hollowness and a frailty about him that suggested he was not well. Of course, Little John was only a shell created to conceal the life force that lay beneath, and any outward indication of illness might be symptomatic of something entirely different from what it appeared. Little John was not a real boy, after all, but a creature of magic.

Yet sitting there as he was, lost in thought, so deeply focused on whatever mind game he was engaged in that he was oblivious to everything else, he seemed as real as any child Ross had ever known. Were gypsy morphs really so different from humans? Little John's life force was housed in his body's shell, but wasn't that so for humans as well? Weren't their spirits housed in vessels of flesh and blood, and when death claimed the latter, didn't the former live on?

Some people believed it was so, and Ross was among them. He didn't know why he believed it exactly. He supposed his belief had developed during his years of service to the Word and had been born out of his acceptance that the Word and Void were real, that they were antagonists, and that the time line of human evolution was their chosen battleground. Maybe he believed it simply because he needed to, because the nature of his struggle required it of him. Regardless, he was struck by the possibility that humans and gypsy morphs alike possessed a spiritual essence that lived on after their bodies were gone.

He leaned on his staff, mulling it over. Such thinking was triggered, he knew, by the inescapable and unpleasant fact that time was running out on all of them. Whatever else was to happen to Little John, Nest, Harper, and himself, it should not be invited to happen here. Nest might wish to remain in her home and to make whatever stand she could in a familiar place. She might believe that the sylvan Pick could spin a protective web of magic about her fortress so that she could not again be attacked by surprise. But John Ross was convinced that their only chance for survival was to get out of there as fast as possible and to go into hiding until the secret of the gypsy morph was resolved, one way or the other. They must slip away this afternoon, as quickly as it could be managed, if they were to have any hope at all. Findo Gask would not wait for Christmas to be over or the holiday spirit to fade. He would come for them by nightfall, and if they were still there, it was a safe bet that someone else was going to die.

Ross listened to the old grandfather clock ticktock in the silence, finding in its measured beat a reminder of how ineffectual he had been in his use of the time allotted him. He knew what was required if he was to resolve the secret of the morph. He had known it from the beginning. It had taken him forever just to get this far, and he had almost nothing to show for it. That the morph had brought him to Nest Freemark was questionable progress. That she believed it wanted something from her was suspect. She was levelheaded and intuitive, but her conclusion had come in the heat of a struggle to stay alive and might be misguided. So much of her thinking was speculative. How much was generated by wishful thinking and raw emotion? Could she really believe that Wraith and the morph were somehow joined? What could Wraith have to do with the morph's interest in Nest? Why would it matter to the morph that the ghost wolf was an integral part of her magic?

Ross considered what he knew, still watching the boy. *Be fair,* he cautioned himself. *Consider the matter carefully.* It might be that there was a problem because the ghost wolf was created substantially out of demon magic. Perhaps the morph couldn't tolerate that presence. Yet morphs had the ability to be anything. Their magic could be good or bad, could be used for any purpose, so that the presence of other magics logically shouldn't have any effect. Was it something about the form of the ghost wolf that bothered the morph? Was Wraith's magic competing with its own in some way?

Ross mulled his questions through. This boy, this boy! Such an enigmatic presence, closed away and so tightly sealed, so inscrutable! Why had the morph become a boy in the first place? The answer to everything was concealed there, in that single question—Ross was certain of it. Everything that had happened flowed directly from the morph's last, final evolution into Little John, the form it had taken before asking for Nest, the form it had taken before their coming here.

His hands tightened about the smooth wood of the staff. What was the gypsy morph looking for? What, that it couldn't seem to find in the woman whose name it had spoken with such need?

The door to the den opened, and Nest came out leading Harper by the hand. Neither said anything as they passed him and went into the kitchen. Ross followed them with his eyes, keeping silent himself. He could tell they had been crying; he could guess easily enough why. Nest poured apple juice into Harper's baby cup and gave it to her, then poured a cup for Little John and carried it to the living room, Harper trailing after her. The children sat together once more and began working the puzzle anew.

Nest was bending down to help, speaking to them in a low voice, when the phone rang. She remained where she was, kneeling on the floor, Harper on one side and Little John on the other.

"John," she called softly without looking up. "Could you get that, please?"

He crossed the hall to the kitchen phone and picked up the receiver. "Freemark residence."

"I guess this just goes to prove how shameless I am, chasing after someone who leaves without a word in the middle of the night," Josie Jackson said.

He rubbed his forehead. "Sorry about that. I'm the one who's shameless. But I got worried about Little John. You looked so peaceful, I decided not to wake you."

"That's probably why you decided not to call this morning either. You wanted to let me sleep in."

"Things have been a bit hectic around here." He considered how much he ought to tell her, then lowered his voice. "Bennett Scott disappeared last night. They found her this morning at the bottom of the cliffs in Sinnissippi Park."

"Oh, John."

"Nest just finished telling Harper. It's hard to know how she's going to deal with this. I think Nest is trying to find out."

"Should I come over?"

He hesitated. "Let me tell Nest you offered. She can call you back if she thinks you should."

"Okay." She was silent a moment. "If I don't come there, will you think about coming here?"

"To tell you the truth, Josie," he said, "I've been thinking about it since the moment I left."

Not that he would go to her, he reminded himself firmly. Because he couldn't do that, not even though he was telling her the truth and badly wanted to. He had already determined what he must do. He must leave Hopewell, and leave quickly—with Little John and Nest and Harper in tow. Maybe he could come back when this business with the gypsy morph was over. Maybe he could stay forever then. Maybe he and Josie could have a chance at a life.

But maybe not.

He was reminded anew of what had happened several months earlier when he had returned to Wales and the Fairy Glen to speak with the Lady. He was reminded anew of how deceptive hope could be.

It was early October when the tatterdemalion came to him. He was still living in Cannon Beach with Mrs. Staples and working at the Cannon Beach Bookstore. Through help from Anson Robbington, he had discovered the cave in which the gypsy morph would appear, and had returned there many times to prepare for the event. He had memorized the cave's layout and begun thinking of how he might trap the morph when it appeared. But he was still unable to conceive of a way in which to snare this elusive creature. He was hoping his dream of the Knight on the cross would come again and show him something new.

He was marking time.

The tatterdemalion appeared to him when he woke from a different dream, a particularly bad one, a dream in which he had witnessed another city's demise and the slaughter of its inhabitants. He could not remember the city's name, which troubled him considerably. He could not even remember which part of the country it was located in. There were people in the dream whose names and faces he knew, but on waking he could remember none of them. He had been fighting on a roadway leading out of the city, a group of women and children and old people under his protection and care. He had gotten them clear of the city, but they couldn't travel fast enough to stay ahead of their pursuers. Finally, Ross had been forced to turn and fight. Once-men and demons quickly surrounded them, and there was nowhere to go. Ross was still engaged in a desperate attempt to break free when he awoke.

For a moment, he could not remember where he was. His head still swam with images from the dream, and the sounds of battle rang in his ears. It was a warm, windless night, strayed somehow from the summer gone, and the windows to his bedroom were open to the air. The tatterdemalion stood by the window closest to the sea, pale and vaguely iridescent, a child of indeterminate sex, very young, with lost, haunted eyes that reflected bits and pieces of a human life best forgotten.

"Are you John Ross?" it asked in a soft, high voice.

Ross blinked and nodded, remembering his situation, the remnants of his dream beginning to fade. "Yes."

"I have a message for you from the Lady. She would speak with you. She wishes you to come to her."

"To the Fairy Glen?" he asked quickly, sitting up now.

The tatterdemalion shimmered faintly. "She wishes you to come at once."

"To the Fairy Glen?" he repeated.

But the tatterdemalion was already fading, its luminescence failing, its lines erasing, its presence turning to memory. In seconds, it had disintegrated entirely, and Ross was alone once more.

He caught a flight out of Portland the next afternoon, flew east to New York, changed planes at Kennedy, and by midday of the following day, he was landing at Heathrow. From there, he took a train to Cardiff, then rented a car and drove north to Betwys-y-Coed. The trip cost him most of what he had earned that summer at the bookstore. He had barely managed to throw together the clothes he needed before going out the door. He was disorganized and exhausted on his arrival, and while his instincts were to go at once to the Fairy Glen, his body thought otherwise, and he collapsed in his bed and slept ten hours.

When he awoke, dream-haunted, but better able to make the decisions that might be required of him, he showered, dressed, and ate lunch in the pub downstairs. Afterward, on a typical Welsh October day—mostly cloudy, some brief rain showers interspersed with glimpses of sun, and a hint of early winter cold in the air—he drove up to the Fairy Glen and walked in from the road.

There were a pair of cars in the tiny parking area, and a handful of people in the glen, climbing over the rocks and wandering the muddied paths. The glen was green and lush, the stream that meandered along its floor swollen from recent rains. Ross descended the trail from the upper road cautiously, taking his time, placing his staff carefully for support. The familiar sounds filled him with excitement and hope—the tumble of the waterfall, the rush of the stream, the whisper of wind through the leaves, and the birdsong. He breathed in the dank rawness of the earth and plants, the rich smell laced with the fragrances of wildflowers and greenery. It was startling how much he felt at peace here, how close to everything that grew about him, as if this was where he really belonged now, as if this was his home.

He knew he would not see the Lady, or the fairy creatures that served her, in daytime. He thought he might see Owain Glyndwr in the familiar guise of a fisherman, but it didn't really matter if Glyndwr appeared to him or not. Mostly, he had come just to see the glen in daylight, to feel once again the lure of this place that had changed his life so dramatically. He descended to its floor and sat on the rocks, looking off at the waterfall and the stream, at the trees and plants and tiny wildflowers, at nothing in particular at all, just the sweep of the hollow and the colors that imbued it.

After a while, he went back to the inn and took a short nap. When he woke again, he walked around the tiny village, then returned for dinner. The innkeeper remembered him from his last visit, and they talked for a time about upheaval and unpredictability in the larger world. Betwys-y-Coed was an island of tranquillity and constancy, and it offered a sense of reassurance to its inhabitants. The innkeeper had lived in the village all his life; he couldn't understand why anyone would want to live anywhere else.

An hour before midnight, Ross returned to the Fairy Glen. The night was black and starless, and the moon peeked through the clouds like an intruder. Ross parked and walked to the gate, then descended the pathway to the glen. The damp air was chilly, and Ross tucked his chin into his heavy coat and watched his breath cloud the air before him. Using his staff, he navigated the uncertain trail to the edge of the stream and stood looking around. He breathed in the night smells and listened to the soft rush of the falls.

Almost immediately, Owain Glyndwr appeared. A Knight of the Word once and servant to the Lady now, he stood as still as stone on the other side of the stream, his greatcoat wrapped about his lean body, his wide, flat-brimmed hat shadowing his face. He held his fishing pole loosely, the line curved away into the flowing waters.

He nodded amiably toward Ross. " 'Tis a good night for watching fairies," he said quietly. "Come to see them, have you?"

"I have," Ross acknowledged, realizing suddenly that it was true, it was a part of the reason he was here.

"Wait a bit, and they'll appear," the other offered. "Your eyes say you need their comfort. Well and good. Those who believe can always find comfort in them."

He shifted his weight slightly, and his face lifted out of the shadows. Ross saw himself in that face, his features more closely mirrored than when he had encountered his ancestor last. He was older, of course, so their ages were closer. But it was more than that. It was as if by living lives as Knights of the Word, their resemblance to each other had increased.

Owain Glyndwr began moving slowly downstream from Ross. He stopped once, casting his line anew. Ross watched him a moment, then looked away in the direction of the falls. When he looked back again, the other man was gone.

Ross stayed where he was, waiting patiently. The glen's darkness was hard and cold about him, but it was strangely comforting as well. It enfolded and welcomed him. It gave him peace. That had not been so on his last visit, when he had returned ten years earlier to tell the Lady he could no longer serve as a Knight of the Word. The glen had felt hostile and forbidding then; it had disdained him. The Lady had not appeared, and he had gone home disconsolate and frustrated in his efforts. He had lost his way without knowing it. As a consequence, he had almost died.

Lights twinkled suddenly in the curtain of the falls, bright and pulsing as they moved through the dark waters. Hundreds of them appeared at once, as if tiny fireflies had migrated out of place and time to welcome him home. He smiled at the sight of them, at the realization the fairies were revealing themselves to him, acknowledging his presence. They grew in number until they filled the waterfall with their light, and Ross thought he would never see anything so wonderful again.

Then he heard his name called softly.

"John Ross."

He knew her voice at once, recognized it as surely as he did the fairies dancing in the waterfall.

"John Ross, I am here."

She was standing where Owain Glyndwr had disappeared, balanced on the surface of the water, suspended on air. She was as young and beautiful and ephemeral as ever, almost not there in the paleness of light that defined her image. She lifted her arms toward him, and the light moved with her, cloaking her in silver, trailing after her in bright streamers. She advanced in an effortless, floating motion, a shifting figure of shadows and moonlight.

"My brave knight-errant," she whispered as she drew close. "You have done well in my service. You are the image of your ancestor in more than appearance. You carry his blood in your veins and his heart in your breast. Six hundred years have passed since his time, but you reflect anew what was best in him."

He was shaking, not from fear or expectation or anything he could readily define, but simply because she was so close to him that he could feel her presence. He could not answer, but only wait on her to speak again.

"John Ross," she whispered through silky blackness and shimmering light. "Brave Knight, your service is almost ended. One more thing must you do for me, and then I will set you free."

He could not believe what he was hearing. He had waited more than twenty-five years for those words. He was fifty-three years old, and he had been a Knight of the Word for half of them. Ten years earlier, he had begged in vain to be released. Now she was offering him his freedom without even being asked. He was stunned.

"You must return to await the appearance of the gypsy morph," she told him. "As in your dream, it will come. As foretold, it will appear. When it does, you must be ready. For the time allotted to it, you must protect it from the Void. You must protect it at all costs. It is precious to me, and you must keep it safe. When it has transformed for the final time, your service to the Word is finished. Then you may come home."

He could barely comprehend what he was being told. His voice failed him when he tried to speak; the words would not form in his mouth.

"Give me your hand," she instructed.

Without thinking, he knelt at her approach, lifting his hand to touch hers. All that she was and all that was the Word filled him with strength and determination. He felt something pressed into his hand, and when her own withdrew, he found himself holding a gossamer net.

"You will use this to take possession of the creature you seek. When it appears and begins to take form, cast the net. The gypsy morph will be yours then—to care for, to protect, and to shepherd as a newborn lamb." The Lady lifted her arm to sweep the air with light. "Give to it the shelter of your magic, your faith, and your great heart. Do not forsake it, no matter how strong the temptation or great the odds. Do this for me."

"I will," he said, the words coming almost unbidden, his voice returned.

"Rise," she said to him, and he did so. "The Word takes pleasure in you, John Ross—as do I. Go now, and serve us well."

He did as he was bid, departing the Fairy Glen, carrying with him the gossamer net that would snare the gypsy morph, resolving that he would do what was necessary so that finally his time of service might be ended.

It was only later, when he was back at Cannon Beach, awaiting Thanksgiving and the gypsy morph's coming, that he began to ponder more closely the Lady's words, and only in the past few days, as time began to narrow down and the demons close about, that he understood how he might have mistaken their meaning.

"Do you mean that, John?" Josie's voice spoke suddenly through the receiver, interrupting his reverie. "Because I wouldn't want you to say so if you didn't. Not to make me feel better, certainly. And not because you think it's the right thing to say after last night."

He brushed aside his thoughts of the Lady and the Fairy Glen. "I'm saying it because it's true, Josie."

"Will you come see me, then? Tonight?"

"If I can." He took a deep breath. "I want to promise you I will. I want to promise you a lot of things. But you were right last night. I didn't come back for that. I'm not in a position to promise anything. Not yet, at least. One day, that could change. I hope it does. I suppose I hope for it more than anything."

There was a long silence from the other end. He stood motionless by the kitchen phone, waiting for her to say something. Hawkeye appeared from somewhere in the back of the house, sauntering down the hallway and into the living room. With barely a glance at Ross, he wandered over to Little John and lay down beside him. The boy reached out at once to begin stroking him. The cat's eyes closed in contentment.

"I love you, John," Josie said suddenly. Her voice caught. "Big surprise, huh? But I had to say it at least once. Funny, it didn't hurt a bit. Call me later, okay?"

She hung up before he could say anything. He stared at the phone for a moment, listening to the dial tone, then placed the receiver back in its cradle. The ache he felt inside was bittersweet, and it left him wanting a resolution he couldn't have. He should call her back. He should tell her he loved her, too. But he knew he wouldn't.

He was still mulling the matter when he caught a glimpse of movement through the kitchen window. When he walked over for a closer look, a sheriff's cruiser was parked in the driveway and Larry Spence was walking toward the house.

Chapter 24

Just from the look on John Ross's face, Nest knew who it was even before she answered the knock at the door. Her impatience and frustration with Larry Spence crowded to the forefront of her thoughts, but she forced herself to ignore them. This visit did not concern her; it concerned Bennett Scott. Because it was necessary to talk with him about Bennett at some point anyway, she was prepared to endure the unpleasantness she was certain would follow.

"Afternoon," he greeted as she opened the door. "Would it be all right with you if I took those statements now?"

As if she had a choice. She managed a weak smile. "Sure. Come on in."

He clumped through the open doorway, knocked the snow from his boots onto the throw rug, and slipped off his uniform coat and hat and hung them on the rack. He seemed ill at ease, as if his size and authority were out of place here, as if they belonged somewhere else entirely and not in her home. She felt better for this, thinking that it wouldn't hurt for him to walk on eggshells for a while.

"Armbruster finished the autopsy," he advised conspiratorially, lowering his voice. "The young lady had enough drugs in her system to float a battleship. But the drugs didn't kill her. She froze to death. The marks on her body were from the fall off the bluff. I'd say she lost her way and wandered off, but it's just a guess."

"Larry," she said quietly, turning him with her hands on his arms so that his back was to the living room. "I don't know anything about Bennett Scott and drugs beyond the fact she was an addict. John knows even less. I didn't even know she was coming back here until she showed up on my doorstep. John, when he came to see me, didn't either. He hasn't been back here in fifteen years. Bennett was five then. All this talk about drug dealing in the park, true or not, does not involve us. Keep that in mind, will you?"

His face closed down. "I'll keep an open mind, I can promise you that." He glanced over his shoulder. "I'll need to see the young lady's room. You don't have to let me, of course, if you don't want to. But it would save me a trip down to the courthouse for a search warrant."

"Oh, for God's sake, Larry!" she snapped. "You can see anything you want!" She sighed wearily. "Come with me. I'll show you where she was staying."

They walked down the hallway past the den and Nest's room to the guest bedroom where Bennett and Harper were staying. The room was gray with shadows and silent. Bennett's clothes were still in her bag in the closet, and Nest had already picked up after Harper and made the bed. She stood in the doorway while Larry Spence poked about, checking the closet and the dresser drawers, looking under the bed and in the adjoining bathroom, and searching Bennett's worn satchel. He didn't seem to find anything of importance, and when he was done he put everything back the way he had found it.

"Guess that'll do," he said without much enthusiasm. "Why don't we do the interviews now, and then I'll be out of your hair?"

"All right," she replied. "Do you want some privacy for this?"

He shrugged his big shoulders, and she could hear the creak of his leather gun belt. "I can interview you and Mr. Ross out in the living room. Do the both of you together. Maybe the children could play back here while we talk."

She shook her head. "I don't want Harper alone in this room just yet. I just finished telling her about her mother." She hesitated. "They can play in my bedroom."

She went past him out the door and down the hall, irritated but resigned, already thinking about the more pressing problem of how she would manage the next twenty-four hours. It wouldn't be easy. Harper would be thinking of her mother. Little John was a weight she could barely shoulder, and yet she had to find a way to do so. Ross would probably be wanting to leave and go into hiding; he hadn't said so, but she could sense he'd made the decision. Whatever she did about any of them, she would second-guess herself later.

She collected Harper and Little John, the puzzle and a few other toys, and took them all into her bedroom. She told the children she had to talk with someone out in the living room, but she would be back to check on them. It wouldn't take long, and they could come back out when she was done.

It felt awkward, but she wanted the space and maneuverability that the living room offered so that she could usher Larry Spence out as soon as the interviews were concluded—sooner, if he started to annoy her—without disturbing the children.

Larry Spence had closed Bennett's bedroom door and was standing in the hallway, waiting for her. He continued to look ill at ease. Leaving her own bedroom door open just a crack, anxious that Harper not hear what might be said, she took him back down the hall to where Ross was waiting. They sat together in the living room, Ross and Nest on the couch, Spence in the easy chair. He produced a small notebook and pen, jotted a few notes, and then asked Nest to begin.

She did so without preamble, detailing the events from the time of their departure from the house until her discovery at Robert's that Bennett was missing. She left out anything about Ross, preferring to let him tell his own story. She also left out everything about the ur'droch, saying instead that she had come back to find the house broken into and the power and phone out.

When she finished her account, she brought out the note that Bennett had left in her coat the night before. "I forgot about this earlier, but I found it this morning before you called. Bennett must have tucked it in my pocket last night before she slipped out of the Hepplers'."

She handed it to Spence, who read it carefully. "Almost sounds as if she thought something was going to happen to her, doesn't it?" he said, mostly to himself. He cleared his throat and shifted to a new position. "Just one or two more questions. Then I'll take Mr. Ross's statement and be on my way."

He ended up asking rather a lot of questions, she thought, repeating himself more than once in the process and annoying her considerably. But she stuck it out, not wanting to have to go through this again later. Once or twice, she got up to peek down the hallway, and each time Larry Spence quickly called her back by saying he was almost done, that he had just a few more questions, as if he was afraid she was going to walk out on him and not come back.

When he was finished with her, he interviewed Ross, a process that for all the noise he had made earlier about drug connections and shady characters took considerably less time than it had with her. He raised an eyebrow when Josie Jackson was mentioned, but said nothing. If she hadn't known better, she would have thought he'd lost interest in Ross completely.

"Guess that's it," he announced finally, checking his watch for what must have been the twentieth time, slapping closed the notebook, and rising to his feet. "Sorry to take so long."

He was still nervous as Nest walked him to the front door, glancing everywhere but at her, looking as if he had something bottled up inside that he was dying to get out. At the door, he gave her a peek at what it was.

"Look, I don't want you to get the wrong idea, girl, but I'm worried about you staying here." He seemed uncertain about where to go with this, his head lowered, his deputy sheriff's hat in his hands. "There's things about this investigation that you don't know. Things I can't tell you."

I could say the same, she thought. She had no time for this. "Well, call me when you can, okay?"

He nodded absently. "If you want to come by the office later—alone—I'll try to fill you in." He shook his head. "I shouldn't do this, you know, I'm not supposed to tell you anything, but I can't just leave you in the dark. You understand what I'm saying?"

She stared at him. "Not really."

He nodded some more. "I suppose not. It's pretty complex, even to me. But you got yourself in the middle of something, girl. I know you don't have any part in what's happening, but I—"

"Not this again, Larry," she interrupted quickly.

"I know how you feel, but—"

"You don't know how I feel," she exploded, "and if you want my honest opinion, you don't know what you're talking about, either! If this has to do with that old man in the black coat with the leather book, I'm telling you for the last time—stay away from him. Don't listen to anything he says and don't do anything he tells you to. He's dangerous, Larry. Trust me. You don't want anything to do with him."

Larry Spence screwed up his face and straightened his shoulders. "He's FBI, Nest!" he hissed softly.

She looked at him as if he had just climbed out of a spaceship. "No, Larry, he isn't. He's not one of the good guys. He's not your friend and he's certainly not mine. He's not anything he seems to be. Have you checked up on him? Have you asked for proof of who he claims to be from someone else?"

"Don't tell me how to do my job, please."

"Well, maybe someone should! Look, do yourself a favor. Call Washington or whoever. Make sure. 'Cause you know what? It's entirely possible that old man is responsible for what happened to Bennett."

"You're way out of line, girl!" Spence was suddenly agitated, combative. "You don't know any of this. You're just saying it to protect Ross!"

"I'm saying it to protect you!"

His face flushed dark red. "You think I'm stupid? You think I can't see what's going on? You and Ross are—"

He caught himself, but it was too late. She knew exactly what he was going to say next. Her mouth tightened. "Get out, Larry," she ordered, barely able to contain her fury. "Right now. And don't come back."

He swept past her with a grunt and went out the door, slamming it behind him. She watched him stomp back to his cruiser, climb in, and drive off. She was so angry she kept watching until he was out of sight, half-afraid he might change his mind and try to come back.

When the phone rang, she was still seething. She stalked into the kitchen and snatched up the receiver. "Hello?"

"Nest? Hi. You sound a little out of sorts. Did I pick a bad time to call?"

She exhaled sharply. "Paul?"

"Yeah. Are you okay?"

She brushed back her curly hair. "I'm fine."

"You don't sound fine."

She nodded at the wall, looking out the window at the empty drive. "Sorry. I just had a visitor who rubbed me the wrong way. How are you?"

"I'm good." He sounded relaxed, comfortable. She liked hearing him like this. "You got my earlier messages, right?"

"I did. Sorry I didn't call back before, but I've been pretty busy. I have some guests for the holiday, and I've . . ."

She ran out of anywhere to go with this, so she simply left the sentence hanging. "Well, it's been hectic."

"That's the holidays for you. More trouble than they're worth sometimes. Especially when you have a houseful."

"It's not so bad," she lied.

"If you say so. Anyway, how would you feel about having another guest, maybe sometime after the first of the year?"

She couldn't tell him how much she wanted that, how much she needed to see him. She was surprised at the depth of the feeling he invoked in her. She knew it was due in part to her present circumstances, to the loneliness and uncertainty she was feeling, to her heightened sense of mortality and loss. She knew as well that she still had strong feelings for Paul. A part of her had never really given up on him. A part of her wanted him back.

"I'd like that." She smiled and almost laughed. "I'd like that very much."

"Me, too. I've missed you. Seems like a million years since I've seen you. Well, since anyone's seen you, for that matter." His voice turned light, bantering. "Good old Hopewell, refuge for ex-Olympians. I can't believe you're still there. Seems like the wrong place for you after all you've done with your life. You still train regularly, Nest?"

"Sure, a little."

"Thinking about competing in the next Olympics?"

She hesitated, confused. "Not really. No."

"Well, either way, you've got a great story to tell, and my editor will pay a lot for it. We can talk about your career, memories, old times, flesh it out with what's happening now. I can use an old picture of you or have the photographer take a new one. It's your choice. But you might get the cover, so a new one makes sense."

She shook her head in confusion. "What are you talking about?"

"Of the magazine. The cover. I want to do a story on you while I'm visiting. Mix a little business with pleasure. It makes sense. Everybody wants to know what's happened to you since the last Olympics. Who can tell your story better than me? We can work on it in our spare time. They'll pay a pretty good fee for this, Nest. It's easy money."

All the breath went out of her lungs, and she went cold all over. "You want to do a story on me?" she asked quietly, remembering the editor from Paul's magazine she had hung up on a month or so earlier.

He laughed. "Sure. I'm a journalist, remember?"

"That's what coming here to see me is all about?"

"Well, no. Of course not. I mean, I want to see you, first and foremost, but I just thought it would be nice if—"

She placed the receiver back in its cradle and severed the connection. She stood where she was, staring down at the phone, unable to believe what had just happened. A story. He wanted to see her so he could do a story. Had the magazine editor put him up to it? Had he thought he could get to her through Paul? Tears flooded her eyes. She fought to hold them in, then gave up. She walked to where Ross couldn't see her and cried silently. The phone rang again, but she didn't answer it. She stood alone in a corner and wished everything and everyone would just go away.

It took her a few minutes to compose herself. Outside, the day was fading quickly toward darkness, and snow was beginning to fall once more in a soft white curtain. Streetlamps and porch lights glimmered up and down Woodlawn Road, and Christmas tree lights twinkled through frosted windows and along railings and eaves. On a snow-covered lawn across the way, a painted wooden nativity scene was bathed in white light.

Ross appeared in the kitchen doorway. "Are you all right?"

Everybody's favorite question. She nodded without looking at him. "Just disappointed."

The phone rang again. This time, she picked it up. "Look, Paul," she began.

"Nest, it's Larry Spence." She heard him breathing hard in the receiver, as if he had run a race. His voice was breaking. "I just wanted to tell you I'm sorry, that's all. I'm sorry. I know you'll probably never speak to me again, but Robinson is right—we can't take chances with this business. You're not thinking straight, girl. If you were, you'd see how much danger you're in and you'd get the hell out of there. I'm just doing what I have to do, nothing more. But I'm sorry it had to be me, 'cause I know you—"

"Go away, Larry," she said, and hung up.

She stared at the phone absently. What was he talking about? She had no idea, but his tone of voice bothered her. He sounded anxious, almost frantic. Apologizing like that, over and over, for asking a few boring questions . . .

Then suddenly, unexpectedly, she thought of the children. She had forgotten about them in the rush of events, of Larry Spence coming and going, of the phone calls. She glanced toward her bedroom. They were being awfully quiet in there.

She walked down the hallway quickly, snapping on lights as she went. She was being silly. She was overreacting. Pick's security net was in place. No one could get in or out of her house without her sensing it. She fought down the impulse to run. No, she kept saying inside her head, trying to reassure herself. No!

"Harper! Little John!"

She reached her bedroom and threw open the door. An orange blur shot past her from under the bed and disappeared down the hall—Hawkeye, hair all on end, hissing in rage and fear. Her eyes swept the room hurriedly. Shadows nestled comfortably in the corners and draped the bed in broad stripes. The puzzle and toys lay scattered on the floor. Harper's cup of apple juice sat half-empty on her nightstand.

But the children were gone.

CHAPTER 25

At first, she could not bring herself to move. She just stood, staring at the empty room, shocked into immobility, frozen with disbelief. A rush of confused thoughts crowded through her mind. The children had to be there. She had put them there herself. She just wasn't seeing them. Maybe they were playing hide-and-seek, and she was supposed to come look for them. Maybe they were under the bed or in the closet. But they couldn't have just disappeared!

She forced herself to look for them because the sound of her thinking was making her crazy. Even though she knew what she would find, she searched under the bed and in the closet and anywhere else she could think to look. As she did, her shock dissipated and her anger began to grow. They were supposed to be safe; her house was supposed to be protected! Nothing was supposed to be able to get inside without her knowing! It was the first time that Pick had let her down, and she was furious at him.

It wasn't until she searched the adjoining rooms, desperate by now for help from any quarter, that she discovered the window in Bennett's bedroom was wide open. Then the telephone call from Larry Spence began to make sense. She had left him alone in that bedroom while she had gone to fetch the children, and he had used the opportunity to open the window from the inside. Pick had warned that the safety net was vulnerable from within. Larry was still under the sway of Findo Gask, and he had given Gask access without her knowing. He had come to her home specifically to help the demon steal the children.

Worried by the silence, Ross came down the hallway to find her. It was he who found the damp outline of the footprint on the carpet. The footprint wasn't human; it resembled that of a large lizard, three-toed and clawed at the tips.

The ur'droch took them, she realized at once. And now the demons had them.

She wanted to curl up and die. She wanted to attack someone. She was conflicted and ravaged by her emotions, and it was all she could do to hold herself together as she stood with Ross in the darkened hallway and discussed the possibilities.

"Gask has them," she insisted quietly, her voice hushed and furtive, as if the walls would convey her thoughts to those who shouldn't hear.

Ross nodded. He stood very tall and still, another shadow carved from the night that gathered outside. "He wants to trade for the morph."

"But he already has the morph."

"He doesn't realize that. If he did, he wouldn't have bothered with Harper." Ross was staring at her, green eyes locked on hers. "He thinks we still have it hidden away somewhere. He's taken the children to force us to give it up. Nothing else has worked—threats, attacks, breaking into the house. But he knows how you feel about the children."

She thought again of Larry Spence. "I was a fool," she said bitterly. She leaned against the wall, running her fingers through her curly hair. "I should have seen this coming. Gask tried for the children last night. I just didn't realize what he was doing. I thought he was attacking them to scare me. He was trying to steal them."

"He was more subtle about it this time. He used the deputy sheriff to open up the house and then distract us."

She made a disgusted noise. "Larry doesn't understand what's happening. John, what are we going to do?"

"Wait." He started back down the hall for the living room. "Gask will call."

The demon did so, fifteen minutes later. They were sitting in the kitchen by then, sipping at hot coffee and listening to the ticking of the grandfather clock in the silence. Outside, the darkness had chased west the last of the daylight and layered the snow-shrouded landscape. Streetlamps and porch lights blazed bravely in the blackness, small beacons illuminating houses adrift in snowbanks and wreathed in icicles. Thick flakes of snow floated through their gauzy halos as the new storm slowly rolled out of the plains.

"Good evening, Miss Freemark," Findo Gask greeted pleasantly when she picked up the phone on the second ring. "I have someone who would like to speak to you."

There was a momentary pause. "Neth?" Harper said in a tiny, frightened voice.

Findo Gask came back on the line. "No more games, Miss Freemark. Playtime is over. You lost. Give me what I want or you won't see these children again, I promise you. Don't test me on this."

"I won't," she said quietly.

"Good. I don't know where you've hidden the morph, but I will give you until midnight to recover it. I will call you back then to arrange a time and place for the exchange. I will call only once. Any delay, any excuses, any tricks, and you and Mr. Ross will spend a very lonely Christmas. Do we understand each other?"

She closed her eyes. "Yes."

He hung up. She placed the receiver back in its cradle and looked at Ross. "You were right," she said. "He wants a trade. The children for the morph."

He nodded without speaking.

"Except we don't have the morph to give him."

"No," he agreed softly. "We don't."

Findo Gask wrapped his fingers carefully about the Book of Names and stood staring off into empty space. Something was wrong. He couldn't put his finger on it, but something wasn't right. It wasn't in the situation, which was progressing just as he had planned, or in Nest Freemark's voice, which was suitably submissive and worried. No, it was something else, something he had overlooked.

"Gramps!" Penny snapped at him impatiently. "What did she say?"

It wouldn't come to him, so he put the matter aside for later consideration. "She'll do what we want."

Penny giggled and twirled about in mock celebration. "Little Miss Track Shoes has run out of tricks! Too bad, too bad! No gold medal for her! Better luck next time!"

She danced around the room, frizzy red hair flying, gleefully singing *tra-la-*

la-la. She danced at Twitch, who just looked at her dumbly, then at the ur'droch where it crouched hidden in a corner. Gask waited her out patiently.

"Make the children some dinner," he said when she had calmed down sufficiently to pay attention. "Don't get cute and don't frighten them."

"What's the difference?" she asked, pouting. "You'll kill them anyway. Why can't I have some fun with them first?"

"Because I say so, Penny," he answered, giving her a steady look. "Is that reason enough for you?"

The redhead's mouth twisted in a hard sneer. "Sure enough, Gramps. Anything your little old heart desires."

She disappeared into the kitchen, humming tunelessly. She was becoming increasingly unstable, less easily controlled. If she went off, as she was certain to do sooner or later, he would have to kill her. Not that he was reluctant to do so, but it was inconvenient. He still might need her help. His adversaries were resourceful, and their desperation would render them less predictable. Penny Dreadful was a valuable counter to such behavior. He might have to agree to give her the children as a reward. She would like that. If she had his promise that she could have them when this was over, she was more likely to stay in line. It was a cheap enough price.

The children were down in the basement in a big, L-shaped recreation room containing an old Lionel train setup, a jukebox and bar, a game table and dartboard, and some couches and chairs situated around a television. There was only one way in or out, down a stairway leading from the back of the house, so it was easy to keep an eye on them.

Nevertheless, he sent the ur'droch down to stand watch without their seeing it. Twitch and Penny were too scary and more likely to do something of which he didn't approve. The ur'droch would just stay hidden.

When the phone rang, he was surprised. No one should be calling. He picked up the receiver guardedly. "Yes?"

"Mr. Robinson?"

It was that sheriff's deputy, what's-his-name Spence. Findo Gask suppressed a grimace. "What can I do for you?"

"We need to talk. The sooner, the better."

"Go ahead, Deputy Sheriff. Talk."

"No, not on the phone. In person. I just need to clarify a few things. About what's going on with John Ross and this drug business. I'm worried about those kids. I want to make sure they're safe. Where can we meet?"

Findo Gask shook his head. Gask could tell by the way Spence spoke. He had been checking, and he had found out that no one knew anything about an FBI assignment in Hopewell or an agent named Robinson. Spence was scared. On Robinson's instructions, he had opened a bedroom window in the Freemark home so that the children could be removed for safekeeping while a sting operation was implemented to collar the dangerous Mr. Ross. Spence was afraid he had facilitated the kidnapping of two children, aiding and abetting the commission of a felony, and he could see his entire career slipping away.

What to do?

"I'm going to give you an address, Deputy Sheriff." Gask looked at Twitch, slumped on the sofa in front of the television, huge and vacant-eyed. "I've been thinking that the children might be better off with the local authorities. If you could pick them up, I would be grateful. We can talk then."

"Yeah, sure, that would be fine." Spence sounded relieved.

Gask gave the deputy sheriff their address. He wasn't worried about Spence descending on him with an army of law enforcement officers; the deputy sheriff would be looking for a way to protect himself from any fallout in this business. If he could get the children back unharmed, things would be fine. That's the way he would look at it. He would come alone.

Findo Gask hung up the receiver. A picture of how this business would end took shape. Newspaper headlines and television trailers scrolled through his mind. A family tragedy was sparked by jealousy and misunderstanding. Two men and a woman were involved, the latter a well-known athlete. Multiple killings of adults and children ensued. Murder and suicide made an unwelcome appearance in tiny Hopewell.

It would make for good reading in other cities.

"What are we going to do, John?" Nest repeated, a hint of desperation creeping into her voice.

Ross limped to the kitchen counter with the aid of his staff and leaned his backside against the lower cabinets, crossing his arms over his chest, embracing the staff possessively. His lean face was lined with fatigue, but his eyes were fierce.

"There's something I haven't told you," he said after a moment's reflection. "Not because I was trying to keep it from you or didn't trust you, but because it didn't have anything to do with you. Except that now it does. I told you that a dream led me to the gypsy morph. But I didn't tell you what the dream was about. In the dream, a Knight of the Word was hung from a cross. Demons and once-men had crucified him. He was dying. Just before I woke, I saw his face. It was my own."

He held up one hand to cut short her startled exclamation. "I wasn't sure at first if the Knight on the cross was me or if I was just supposed to see myself in him. I was hoping I would learn the answer from the Lady when she summoned me to Wales two months ago. I didn't, but I learned something more important. I learned that if I was successful in protecting the gypsy morph through its final transformation, I would be released forever from my commitment to the Word."

"John!" she breathed.

He nodded. "I know. I fought so hard for it ten years ago when it wasn't permitted, and then it's offered to me without my even having asked. I want it, Nest. I'll admit that. I've seen too much, living in both the present and the future. I'm tired of death and chaos and destruction. I'm tired of fighting to stay alive. Hell, I'm just plain tired. I've been a Knight of the Word for twenty-five years. Half my life. It's all I can remember anymore. It seems like the only existence I've ever known. I need to give it up. I need to rest."

"But you can do that now!" she exclaimed quickly. "You've done what was asked of you. The morph hasn't changed in days. Its time is almost up, and it's still a little boy. It's finished changing, isn't it?"

"Maybe. Maybe not. I'm not sure. It hasn't bonded with you the way I expected. It seems to be looking for something. I don't know what, but the way it responded to you last night when Wraith came out suggests it's still waiting for something to happen. It might be another change."

She studied him a moment. "All right. So what do we do?"

"We let Findo Gask call us back and set up the exchange. We meet with him. We find a way to separate Harper from the demons. Your job is to get her safely out of there. Mine is to do what I can to save the morph."

She walked to the kitchen window and looked out into the night. It was snowing heavily again, thick flakes drifting out of the clouded skies, a fresh blanket of white gathering over the earth. "They'll be expecting something like that," she said quietly.

"I know."

"You'll lose the morph anyway. And your life as well."

"Maybe."

"We'll have accomplished nothing."

"We'll have saved Harper."

She thought about it some more. Gask would pick a place for the exchange that would favor the demons. He would have his companions hidden all about them. He would make certain she and Ross were rendered helpless in the event they tried to surprise him. Her mind spun out possible scenarios, all bleak and hopeless. Nothing she envisioned had a happy ending.

Then a dark realization swept over her. She wasn't seeing this right. There wouldn't be any trade. There wasn't any reason for one. Why would Findo Gask leave any of them alive when he didn't have to? It made perfect sense, in demon terms, not to let them go, but to kill them.

Don't underestimate him!

She had to find a way to get one step ahead of him. Where was he now? Where was he hiding Harper and Little John? If she only knew that—

She caught herself. But she did know. She had known all along, even without realizing it. She knew exactly where they were.

The phone rang, interrupting her train of thought. She walked over and snatched it up. "Hello?"

"Nest, it's Robert. I just heard about Bennett Scott." He sounded shaken. "I'm really sorry."

She put her hand over her eyes wearily. "Thanks, Robert."

"I'm sorry about her dying, and I'm sorry for all the things I've said about her. And about John Ross. You didn't need to hear that kind of junk from me. I wish I'd never said any of it, but I did, and it's too late to take it back. That's been a problem for me all my life."

"It's okay, Robert."

"I know things must be tough over there, especially for the little ones. Amy and I want you to think about coming over here Christmas Day. All of you, Ross included. You don't have to come for the whole day, just as much of it as you want. But it would be good for the kids to have other kids to play with. It would be good for all of you to be with other people."

She didn't say anything, her throat and chest tight with sudden grief and despair. All she could think about was losing Harper and Little John to the demons and not being able to get them safely back.

"Nest?" he said.

She felt everything break apart inside like deadwood and then come back together again, the broken pieces bound together by iron forged in the furnace of her determination. "You're a good guy, Robert," she said quietly. "Tell Amy how much your invitation means to me. Let me think about it, and I'll call you tomorrow morning."

She hung up the phone, stared off into space for a moment, and then looked at Ross. "What do you say, John? I'm tired of being pushed around. Let's not wait on Findo Gask and his phone call. Let's go get the children back right now."

CHAPTER 26

It took a considerable amount of effort on Nest's part to persuade Ross that she was right. If they let Findo Gask dictate the conditions of any trade, she argued, he would put them in a box. He would create a situation where they had no hope of freeing either Harper or Little John. Besides, he would not make the exchange in any case, not even if they revealed to him that he had the gypsy morph in his possession already. He would simply kill them. If they wanted to have any chance at all, they had to act now, while Gask thought them paralyzed and helpless. They had to go after the demons on their own ground.

Ross was not averse to the idea of a preemptive strike; it rather appealed to him. He had taken on a fatalistic attitude regarding his own future, and his sole concern was for the children. But he was adamant that their best approach was to keep Nest out of the picture entirely. He would go by himself, confront Gask, and free the children if he could. If there were any sacrifices required, they would come from him.

"John, you can't do it alone," she pointed out reasonably. "You don't even know how to get to where you need to go. I'll have to drive us. Listen to me. When we get there, one of us will have to distract the demons while the other frees the children. It will be hard enough with two of us working together. It will be impossible if you try it alone."

There were at least four demons, she added. Findo Gask, the girl Penny, the ur'droch, and a giant albino called Twitch. That was too many for him to try to take on by himself.

"I have as much stake in this as you do, John," she said quietly. "Harper is my responsibility. Bennett gave her into my safekeeping. And what about Little John? He asked for me, brought you to me, and last night called me *Mama* as if I had it in me to give him the one thing he most needs. I can't ignore that. I can't pretend it didn't happen or that it doesn't mean anything, and it's wrong of you to ask me to do so."

"You're not equipped for this, Nest," he insisted angrily. "You don't have the tools. The only real weapon you have is one you don't want to use. What's going to happen if you have to call Wraith out to defend you? What if you can't? The demons will kill you in a heartbeat. I have the magic to protect myself, but I don't think I can protect us both.

"Besides," he said, shaking his head dismissively. "You aren't the one who was asked to protect the morph. I was. This isn't your fight."

She smiled at that. "I think it's been my fight since the day Findo Gask appeared on my doorstep and told me what would happen if I took you in. I don't think I've got a choice."

In the end, he agreed. They would go together, but only if she promised that once she had possession of the children she would get out of there and that she would not expose herself to any more danger than was absolutely necessary.

As *if*, she wanted to say, but agreed.

The children, she told him, were in an old house on Third Street, down by the west plant of MidCon Steel. She had gone to that house with church carolers earlier on the same night he had appeared at her door.

In the wake of everything else that had happened, Nest had all but forgotten the incident with Twitch and Allen Kruppert. She had suspected that something wasn't right with that house and the strange people in it, but she hadn't given the matter any further thought after Ross appeared with the morph. It wasn't until now she remembered Bennett saying, when pressed, that Penny claimed to be Findo Gask's niece.

"If the connection is real," she explained to Ross, "they're all staying in that house on Third. That's where they'll have the children. Gask wasn't there that night, or at least he didn't show himself. I think he was testing me, John, trying to see how strong I was, how easily I would frighten. But he was being careful to stay hidden from me in the process. I don't think he has any idea we know about his connection to that house."

"Maybe," Ross acknowledged grudgingly. "But even if you're right, we won't be able to just walk in there. If you were smart enough to have Pick throw a protective net over your house, won't Gask have done something like it to his?"

She had to agree that he would. How would they get past whatever safeguards he had installed? For that matter, how would they even know where to look for the children? If she couldn't get to them before the demons discovered what they were about, the children's lives were over. Even a distraction by Ross probably wouldn't be enough to save them. At least one demon would get there first.

It was still snowing heavily outside, and the snowplows were beginning to make their runs up and down the nearby streets, metal blades scraping loudly in the snowfall's hushed silence. Pick might have the solution to their dilemma, knowing what he did about magic's uses, but she was unlikely to find him out on a night like this. Pick might be able to throw his voice from great distances to speak with her, but she could not do the same to summon him. Ross, when pressed, admitted he lacked any sort of magic that would enable him to bypass a demon security web. The way matters stood, if they went to the house on Third Street, any attempt at an entry would probably result in failure.

Nest felt time and opportunity slipping away. It was already edging toward eight o'clock. They had little more than four hours in which to act. The weather was worsening, the streets would soon be impassable where the snowplows hadn't reached, and even getting to where they had to go would become difficult.

Hawkeye had reappeared from wherever he had been hiding and taken up a position on the living-room couch. The hair along the ridge of his spine was spiked, and his green eyes were fierce and angry and resentful. She watched him for a time as she stood in the kitchen doorway, thinking. He must have had a close encounter with the ur'droch when it took the children out of her bedroom. He was probably lucky to be alive.

An idea came to her suddenly, but it was so strange she could barely bring herself to allow it to take shape. In fact, it was more than strange—it was anathema.

Under any other circumstances, she wouldn't have even considered it. But when you are desperate, you will go down some roads you would otherwise avoid.

"John," she said, drawing his attention. "I'm going outside for a little bit." She spoke quickly, before she could think better of it, before she had time to reconsider. "I'm going to try something that might help. Wait here for me."

She pulled on her hooded parka, scarf, gloves, and boots, and she laced, buttoned, and zipped everything up tight. She could hear Ross saying something behind her, but she didn't answer. She didn't trust herself to do so. When she was sufficiently bundled up, she went out the back door into the night.

It was cold and snowing, but the wind had died away, and the air didn't have last night's bite. Sending clouds of breath ahead of her, she walked to the hedgerow at the end of her backyard and passed through the tangle of brittle limbs to where the service road lay. Lights blazed from the windows of distant houses, but it was the eyes of the feeders who quickly gathered that drew her attention. There were dozens of them, slinking through the shadows, appearing and disappearing in the swirl of falling snow. They had come to her to taste the magic she was about to unleash, sensing in that way they had what she intended to do.

Her plan was simple, if abhorrent. She intended to release Wraith and send him into the park in search of Pick. Her own efforts would be wasted, because her presence alone would not be enough to summon the sylvan from wherever he was taking shelter. Moreover, it would take time she did not have. But Wraith was all magic, and magic of that size roaming Pick's woodland domain would alert the sylvan instantly. It would draw him out and bring him in search of her.

The problem, of course, was that this plan she had stumbled on required that she release Wraith, something she was loath to do under any circumstance and particularly where she was not personally threatened. The difficulties she faced in releasing Wraith were daunting. She did not know for certain that she could control what he might do or how far away from her he might venture once released, or if she could bring him back inside once he was out. She did not know how much energy she would have to expend on any of this, and she was looking at a night ahead when she might need that energy to stay alive.

But without Pick's help, she did not stand a chance of bypassing any security net Findo Gask might have set in place or of finding where the children were concealed. Without Pick's help, her chances of succeeding were minimal.

It was a risk worth taking, she decided anew, and hoped she was thinking clearly.

She found a patch of deep shadow amid a cluster of barren, dark trees and bushes near the far end of the Peterson yard and placed herself there. The feeders were clustered all about her, but she forced herself to ignore them. They were no threat to her if she stayed calm.

Closing her eyes, she reached down inside in search of Wraith. It was the first time she had ever done so consciously. She was not sure about what she was doing and found herself groping as if blind and deaf. There were no pathways to follow, and she lacked anger and fear as catalysts to spark his interest. She searched, and nothing happened. She hunted, but found only silence and darkness.

She opened her eyes and frowned. It wasn't working.

Briefly, she considered giving up, abandoning her search, going back into the house, and collecting Ross. But she was stubborn by nature, and she was curious about why she was struggling so. There should have been at least some sign of the ghost wolf. There should have been some small hint of his presence. Why wasn't there?

Brushing at the snowflakes that settled on her eyelashes, she tried again. But this time she went looking for what she knew she could find—her own magic, the magic she had been born with. She found it easily and called it forth with a confidence born of familiarity. A syrupy warmth spread from her body into her limbs, tingling like a charge of electricity.

Sure enough, the summoning of her own magic brought out Wraith as well. She felt him surge inside, a massive jolt that staggered her. He was there all at once, brutal and powerful, waking to confront whatever threatened, emerging to investigate, feral instincts and hunger washing through her like fresh blood.

He came out of her in a rush—without her asking him to do so, without her being under threat, without any visible danger presenting itself. In a heartbeat, her worst fears were confirmed. She could not control him. She was the vessel that housed him, but she had no power over him. Her certainty about it was visceral. It left her feeling helpless and small and torn with doubt. She wanted his protective presence, but she did not want the responsibility for what he might do. Her nearly overpowering, instinctual wish was that he might be gone from her forever. But her need for his help was stronger still and thrust her repulsion aside.

The feeders fell away from her in a whisper of scattered snow, their lantern eyes disappearing back into the night.

Wraith began to run. With a surge, he bounded into the park, a low, dark shape powering through the new snow, legs churning, lean body stretched out. She didn't ask it of him, didn't direct him to go, but he seemed to sense all on his own what was required of him and responded. Something of her went with him, feeling what he felt, seeing through his eyes. She was trapped inside his wolf's body, crossing swiftly over snowfields, past the dark trunks of trees, and over hillocks and drifts. She felt nothing of the cold and snow, for Wraith was all magic and could only wax or wane in power and presence; he would never be affected by the elements. She felt his brute strength and great heart. She felt the fury in him that burned just below the surface of his skin.

Most of all, she felt her father's magic, white-hot and capable of anything, unburdened by moral codes and reason, shot through with the iron threads of the cause for which Wraith had been created when she was still a child—to protect her, to keep her safe from harmful magic, to bring her safely to maturity, and, ultimately, to deliver her into her father's hands.

Everything had changed with time's passage, shifted around and made new. Her father was dead. She was grown and become her own person. But Wraith was still there.

He bounded on across the snow-blanketed flats and into the trees, tiger face fierce and spectral. No one was in the park to see him, and it was just as well. Nightmares are born of such encounters. Nest felt herself enveloped in a haze of emotions she could neither define nor separate, emotions born of the ghost wolf's freedom and raw power, emotions that emerged in a rush as he neared the deep woods.

Faster Wraith ran, deeper into the night.

Then, abruptly, Nest felt something snap all the way down inside her body where her joining with Wraith began. She gasped in shock, and for a long, painful moment, everything went black and silent.

When she could see again, she was back inside her own body, standing alone in the patch of shadows at the end of the Petersons' backyard. The feeders had dispersed. Snow fell wet and cold on her face, and the park stretched away before her, silent and empty.

Her realization of what had happened came swiftly and left her stunned. She could no longer see through Wraith's eyes. She was no longer connected to him.

The ghost wolf had broken free.

Larry Spence pulled the cruiser into the driveway of the old Victorian on West Third and shut off the engine. In the ensuing silence, he sat in the car and tried to think matters through, to decide how he should approach this business. But it was hard; his head throbbed and there was a persistent buzz in his ears. He wasn't sure how long he'd had the headache and buzzing; he couldn't remember when they had begun. But they assailed him unrelentingly, making it almost impossible for him to concentrate.

Everything seemed so difficult all of a sudden.

He knew he had made a mistake about the children. He knew he had placed his career in jeopardy by allowing Robinson to take them out of Nest's home. His betrayal of Nest was almost unbearable. It no longer mattered that he thought he was doing the right thing at the time; he had allowed himself to be manipulated and deceived. He was furious about this, but oddly impotent as well. He should do something, but even now, parked in the drive of Robinson's safe house, he was uncertain what that something should be.

He exhaled wearily. At the very least, he had to get the children back. Whatever else happened, he could not leave here without them. He did not know for sure what was going on, but he knew enough to realize he would have been better off if he had thrown Robinson out the door of his home on that first visit. Thinking back on it, he couldn't understand why he hadn't.

The headache throbbed at his temples and the buzzing hummed in his ears. He squeezed his eyes shut momentarily. He just wanted this business to be over with.

Taking a deep, steadying breath, he climbed out of the car and walked up the snowy drive to the front porch, mounted the steps, and knocked on the door. Inside, it was silent. There were lights, but no movement behind the drawn curtains. The neighborhood of once-grand homes had the feel of a graveyard. The street, in the wake of the storm, was deserted.

I'll make this quick, he told himself. *I'll take those children out of here and be rid of these people.*

The door opened, and the man who called himself Robinson was standing there, smiling. "Come in, Deputy Sheriff." He stepped back.

Careful, now, Larry Spence warned himself. *Take it slow.*

He entered and looked around cautiously. He stood in a large entry. A stairway climbed into darkness to one side. A door stood closed on the other. The living room opened up ahead, bright and quaint with turn-of-the-century furniture and fading wallpaper that hung from wainscoting to mopboards in a field of yellow flowers.

"Take off your coat, Deputy Sheriff," Robinson said. It almost sounded like an order. "Sit down for a moment."

"I won't be staying that long." Larry shifted his gaze to Robinson, then back to the living room, where Penny sat with her legs curled up on the couch next to a giant, nearly hairless albino, both of them staring at a television set. Penny saw him and gave a small wave and smile. He nodded stone-faced in response.

"Where are the children, Mr. Robinson?" he asked. His head was pounding, the pain much worse, the buzzing so insistent it threatened to scramble his thoughts completely.

"Playing downstairs." The other man was watching him carefully.

"I'd like you to bring them up here, please."

"Well, things have changed a bit." Robinson seemed genuinely apologetic. "I need to ask you for one more favor."

"I think I've done enough favors for you."

Robinson smiled anew. "I'm not asking much. Just take a short ride with us in a little while. The children can go, too. Afterward you can have them back."

Larry could already feel something wrong with things, could sense a shift in attitude that signaled this was not going to go the way he wanted. He had been a sheriff's deputy for better than fifteen years, and he trusted his instincts. He needed to get the upper hand on these people right away, not take any chances.

"I've been doing some checking," he said, deciding to force the issue. "I called the FBI's Chicago field office and asked about you. They never heard of you. They don't know anything about a drug operation in this area."

Robinson shrugged. "They don't know we're here. We operate out of Washington. What is the problem, Deputy?"

"Is that one of your operatives?" Larry pressed, staying calm, pointing at the strange man on the couch.

Robinson glanced over his shoulder, then back at Spence. "Yes, he's a local—"

Larry had his .45 out and pointed at Robinson's midsection. "Stand easy," he advised. "Keep your hands where I can see them." He reached forward and patted the old man's coat pockets and sides, then stepped away. "I checked with Washington as well. No one there knows who you are, either."

The man who called himself Robinson said nothing.

"So who are you?" Larry pressed.

The other man shrugged. "It doesn't matter."

Penny looked up from the television. When she saw the gun in Larry's hand, she started to rise.

"Sit down!" Larry ordered sharply. She hesitated, then did so. But she was grinning broadly. "What's going on here?" Larry demanded of everyone in general.

Robinson smiled. "Figure it out for yourself, Deputy Sheriff. You seem pretty clever."

"Your being here doesn't have anything to do with drugs, does it?"

Robinson pursed his lips. "No, Deputy Sheriff, it doesn't. But it does have to do with addiction. I am a specialist in addictions, did you know that? Addictions that beset the human race. There are hundreds of them. Thousands. Human beings are enslaved by their addictions, and I find that by determining the nature of the addictions that rule them, I can influence the course of action they take."

He cocked an eyebrow at Spence. "Take yourself, for instance. I knew almost from the beginning that if I wanted something from you, all I had to do was link my request to your very obvious attraction to Miss Freemark. You were blinded to everything when focused on her. Silly, really, since she doesn't care the weight of a paper clip for you. But you see her as your future wife and the mother of your children and so you do the things you think will further the happening of those events."

Larry flushed angrily. "That's not an addiction. What the hell are you talking about?"

"Addictions come in all sizes and shapes," Robinson continued mildly, "and the people who have them always think they're something else. Dependencies, Deputy Sheriff. They give an illusion of control you lack. Yours is a small dependency, but deeply ingrained, and it rules you. It's why you've been so helpful to me. I give you the illusion of control over your need to influence Miss Freemark and you're ready to walk over coals."

The headache and buzzing were attacking Larry Spence with such ferocity that he could barely focus on what Robinson was saying. "Let's get those children up here right now!" he snapped, suddenly furious.

"Let's not," Robinson replied calmly.

Larry stared at him. What was he thinking? That Larry wouldn't shoot, that he wouldn't use the gun he was holding if the other man made even the slightest move to stop him? Did he think Larry wasn't in charge of this situation, that he wasn't able to do what was needed just because he had allowed himself to be tricked earlier?

Then he looked into Robinson's eyes, and he saw the truth. His gun didn't mean anything. Or his badge of office, or the weight of the law, or even Larry himself. None of it mattered. Those eyes were dead to everything. They had been dead a long time.

Larry went cold and hot in rapid sequence, and suddenly all he wanted to do was to get the hell out of there as quickly as he could. But he knew it was too late, that he couldn't, that he was trapped as surely as if Robinson was holding the gun on him.

"Oh, my God," he breathed softly.

His hand was frozen. Suddenly terrified, he tried to pull the trigger, but his fingers refused to work. Robinson came forward, took the gun out of his hand, and slipped it back into its holster. Larry couldn't do anything to stop him. Nothing. He was paralyzed by the buzzing in his ears and the throbbing in his head and by a cold certainty that he was completely helpless. He stood in front of Robinson with his hands empty and his options all used up. He wanted to scream, but he couldn't. Tears leaked from his eyes, and his big frame shook as he began to cry.

"Please," he begged, unable to help himself. "Please."

Robinson smiled, but his smile held no warmth.

Silence.

Nest stood paralyzed in the frigid darkness at the edge of Sinnissippi Park, trying desperately to regain her scattered thoughts. The enormity of what had just happened threatened to overwhelm her. She had lost Wraith! Somehow, some way, she had lost him. She hadn't meant to do so, hadn't even suspected it was possible. It was true that he had emerged from her body only a handful of times since he had taken up residence, but there had never been any indication that he might break free. She felt empty and bereft in a way she had never expected. She saw all her hopes of saving the children from the demons drifting away on the backs of snowflakes.

What had she done?

For a long time, she just stood there, unable to move, trying to decide what she should do. She couldn't go back into the house. She had to find Wraith and get him back under her control. She had to! She stared out at the black-and-white expanse of the park and realized how hopeless her task was. Wraith could move so much faster than she could. He would never be found if he didn't wish it. She could search forever, and she wouldn't even see him. He didn't even have to outrun her. He could simply disappear, the way he did when she was little. He could vanish as completely as last summer's warmth, and she had no way to bring him out again.

Despair staggered her; it left her frantic. She held on only through sheer force of will. She could not afford to give in to what she was feeling. If she did, there would be no chance for any of them.

Then a shadow soared out of the darkness ahead, gliding smooth and silent through the falling snow, materializing from out of the tangled limbs and trunks of the trees. She recognized Jonathan, great wings stretched wide, and as he drew closer, she saw Pick astride him. Grasping at the faint hope the sylvan's appearance offered, she detached herself from the shadows. Jonathan swept past her, circled back around, passed over her again, but closer this time, and suddenly Pick was standing on her shoulder.

"Criminy, what are you doing out in this weather?" he demanded disgustedly. But there was concern in his voice as well; he knew something wasn't right.

"Oh, Pick, everything's gone wrong!" she blurted out, cupping her gloved hands so he could jump down into them.

He did so, grumbling vehemently. "I thought as much when I felt a disturbance in the magic of the park, and there was Wraith, running through the deep woods as if possessed. Hah, which I guess he is, in a manner of speaking!"

She started. "You saw Wraith? Where is he? Why isn't he with you?"

"Would you settle down?" he snapped, putting up his twiggy hands defensively. "Since when am I in charge of keeping track of Wraith? What do I look like, anyway? He's your pet!"

"He broke away from me!" she exclaimed. "I sent him into the park to find you, and he broke away! Why would he do that? He's gone, and I don't know how to get him back!"

She sounded like a little girl, but she couldn't help herself. Pick didn't seem to notice. He brushed at a flurry of stray snowflakes that fell into his face. "Would you mind stepping out of the weather a bit?" he asked irritably. "Would that be asking too much?"

She retreated back into the shelter of the trees and brush where the big limbs and trunks deflected most of the falling snow. Shadows enfolded them, and a scattering of feeder eyes appeared.

"Start at the beginning," he ordered, "and let's see if I can make any sense out of what you've got to say!"

She told him everything that had happened from the time Larry Spence had appeared at the house—the breaching of the sylvan's security net, the children's disappearance, Findo Gask's phone call, and her effort to send Wraith into the park in search of him. She told him that she would try to free the children from where Findo Gask had concealed them in the old house on West Third, hoping to catch the demons off guard.

"But I need someone to check for traps he might have set to warn of anyone trying to get into the house. I need someone to go inside and find out where the children are hidden. I need you, Pick."

He was uncharacteristically silent in the aftermath of her plea. He sat in the cup of her hands, worrying stray threads of his mossy beard with his mouth and mumbling inaudibly. She let him be; there was nothing more she could say to persuade him.

"Too bad about that fellow opening your bedroom window," he said finally. "But if Gask wanted the children that bad, he probably would have come after them anyway. That was what he was trying to do last night. I don't expect the security net would have stopped him."

She nodded silently.

"Demons," he muttered.

She waited.

"I don't like going out of the park," he declared. He held up his hands quickly when she tried to speak. "Not that I don't do so now and then, when there's need for it." He huffed. "I don't much like going into strange houses, either. You sure you don't want to let go of this thing? You might be better off if you did. Four demons are a lot to overcome, even with a Knight of the Word helping out. I know you. You're stubborn. But you can't fight everyone's battles. You can't save the entire world."

"Pick," she said softly, bending close to him, so she could see his pinprick eyes. "I can't explain exactly why I have to do this, but I do. I feel it the way you feel a breach in the magic. I know it's the right thing. Harper's all alone, and there's something about Little John, something that has to do with me."

He snorted.

"This is important to me, Pick. I have to go after those children. With or without your help, I have to."

"Since when have you ever done anything where demons and magic were concerned without my help?" he demanded in exasperation. "Look, I'll do this. I'll sweep the grounds and walls and doors and windows for traps and snares and have a look inside to find those kids. But when I'm finished, if I tell you it can't be done, that's the end of it. Fair enough?"

"Deal," she said.

He spit over his shoulder. "Now, what's this nonsense about losing Wraith? You can't lose magic once it's given to you. It doesn't just go wandering off by itself. You have to use it up or pass it on or set it free or cast it away. Did you do any of those?"

She shook her head. "I don't think so. I didn't do anything. I just sent him out to attract your attention, then there was this snapping inside, this feeling of something breaking loose, and I couldn't feel him anymore."

Pick shrugged. "Well, I don't know about that, but I do know he's standing right over there, looking at you."

She glanced quickly to where he was pointing. Sure enough, Wraith was standing in the shelter of the trees in the Peterson backyard, as still as stone, tiger face lowered, bright eyes staring at her. She stared back in surprise and disbelief. What was he doing?

"Pick?" she said softly.

"I know, I know," he muttered in response, fidgeting in her palm. "He's backed off of you for some reason. Are you sure you didn't do anything to him?"

"What would I do?" she snapped angrily.

"I don't know! Call him! See what he does!"

She did, speaking his name softly, then more firmly. But Wraith didn't move. Snow gathered on his dark, bristling fur, pinpricks of white. All around, the night was silent and cold.

"Maybe he doesn't want to come back inside you just yet," Pick mused. He shifted in her palm, a bundle of sticks. "Maybe he wants to stay out there awhile."

"Fine with me," she declared quickly, frustrated and confused. "I'm not too happy with him living inside my skin anyway. I never have been."

Pick looked at her. "Maybe he senses that."

"That I don't want him to come back inside me?"

"Maybe. You made it plain enough to me. You probably made it plain enough to him."

She shook her head. "Then why didn't he leave sooner? Why didn't he just—"

Then suddenly she realized why. Suddenly, she knew. Her revelation was instantaneous and stunning. He had stayed not because he wanted to, but because she wouldn't let him go. He was living inside her body because she demanded it. It might not have been that way in the beginning, when she was still just a girl. He might have been responding freely to her need, which was genuine and compelling. But at some point, the relationship had changed. Subconsciously, at least, she had decided she could not give him up. She hadn't been aware of what she had done, of the chain she had forged to keep him close. She had thought him gone, after all. It wasn't until he had revealed himself in Seattle ten years ago, that she had even realized he was still there.

She was staggered by the enormity of her discovery, thinking at first she must be wrong. She had wanted him gone for so long that it seemed ridiculous to believe she could have bent him to her will, even in the most subliminal way, that she could have imprisoned him inside her without realizing it. But his magic belonged to her; her father and grandmother had given it to her. It was the way Pick said: magic didn't just wander off of its own accord. Wraith was hers, and the strength of her need had persuaded her that she must keep him close, always and forever.

She stared at him now through the night shadows with fresh eyes, seeing the truth. "It was me," she told Pick softly.

"What are you talking about?" he demanded.

"Don't you see? I wouldn't let go of him. I didn't intend it. I didn't mean for him to become a part of me. But I made it happen without ever realizing what it was I was doing. I thought it was his choice. But it wasn't. It was mine. It was always mine."

Pick rubbed his beard. "That doesn't make any sense. You haven't been happy about him living inside you for years. He must have known, yet he didn't do a thing about it. So why is he standing up to you now? If he couldn't or wouldn't break free before, why is he doing so now? What's changed?"

She looked back at Wraith, at his tiger face, fierce and challenging, at his gleaming eyes fixed on her as if they could see what she could not. "The morph," she whispered.

"What?" Pick was confused. "Speak up!"

"The gypsy morph," she repeated. "That's what's changed."

She could almost see it then, the truth she had been searching for since John Ross and the morph had appeared on her doorstep three days ago. It was a shadowy presence that darted across her consciousness in the blink of an eye and was gone. It whispered to her of Little John, of why he took the form of a four-year-old boy and spoke her name and came to find her and called her *Mama.* It whispered to her of a revelation waiting to be uncovered if she would just believe.

She thought suddenly of the Freemark women, of the way the magic passed from one generation to the next. She thought of Gran, and the sacrifice she had made for Nest so many years ago.

When she spoke, her voice was distant and searching. "Pick, if I set Wraith free, will I lose him? Will I lose his magic?"

Pick was silent for a long time. "I don't know," he said finally. "Maybe."

She nodded slowly. "I'll have to chance it. I'm leaving him out there to do what he wishes. I won't take him back inside me." She took a deep breath and turned away from the ghost wolf. No words were necessary. Wraith would know.

"Call Jonathan," she ordered Pick. "Fly to the house on West Third and start checking. But be careful. I'll take John in the car and meet you there."

Pick grumbled to himself for a moment, then whistled sharply. The barn owl reappeared out of the trees, gliding past Nest's outstretched hand, his great wings brushing her shoulder softly. The sylvan jumped onto his back, and in seconds they were gone, winging away into the night.

Nest watched them fade into the snowfall, keeping her back to Wraith. When they were gone, she turned to see if he was still there. He wasn't. The ghost wolf had vanished. She stared at the space he had occupied, then glanced around quickly. There was no sign of him.

"Good hunting, Wraith," she whispered.

Then she was running for the house and John Ross.

Chapter 27

They drove through the mostly deserted streets of Hopewell, Nest at the wheel and Ross beside her in the passenger seat. Neither spoke. Snow continued to fall in a curtain of thick, soft flakes, and everything was blanketed in white. The main streets had been cleared by the plows on their first pass, but the side streets were mostly untouched, the snow spilling over onto sidewalks and lawns in a smooth, unbroken carpet, the metal roofs of parked cars lifting out of the winterscape like the humped backs of slumbering beasts. Streetlights glistened off the pale crust in brilliant bursts that spread outward in halos of diminishing radiance. Everywhere, there was a deep, pervasive, and enveloping silence.

As she steered through the shaken-snow-globe world, Nest was shot through with doubt. She could not fathom doing what she knew she must without Wraith to stand beside her, even though she had accepted that it might be necessary. She tried not to dwell on the enormity of the task that lay ahead—getting into the demon lair, finding the children, and getting them out safely, all without having Wraith's magic to aid her. She tried not to question her belief that giving up Wraith was somehow necessary in order to discover the secret of the gypsy morph, even though that belief was essentially blind and deaf and paper thin. She had not told Ross of it. She had not told him of freeing Wraith. If he had known, he would never have let her come with him. She had told him only what she felt necessary—that Pick had gone on ahead to scout the grounds and entrances to the demon house in order to find a way in. What happened from here forward must be on her conscience and not made a burden on his.

When they reached the intersection of West Fourth Street and Avenue G, Nest pulled the Taurus into the mostly invisible parking lot of a dry-cleaning service two blocks away from and out of sight of their destination. From there, they walked through the deep snow, down unplowed walks and across deserted side streets until the old Victorian came in sight. West Third was plowed, but empty of traffic, and the old houses were mostly dark at the ends of their snow-covered lawns and long drives. Even the one in which Findo Gask and his demons took shelter had only a few lights burning, as if electricity were precious and meant to be rationed.

They were almost in front of the house, keeping to the shadows and away from the pale glow of the streetlamps, when they saw the sheriff's cruiser parked in the drive.

Nest shook her head at Ross as they paused beneath a massive old hickory. "Larry Spence." She spoke his name with disgust and frustration. "He just can't manage to keep out of this."

Ross nodded, eyes fixed on the house. "We can't do anything about him now. We have to go in anyway."

She took a deep breath, thinking of all the chances she'd had to put Larry out of the picture, to scare him so badly he wouldn't dream of involving himself further. It might have spared them what they were about to go through. It might have changed everything. She sighed. That was the trouble with hindsight, of course. Always perfect. She hadn't even considered doing harm to Larry. She had always thought he would lose interest and drop out of the picture on his own. But maybe that was never an option. Maybe the demons had gained too tight a hold over him for that to be possible.

She glanced at the cruiser one final time and dismissed the matter. She would never know now.

They worked their way along the edge of a hedgerow separating the old Victorian from an English manor knockoff that was dark and crumbling. They drew even with the front entry and paused, kneeling in the snow, staying low to the ground and the shadows.

If I'm wrong about this, Nest kept thinking, unable to finish the thought, but unable to stop repeating herself either.

She didn't see where Pick came from. He just appeared, dropping out of nowhere to land on her shoulder, giving her such a fright that she gasped aloud.

"Criminy, settle down!" the other snapped irritably, grasping her collar to keep from being shaken off. His mossy beard was thick with snowflakes, and his wooden body was damp and slick. "Took your time getting here, didn't you?"

"Well, navigating these streets isn't like sailing along on the open air!" she snapped back, irritated herself. She exhaled a cloud of breath at him. "What did you find?"

He sniffed. "What do you think I found? There's traps and trip lines formed of demon magic all over. The place stinks of them. But those are demons in there, not sylvans, so they tend to be more than a little careless. No pride of workmanship at all. There are holes in that netting large enough to fly an owl through—which is exactly what I did. Then I slipped through a tear in the screen on the back porch, which they forgot about as well, and got inside through the back door. They've got the children down in the basement in a big playroom. You can get to them easy."

He scrunched up his face. "The bad news is that something's down there with them. I don't know what it is. Might be a demon, might be something else. I couldn't see it, but I could sure as heck smell it!"

Nest nodded. She knew what it was. She glanced at Ross, then back at Pick. "Could you tell exactly where it was? I mean, where in the room?"

"Of course I could!" he snapped. "You could tell, too, if you had my nose!"

"Which is my point," she went on quickly. "Will you go back inside with me and show me exactly where it's hiding?"

There was a long silence as he considered the matter, rubbing at his beard and muttering to himself furiously. *Don't say anything about Wraith,* she begged him silently, knowing he would be thinking about doing exactly that.

He surprised her by merely shrugging and saying instead, "Well, you probably can't do it by yourself. Let's get on with it."

They conversed in low tones for a few moments more, she and the sylvan and John Ross, setting up their plan of attack. It was agreed that Nest would slip in through the back door with Pick, then hide while Pick checked out the basement once more, located whatever was down there, and gave Nest whatever chance he could to reach the children first. Twenty minutes would be allotted. At the end of that time, Ross would come in through the front door and attack the demons, distracting them long enough for Nest and the children to escape out the back.

They stood staring at the old house for long moments, statues in the falling snow. Its walls rose black and solitary against the backdrop of the steel mill and the river, rooflines softened by the snowfall, eaves draped in icy daggers. Nest wondered if she was committing suicide. She believed that Wraith would come if she needed him, that he would not deny her the protection of his magic. She believed it, yet she could not be certain. Not until it was too late to do anything about it if she was wrong. Everything she was about to do was built upon faith. Upon trust in her instincts. Upon belief in herself.

"Okay, Pick," she said finally.

They skirted the hedgerow to where it paralleled the back of the old house, then cut swiftly across the snow. Pick guided her, whispering urgent directions in her ear, keeping her clear of the snares the demons had set. They reached the back porch, where Pick directed her to the gap in the screen. She widened it carefully, rusted mesh giving way easily to a little pressure, and climbed through. She stood on the porch, a dilapidated, rotted-out veranda that had once looked out on what would have been a long, flowing, emerald green lawn. She moved to the back door, which was closed, but unlocked. With Pick settled on her shoulder, she stood listening, her ear pressed against the door.

She could just make out the faint sound of a television playing in the background. She checked her watch. She had used seven of her twenty minutes.

Cautiously, she opened the back door and stepped inside. She was at the end of a long hallway in an entry area that fed into the rest of the house. Coat hooks were screwed into an oak paneled wall, and a laundry room opened off to the left. Ahead and to the right, a stairwell disappeared downward into the basement. Light shone from the room below, weak and tiny against the larger, deeper blackness of the well.

She looked for Pick to tell him to be off, but he was already gone. She stood motionless and silent in the entry, listening to the sounds of the house, creaks that were faint and muffled, the low hum of the oil furnace, and the drip of a faucet. She listened to the sounds of a program playing on the television set and, once or twice, to one of the demons speaking. She could tell the difference between the two, the former carrying with it a hint of mechanical reproduction, the latter low and sharp and immediate. She forced herself to breathe slowly and evenly, glancing at her watch, keeping track of the time.

When Pick reappeared, she was down to three minutes. He nodded and gestured toward the basement. He had found the children and whatever watched over them.

It was twenty-five minutes to midnight.

She took off her boots, coat, gloves, and scarf, and in her stocking feet, she started down the stairs. Slowly, carefully, placing one foot in front of the other to test her weight on the old steps, she proceeded. Carpet cushioned and muffled her stealthy advance, and she made no sound. Pick rode her shoulder in silence, wooden face pointed straight ahead, eyes pinprick bright in the gloom.

At the bottom of the stairs, she was still in darkness. A solitary table lamp, resting atop an old leather-wrapped bar, lit the large L-shaped room before her. The children sat together in an easy chair close by, looking at a picture book. Harper was pretending to read, murmuring softly to Little John, who was looking directly toward the stairs at Nest.

He knows I'm here, she thought in surprise.

Pick motioned toward the darkness at the open end of the bar, back and behind where the children sat. Whatever stood guard was concealed there. Nest felt a sudden rush of hope. Her path to the children lay open.

She took a deep, slow breath. What to do now?

The problem was solved for her by the explosion that ripped through the house upstairs.

John Ross stood watching as Nest and Pick crept down the concealing wall of the hedgerow, across the side yard and into the back of the house. He listened carefully for any response from within, but there was none. He waited patiently for ten of the twenty minutes allotted, then made his way across the yard to the sheriff's cruiser and crouched next to it in the darkness. He had been in a lot of battles in his time as a Knight of the Word, both in the present and in the future, awake and in his dreams, and he knew what to expect. The demons would react instinctively, but for a few moments at least, they would be confused. If he struck at them quickly enough, they would not be able to use their numbers to overwhelm him.

He studied the windows of the house for movement. There was none. He looked at his watch. He had less than five minutes. A whisper of fear swept through him, and he tightened his grip on the black staff. The house would be warded by demon magic; he could not hope to get past it as Nest had done. His best bet was to get as close as possible, then move quickly from there. He tried to think where the warding would begin. At the edge of the porch, he decided. It probably did not extend out into the yard.

But there was only one way to find out.

He waited until he had two minutes remaining, then left the cover of the sheriff's cruiser and advanced quickly toward the front entry. He crossed the yard to the lower steps and stopped, watching the house and its windows as he did. Nothing moved. Nothing changed.

His watch said Nest's twenty minutes were up. He braced himself. There was no more time to think, and nothing left to think about.

He went up the steps swiftly, using the railing and his staff to lever himself onto the porch, set himself in place, and hurled his magic into the door with such force that he blew it right off its hinges. He was through the opening and into the house in seconds, taking in the scene beyond. A living room was visible directly ahead through a veil of smoke, lights bright against the entry darkness. A television screen flickered with muted images. Figures moved through the roiling haze, swift and purposeful. In a wing chair to his right, Larry Spence sat stiff and unmoving in his sheriff's uniform, staring at nothing.

Ross slid to one side of the entry, crouching low. The girl Penny flashed across his vision, face contorted, eyes wild, throwing knives in both hands. She flung them at him with a shriek but, deflected by the staff's magic, they sailed wide. He turned the magic on her then, knocking her backward. She tumbled away, her cry high-pitched and laced with rage. Frock coat trailing as he slid along the wall, Findo Gask moved to attack. Ross struck out at the demon instantly, caught him a solid blow, and knocked him flying, flat-brimmed hat sailing away, arms windmilling helplessly.

Then Twitch, materializing from the other side of the entry, was on top of him, voice booming as he lumbered forward. The giant slammed into Ross, knocking the wind from his lungs, sending him sprawling against the wall. Ross scrambled up, fighting for air, and sent the staff's fire hammering into the albino. Enraged, Twitch was shouting unintelligibly as he advanced. Ross burned him with the magic again, more fiercely this time, and the giant reeled away in pain and anger, clawing at the air.

Ross went by him quickly, into the living-room light, determined to place himself where he could keep them from reaching Nest. But Gask was back on his feet, white hair wild, a cottony halo about his leathery face. He gestured toward Ross, throwing his arms forward, and Ross brought up his staff protectively. But it was Larry Spence who responded, grabbing him from behind, pinning his arms and staff to his sides. A puppet to Gask's gestures, the deputy sheriff turned Ross toward Penny, as she uncoiled from the wall, both arms cocked. Another pair of the slender throwing knives streaked through the air so swiftly there was barely time to register their presence. With Spence still clinging to him, Ross twisted desperately, hands tightening about the staff, and the Word's magic flared protectively. Larry Spence grunted in pain, released him abruptly, and staggered back, Penny's blades buried in his shoulder and side. Dropping to one knee, he fumbled for his .45, dragged it from his holster, and began shooting at everything around him, people and furniture alike. Ross caught a glimpse of his face as he did so. His eye sockets were bleeding and empty. The eyes had been gouged out.

Then Penny catapulted out of the haze, another deadly knife in hand. Screaming and spitting, she raked at his midsection. Buttressed by demon magic, the slender blade broke through his defenses and pierced his side. He gasped from the force of the blow and the sudden pain. Penny yanked the knife free and stabbed at him again, but he deflected the second blow and sent her spinning away.

Almost immediately, Twitch reappeared. Reaching down, he fastened both massive hands about Ross's neck and began to squeeze.

When she heard the front door explode off its hinges, Nest called to Pick, "Hang on."

She broke from the darkness of the stairwell into the light and raced for the children. But she had forgotten she had removed her shoes, and she couldn't find sufficient purchase in her stocking feet. She was sliding on the tile floor almost instantly.

Harper was clinging to Little John, both of them frozen in place, uncertain what was happening.

"Run!" she shouted at them.

She was expecting the guard demon to come at her, had readied her magic to combat it, and still wasn't prepared when the ur'droch hurtled out of the shadows. A blur of darkness, it crossed in front of the children to intercept her, pushing through her magic as if it wasn't there. It slammed into her with stunning force, unexpectedly solid for something that seemed so insubstantial. The blow spun her sideways into the wall, where she sagged to her knees. Pick went flying off her shoulder and disappeared.

Wheeling back, keeping to the shadows until the last moment, the ur'droch attacked again. Dazed and gasping for air, she sent her small magic lancing into it, to gain a moment's respite. The demon was staggered this time, and it careened into the sofa, knocking it askew. Swiftly, it slid back into the gloom.

Nest looked quickly for the children. Harper and Little John were hanging on to each other only a few yards away.

"Run!" She screamed again.

Overhead, the ceiling shuddered from the impact of colliding bodies and expended magic. The lamp shade on the bar counter tilted crazily, and the dim light sprayed the darkness, casting strange shadows that rocked and swayed.

Nest braced herself against the wall, willing herself to remain upright. Everything in her body felt broken. The children were running to reach her, arms outstretched. The ur'droch shot out of the darkness in pursuit, a roiling black shadow. Nest threw her magic at it, trying again to keep it at bay. But she had little strength left and almost no focus she could bring to bear, and she could feel both crumble in the face of the other's determined assault.

Then Wraith appeared, suddenly, explosively, in response to her desperate need, in answer to her unspoken prayer, launched from the layered darkness as if from a nightmare's epicenter. Tiger-striped muzzle drawn back, the big ghost wolf hammered into its enemy and sent it flying into the shadows. Barely pausing, it gave pursuit. Seconds later, they emerged in a ball of dark fury, tearing at each other, emitting sounds that were primal and blood-chilling. Across the shadowy room they surged, back and forth, locked in their life-and-death struggle.

The children reached Nest safely and latched on to her legs. She was so weak, she almost went down again. Her head spun. She had to get them out of there, but she had no strength to do so.

And she couldn't leave Wraith. Not after he had come back for her. Not without trying to help.

The ghost wolf and the ur'droch wheeled and lunged through the pale spray of tilted lamplight, through the hazy gloom, back and forth across the furniture's debris.

Harper was sobbing and clutching tightly at her legs, and Little John was saying "Mama, Mama," over and over.

Get them out! Wraith is only something made of magic! He isn't real! It doesn't matter what happens to him! Get the children out!

She hugged them against her in paralyzed confusion, eyes riveted on the battle taking place before her.

Do something!

The ur'droch continually tried to carry the fight into the shadows, to maneuver at every opportunity toward the room's shadowy edges. It dragged at Wraith, hauling him out of the light . . .

Impulsively, Nest stumbled toward the stairway and the bank of wall switches she had passed coming in. When she reached them, she threw them all on.

Light blazed the length and breadth of the rec room, flooding through the shadows, and suddenly there was no more darkness to be found. The ur'droch wheeled about in confusion, and Wraith took advantage. Boring in with single-minded fury, he fastened his jaws on some part of the demon that Nest could not identify and began to shake his enemy. The ur'droch jerked from side to side as if made of old rags. Bits and pieces of it began to come loose. It made no sound, but things that might have been clawed feet scrabbled at the tile floor and flailed at the air. Still Wraith shook it, braced on all fours, tiger face lifted to hold it aloft.

Then abruptly the ur'droch exploded into black smoke and disintegrated into ash. The small, winged creature that was its withered soul made a futile effort to escape, but Wraith had it in his massive jaws instantly, crushing it to pulp.

With a rush of air and billowing, inky smoke, the ur'droch was gone.

At that same moment, John Ross was struggling to break loose from the giant Twitch. Magic from his staff lanced into the big albino's midsection, burning through him. The massive hands that were fastened about his neck released, but the tree-trunk arms closed about his chest. Ross felt his ribs crack as even the Word's magic was unable to protect him. In desperation, he slammed his forehead into the bridge of the albino's nose. Twitch roared and shook himself, and his arms loosened just enough for Ross to twist free.

Tumbling to the floor, he rolled away from the flailing giant into Penny, who stabbed at him again and again with her knives, her face streaked with blood and her eyes wild. He fended her off with a solid kick, then struck at her with the staff. He caught her across the ankles with a sweeping blow and dropped her to her knees. She dug into the floor with her knives, tearing at the carpet, consumed by madness and blood-lust. Larry Spence staggered past, still pulling the trigger on his empty .45, *click, click, click,* and with a wicked, sideways slash of her blade, Penny cut him open to his backbone.

Larry Spence fell to the floor, dying, as Ross brought the length of his staff across Penny's face, shattering her skull into pieces. Faceless and groping, knives gone, fingers become claws, still she fought to reach him, until his magic burned through the core of her body to her twisted, black soul and turned both to ash.

A fresh gout of fire spurted up the curtains and along the length of the west wall. Leather-bound book clutched to his dark chest, Findo Gask was crouched by the old fireplace, laughing. Ross tried to reach him, but Twitch reappeared in his path, all size and lumbering destruction, tearing at the air and furniture indiscriminately. Ross held his ground, summoning what remained of his strength, calling up the magic one final time. Twitch reached for him, and Ross jammed one end of the staff into the giant's throat and sent the magic skimming along its length. Twitch reared back, body shaking as if he had touched a live wire, voice booming with rage. Ross pushed him back into the closest wall and pinned him there, refusing to let him escape. Fire spurted from the giant's ears and mouth and nose, and his huge body convulsed.

When the demon collapsed finally, Ross found that tiny bat of wickedness that formed its core as it tried to break free of the giant's dead, hollow shell, slammed it to the floor, and burned it away.

With everyone around him dead, Ross sagged to one knee and stared across the room at Findo Gask. The demon stared back. For an instant, neither moved. The room flickered with shadows as the fire sparked by the combatants' magic continued to consume the old house. The fire shone quicksilver and eerie against the darkness beyond, as if something come alive to challenge the night.

"Mr. Ross!" Gask shouted at him.

Ross tried to rise and fell back. He had no strength.

"You're dying, Mr. Ross!" Findo Gask said, and laughed.

His leathery face was streaked with sweat and grime, and his black coat was torn. He began easing his way slowly along the wall toward the back of the house. Again, Ross tried unsuccessfully to climb back to his feet. Nothing seemed to work. He summoned his magic to support him, but he had almost nothing left to call on.

"Demon poison, Mr. Ross!" Gask spit at him. There was venom and rage in his voice. "Just a scratch would be enough for normal men. But a blade's length plunged inside the stomach wall will put an end even to a Knight of the Word!"

Ross reached down and touched his damaged midsection, willing the wound to heal over and the blood flow to stop. He kept his eyes on Findo Gask the entire time.

"I'll be leaving now, Mr. Ross!" the demon taunted. "Time to check on Miss Freemark. Down in the basement, isn't she? Don't bother getting up to show me the way. I'll find it on my own. Get on with the business of dying, why don't you?"

He was almost to the darkened hallway when he turned back one last time. "It was all for nothing, Mr. Ross! All of it! You've lost everything!"

Then he wheeled away and was gone.

In the hushed aftermath of the ur'droch's destruction, Nest knelt before Harper and Little John and touched their faces gently. "It's all right," she told them. "Everything is all right."

Wraith prowled through the scattered remains of the demon, big head lowered as he sniffed at the ashes. Little John watched him intently. Overhead, the battle continued, violent and unabated.

"Come here, peanut," Nest urged Harper, and when the little girl did, she took her in her arms and held her, cooing softly. "It's all right, it's all right."

Little John looked at them, eyes suspicious and uncertain. Nest held out her hand to him, but he refused to come. She gestured with her fingers. He stayed where he was.

Gently, she eased Harper away from her, folding the little girl down against her thigh, freeing both arms. "Little John," Nest said softly. "It's all right."

The boy stared at her with such longing that it was all she could do to keep from bursting into tears. His need was naked and compelling, but he could not seem to free himself from the indecision or doubt or whatever it was that kept him at bay. She held his gaze, her arms outstretched, patiently waiting him out. She noticed for the first time how much the color of his hair and skin were like her own. She was surprised at how similar their features were. *Odd,* she thought. She had not remembered that his eyes, like hers, were green. They had always seemed so blue . . .

In fact, she amended suddenly, they had been blue.

"Oh, my God!" she whispered.

He was changing right in front of her, just a little, barely enough to tell that anything was happening. It was his face that was transforming now, beginning to mirror her own in small, almost negligible ways—just enough that she could not fail to see what he was doing, what he was trying to make happen.

Mama he had called her. *Mama.*

"Do you want me to be your mother, little boy?" she asked him quietly. "Is that what you want? I want that, too. I want to be your mother more than anything. You and me and Harper. We can be a family, can't we?"

"Luv 'ou, Neth," Harper murmured without looking up, keeping her face lowered against Nest's thigh.

"Come here, Little John," Nest urged again. "Come let me hold you, sweetie."

The gypsy morph glanced over at Wraith. The big ghost wolf lifted his head immediately and stared back. After a moment, he took a step toward the morph, and Little John instantly reached for Nest, cringing. Nest took him into her arms at once, pulling him against her, stroking his hair.

"It's all right, Little John," she told him. "He won't hurt you. He isn't coming over here. He's staying right where he is."

She glared in warning at Wraith, as if the look alone could convey what she wanted. The ghost wolf merely stared back at her, eyes bright and fierce, revealing nothing of his thoughts. When he turned away again, it was almost as an afterthought.

"Little boy," she cooed to the gypsy morph. "Tell me what you want. Please, little boy."

His head lifted, and he glanced over to make certain that Wraith was not trying to approach.

"He's not coming back to me, not like he was, not inside me. He doesn't belong there. He doesn't even want to be there. It was my fault, Little John. I made him be there. But he won't come back again. I won't let him. It's all right now. It's only you and me."

It had gone quiet upstairs, but she could smell smoke and feel the heat of flames. The house was on fire, and she was out of time. If she didn't break through to him now, she never would. She had to take him out of there, but she didn't want to interrupt what was happening. She was as close to him as she would ever be. She could feel that he was ready to reveal himself to her. Something crashed overhead, and she wondered suddenly what she would find waiting for her when she finally took the children back up.

"I love you, Little John," she whispered, a twinge of desperation creeping into her voice.

She felt him stir, worming more tightly into her.

"Tell me what you want, little boy," she begged.

When he did, it was not at all what she had expected, but ever so much more than she had any right to hope.

CHRISTMAS

CHAPTER 28

Battered and disheveled, his black clothes stained and torn, Findo Gask made his way slowly down the back hallway of the old Victorian in search of Nest Freemark. He had lost his flat-brimmed hat and a good chunk of his composure. He kept his Book of Names clutched tightly to his chest. Behind him, flames climbed the walls and ate through the ceiling, consuming hungrily. His strange, gray eyes burned with the intensity of the fire he turned his back on, reflecting the mix of anger, frustration, and disappointment he was battling.

John Ross and Nest Freemark had been much stronger and more daring than he had anticipated. He could not believe they'd had the temerity to come for him, much less the courage to attack in spite of such formidable odds. It wasn't the loss of Twitch and Penny and most probably the ur'droch that bothered him. They had all been expendable from the beginning. It was his loss of control over the situation. It was the effrontery Ross and Nest Freemark had displayed in attacking him when he had believed them so thoroughly under his thumb. He prided himself on being careful and thorough, on never getting surprised, and the night's events had knocked his smoothly spinning world right out of its orbit.

His seamed face tightened. There was no help for it now. The best he could do was to set things right again. He would have to make certain that Nest Freemark, if she was still alive, did not stay that way. Then he would have to find the gypsy morph and, at the very least, put an end to any possibility that its magic might one day serve the Word.

When he reached the top of the basement stairs, he paused. It was brightly lit below, but devoid of movement and sound. Whatever was down there that was still alive was keeping very quiet. Then he heard someone stirring, heard a child's voice, and knew they had not escaped him. Footsteps approached the stairwell, and he moved swiftly back into the shadows. When he saw Nest Freemark at the bottom of the stairs, he backed into the hall. Where to deal with her? She would attempt to slip out the back, of course, bringing the children with her. It was the children she would think of first, not Ross. It was the children she had come to save, surmising correctly that waiting to make any kind of trade for the morph would get them all killed.

She was intelligent and resourceful. It was too bad she wasn't more her father's daughter. In all the years he had worked in the service of the Void, he had never come across anyone like her.

He sighed wearily. He would wait for her outside, he decided, where he would put an end to her for good.

When she emerged onto the back porch, he was standing in the shadows by the hedgerow across the way. He could see her clearly in the light of the flames. She carried the little girl in her arms, and the sylvan rode her shoulder. There was no sign of the boy.

When she came down the porch stairs, he stepped out to confront her.

"Miss Freemark!" he called out sharply, bringing her head around. "Don't be so quick to leave! You still have something that belongs to me!"

She stopped at the bottom of the steps and stared at him wordlessly. She didn't panic. She didn't turn back or try to move away. She just stood there, holding her ground.

"We're finished, you and I, Miss Freemark," he said, coming forward a few steps, closing the distance between them. "The game is over. There's no one left but us." He paused. "You did destroy the ur'droch, didn't you?"

Her nod of acquiescence was barely discernible. She seemed to be trying to make up her mind about something. "Congratulations," he offered. "I wouldn't have thought it possible. The ur'droch was virtually indestructible. So that accounts for everyone, doesn't it? Mr. Ross disposed of Twitch and Penny, and they disposed of Mr. Ross and the deputy sheriff. That leaves just us."

To her credit, she didn't react visibly to his words. She just stood there, silent and watchful. He didn't like it that she was so unmoved, so calm. She was made of fire and raw emotion, and she should be responding more strongly than this.

"Think how much simpler it would have been if you'd listened that first day when I asked for your help." He sighed. "You were so stubborn, and it has cost you so much. Now here we are, right back where we started. Let's try it again, shall we, one last time? Give me what I want. Give me the gypsy morph so that I can be out of your life forever!"

The faintest of smiles crossed her lips. "Here's a piece of irony for you, Mr. Gask. You've had what you wanted all night, and you didn't realize it. It's been right under your nose. Little John was the gypsy morph. That boy was what you were looking for. In his last transformation before coming here, that's what he became. How about that, Mr. Gask?"

Findo Gask quit smiling. "You're lying, Miss Freemark."

She shook her head. "You know I'm not. You can tell. Demons recognize lies better than most; it's what they know best. No, Mr. Gask, you had the morph. That was one of the reasons John and I came here tonight—because we didn't have it to trade for the children and had no other way to get them back."

She shifted the little girl in her arms. The child's head was buried in her shoulder. "Anyway, he's lost to both of us now. Another piece of irony for you. You notice I don't have him with me? Well, guess what? He ran out of time. His magic broke apart down there in the basement. He disappeared. Poof! So it really is just you and me, after all."

Findo Gask studied her carefully, searching her face, her eyes, sifting through the echoes of her words in his mind. Was she lying to him? He didn't think so. But if the morph had self-destructed, wouldn't he have sensed it? No, he answered himself, magic was flying everywhere in that house, and he wouldn't have been able to separate the sources or types.

"Look in my eyes, Mr. Gask," she urged quietly. "What do you see?"

What he saw was that she was telling the truth. That the morph had been the boy all along, and now the boy was gone. That the magic had broken apart one final time. That it was beyond his reach. That was what he saw.

He felt a burning in his throat. "You have been a considerable source of irritation to me, Miss Freemark," he said softly. "Maybe it is time for you to accept the consequences of your foolish behavior."

"So now you want to kill me, too," she said. "Which was your plan all along anyway, wasn't it?"

"You knew as much. Isn't that another reason why you came here instead of waiting on my call?"

He took a step toward her.

"I wouldn't come any closer if I were you, Mr. Gask," she said sharply. "I can protect myself better than most."

She glanced to her right, and Gask followed her gaze automatically. The big ghost wolf the ur'droch had encountered at her home the night before stood watching him from the shadows, head lowered, muzzle drawn back, body tensed. Gask studied it a moment, surprised that it was still alive, that it hadn't been forced to exchange its own life for that of the ur'droch. He had thought the ur'droch a match for anything. Well, you never knew.

"I don't think your friend is strong enough to stop me," he said to Nest Freemark, keeping his eyes fixed on the beast.

"I've lost a lot in the past few days, Mr. Gask," she replied. "This child in my arms is one of the few things I have left. I promised her mother I would look after her. If you intend to keep that from happening, you're going to have to do it the hard way."

Gask continued to measure the ghost wolf. He did not care for what he saw. This creature had been created by a very powerful demon magic that had been strengthened at least once since. It was not hampered by the rules that governed the servants of the Word. It would fight him as a demon would fight him. Most likely it had already destroyed the ur'droch. Findo Gask was stronger and smarter than his late companion, but he was not indestructible. He might prevail in a battle with this creature, but at what cost?

In the distance, the wail of fire engines rose out of the silence. Lights had come on in the surrounding homes. On the street, a cluster of people had begun to gather.

He let the tension drain from his body. It was time to let go of this business, time to move on. He could not afford to let personal feelings interfere with his work. There would be other days and more important battles to fight.

A shawl of snowflakes had collected on the shoulders and the lapels of his frock coat. He brushed them away dismissively. "What is the worth of the life of a single child here or there?" he asked rhetorically. "Nothing. The end will be the same. Sooner or later, the Void will claim them all."

"Maybe," she said.

He backed away slowly, still watching the ghost wolf, still wary. "You've failed, Miss Freemark. People died for you, and what do you have to show for it? Mr. Ross gave up his life, and what did he gain by doing so? What was the point of any of it? What did you accomplish?"

The yellow eyes in the tiger-striped face glowed like live coals as they tracked his retreat. Findo Gask backed all the way across the side yard and through the barren-limbed hedge before turning away.

He walked to the street without looking back, fighting to stay calm, to keep his frustration and rage from making him do something foolish. He could go back after her, he knew. He could find a way to get to her, sooner or later. But it was pointless. She had nothing left he wanted. His battle with her was finished. There were other causes to attend to. It made no difference to him that he had failed to secure the morph's magic. It mattered only that it could never be used in the service of the Word. By that measuring stick, he had won. It was enough to satisfy him.

When he reached the street, he saw a pair of fire engines wheeling around the corner and coming for the house. He turned the other way, walking quickly. At the corner, he paused. Standing beneath the streetlight, he opened the Book of Names and looked at the last entry.

The name *John Ross* was faintly legible against the aged parchment. Even as he watched, the name turned a shade darker.

You take away what you can from these battles, he thought. The life of a Knight of the Word was a reasonable trophy.

He closed the book and walked on. In seconds, his tall, dark figure had vanished into the night.

Nest Freemark remained where she was until she could no longer see Findo Gask. Harper nestled against her breast, fast asleep. Pick sat on her shoulder, twiggy fingers wrapped in her parka collar, a silent presence.

Wraith had faded away into the ether, free to go where he wished, but never, she believed, to go too far from her.

"He did a fine job of convincing himself, didn't he?" Pick said finally, gesturing after Findo Gask.

Nest nodded. "He believed what he saw in my eyes."

"You didn't lie."

"I didn't have to."

"I guess he was looking hard enough that if he was ever going to find out, he would have found out now."

"I guess."

The flames from the burning house were growing hotter as the fire spread to the roof. On the front lawn, the firemen were scrambling to contain the blaze, their efforts directed primarily at protecting the surrounding homes. It was clear there was nothing they could do to save the Victorian or anyone in it.

"You think he was telling the truth about John Ross?" Pick asked suddenly.

She watched the activity out front without speaking for a moment, then nodded. "Yes."

"I could try to get back inside for a quick look."

The entire front half of the house was engulfed in flames and the fire was spreading quickly. Any attempt at going back inside would be foolish. Her heart could not accept that John Ross was really dead, but she knew it was so. If he was still alive, he would have come for her by now.

"Let it go, Pick," she said softly.

Pick went silent, absorbing the impact of her words. In her arms, Harper stirred. The little girl was growing heavy, but Nest refused to put her down. She was reminded of the time she had carried Bennett home from the cliffs of Sinnissippi Park fifteen years earlier after saving her from the feeders. She hadn't put Bennett down either that night, not until she was safely home in bed. She would do the same now with Harper. Maybe this time, it would make a difference.

"You better get going," Pick said finally.

She nodded. "You better get going, too."

He hesitated. "Don't you be second-guessing yourself later," he snapped at her suddenly. "You did everything you could! More than everything, in fact! Criminy, you should be proud of yourself!"

He jumped from her shoulder and disappeared into the tangle of the shrubbery. Moments later, she caught a glimpse of a barn owl winging its way toward the river through the snowfall and the night.

Safe journey, Pick, she wished him.

She turned and walked back toward the street, angling diagonally across the front yards of the old houses, keeping to the shadows of the trees and porches, holding Harper tightly against her. She glanced back once at the burning house, and when she did so, her eyes filled with tears. She began to cry silently, realizing what she was leaving behind, thinking of John Ross. She thought of all they had shared over the past fifteen years. She thought of what he had endured in his twenty-five years as a Knight of the Word. He had given everything in his service to the Lady. In the end, he had even given his life.

She brushed at her eyes with the back of her gloved hand. John Ross might have died for her and for the children, but he hadn't died for nothing. And neither of them had failed in what they had set out to do.

She fought to compose herself as she crossed down a side street and came in view of her car. She wished he could have lived to see the baby. *John Ross Freemark* she would name him. He would be born next fall, another of those children Findo Gask was so quick to dismiss as unimportant. But this one could surprise him. Created of wild magic and born to a woman for whom magic was a legacy, he could become anything. She felt him inside her, deep in her womb, transformed into what he had sought to become all along—her baby-to-be, her future child. She did not know his plan, nor perhaps did he know it himself. Even the Word might not know. They must bide their time, all of them; they must wait and see.

She climbed into the car and placed Harper on the seat beside her. The little girl curled into a ball, her head resting on Nest's lap. Nest started the car and let it warm up for a moment. She felt the inevitability of what had happened with the gypsy morph stir in her memories. She looked back and saw clearly all the workings of its transitions and of its journey to reach her. She could feel its final moments outside her body, pressing against her, then into her, then transforming for the last time. She could understand why Wraith had been such an obstacle to its needs. For the gypsy morph to become what it wanted, Wraith could not remain inside her. Her body must belong to her unborn child alone. It had needed to know she wanted this as much as it did. It had needed a sacrifice from her that she herself did not know until tonight she was capable of making.

Why had it chosen to become her child? There was no answer to that question, none that she could discover for a while, if ever. It must be enough that it had made such a choice, that its need matched her own, and that their joining felt good and right.

A child. Any child. It made all the difference in the world. Findo Gask was wrong about what that was worth. One day, he would learn his mistake.

She pulled the car out of the parking lot onto West Third and began driving back through Hopewell. She would take Harper home now and put her to bed. Tomorrow, when she woke, they would open their presents. Then they would go to Robert's to visit Amy and the kids and have dinner.

It would mark the beginning of a new life.

It would be a bright and joyous Christmas Day.

Sprawled on the living-room floor, flames climbing the walls all around him, John Ross fought the poison that seeped through his system, bringing all that remained of his strength and magic and heart to bear. He got to his feet and staggered down the hall after Findo Gask. It took him a long time. His only thought was to get to the demon before the demon got to Nest. He was too late. By the time he reached the back door, the confrontation between them had already occurred. Gask had disappeared, and Nest was moving away. She did not appear to have been harmed.

He had thought momentarily of going after her and decided he was too weak. It was best just to let her go. He watched her from the doorway, the flames consuming the house around him, working their way down the hall at his back. He watched until she was several houses down, then slipped out the door and into the night.

He would go to Josie instead, he decided. He would make his way to her home, and she would care for him. He would mend eventually, and then they would be together for the rest of their lives.

He did not know where he went after that. His instincts took over, and he did as they directed. He lurched and staggered through backyards, through clusters of trees and along fences and walls, in the shadow of buildings and across snowy stretches, all without seeing or being seen by another living soul. It was after midnight, and apart from those gathered at the scene he had departed, the world was asleep. He leaned on his staff and drew from it the strength he required to go on. He was crushed and broken inside, and his wound from Penny's knife burned and festered beneath his clothing. He was growing colder.

When he reached the banks of the Rock River, close by the dark span of the Avenue G bridge where it crossed to Lawrence Island, he was surprised to find himself so far from where he had intended to go. Josie's house, he knew, was in the other direction. He sagged down against the rough-barked trunk of an old oak and stared out at the night. The river was frozen everywhere but at its center, where the current was strong enough to keep the ice from closing over. He watched the dark water surge, its surface reflecting the lights of the bridge overhead. It would be all right, he knew. It was quiet here. He was at peace.

Soon a fresh brightness appeared on the crest of the flowing water, a light that broadened and spread. The Lady appeared, come out of the darkness in her flowing, gossamer robes, her fine, soft features pale and lovely. She crossed the ice on her tiny feet to where he sat and bent to him.

"Brave Knight, you have done well," she said softly. "You have done all that I asked. You have fulfilled your promise and your duty. You have completed your service to the Word. You are released. You are set free."

A great weariness filled him. He could not speak, but he smiled in acknowledgement. He was satisfied. It was what he had worked so long for. It was what he had wanted so much.

"Brave Knight," she whispered. "Come home with me. Come home where you belong."

She reached out her hand. With great effort, he lifted his own and placed it in hers. The light that surrounded her flowed downward through his body and enfolded him as well.

As he came to his feet, he was renewed and made whole again. The black staff fell away from his hand.

Seconds later, he was gone.

The staff lay where it had fallen. In the deep silence of the night, the snowfall began to cover it over. Little by little, it began to vanish beneath a white blanket.

Then a figure appeared from out of the shadows, a big man with copper skin and long black hair braided down his back, a man who wore army fatigues and combat boots. He walked to where the staff lay and stooped to retrieve it. He brushed the snow from its dark length and held it before him thoughtfully.

A solitary warrior and a seeker of truth, he looked out across the ice to where the open water flowed, and then beyond, to where the Word's battle against a sleeping world's ignorance and denial still raged.

ABOUT THE AUTHOR

A writer since high school, Terry Brooks published his first novel, *The Sword of Shannara,* in 1977. It became the first work of fiction ever to appear on the *New York Times* Trade Paperback Bestseller List, where it remained for more than five months. He has published fifteen consecutive bestselling novels since, including the novel based upon the screenplay and story by George Lucas: *Star Wars*®: Episode I *The Phantom Menace*™. His novels *Running with the Demon* and *A Knight of the Word* both won the annual "Rocky Award" given by *The Rocky Mountain News* for the year's best fantasy novel.

The author was a practicing attorney for many years, but now writes full-time. He lives with his wife, Judine, in the Pacific Northwest and Hawaii.

THE Science Fiction BOOK CLUB®

If you enjoyed this book...
Come visit our Web site at

www.sfbc.com

and find hundreds more:
• science fiction • fantasy
• the newest books
• the greatest classics

THE SCIENCE FICTION BOOK CLUB
has been bringing the best of science fiction and fantasy
to the doors of discriminating readers for over 50 years.
For a look at currently available books and details on how to join,
just visit us at the address above.